THE CROWN OF GILDED BONES

Also From Jennifer L. Armentrout

Fall With Me
Dream of You (a 1001 Dark Nights Novel)
Forever With You
Fire In You

By J. Lynn
Wait for You
Be With Me
Stay With Me

A Blood and Ash Novel
From Blood and Ash
A Kingdom of Flesh and Fire
The Crown of Gilded Bones

The Covenant Series
Half-Blood
Pure
Deity
Elixer
Apollyon
Sentinel

The Lux Series
Shadows
Obsidian
Onyx
Opal
Origin
Opposition
Oblivion

The Origin Series
The Darkest Star
The Burning Shadow

The Dark Elements
Bitter Sweet Love
White Hot Kiss

Stone Cold Touch
Every Last Breath

The Harbinger Series
Storm and Fury
Rage and Ruin

A Titan Novel
The Return
The Power
The Struggle
The Prophecy

A Wicked Novel
Wicked
Torn
Brave
The Prince (a 1001 Dark Nights Novella)
The King (a 1001 Dark Nights Novella)
The Queen (a 1001 Dark Nights Novella)

Gamble Brothers Series
Tempting The Best Man
Tempting The Player
Tempting The Bodyguard

A de Vincent Novel Series
Moonlight Sins
Moonlight Seduction
Moonlight Scandals

Standalone Novels
Obsession
Frigid
Scorched
Cursed
Don't Look Back
The Dead List
Till Death
The Problem With Forever
If There's No Tomorrow

Anthologies

Meet Cute

Life Inside My Mind

Fifty First Times

THE CROWN OF GILDED BONES

#1 *NEW YORK TIMES* BESTSELLING AUTHOR
JENNIFER L. ARMENTROUT

The Crown of Gilded Bones
A Blood and Ash Novel
By Jennifer L. Armentrout

ISBN: 978-1-952457-78-4

Published by Blue Box Press, an imprint of Evil Eye Concepts, Incorporated

Acknowledgments from the Author

Thank you to Liz Berry, Jillian Stein, and MJ Rose, who fell in love with these characters and world as much as me. Thank you to my agent Kevan Lyon, and to Chelle Olson, Kim Guidroz, the team at Blue Box Press, Jenn Watson, and my assistant Stephanie Brown for your hard work and support. Mega thanks to Hang Le for creating such beautiful covers. A big thank you to Jen Fisher, Malissa Coy, Stacey Morgan, Lesa, JR Ward, Laura Kaye, Andrea Joan. Sarah Maas, Brigid Kemmerer, KA Tucker, Tijan, Vonetta Young, Mona Awad, and many more who have helped keep me sane and laughing. Thank you to the ARC team for your support and honest reviews, and a big thank you to JLAnders for being the best reader group an author can have, and the Blood and Ash Spoiler Group for making the drafting stage so fun and being utterly amazing.

None of this would be possible without you, the reader. Thank you.

Dedication

Dedicated to the heroes—the healthcare workers, first responders, essential workers and researchers who have worked tirelessly and endlessly to save lives and to keep stores open all around the globe, at great risk to their own lives and the lives of their loved ones, thank you.

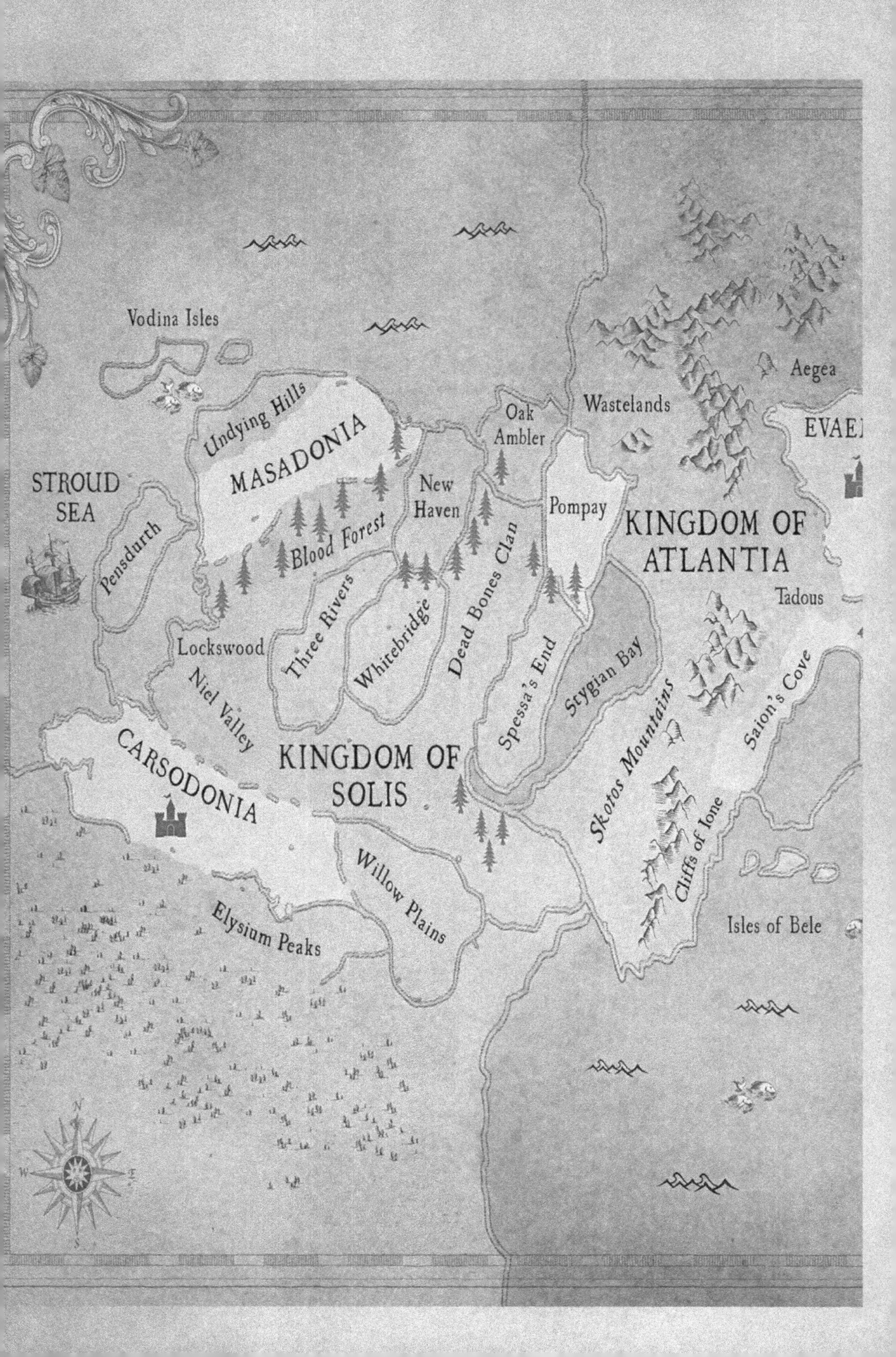

Vodina Isles
Undying Hills
MASADONIA
STROUD SEA
Pensdurth
Blood Forest
Oak Ambler
New Haven
Wastelands
Aegea
EVAE
Pompay
KINGDOM OF ATLANTIA
Tadous
Three Rivers
Whitebridge
Dead Bones Clan
Lockswood
Niel Valley
Spessa's End
Stygian Bay
Saion's Cove
Skotos Mountains
CARSODONIA
KINGDOM OF SOLIS
Cliffs of Ione
Willow Plains
Elysium Peaks
Isles of Bele
N
W
E
S

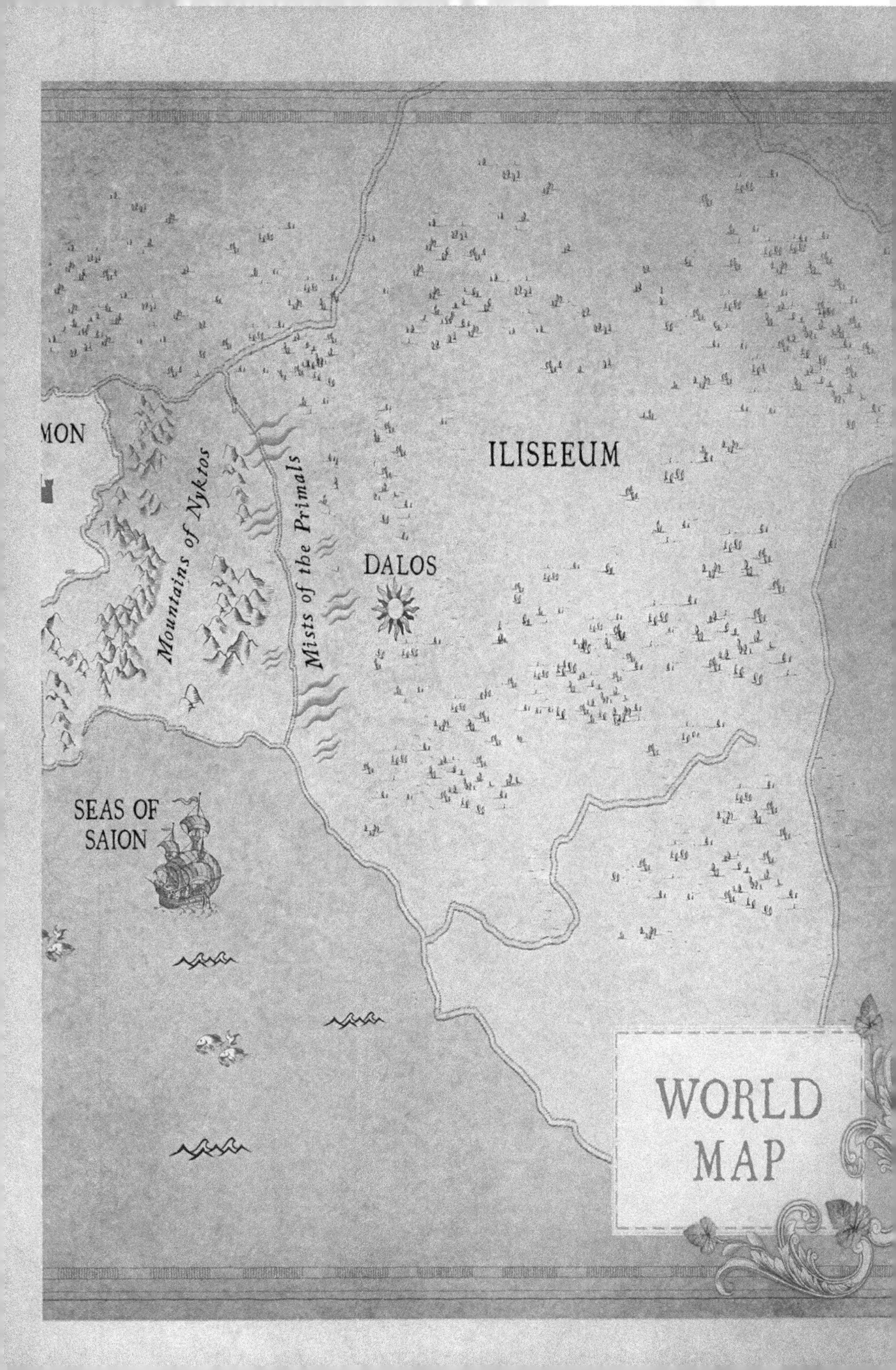
MON
Mountains of Nyktos
Mists of the Primals
ILISEEUM
DALOS
SEAS OF SAION
WORLD MAP

Chapter 1

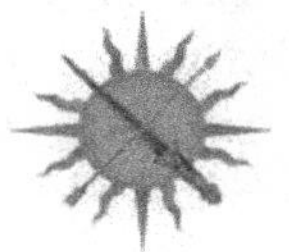

"Lower your swords," Queen Eloana commanded, her hair shining a glossy onyx in the sun as she sank onto one knee. The raw emotion pouring out of her seeped into the Temple floors of the Chambers of Nyktos, bitter and hot, tasting of anguish and a helpless sort of anger. It stretched out toward me, needling my skin and brushing against this...*primal* thing inside me. "And bow before the...before the *last* descendant of the most ancient ones. She who carries the blood of the King of Gods within her. Bow before your new Queen."

The blood of the King of Gods? Your new Queen? None of that made sense. Not her words or when she had removed her crown.

A too-thin breath scorched my throat as I looked at the man standing beside the Queen of Atlantia. The crown was still upon the King's golden-haired head, but the bones had remained a bleached white. Nothing like the gleaming, gilded one the Queen had placed at the feet of the statue of Nyktos. My gaze skipped over the terrible, broken things scattered about the once pristine, white floors. I'd done that to them, adding their blood to what had fallen from the sky, filling the thin fissures in the marble. I didn't look at that or anyone else—every part of my being focused on *him.*

He remained on one knee, staring up at me from between the vee of the swords he'd crossed over his chest. His damp hair, blue-black in the Atlantian sunlight, curled against the sandy-hued skin of his forehead. Red streaked those high, angular cheekbones, the proud curve of his jaw, and ran down lips that had once shattered my heart.

Lips that had pieced those broken shards back together with the truth. Bright, golden eyes locked with mine, and even bowed before me, so motionless I wasn't sure he breathed, he still reminded me of one of the wild and strikingly beautiful cave cats I'd once seen caged in Queen Ileana's palace as a child.

He had been many things to me. A stranger in a dimly lit room who'd been my first kiss. A guard who had sworn to lay down his life for mine. A friend who had looked beyond the veil of the Maiden to truly see me underneath, who'd handed me a sword to protect myself instead of forcing me into a gilded cage. A legend cloaked in darkness and nightmares that had plotted to betray me. A Prince of a kingdom believed to have been lost to time and war, who had suffered unimaginable horrors and yet managed to find the pieces of who he used to be. A brother who would do anything, commit any deed to save his family. His people. A man who bared his soul and stripped open his heart to me—and only me.

My first.

My guard.

My friend.

My betrayer.

My partner.

My husband.

My heartmate.

My *everything.*

Casteel Da'Neer bowed before me and stared up at me as if I were the only person in the entire kingdom. I didn't need to concentrate like before to know what he was feeling. Everything he felt was wide-open to me. His emotions were a kaleidoscope of ever-shifting tastes—cool and tart, heavy and spicy, and sweet like chocolate-dipped berries. Those unyieldingly firm and unrelentingly tender lips parted, revealing just the hint of sharp fangs.

"My Queen," he breathed, and those two smoky words soothed my skin. The lilt of his voice quelled the ancient thing inside me that wanted to take the anger and the fear radiating from all the others and twist it, turn it back, truly give them something to fear, and add to the shattered things thrown about the floor. One side of his lips curled up, and a deep dimple appeared in his right cheek.

Dizzy with relief at the sight of that infuriatingly stupid—and adorable—dimple, my entire body shuddered. I feared that when he saw what I'd done, he'd be afraid. And I couldn't blame him for that.

What I'd done should terrify anyone, but not Casteel. The heat that turned his eyes the color of warmed honey told me that fear was very much the furthest thing from his mind. Which was also a little disturbing. But he was the Dark One, whether he liked being called that or not.

Some of the shock faded, and the pounding adrenaline eased. And when it left, I realized I *hurt.* My shoulder and the side of my head throbbed. The left side of my face felt puffy, and that had nothing to do with the old scars there. A dull ache pulsed in my legs and arms, and my body felt funny, as if my knees were weakening. I swayed in the warm, salty breeze—

Casteel rose quickly, and I shouldn't have been surprised by how fast he moved, but I still was. In a heartbeat, he'd gone from kneeling to standing, a foot closer to me, and several things happened at once.

The men and women behind Casteel's parents, the ones wearing the same white tunics and loose pants of those lying on the floor, also moved. Light reflected off the golden armbands adorning their biceps as they lifted their swords, shifting closer to Casteel's parents, protecting them. Some reached for crossbows strapped to their backs. They had to be guards of some sort.

A sudden growl of warning came from the largest wolven I'd ever seen. Kieran and Vonetta's father stood to my right. Jasper had officiated the marriage between Casteel and me in Spessa's End. He'd been there when Nyktos showed his approval by briefly turning day to night. But now, the steel-hued wolven's lips peeled back, baring teeth that could tear through flesh and break bone. He was loyal to Casteel, and yet instinct told me that it wasn't just the guards he warned.

Another snarl came from my left. In the shadows of the blood tree that had sprouted from where my blood had fallen and then grew to a massive height within seconds, a fawn-colored wolven crept into my line of sight, head dipped low, and wintery blue eyes iridescent. *Kieran.* He stared down Casteel. I didn't understand why either of them would behave this way toward the Prince, but especially Kieran. He had been bonded to Casteel from birth, meant to obey and protect him at all costs. But he was more than a bonded wolven to Casteel. They were brothers, if not by blood then by friendship, and I knew they loved each other.

Right now, nothing about the way Kieran's ears were pinned back was *loving.*

Unease skipped its way through me as Kieran sank down, the sleek muscles of his legs tensing as he prepared to attack…Casteel.

My stomach plummeted. This wasn't right. None of this was right. "No," I rasped, my voice hoarse and barely recognizable, even to my ears.

Kieran didn't appear to hear me or care. If he had been acting normally, I would've just assumed he was attempting to ignore me, but this was different. *He* was different. His eyes were brighter than I ever remembered seeing, and they weren't right because they…they weren't just blue now. His pupils glowed silvery-white, an aura that seeped out in wispy tendrils across the blue. My head jerked to Jasper. His eyes had changed, too. I'd seen that strange light before. It had been what my skin had done when I healed Beckett's broken legs—the same silvery glow that had radiated from me minutes earlier.

Icy bursts of surprise raced through Casteel as he eyed the wolven, and then I felt…*relief* radiate from him.

"You all knew." Casteel's voice filled with awe, something no one standing behind him felt. Even the easy grin was absent from the auburn-haired Atlantian. Emil looked at us with wide eyes, broadcasting a healthy dose of fear, as did Naill, who had always appeared utterly unfazed by everything—even when he'd been outnumbered in battle.

Casteel slowly sheathed his swords at his sides. Hands empty, he kept them down. "You all knew something was happening to her. That's why..." He trailed off, his jaw hardening.

Several of the guards moved to the front of the King and Queen, surrounding them fully—

A shock of white fur shot forward. Delano tucked his tail back as he pawed at the marble. He lifted his head and howled. The eerie yet beautiful sound raised the tiny hairs all over my body.

Off in the distance, the faint sounds of yips and barks answered, growing louder with each second. The leaves on the tall, cone-shaped trees separating the Temple from Saion's Cove trembled as a rolling rumble echoed from the ground below. Blue-and-yellow-winged birds took flight from the trees, scattering to the sky.

"Godsdamn." Emil turned to the Temple steps. He reached for the swords at his sides. "They're summoning the whole damn city."

"It's her." The deep scar slicing across the older wolven's forehead stood out starkly. Potent disbelief rolled off Alastir as he stood just outside the circle of guards who'd formed around Casteel's parents.

"It is not her," Casteel shot back.

"But it is," King Valyn confirmed as he stared at me from a face that Casteel's would one day become. "They're responding to her. That's why the ones on the road with us shifted without warning. She called them to her."

"I…I didn't call anyone," I told Casteel, voice cracking.

"I know." Casteel's tone softened as his eyes locked with mine.

"But she did," his mother insisted. "You might not realize it, but you did summon them."

My eyes darted to her, and I felt my chest wrench. She was everything I'd imagined Casteel's mother to be. Stunning. Regal. Powerful. Calm now, even as she remained on one knee, even when she had first seen me and demanded of her son—*What have you done? What have you brought back?* I flinched, fearing those words would stay with me long after today.

Casteel's features sharpened as golden eyes swept over my face. "If the idiots behind me actually laid down their swords instead of lifting them against my *wife*, we wouldn't have an entire colony of wolven about to descend on us," he bit out. "They are only reacting to the threat."

"You're right," his father agreed as he gently guided his wife to her feet. Blood soaked the knee and the hem of her lilac gown. "But ask yourself why your bonded wolven is guarding someone other than *you*."

"I really couldn't care less at the moment," Casteel responded as the sound of hundreds—if not more—of paws pounding the earth grew even closer. He couldn't be serious. He had to care, because that was a damn good question.

"You need to care," his mother cautioned, a thin quiver in her otherwise steady voice. "The bonds have broken."

The bonds? Hands trembling, my wide eyes shot to the Temple steps, to where Emil slowly backed away. Naill had his swords in his hands now.

"She's right," Alastir uttered, the skin around his mouth appearing even whiter. "I can… I can feel it—the Primal *notam*. Her mark. Good gods." His voice trembled as he stumbled back, nearly stepping on the crown. "They've all broken."

I had no idea what a *notam* was, but through the confusion and the blossoming panic, there was something odd about what Alastir had stated. If it was true, then why wasn't he in his wolven form? Was it because he'd already broken his wolven bond with the former King of Atlantia all those years ago?

"Look at their eyes," the Queen ordered softly, pointing out what I'd seen. "I know you don't understand. There are things you never needed to learn, Hawke." Her voice cracked then, thickened at the use of his nickname—a name I'd once believed to be nothing more than a lie. "But what you need to know now is that they no longer serve the elemental bloodline. You are not safe. Please," she begged. "Please. Listen to me, Hawke."

"How?" I croaked. "How could the bond break?"

"That doesn't matter right now." The amber of Casteel's eyes was nearly luminous. "You're bleeding," he said as if that were the most important issue at hand.

But it wasn't. "How?" I repeated.

"It's what you are." Eloana's left hand balled into the skirt of her gown. "You have the blood of a god in you—"

"I'm mortal," I told her.

A thick lock of dark hair tumbled from her knot as she shook her head. "Yes, you are mortal, but you are descended from a deity—the children of the gods. All it takes is a drop of god's blood—" She swallowed thickly. "You may have more than just a drop, but what is in your blood, what is in *you*, supersedes any oath the wolven have taken."

I remembered then what Kieran had told me in New Haven about the wolven. The gods had given the once-wild kiyou wolves mortal form to serve as guides and protectors to the children of the gods—the deities. Something else Kieran had shared then explained the Queen's reaction.

My gaze shot to the crown lying near Nyktos's feet. A drop of deity blood usurped any claim to the Atlantian throne.

Oh, gods, there was a good chance I really might pass out. And how embarrassing would that be?

Eloana's gaze shifted to her son's rigid back. "You go near her? Right now? They will see you as a threat to her. They will rip you apart."

My heart stuttered to a panicked stop. Casteel looked as if he might do just that. Behind me, one of the smaller wolven lurched forward, barking and snapping at the air.

Every muscle in my body tensed. "Casteel—"

"It's okay." Casteel's eyes never left mine. "No one is going to harm Poppy. I will not allow that." His chest rose with a deep, heavy breath. "And you know that, right?"

I nodded as each breath came too fast, too shallowly. It was the only thing I understood at the moment.

"Everything's all right. They're just protecting you." Casteel smiled for me then, but it was tense and tight. He looked to my left, at Kieran. "I don't know everything that is going on right now, but you—all of you—want to keep her safe. And I'm all about that. You know I would never hurt her. I would tear out my own heart before I did that. She's injured. I need to make sure she's okay, and nothing is going to stop me from doing that." He didn't blink as he held Kieran's stare, as the rolling thunder of the other wolven reached the Temple steps. "Not even you. Any of you. I will destroy every single one of you who stands between her and me."

Kieran's growl deepened, and an emotion I'd never felt from him before poured into me. It was like anger, but older. And it felt like that buzz in my blood had. Ancient. Primal.

And in an instant, I could see it all playing out in my mind as if it were happening before me. Kieran would attack. Or maybe it would be Jasper. I'd seen what kind of damage a wolven could inflict, but Casteel wouldn't go down easily. He would do just as he'd promised. He'd tear through all that stood between him and me. Wolven would die, and if he harmed Kieran—if he did worse than that, the wolven's blood wouldn't just be on Casteel's hands. It would mark his soul till the day he died.

A wave of wolven crested the Temple's stairs, both small and large, in so many different colors. Their arrival brought terrifying knowledge. Casteel was incredibly strong and unbelievably fast. He would take down many. But he would fall with them.

He would die.

Casteel would die because of me—because I called to these wolven and didn't know how to make it stop. My heart thumped erratically. A wolven near the steps stalked Emil as he continued backing up. Another tracked Naill as he spoke softly to the wolven, attempting to reason with the creature. The others had zeroed in on the guards surrounding the King and Queen, and a few... Oh, gods, several of them crept up behind Casteel. This had slipped into chaos, the wolven beyond control of any of them...

I sucked in a sharp breath as my mind raced, breaking free of the pain and turbulence. Something had happened within me to make that drop of god's blood break the bonds. I superseded their previous oaths, and that had...it had to mean that they now obeyed *me*.

"Stop," I ordered as Kieran snapped at Casteel, whose own lips were now peeled back. "Kieran! Stop! You will not hurt Casteel." My voice rose as a soft hum returned to my blood. "All of you will stop. Now! None of you will attack."

It was like a switch had been thrown in the wolven's minds. One second they were all poised to attack, and then they were sinking onto their bellies, lowering their heads between their front paws. I could still feel their anger, the old power, but it had lessened already, was fading in steady waves.

Emil lowered his sword. "That…that was timely. Thank you for that."

A ragged breath left me as a tremor traveled up and down my arms. I almost couldn't believe it'd worked as I scanned the Temple, seeing all the wolven lying down. My entire being wanted to rebel against further confirmation of what the Queen had claimed, but gods, there was only so much I could deny. Throat dry, I looked at Casteel.

He stared at me, his eyes wide once more. I couldn't breathe. My heart wouldn't slow enough for me to make sense of what he was feeling.

"He will not hurt me. You all know that," I said, my voice shaking as I looked at Jasper and then Kieran. "You told me that he was the only person in both kingdoms that I was safe with. That hasn't changed."

Kieran's ears twitched, and then he rose, backing up. He turned, nudging my hand with his nose.

"Thank you," I whispered, briefly closing my eyes.

"Just so you know," Casteel murmured, thick lashes lowered halfway, "what you just did? Said? It has me feeling all kinds of wildly inappropriate things at the moment."

A weak, shaky laugh left me. "There's something so wrong with you."

"I know." The left side of his lips curved, and his dimple appeared. "But you love that about me."

I did. Gods, I really did.

Jasper shook out his fur as his large head swung from me to Casteel. He turned sideways, making a rough, huffing sound as he did. The other wolven moved then, coming out from behind the blood tree. I watched them trot past me—past Casteel and the others—ears perked and tails wagging as they joined those descending the steps and left the Temple. Of the wolven, only Jasper, his son, and Delano remained, and the feeling of chaotic tension lifted.

A thick lock of dark hair fell over Casteel's forehead. "You were glowing silver again. When you ordered the wolven to stop," he told me. "Not a lot, not like before, but you looked like spun moonlight."

Had I been? I glanced down at my hands. They looked normal. "I...I don't know what's happening," I whispered, my legs shaking. "I don't know what's going on." I lifted my eyes to his and watched him take a step forward, and then another. There were no snarls of warning. Nothing. My throat started to burn. I could feel it—tears creeping into my eyes. I couldn't cry. I *wouldn't.* Everything had already turned into enough of a mess without me sobbing hysterically. But I was so tired. I *hurt*, and it went beyond the physical.

When I first stepped into this Temple and looked out over the clear waters of the Seas of Saion, I'd felt like I was *home.* And I knew things would be hard. Proving that our union was real wouldn't be nearly as difficult as gaining the acceptance of Casteel's parents and that of his kingdom. We still needed to find his brother, Prince Malik. And mine. We had to deal with the Ascended Queen and King. Nothing about our future would be easy, but I had hope.

Now, I felt foolish. So naïve. The older wolven in Spessa's End, the one I'd helped heal after the battle, had warned me about the people of Atlantia. *They did not choose you.* And I now doubted they ever would.

I drew in a stuttering breath and whispered, "I didn't want any of this."

Tension bracketed Casteel's mouth. "I know." His voice was rough, but his touch was gentle as he placed his palm over the cheek that didn't feel swollen. He lowered his forehead to mine, and the shock of awareness his flesh against mine brought was there, rippling through me as he slid his hand into the tangled mess of my hair. "I know, Princess," he whispered, and I squeezed my eyes shut against a stronger rush of tears. "It's okay. It will all be okay. I promise you that."

I nodded, even though I knew it wasn't something he could guarantee. Not anymore. I forced myself to swallow the knot of emotion that rose.

Casteel kissed my blood-streaked brow and then lifted his head. "Emil? Can you retrieve clothing from Delano's and Kieran's horses so they can shift and not scar anyone?"

"I'll be more than happy to do that," the Atlantian answered.

I almost laughed. "I think their nakedness will be the least scarring thing to happen today."

Casteel said nothing as he touched my cheek again, gently tilting my head to the side. His gaze then dropped to several of the rocks still littering the ground at my feet. A muscle popped along his jaw. His eyes lifted to mine, and I saw his pupils were dilated, only a thin strip of amber visible. "They tried to *stone* you?"

I heard a soft gasp I thought had come from his mother, but I didn't look. I didn't want to see their faces. I didn't want to know what they felt right now. "They accused me of working with the Ascended, and they called me a Soul Eater. I told them I wasn't. I tried to talk to them." Words spilled out in a rush as I lifted my hands to touch him, but I stopped. I didn't know what my touch would do. Hell, I didn't even know what I would do *without* touching someone. "I tried to reason with them, but they started throwing stones. I told them to stop. I said it was enough, and…I don't know what I did—" I started to look over his shoulder, but Casteel seemed to know what it was I searched for. He stopped me. "I didn't mean to kill them."

"You were defending yourself." His pupils constricted as he caught my stare. "You did what you had to do. You were defending yourself—"

"But I didn't touch them, Casteel," I whispered. "It was like in Spessa's End, during the battle. Remember the soldiers who surrounded us? When they fell, I felt something in me. I felt that again here. It was like something inside me knew what to do. I took their anger and I—I did exactly what a Soul Eater *would* do. I took it from them and then gave it back."

"You are not a Soul Eater," Queen Eloana said from somewhere not too far away. "The moment the eather in your blood became visible, those who attacked you should've known exactly what you were. What you are."

"Eather?"

"It's what some would call magic," Casteel answered, shifting his stance as if he were blocking his mother from me. "You've seen it before."

"The mist?"

He nodded. "It's the essence of the gods, what's in their blood, what gives them their abilities and the power to create all that they have. No one really calls it that anymore, not since the gods went to sleep, and the deities died off." His eyes searched mine. "I should have known. Gods, I should've seen it…"

"You can say that now," his mother spoke. "But why would you have even thought that this would be a possibility? No one would've expected this."

"Except for you," Casteel said. And he was right. She'd known, without a doubt. And, granted, I had been glowing upon her arrival, but she'd known with unquestioned certainty.

"I can explain," she said as Emil appeared, carrying two saddlebags. He gave all of us a wide berth as he dropped them near Jasper and then backed away.

"Apparently, a lot needs to be explained," Casteel remarked coolly. "But it will have to wait." His gaze touched on my left cheek, and that muscle throbbed along his jaw again. "I need to get you somewhere safe where I can… Where I can take care of you."

"You can take her to your old rooms at my place," Jasper announced, startling me. I hadn't even heard him shift. I started to look over at him but saw skin as he reached for the saddlebag.

"That will do." Casteel took what appeared to be a pair of breeches from Jasper. "Thank you."

"Will it be safe for you there?" I asked, and a wry grin tugged at Casteel's lips.

"He'll be safe there," Kieran answered.

So shocked by the sound of Kieran's voice, I turned. And didn't stop. There was a whole lot of tawny skin on display, but he stood there like he wasn't naked in front of all who remained. For once, I really had no problem ignoring the fact that he was nude. I looked at his eyes. They were normal—a vivid, striking blue without the silvery-white aura. "You were going to attack Casteel."

Kieran nodded as he took the pants from Casteel.

"He most definitely was," Casteel confirmed.

I looked back at my husband. "And you threatened to destroy him."

The dimple in his left cheek appeared again. "I did."

"Why are you smiling? That isn't something that should make you smile." I stared at him, stupid tears burning my eyes. I didn't care that we had an audience. "That can never happen again. Do you hear me?" I twisted to Kieran, who arched a brow as he pulled his breeches up over his lean hips. "Do you both hear me? I won't allow it. I won't—"

"Shh." Casteel's light touch to my cheek drew my gaze back to his as he stepped into me. He was close enough that his chest brushed mine with each breath. "It won't happen again, Poppy." His thumb quickly swiped under my left eye. "Right?"

"Right." Kieran cleared his throat. "I don't…" He fell quiet.

His father didn't. "As long as the Prince doesn't give any of us a reason to behave differently, we will protect him as fiercely as we will protect you."

We. As in the entirety of the wolven race. That's what Alastir had meant when he'd said that all the bonds had broken. I had a lot of questions, but I plopped my head on Casteel's chest. It didn't feel that great, sending a flare of pain across my head. I didn't care because when I inhaled, all I smelled was lush spice and pine. Casteel carefully folded an arm around my upper back, and I thought… I thought I felt him shudder against me.

"Wait," Kieran said. "Where is Beckett? He was with you when you walked off."

Casteel drew back slightly. "That's right. He offered to show you the Temple." His eyes narrowed as he stared down at me. "He led you here."

A wave of goosebumps pimpled my skin. *Beckett.* Pressure clamped down on my chest, squeezing tightly as I thought of the young wolven who'd spent the vast majority of the trip here chasing butterflies. I still couldn't believe that he had led me here, knowing what awaited. But I remembered the bitter taste of his fear that day in Spessa's End. He'd been terrified of me.

Or had he been terrified of something else?

His emotions had been all over the place. He'd gone from being normal around me, happy and grinning, to suddenly afraid and anxious, as he had been when he brought me up here.

"He disappeared before the others showed up," I told Casteel. "I don't know where he went."

"Find Beckett," he ordered, and Delano, still in his wolven form, tilted his head. "Naill? Emil? Go with him. Make sure Beckett is brought to me alive."

Both Atlantians nodded and bowed. Nothing about Casteel's tone suggested that the *alive* part was a good thing. "He's just a kid." I watched Delano rush off, quickly disappearing with Naill and Emil. "He was scared. And now that I think about it—"

"Poppy." Casteel placed the tips of his fingers against my cheek, just below a spot that ached. He dipped his head, brushing his lips over the cut. "I have two things to say. If Beckett had anything to do with this, I don't care what or who he is, and I sure as fuck don't care about what he was feeling." His voice rose until all who remained at the Temple could hear him, including his parents.

"A move against my wife is a proclamation of war against *me*. Their fate is already sealed. And, secondly?" He lowered his head even farther. This time, his lips brushed over mine in a featherlight kiss. I could barely feel it, but it somehow still managed to twist my insides into knots. He then lifted his head, and I saw it in his features—the stark stillness of a predator locking onto its prey. I'd seen it before, right before he'd torn out Landell's heart back in New Haven.

Casteel turned his head to the side, looking at the only wolven who remained, now standing on two legs. "*You*."

Chapter 2

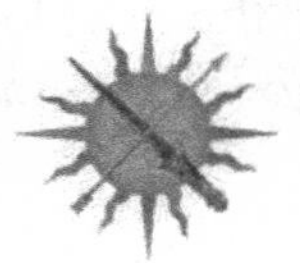

Alastir Davenwell was Casteel's parents' advisor. And when King Malec had Ascended his mistress, Isbeth, it was Alastir who had alerted Queen Eloana, breaking the bond between him and the now exiled—most likely dead—King. Only the gods knew how many Atlantians Alastir had saved throughout the years by helping them escape Solis and the Ascended, who used their blood to make more vamprys.

Who knew how different things would've turned out for my family if they had found Alastir? They could still be alive, living a happy and whole life in Atlantia. And my brother Ian would be there, too. Instead, he was in Carsodonia and was likely now one of them—an Ascended.

I swallowed hard, shoving those thoughts aside. Now was not the time for that. I liked Alastir. He had been kind to me from the beginning. But more importantly, I knew that Casteel respected and cared for the wolven. If Alastir had played a role in this, it would cut Casteel deeply.

Honestly, I hoped that neither Alastir nor Beckett had had anything to do with this, but I had long stopped believing in coincidences. And the night the Ascended had arrived at Spessa's End? I had realized something about Alastir that hadn't sat well with me. It had fallen to the wayside when the Ascended arrived and with everything that had happened afterward, but it took center stage once more.

Casteel had once planned to marry Shea—Alastir's daughter—but then Casteel had been captured by the Ascended, and Shea had betrayed him and his brother in an attempt to save her life. Everyone, including Alastir, believed that Shea had died heroically, but I knew the true tragedy of how she'd perished. However, Alastir also had a great-niece, a wolven that both he and King Valyn hoped Casteel would marry upon his return to the kingdom. It was something he'd announced at dinner, claiming he believed that Casteel had already told me. I wasn't so sure he truly believed that, but that was neither here nor there.

I couldn't be the only person who found the whole thing…weird. Alastir's daughter? And now his great-niece? I doubted there weren't plenty of other wolven or Atlantians that would've also been well suited to marry Casteel, especially since Casteel had given no indication that he'd be interested in such a union.

None of that made Alastir guilty, but it *was* strange.

Now the wolven looked absolutely thunderstruck as he stared back at Casteel. "I don't know what you think Beckett did or how it has anything to do with me, but my nephew would never be involved in something like this. He's a pup. And I would—"

"Shut the hell up," Casteel growled as I peeked around his shoulder.

The wolven blanched. "Casteel—"

"Do not make me repeat myself," he interrupted, turning to the guards. "Seize Alastir."

"What?" Alastir exploded as half the guards turned to him, while the others nervously glanced between Casteel and the only King and Queen they knew.

The King's eyes narrowed on his son. "Alastir has committed no crime that we know of."

"Maybe he hasn't. Maybe he is completely innocent, as is his great-nephew. But until we know for sure, I want him held," Casteel stated. "Seize him, or I will."

Jasper prowled forward, growling low in his throat as his muscles strained under his mortal skin. The guards shifted nervously.

"Wait!" Alastir shouted, his cheeks mottling as anger pulsed around him. "He does not have the kind of authority required to make demands of the Guards of the Crown."

I imagined the Crown Guard was a lot like the Royal Guard that served the Ascended. They only took orders from Queen Ileana and King Jalara, and whatever Royal Ascended were seated to lord over a city or town.

"Correct me if I'm wrong. I don't think I am, but stranger things have happened," Casteel said, and my brows puckered. "My mother removed the crown and told everyone here to bow before the new Queen—who happens to be my wife. Therefore, according to Atlantian tradition, that makes me the King, no matter what head the crown rests upon."

My heart tumbled. King. Queen. That couldn't be us.

"You never wanted the throne or the trappings that come with that crown," Alastir spat. "You spent decades seeking to free your brother so he could take the throne. And yet now you seek to claim it? You've truly given up on your brother then?"

I sucked in a sharp breath as anger flooded me. Alastir, of all people, knew how much finding and freeing Malik meant to Casteel. And his words had cut deep. I felt from Casteel then what I'd sensed the very first time I ever laid eyes on him—a rawness that felt like shards of ice against my skin. Casteel was always in pain, and even though it had lessened a little with each passing day, the agony he felt over his brother was never far from the surface. He'd just recently allowed himself to feel something other than the guilt, the shame, and the anguish.

I didn't even realize I had moved forward until I saw that I was no longer under the shade of the blood tree. "Casteel hasn't given up on Malik," I snapped before I could find my damn dagger and throw it across the Temple. "We will find him and free him. Malik has nothing to do with any of this."

"Oh, gods." Eloana pressed her hand to her mouth as she turned to her son. Pain tightened her features, and in an instant, soul-deep sorrow rolled off her in potent waves. I couldn't see it, but her grief was a constant shadow that followed her, just as it did for Casteel. It hammered at my senses, scraping my skin like frozen, broken glass. "*Hawke,* what have you done?"

My focus darted to Valyn as I shut down the connection with Casteel's mother before it overwhelmed me. A jagged pulse of grief surrounded him, pierced by a surge of peppery, desperate anger. But he locked it down with a strength that I couldn't help but admire and envy. He bent and whispered in his wife's ears. Closing her eyes, she nodded at whatever he said.

Oh, gods, I shouldn't have said that. "I'm sorry." I clasped my hands together tightly. "I didn't—"

"You have nothing to apologize for," Casteel said, looking over his shoulder at me and finding my gaze with his. What radiated from him was warm and sweet, overshadowing the icy ache a bit.

"It is I who should apologize," Alastir stated gruffly, surprising me. "I shouldn't have brought Malik into this. You were right."

Casteel eyed him, and I knew he didn't know what to do with Alastir's apology. Neither did I. Instead, he focused on his parents. "I know what you're likely thinking. It's the same thing Alastir believed. You think my marriage to Penellaphe is yet another fruitless ploy to free Malik."

"It's not?" his mother whispered, tears filling her eyes. "We know you took her to use her."

"I did," Casteel confirmed. "But that's not why we married. That's not why we're together."

Hearing all of this used to bother me. The truth of how Casteel and I had gotten to this place was an uncomfortable one, but it no longer made me feel as if my skin no longer fit. I looked down at the band around my pointer finger and the vibrant golden swirl across my left palm. The corners of my lips turned up. Casteel had come for me with plans to use me, but that had changed long before either of us realized it. The *how* no longer mattered.

"I want to believe that," his mother whispered. Her concern was oppressive, like a coarse, too-thick blanket. Maybe she *wanted* to believe it, but it was clear that she didn't.

"That is something else we need to discuss." Valyn cleared his throat, and it was clear that he too doubted his son's motivations. "As of right now, you are not the King, nor is she the Queen. Eloana had a very impassioned moment when she took off her crown," he said, squeezing his wife's shoulders. The way her entire face pinched in response to her husband's comment was something I felt deep in my soul. "A coronation would have to take place, and the crowning would have to go uncontested."

"Contest *her* claim?" Jasper laughed as he folded his arms over his chest. "Even if she wasn't married to an heir, her claim cannot be contested. You know that. We all know that."

My stomach felt as if I were back on the edge of the cliff in the Skotos Mountains. I didn't want the throne. Neither did Casteel.

"Be that as it may," Valyn drawled, eyes narrowing, "until we discover who was involved in this and have had time to speak, Alastir should be kept somewhere safe."

Alastir turned to him. "That's—"

"Something you will accept, graciously." Valyn silenced the wolven with one look, and it was quite clear exactly where Casteel had gotten that ability from. "This is as much for your benefit as it is for everyone else. Fight this, and I'm sure Jasper, Kieran, or my son will be at your throat in a heartbeat. And at this moment, I cannot promise that I would move to stay any of them."

Casteel's chin lowered, and his smile was as cold as the first breath of winter. The tips of his fangs appeared. "It'll be me."

Alastir glanced between Jasper and his Prince. Lowering his hands to his sides, his chest rose with a heavy breath. His wintry blue eyes fixed on Casteel. "You are like a son to me. You would've been my son if fate hadn't had something else in store for all of us," he said, and I knew he was thinking of his daughter. The sincerity in his words, the rawness of the pain he felt sliced into him, cutting deeply, and fell like icy rain, only increasing when Casteel said nothing. How he'd kept that level of pain hidden from me was stunning. "The truth of what is happening here will be revealed. Everyone will know I am not the threat."

I felt it then as I stared at Alastir. A surge of…determination and steely resolve pumping hotly through his veins. It was quick, but instinct flared inside me, screaming out a warning I didn't fully understand. I stepped forward. "Casteel—"

I wasn't quick enough.

"Protect your King and Queen," Alastir commanded.

Several of the guards moved, surrounding Casteel's parents. One of them reached behind his back. Valyn spun around. "Don't!"

Jasper shot forward, shifting in mid-leap as Eloana screamed out a hoarse cry. "No!"

An arrow struck the wolven in the shoulder, stopping him in midair. He went down, slipping back into his mortal form before he slammed into the cracked marble. I stumbled back, shocked as Jasper went still, a pale, gray color sweeping across his skin. Was he—?

My heart froze at the sound of high-pitched yelps and snarls coming from below the Temple. The other wolven—

An arrow zinged through the air, striking Kieran as he leapt toward me. A scream caught in my throat as I lurched toward him. He caught himself before he fell, his back jerking straight and then bowing. The tendons in his neck stood out starkly as my eyes locked with his. The irises were a luminous blue-silver as he reached for the arrow protruding from his shoulder—a thin shaft leaking a grayish liquid. "Run," he snarled, taking a stiff, unnatural step toward me. "*Run.*"

I ran toward him, grabbing his arm as one of his legs buckled. His skin—gods, his skin was like a chunk of ice. I tried to hold him, but his weight was too much, and he hit the ground on his back as Casteel reached my side, folding an arm around my waist. Horrified, I watched the gray pallor sweep over Kieran's tawny skin, and I…I felt nothing. Not from him. Not from Jasper. They couldn't be…this couldn't be happening. "Kieran—?"

Casteel suddenly spun me behind him, a roar of fury exploding from him, tasting of icy-hot rage. Something hit him, knocking him away from me. His mother screamed, and my head jerked up in time to see Queen Eloana shoving her elbow into a guard's face. Bone cracked and gave way as she rushed forward, but another guard grabbed her from behind.

"Stop! Stop this now!" Eloana ordered. "I command you!"

Terror sank its claws into me as I saw the arrow jutting out of Casteel's lower back—also leaking that strange, gray substance. But he still stood in front of me, sword in one hand. The sound that rumbled out of him promised death. He stepped forward—

Another arrow came from the Temple's entrance, striking Casteel in the shoulder as I saw Valyn shove a sword deep into the stomach of a man holding a bow. The projectile pierced Casteel's leg, throwing him back. I caught him around the waist as his balance faltered, but like Kieran, his weight was too much. The sword clattered off the marble as he went down hard, the long length of his body straining as he kicked his head back. The tendons in his neck bulged as I dropped beside him, not even feeling the impact on my knees. Gray liquid poured from the wounds, mingling with blood as his lips peeled back from his fangs. Veins swelled and darkened under his skin.

No. No. No.

I couldn't breathe as his wild, dilated eyes met mine. *This isn't happening.* Those words repeated themselves over and over in my mind as I bent over, clutching his cheeks with shaking hands. I cried out at the feeling of his too-cold skin. Nothing alive felt this cold. Oh, gods, his skin didn't even feel like flesh anymore.

"Poppy, I…" he gasped out as he reached for me. A gray film crept across the whites of his eyes and then the irises, dulling the vivid amber.

He went still, his gaze fixed on some point beyond me. His chest didn't move.

"Casteel," I whispered, trying to shake him, but his skin—his entire body—had…it had hardened like stone. He was frozen, his back arched and one leg curled, an arm lifted toward me. "*Casteel.*"

There was no answer.

I opened my senses wide to him, desperately seeking any hint of emotion, anything. But there was nothing. It was like he had entered the deepest level of sleep or was…

No. No. No. He couldn't be gone. He couldn't be dead.

Only a handful of seconds had passed from the time Alastir had issued his initial command to Casteel lying before me, his body drained of the vibrancy of life.

I quickly looked over my shoulder. Neither Jasper nor Kieran moved, and their skin had deepened to a dark gray color, the hue of iron.

Panic-fueled agony flooded me, entrenching itself in the area around my pounding heart as I slid my hands to Casteel's chest, feeling for a heartbeat. "Please. Please," I whispered, tears gathering in my eyes. "*Please.* Don't do this to me. Please."

Nothing.

I felt nothing in him, Kieran, or Jasper. A hum whirred within the very core of my being as I stared down at Casteel—at my husband. My heartmate. My *everything.*

He was lost to me.

My skin began to vibrate as a dark and oily, soul-deep rage rose within me. It had a tang like metal in the back of my throat and burned like fire in my veins. It tasted like *death.* And not the kind that occurred here—the final kind.

Fury swelled and expanded until I could no longer contain it. I didn't even try to stop it as tears tracked down my cheeks and fell on Casteel's iron-colored skin. The rage lashed out, pounding the air and seeping into the stone. Under me, I felt the Temple begin to faintly tremble once more. Someone shouted, but I was past hearing words.

Leaning over Casteel, I picked up his fallen sword as I brushed my lips over his still, stone-cold lips. That *ancient* thing inside me pulsed and throbbed as it had done before as I rose above my husband and turned. A sharp wind whipped across the Temple floor, extinguishing the fire of the torches. The leaves of the blood tree rattled like dry bones as my grip on the short sword tightened. I didn't see Casteel's parents. I didn't even see Alastir.

Dozens stood before me, all garbed in white, holding swords and daggers. Familiar metal masks, those worn by the Descenters, hid their faces. Seeing them now should've terrified me.

It only *enraged* me.

That primal power surged, invading all of my senses. It silenced every emotion inside me until only one remained: *vengeance.* There was nothing else. No empathy. No compassion.

I was me.

And yet, I was something else entirely.

The sky above was free of clouds, remaining a stunning shade of blue. Blood didn't rain, but my flesh *sparked.* Silvery-white embers danced over my skin and crackled as wispy cords stretched out from me, swathing the columns like glistening spiderwebs and flowing across the floor in a network of shimmering veins. My rage had become a tangible entity, a living, breathing force that could not be escaped. I stepped forward, and the top layer of stone shattered under my boot.

Tiny pieces of stone and dust broke away, drifting down. Several of the masked attackers moved back as thin fissures appeared in the statues of the gods. The cracks along the floor grew.

A masked attacker broke from the line, rushing me. Sunlight reflected off the blade of his sword as he lifted it into the air. I didn't move as the wind picked up the tangled strands of my hair. He yelled as he brought the hilt of the weapon's handle down on me—

I caught his arm, halting the blow as I shoved Casteel's blade deep into his chest. Red poured across the front of his tunic as he shuddered, falling to the side. Four more charged me, and I spun under the arm of one as I thrust up the blade, slicing open another's throat. Blood sprayed as I whipped around, swinging the sword through the metal mask. A sharp, stinging pain raced across my back as I planted my foot in the center of the man's chest and pushed off as I yanked the blade free of his skull.

A hand grabbed me, and I twisted, slamming the blade deep into the attacker's belly. I jerked the hilt of the sword sharply as I dragged it through the man's stomach, voicing the rage inside me with a scream. That rage pulsed into the air around me, and a statue near the back of the Temple broke in two. Chunks of stone crashed to the floor.

Another ripple of pain flowed over my leg. I turned, sweeping the sword in a high arc. The blade met little resistance. A dagger fell into my hand as a head and mask rolled in opposite directions. Out of the corner of my eye, I saw one of the Descenters grab Kieran's stiff body by the arms. Flipping the dagger in my hand, I cocked back my arm and threw it. The blade struck under the mask, and the attacker pinwheeled backward, clutching at his throat.

Movement caught my attention. A wave of masked assailants raced across the Temple. Silvery-white light edged into my vision as I heard a voice—a woman's voice—whispering inside me. *It wasn't supposed to be this way.*

In a flash, I saw her, hair like moonlight as she thrust her hands deep into the ground. Some inherent knowledge told me that she was where this Temple now stood, but in a different time, back when the world was an unknown place. She threw back her head, screaming with a kind of pained fury that throbbed relentlessly inside me. Silvery-white light drenched the soil, radiating out from where she touched. The ground cracked open, and thin, bleached-white fingers dug out from the dirt all around her, nothing more than bones. Her words reached me once more. *I am done with this, all of this.*

As was I.

I shuddered, the image of the woman fading as I tossed the sword aside. In the emptiness of my mind, I pictured the glittering cords peeling off the columns. They did so before me, draping over a dozen of the attackers like fine webbing. I wanted them to feel as I did inside. Broken. Twisted. Lost.

Bone cracked. Arms and legs snapped. Backs broke. They fell like shattered saplings.

Others turned away from me, to run. Flee. I would not allow that. They would pay. All of them would taste and drown in my wrath. I would bring this structure down and then rip the entire kingdom apart to ensure it. They would feel what was inside me, what they wrought. Threefold.

Rage poured from me in another scream as I stalked forward, lifting my arms. The cords rose from the floor. In my mind, they grew and multiplied, stretching out beyond the Chambers of Nyktos to the trees and the city below. I started to rise—

In the chaos, I saw *him*. Alastir stood near the front of the Temple, just out of reach of the pulsating rage and energy. I didn't sense fear from him. Just acceptance as he stared at me as if he'd expected this.

Alastir met my gaze. "I'm not the threat to Atlantia," he said. "You are. You have always been the threat."

Pain exploded along the back of my head, so sudden and so overwhelming that nothing could stop the darkness from rushing me.

I fell into nothing.

Chapter 3

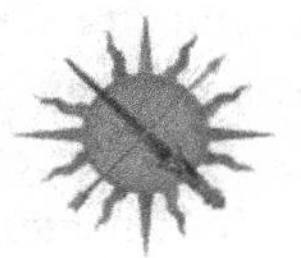

What a pretty little flower.

What a pretty poppy.

Pick it and watch it bleed.

Not so pretty any longer.

I came to, gulping in a deep breath of air that smelled of damp soil and old decay. The horrible rhyme echoed in my aching head as I opened my eyes and gasped, choking on a scream.

Dark, empty eye sockets stared back at me from a dusty, dirty skull.

Heart slamming against my ribs, I shot upright and scuttled back. I made it about a foot when something tightened painfully, sharply jerking my arms and legs. I ground my teeth, stifling a whimper as the skin of my wrists and below my knees burned. Someone had removed my sweater and left me in only the too-thin slip I'd worn under the top. Any concern I might've felt over where my sweater and pants had gone, or how the cinched bodice of the slip did very little to hide anything, fell away as I stared at my hands.

Bones… Polished, ivory bones were twisted around my wrists. Bones and…and vines. And some part of them dug into my skin. I carefully drew up one leg, chest rising and falling rapidly as I saw the same just below my knees. Upon closer inspection, I saw that they weren't vines. They appeared to be some kind of root. Dried blood streaked my calves as I reached for the manacle—

Fiery pain branded my wrists, stopping me. "Gods," I hissed through my teeth as I carefully leaned back against something hard, damp, and cold. A wall?

Throat dry, my gaze followed the twist of bone and roots to where it connected with the wall. My breath came out in short, uneven pants as I glanced back at the…the *thing* beside me. Patches of thin, stringy, blond hair hung in clumps from the skull. Only pieces of tattered clothing remained, darkened by age and dirt. I had no idea if it had been male or female, but it had clearly been here for decades—maybe even centuries. Some kind of spear rested against the corpse's chest, the blade a chalky black. Ice drenched my entire being as I saw the same knotted bones and roots encircling its wrists and ankles. Air lodged in my throat as my gaze lifted to what sat on the other side of the body. More remains, bound in the same manner. And there was another, and another—propped against the entire length of the wall—dozens of them.

Oh, gods.

My wide gaze darted wildly around. Torches jutted out from gray-black columns in the center of the space and farther back, casting an orange glow across…

Horror filled me as I saw several raised stone slabs—long and square boxes situated between two rows of pillars. Oh, gods. I knew what they were. *Sarcophagi.* Sarcophagi smothered by coiled bone and root chain, the bindings draped over each one.

I was in a crypt.

And it was clear that I wasn't the first to be held here.

Panic crept up my throat, making it even harder to breathe in the cold, dank air. My pulse pounded sickeningly fast. Nausea rose, cramping my stomach as I searched the shadows beyond the sarcophagi and pillars. I had no recollection of how I'd arrived here or how long I'd—

Casteel.

An image of him formed in my mind, reaching for me as his skin turned gray and hardened. Pressure clamped down on my chest, grinding my heart. I squeezed my eyes shut against the rush of dampness rising, but it was no use. I still saw him, his back arched and body contorted, his eyes dulling, his gaze fixing. He couldn't be gone. Neither could Kieran or Jasper. They had to be fine. I just needed to get out of here and find them.

I moved to stand—

The bindings snapped against my skin, digging in deeper. A hoarse cry parted my dry lips as I fell back against the wall. Inhaling deeply, I lifted my arm to get a better look at the chain. Spurs. The bones had sharpened spurs on them.

"Shit," I whispered, wincing at the sound of my voice.

I needed to calm. I couldn't panic. The wolven…they would hear me, right? That's what it had sounded like Casteel and the others were saying. That they'd heard or felt my distress before and had answered. I was *definitely* distressed now.

But I'd heard them yelping in pain after Jasper and Kieran were shot. None of them had reached the top of the Temple after that. What if they too were—?

I lifted my hands to my face. The chain had enough give to do so without pain. "Stop," I told myself. They couldn't have killed all the wolven.

They.

Namely, Alastir.

Anger and disbelief warred inside me as I focused on steadying my breathing. I would get out of here. I would find Casteel and Kieran and the others. All of them had to be okay.

Then I would kill Alastir. Slowly and painfully.

Holding that promise close to my heart, I forced out a slow, even breath and lowered my hands. I'd been chained before. That time in New Haven had not been as bad as this, but I'd been in bad situations before with Duke Teerman and Lord Mazeen. Like in the carriage with Lord Chaney, who had been bordering on bloodlust, I had to stay calm. I couldn't cave to panic. If I did, I would lose myself.

Like I'd lost myself at the Chambers of Nyktos.

No. I hadn't lost myself when I killed those people. I'd still been there. I just hadn't…I hadn't cared to hold back, to curtail whatever power had come alive inside me. I didn't even feel guilt now. I didn't think I'd feel remorse later, either.

My legs and back stung from the wounds those blades had left behind as I looked at where my bonds connected with the wall. No ring held the chain in place. It wasn't just fused to the wall, it was a *part* of it—a growth.

What in the hell kind of crypt was this?

I couldn't break stone, but bone…bone and roots were fragile in comparison. Carefully, I twisted my wrist to create tension that didn't press against my skin. I gripped the other length of bone and root with my other hand—

"I wouldn't do that."

My head snapped in the direction of the male voice. It came from the shadows beyond the lit pillars.

"Those aren't normal bones you're handling," the male voice continued. "They're the bones of the ancients."

My lip curled as I immediately loosened my grip.

A deep chuckle rose from the shadows, and I stilled once more. That laugh…it sounded a little familiar. So did the voice.

"And because they're bones of the deities, they carry Primal magic—the eather—within them," he added. "Do you know what that means, Penellaphe? Those bones are unbreakable, imbued by another who carries the blood of the gods within them." The voice drew closer, and I tensed. "It was a rather archaic technique crafted by the gods themselves, designed to immobilize those who had become too dangerous—too much of a threat. They say it was Nyktos himself who bestowed the power on the bones of the dead. An act he carried out when he ruled over the dead in the Shadowlands. When he was the Asher, the One who is Blessed, the Bringer of Death, and the Guardian of Souls. *The* Primal God of Common Men and Endings."

The…the Shadowlands? Ruled over the dead? Nyktos was the God of Life, King of all the gods. Rhain was the God of Common Men and Endings. I had never heard of the Shadowlands before, but with that name alone, it sounded like a place I didn't want to learn more about.

"But I digress," he said, and I saw the hazy dark outline of a man in the gloom. I squinted, focusing on him, but I…I sensed nothing from him. "You pull on those bindings, they will simply tighten. You keep doing it, they will cut through your flesh and into your bone. Eventually, they will sever your limbs. Don't believe me, take a closer look at the one beside you."

I didn't want to look, to take my eyes off the shadowy form, but I couldn't help myself. I glanced at the body beside me and looked down at its side. The skeletal remains of a hand lay beside it.

Oh, gods.

"Lucky for you, you only carry the blood of the gods in you. You're not a deity like them. You would bleed out and die rather quickly. The deities like the one beside you?" the man said, and my attention shot back to him. The shadowy mass was closer now, having stopped at the edges of the fiery glow. "He…well, he grew weaker and hungrier until his body started to cannibalize itself. That process alone most likely took centuries."

Centuries? I shuddered.

"You must be asking yourself what he could have done to warrant such a horrid punishment. What did he and the others lining the walls and in their coffins do?" he asked. And, yeah, a part of me wondered just that.

"They became too dangerous. Too powerful. Too…unpredictable." He paused, and I swallowed hard. It took no leap of logic to assume that those against the wall and before me were deities. "Too much of a threat. Just like you."

"I'm not a threat," I snarled.

"You're not? You killed many."

My fingers curled inward. "They attacked me for no reason. They hurt—" My voice cracked. "They hurt the wolven. Their Prince. My—"

"Your heartmate?" he suggested. "A union of not only the hearts but also of the soul. Rare and more powerful than any bloodline. Many would consider such a thing a miracle. Tell me, do you think it's a miracle now?"

"Yes," I growled without hesitation.

He laughed, and yet again, something tugged at the recesses of my memories. "You will then be relieved to know that they are all safe. The King and Queen—those two wolven, even the Prince," he said, and I might've stopped breathing. "If you don't believe that, you can trust the marriage imprint."

My heart stuttered. I hadn't even thought of that. Casteel had told me that the imprint faded upon the death of one of the partners. That was how some had learned of their heartmate's demise.

Part of me didn't want to look, but I had to. A hollowness filled my stomach as my gaze shifted to my left hand. It trembled as I turned it over. The golden swirl across my palm glimmered faintly.

Relief cut so swiftly through me that I had to clamp my mouth shut to stop the cry from rising up from the very depths of my being. The imprint was still there. Casteel was alive. I shuddered again, tears scorching my throat. He was *alive*.

"Sweet," he whispered. "So very sweet."

An uneasy sensation crept over my skin, stealing bits and pieces of the relief.

"But he would've been greatly injured if you hadn't been stopped," he said. "You would've brought the whole Temple down. He would've fallen with it. Maybe you would've even killed him. It is possible for you to do that, you know? You have the power within you."

My heart skipped a beat in my chest. "I would never hurt him."

"Maybe not intentionally. But from what I've gathered, you seem to have very little control over yourself. How do you know what you would've done?"

I started to deny what he'd said, but I tipped my head back against the wall, unsettled. I…I wasn't sure what I had become in that Temple, but I had been in control. I had also been full of vengeance, just like the strange flash of the woman I'd seen in my mind. I had been prepared to kill those who ran from me. I'd been prepared to tear apart the entire kingdom. Would I have done that? Saion's Cove was full of innocent people. Surely, I would've stopped before it got to that point.

I was lying to myself.

I'd believed that Casteel had been gravely injured, if not killed. I wouldn't have stopped. Not until I'd sated that need for vengeance. And I had no idea what it would've taken for that to happen.

The air I breathed turned sour, and it was an effort to file that realization away to stress over later. "What did you do to him? To the others?"

"I did nothing."

"Bullshit," I snapped.

"I fired no arrows. I wasn't even there," he replied. "What *they* did, was use a toxin derived from the shadowshade—a flower that grows in the most eastern regions of the Mountains of Nyktos. It causes convulsions and paralysis before hardening the skin. Quite painful before they enter into the deep sleep. The Prince will take a bit longer than normal to awaken from what I hear. A few days. So, I imagine tomorrow, perhaps?"

A…a few days? Tomorrow? "How long have I been out?"

"Two days. Maybe three."

Good gods.

I didn't even want to think about the damage done to my head that would have knocked me out for that long. But the others hadn't been struck as many times as Casteel. Kieran would likely be awake now. So would Jasper. And maybe the other—

"I know what you're thinking," the male cut into my thoughts. "That the wolven will feel your call. That they will come for you. No, they won't. The bones nullify the Primal *notam*. They also negate any and all abilities, reducing you to what you are at your very core. Mortal."

Was that why I felt nothing from this man? That wasn't exactly what I'd wanted to hear. Panic threatened to dig its claws into me once more, but the shadowy form moved closer, stepping into the glow of the torch.

My entire body went rigid at the sight of the man dressed in all black. Every part of me rebelled at what I saw. It didn't make sense. It was impossible. But I recognized the dark, buzzed hair, the hard-set jaw, and thin lips. Now I knew why his laugh sounded so familiar.

It was the commander of the Royal Guard.

Commander Jansen.

"You're dead," I breathed, staring up at him as he drifted between the pillars.

A dark eyebrow rose. "Whatever gave you that impression, Penellaphe?"

"The Ascended discovered that Hawke wasn't who he said he was shortly after we left." What Lord Chaney had told me in that carriage resurfaced. "They said the Descenters infiltrated the highest ranks of the Royal Guard."

"They did, but they didn't catch me." One side of Jansen's lips curved up as he strolled forward, his fingers skating over the side of a coffin.

Confusion swirled through me as I stared up at him. "I…I don't understand. You're a Descenter? You support the Prince—?"

"I support Atlantia." He moved fast, crossing the distance in less time than it took a heart to beat. He knelt so we were at eye-level. "I am no Descenter."

"Really?" His superspeed sort of gave that away. "Then what *are* you?"

The tight-lipped smile grew. His features sharpened, narrowed, and then he *changed*. Shrinking in height and width, the new body drowned in the clothing Jansen had been wearing. His skin became tanner and smoother. In an instant, his hair darkened to black and became longer, his eyes lightening and turning blue.

Within seconds, Beckett knelt before me.

Chapter 4

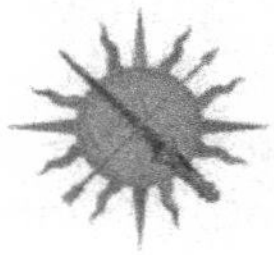

"Good gods," I croaked, pressing away from this—this *thing* before me.

"Did I startle you?" Jansen/Beckett asked in the young wolven's voice—coming from a face identical to Alastir's great-nephew.

"You're...you're a changeling."

He nodded.

I couldn't stop staring at him, my brain unable to reconcile the knowledge that it was Jansen before me and not Beckett. "I...I didn't know they could make themselves look like other people."

"Most of the changeling bloodlines that are left are only able to shift into animal form or have...other skills," he said. "I'm one of the very few who can do it and hold another's form for long periods of time. Want to know how?"

I really did, but I said nothing.

Lucky for me, he was in a talkative mood. "All I need is something of them on me. A strand of hair is typically enough. The wolven are incredibly easy to replicate."

No part of me could comprehend how anyone could be easy to replicate. "And would they...know that you'd done this? Taken on their appearance?"

Still smiling with Beckett's boyish features, Jansen shook his head. "Not usually."

I couldn't even begin to process what it would be like to take on another's identity or how someone could do so without the other's permission. It felt like a great violation to me, especially if done to trick someone…

Realization swept through me in a wave of fresh anger. "It was *you*," I seethed. "Not the real Beckett who led me into the Temple. You."

"I've always known a clever girl lived behind the veil," he remarked and then shifted once again into the features that belonged to him. It was a feat no less shocking than the time before.

The knowledge that it hadn't been the young, playful wolven who'd led me into a trap brought forth a decent amount of relief. "How? How did no one know? How had I—?" I cut myself off. When I read his emotions in the Temple, they had felt just like Beckett's.

"How did you or our Prince not know? Or even Kieran or Jasper? When changelings assume the identity of another, we take on their characteristics to the point where it's extremely difficult to decipher the truth. Sometimes, it can even become hard for us to remember who we truly are." A troubled look crept across his features but vanished so quickly that I wasn't sure I'd seen it. "Of course, our Prince knew I was a changeling. As do many others. But, obviously, no one expected such a manipulation. No one was even looking for one."

"Is Beckett okay?"

Jansen looked away. "He should have been. He was given a sleeping draft. That was the plan. For him to sleep long enough for me to take his place."

My heart twisted. "But that didn't happen?"

"No." Jansen briefly closed his eyes. "I underestimated how much potion a young wolven needed to remain asleep. He woke when I entered his room." He leaned back, scrubbing a hand down his face. "What happened was unfortunate."

Bile crept up my throat. "You killed him?"

"It had to be done."

Disbelief stole my breath as I stared at the changeling. "He was just a kid!"

"I know." He lowered his hand. "It wasn't something any of us enjoyed, but it had to be done."

"It didn't have to be done." Tears crowded my eyes. "He was a kid, and he was innocent."

"Innocents die all the time. You spent the entirety of your life in

Solis. You know that to be true."

"And that makes it okay to harm another?"

"No. But the end justified the means. The people of Atlantia will understand that," Jansen countered. I couldn't fathom how anyone could *understand* the murder of a child. "And why do you even care? You stood by and witnessed people being starved, abused, and given over to the Rite. You did nothing."

"I didn't know the truth then," I spat, blinking back tears.

"And does that make it okay?"

"No. It doesn't," I said, and his eyes widened slightly. "But I didn't always stand by and do nothing. I did what I could."

"It wasn't enough."

"I didn't say it was." I drew in a ragged breath. "Why are you doing this?"

"It is my duty to stop any and all threats to Atlantia."

A hoarse laugh of disbelief left me. "You know me. You've known me for years. You know I'm not a threat. I wouldn't have done anything in that Temple if I hadn't been threatened."

"That is what you say now. One day, that will change," he said. "Strange how small the world is, though. The whole purpose of assuming the role I did was to ensure an open pathway between Casteel and you. I spent years living a lie, all so he could capture the Maiden and use her to free his brother and gain back some of our stolen land. I had no idea what you were or even why you were the Maiden."

"And him marrying me felt like a betrayal to you?" I surmised.

"Actually, no," he replied, surprising me. "He could still accomplish what he intended. Probably would've been even better positioned to do so with you as his wife and not his captive."

"Then why? Because I'm…because I have a drop of god's blood in me?"

"A drop?" Jansen laughed. "Girl, I know what you did in that Temple. You need to give yourself more credit."

My temper spiked, and I welcomed it, holding onto the rage. It was far better company than the welling grief. "I haven't been a *girl* in years, so do not call me one."

"My apologies." He bowed his head. "I would be willing to bet you have far more than a drop. Your bloodline must've remained very clean for you to exhibit those kinds of godly abilities." He moved suddenly, grasping my chin. I tried to pull free, but he held me in place. His dark eyes swept over my face as if he were searching for something. "Strange that I never saw it before. I should have."

I reached up, gripping his forearm. The manacle on my wrist tightened in warning. "Remove your hand from me."

"Or what, Maiden?" His smile kicked up a notch as my anger flared hotly. "There is nothing you can do to me that will not result in you harming yourself. I just said you were always clever. Don't make a liar out of me."

Helpless anger prodded at the deeply rooted desperation I felt at not being able to defend myself. "Let go of me!"

Jansen released his grip and rose suddenly. He glanced over at the pile of bones beside me as I dragged in deep breaths. My heart pounded way too fast. "I knew it wouldn't be wise for me to linger in Masadonia," he said. "So, I left shortly after you did. I met up with Alastir on the road to Spessa's End. It was then that I learned what you were."

My fingernails pressed into my palms. "So, Alastir knew what I was?"

"Not when he first saw you." He nudged something with his toe, kicking it across the dusty floor. It was the dismembered hand. My stomach roiled. "I remained hidden until it was time and then assumed Beckett's identity."

"You stood by when we were nearly overtaken by the Ascended armies. People died, and you just stood by?" Scorn dripped from my tone.

His gaze snapped back to mine. "I'm not a coward."

"You said it." My smile was thin. "Not me."

He didn't move for a long moment. "Watching those armies descend on Spessa's End wasn't easy. Staying hidden was one of the hardest things I've ever done. But unlike those false Guardians, I am a Protector of Atlantia, a true Guardian of the realm. I knew my purpose was far greater than the potential fall of Spessa's End or even the death of our Prince."

"True Guardian?" I thought of the women who had descended from a long line of warriors—women who had leapt from the Rise surrounding Spessa's End and wielded swords more fearlessly than I'd ever seen the commander do. I laughed harshly. "You're pale and pathetic compared to the Guardians."

Pain erupting across the side of my cheek and face was the only warning that he'd moved—that he'd lashed out. A metallic taste filled my mouth.

"I understand that things must be very confusing and stressful for you," he said, his tone heavy with false sympathy as he rose and took a step back. "But if you insult me one more time, I will not be responsible for my actions."

An icy-hot feeling flowed over my skin. My cheek throbbed as I turned my head back to him and met his gaze. "You will die," I promised, smiling at the red blush of anger staining his cheeks. "It will be by my hand, and it will be a death befitting a *coward* like you."

He shot toward me. This time, darkness came with the biting pain, one I couldn't escape no matter how hard I tried.

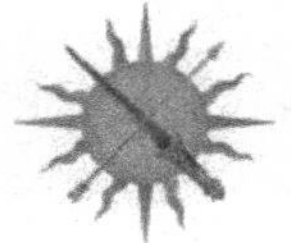

Gritting my teeth against the pressure of the bindings around my wrist, I slowly inched my hand to the left as I stared at the spear on the skeleton's chest. Fresh blood dripped onto the stone, and I stopped, breathing raggedly.

I waited, having learned that with each inch gained, the bindings loosened a little. Gaining that knowledge had been a painstakingly slow process.

Focusing on deep, steady breaths, I rested the side of my head against the wall as my entire arm throbbed. I had no idea how much time had passed since I'd lost consciousness. It had to be hours. Maybe longer as my pangs of hunger had gone from sporadic waves to a low, steady gnawing ache in my gut. And I was cold—every part of my body felt chilled.

My gaze crept over the stone coffins. Why had they been given the honor of a proper resting place while the ones against the walls hadn't? That was only one of the many questions I had. Granted, it wasn't nearly the most important one, but I'd rather think about that than wonder why I was still alive.

Jansen had claimed that I was a threat. And maybe whatever had awakened in me at the Temple was. Perhaps I *was* a threat. But why keep me alive? Or was this what they'd planned all along? To just shove me into this crypt and leave me here until I died of hunger or starvation, becoming nothing but another dusty pile of bones against the wall.

Panic was a vise around my throat, making it harder to breathe. I shut it down, though. I couldn't let myself give in to the fear that had formed a haunting shadow in the back of my mind. I would get out of here—either on my own, or Casteel would find me.

I knew he had to be searching for me. Likely started the moment he woke. And he would tear the entire kingdom apart if necessary. He would find me.

I would get out of here.

But first, I needed a weapon.

Bracing myself for pain, I slowly stretched out my arm. My fingers brushed the dusty handle of the spear. Excitement thrummed as the bindings snapped tighter around my wrist, digging into my flesh. Pain spiked—

Stone slid against stone somewhere in the darkness of the crypt, halting my attempt. Ignoring the intense throbbing in my limb, I drew my hand back to my lap, where fresh blood gathered, soaking my slip. I stared into the shadows, straining to see who had arrived.

"I see you're finally awake."

My hands curled into fists at the sound of Alastir's voice.

A moment later, he passed under the glow of one of the torches. He looked the same as he had in the Temple, except his black tunic, threaded with gold, was sleeveless. "I checked on you earlier, but you were asleep."

"You traitorous son of a bitch," I spat.

Alastir stopped between two of the stone tombs. "I know you're angry. You have every right to be. Jansen confessed that he lost his temper and struck you. I apologize for that. Hitting anyone who cannot defend themselves is not part of the oath we took."

"I don't care that he hit me," I hissed, glaring up at Alastir. "I care about how you betrayed Casteel. How you had a hand in the death of your own great-nephew."

His head tilted, and the shadows hid the jagged scar across his forehead. "You see what I have taken part in as a betrayal. I see it as a messy necessity to ensure the safety of Atlantia."

Fury burned through my chest and my blood. "Like I told Jansen, I only defended myself. I only defended Casteel and Kieran and Jasper. I would—"

"You would never have done what you did unless you believed that kind of reaction was warranted?" he interrupted. "You were forced to use the power in your blood against others?"

My chest rose and fell heavily. "Yes."

"Long ago, when the gods of names long forgotten were awake and coexisted with mortals, rules governed the mortals' actions. The gods acted as their protectors, aiding them in times of crisis, and even granted favors to the most faithful," he said.

"I couldn't care less about this history lesson if my very life depended on it," I fumed.

"But they also acted as the mortals' judge, jury, and executioner if the mortals' actions were deemed offensive or unwarranted," Alastir continued as if I hadn't spoken. "The problem with that was that only the gods chose what was and wasn't a punishable act. Countless mortals died at the hands of those gods for offenses as small as raising the ire of a god. Eventually, the younger brethren rose against those gods. But the tendency to react without thought, often fueled by passion or other volatile, unpredictable emotions, and to react with violence, was a trait even the gods fell prey to—especially the eldest among them. It was why they went to sleep."

"Thanks for sharing," I snapped. "But you still haven't explained why you betrayed the Prince. Why you used Beckett to carry this out."

"I did what I needed to because the gods' violent trait was passed onto their children," he stated. "The deities were even more chaotic in their thoughts and manners than their predecessors. Some believed it was the mortal influence, as the gods before them had coexisted with mortals but did not live among them. They remained in Iliseeum, while their children lived in the mortal realm."

Iliseeum? The Shadowlands? All of this sounded delusional, and my patience was already barely hanging on by a thin thread. I was *this* close to risking losing a hand so I could grab the spear and launch it at the bastard.

"I don't know if it was mortal influence or not, but after the gods chose to sleep, the deities became—"

"Too powerful and too dangerous," I cut in. "I know. I've already heard this."

"But did Jansen tell you what they did to deserve that fate? I'm sure you've realized by now that all those entombed here are deities." He lifted his arms, gesturing toward the sarcophagi and the bodies. "Did he tell you why the elemental Atlantians rose against them, just like their forefathers rose against the original gods? Did he tell you what kind of monsters they became?"

"He was too busy hitting me to get to that point," I sneered. "So, no."

"I feel I must apologize for that once more."

"Fuck you," I choked out, hating his apology—the apparent sincerity of his words. And he legitimately meant them. I didn't need my ability to know that.

His brows lifted, and then his expression smoothed out. "The deities built Atlantia, but they almost destroyed it in their greed and through their thirst for life—their unquenchable desire for more. Always *more*. They knew no limits. If they wanted something, they took it or created it. Sometimes, to benefit the kingdom. A lot of the internal structure you see here exists because of them. But more often than not, their actions only benefited them."

What he said reminded me an awful lot of the Ascended. They ruled with their desires at the forefront of each thought.

I stared up at him. "So, I'm a threat that must be dealt with because I'm descended from a deity, who may or may not have had anger-management issues?" A strangled laugh parted my lips. "As if I have no autonomy and am just a byproduct of what is in my blood?"

"That may sound unbelievable to you now, Penellaphe, but you've just entered into the Culling. Sooner or later, you will start to show the same chaotic and violent impulses as they did. You are dangerous now, but you will become something else entirely eventually."

An image of the strange woman with the moonlight hair flashed before me.

"Worse yet, at the heart of you, you are mortal—far more easily influenced than an Atlantian or a wolven. And because of that mortality, you will be even more prone to impulsive choices."

The woman faded from my mind as I stared at him. "You're wrong. Mortals are far more cautious and protective of life."

He arched a brow. "Even if that was the case, you descended from the ones born of the flesh and fire of the most powerful gods. Your abilities are strikingly reminiscent of those who, if angered, could quickly become catastrophic, their tempers all-consuming. Families were decimated because someone offended one of them. Towns laid to waste because one person committed a crime against them. But all paid the price—men, women, and children," he told me, and unease grew under my anger.

"Then they began turning on one another, picking each other off as they fought to rule Atlantia. And in the process, they eradicated entire bloodlines. When the descendants of Saion were killed, the ceeren rose against the deities responsible. They didn't die because they fell into depression, nor did their bloodline simply become so diluted that it eventually died out. Another deity killed them. Many of those bloodlines died at one deity's hand—the one that so many believed was different." Anger tightened the lines of his mouth. "Even I did at one time. How could I not believe that he was different? After all, he'd descended from the King of Gods. He couldn't be like the others."

"Malec?" I guessed.

Alastir nodded. "But a lot of people were wrong. *I* was wrong. He was the worst of them all."

Tensing, I watched him come forward and lower himself to the stone floor before me. He sat with a heavy sigh, resting an arm on a bent knee as he studied me. "Not many people knew what Malec was capable of. What his godly powers were like. When he used them, he left very few witnesses behind. But I knew what he could do. Queen Eloana knew. King Valyn did." His cool blue eyes met mine. "His abilities were a lot like yours."

I sucked in a short breath. "No."

"He could sense emotion, like the empath bloodline. It was believed that their line branched off from the one that birthed Malec, having mingled with a changeling line. Some believe that was why the gods favored the empaths. That they had more eather in them than most," he continued.

"Malec could heal wounds with his touch, but he rarely did it because he was not only descended from the God of Life, he was also a descendant of the God of Death. Nyktos. The King of Gods is both. And Malec's abilities had a dark side. He could take emotion and turn it back on others, like the empaths. But he could do so much more."

There was no way.

"He could send his will into others, breaking and shattering their bodies without touch. He could *become* death." Alastir held my gaze as I shook my head. "I like you. I know you may not believe that, and I understand if you don't. But I am sorry because I know that Casteel cares for you deeply. I didn't in the beginning, but I know now that your relationship is real. This will hurt him. But that is the blood you carry in you, Penellaphe. You are descended from Nyktos. You carry the blood of King Malec inside you," he said, watching me. "I belong to a long line of people who swore an oath to protect Atlantia and her secrets. That was why I was willing to break my bond with Malec. And it is why I cannot allow you to do what he almost succeeded in."

It was hard for me to fully comprehend that I carried any godly blood in me. Obviously, I couldn't deny that I wasn't just half-Atlantian and half-mortal. One of mixed heritage couldn't do what I had done. Not even an elemental Atlantian was capable of that. But someone descended from Nyktos? From King Malec?

The deity who had created the very first Ascended? His actions had led to thousands of deaths, if not more.

That was in my blood?

I couldn't believe what Alastir was saying. It sounded as impossible as what Duchess Teerman had claimed about the Queen of Solis being my grandmother. That *was* impossible. The Ascended couldn't bear children.

"How could I descend from Malec?" I asked, even if it sounded impossible.

"Malec had many mistresses, Penellaphe. Some were mortal. Some weren't," he told me. "And he had children with some of them—offspring who spread across the kingdom, settling in areas far west from here. It is not at all impossible. There are many others like you—those who never reached the age of the Culling. You are his descendant."

"Others who never reached…." I trailed off, a whole new horror beginning to take shape in my mind. Good gods, were Alastir and Jansen—and who knew how many others—responsible for the deaths of…of children over the course of the centuries?

"But it's not just the bloodline, Penellaphe. We were warned about you long ago. It was written in the bones of your namesake before the gods went to sleep," Alastir said. My skin pimpled.

"'*With the last Chosen blood spilled, the great conspirator birthed from the flesh and fire of the Primals will awaken as the Harbinger and the Bringer of Death and Destruction to the lands gifted by the gods. Beware, for the end will come from the west to destroy the east and lay waste to all which lies between.*'"

I stared at him in stunned silence.

"You are the Chosen, birthed of the flesh and fire of the gods. And you come from the west, to the lands the gods have gifted," Alastir conferred. "You are who your namesake warned about."

"You…you're doing all of this because of my bloodline and a *prophecy*?" A harsh laugh rattled from me. There had been old wives' tales about prophecies and tales of doom in every generation. They were nothing but fables.

"You don't have to believe me, but I knew—I think I always did."

He frowned as his eyes narrowed slightly. "I sensed it when I looked into your eyes for the first time. They were old. Primal. I saw death in your eyes, even all those years ago."

My heart stuttered and then sped up. "What?"

"We met before. You were either too young then to remember or the events of the night were too traumatic," Alastir said, and every part of me flashed hot and then cold. "I didn't realize it was you when I saw you for the first time in New Haven. I thought you looked familiar, and it kept nagging at me. Something about your eyes. But it wasn't until you said your parents' names that I knew exactly who you were. Coralena and Leopold. Cora and her *lion*."

I jolted, feeling as if the floor of the crypt had moved under me. I couldn't speak.

"I lied to you," he said softly. "When I said that I would ask to see if any others had known of them or had potentially tried to help them escape to Atlantia, I never planned to ask anyone. I didn't need to because it was me."

Heart pounding fast, I snapped out of my stupor. "You were there that night? The night the Craven attacked the inn?"

He nodded as the torches flickered behind him.

A picture of my father formed in my mind, his features hazy as he kept glancing out the window of the inn, looking and searching for something or someone. Later that night, he'd said to someone who lingered in the shadows of my mind, "*This is my daughter.*"

I couldn't…I couldn't breathe as I stared at Alastir. His voice. His laugh. It had always sounded so familiar to me. I'd thought it reminded me of Vikter. I'd been wrong.

"I came to meet them, give them safe passage," he said, his voice growing weary.

"She doesn't know," my father had told that shadow in my memory that I could never fully latch on to. Images flashed rapid-fire behind my eyes, snapshots of memories—recollections I wasn't sure were real or fragments of nightmares. My father…his smile had been all wrong before he looked over his shoulder. "*Understood*," was the phantom voice's response. Now I knew who that voice had belonged to.

"Your parents should've known better than to share what they knew with anyone." Alastir shook his head again, this time sadly. "And you were right to assume that they were attempting to flee Solis, to get as far away from the kingdom as they could. They were. They knew the truth. But you see, Penellaphe, your mother and father always knew exactly what the Ascended were."

I jerked back, barely feeling the pain in my wrists and legs. "No."

"Yes," he insisted. But there was no way this was the truth. I knew my parents were good people. I *remembered* that. Good people wouldn't have stood by, doing nothing, if they knew the truth of the Ascended. Realized what happened when children were given over during the Rite. Good people didn't stay silent. They were *not* complicit.

"Your mother was a favorite of the counterfeit Queen, but she was no Lady in Wait destined to Ascend. She was a Handmaiden to the Queen."

Handmaiden? Something about that struck a chord of familiarity. Out of the churning chaos of my mind, I saw…women who were always with the Queen. Women in black who never spoke and wandered through the halls of the palace like shadows. They…they'd scared me as a child. *Yes.* I remembered that now. How had I forgotten about them?

"Her Handmaidens were her personal guards." Alastir's brows knitted, and the scar on his forehead deepened. "Casteel knows they were a unique sort of nightmare."

I lifted a hand and froze. Casteel had been held by the Queen for five decades, tortured and used by her and others. He'd been freed before my mother was born, but his brother took his place.

But my mother, my gentle, soft, and helpless mother couldn't have been like that. If she were one of the Queen's personal guards, nightmare or not, she would've been trained to fight. She would've—

She would've been able to defend herself.

I didn't understand. Didn't know if any of that was true. But I knew what *was.* "You," I breathed, my entire being turning numb as I stared at the man I'd befriended. That I'd trusted. "It was you. *You* betrayed them, didn't you?"

"It wasn't me who struck down your father. It wasn't me who betrayed your mother," he replied. "But in the end, it doesn't matter. I would've killed them anyway. I would've killed you."

A harsh laugh erupted from me as rage and disbelief twisted my insides. "If it wasn't you, then who was it? The Craven?"

"There were Craven there that night. You carry their scars. They were led right to the doors of the inn." He didn't blink. Not once. "*He* led them there. The Dark One."

"Liar!" I shouted. "Casteel had nothing to do with what happened."

"I never said Casteel did. I know it wasn't him, even though I never saw the face behind the cloak and hood he wore when he came to that inn," Alastir replied. "Other things were at play that night. Darkness that moved outside of my influence. I was there to help your parents. That is what I did back then. But when they told me what you could do, I knew—I *knew* who you came from. So, when the darkness came to those doors, I let it in."

I didn't know if I believed him or if it even mattered if my parents had died by his hand or not. He had still played a role in my parents' deaths, leaving Ian and I and everyone else there to die, as well. Leaving me to be torn apart by claws and teeth. That pain. That night. It had haunted me for my entire life.

A breath shuddered out of him. "I let it in and walked away, believing that the dirtiest part of my duty was done. But you survived, and here we are."

"*Yes.*" The word rumbled out of me in a growl that would've surprised me at any other time. "Here I am. Now what? You going to kill me? Or leave me here to rot?"

"If only it were that simple." He leaned on one hand. "And I would never leave you here to die such a slow death. That is far too barbaric."

Did he even hear himself? "And chaining me in these bones and roots isn't? Leaving my family and me to die isn't barbaric?"

"It was a necessary evil," he stated. "But we can't just kill you. Maybe before you arrived—before the Primal *notam* locked into place. But not now. The wolven have seen you. They've felt you."

My gaze sharpened on him. "Why didn't you change like the others? The way the King and Queen spoke, it was like they had no control over their forms. They had to answer my call."

"It's because I can no longer shift into my wolven form. When I broke my oath to King Malec, I severed the connection between myself and my wolven side. So, I wasn't able to feel the Primal *notam*."

Shock flickered wildly through me. I hadn't known that. "Are you…are you still a wolven, then?"

"I still have the lifespan and the strength of a wolven, but I cannot shift into my true form." His gaze clouded over. "Sometimes, it feels like a missing limb—the inability to feel the change come over me. But what I did, I carried out knowing full well what the consequences would be. Not many others would've done that."

Gods, that had to be unbearable. It had to feel like…I had when they forced me to wear the veil. Part of me was impressed by Alastir's loyalty to Atlantia and to the Queen. And that said a lot about his character—who he was as a man, a wolven, and what he was willing to do in service to his kingdom.

"You did that, but you won't kill me?"

"If we were to kill you, you would become a martyr. There would be an uprising, another war, when the real battle lays to our west." He was talking about Solis—about the Ascended. "I want to avoid that. Avoid creating even more problems for our kingdom. And soon, you will no longer be our problem."

"If you're not going to kill me or leave me in here to die, I'm a little confused by what you plan to do," I bit out.

"I will give the Ascended what they were so desperate to keep," he said. "I will give them you."

Chapter 5

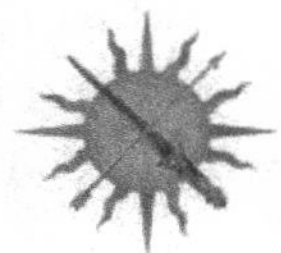

I couldn't have heard him right. There was no way he planned to do what he'd stated.

"None will be the wiser until it's too late," he said. "You will be beyond their reach, like all the others the Ascended have taken."

"That…that doesn't even make sense," I said, stunned when I realized that he was serious.

"It doesn't?"

"No!" I exclaimed. "For several reasons. Starting with how you plan to get me there."

Alastir smiled at me, and my unease grew. "Penellaphe, dear, you're no longer within the Pillars of Atlantia. You're in the Crypt of the Forgotten Ones, deep within the Skotos Mountains. If anyone even learns that you are here, they will not find you. We will already be gone by then."

My insides chilled as disbelief rose. "How did you get past the Guardians?"

"Those who were unaware of our presence felt the kiss of the shadowshade."

"And those who weren't?" I asked, already guessing what'd happened to them. "You killed Guardians?"

"We did what needed to be done."

"Gods," I whispered, swallowing the anger and panic that swirled within me. "They protected Atlantia. They—"

"They were not the true Guardians of Atlantia," he cut me off. "If they were, they would've struck you down the moment you appeared."

My lip curled as I forced my breathing to remain even. "Even if you hand me over to them, how will I not be Atlantia's problem if you give me back to the people who plan to use my blood to make more vamprys?"

He lifted his weight from his hand and sat straight. "Is that what they plan?"

"What else would they plan to do?" I demanded. All of a sudden, I remembered Duchess Teerman's words at Spessa's End. She had claimed that Queen Ileana would be thrilled to learn that I had married the Prince. That I would be able to do what she'd never been able to do—destroy the kingdom from within. Before I could allow those words to mix with what Alastir had said about me being a threat, I shoved them aside. Duchess Teerman had told a lot of lies before she died, starting with what she'd said about Queen Ileana, a vampry incapable of bearing children, being my grandmother. She'd also claimed that Tawny had gone through the Ascension, using Prince Malik's blood. I couldn't believe that, either.

Alastir eyed me silently for a moment. "Come now, Penellaphe. Do you really think the Ascended have no idea that they had the descendant of Nyktos in their grips for nearly nineteen years? Longer?"

Ian.

My breath caught. He was talking about Ian. "I was told Ian Ascended."

"I would have no knowledge of that."

"But you think Queen Ileana and King Jalara knew that we're Nyktos's descendants?" When he said nothing, I fought the urge to launch myself at him. "What does that knowledge change anyway?"

"They could use you to make more vamprys," he agreed. "Or, they know what you're capable of. They know what was written about you, and they plan to use you against Atlantia."

My stomach hollowed. The idea of being handed over to the Ascended was terrifying enough. But to be used against Atlantia—against Casteel? "Then let me ask you again, how is that not Atlantia's problem if they…?" I jerked back against the wall, my eyes widening.

"Wait a minute. You said very few people knew what Malec could do—that my gifts were like his. They could've guessed that Ian and I had god's blood in us, but how would they know our lineage?" I leaned forward as far as I could. "You're working with the Ascended, aren't you?"

His lips thinned. "Some Ascended were alive when Malec ruled."

"By the time Jalara fought the Atlantians at Pompay, Malec no longer sat on the throne," I said. "Not only that, but he was able to keep the vast majority of the Atlantians in the dark about his abilities—about who he descended from. But some random Ascended knew? One who managed to survive the war? Because it sure as hell wasn't Jalara or Ileana. They came from the Vodina Isles, where I'm willing to bet they Ascended." My lip curled in disgust. "You claim you're a true Protector of Atlantia, but you've plotted with its enemies. The people who held both of your Princes captive? The people—"

"This has nothing to do with my daughter," he said, and I pressed my lips together. "Everything I have done, I have done for the Crown and for the kingdom."

The Crown? A horrible coldness spread in my chest as my mind reeled from one discovery after another. I opened my mouth and then closed it before asking the question I wasn't sure I wanted to know the answer to.

"What?" Alastir asked. "There's no need to play the quiet one now. We both know that's not who you are."

My shoulders tightened as I lifted my gaze to his. "Did Casteel's parents know you were going to do this?" They'd fought back in the Temple, but that could've been an act. "Did they know?"

Alastir studied me. "Does it matter?"

It did. "Yes."

"They do not know about this," he said. "They may have speculated that our…brotherhood had risen once more, but they had no hand in this. They won't like what I've been a part of, but I believe they will come to see the necessity of it." He inhaled deeply through his nose, tilting his head back. "And if they don't, then they too will be treated as a threat."

My eyes widened once more. "You…you're staging a coup."

His gaze shot back to mine. "No. I am saving Atlantia."

"You're saving Atlantia by working with the Ascended, putting the people of the kingdom in even more danger, and overthrowing or doing something worse to the Crown if they disagree with your actions? That is a coup. That is also treasonous."

"Only if you've sworn allegiance to the heads the crown sits upon," he countered. "And I don't think it will come to that. Eloana and Valyn both know that protecting Atlantia may mean engaging in some most unsavory deeds."

"And you think Casteel will go along with this?" I demanded. "That after you hand me over to the Ascended, he'll just give up and move on? That he'll marry your great-niece after your daughter—" I cut myself off before exposing what Shea had really done. Withholding that wasn't for his sake. Gods, no. The desire to see his face when he learned the truth of what his daughter had done savagely burned through me, but I stopped out of respect for Casteel—for what he'd had to do.

Alastir stared at me, his jaw tight. "You would've been good for Casteel, but you never would've been my daughter."

"Damn straight," I said, my nails digging into my palms. It took me several moments to trust myself before I spoke again. "Casteel chose me. He's not going to turn around and marry your great-niece or another family member you can drag out before him. All you're doing is causing him to risk his life and the future of Atlantia. Because he will come for me."

Pale eyes met mine. "I don't think it will come to that."

"You're delusional if you believe that."

"It's not that I believe he'll give up on you," he said. "I just don't think he'll get the chance to stage a rescue attempt."

My entire body locked up. "If you hurt him—"

"You will do nothing, Penellaphe. You're not in a position to do anything," he pointed out, and I swallowed a scream of rage and frustration. "But I have no plans to harm the Prince. And I pray to the gods that it doesn't come to that."

"Then what…?" It occurred to me then. "You think the Ascended will kill me?"

Alastir said nothing.

"You *are* delusional." I tipped my head back against the wall. "The Ascended need me. They need Atlantian blood."

"Tell me, Penellaphe, what will you do when you're in their hands? The moment you are free of the bones. You'll attack them, won't you? You'll kill as many of them as you can to get free and return to our Prince."

He was right.

I would kill any and all who stood between Casteel and me because we deserved to be together. We deserved a future, a chance to explore each other's secrets. To love one another. We deserved to simply…*live*. I would do anything to ensure that.

Alastir continued watching me. "And what do you think is the only thing the Ascended value above power? Survival. They will not have these bones to hold you. And if they believe they can't control you, think that you're too much of a risk, they will end you. But before that happens, I imagine you will take many down with you."

Sickened, I forced my hands to relax. "Kill two birds with one stone?"

He nodded.

"Even if you're successful, your plan will still fail. You think Casteel won't know that you and every other so-called Protector handed me over to them? That the wolven won't know?"

"There is still a risk of an uprising," he admitted. "But it is a small one. You see, we will lead them to believe that you escaped your captivity and fell into the Ascended's hands. They will never know that we gave you to them. They will turn their anger on the Ascended, where it should have always been. Every Ascended will be killed, and any who support them will fall beside them. Atlantia will take back what belongs to us. We will become a great kingdom again."

Something about how he spoke told me that I would sense pride and arrogance in him if I could use my gift. I also had a feeling I'd feel the thirst for *more.* I didn't, for one second, believe that his only motivation was to save Atlantia. Not when his plan put the kingdom at further risk. Not when his plan could possibly benefit him if he survived this.

"I have a question," I asked as my empty stomach grumbled. He arched a brow. "What happens to you if Malik or Casteel becomes king? Will you still be an advisor?"

"It would be whoever the King or Queen chooses. Usually, it's a bonded wolven or a trusted ally."

"In other words, it wouldn't be you?" When Alastir fell silent, I knew I was onto something. "So, whatever influence you have on the Crown—over Atlantia—could be lessened or lost?"

He remained silent.

And since Jasper was the one who spoke for the wolven, what effect would Alastir have? And what kind of power did he want to wield?

"What are you getting at, Penellaphe?"

"Growing up among the Royals and other Ascended, I learned from a very young age that every friendship and acquaintance, every party or dinner a person was invited to or hosted, and every marriage ordained by the King and Queen were all power moves. Each choice and decision was based on how one could either retain power or influence or gain it. I don't think that is a trait just to the Ascended. I saw it among the wealthy mortals. I saw it among the Royal Guards. I doubt the wolven or Atlantians are different."

"Some are not," Alastir confirmed.

"You believe I'm a threat because of the blood I carry, and because of what I can do. But you haven't even given me a chance to prove that I am not just the sum of what my ancestors did. You can choose to judge me based on what I've done to defend myself and those I love, but I do not regret my actions," I told him. "You may not be able to feel the Primal *notam*, but if you planned for Casteel to marry your great-niece to bring the wolven and the Atlantians together, then I can't see why you wouldn't support this union. Give it a chance to strengthen the Crown and Atlantia. But that's not all you want, is it?"

His nostrils flared as he continued staring at me.

"Casteel's father wants retribution, just as you do. Right? For what they did to your daughter. But Casteel doesn't want war. You know that. He's trying to save lives even as he gains land. Just like he did with Spessa's End."

That was what Casteel had planned. We would negotiate for land and the release of Prince Malik. I would find my brother and deal with what he may or may not have turned into. King Jalara and Queen Ileana wouldn't remain on the throne, not even if they agreed to everything Casteel set before them. They couldn't. He would kill them for what they'd subjected his brother and him to. Strangely, the idea of that no longer made me squirm with conflict. It was still hard to reconcile the Queen who'd cared for me after my parents died with the one who had tortured Casteel and countless others, but I'd seen enough to know that her treatment of me wasn't enough to erase the horrors she had inflicted on others.

But now, if Alastir had his way, that plan could never become a reality.

"What he did with Spessa's End was impressive, but it's not enough," Alastir stated, his voice flat. "Even if we were able to reclaim more land, it wouldn't be enough. King Valyn and I want to see Solis pay, not only for our personal losses but for what the Ascended have done to many of our kind."

"That's understandable." Realizing what Ian could have become was hard enough. But Tawny, too—my friend who was so kind and full of life and love? If they'd turned her into an Ascended as Duchess

Teerman claimed, it would be hard for me not to want to see Solis burn. "So, you're not a supporter of Casteel's plan. You want blood, but more importantly, you want the influence to get what you want. And you see that power slipping through your fingers even though I haven't made a single claim to the Crown."

"It doesn't matter if you want the Crown or not. So long as you live, it's yours. It is your birthright, and the wolven will ensure that it becomes yours," he said, speaking of his people as if he were no longer one of them. And maybe he didn't feel like he was. I didn't know, and I didn't care. "Just like it was Casteel's. It doesn't matter if you detest the responsibility as much as the Prince does."

"Casteel doesn't detest responsibility. I'm sure he has done more for the people of Atlantia in his lifetime than you've done since you broke your oath to Malec," I shot back, infuriated. "He just—"

"Refuses to believe his brother is a lost cause, and therefore, refuses to assume the responsibility of the throne—what would've been in the best interest of Atlantia." A muscle ticked in his jaw. "So, it is up to me to do what's best for the kingdom."

"You?" I laughed. "You want what is best for yourself. Your motivations aren't altruistic. You're no different than anyone else who's hungry for power and vengeance. And you know what?"

"What?" he barked as his façade of calm began to crack.

"This plan of yours will fail."

"You think so?"

I nodded. "And you won't survive this. If not by my hand, then by Casteel's. He's going to kill you. And he won't tear your heart from your chest. That will be too quick and painless. He'll make your death hurt."

"I've done nothing that I'm not willing to accept the consequences for," he replied, lifting his chin. "If death is my fate, so be it. Atlantia will still be safe from you."

His words would've unsettled me if I hadn't seen the way his mouth tightened or how he swallowed. I smiled then, just like I had when I'd stared down Duke Teerman.

Alastir rose suddenly. "My plan might fail. That is possible. I would be foolish not to take that into consideration. And I have." He stared down at me. "But if it fails, you will not be free again, Penellaphe. I would rather see a war among my people than have the crown sit upon your head, and you unleashed upon Atlantia."

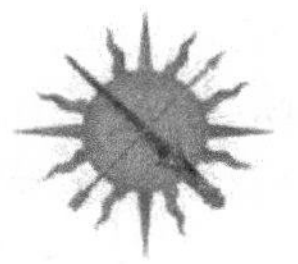

At some point, food was brought to me, carried in by either a man or woman wearing the bronze mask of a Descenter. They placed the tray just within my reach and then quickly backed out without saying a word, leaving me to wonder if Alastir and these *Protectors* had played a role in the attack on the Rite. Casteel hadn't ordered the attack carried out in the name of the Dark One, but it had been organized and well planned regardless. Someone had set a fire to draw many of the Rise Guards away—something Jansen could've ensured happened.

I clenched my jaw as I stared at the hunk of cheese and the lump of bread wrapped in a loose cloth next to a glass of water. When Casteel learned that not only had Alastir betrayed him but that Jansen had, as well, his rage would be unyielding.

And his pain?

It would be just as ruthless.

But what I felt when I thought about Alastir's involvement the night my parents died? The rage scorched my skin. He'd been there. He'd come to help my family and had betrayed them instead. And what he'd said about my parents knowing the truth about the Ascended? Obviously, they had learned the truth and escaped. That didn't mean they knew for years as they stood by and did nothing.

And my mother? A Handmaiden? If that was true, why didn't she fight back that night?

Or had I just not remembered that she had?

There was so much I couldn't remember about that night, things I couldn't decipher as real or only nightmares. I couldn't believe I'd forgotten them. Had I blocked them out because I was scared of them? What else had I forgotten?

Regardless, I had no idea if the Queen's Handmaidens were guards or not. And I didn't believe that any darkness—besides Alastir—was involved with that night. His twisted sense of honor and righteousness prevented him from owning up to what he'd done. Somehow, he'd led those Craven to us and then left everyone in that inn to die. All because I carried the blood of the gods within me.

All because I was King Malec's descendant.

A part of me still couldn't believe any of it—the old part of me that hadn't been able to understand what about me, beyond a gift I hadn't been allowed to use or being born in a caul, had made me special enough to be the Chosen. Blessed. The Maiden. And that part reminded me of when I was a child and used to hide behind Queen Ileana's throne instead of going to my room at night because the darkness had scared me. It was the same part that had enabled me to spend afternoons with my brother, pretending that my parents were out walking together in the garden instead of being gone forever. It felt incredibly young and naïve.

But I wasn't that little girl anymore. I wasn't the young Maiden. The blood in me explained the gifts I'd been born with and why I'd become the Maiden—how my gift had grown, and why my skin glowed. It also explained the disbelief and agony I'd felt from Queen Eloana. She'd known exactly who I descended from, and it must have made her sick to think that her son had married the descendant of a man who'd repeatedly betrayed her and nearly destroyed their kingdom in the process.

How could she ever welcome me, knowing the truth?

Could Casteel ever look upon me the same?

My chest twisted painfully as I stared at the food. Would I even get the chance to see Casteel again? Seconds turned into minutes as I tried to keep my thoughts from straying toward what Alastir planned. I couldn't let myself dwell too long on it—to think about the worst-case scenario playing out in my mind. If I did, the panic I'd been fighting off would seize control of me.

I wouldn't let Alastir's plan succeed. I *couldn't.* I needed to either escape or fight back the second I could. Which meant, I needed my strength. I had to eat.

Reaching out carefully, I broke off a piece of the cheese and gingerly tasted it. There was little flavor to it. The section of bread I tried next was most definitely stale, but I quickly ate both and then drank the water, trying not to think about the gritty taste or how dirty it likely was.

Once I finished, I turned my attention to the spear. I wouldn't be able to hide it, even if I were able to free it from the poor soul beside me. But if I could break off the blade, I might have a better chance. Drawing in a breath that felt…oddly heavy, I inched my hand toward the spear and stopped suddenly. It wasn't the bindings. They hadn't tightened.

I swallowed, and my heart skipped a beat. A strange, sweetness coated the back of my throat and my…my lips tingled. I pressed the tips of my fingers to them and didn't think I felt the pressure. I tried to swallow again, but it felt weird—as if the mechanics of my throat had slowed.

The food. The *gritty* taste of the water.

Oh, gods.

That sweet taste. The sleeping drafts the Healers made in Masadonia had a sugary-sweet aftertaste. There was a reason I'd refused the drafts, no matter how little sleep I got. They were powerful and rendered you completely unconscious for hours and hours—leaving you entirely helpless.

They'd drugged me.

This was how Alastir planned to move me. How he planned to deliver me to the Ascended. He'd be able to remove the bindings safely when I was unconscious. And when I came to…

There was a good chance I'd be in the Ascended's hands once again.

And Alastir's plan would likely come to fruition because I would never allow the Ascended to use me for *anything.*

Anger at them—and myself—exploded within me and then quickly gave way to panic as I staggered to the wall. I barely felt the pain of the bindings tightening. Desperate, I reached for the spear. If I could get that blade, I wouldn't be weaponless, even with the damn bone and root bindings. I tried to seize it, but my arm wouldn't lift. It didn't feel as if it were a part of me any longer. My legs became heavy, numb.

"No, no," I whispered, fighting the insidious warmth seeping into my muscles, my skin.

But it was no use.

Numbness swept through my body, deadening my eyelids. There was no pain when the nothingness came for me this time. I simply fell asleep, knowing I would wake to a nightmare.

Chapter 6

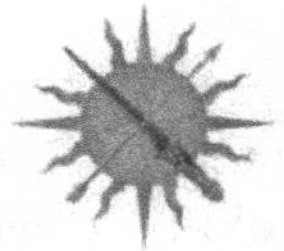

Twinkling lights blanketed the ceiling of the crypt when I opened my eyes. My lips parted as I dragged in deep gulps of…fresh, clean air. That wasn't the ceiling or lights I saw. They were stars. I was outside, no longer in the crypt.

"Dammit," a man to my right swore. "She's awake."

My body immediately reacted to the sound of the voice. I reared up—

Pressure pressed down all over my body, followed by a sharp, stinging wave. My jaw clamped shut against the cry of pain as my head lifted off a flat, hard surface. Ivory bones entwined with thick, dark roots lay across me from my chest to my knees.

"It's okay. She's not getting free."

My gaze swept in the direction of the voice. Commander Jansen stood to my left, a silver wolven mask hiding his face. He angled his body toward mine. Beyond him, I saw the crumbling remains of a stone wall bathed in moonlight, and then nothing but darkness beyond. "Where am I?" I rasped.

His head tilted to the side, his eyes nothing but shadows inside the thin slits of the mask. "You're in what remains of the city of Irelone. This," he answered as he swept his arms out widely, "is what is left of the once-great Castle Bauer."

Irelone? That sounded vaguely familiar. It took a couple of moments for my mind to clear enough for the old maps with their faded ink, created before the War of Two Kings, to form. Irelone…

Yes, I knew that name. It had been a port city to the north and east of where Carsodonia was now. The city had fallen before Pompay during the war. Good gods, that meant…

I was in the Wastelands.

My heart thundered in my chest. How long had I been asleep? Hours or days? I didn't know where the Crypt of the Forgotten Ones had been in the Skotos Mountains. For all I knew, the crypts could've existed in the foothills of the mountains, a half a day's ride north of the outer reaches of the Wastelands.

Throat dry, I lifted just my head to look around. Dozens of the so-called Protectors stood in the center of what could've been the castle's Great Hall at one time and around the edges of the decaying structure, all hidden behind gleaming bronze masks. It was the kind of sight conjured from the depths of the darkest nightmares. Was Alastir among them?

In the darkness beyond the ruins, a single torch flared to life. "They're here," a masked man announced. "The Ascended."

Air halted in my throat as several more torches caught fire, casting an orange glow over heaps of fallen stone and earth that had refused to house new life in the hundreds of years that had passed. Shadows formed, and I heard the sounds of hooves and wheels on packed earth.

"Believe it or not,"—Jansen drew closer, placing his hands on the stone as he leaned over me—"I wouldn't wish your fate upon anyone."

My gaze shot to his as anger coated my insides. "I'd be more worried about your fate than mine."

Jansen stared down at me for a moment and then reached into the pocket of his pants. "You know," he said, lifting his hand now filled with a bundle of cloth, "at least you knew when to keep your mouth shut when you were the Maiden."

"I'm going—" He shoved the wad of fabric into my mouth, securing the ends behind my head and effectively silencing my threats. Nausea churned at the taste and the spike of helplessness I felt.

He arched a brow at me before pushing away from the stone slab, his hand falling to the hilt of a short sword. His shoulders tensed, and I wished I could see his expression. He turned from me as others drew swords. "Keep alert," he barked. "But do not engage."

The masked men moved out of my line of sight as the creak of carriage wheels ceased. I couldn't allow myself to think beyond the next second, that very moment, as I watched the torches drift forward, thrust into the ground around the broken remains of Castle Bauer. My heart pounded. I couldn't believe this was happening. I twisted my head to the side, hoping to dislodge the bindings, but they didn't move.

Panic swelled as a dark shadow drifted closer to what remained of the steps, then climbed them slowly. A cloaked figure in black and red stood in the middle of the half-fallen walls. I stopped moving, but my heart continued throwing itself against my chest.

This couldn't be happening.

Two pale hands lifted the hood of the robe, lowering the material to reveal a woman I didn't recognize, one with hair the color of sunlight, swept back from a face that was all cold angles. She strode forward, the heels of her shoes clicking on the stone. She never once spared a single look at the others. She seemed utterly unafraid of their presence and the swords they held. Her entire focus was on me, and I wondered how either side could share the same space as the other. Could these pretend Protectors' need to be rid of me, and the desire for the Ascended to reclaim me, be that great? And would the Ascended take me and not attempt to capture all the Atlantians standing among them, all so full of the blood they craved so desperately?

Gods, a sick part of me hoped this was a trap. That the Ascended would turn on them. It would be so very fitting.

I forced myself to show no reaction as the Ascended passed my legs, her lip curling as she flicked her gaze over the bone and root chains. "What is this?" she demanded coolly.

"It's to keep her…calm," Jansen answered from somewhere behind me. "You will need to remove them. The gag? Well, she was being quite rude. I suggest you keep that one on for as long as possible."

Bastard, I seethed silently, watching the Ascended as she came closer.

"She appears quite calm now." She stared down at me, at my scars, with eyes that swallowed the night. A breath shuddered out of her. "It is her," she called out to whoever remained in the darkness as she reached for me. Cold fingers brushed my brow, causing me to flinch. Blood-red lips formed a smile. "It will all be okay now, Maiden. We will take you home. Where you belong. Your Queen will be so very—"

The Ascended jerked back without warning as something wet and warm sprayed my face and neck. She looked down at the same time I did, my eyes and hers widening at the sight of the thick bolt now embedded deep in her chest.

Her lips peeled back, and she let out a high-pitched snarl, revealing jagged fangs. "What in the—?"

Another bolt tore through her head, shattering bone and tissue. The sight was so unexpected and so sudden that I didn't even hear the shouts at first. All I could do was stare at the spot where she'd stood—where her head *had* been. Suddenly, something large and white leapt into my line of sight, taking down a masked man.

Delano.

A wealth of relief rose so swiftly within me that I cried out, the sound muffled by the gag. They were here. They'd found me. I cranked my head to the side and back, straining to look as far as I could see. Another wolven raced forward, this one large and dark. It shot across the castle ruins' floor, its powerful muscles tensing as it launched over one of the half-fallen walls. The wolven disappeared into the night, but a sharp screech from the darkness followed. The wolven had captured an Ascended.

"*Poppy.*"

My head whipped to the right, and I shuddered at the sight of Kieran. He looked nothing like the last time I'd seen him, his skin now a warm shade of brown against the black of his clothing. I started to reach for him, and the action ended in a hiss of pain.

With a curse, he grabbed hold of the gag and pulled it free from my mouth as his pale eyes swept over me. "How badly are you injured?"

"I'm not." I forced myself to remain still as I ignored the cottony feeling the gag had left behind in my mouth. "It's these bonds. They're—"

"The bones of a deity." Disgust curled his lip as he reached for the one lying just below my throat. "I know what they are."

"Careful," I warned. "They have spurs in them."

"I'll be fine. You just…don't move," he ordered, the muscles of his bare arm straining as he pulled on the first row of bindings.

A thousand questions rose, but the most important one came out first. "Casteel—?"

"Is currently disemboweling some idiot in a godsdamn Descenter mask," he answered, gripping the bone and roots with both hands. Even though that sounded extremely grotesque, I turned my head to the other side, trying to find him—

"Keep still, Poppy."

"I'm trying."

"Then try harder," Kieran snapped, his eyes narrowing on the ravaged skin of my wrists. "How long have you been in these things?"

"I don't know. Not that long," I said. The look Kieran shot me told me that he knew I lied. "Are all of you okay? Your father?"

He nodded as a broad-shouldered male appeared several feet behind Kieran, the man's blond hair pulled back in a knot at the nape of his neck. Shock trickled through me as the male turned to the side, shoving his sword into a man's chest as he ripped off the Descenter mask.

It was Casteel's father. He was here. Maybe it was hunger or the residual panic of being seconds away from being in the clutches of the Ascended once more. Perhaps it was everything that Alastir had told me. Either way, tears climbed my throat as I stared at King Valyn. He was here, fighting to free me.

"I think my father is currently venting his anger by tearing through the Ascended with Naill and Emil," Kieran told me.

"It looks like Casteel's father is doing the same." I breathed through the raw emotions coursing through me. I couldn't believe Valyn was here. It was incredibly dangerous for him to be this far from Atlantia. If any of the Ascended knew it was him dressed in all black, they would swarm him. He had to know the risks, but still he was here, helping Casteel. Helping *me*.

Kieran snorted. "You have no idea."

I still had so many questions, but I needed to make sure Kieran knew what they were dealing with. "It wasn't just Alastir. I don't know if he's here, but Commander Jansen is. He's in a silver Descenter mask."

Kieran's jaw hardened as he snapped the binding in two. The ends fell to the sides. "Anyone else you recognized?"

"No." My heart thudded. "But…Beckett—it wasn't him at the Temple. He's—" My voice cracked. "It wasn't him."

Kieran gripped the second row of bindings. "Poppy—"

"Beckett's dead," I told him, and his gaze shot to mine as he froze. "They killed him, Kieran. I don't think they planned to, but it happened. He's dead."

"Fuck," he growled, moving once more.

"Jansen took Beckett's form. He left Spessa's End with us. Not Beckett. Jansen admitted to it all, and Alastir said he planned to give me to the Ascended."

"Obviously," Kieran replied wryly, breaking another set of bones and roots. "What a fucking idiot."

I laughed, and it sounded hoarse and all wrong amidst the shouts of pain and snarls of anger. It felt just as wrong yet strangely wonderful that I could laugh again. It faded as I stared at the slash of Kieran's brows. What I said came out as a whisper. "Alastir said I'm descended from Nyktos. That I'm related to King Malec, and that he was there the night my parents died. It was—" Movement beyond Kieran's shoulder snagged my attention. A masked man raced toward us—

Before I could shout a warning to Kieran, *he* was there, tall and as dark as the night creeping into the ruins, his blue-black hair windblown. Every part of my being zeroed in on Casteel as his crimson sword plunged through the Protector's stomach, embedding itself in the wall behind the masked figure. Casteel turned, catching the arm of another. A dark rumble escaped from his throat as he dragged the man toward him. Teeth bared, he snapped his head down on the man's throat, tearing through skin as he thrust his hand *through* the man's chest. Lifting his head, he spat a mouthful of the man's blood into the Protector's face.

Casteel tossed the body to the ground and looked up at another man, blood streaming from his mouth. "What?"

The masked man spun and ran.

Casteel was faster, reaching him in the blink of an eye. He shoved his fist into the man's back and jerked his arm back sharply, pulling out something white and smeared with blood and tissue. His spine. Dear gods, it was the man's *spine.*

Kieran's eyes met mine. "He's a little angry."

"A little?" I whispered.

"Okay. He's really angry," Kieran amended, reaching for the bindings just below my breasts. "He has been going crazy looking for you. I've never seen him this way." His hands trembled slightly as they folded over the bone and root chains. "*Never*, Poppy."

"I…" I trailed off as Casteel spun around. Our gazes locked, and Nyktos himself could have appeared before me, and I wouldn't have been able to look away from Casteel. There was so much rage in the sharp set of his features and his eyes. Only a thin strip of amber was visible, but I also saw relief and something so potent, so powerful in his stare that I needed no gift to feel it.

The wind lifted the edges of his cloak as he started toward me. A guard flew out from the darkness—one who wore the black uniform of the Rise Guard and had come with the Ascended. Casteel pivoted, catching the guard by the throat as he shoved the blade into the man's chest.

"I love him," I whispered.

Kieran paused by my legs. "Are you just now figuring that out?"

"No." My stare followed Casteel as he unsheathed a dagger from his side and threw it out into the night. A sharp, too-quick scream told me that he'd hit his target. Every part of me buzzed with the need to touch him, to feel his flesh under mine so I could erase the memory of what his skin had felt like the last time I'd touched him. The breath I let out was shaky. "How did you all find me?"

"Casteel knew others in the Crown Guard had to be involved," Kieran explained. "He made it very clear that if he didn't find out who, he would start killing all of them."

My stomach dipped as my gaze shot to Kieran's. I didn't have to ask.

"He used compulsion. Ferreted out four of them that way, but only one really knew anything," he said. "He told us where you were being held and what was planned. We got to those crypts only a few hours after you left, but we didn't come up empty-handed."

I was too hopeful to even ask, but I did. "Alastir?"

A savage grin appeared. "Yes."

Thank the gods. My eyes closed briefly. I hated the betrayal Casteel must feel, but at least Alastir wasn't out there.

"Poppy?" Kieran's hands were on the last of the bone bindings. "I'm going to assume that even if I ask you nicely to sit this fight out, you won't listen to me, will you?"

I sat up tentatively, expecting pain. Instead, there was nothing but the previous aches. "How long have they had me?"

Kieran's nostrils flared. "It's been six days and eight hours."

Six days.

My chest rose sharply. "They kept me chained to the wall of a crypt full of the remains of deities. They drugged me and planned to hand me over to the Ascended," I told him. "I'm not sitting this out."

"Of course, not." He sighed.

The last bone broke, and then Kieran pulled it away. The moment it was gone, a wave of tingles swept over the back of my head and down my spine, branching out and following the pathways of my nerves. The center of my chest warmed, and I hadn't realized until that moment that the coldness I'd felt wasn't only due to the damp iciness of the crypt. It had also been because of the bones. It was like my blood rushed back to parts of me that had gone numb. But it wasn't the blood, was it? It was the…the eather. The tingling sensation wasn't at all painful, though; more like a wave of release.

The center of my chest started to hum, the sound vibrating out through my lips. My senses opened wide and stretched out, connecting with those around me. I tasted bitter, sweat-drenched fear and the hot acidic burn of hatred. I didn't try to stop it. I let instinct—the Primal knowledge that had woken in the Chambers of Nyktos—take hold. I swung my legs off the raised surface as Casteel took down what appeared to be an Ascended, his father fighting alongside him. I stood, feeling a rush of power just from being able to stand after being held down by the bones and roots for so long.

Kieran picked up a fallen sword, his brow furrowing as he stared at the blade. "Here," he offered the weapon to me.

I shook my head as I took a step, my legs trembling slightly from not holding my weight for so long. The hum in my chest grew, the eather in my blood intensifying as I kept my senses open wide. These people wanted to hurt me. They *had.* And they had harmed Casteel, Kieran, and everyone else. They'd killed Beckett. None of them deserved to live.

The corners of my vision turned white, and in my mind, the thin, silvery-white cords slipped out from me, crackling off the floor and reconnecting with the others. My anger joined the pounding emotions now flooding my senses. I drew in a deep breath, taking in everybody's feelings, letting their hatred, fear, and twisted sense of righteousness seep into my skin and become a part of me. Those emotions twined with the cords in my mind. I took it all in, feeling the toxic storm thrumming inside me. There wouldn't be time for them to regret what they took part in. I would destroy them. I would obliterate them—

Alastir's words came back to me at that moment. "*You are dangerous now, but you will become something else entirely later.*"

Unease exploded in my gut, dispersing the silver cords in my mind. These people deserved whatever I dealt to them. What Alastir had said didn't matter. If I killed them, it wouldn't be because I was unable to control myself. And it wasn't because I was unpredictable or chaotically violent like the deities were supposed to be. I just wanted them to taste their emotions, for that ugliness to be the last thing they felt. I wanted that more than—

I wanted that too much, when I shouldn't want it at all.

I didn't enjoy killing, not even the Craven. Killing was merely a harsh reality, one that shouldn't be desired or enjoyed.

Unsettled, I sucked in dry air and did what I had to when I was in a crowd or around someone who projected their emotions into the space around them. I shut my senses down, forcing the silvery webbing of light from my mind. The hum in my chest calmed, but my mind didn't. I'd stopped myself. That's all I needed to know to prove that what Alastir had said wasn't true. I wasn't a chaotic, violent entity incapable of controlling myself.

Kieran came to my side, angling his body so he could see me and everything happening around us. He unhooked his cloak. "Are you okay?"

"I'm not a monster," I whispered.

He stiffened. "What?"

Swallowing hard, I shook my head. "N-nothing. I…" I watched King Valyn strike down another masked man. He and his son fought with the same kind of gracefully brutal force. "I'm fine."

Kieran draped the soft material over my shoulders, startling me. "You sure about that?"

"Yes." My gaze flicked to his as he secured the button just below my neck. It was then that I remembered I wore nothing but the thin, bloody slip. He pulled the halves together. "Thank you. I'm…I'm going to sit this one out."

"I want to thank the gods," Kieran muttered. "But now you really have me worried."

"I'm okay." My gaze followed Casteel as he spun, knocking a sword from a Protector's hand. The blade clattered on the stone floor as Casteel drew his sword back, prepared to deliver a fatal blow. Moonlight glinted off the man's facial covering—a silver mask.

Jansen.

"Casteel, stop!" I shouted. He halted, his chest rising and falling with his heavy breaths as he leveled his sword at Jansen. Later, I would marvel over the fact that he had stopped without hesitation. Without question. I walked forward. "I made him a promise."

"Thought you were sitting this one out," Kieran stated as he kept pace with me.

"I am," I told him. "But he's different."

Casteel stiffened at my words and shot forward so quickly that I thought he might deliver the fatal blow anyway. But he didn't. He gripped the front of the silver mask and ripped it aside.

"Son of a bitch." He tossed the mask to the floor.

Jansen's eyes darted between Casteel and his father. "She will—"

"You need to shut the fuck up," Casteel snarled as he stepped to the side.

I stalked forward, the stone cool under my bare feet as Kieran followed. As I passed Casteel, he pressed the hilt of his sword into my palm, and his bloodied lips touched my cheek.

"Poppy," he said, and the sound of his voice punched a small hole in the wall I had built around my gifts. Everything he felt in the moment reached me. The hot acidity of rage, the refreshing, woodsy feeling of his relief, and the warmth of everything he felt for me. And given what he'd experienced before, the bitterness of fear and panic.

I shuddered as I stared at Jansen. "I'm okay."

Casteel squeezed my hand that now held his sword. "None of this is okay."

He was right.

It really wasn't.

But I knew what would make it a little okay, right or wrong.

I pulled free from Casteel. "What did I promise you?" I asked Jansen.

The Royal Guard commander reached for his fallen sword, but I was faster, thrusting the sword out. Grunting, he staggered back, dropping to his knees. Glaring up at me, he folded his hands over the blade as if he could actually stop what was about to happen. "I told you that I'd be the one to kill you." I slowly pushed the blade into his chest, smiling as I felt his bones break under the pressure of the sword as it met softer tissue. Blood bubbled out of the corner of his mouth. "I keep my promises."

"As do I," he rasped, the life fading from his eyes as his hands slipped from the blade, the skin of his palms and fingers torn open by the sharp edges.

As do I?

Without warning, something jerked me back with such force that fiery pain erupted in my chest. I lost my grip on the sword. The movement was so sudden, so intense, that I felt nothing for a moment as if I'd become detached from my body somehow. Time stopped for me, but people were still moving, and I saw a flash of Jasper as he leapt onto a Protector's back, his teeth clamping down on the masked man's throat. Something fell from the man's hand. A bow…a crossbow.

Slowly, I looked down. Red. So much red everywhere. A bolt protruded from my chest.

Chapter 7

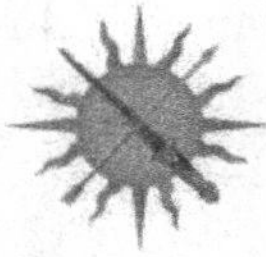

Stunned, I looked up, my eyes locking with Casteel's. There was barely any amber visible as the kind of horror I'd never seen before settled into his features. His shock blasted through my protective walls, overwhelming my senses.

I opened my mouth and tasted an awful metallic taste in the back of my throat. Viscous liquid bubbled up with each breath I tried to take, spilling over my lips. "Casteel…?"

Pain surged through my entire body, all-consuming and total. The agony came in wave after wave, shortening each breath I took. I'd never felt anything like this. Not even the night at the inn. All my senses shorted out, shutting down my gift. I couldn't feel anything beyond the searing misery burning through my chest, my lungs, and every nerve ending.

Oh, gods, this kind of pain brought a razor-edged terror with it. A knowledge that I couldn't escape. I felt slippery, wet, and cold *inside.* I took a breath as I reached for the bolt. Or tried to. Whatever air I sucked in, I choked on, and what made it past my throat crackled and bubbled in my chest. My fingers slipped on the smooth surface of the bloodstone bolt, and my legs—they just *disappeared.* Or seemed to. My knees buckled.

Arms caught me, stopping my fall, and for a heartbeat, the scent of lush spice and pine overshadowed the iron-rich smell of blood pumping from the wound. I lifted my head.

"I've got you. It's okay. I've got you." Wide, dilated, amber eyes locked with mine—wild. His gaze was *wild* as he quickly glanced down at my chest. When he refocused on my face, he said, "You're going to be okay."

I didn't feel okay. Oh, gods, I didn't feel right at all.

Movement stirred the air as Kieran appeared at our side, his normally dusky skin so, so pale. He placed his hand on the base of the bolt, trying to stanch the blood.

The touch was torment. I twisted, trying to move away. "It…it *hurts*."

"I know. I'm sorry. I know it hurts." Casteel glanced at Kieran. "Can you see how far it went in?"

"I don't see the ridges on the bolt," he said, looking over my shoulder. I shuddered, knowing these bolts were like the jagged stems of some of the arrows I'd fired before, ones created to cause maximum damage. "The blood, Cas. It's too much."

"I know," Casteel bit out as a snapping, snarling, *fleshy* and *wet* sound from somewhere behind us blocked out what he said next.

Kieran gripped my left shoulder, and my entire body spasmed with pain. I screamed. Or maybe it was only a gasp. Warm wetness splattered across my lips, and that was bad. My wide gaze moved between Casteel and Kieran. I knew this was bad. I could feel it. I could feel the bolt, and I couldn't take deep breaths, and…and I couldn't feel my fingertips.

"I'm sorry. I'm trying to keep your body stable so we don't move the bolt. I'm sorry. I'm sorry, Poppy," Kieran said again and again. He kept saying that, and I wanted him to stop because he sounded too breathy, too rattled. He never got rattled. He sounded like he already knew what my body was trying to tell me.

Casteel started to move, and I tried to curl in on myself, to turn away from the pain, to use my legs. But I... My pulse skittered, and my eyes rolled frantically as panic fluttered through me. "I…I can't feel…my legs."

"I'm going to fix that. I promise. I'm going to fix all of this," Casteel swore, and over his shoulder, I stared at the night sky—at each diamond-bright star disappearing.

Casteel sank to his knees and lowered me slowly. He angled my body so his chest cradled my right side.

"How bad is it?" Casteel's father appeared behind him, his familiar features stark as he stared down, his eyes wide.

"We can't pull it out," Casteel said.

"No," Kieran agreed, his voice thick and heavy and somehow tight. Now, the clouds that covered the stars were pitch-black. Kieran's hand slipped on my chest, and he quickly replaced his palm. This time, it didn't hurt as much. "Cas, man—"

"It didn't get her heart," Casteel cut him off. "She wouldn't be—" His voice cracked, and I flinched, forcing myself to focus on him. His skin had leached of all color. "It didn't get her heart."

"Cas—"

He shook his head as he touched my cheek, wiping under my mouth. "I can give her blood—"

"*Cas*," Kieran repeated as King Valyn placed his hand on Casteel's shoulder.

"You're going to be okay," he said to me. "I'm going to take the pain away. I promise you." The hand on my chin trembled, and Casteel…he rarely ever shook, but his entire body did now. "I promise you, Poppy."

I wanted to touch him, but my arms felt weighted down and useless. The breath I forced myself to take was wet and reedy. "I…I don't hurt so…much."

"That's good." He smiled—or tried to. "Don't try to talk. Okay? I'm going to give you some blood—"

"Son," his father started. "You can't. And even if you could—"

Casteel's lips pulled back over his fangs as he shrugged off his father's grip. "Get the fuck away from us."

"I'm sorry," King Valyn whispered, and then Jasper was there, snarling and snapping, forcing Casteel's father back. Lightning streaked across the dark sky. "I didn't want this for you—for either of you. I'm sorry…"

"Cas," Kieran rasped, pleading now.

Casteel bit into his wrist, tearing the skin. Bright red blood welled, and it struck me then as I watched the streaks of silvery-white lightning slice across the sky that I felt no pain at all now. My body was numb and… "*Cold.* I'm…cold again."

"I know." Fresh blood smeared Casteel's lips and chin. He lowered his wrist to my mouth as he shifted my head so it rested in the crook of his elbow. "Drink, Princess. Drink for me."

His blood touched my lips, warm and lush. It reached the back of my throat, but I couldn't taste it, couldn't swallow it. There was so much stuff in there already. Panic spread.

"Cas—"

"What?" he thundered.

"Listen to me. Please, Cas. Listen to me. It didn't get her heart." Kieran leaned in, clasping the back of Casteel's neck. "Look at the blood. It got an artery and at least a lung. You know that—"

A flash of intense light exploded over the ruins, momentarily blinding me, followed by a loud boom. Stone cracked. Someone shouted. I heard a scream. The stone floor shuddered as whatever the lightning had struck fell.

"*No. No. No.* Open your eyes," Casteel begged. They had closed? "Come on. Don't do this. Don't do this to me. *Please.* Open your eyes. Please, Poppy. Drink." He curled over me, pressing his wrist against my mouth. "Please. Poppy, drink."

Casteel's features pieced themselves back together, but they were hazy as if the lines and angles had been smudged. I blinked rapidly, trying to clear my vision.

"There you are," he said, his chest rising and falling too fast. "Stay with me. Okay? Keep your eyes open. Stay with me."

I wanted to. Gods, I wanted to more than anything, but I was tired. Sleepy. I whispered that. At least, I thought I did. I wasn't sure, but it didn't matter. I concentrated on his face, on the lock of dark hair, the winged, expressive brows. I soaked in the thick fringe of lashes and the high, angular cheekbones. I studied every inch of his striking features, from the hard curve of his jaw to his full, well-formed mouth, committing them to memory. Because I knew…I knew when my eyes closed again, they wouldn't reopen. I wanted to remember his face when the world turned dark. I wanted to remember what it felt like to be in his arms, to hear his voice and feel his mouth against mine. I wanted to remember the way he smiled when I threatened him, and how his eyes lit up and warmed whenever I challenged him. I wanted to remember the pride I felt from him whenever I silenced those around me with words or by blade. I wanted to remember how he touched my scars reverently as if he wasn't worthy of them—of me.

Another bolt of lightning streaked overhead, striking the ground and charging the air. Chunks of stone flew into the sky. Casteel's father shouted, and I heard a chorus of howls coming from all around. But I focused on Casteel. His eyes were glossy, and his lashes were wet.

He was crying.

Casteel was *crying.*

Tears streaked his cheeks, creating glistening tracks in the dried blood as they rolled and rolled…and I knew…I knew I was dying.

Casteel knew it, too. He had to. There was so much I wanted to say, so much I wanted to do with him and change. His brother's future. Ian's. That of the people of Atlantia and Solis. *Our* future. Did I ever thank him for seeing past the veil? Or for never once forcing me to stand down? Did I tell him how much he'd changed my life, how much that meant to me, even when I thought I hated him—even when I *wanted* to hate him? I think I did, but it didn't feel like it was enough. And there was more. I wanted one more kiss. One more smile. I wanted to see his stupid dimples again, and I wanted to kiss them. I wanted to prove to him that he was worthy of me, of love and life, no matter what had happened in his past or what he'd done. But, oh gods, there wasn't enough time.

I pushed past the panic and the fading, drowning feeling, the sensation that none of this felt real. My lips moved. I made them, but no sound came out.

Casteel…*broke*.

He threw back his head and roared. He *roared*, and the sound echoed around us, through me. Under me, the stone cracked and opened. Thick, ropey roots spilled out, the color of ash. Kieran fell back on his ass as they came down over my legs, over Casteel's back. A tree grew. It grew so fast. Lightning tore through the sky again, one strike after another, turning night to day as thick, glistening bark stretched high, forming hundreds of branches. Tiny golden buds sprouted, filling the branches. They blossomed, unfurling into blood-red leaves.

Casteel's head snapped down, his eyes feral and lost as they'd been the morning he woke from the nightmare. He caught one of the roots as it fell over my stomach and stared at it for a moment before he broke it, tossing it aside. "I cannot let you go. I won't. Not now. Not ever." His hand moved to my cheek, but I barely felt it. "Kieran, I need you to pull the bolt out. I—I can't—" His voice shattered. "I need you. I can't do that."

"You're going to…" Kieran rocked forward. "Fuck. Yeah. Okay." He tore through the roots. "Let's do this."

Do…do what?

Kieran gripped the bolt. "Good gods, forgive us," he uttered. "You've got to be fast. You'll have seconds if you're lucky, and then…"

"Then I will deal with what comes next," Casteel stated bluntly.

"No," Kieran argued. "*We* will deal with what comes next. Together."

"Casteel, stop!" his father yelled. "I'm sorry, but you can't do this!" I heard panic. So much panic filled his voice, it flooded the air. "You know what will happen. I won't allow this. You can hate me for the rest of your life, but I will not allow this. Guards, seize him!"

"Get them away from me," Casteel snarled. "Get all of them away from us, or I swear to the gods, I will rip their hearts from their chests. I do not care if a heart belongs to one who gave me life. You will not stop me."

"Look around you!" his father shouted. "The gods are speaking to us right now. You cannot do this—"

"The gods will not stop me, either," Casteel swore.

The rolling rumble shook the ground, but it was faster and greater. Howls and yips exploded between blasts of thunder. There were…there were *screams*. High-pitched wails of pain, and throaty, vibrating growls. Jasper prowled into my line of sight, crouching so he was over my legs, standing between Kieran and Casteel. I caught a glimpse of white fur, circling and circling. The sounds the wolven made—the keening, mournful howls—haunted every too-thin, too-short breath I managed.

"No one is getting close to us." Kieran shifted forward. "If they do, they won't be standing for long."

"Good," Casteel said. "I'm not going to be much of a…" A veil of darkness slipped over me, and I felt as if I were starting to fall. He faded out and then came back. "…she may be different… Promise me you will keep her safe."

"I will make sure *both* of you are safe," Kieran told him.

The next thing I heard was Casteel's voice. "Look at me," he ordered, turning my head toward his. My eyelids were too heavy. "Keep your eyes open and look at me."

My eyes opened, answering his will, and I… I couldn't look away as his pupils constricted.

"Keep looking at me, Poppy, and listen." His voice was soft and deep, and it was *everywhere*, all around me and inside me. All I could do was obey. "I love you, Penellaphe. *You*. Your fierce heart, your intelligence and strength. I love your endless capacity for kindness. I love your acceptance of me. Your understanding. I'm in love with you, and I will be in love with you when I take my last breath and then beyond in the Vale." Casteel lowered his head, pressing his lips against mine. Something wet glanced off my cheek. "But I have no plans to enter the Vale anytime soon. And I will *not* lose you. *Ever*. I love you,

Princess, and even if you hate me for what I'm about to do, I will spend the rest of our lives making up for it." He jerked back, exhaling heavily. "Now!"

Kieran yanked the bolt free, and that—*that* pierced the cold numbness that had enveloped my body. My entire body jerked, and it kept jerking and twitching. Pressure clamped down on my skull, my chest, expanding and twisting—

Casteel struck as fast as the lightning. He pulled my head back and sank his teeth into my throat. Confusion rose. Hadn't I already lost enough blood? My thoughts were murky, and what Casteel was doing was slow to make sense. He was....

Oh, gods, he was going to Ascend me.

Terror dug its claws into me. I didn't want to die, but I didn't want to turn into something inhuman, either. Cold and violent and without a soul. And that's what the Ascended lacked, wasn't it? That's why I couldn't feel anything from them. There was no soul to fuel the emotions. They were incapable of even the most basic feelings. I didn't—

Red-hot pain scattered all my thoughts, shocking my already faltering heart. The sting of his bite didn't ease when he closed his mouth over the wound. It wasn't replaced by the sensual, languid pull as he drew my blood into him. There was no glorious, seductive heat building. There was only fire on my skin and inside me, burning through every cell. It was way worse than when I'd been trapped in the carriage with Lord Chaney, but I couldn't fight back now. Nothing worked. I couldn't move away from the pain. It was too much, and the scream I couldn't give breath to bounced off my skull and exploded in the sky, in silvery lightning that streaked from cloud to cloud and slammed down onto the ruins of the castle and all around it. The entire world seemed to shudder as crimson leaves drifted from the tree, falling on Casteel's shoulders, blanketing the length of Kieran's back and settling in Jasper's silver fur.

My heart—it faltered. I felt it. Oh, gods, I felt it miss a beat, skipping two, and then sluggishly trying to keep up, to restart. And then it failed. Everything seized in me. My lungs. My muscles. Every organ. My eyes were wide, my gaze fixed as my entire body strained for breath, for relief, and then...death swept in so sweetly, it swallowed me whole. I drowned in its lush, dark spice.

Chapter 8

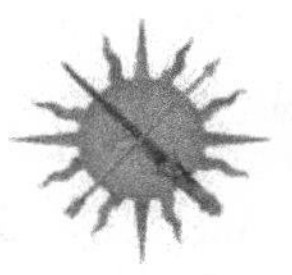

There was no light, no color, and I floated in there for a while, untethered, hollow and cold. I didn't think. I didn't feel. I just existed in the nothingness…

Until I saw a speck of silvery light that seemed a world away from me. The illumination throbbed, and with each beat, it expanded. Wispy tendrils seeped out from the edges, stretching across the void. Slowly, I drifted toward it.

Sound came back without warning. A voice so deep and powerful that it found me in the nothing, caught hold of me so I was no longer slipping toward the silvery light. The voice held me captive.

"Drink. Keep drinking," it ordered. "That's it. Keep swallowing. Drink, Princess, drink for me…"

The words repeated themselves over and over for what felt like an eternity before they faded away, and I was once again in the stillness. There was no silvery light now. Nothing but a warm and empty darkness with the sweet, comforting scent of…lilacs.

I stayed there until flashes of muted color surrounded me. Reds. Silvers. Golds. They swirled together, and I slipped through them, falling back through the nights, through the years, until I was small and helpless, standing before my father.

I could see him clearly, his hair a coppery red in the lamplight. His square jaw covered in several days-worth of a beard. Straight nose. Eyes the color of pine.

"What a pretty, little flower. What a pretty poppy." Papa leaned in, kissing the crown of my head. "I love you more than all the stars in the sky."

"I love you more than all the fish in the sea."

"That's my girl." Papa's hands trembled on my cheeks. "Cora?"

Momma came forward, her face pale. "You should've known she would find a way down here." She glanced over her shoulder. "You trust him?"

"I do," he said as Momma took my hand in hers. "He's going to lead us to safety…."

Wind roared like thunder through the inn, coming from a place that was not here. Voices rose, ones that didn't come from Papa or Momma, but from above, somewhere beyond the whirlpool of colors at the other end of the nothingness.

"Who remains?" a male voice reached me, the same one that had found me when I was drifting toward the silvery light, but it was now hoarse and faint, weary and weakened.

"Just us," another deep voice replied, this one strained. "We don't have to worry about the guards. I think Jasper decided it would be best if they were…no more."

"My father?"

"Not an issue for now." There was a pause. "We won't make it back to the Cove, but there is…" He faded out briefly. "We'll have to make it work just in case she… Do you think you can move?"

There wasn't an answer for a long moment. "I…I don't know."

I fell again, slipping back through the years once more.

"Stay with your momma, baby." Papa touched my cheeks, drawing me away from the voices. "Stay with her and find your brother. I'll be back for you soon."

Papa rose and turned to the door—to the man who stood there, watching from the small crack between the panels. "Do you see him?"

The man at the door, whose hair reminded me of the beaches of the Stroud Sea, nodded. "He knows you're here."

"He knows she's here."

"Either way, he's leading them here. If they get in here…"

"We don't let that happen," Papa said, reaching for the hilt of a sword. "They can't have her. We can't let that happen."

"No," the man agreed softly, looking over his shoulder at me with strange blue eyes. "I won't."

"Come, Poppy." Momma pulled on my hand—

The voice pulled me beyond the colors and the nothing.

"I don't know what will happen from here." He sounded closer, but even more tired than the last time his voice had reached me. Each word seemed to require an effort that he was quickly losing the ability to give. "She breathes. Her heart beats. She lives."

"That is all that matters," the other voice said, less strained. "You need to feed."

"I'm fine—"

"Bullshit. You were barely able to get on your horse and stay on it. You've lost too much blood," the other argued. "She's going to wake eventually, and you know what will happen. You won't be able to take care of her. Would you like Naill or Emil to service you, or would you prefer that they service—?"

"Naill," he barked out. "Get Naill, dammit."

There was a rough chuckle, and I slipped away, only to hear sometime later, "Rest. I will watch over both of you."

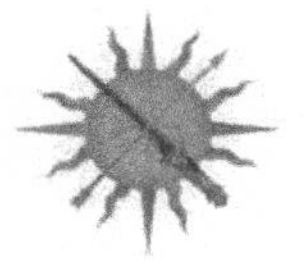

I was gone again, but this time was different. I slept. I slept deeply, where only fragments of words reached me. But in that place, I became…aware that I had parts. A body. There was a warm, damp touch to my brow, my cheek. It was soft. A cloth. It swept over my lips and under them, along the side of my throat and between my breasts. It disappeared, and then there was sound. A trickling of water, and then the cloth returned, gliding over my bare arms and between my fingers. The touch felt nice. It lulled me, letting me slip back into the heavy sleep and fall once more.

I was that child again, grasping at my mother's bloodied arm. *They had gotten inside, just like the man had warned. The screams. There were so many screams, and the shrieks of those things outside the window, scratching and clawing at it.*

"You've got to let go, baby. You need to hide, Poppy—" Momma stilled and then wrenched her arm free.

Momma reached into the kid leather boots I liked to shuffle around in, pretending that I was older and bigger. She pulled something out, something black as night and slender and sharp. She moved so fast—faster than I'd ever seen her move before, spinning around as she rose, the black spike in her hand.

"How could you do this?" Momma demanded as I scooted to the edge of the cupboard.

And then I was above the colors, in the nothingness once again, but I wasn't alone.

A woman was there, her hair long and floating around her, the color so pale it was like spun moonlight. Her features were familiar. I'd seen her before in my mind while in the Temple. But now I thought she looked a bit like me. There were freckles across the bridge of her nose and on her cheeks. Her eyes were the color of dew-kissed grass, but behind the pupils, there was a light. A silvery-white glow that seeped out, fracturing the vibrant green.

Her lips moved, and she spoke. Her lashes swept down, and a tear fell from the corner of one eye—a blood-red tear. Her words sent a jolt of icy shock through me. But then she was gone, and so was I.

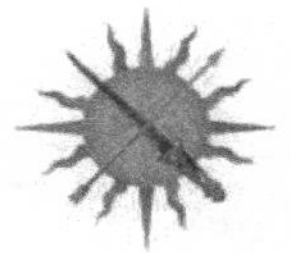

A pins-and-needles sensation was the first thing I became aware of. It started in my feet and then crawled up my calves to spread over the rest of my body. Heat followed. A fever swept through me, drying my already parched throat. Thirsty. I was so *thirsty.* I tried to open my mouth, but my lips felt sealed together.

My toes curled, and I didn't like the feeling at first. It caused the rest of my flesh to become aware of the blanket lying on me and the mattress under me. My skin felt too sensitive, the material too scratchy.

I was so thirsty.

My fingers twitched against my bare stomach. The skin felt jagged, uneven. I concentrated on my mouth, willing my lips to part. If I could open them, I could ask for…for water. No. I didn't want water. I wanted something else.

I wasn't thirsty. I was…hungry. *Starving.* I forced my lips to part, and a shallow breath worked its way in. There were scents. Fresh pine. Something wild. My skin started to tingle and grow tight, becoming even more sensitized. My ears vibrated with sound. A whisper of a breeze. A fan churning lazily. The sound was pleasant, but I was hollow, an empty void.

I was so hungry.

I was so hungry, I *ached.* The inside of my mouth throbbed, and everything inside me felt as if it were drying out, becoming shriveled and brittle. My muscles cramped as I struggled to open my eyes. They felt sewn shut, but I was hungry, and I needed to open my eyes. What felt like a lifetime passed before I managed to pry my lashes apart.

Everything was a hazy, fuzzy array of shadows and splotches of light. I blinked several times, half-afraid my eyes wouldn't open again, but they did. My vision cleared. Soft light from a gas lamp flowed across gray walls and an old, worn chair—

A chair that wasn't empty.

A male was slumped in it, his skin a beige-brown, his dark hair cropped close to the skull. He rubbed at his eyes, and a strange feeling took root in my chest, a sensation I tried to grasp. But whatever it was kept slipping through my fingers. I was too starved to concentrate. I needed…

The male sighed and my muscles tensed. My legs curled up, and the ache in the pit of my stomach and my chest grew and grew. Throat constricting, my heart started to thud heavily against my ribs as the hunger seized me. I wasn't aware of moving, of sitting up, until hair fell over my shoulders, causing my skin to pinch. The man lowered his hand.

Shock splashed across his features and against my heated skin like an icy rain shower. My legs tucked under me, tensing.

He leaned forward, gripping the arms of the chair until the tendons popped, and his veins… "I can still feel your *notam*."

His words didn't matter. Hunger pierced my chest as my chin dipped, and my lips peeled back. My entire being focused on his throat, on where I swore I saw his pulse pounding.

"Shit," he whispered, rising.

I shot off the bed and launched myself at him. Stumbling back, he caught my wrists. The back of his knees hit the chair. Off-balance, he fell into the seat, and I went with him, straining forward as I scrambled into the chair. "Gods. You're fast. And you're really strong," he grunted, his arms trembling as he held me back. Strands of coppery-red hair fell across my face as I lifted my head.

He gasped, his blue eyes widening. "Holy shit."

I threw myself onto him. The chair groaned under our combined weight. One of his arms caved, and I went for his throat, my mouth stretching wide, stomach clenching—

An arm folded around my waist, catching me. Another banded across my breasts, hauling me back against hard, warm skin. A static charge passed during the contact, startling me. That feeling…that smell of spice and pine. A keening, whimpering sound tore its way from my throat as I stretched out, trying to grasp the male as he jumped from the chair, his black tunic wrinkled and stained with…with something. Blood? My blood. I stared at him, sensing that he was not mortal. He was something *else*. Something that belonged to me.

"You don't want him," a voice danced over my ear. "He won't be as tasty. You want me."

"In any other situation," the male with wintry blue eyes said, "I might be offended."

Hunger lashed at my insides. Desperation blistered my skin. I was starving, and it hurt. Everything *ached*. My skin, my bones, my muscles. My hair. A low, humming sound came from deep within me, finally forming rough, guttural words. "It *hurts*."

"I know. You're hungry. But you can't eat Kieran. That would make me a little sad."

I didn't care if it made him sad. I threw my head back, connecting with his jaw. He grunted, but his hold on me didn't loosen. It only tightened.

"Careful," the one called Kieran said. "She's stronger."

"I got her," he bit out, holding me tight to his front. "You should probably put some distance between you and her."

The other didn't move as the one who held me shifted an arm, lifting his wrist over my shoulder. A scent hit the air. My heart sped up as I stilled, breathing deeply. It smelled *wonderful*, lush and decadent. The gnawing ache intensified.

"Her eyes," the other said as the one holding me lowered his arm—his wrist. His *bleeding* wrist. "They're not black. They're still green."

The male stiffened against me. "*What*?"

Forgetting about the one in front of me, I grabbed the arm and struck, closing my mouth over the two open wounds and drawing in deeply. The male jerked and gasped. "*Gods*."

The first taste of his blood was a shock to my senses, tart and sweet. His blood coursed down my throat, warm and thick. It hit the hollowness in my chest, the empty pit in my stomach, easing the ache. I moaned, shuddering as the cramping in my muscles began to fade. The red-tinted shadows in my mind started to thin, and fragments of thought began to break through the hunger. Pieces of—

A hand curled under my jaw, lifting my mouth from his wrist. "No!" I panicked. The painful hunger surged back to life. I needed—I needed *more.*

"Look at me."

I fought against his grip, bucking against his hold, but he was *strong.*

The male turned my head. "*Stop.*" His breath danced over my lips, and something about his words was different, softer, deeper. It echoed through me. "Stop fighting me and open your eyes, Penellaphe."

His voice pierced through the hunger as it had before when I was drifting in the darkness. My breathing slowed as my body obeyed his command. Amber eyes stared into mine, bright and churning with golden flecks. I couldn't look away—couldn't move even as a barb-edged surge of anguish flooded me.

"*Poppy,*" he whispered, those strange, churning eyes glimmering with dampness. "You didn't Ascend."

I knew his words should make sense. A distant, fragmented part of me knew that I should understand. But I couldn't think past the hunger—couldn't focus on anything but that.

"I don't understand," the other male said. "Even with the blood of the gods in her, she was still mortal."

The one who held me shifted his hand from my chin and touched my lips. The urge to snap down on his finger rode me hard, but I couldn't fight him. The hold he had on me wouldn't allow it as he gently pushed back my upper lip.

"She doesn't have fangs," he said, his gaze quickly returning to mine. I felt…I felt the tartness of his confusion give way to the earthy, woodsy sensation of relief. "I know what this is. It's bloodlust. She's experiencing bloodlust, but she didn't Ascend. That's why you still feel the Primal *notam.*" He slipped his thumb away and shuddered. "Feed," he whispered, letting go.

Bindings I couldn't see or feel left me. I could move. He lifted his wrist once more, and I latched on to him. My mouth sealed over his wound again. The blood wasn't flowing as freely as before, but I drank deeply anyway, drawing him into me.

"Careful," the other…the wolven warned. "You've given a lot of blood and haven't nearly taken enough."

"I'm fine. You should leave."

"Not going to happen," the wolven growled. "She may hurt you."

The one who fed me let out a rough chuckle. "Shouldn't you be more concerned about her well-being now?"

"I'm concerned about both of you."

The male sighed. "This could get…intense."

There was a beat of silence. "It already is."

Something about what the wolven said and the raggedness in the way the one I fed from spoke should have concerned me. And it did a little. I wasn't sure why, but I was lost again in the one who held me, in his taste and his essence. I barely felt him move, sitting down and gathering me close in his lap, cuddling me against his chest as he kept his wrist against my mouth. All that mattered was his blood. It was an awakening. A *gift* sparking through my veins, filling that empty hollowness once more and reaching into the darkness of my mind. The thick film of blackness there cracked, and tiny pieces of *me* trickled in.

His fingers grazed my cheek, catching the strands of my hair and tucking them back over my shoulder. I tensed, but when he didn't pull me away, I relaxed. He touched me again, gliding his fingers through my hair in soothing, comforting caresses. I liked that. Touch was…it was special to me. It had once been forbidden, but he…*he* had shattered that rule from the beginning.

"Poppy," he whispered. *Poppy*. That was me. "I'm sorry," he said, his voice ragged. "I'm sorry that you woke in this state and I wasn't here. I think I…I must've passed out. I'm so damn sorry. I know what bloodlust feels like. I know that you can lose yourself in it. But you'll find yourself again. I don't doubt that for one second. You're so strong." His fingers continued moving along my scalp, and my grip on his arm loosened as he spoke. The taste of his blood was everything, and with each swallow, the void in me lessened, and the shadows in my mind cracked even more.

"Gods, I hope you truly understand how strong you are. I'm constantly in awe of you. I've been in awe of you since the night in the Red Pearl."

The ragged breaths evened out. The racing of my heart and pulse started to slow, and behind my eyes, I saw colors—a blue, cloudless sky and warm sunlight. Black waters that shimmered like pools of obsidian, and sandy dirt warm under my feet. Palms joined, and him whispering: "*Unworthy*." These images, these thoughts were his as he spoke softly.

"You're brave, so damn brave. I realized that at the Red Pearl. To be the Maiden, to be raised as you were, and to still want to experience life told me that you were brave. That night on the Rise, when you went up there in that…that damn nightgown?" His chuckle was rough. "You didn't hide. Not then, and not when you went out to ease the pain of those cursed by the Craven. You've chosen things for yourself longer than you realize, Poppy—longer than you give yourself credit for. You always did when it mattered the most, and did so knowing the consequences. Because you're brave. You were never the Maiden. You were never truly helpless. You were smart, strong, and brave."

He exhaled heavily. "I don't think I've told you this. I didn't get the chance yet. When you asked me to kiss you under the willow? Deep down, I knew then that I would give you anything you asked for. I still will. Whatever you want," he promised roughly, his fingers tangling in my hair. "You can have it. Anything. Everything. You can have it all. I will make sure of it."

Warmth buzzed through me, erasing the prickly sensation in my skin. I swallowed the rich essence of him and then I took what felt like my first real breath. It didn't burn or open that empty feeling again. It did something entirely different. *The* blood…

His blood…

It was like liquid fire, stroking to life a different kind of need, one I fell headfirst into. I tilted forward, pressing my breasts against his bare chest. The contact left me hungry in a way much different from earlier but just as potent. I shifted in his lap. We both groaned. Instinct took over, my body knowing what I wanted—what I *needed*—as I drank from his wrist. I rolled my hips against his, shaking at the intense curling sensation deep in my lower stomach.

His blood…gods. My skin tingled now, becoming overly sensitive. The tips of my breasts ached as they brushed against the fine dusting of hair across his chest. I whimpered, pressing down against the hardness straining through thin pants. I wanted…no, I needed *him*.

"Whatever you want," he said, his words a vow. "I will give it to you."

Him. I wanted him.

Keeping his wrist to my mouth, I planted my hand on his chest and pushed—pushed hard. He fell onto his back as I tilted my hips, rubbing against his length. With shocking strength, he lifted both of us just enough to shove his pants down to his thighs with one hand. The feel of him hot and hard against my lower body dragged a thready moan from me.

"Fuck," he gasped, his large body shaking. And then he moved again, lifting me in one fluid motion and angling my hips. He brought me down onto him, sliding deep inside me. His wrist smothered my cry of surprise as his hips flexed and thrust upward. Toes curling, I pushed down, matching his pace as I curled myself around his arm, drinking deeply.

"She's taking too much," the other man said, his voice closer. "You've got to stop her."

Even in my lust-addled mind, even as tension coiled tighter and tighter inside me, I knew the one who moved under me and in me wouldn't stop me. He'd let me take it all. He'd let me drain him dry. He'd do that because he...

"For fuck's sake," the wolven snarled. A heartbeat later, I felt his arm clamp down on my waist as his fingers pressed into the skin under my jaw. He pulled my head back, but I didn't fight him because this male's blood was everything to me.

The one under me sat up, curling an arm around my hips, just below the other's arm. A sharp swirl of tingles rushed through me. He reached around the wolven's grip, fisting my hair as he pressed his forehead to mine. Under me, he moved his magnificent body at a furious rhythm. My entire body stiffened and then lightning flew through my veins. My muscles clamped down on him, spasming. My cry mixed with his rough shout as his hips pumped furiously, and he followed me into the wild, mindless bliss that wracked my entire body. Slowly, the tension poured out of me, turning my muscles to liquid. I didn't know how much time passed, but finally, the hand under my jaw eased, and one of the arms slid away from me. My cheek fell to a warm shoulder, and I sat there, eyes closed and breathing shallowly as he held me tightly to his chest, his hand still tangled in my hair at the back of my head. He nodded, and the wolven left. The click of a nearby door signaled his departure, but I remained, sated and relaxed. The heat of the blood coursing through me cooled. His blood…

Hawke's blood.

Casteel's blood.

The nothingness in my mind shattered in an instant. Thoughts flooded me, connecting with memories. They reached into the deepest parts of me, linking with a sense of self. Shock found me first—utter disbelief and anguish over what Alastir had done while we stood at the Chambers of Nyktos and everything that had happened after that.

I'd trusted him.

I…I'd wanted acceptance from the people at the Temple, but they'd called me a Soul Eater. They'd called me a *whore*. They…they'd called me the Maiden, and I was none of those things. Anger crowded out the horror. A rage that carved itself into every bone in my body. Fury hummed at my very core, striking against the wildness growing inside me. They would pay for what they had done to me. Every single one of them would discover exactly what I was. I would never be struck down like that again. They wouldn't succeed…

But hadn't they already?

I could still feel the bolt striking my flesh, tearing through vital parts of me. I'd tasted death. *Felt* it—the breath I couldn't take, the heart that no longer beat, and the words I couldn't speak. I'd been dying, but there had been a different pain, too, a fiery one that had ripped through me. *Drink. Keep drinking. That's it. Keep swallowing. Drink, Poppy, keep drinking for me…* The taste of citrus and snow still coated the back of my throat, my lips. Still warmed and filled that gnawing, painful hollowness inside me. I shuddered, and the hand on the back of my head stilled. Oh, gods, they succeeded. He'd…Ascended me.

What had he been thinking? *I will not lose you. Ever. I love you, Princess.* He hadn't been thinking. He'd simply been…feeling.

Suddenly, it was like a chest in my mind unlocked, and the lid was thrown off. Emotions poured into me—nearly nineteen years-worth of them that went beyond what had happened in the Temple, the memories and beliefs, experiences and feelings. Nightmares came, too, heavy with desperation and hopelessness. But so did dreams full of such wonder and possibility. Dreams bursting with need and want and *love*.

I sat back so quickly I lost my balance. An arm dropped to my waist, stopping me before I toppled out of his lap. Through the messy strands of my hair, I saw him, really saw *him*.

Dark, disheveled hair tumbled across his forehead. Tension bracketed the corners of his mouth, and shadows smudged the skin under his eyes, but they were a bright topaz as they held mine. Neither of us moved or spoke as we stared at one another. I had no idea what he was thinking, and I barely knew *my* thoughts in that moment. So much had happened, so many things I didn't understand. Namely, how I was in here after I had Ascended. After he'd done the unthinkable to save me. I remembered the panic in his father's voice as he pleaded with him not to do it—not to repeat history. But he'd risked—gods, he'd risked everything. And I was alive because of him. I was here because of him. But none of this made sense.

The Ascended were uncontrollable after being turned, dangerous for mortals, let alone an elemental Atlantian. It could take them years to control their thirst, but more unbelievable was that I could still feel all those heady and exhilarating and terrifying emotions within me. I could feel *love*, and I didn't think any Ascended was capable of feeling such a miracle. I didn't understand. Maybe this was some sort of dream? Perhaps I had passed and was in the Vale, an eternity of paradise awaiting me. I wasn't sure if I wanted to know if that was the case.

I lifted my trembling hand and pressed my fingers to the warm skin of his cheek. "*Casteel*."

Chapter 9

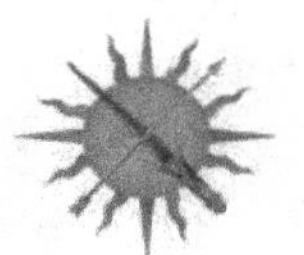

Casteel shuddered as he whispered, "Poppy."

"Is this real?" I asked.

The golden flecks in his eyes churned fiercely. "There's nothing more real than right now."

I don't know who moved first. Me. Him. Both of us at the same time? It didn't matter. Our mouths met, and there was nothing gentle about the way we came together. He grasped the back of my head, his hand fisting in my hair. I held onto him, my fingers digging into the skin of his shoulders. It was a wrecking sort of kiss, demanding and raw. We claimed each other. Our lips mashed together. Our teeth clashed. Our arms wrapped fiercely around one another, and the kiss, the way we held each other, became something else entirely. His hands slid down my sides to my hips as he pulled me against him, where I felt him hardening against me once more.

"I need you," he groaned against my lips. "I need you, Poppy."

"You have me," I told him, echoing the words I'd said to him once before. Now, they felt like an unbreakable vow. "Always."

"Always," he repeated.

Lifting me from his lap, he stood and then turned, placing me on the center of what I realized was a fairly narrow bed. I got a brief glimpse of the dark walls and fractured sunlight seeping through the cracked boards of a door in the room, but then all I saw was him.

Casteel.

My husband.

My heartmate.

My savior.

Gods, he…he *had* saved me, believing he'd committed the forbidden act of Ascension. He'd taken that risk, understanding that I would become a vampry. His father hadn't been able to stop him. Neither had the gods. No one could because he wouldn't let me go. He refused to lose me.

Because he loved me.

And now he climbed over me, his attention feral and possessive. Every muscle in my body tensed. My leg curled as he slid his hand up my thigh, the rough skin of his palm creating delicious friction. I couldn't look away from the vivid burn of his eyes. I was absolutely transfixed by them—by him. Slipping an arm under my waist, he flipped me onto my belly. Surprise flickered through me. I started to rise, but the heat of his body against my back pressed me down to the rough blanket. Casteel rained kisses down my spine, over my hips, and then to the swell of my rear, eliciting a shiver from me.

"If you ever tell me to kiss your ass," he said, "remember that I already have."

A throaty laugh parted my lips, the sound and act surprising. "I don't think I'll forget that."

"Good." He lifted me to my knees, using his thigh to urge my legs farther apart. My fingers dug into the coarse material as a tremble of anticipation rolled through me. "I'm not going to last very long," he warned. "But neither will you."

I couldn't think, couldn't breathe with him curling his arm around my waist as his other hand clamped down on my hip. He didn't move. My pulse thrummed.

"Cas—" His name ended in a sharp cry as he thrust into me.

He pulled me back against him as he plunged into me, over and over, his pace wickedly savage. Pulling my back flush to his chest, he ground his hips against my rear as his hand left my hip and folded over the base of my throat. He pressed his lips to my damp temple. "I love you."

I broke apart, shattering into a thousand tiny pieces as my release crashed through me with such force that a growl rumbled from his chest. His arms tightened around me. One more deep thrust, and he came, shouting my name. Panting and slick with a fine sheen of sweat, he brought us both to the bed. The blanket scratched my skin, but I was sated, boneless, and so damn relieved to be alive that I couldn't actually worry about the irritation of the material. I didn't know how long we stayed where we were, me on my belly, and Casteel lying half on me, but the sensation of his weight enthralled me, as did his wildly beating heart against my back.

Sometime later, I once more ended up seated in his embrace, cradled against him. We were at the head of the narrow bed now. I didn't remember how we'd even gotten there, but he held me as he dragged a trembling hand over my head and through my hair. We stayed that way for so long—hours, it seemed.

"How are you feeling?" Casteel asked, his voice rough. "Does anything hurt?"

I gave a small shake of my head. "Not really." There were aches, but they were nothing. "I…I don't understand. I was dying." Lifting my head, I looked down at my chest as I scooped the tangled strands of my hair to the side. I saw shiny, pink skin in the shape of a rough circle between my breasts. The bolt had gone through me. "And you…you took my blood until I felt my heart fail and then gave me yours."

"I did." He pressed his fingers just below the barely noticeable injury, and a wave of awareness skittered through me. "I couldn't let you go. I wouldn't."

My gaze flew to his, but he was staring at the wound, his brow furrowed. "But I'm not in bloodlust—well, I *was*. I was so hungry. I've never felt that hungry before." I swallowed hard, wanting to forget what that had felt like. Wanting to forget that Casteel had experienced that over and over for decades. How had he found himself? I was in awe of him, and I was in love with him.

I love you. Those words repeated themselves over and over in my mind—words that were tattooed on my skin and carved into my bones. What I felt for him was far more powerful than words, but words were important. Of all people, I knew the power of speaking up, of being able to do so honestly and openly without hesitation. I knew the importance of not holding back now because when I'd lain there in those ruins, with my blood leaking out of my body, I'd never thought I would have the chance to say those words to him.

My fingers curled around his side as I met his gaze once more. "I love you."

Casteel's hand halted its movements under my hair and halfway up my back. "What?" he whispered. His eyes had widened slightly, and his pupils were dilated a little. I could see his surprise and felt it like a rush of cold air against my skin. Why did he seem so astonished? He had to know.

But Casteel couldn't read emotions like I could. I had told him how he made me feel and showed it when I held the blade to my throat during the battle at Spessa's End—more than ready to end my life if it meant saving his. But I'd never said the words.

And I needed to. Desperately.

I pressed the tips of my fingers against his cheek as I drew in a shallow breath. "I love you, Casteel," I said. His chest stilled against mine and then rose sharply. "I love—"

Casteel kissed me, his lips moving over mine so gently, so tenderly. It was a sweet and slow kiss as if it were the very first time our lips had ever come together, as if he were learning the shape and feel of my mouth against his. He shuddered, and a wave of tears reached my eyes.

He drew back enough that his forehead rested against mine. "I didn't…" He cleared his throat as I ran my fingers along his jaw. "I mean, I…I thought you did. I believed that—or maybe I needed to believe it—but I don't think I really knew." His voice roughened again as he reached between us, wiping away a tear that had escaped. A moment passed, and his chest rose with a sharp breath. All the many masks Casteel wore cracked and fell away then, as they had in the ruins when he'd thrown his head back and screamed. "I knew you cared for me. But love? I just didn't know if you could after…everything. I wouldn't have blamed you if you were unable to feel that for me. Not after what—"

"It doesn't matter what was done in the past. I understand why you did those things. I've moved past that." My fingers tangled in the soft strands of his hair at the nape of his neck. "I love you. I would"—I swallowed—"I would do anything for you, Cas. Like you did for me. Anything—"

His mouth found mine again, and this time…oh, gods, the kiss went deeper. I melted into him as his tongue stroked my lips, parting them. Tiny shivers erupted all over my body, and we kissed until we were both breathless.

"*Cas*," he echoed against my lips. "You have no idea how long I've waited to hear you call me that."

"Why?" I hadn't even realized I had used the nickname.

"I don't know. Only those I trust most call me that." His laugh was soft, and then he drew back farther, clasping my cheeks carefully. "You know, don't you?" He searched my eyes with his. "What you mean to me? What I feel for you?"

"Yes."

He wiped away another tear with his thumb. "I never knew it could feel like this. That I could feel this for someone. But I do—I love you."

I trembled as my chest swelled with love, hope, anticipation, and a hundred other wild emotions that felt so strange after everything that had happened. And yet, they felt so right. "I think I might start crying harder."

He dipped his head, kissing away a tear that had wiggled free. I managed to pull myself together as he pressed a kiss to my temple, to my forehead, and then to the bridge of my nose as he picked up my left hand. His eyes were closed as he dropped tiny kisses along the length of the golden marriage imprint. I watched him in silence for several moments, a little lost in him.

He touched the band around my forefinger. "I…I didn't want your first glimpse of Atlantia, of *your* home, to be something horrific. I wanted you to see the beauty of *our* home, of our people. I knew it wouldn't be easy." He swallowed thickly. "Alastir was right when he said that some of our people are superstitious and wary of newcomers, but I wanted you to feel welcomed. Above all, I wanted you to feel safe. I hate that this happened, and I'm sorry. I'm so damn sorry."

"It's not your fault. You did everything to make sure I was safe."

"Did I?" he countered. "I knew there could be resistance. I knew there would be people hungry for revenge. I overestimated their desire to survive. I shouldn't have let you walk off like that. I should've been there. I failed to protect you—"

"Stop." I tipped forward, cupping his cheek with the hand he didn't hold. "It wasn't your fault," I repeated. "Please, don't think that. I…" I inhaled sharply. Sharing my feelings had never been easy, not even after speaking those incredibly powerful words. How could it be when I'd been groomed to never do so? But I needed to continue to breathe these words. I had to because I could feel the sour bite of guilt. "I couldn't bear it if you thought you were responsible. I don't want that to eat away at you. You haven't failed me. I don't know where I would be right now if it weren't for you. I don't even know if I would be alive."

He said nothing as he closed his eyes, turning his head so his cheek pressed into my palm.

I dragged my thumb along his bottom lip. "But I do know that I would be… I would be *less*. I wouldn't feel like this—like I'm whole. And that's because of you." I took another breath. "When I first saw the Pillars and stood in the Chambers, I did feel like this was home. It was like a sense of rightness—like what I feel for you. It felt *right* to be here. And maybe that has to do with my ancestry. I…I don't know what Atlantia is to me now or what it will become, but that doesn't matter." I realized how true that statement was in the moment, and the sudden knowledge of that lifted so much weight from me. Having Atlantia's acceptance and that of Casteel's parents would be wonderful, but our acceptance of one another was so much more important. That was what mattered when I closed my eyes at night and opened them again in the morning. "You are the foundation that helps me stand. You are my walls and my roof. My shelter. *You* are my home."

His lashes swept up, the amber of his eyes churning wildly. "As you are mine, Poppy."

"Then please don't blame yourself. Please. If you do, I'll…I don't know what I'd do, but I'm sure you wouldn't like it."

"Does it involve stabbing?"

I stared at him.

"Because I'd probably like that."

I sighed. "Cas."

A faint smile appeared. "I will try not to blame myself. Okay? The guilt that I feel isn't something that will go away immediately, but I will try. For you."

"For us," I corrected.

"For us."

Exhaling softly, I nodded even though I wanted it to go away immediately. "I knew I would see you again, even as I was held captive." I slid a hand down the satiny hardness of his chest. "I knew I would either get free, or you would find me. And you did. You found me."

"How could I not?" he asked. "I will always find you. No matter what."

My heart squeezed as I cupped his cheek. "But when that bolt struck me, and I was lying there? I thought I would never get to feel you hold me again. That I would never feel your kiss or see your stupid dimples."

He grinned, and the dimple on his left cheek appeared. "You love my dimples."

I drew my thumb over the indent. "I do." Dipping my head, I

placed my lips where my thumb had been. "What I felt when I woke up earlier, when I was…hungry. I've never felt anything like that before. That need? It was terrifying, and I…" I briefly closed my eyes. "You know exactly how that feels. You were driven to that point time and time again when the Ascended held you. I don't know how you dealt with that." My eyes met his. "You said I'm strong, but you…you are the strongest person I know."

"I hate that you had to learn what that felt like. I knew that would happen, especially if you Ascended. I should've—"

"You were there. You would've let me keep feeding."

His gaze continued to hold mine. "I would have given you the last drop of blood in my body if that was what you needed."

My breath seized. "You can't do that. You shouldn't have let me drink for as long as I did. You had to be given blood, didn't you?" I remembered the conversation now. "You…you fed from Naill."

"I did, and I'm fine. My blood replenishes itself quickly," he said, and I wasn't sure if I believed him or not. His chest rose with a deep breath. He placed his hand over mine, lifting it and placing a kiss to the center of my palm. "Are you still hungry?"

"No. I don't feel that way now. All I feel is you."

"My blood—"

"No. Not that." Well, I could feel his blood in me, dark and lush, but it had cooled. It no longer drove me—drove both of us with reckless abandon…

Oh, my gods.

I realized then that Kieran had been there. He'd been in the room when we—when Casteel and I came together the first time. He had stopped me from taking too much blood. Spine stiffening, I looked over my shoulder, half-expecting the wolven to be standing there. I didn't recognize the room at all.

"Kieran left," Casteel said, splaying his fingers against my cheek. He drew my gaze back to him. "He stayed because he was worried."

"I…I know." I remembered. *I'm concerned about both of you.* I waited for shame to drown me, and embarrassment did settle over me, but it had nothing to do with what Kieran had witnessed. "I…I tried to eat Kieran."

"He won't hold it against you."

"I tried to eat Kieran while I was naked."

"That's probably why he won't hold it against you."

"That's not funny." I stared at him.

"It's not?" One side of his lips curved up, and his dimple appeared in his cheek.

That stupid, stupid dimple.

"I don't understand. How did I go from trying to eat Kieran, to eating you, to this? I mean, I feel emotion. I feel *normal.* That's not how a recently made vampry feels, right? Or is it because I fed from you?" My heart thumped heavily. "Does my skin feel cold to you? Do I have fangs?" I vaguely remembered hearing one of them say that I didn't, but I reached for my mouth anyway, just to be sure.

Casteel caught my hand, pulling it away from my face. "You don't have fangs, Poppy. And your eyes… They are still the color of an Atlantian spring. Newly turned vamprys cannot get enough blood, no matter how much they feed. I know. I've seen them in the hours and days after they're turned," he told me, and I hated that he had experienced any of that. "You would be going at my throat right now if you were a vampry. You wouldn't feel warm and soft in my arms or around my cock," he said, and I flushed a hot pink. "You didn't Ascend."

"But that doesn't…" My gaze traveled past the bed to the doors. *Sunlight.* The Ascended could be in indirect sunlight without injury. But direct sunlight?

Totally different story.

I moved before I even realized what I was doing, launching myself out of Casteel's lap. I must've caught him off guard because he reached for me, but I slipped past his grip. Or maybe I was just that fast. I didn't know.

"Poppy!" Casteel shouted as I reached the door. "Don't you dare—"

Gripping the handle, I threw the door open. Cold air poured in as I stepped out onto a small porch. Sunlight streamed in, drenching the cracked stone of the floor with cool light. I stretched out an arm as Casteel's curse blistered my ears. Light fell over my fingers and then my hand.

Casteel wrapped an arm around my waist, hauling me back against his chest. "Godsdamnit, Poppy."

I stared at my hand, at my skin, and waited for it to do something terrifying. "Nothing's happening."

"Thank the gods," he growled, squeezing me tightly. "But I might be having a heart attack."

My brows pinched. "Can Atlantians have heart attacks?"

"No."

"Then you're fine," I replied, biting down on my lip as I became aware of the dampness between my thighs.

His forehead pressed against the side of my head. "That's debatable. I feel like my heart is about to come out of my chest at the moment."

A rough, huffing noise came, drawing my gaze up to the thick line of half-dead trees. It had sounded an awful lot like a laugh. For a moment, I forgot all about what I'd been doing. My eyes narrowed on the bare, corpse-like branches hanging low and sweeping the ground. A pure white wolven crouched among the trees.

Delano.

His ears perked as he tilted his head to the side.

And that was roughly the time I realized there wasn't a stitch of clothing on me. "Oh, my gods." A flush swept over my entire body. "I'm naked."

"Very," Casteel murmured, angling his body so he shielded me. He caught hold of the door. "Sorry about that," he said to Delano.

The wolven made that rasping, laughing sound again as Casteel closed the door. Immediately, he spun me around so I faced him. "I can't believe you did that."

"I can't believe yet another random person just saw me naked," I muttered, and Casteel stared at me like my priorities were all wrong. And maybe they were. I refocused. "But you said I didn't Ascend—"

"That doesn't mean I know exactly what happened. I had no idea what would occur if you stepped out into the sun." He gripped my shoulders, and my scattered senses connected with his emotions. I felt the heavy feeling of concern mixed with the freshness of relief. Underneath, a spicy, smoky flavor threaded with sweetness. "Nothing could've happened. Or your skin could've started to decay, and I would've lost you *again.*" His chest rose sharply as the gold specks in his eyes burned brightly. "Because I *did* lose you, Poppy. I felt your heart stop. The imprint on my palm started to fade. I was losing you, and you are my everything."

I shuddered. "I'm sorry."

"Don't apologize," he told me. "None of what happened was your fault, Poppy. I just…I can't feel that again."

"I don't want you to." I stepped in close to him, and he slid his arms around me. "And I didn't mean to make you feel that again."

"I know." He kissed my temple. "I know. Let's just sit. Okay?" He led me back to the bed.

I sat while he bent, picking up his breeches. I bit down on my lip as I watched him pull them up, leaving the flap unbuttoned. They hung indecently low on his waist as he turned. There was another chair in the room, a wooden one, and I saw a small lump of clothing there.

"Jasper found some clothing and boots he thought you could wear. It's a slip, a pair of breeches, and a sweater. I honestly don't know where he found them, and I'm not quite sure I want to know." He brought the slip to me and a dark brown sweater. "But they're clean."

"Where are we?" I asked as he motioned for me to lift my arms. I did as he requested. "We were in…Irelone, right? That's where they took me?"

In the dim light, I saw a muscle flex in his jaw as he lowered the slip over my head. The cloth was soft and smelled of fresh air. "We're no longer in Irelone or the Wastelands. We're in the Skotos foothills. This is an old hunting cabin we sometimes use when we're traveling in and out of the Skotos. We're actually not too far from Spessa's End, but we didn't want to…"

Casteel didn't finish what he was saying as I rose to my knees and let the slip slide into place. I knew what he was thinking. They didn't want to take me into Spessa's End, just in case I had Ascended and became uncontrollable.

Still utterly dumbfounded by the fact that I was alive and wasn't a vampry, I said nothing as he tugged the thick sweater on over my head. It was a little scratchy but warm. I lifted the collar, giving it a small sniff. The garment smelled a little of woodsmoke, but for some reason, I thought it also smelled of…lilacs.

I *remembered.*

Looking up, I found Casteel watching me with a raised brow as he finally buttoned the flap on his breeches. I dropped the sweater. "When you gave me your blood the very first time in New Haven, I think…I think I saw your memories. Or felt your emotions. I smelled lilacs then, and I smelled them again," I told him, thinking of the flowers that drenched the cavern in Spessa's End. "Were you thinking of when we were married when I…when I drank your blood this time?"

"I was."

"How did I see your memories, though? Before and now? That's not the same as reading emotions."

"It can happen when two Atlantians feed." He dipped his head, brushing his lips over my brow. "Each can pick up on memories. I think that's what happened."

I thought about the first time in New Haven. He'd stopped me just as I reached his memories.

He hadn't stopped me this time.

"Could you read any of mine?" I wondered.

"I've never fed from you long enough to try," he answered, and I felt a strange little tumble of anticipation. "But right now, I wish I knew what you were thinking."

"I was thinking…" I drew in a deep breath. Gods, I was thinking about everything. My thoughts bounced from one event, one conversation to another. "Do you know what I did in the Chambers? After…after you were attacked?"

He sat beside me. "I heard."

I lowered my hands to where the sweater pooled in my lap. They looked normal. "When we were in the Chambers of Nyktos and that arrow struck you, and your body turned cold and gray, I thought you died. I didn't think I would be okay again. I forgot about the imprint," I admitted, turning my hand over. There it was, the golden swirl glimmering softly. "I kind of…I don't know. I lost it."

"You defended yourself," he corrected. "That's what you did."

I nodded, still staring at the imprint as my mind skipped from the Temple to the crypts, to Alastir so confident that I would be just as chaotically violent as the ancient ones.

Chapter 10

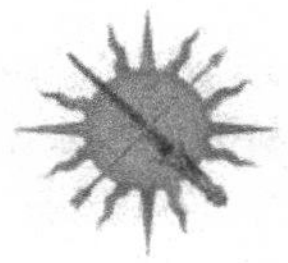

"I know a lot has happened," Casteel said, gently catching a strand of my hair and tucking it behind my ear. "And I know things are confusing as fuck right now, but do you think you can tell me what happened? I know some things," he told me. "I was able to get some information out of Alastir and the others by using compulsion, but it's not like it's a truth serum or I can force them into telling me everything. I have to be exact in what I ask, and I was mostly concerned about finding you and who else could be involved. So, I want to hear it from you. I think that is the only way we can begin to figure out what has happened here, tackling everything one step at a time."

Dragging my gaze from my hands, I looked over at him. "I can tell you."

He smiled at me as he touched my cheek. "You okay with me bringing Kieran in? He will need to hear this information."

I nodded.

Casteel kissed where his fingers had touched seconds before and then rose, walking to the door as my gaze returned to my hands. Only a handful of moments passed before Kieran slipped back into the room. I peeked at him, tentatively reaching out with my senses as he stared at me and approached the bed. I didn't know what I expected to feel from him, but all I felt was the heaviness of concern and a freshness that reminded me of spring air. Relief.

Kieran knelt in front of me as Casteel returned to sit beside me. "How are you feeling?"

"Okay, and a little confused," I admitted. "I have a lot of

questions."

One side of the wolven's lips tipped up. "I'm so shocked," he murmured, pale eyes gleaming with amusement.

"I'm sorry for trying to eat you." I felt my cheeks warm.

Kieran smiled then. "It's okay."

"Told you he wouldn't hold it against you," Casteel said.

"Wouldn't be the first time a hungry Atlantian tried to eat me," Kieran said, and my brows lifted. I now had more questions, but a memory surged through me.

When I woke, I'd been too lost to the bloodlust to realize that I hadn't been covered in blood. And I should've been. There had been so much blood from the wound. "You cleaned me, didn't you? You wiped away the blood."

"It didn't feel right letting either of you lay in your blood," he said with a shrug as if the act was nothing. "I didn't want either of you seeing that when you woke up."

Emotion clogged my throat as I stared at Kieran. I reacted without much thought, pitching forward. I didn't know if he sensed what I was about to do or if he was worried that I was about to attempt to rip his throat out again, but he caught me without falling over, even though he did wobble a bit. He folded his arms around me without a heartbeat of hesitation, holding me just as tightly as I held him. I felt Casteel's hand on my lower back, just under Kieran's arms, and the three of us stayed like that for a little while. "Thank you," I whispered.

"You don't need to thank me for that." He dragged a hand up to the back of my head and leaned away enough that his gaze met mine. "It was the least I could do."

"But that wasn't all you did," Casteel said, reaching over and clasping a hand on the wolven's shoulder. "You made sure we got here safely and kept watch. You did everything we needed and more. I owe you."

Kieran lifted his hand from the back of my head and clasped Casteel's forearm as his pale gaze met my husband's amber one. "I did all that I could," he reiterated.

Seeing them together caused another swell of emotion. I remembered what had been said in the Chambers of Nyktos about the bonds breaking. An ache started up in my chest as I disentangled myself from Kieran and glanced between them. "Is the bond really broken?" I asked. "Between you two?"

Casteel stared at Kieran, and a long moment passed. "It is."

The ache in my chest grew. "What does that mean? Really?"

Kieran glanced at me. "That conversation can wait—"

"The conversation can happen now." I crossed my arms. "Alastir and Jansen said some stuff while I was in the crypts," I told them, inwardly cringing as I felt twin bursts of anger against my skin. "I don't know how much of it was true, but neither really explained how me being a descendant of a deity…." I sucked in a sharp breath as I thought of who Alastir had claimed was part of my heritage. Did Casteel already know that? "I don't understand how that supersedes something that has been around for ages. I'm not a deity."

"I don't think we know what you are exactly," Casteel stated.

"I'm not a deity," I protested.

"The fact that you are here and not a vampry means that nothing is off the table," Kieran added. I was *so* taking that off the table. "But either way, you are a descendant of the gods. You are the only living one. You have—"

"If I hear I have the blood of a god inside me one more time, I might scream," I warned.

"Okay, then." Kieran scratched his face as he rose and then sat on the other side of me. There was a faint days-worth of scruff on his jaw. "Because of the blood you carry, the kiyou were given mortal form. Not to serve the elemental bloodlines, but to serve the children of the gods. If the deities hadn't…" He trailed off with a shake of his head. "When the gods gave the kiyou mortal form, we were bonded to them and their children on an instinctual level that is passed down generation after generation. And that instinctive bond recognizes you."

I understood what he was saying on a technical level, but fundamentally, it was utterly insane to me. "That's just… I'm just Poppy, blood of the gods or not—"

"You're not just Poppy, and that has nothing to do with you not becoming a vampry," Casteel placed a hand on my shoulder. "And I mean it, Princess. I can't say for sure that you're not some sort of deity. What I saw you do? What I've *seen* and heard that you have done? You're unlike any of us, and I still can't believe I didn't put it together when I first saw that light around you."

"How did you not know?" I looked up at Kieran. "If my blood really is that potent, how did no wolven know what I was?"

"I think we did, Poppy," Kieran answered. "But just like Casteel, we didn't connect what we were seeing or feeling when we were around you."

Understanding crept into me. "That's why you said I smelled like something dead—"

"I said you smelled *of* death," Kieran corrected with a sigh. "Not that you smelled like something dead. Death is power, the old kind."

"Death is power?" I repeated, not entirely sure at first how that made sense. But then it occurred to me. "Death and life are two sides of the same coin. Nyktos is…"

"He's the God of Life and Death." Kieran's gaze flicked to Casteel. "And this explains why you thought her blood tasted old."

"Ancient," Casteel murmured, and I started to frown. "Her blood tastes ancient."

I really didn't want them to continue discussing what my blood tasted like. "Delano thought he heard me calling him when I was imprisoned in that room in New Haven—"

"For your safety," Casteel tacked on.

I ignored his comment, still annoyed at being kept in that room. "I was feeling rather…emotional at the time. Is that what the summoning thing is? Were you reacting to my emotions?"

Kieran nodded. "In a way, yes. It's similar to the bond we have with the Atlantians. Extreme emotion was often an alert that the one we were bonded to was threatened. We could sense that emotion."

I thought about that. "There were shocks of static whenever some wolven touched me," I murmured. The signs had been there, but like Casteel's mother had said, why would anyone suspect this when the last of the deities had died out ages ago? It seemed to have even confused Alastir—the extent of my…powers. But how could I not have other amazing abilities if I was indeed a descendant of the King of Gods?

Well, killing people by turning their emotions back on them would probably count as an amazing ability—a scary one—but why couldn't I morph into something like a dragon?

That would be incredible.

"Am I really descended from Nyktos? Alastir said I was, but since Nyktos is the father of the gods—"

"That is the figure of speech," Casteel corrected. "Nyktos isn't the actual father of the gods. He is the King of them. Alastir spoke the truth, or at least he spoke what he believed to be true," he said, his jaw hardening.

I exhaled heavily. "Why could I even do what I did in the Chambers? What changed? The Culling?" I asked, referencing the process the Atlantians went through when they no longer aged like mortals and began to develop heightened senses, along with undergoing numerous physical changes. It was why Casteel believed that the Ascended had waited until now to have me go through my Ascension. My blood would be of more use to them now, capable of making more Ascended.

Had the Ascended known about the blood I carried? Had Queen Ileana known the entire time? Alastir had been in contact with the Ascended. I believed that. Would my blood even work now that I had…?

I had nearly died.

And maybe I had a little. I remembered floating toward a silvery light, without body or thought. And I knew if I made my way to it, not even Casteel would be able to reach me.

"I think so," Casteel said as the warmth of his body pressed against my side, drawing me from my thoughts. "I think being on Atlantian land combined with the blood I've given you played a role in strengthening the blood in you."

"And I guess what happened at the Chambers of Nyktos just tipped it all over the edge?" I leaned into Casteel. "Waking this…thing up inside me?"

"What is in you is not a *thing*, Poppy." Casteel looked down at me. "It is a power. Magic. It is the eather waking up inside you, becoming a part of you."

"I'm not sure that makes me feel any better."

A lopsided grin appeared. "It would if you stopped thinking of your ancestry as a thing. But considering everything that has happened, you really haven't had any time to come to terms with any of this."

I wasn't sure how I could come to terms with it even when I had time. "I don't…"

"You don't want this," Kieran finished for me, his wintry gaze meeting mine.

"I don't want"—I briefly closed my eyes—"I don't want to come between you two. I don't want to come between any wolven and the Atlantian they were bonded to." I don't want to be the monster that Alastir warned me I'd become.

"Poppy," Casteel started.

"You can't tell me that having your bond with Kieran broken hasn't affected you," I cut in. "You guys were ready to tear each other apart at the Temple. That didn't feel right." A knot of emotion choked me. "I didn't like it."

"If you knew us when we were younger, you probably would've thought we hated each other." Casteel gently squeezed my shoulder. "We've come to blows over far less important things than you."

"Is that supposed to make me feel better?" I asked. "Because you're doing a really terrible job at that right now."

"I guess not." Casteel touched my cheek, tipping my head back so our eyes met. "Look, knowing the bond isn't there is weird. I'm not going to lie. But knowing that the bond has shifted to you—that not just Kieran, but all the wolven will protect you, is a relief. That is part of how we tracked you to the crypts in the Skotos Mountains and to the Wastelands. They felt you. If they hadn't been able to, we wouldn't have gotten to you in time," he said, and all of it made my stomach twist. "I can't be mad about that or upset. Not when I know the limits Kieran will go to to ensure that you remain safe."

My lower lip trembled. "But he's your best friend. He's like a brother to you."

"And I still am. Bonds are strange things, Poppy." Kieran placed his hand over the top of where Casteel's remained on my shoulder. I shuddered. "But my loyalty to Cas has never been about a bond created when neither of us was old enough to walk. It never will be. You have nothing to worry about when it comes to us. And I doubt that you have much to worry about when it comes to any of the other bonded wolven. Most of us have fostered friendships that can't break. So, we just…we just made room for you."

Made room for me.

"I…I like the sound of that," I whispered hoarsely.

Kieran patted my shoulder, or rather Casteel's hand. Maybe both.

"You think you can tell us what you remember?" Casteel asked after a moment, and I told him I could. "I need to know exactly what happened at the Temple. What you and that son of a bitch Jansen may have talked about when he was masquerading as Beckett. How he acted. I want to know exactly what those people said to you." He met my gaze. "I know it won't be easy, but I need to know anything you can remember."

I nodded. I told him everything, and it was easier than I thought it would be. What had happened had caused an ache in the center of my chest, but I didn't let that feeling grow or get in the way. Casteel wouldn't let it. I felt next to nothing from him as I talked. Now was not the time for emotion. Only facts were needed.

"That prophecy he spoke of?" I said, looking between them.

"Have either of you heard of that?"

"No." Casteel shook his head. "It sounded like a load of bullshit, especially the part about the Goddess Penellaphe. Sort of insulting to attach that nonsense to the Goddess of Wisdom."

I couldn't agree more. "But could it be something you haven't heard?"

"No. We don't have prophecies," Kieran confirmed. "We don't believe in them. It sounds like a mortal thing."

"They're not widely believed in Solis, but they do exist," I told them. "I didn't believe it either. It all sounded too convenient and exact, but there's a lot of things I don't know or believe."

"Well, that is one thing I don't think you have to worry about," Casteel stated.

I nodded, my thoughts shifting. "When the sky started to rain blood, they said it was the tears of the gods," I told him. "They took it as a sign that what they were doing was right."

"They were wrong."

"I know," I said.

"Do you know how you were able to stop them?" Kieran asked. "How you used your abilities?"

"That is a hard question to answer. I…I don't know how to explain it other than to say it was like I knew what to do." My brows knitted as I pressed my palm to the center of my chest. "Or like it was some instinct I didn't realize I had. I just knew what to do."

"Eather," Casteel corrected softly.

"Eather," I repeated. "I sort of…saw it in my mind, and it happened. I know that sounds bizarre—"

"It doesn't." He returned to stand in front of me. "When I use compulsion, the eather gives me the ability to do so. I see in my mind what I want the person to do as I speak it."

"Oh. So, it's…it's kind of like projecting your thoughts?"

He nodded. "Sounds like what you did is the same. It's also how we can tell if we're dealing with an elemental or another bloodline—based on the amount of eather we feel."

"It was written that the gods could sense it, too, whenever it was used," Kieran said. "It felt like a seismic shift to them."

I thought over everything they'd said. "It's weird, though. When I ease someone's pain, I think happy thoughts—good ones. And then…" I rolled my eyes as I sighed. "Then I projected those feelings into the person."

Casteel grinned at me.

"I guess it's not that much different."

He shook his head. "You think you can do it again?"

My stomach tumbled a bit. "I don't know. I don't know if I want to—"

"You should," he said, his jaw hardening as he held my gaze. "If you are ever in a situation like that again, any situation where you cannot physically defend yourself, do not hesitate. Listen to that instinct. Let it guide you. It will not steer you wrong, Poppy. It will keep you alive, and that is all that matters."

"I agree with everything Cas just said," Kieran chimed in. "But I know you can use those powers. That you know how. You were going to do it back at the ruins before you saw Jansen, but you stopped yourself." His gaze searched mine. "You stopped yourself and said that you weren't a monster."

An unnatural stillness came from the other side of me. "Why?" Casteel demanded. "Why would you say something like that?"

Kieran was right. I knew how to use the eather. All I had to do was picture it in my mind. The knowledge existed like some ancient instinct.

"Poppy," Casteel said, his tone gentler. "Talk to me. Talk to us."

"I…" I wasn't sure where to begin. My thoughts were still so damn scattered. I looked between the two of them. "Did you go into the crypts?"

"We did," Casteel confirmed. "Briefly."

"Then you saw the deities chained there, left to die?" Their fate still made me sick to my stomach. "I was kept with them. I don't know for how long. A couple of days? Alastir and Jansen said that the deities had become dangerous." I told them the story, repeating what Jansen and Alastir had told me about the children of the gods. "They said that I too would be dangerous. That I was a threat to Atlantia, and that was why they were…doing what they were. Were the deities really that violent?"

Kieran's gaze touched Casteel's over my head as he said, "The deities were gone by the time we were born."

"But?" I persisted.

"But I've heard they could be prone to acts of anger and violence. They could be unpredictable," Casteel stated carefully, and I tensed. "They weren't always like that, though. And not all of them were. But it had nothing to do with their blood. It was their age."

I frowned. "What do you mean?"

Casteel exhaled heavily. "You think an Atlantian's lifespan is unthinkable, but a deity is like a god. They are immortal. Instead of living two and three thousand years, they lived double and triple that," he said, and my heart stuttered. "Living that long would make anyone apathetic or bored, impatient and intolerant. They…simply grew too old and became cold."

"Cold? Like the Ascended?"

"In a way, yes," he said. "It's why the gods went to sleep. It was the only way they could keep some sense of empathy and compassion. The deities never chose to do that."

"So even if that were to happen to you," Kieran began, drawing my gaze to his, "you would have thousands of years before it came time to take a very nice, long nap."

I started to frown, but what Kieran said slammed into me with the speed and weight of an out-of-control carriage. My heart started racing as I stared at him first and then turned to Casteel. A tingling sensation swept over my skin as my mouth tried. "Am I…am I immortal now?"

Chapter 11

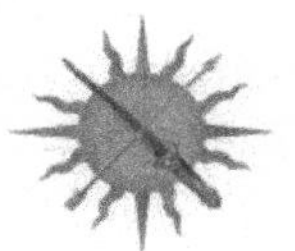

Casteel's chest rose with a deep breath. "What I know is that I took what was left of the blood in your body. And when I felt your heart stop," he said, clearing his throat, "I gave you mine. It was my blood that restarted your heart and kept it beating, and it was my blood that fed your body. There isn't a drop of mortal blood in you."

My lips parted as I tried to wrap my head around what he was saying—and what it meant.

"And that is not all I know," he continued, and a fine tremor danced through my body. "You…you don't feel mortal to me."

"You don't feel that way to me either," Kieran added. "You don't smell mortal any longer."

"What…what do I feel like? What do I smell like?" I asked, and Kieran looked like he didn't want to answer that question. "Do I smell more like death?"

He blinked slowly. "I wish I'd never said that."

"Do I?" I demanded.

Kieran sighed. "You smell of more power. Absolute. Final. I've never smelled anything like it."

"You don't feel like an Atlantian or an Ascended," Casteel said, curling his fingers around my chin and guiding my eyes to his. "I've never felt anything like you before. I don't know if that means you feel like a deity. My parents would know. Maybe even Jasper, but he was very young when he was around any of the deities so I'm not sure about him."

Before I could demand that he find Jasper immediately, he continued, "And I don't even know if you will continue to need blood."

Oh, gods.

"I hadn't even thought of that." My newly restarted heart was going to give out on me. Vamprys needed blood—mortal or Atlantian—nearly every day, while an Atlantian could go weeks without feeding. I didn't know about deities and the gods. Wasn't sure if they needed blood or not. No one had really specified that, nor had I even thought of it. "Do deities and gods need blood?"

"I don't think so," Casteel answered. "But the deities were guarded when it came to their weaknesses and needs. The gods even more so. It's possible."

I bet his mother would know. But even if they needed blood, it truly didn't matter. I was neither of those things.

"I don't even know if I can think of that right now. Not because I find it repulsive or anything..."

"I know. It's just different, and it's a lot to add on top of a lot. But we will figure it out together." He tucked a strand of hair back from my face. "So, I don't know if you're immortal or not, Poppy. We'll have to take that question day by day."

Immortal.

Living thousands and thousands of years? I couldn't process it. I couldn't even fully comprehend it when I had been the Maiden and believed I would go through an Ascension. The idea of living for hundreds of years had frightened me then. A lot of that had to do with how cold and untouchable the Ascended were. I knew that the Atlantians and the wolven weren't like that, but it was still a lot to wrap one's head around.

And if I ended up immortal, Casteel wasn't, even though he could live like a hundred or more mortal lifetimes before he truly began to age. He still would. He would eventually die. And if I was something…else, I wouldn't.

I shut down the unnecessary panic so I could freak out about it another day—like maybe after I learned if I truly was immortal.

I nodded, feeling rather logical at the moment.

"Okay," I said, taking a nice deep and slow breath. "We'll take that day by day." Something occurred to me then, and I looked at Kieran. "You're going to be happy to hear this. I have a question."

"I am so thrilled." Only the light in Kieran's eyes told me that he was glad I was alive and able to ask questions.

"If the wolven were bonded to the deities, how did they not protect the deities during the war?" I asked.

"Many did, and many died in the process," Kieran said, and my shoulders tightened. "Not all deities were killed, though. There were several left after the war, ones who had no interest in ruling. The wolven became very protective of them, but there was a rough period after the war where relations between the wolven and Atlantians were tense. According to our history, an ancestor on your husband's side handled it."

"What?" I looked at Casteel.

"Yep. It was Elian Da'Neer. He summoned a god to help smooth things over."

"And the god answered?"

"It was Nyktos himself, along with Theon and Lailah, the God of Accord and War and the Goddess of Peace and Vengeance," he told me, and I knew my eyes were wide. "They spoke with the wolven. I have no idea what was said, I'm not even sure if the wolven alive today know, but the first bonding between the wolven and an Atlantian came out of that meeting, and things calmed down."

"Was your ancestor the first to be bonded?"

Casteel grinned as he nodded. "He was."

"Wow." I blinked. "I really wish we knew what was said."

"Same." His gaze met mine and he smiled again, but it didn't reach his eyes as he studied me. "Poppy."

"What?" Wondering if I was starting to glow, I glanced down at my skin and saw that it appeared normal.

"You're not a monster," he said, and that nice, deep breath got lodged in my throat. "Not today. Not tomorrow. Not an eternity from now, if that is the case."

I smiled at his words, my heart swelling. I knew he believed that. I could taste his sincerity, but I also knew that when Alastir had spoken of the deities, he hadn't been lying. He'd told the truth, whether or not it was the one he believed or the real story. Still, others alive today had been around the deities. They would know if it truly was because they had grown too old and too embittered—or if it was something else.

Casteel's parents would know.

"I know it's a little hard to move on from that topic," Kieran began, and for some reason, I wanted to laugh at the dryness of his tone.

"No, I want to move on from that," I said, pushing some hair back that had fallen once more. "I kind of need to so my head doesn't explode."

A wry grin appeared on Kieran's face. "We wouldn't want that to happen. It would be far too messy, and there are no more clean towels," he said, and I laughed lightly. His pale eyes warmed. "Did Jansen speak of anyone else who could be involved? Cas compelled Alastir to tell us all he knew, but either he truly had no idea of who else was involved, or they were smart enough to make sure most of their identities weren't known."

"As if they had planned for someone to use compulsion?" I said, and they nodded. That was smart.

Pressing my lips together, I thought through the conversations with them. "No. No one by name, but both spoke as if they were a part of an…organization or something. I don't know. I think Alastir mentioned a brotherhood, and all of the ones I saw, except for when I first arrived in the Chambers, were male—at least from what I could tell. I don't know if they were truly a part of what Alastir spoke of or if they were somehow manipulated into their actions. But I do know that Alastir must have been working with the Ascended. He insinuated that they knew what I was capable of and that they planned to use me against Atlantia." I told them what Alastir believed the Ascended would do, my mind always drudging up the memory of the Duchess.

"He figured that the Ascended would kill me when I attacked them, but he also had a backup plan. I didn't get it when he said that I would never be free again. He must've given the others an order to kill me if the plan with the Ascended failed. He said he'd rather see a war among his people than have me…unleashed upon the people."

"He's a fucking idiot," Casteel growled, rising from the bed. "Part of me wanted to give Alastir the benefit of the doubt at first in the Chambers. That he wouldn't be that fucking stupid."

"I don't think any of us thought he'd do something like this," Kieran said. "To go as far as to betray you—your parents. Kill Beckett? That's not the man I know."

Casteel cursed again, dragging a hand through his hair. Sadness settled on my shoulders. I couldn't stop the image of Beckett in his wolven form, tail wagging as he bounded alongside us as we arrived in Spessa's End. Anger mixed with the distress. "I'm sorry."

Casteel turned to me. "What do you have to apologize for?"

"You respect and care for Alastir. I know it has to bother you."

"It does, but it is what it is." He tilted his head to the side. "But it would not be the first betrayal by one who shares his blood."

An ache pierced my chest, even though he had his emotions locked down. "And that makes me even more sorry because you spent the last several decades protecting him from the truth."

A muscle flexed in Casteel's jaw, and a long moment passed before Kieran said, "I believe Alastir cares for your family, but he is loyal to the kingdom first and foremost. Then to Casteel's parents, and then to himself and Malik. The only reason I can come up with for why he'd be involved in something like this is that he somehow realized what you were before anyone else did, and he knew what that meant for Atlantia and for the Crown."

I hadn't told them about Alastir's involvement, and I didn't think that was something that would've even come during compulsion. My stomach tightened, and the center of my chest hummed.

"It's because he did know."

Both of them stared at me.

"He was there the night the Craven attacked the inn. He was there to help my parents relocate to Atlantia," I said, shaking my head. "They trusted him. Told him what I could do, and he knew then what it meant. He said that my parents knew what the Ascended were doing—that my mother was a…a Handmaiden." I looked at Casteel to see that he'd stilled.

"I didn't remember them until he mentioned them, but then I recalled seeing these women dressed in black that were often around Queen Ileana. I don't know if that memory was true."

Tension bracketed Casteel's mouth. "The Handmaidens are real. They are the Blood Queen's private guards and cohorts," he said, and I shuddered. "I don't know if your mother was one of them. I don't see how she could have been. You said she didn't defend herself, and those women were trained in every manner of death known."

"I don't know," I admitted. "I don't remember her fighting, but…" I had gotten those glimpses of her holding something in her hand that night. "I really don't know, but Alastir said that he didn't kill them. That something else led the Craven there. He said the Dark One did. Not you, but someone else."

"That sounds like a load of bullshit," Kieran muttered. "Also sounds like he got lucky with the Craven showing up to do his dirty work."

I agreed, but again, there were those glimpses that lingered on the fringes of my consciousness. They were like smoke, though. When I tried to grab them, they slipped through my fingers.

I sighed. "Much of the way he behaved toward me was an act." That hurt, because Alastir…he reminded me a little bit of Vikter. "He came to me more than once to ask if I wanted aid in escaping. That he wouldn't be party to me being forced into a marriage. I thought that meant he was a good man."

"It could've been a genuine offer at first," Kieran said. "Who knows?"

"And his offer held an ulterior motive later?" I looked over at Casteel. "Do you not find it odd that he wanted you to marry his great-niece?"

"It wasn't just him," Casteel stated. "It was also my father."

"And he is your father's advisor," I pointed out. "It's just strange to me that he would want that when you were engaged to his daughter. Maybe it's not that odd since so many years have passed, but I just…it's weird to me."

"It is odd but not unheard of." His eyes squinted thoughtfully. "I can think of several examples of widows and widowers becoming involved with siblings of the deceased years later."

I couldn't even fathom that. Not because I would judge someone in that situation, but I would be so concerned that the other might worry they were a replacement. "I know that he would have more control over the Crown if you were to marry someone he had control of. That he was on the verge of losing whatever influence he had over Atlantia with you marrying me, and him knowing the truth of what I was. I don't think for one moment that his motives were purely centered around protecting Atlantia. I think he wanted to maintain control, and he was virtually staging a coup. I told him I thought as much, too."

A slow, shadowy smile crossed Casteel's features. "Did you?"

"Yeah." A tiny grin pulled at my lips. "He wasn't too happy about that. Protested a lot."

"Protested too much?" Kieran said.

I nodded. "I think he believed he was doing the right thing, but I think he wanted to keep his influence, and he wanted revenge."

"That makes sense," Casteel said. "My father wants retribution, just as Alastir does. Malik wouldn't have wanted war, and he knew that I don't either. Both my father and Alastir were impressed with what was done with Spessa's End."

"But Alastir didn't believe it was enough," I said, recalling how Alastir had responded. "He said it wasn't enough for your father, either."

"It hasn't been," Casteel admitted. "And Alastir wasn't a fan of my plan to negotiate. He wants blood from Solis. My father wants the same. Alastir believes that my brother is a lost cause." He folded his arms over his chest, and I felt the tangy spike of anguish. I started moving to him to take away his pain. I forced myself to stop because he had asked me once before not to do that. I clasped my hands together as he continued. "And perhaps he thought with Gianna as my bride, he would be able to wield his influence."

Gianna.

I wasn't sure what to think of the female wolven I'd never met or seen, as far as I knew. Casteel had never intended to marry her, and according to him, she hadn't shown any interest in him, either. She wasn't to blame for what his father or Alastir wanted. At least, that was what I kept telling myself. Alastir hadn't mentioned her at all.

"Whatever his motivations were," Kieran said, "it really doesn't matter now."

I supposed it didn't. Because Casteel had found him, and I knew the wolven no longer breathed.

Casteel came forward then, kneeling in front of me. He took my hands, and as I stared down at him, I felt his anger at himself and his family. But his anger for what had been done to me, his concern, overshadowed it. "I'm sorry you had to find out the truth like that." He picked up my hands, holding them in his. "I can't imagine what you must have felt."

"I wanted to kill him," I admitted. He lowered his lips to my hands, kissing the top of both of them. "Well, Princess, do you remember when I said I would give you whatever you wanted?"

"Yeah?"

He smiled again, and this time, it was a smile that promised blood. "Alastir is still alive."

"What?" I whispered.

"We made sure he was imprisoned before we headed to the Wastelands," Kieran said. "We figured it was best to keep him alive just in case we didn't get to you in time."

Casteel's gaze captured mine. "He's all yours, Poppy."

I learned that we would travel straight through the Skotos, not stopping. According to Kieran, we would reach the other side by nightfall because of how close we already were to the mountains. I was relieved to hear that as I didn't look forward to spending another night in the mountains with the mist. The fact that I'd almost walked off a cliff the last time still haunted me, and I really didn't need a repeat of that right now.

My mind was still skipping all over the place when Kieran left to ready the rest of the wolven and the Atlantians who remained—my memories jumping from one discovery to another. There were three things I was not thinking about as I made use of the small bathing chamber and returned to the sparse room.

The immortality thing and everything with that. Surprisingly, it wasn't hard not to think about it because I didn't feel any different than I had before the bolt struck me in the chest. And I didn't think I looked any differently. There was no mirror in the bathing chamber to confirm, but Casteel hadn't mentioned anything. I felt like myself.

I wasn't allowing myself to think about the whole Queen thing, either, which was something neither Kieran nor Casteel had brought up, thank the gods. I would have probably ended up in the corner of the hunting cabin if they had.

The third thing, I was failing at not thinking about. Who Alastir claimed I was related to kept popping up in my head every couple of moments. I watched Casteel pull on a thick tunic. Did he know? Had Alastir told him when he captured the wolven? Maybe he hadn't. I didn't have to say anything. If Casteel didn't know, that was probably for the best. Because how would he feel to know that he was married to the descendant of the King who'd nearly destroyed Atlantia? And his mother? My stomach twisted and churned. What would she think?

Or did she already know? Was that why she had asked Casteel what he'd brought home with him? King Valyn had fought beside him, but that didn't mean he didn't know. Alastir had arrived before us, and even if his parents hadn't been involved, they still could know who I was related to.

And his father… I remembered him shouting at Casteel to stop—

to not give me his blood. His father had known what Casteel had been about to do, and gods, it was what Malec had done all those hundreds of years ago, turning his mistress Isbeth into the first vampry out of an act of desperation.

It was like a tragic replay of history, except I hadn't become a vampry.

But King Valyn didn't know that.

"Where is your father?" I asked as I picked up one of the boots Jasper had found.

"Emil and a few others escorted him back to Atlantia. They're currently keeping him under watch," he answered.

I looked up from my boot. "Do you think that's necessary? To keep him under watch?"

Casteel nodded as he sheathed one of his swords at his side. "He's most likely under the assumption that I've turned you into a vampry," he parroted my earlier thoughts. "If we just sent him back to Atlantia, he would've immediately come back here."

"To do what?" I pulled on the soft, worn leather boot. It was a little snug around the calf but would work. "Cut off my head?" I asked, only half-joking.

"He would try and die trying," he stated bluntly.

I froze. "Casteel—"

"I know that sounds harsh." He bent, swiped up the other boot, and brought it over to where I sat on the edge of the wooden chair. "But even if you were a bloodthirsty Ascended, trying to rip the throats out of everyone who came near you, I would still destroy anyone who sought to harm you."

My heart skipped a beat and turned over heavily as I stared up at him. "I don't know if I should be worried about that or flattered."

"Let's go with flattered." He knelt, holding my boot. "And be thankful that it won't come to that. When he sees you, he'll know you haven't Ascended—at least not into a vampry."

But into what? I hoped he or someone could answer. "I can put my own shoes on."

"I know. But it makes me feel useful. Let me be useful, please."

"Only because you said, 'please,'" I murmured, lifting my leg.

He sent me a quick grin. "How are you feeling? Honestly? And I'm not talking about just physically."

I held still as he slid the shaft of the boot up. "I…I'm okay," I said, staring at the dark locks on his bowed head. "It's just a bit weird because I…I feel the same. I don't feel like anything has changed. I mean, maybe nothing really changed?" I said. "Maybe you just healed me—"

"I didn't just heal you, Poppy." He looked up at me as he tugged the boot into place. "Your heart stopped. If I had been a second or two too slow, you would've passed on." His gaze held mine as my stomach dipped. "You don't feel the same."

I gripped the edge of the chair. "I really don't understand what that means. I feel the same."

"It's hard to explain, but it's like a combination of scent and instinct." He placed his hands on my knees. "When I touch you, I recognize the feel of your skin in my soul and in my heart. You are still Poppy, but I don't sense mortal blood in your veins, and you no longer feel the same on an instinctual level."

"Oh," I whispered.

He stared at me for a moment. "Is that all you really have to say to that?"

"It's all I can come up with now."

His gaze searched mine as he nodded. "I can't even begin to imagine all the things that must be racing through your mind right now."

I coughed out a dry laugh. "So much. Some of it I can sort of table for later to freak out over. But…"

"What?" Casteel prodded quietly.

I opened my mouth, then closed it, and then tried again. A part of me still wanted to remain quiet, to not bring up King Malec, but I…I didn't want anything unspoken to linger between us. Not after what had happened. Not after what he'd risked for me. Not after we'd come so close to losing each other.

And even if what I had to say shocked him, I couldn't believe that it would drive a wedge between us. We were…together. We were too strong for that.

My grip tightened on the edge of the chair. "Did Alastir say anything to you when you caught up with him? About me? Other than the whole I'm-a-danger-to-Atlantia thing—which I'm sure he said."

"He said some things," he told me. "But there wasn't a lot of time, nor was I in the mood to listen to much beyond what I needed to know to find you." He squeezed my knees. "Why?"

I swallowed thickly. "He told me that I was descended from Nyktos and that I…I'm also descended from King Malec."

No wave of shock or horror radiated off Casteel as he stared at me. "He said as much to me, too."

"He did?" When Casteel nodded, I asked, "And that doesn't bother you?"

His brows lowered. "Why would that bother me?"

"Why?" I repeated, a little dumbfounded. "He was the one who created the first vampry. He betrayed your mother—"

"Yeah, *he* did those things. Not you." He slid his hands off my knees and placed them over mine. Slowly, he pried my fingers loose. "We don't even know if that's true."

"He said that Malec's abilities were a lot like mine—that he could heal with his touch and use his abilities to hurt people without even touching them," I said.

"I've never heard that." Casteel threaded his fingers through mine.

"He said that only a few people knew what he was truly capable of. That your parents did."

"Then we need them to confirm it."

I tensed. "Your mother—"

"My mother will not hold who you are descended from against you," he interrupted. "It may be a shock to her. It may even make her think of things she has worked to forget, but she will not hold you responsible for what someone distantly related to you did."

I wanted so badly to believe that. And maybe he was right. He knew his mother, but how she'd stared at me when she first saw me kept replaying in my head as well as what she'd said. But that could've just been shock. "Why haven't you said anything about that?"

"Because I honestly didn't think it mattered," he said, and the sincerity of his words tasted like vanilla. "I had no idea if he said it to you or if it's true. To be honest, it doesn't make sense to me. It doesn't explain your abilities or how strong they are, as far as I know. Just because you share similar gifts doesn't mean that you are descended from him."

Rising, he pulled me from the chair and then looped his arms around my waist. "But even if you do share his bloodline, it doesn't matter. It doesn't change you." His eyes were a bright amber as he looked down at me. "Did you really think it would bother me?"

"I didn't think it would come between us," I admitted. "I just…I don't want to be related to him. I don't want to make your mother uncomfortable more than I already have and am going to."

"I can understand that, but you know what?" He dropped his

forehead to mine. "I'm not worried about how she'll feel. I'm concerned about you—about everything that has happened to you. You have been so damn strong. You were attacked, taken captive, and then you almost lost your life." He placed a hand against my cheek, just over the scars there. "We have no idea why you haven't Ascended, or if you did and we just don't know into what yet. And, on top of all of that, you have had one shock after another—from learning the truth about the Ascended, to fearing for your brother and Tawny, to now learning that you have god's blood in you.

"Well, when you list it all out like that, I think I may need to sit down," I commented.

He kissed the bridge of my nose. "But you're not. You're standing. You're dealing with it, and fuck if I'm not in awe of you right now. But I also know none of this has hit you yet, and that concerns me. You keep telling me you're okay every time I ask how you are, and I know that can't be true."

"I am okay." *Mostly.* I rested my cheek against his chest. I needed to be okay because none of what had happened from the moment I stepped into the Chambers of Nyktos changed the fact that we needed to find his brother and mine—

Ian.

I jerked back, my eyes going wide. "Oh, my gods. I haven't even thought about this." Hope exploded deep inside me, loosening tense muscles. "If I didn't become a vampry, then that means Ian might not have, either. He could be like me. What I am. He might not be like them."

Wariness echoed through Casteel. "That's possible, Poppy," he began, his tone cautious. "But he's only been seen at night. And he's married to an Ascended."

The rest of what he wouldn't say hung unspoken in the air of the dusty hunting cabin. Ian may not be my brother by blood, or we may not share the same parent that carried the eather within them. I didn't know. But just because Casteel hadn't seen Ian during the day or just because he was married to an Ascended didn't mean that Ian had become one. The hope I felt now wasn't nearly as flimsy and naïve as it had been a week ago, and that was something to hold onto.

So, I did.

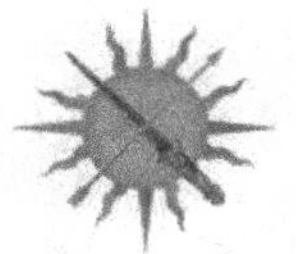

Casteel made sure I didn't run out into the late-morning sun when we stepped out onto the small alcove of a porch and saw Kieran waiting between a massive black horse—Setti—and a brown one. Setti neighed softly, shaking his glossy, black mane. Casteel slowed my steps, gradually letting me walk into the sun.

Other than enjoying the feel of it against my face, nothing happened.

I petted Setti for a moment, scratching him behind his ear as I scoured the trees around the cabin. Every so often, I saw a flash of silver or white or black among the low-hanging, gnarled branches. Brown, curled leaves and brighter, greener ones blanketed the woods surrounding the cabin. It was as if an extreme cold snap had come through, shocking the foliage. But we were in the Skotos foothills, and I could see the mist-drenched mountains looming above the trees. Wouldn't the plant life here be used to the chilly air?

Gripping the saddle as Casteel finished strapping down the saddlebags, I lifted myself onto Setti. Once I'd situated myself, I looked over to find not only Kieran and Casteel staring at me but also a dark-skinned Atlantian. Naill had come around the side of the hunting cabin. The three of them stared as if I had done a backflip onto the horse.

"What?" I asked, touching the mess that was my hair. There had been no comb inside, and I was sure I looked as if I'd been caught in a wind tunnel.

Naill's brows lifted as he blinked slowly. "That was…impressive."

My brows knitted. "What was?"

"You just hoisted yourself onto Setti," Casteel said.

"So?" The corners of my lips turned down.

"You didn't use the stirrup," Kieran pointed out as Naill mounted the horse that Kieran stood beside.

"What?" My frown increased. "Are you sure I didn't?" I must have. There would've been no way for me to seat myself on Setti without placing my foot in the stirrup or without aid. The horse was far too tall for me to have done that, nor did I have the kind of upper body strength required for that kind of feat without a nice running start.

And I would've probably failed spectacularly.

"You totally didn't," Naill confirmed. He stared at me with a bit of wonder that I figured had more to do with the fact that I wasn't a vampry.

"Here." Casteel stretched up, wiggling his hands. "Get down here for a moment."

"I just got myself up here."

"I know, but this will only take a second." He wiggled his fingers again. "I want to see something."

Sighing, I placed my hands in his and let him lift me off Setti, who watched us with an air of curiosity. I really hoped that none of them expected me to seat myself again with all of them watching. "What?"

Casteel dropped my hands and stepped back. "Hit me. Hard. Like you mean it."

My forehead creased. "Why do you want me to hit you?"

Naill folded his arms over the pommel of the saddle. "That's a good question."

"Hit me," Casteel urged.

"I don't want to hit you."

"That would be a first," he replied, his eyes twinkling in the sunlight.

"I don't want to hit you *right now*," I amended.

Casteel was quiet for a moment and then turned to Kieran and Naill. "Did I ever tell you guys about that time I discovered Poppy perched outside a window, clutching a book to her chest?"

My eyes narrowed as Naill said, "No, but I have a lot of questions."

"Cas," I started.

He shot me a slow smile of warning. "She had this book—it's her favorite. She even brought it with her when we left Masadonia."

"I did not," I stated.

"She's embarrassed about it," he went on, "because it's a sex book. And not just any sex book. It's full of all kinds of dirty and unimaginable—"

I snapped forward, punching him in the stomach.

"Fuck," Casteel doubled over with a grunt as Naill let out a low whistle. "Gods."

I crossed my arms. "Happy now?"

"Yeah," he exhaled raggedly. "I will be once I can breathe again."

I rolled my eyes.

"Damn." Casteel looked up at me, his eyes slightly wide. "You are…strong."

"Told you," Kieran commented. "I told you she was strong."

A memory of Kieran telling Casteel that after I'd tried to eat him flashed. My stomach dropped as my arms loosened and fell to my sides. "You think I've gotten stronger?"

"Think?" Casteel laughed. "I know. You've always been able to hit hard, but that was something else."

"I actually didn't hit you as hard as I could," I said.

He stared at me. "Well, damn."

"Do not ask me to hit you again. I'm not going to do it," I told him.

A slow smile crept over his face, and I tasted…lush spice against my tongue. "There is something so wrong with you," I muttered.

A dimple appeared in his right cheek as I turned away from him. Not even a second later, he was next to me, kissing the corner of my lips. "I like that," he said, placing his hands on my hips. "A lot."

Flushing to the roots of my hair, I said nothing as I gripped the saddle. This time, Casteel gave me the boost I may not have needed. He swung up behind me, taking the reins. I honestly didn't know what to think about the possibility that I was stronger. I didn't have the headspace for it. So, I added that to the list of things to dwell on later as I turned to Naill. "Thank you."

He stared at me, his forehead creasing. "For what?"

"For helping Casteel in Irelone. For helping me," I said.

A grin appeared as he glanced between Casteel and I, shaking his head. "You're welcome, Penellaphe."

"You can call me Poppy," I said, thinking that all who aided were those I could consider friends. It didn't matter if they had helped because they felt obligated to Casteel or not. It didn't matter to me.

His grin grew into a striking smile. "You're welcome, *Poppy.*"

Feeling my cheeks heat again, I looked around. "Where are Delano and Jasper?" I asked as Casteel steered Setti toward the woods. "And the rest?"

"They're all around us," Casteel said, nudging Setti forward.

"They don't have horses?" I frowned at the top of Kieran's head. "Where is your horse?"

Kieran shook his head. "The trip through the Skotos will be fast and hard. It takes less energy for us to be in our wolven forms. Plus, we cover much more ground this way."

Huh. I hadn't known that. I watched Kieran walk ahead of us. As he neared the trees, he reached down and gripped the hem of his tunic. I realized that he was already barefoot. He pulled the tunic over his head and off. Lean muscles along the length of his back bunched, and his arm tensed as he tossed the shirt aside.

"That seems wasteful," I muttered, watching the black tunic float for a few moments before it slowly drifted to the ground. His breeches joined it seconds later.

Naill sighed as he moved his horse forward. Shifting sideways on the saddle, he stretched out an arm as he hung low and swiped up the discarded clothing. "I should've just left them there so you could return to the kingdom buck-ass naked."

Out of the corner of my eye, I saw Kieran raise an arm and extend a middle finger. I told myself not to look but I knew he was about to shift, and there was something utterly fascinating about that. I couldn't stop myself. I peeked, keeping my gaze northwards.

Not like that did any good.

Kieran pitched forward, and for a moment, I saw way more than I should have. Then he changed, his skin thinning and darkening. Bones cracked and stretched, fusing back together. Fawn-colored fur sprouted along his back, covering the muscles as they thickened and grew. Claws slammed into the ground, stirring up leaves and dirt. Seconds. It had only taken seconds, and then Kieran prowled ahead of us in his wolven form.

"I don't think I'll ever get used to seeing that," I whispered.

"Which part?" Casteel asked. "The shifting, or Kieran stripping?"

Naill snorted as he righted himself on the saddle, shoving Kieran's clothing into his bag.

"Neither," I admitted, my gaze lifting to the trees as we entered the woods. The tops were deformed, the limbs twisted downward as if a great hand had landed over top of them, attempting to push them into the ground. "Are the trees like this always?"

"They were like that when we arrived at the cabin," Casteel answered, curling his arm around my waist as leaves and thin branches crunched under Setti's hooves. "But they never looked like that before."

"What could've caused that?"

"A hell of a storm must have come through here," he said, and when I glanced at Naill, he was looking up at them, too. As far as we could see, the trees were bent and misshapen.

What kind of storm could do that? Unsettled by the sight, I fell quiet as we traveled forward. It didn't take long for us to reach the mist obscuring the mountains. It was so thick and white that it was like soup. Even though I knew it wouldn't hurt me, I still tensed as Kieran loped through. I noticed the other wolven then, streaking out of the haunting woods around us and entering the mist with hesitation. I spotted Jasper and Delano as they came to our sides, joining the two horses. Wispy tendrils of mist curled around their legs and bodies.

Delano lifted his head as he prowled between Naill's horse and Setti, looking up at me. I gave him an awkward wave as I thought of Beckett disappearing into the mist the first time I'd entered the Skotos.

But that hadn't been Beckett.

Heart heavy, I faced forward, bracing myself to enter the opaque nothingness. My eyes narrowed. The mist didn't seem as thick as I remembered. Or it *moved*, swirling and thinning.

"That's different," Casteel noted, and his grip around my waist tightened.

The mist scattered as we entered, spreading out and opening a clear path for us. I twisted, looking behind us. The mist came together again, sealing into a thick, seemingly impenetrable mass. Turning around, I spotted several of the wolven ahead, their fur glossy in the sunlight.

Eager to see the stunning display of the golden trees of Aios, I looked up as soon as we cleared what was left of the mist.

"My gods," Naill whispered.

Casteel stiffened behind me as Setti slowed, the horse shaking his head nervously. Ahead of us, the wolven had come to a stop, as well, their bodies rigid with tension as they too looked up. My lips parted as a wave of shivers erupted across my skin.

Red.

Deep crimson leaves gleamed like a million pools of blood in the sunlight.

The golden trees of Aios had all become blood trees.

Chapter 12

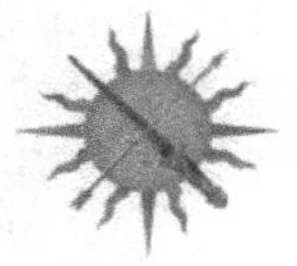

Under a canopy of glittering ruby instead of gold, we climbed the Skotos Mountains at a harsh pace that left little room to question what had happened to the trees of Aios. Not that either Casteel or Naill had an answer. I could feel their shock and unease just as strongly as I felt the same emotions radiating from the wolven as red instead of gold glistened from the bark of the magnificent, sweeping trees.

We split into groups as before, even though there were only faint wisps of mist seeping through prickly shrubs and curling along the thick moss covering the forest floor on the mountain. Kieran and Delano stayed with us as we moved steadily up. There were no sounds of birds or any animals, and while the branches, heavy with gleaming crimson leaves, swayed above us, there was no echo of wind, either. No one spoke beyond Casteel asking if I was hungry or Naill offering his flask, claiming the whiskey would help keep us warm the farther we traveled. Hours into the journey, we stopped long enough to take care of personal needs, feed the horses, and for both Naill and Casteel to don their cloaks. Once I was basically swaddled in the blanket Casteel had brought from the cabin, we continued on in the mountains that were still beautiful in a quiet, unsettling way. I couldn't stop staring at the leaves above me and the deep red ones that had fallen to the ground, peeking out from behind rocks and shrubs. It was as if the entire mountain had turned into one massive Blood Forest—one absent of the Craven.

What had changed the golden trees that had grown through the foothills and the entire mountain range after the goddess Aios had gone to sleep somewhere in the mountain? That question haunted me with each hour that passed. I may enjoy dabbling in denial every now and again, but there could be no coincidence between the change that had occurred here and what had happened to me. Three times now, a tree had grown rapidly where my blood had fallen, and in the ruins of Castle Bauer, the roots of that tree had seemed to gather around me—around Casteel and I both, as if the tree had tried to pull us into the ground or shield us. I didn't know, but I clearly remembered Kieran tearing through the slick, dark gray roots.

Roots that had been identical to the ones that had wrapped around the bone chains.

Had my near-death done this to the trees here? And the deformed woods outside of the hunting cabin? Had the potential loss of my mortality been the storm that swept through the woods and changed the trees of Aios to blood trees? How, though? And why? And had it impacted the goddess who slept here somehow? The one who Casteel and Kieran believed had awoken to stop me from plummeting to my death?

I hoped not.

Despite the uneasy nature of the mountains and the brutal pace, exhaustion dogged me, and I began to sink farther and farther into Casteel's embrace. Each time I blinked, it became harder to reopen my eyes to the beams of sunlight streaking through the gaps in the leaves overhead.

Under the blanket, I curled my fingers loosely around Casteel's arm as I shifted my gaze to where Kieran and Delano ran side by side ahead of us. My thoughts wandered as my eyes started to drift closed. I had no idea how long I'd slept after Casteel gave me his blood and we arrived at the cabin. I hadn't thought to ask, but it felt like I'd slept for a while. But that sleep hadn't been deep. Not all of it anyway because I had dreamed. I remembered that now. I had dreamt of the night my parents died, and those dreams had been different than the ones before. My mother had pulled something from her boot—something long, slender, and black. I couldn't see it now, no matter how hard I tried to remember, but someone else had also been there—someone she'd spoken to, who had sounded nothing like the voice I'd heard in the past—the one who had spoken with my father that I now knew belonged to Alastir. This had been a figure in black. I knew I had dreamed more, but it kept slipping out of reach within my tired mind. Was whatever I dreamed old memories that were finally revealing themselves? Or had they been implanted there, becoming a part of my imagination because of what Alastir had claimed about the Dark One?

But what hadn't felt like a dream, what had felt real, was the woman I'd seen. The one with the long, silvery-blonde hair, who'd filled my mind when I was in the Chambers of Nyktos. She had appeared when I was no longer a body, without substance or thought, floating in the nothingness. She had looked like me a little. She had more freckles, her hair was different, and her eyes were odd—a fractured green and silver, reminding me of how the wolven's eyes had looked when they came to me in the Chambers.

A bloody tear had slid down her cheek. That meant she had to be a god, but I knew of no female gods who were depicted with such hair or features. A weary frown pulled at my lips as I tried to sit up straighter. She had said something to me, too—something that had been a shock. I could almost hear her voice in my mind now, but just like with the dreams of the night at the inn, clarity frustratingly existed on the fringes of my consciousness.

Casteel shifted me so my head rested more fully against his chest. "Rest," he urged in a soft voice. "I've got you. You can rest."

It didn't seem right for me to do so when no one else could, but I couldn't fight the lure. It wasn't the deepest of sleep. Things I wanted to forget followed me. I found myself back in the crypts, chained to the wall. Bile crept up my throat as I turned my head to the side.

Oh, gods.

I came face to face with one of the corpses, its empty eye sockets tunnels of nothingness as it *shuddered.*

Dust sifted through the air as its jaw loosened, and a raspy, dry voice came out of the lipless mouth. "You're just like us." Teeth fell from its jaws, crumbling apart as they did. "You will end up just like us."

I pressed back as far as I could go, feeling the bindings tighten on my wrists and my legs. "This isn't real—"

"You're just like us," another echoed as its head jerked toward me. "You'll end up just like us."

"No. No." I struggled against the bindings, feeling the bones cut through my skin. "I'm not a monster. I'm not."

"You're not," a soft voice intruded, coming from everywhere and nowhere as the corpses along the wall continued shuddering and moving, their bones rubbing and grinding together. The voice sounded like… Delano? *"You are meyaah Liessa. Wake up."*

The thing beside me's mouth fell open in a scream that started silently but turned into a long, keening howl—

"Wake up. Poppy. You can wake up. I've got you." *Casteel.* His arm was tight around me as he gathered me as close as he could to his chest while Setti's powerful muscles moved under us. "You're safe. No one is going to hurt you." His mouth pressed against my temple, warm and comforting. "Never again."

Heart thumping erratically, I dragged in deep breaths. Had I screamed? I blinked rapidly as I struggled to free my hands from where they were tucked between Casteel's arms and the blanket. I managed to pull one free and hastily wipe at my cool cheeks as my eyes adjusted to the faint traces of pale sunlight and the dark, almost-black leaves above us. Swallowing hard, I glanced to where Naill rode, facing straight ahead, and then before us. The white wolven ran beside the fawn-colored one, turning his head to look back at us, his ears perked. For a brief second, our gazes connected, and I felt his concern. The buzz in my chest hummed as a singular pathway opened along the connection to the wolven's emotions, a clearer cord that fed something other than feeling. A springy, featherlight sense that had nothing to do with relief. It was almost like a brand—an imprint of Delano, of who he was at his core—unique only to him.

The wolven broke eye contact as he loped over a boulder, moving ahead of Kieran. I let out a ragged breath.

"Poppy?" Casteel's fingers brushed my chin and then the side of my neck. "Are you okay?" he asked, his voice low.

Pulling my gaze from Delano, I nodded. "I'm fine."

His fingers stilled, and then he lowered his hand, picking up the strands. "What were you dreaming about?"

"The crypts," I admitted, clearing my throat. "Did I…did I scream? Or speak?"

"No," he said, and I silently thanked the gods. "You started to squirm around a bit. You were flinching." He paused. "Want to talk about it?"

I shook my head.

He was silent for a few moments and then he said, "They felt you. Felt whatever you were dreaming. Both Kieran and Delano. They kept looking back here," he told me as my gaze tracked back to the two wolven. They raced over the ground—ground that was no longer as mossy. "Delano started howling. That's when I woke you."

"I…do you think it's the Primal thing?" I asked, wondering if I had really heard Delano's voice. That didn't make sense because he had answered what I'd said in my dream.

"The Primal *notam*? I imagine so."

Leaning into Casteel, I looked up. The trees were thinning, and I could see patches of the sky now painted intense shades of pink and deep blue. "Have we crossed the Skotos?"

"We have," he confirmed. The air wasn't nearly as cold as it had been before I'd fallen asleep.

We rode on, the sky turning dark, and the land under us smoothing and leveling out. Casteel loosened the blanket around me as we broke free of the last of the trees, and the remaining wolven poured out from our sides, joining the group. I twisted at the waist and looked behind Casteel, but it was too dark to see the trees of Aios.

I didn't even want to think what the people of Atlantia felt when they saw the trees change. My heart tripped over itself as I faced forward again, scanning the rocky and jagged terrain. I didn't recognize the land, even though the air seemed to warm with each passing moment.

"Where are we?" I asked as I caught sight of the large silver wolven moving ahead. Jasper easily navigated the boulders, leaping from one to another as the other wolven followed.

"We came out a bit farther south of Saion's Cove," Casteel explained. "Closer to the sea, at the Cliffs of Ione. There's an old Temple here."

"You might've been able to see the Cliffs from the Chambers," Naill advised as he slowed his horse when the terrain became more uneven. "But probably not the Temple."

"This is where my father is waiting, and Alastir is being kept," Casteel told me.

I sat straighter, catching the blanket before it fell and tangled around Setti's legs. Tall cypress trees dotted the landscape, thickening in the distance. The air carried the distinctive scent of salt.

"We can stop here, or we can travel onward to Saion's Cove," Casteel said. "We can deal with Alastir now or later. It is up to you."

I didn't hesitate, even though dealing with Alastir meant facing Casteel's father. "We deal with this now."

"You sure?"

"Yes."

Something akin to pride drifted from Casteel to me as his lips touched my cheek. "So strong."

To our left, the sound of running water reached us. In the moonlight, water glistened from the face of the Skotos Mountains and rushed across the wide strip of land. The water tumbled and spilled off the cliffs, reaching the rocks below.

Stars shone across the sky as the rippling light of numerous torches became visible through the soaring trees, casting an orangey glow over columned sides nearly as tall as the surrounding cypress.

Kieran joined his father as they darted between the trees, racing toward the wide steps of the enclosed Temple. People stood on the colonnade, dressed in black, and I knew without asking that these were Casteel's men and Guardians of Atlantia. Those he trusted.

As several of the wolven climbed the steps, Casteel slowed Setti. "We will most likely see my father first. He needs to see that you didn't Ascend."

I nodded as nervous energy and something rawer buzzed within me.

"*Then* we will handle Alastir," Casteel continued, the arm around my waist shifting. His hand slid across my stomach, leaving shivers in its wake. "I've gotten all I can get out of Alastir that will be of use to us, so you know how tonight will end?"

Nervousness settled as resolve crept over me. I knew how tonight would end. Determination inked itself onto my skin, carving its way into my bones and filling the center of my chest. My chin lifted. "With death."

"By your hand or mine?" he asked, his lips grazing the curve of my jaw.

"Mine."

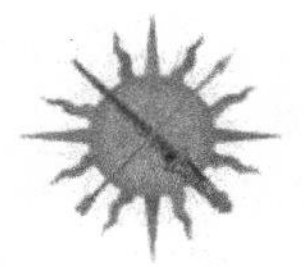

Casteel and I climbed the steps to the Temple of Saion, our hands joined. Nearly two dozen wolven prowled the colonnade while Jasper and Kieran stood in front of doors as black as the sky and nearly as tall as the Temple.

The tartness of uncertainty and the fresher, lemony flavor of curiosity saturated the air as those waiting between the columns took notice of Casteel and then me. Whatever Casteel had sensed that was different about me, they felt it, too. I saw it in the way the Guardians stiffened, their hands reaching for their scabbards and then halting as their heads tilted to the side while they tried to understand what it was they sensed. I felt no fear from any of them, not the Guardians or the others. I wanted to ask one of them what they felt when they looked at me—what made them first go for their swords but then stop. However, Casteel's grip tightened on my hand, preventing me from wandering over to one of the women—which I had apparently been in the process of doing.

Then again, only the gods knew what I looked like at the moment with my hair a curly, knotted mess, the too-tight breeches and boots, and Casteel's cloak over a too large, borrowed tunic. It was quite possible they thought I was a Craven.

One of the Atlantians stepped forward as we reached the top of the steps. It was Emil, his auburn hair redder in the torchlight as his gaze slid from Casteel to me. His nostrils flared as his throat worked on a swallow. His handsome face paled slightly as he clasped the hilt of his sword, bowing slightly at the waist. "I am relieved to see you here, Your Highness."

I gave a small jerk. The use of the formal title caught me a little off guard, and it took me a moment to remember that as Casteel's wife, that was my formal title. It had nothing to do with the whole issue with the Crown. "As am I," I said, smiling. Another ripple of shock came from Emil as he looked at me as if he couldn't quite believe I was standing there. Considering the state I had been in the last time he'd seen me, I couldn't blame him for that. "Thank you for your help."

The same look Naill had given me earlier when I'd thanked him crossed the Atlantian's face, but he inclined his head with a nod. He turned to Casteel. "Your father is inside and isn't exactly thrilled."

"I bet," Casteel murmured.

One side of Emil's lips curved up as Naill joined us. "And neither are the handful of Atlantians and mortals who found their way here, attempting to free Alastir."

"And how did that go?" Casteel demanded.

"It was a little…bloody." Emil's eyes glowed in the torchlight as he looked at his Prince. "Those who are still alive are being kept with Alastir for your…enjoyment."

A tight, dark smile appeared as Casteel tipped back his head. "Has anyone else become aware that my father's being held here?"

"No," Emil answered. "Your mother and the Guards of the

Crown believe he is still with you."

"Perfect." Casteel looked over at me. "Ready?"

I nodded.

Emil started to step back but stopped. "I almost forgot." He reached to his side and under his tunic. I stiffened at the low rumble of warning as Jasper took a step forward, his head lowering. Casteel shifted ever so slightly beside me, his body tensing. The Atlantian shot a nervous glance over his shoulder at the large wolven. "This belongs to her," he said. "I'm just giving it back."

I looked down to see him withdraw a blade—one that gleamed reddish black in the firelight. Air lodged in my throat as he flipped it over, offering me the bone handle. It was my bloodstone dagger. The one Vikter had gifted me on my sixteenth birthday. Other than the memories of the man who risked his career and most likely his life to make sure I could defend myself, it was the only thing I had left of him.

"How…?" I cleared my throat as I closed my fingers around the cold wolven bone. "How did you find it?"

"By pure luck, I think," he said, immediately stepping back and nearly bumping into Delano, who had silently crept up behind him. "When I and a few others went back to look for evidence, I saw it lying under the blood tree."

I swallowed the knot in my throat. "Thank you."

Emil nodded as Casteel clasped the Atlantian on the shoulder. I held onto the dagger, slipping it under the cloak I wore as we walked forward, crossing the wide colonnade. A young, slim male stood against the wall, and I almost didn't recognize the somber, soft, almost fragile lines of Quentyn Da'Lahr's face. He wasn't smiling—he wasn't chattering away, brimming with energy like he normally was as he came toward us with hesitant steps. The moment my senses connected with his emotions, the tang of his anguish took my breath. There was uncertainty in him and the sourness of guilt, but there was also an undercurrent of something…bitter. *Fear.* My chest seized as my senses rapidly attempted to decipher whether his fear was directed at me or… Then I remembered that he had been close to Beckett. The two had been friends. Did he know what had happened to his friend? Or did he still believe that Beckett had been involved in the attack? I wasn't sure, but I couldn't believe that Quentyn had been involved. He wouldn't be standing here if he were.

Casteel's cool amber gaze shifted to the young Atlantian, but before he could speak, Quentyn dropped to one knee, bowing his golden head before us. "I'm sorry," he said, his voice carrying a slight tremor. "I did not know what Beckett was going to do. If I had, I would've stopped—"

"You have nothing to apologize for," I spoke, unable to allow the young Atlantian to carry guilt that was so very wrongly placed. I realized that the others must not have learned what had truly happened. "Beckett was guilty of nothing."

"But he…" Quentyn lifted his head, his golden eyes wet. "He led you to the Chambers and—"

"That wasn't him," Casteel explained. "Beckett committed no crime against Penellaphe or me."

"I don't understand." Confusion and relief echoed through the Atlantian as he rose unsteadily to his feet. "Then where has he been, Your Highness—I mean, Casteel? Is he with you?"

My hand squeezed Casteel's as the muscle in his jaw ticked. "Beckett never left Spessa's End, Quentyn. He was killed by those who conspired with his uncle."

If the others had any reaction to the young wolven's death, I wasn't sure. All I could feel was the rising tide of sorrow as it quickly rose in the Atlantian, following a brutal punch of denial. His pain was so raw and potent that it exploded into the salty air around us, thickening as it settled on my skin. I heard Casteel telling him that he was sorry, and saw Quentyn shaking his head. His pain…it was extreme, and a distant part of me wondered if this was the first real loss he'd experienced. He was older than I was, even though he appeared younger. But by Atlantian years, he was still so very young. He struggled not to show his pain, pressing his lips together, his back stiffening unnaturally. He was trying to hold it together as his Prince spoke to him, and as the wolven, Atlantians, and Guardians surrounded him. Sadly, he was losing the battle as anguish pulsed in waves through him. If he lost it, Casteel wouldn't hold it against him, but I could sense that he wanted to be seen as brave and strong. And I hated that. Hated those who were responsible even more for the pain they had inflicted on others and the lives they had stolen.

I reacted without thought, only instinct. Later, I would obsess over everything that could've possibly gone wrong since I had no idea what my touch would do now. I slipped my hand free from Casteel's and placed it on the Atlantian's arm. His wide eyes shot to mine. Tears clung to his lashes.

"I'm sorry," I whispered, wishing there was something better to say, something more helpful, more inspiring. But words were rarely good enough to ease the pain of loss. I did what I knew, pulling on my happy moments—warm and hopeful emotions. I thought of how I felt when Casteel told me he loved me, how I felt when I realized that he did in Spessa's End. I took those emotions and I let them flow through my body into Quentyn's.

He jerked as I felt his grief and disbelief pulse intensely and then rapidly fade. The skin around his mouth eased, and the tension in his shoulders relaxed. He exhaled heavily, and I felt no more sorrow. I released his arm, knowing the reprieve wouldn't last forever. Hopefully, it could give him some time to come to terms with his friend's death in private.

"Your eyes," Quentyn whispered, blinking slowly. "They're strange—" His cheeks flushed under the torchlight. "I mean, they're really pretty. Strange in a pretty way."

My brows rose as I looked at Casteel.

The lines and angles of his face had softened. "They're glowing," he murmured, leaning in slightly. "Actually, it's not your entire eye that is." His head tilted to the side. "There are wisps of light. Silvery light throughout your irises."

Fractured eyes.

Casteel looked to where Kieran and Delano waited and saw what I did. Eyes a pale blue streaked with luminous silver-white.

Eyes like those of the woman I'd seen in a dream that I knew was no dream—the woman who had spoken to me. Every part of my being at that moment knew that what she had said was the *answer* to everything.

Chapter 13

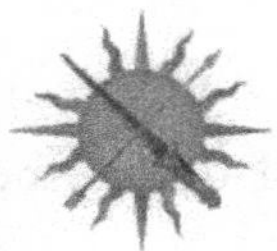

Turning back to me, Casteel took my hand once more, lifting it to his mouth. "They're no longer glowing." He placed a kiss on my knuckles, and that single act eased a lot of the tension already creeping into me. He bowed his head, placing his mouth near my ear as he whispered, "Thank you for what you did for Quentyn."

I shook my head, and he kissed the uneven line of skin along my cheek. Keeping his fingers threaded through mine, he motioned to the Guardians.

Two came forward, placing their hands over their hearts and bowing as they each grasped a handle of the black doors. Stone scraped as they pulled them open. Candlelight spilled out onto the colonnade as Jasper prowled inside, his silver fur gleaming in the light. His son and then Delano followed as Casteel and I walked forward, the wolven dagger still clutched in my grip, hidden by the cloak. The remaining wolven flanked us, streaming along the thick columns lining the four walls of the interior chamber—black stone columns as reflective as the Temples in Solis. I watched the wolven roam between those glossy pillars, their ears lowered and eyes a luminous winter blue as they stalked the chamber, circling the tall, broad-shouldered male sitting on one of the numerous stone benches lining the center of the Temple of Saion, his back to us. His back was rigid as his head followed the wolven's path.

"Father," Casteel called as the door closed behind us with a soft thud.

The King of Atlantia rose slowly, cautiously, and then turned, his hand drifting to his side where his sword would've been sheathed. The man had been hard to read at the Chambers of Nyktos, but now he didn't have nearly as much control over his emotions as his gaze shifted from his son to me.

He jerked back a step, his legs bumping into the bench behind him. "You didn't…" He trailed off as a blast of icy shock chilled my skin. His eyes were wide, pupils dilating so fast that only a thin strip of gold was visible as he stared at me, his lips parting.

My mouth dried as I fought the urge to close down my senses. I kept them open as he took a step forward. Kieran's head snapped in his direction, and a low growl rumbled through the chamber, but Casteel's father appeared beyond hearing as he said hoarsely, "You were dying."

I shivered at the reminder. "I was."

Strands of light hair fell against the rough growth of hair along his jaw and cheeks. "You were beyond saving," he rasped as Kieran appeared to relax, inching back even though Casteel's father took another tentative step toward us. "I saw you. I saw your wound and how much you bled. You were beyond saving unless—"

"I took what was left of her blood and gave her mine," Casteel said. "That is how she stands here. I Ascended her."

"But…" The King appeared at a loss for words.

I drew in a shallow breath and found my voice. "I can walk in the sun—we actually rode all day through it. I don't feel cold to the touch, and I have emotions," I told him. "And I don't feel the need to tear out anyone's throat."

Casteel's gaze slid to mine as a faint thrill of amusement reached me.

"What?" I whispered. "I feel that's necessary to point out."

"I didn't say anything."

I narrowed my eyes at him and then returned my attention to his father. "What I'm trying to say is that I'm not a vampry."

King Valyn's chest rose with a deep inhale, and with that breath, I felt his shock retreat with each passing second, becoming fainter. But I didn't believe that he'd overcome his surprise that quickly. He was tucking his emotions away, hiding them where I couldn't easily reach them—doing the same thing his son did when he didn't want me to know his emotions. A part of me, in the center of my chest, hummed with energy and wanted to dig into those walls he'd built, find the fragile seams, and peel them apart, exposing—

No.

I didn't want that.

I didn't want that for a multitude of reasons, namely for the fact that it would be a massive violation. If someone shut me out, that was their right. That was the only reason that mattered, but I wasn't even sure I could do something like that.

His father cleared his throat, snapping my attention back to him. "I can't believe you did it, Casteel." He backed up and then sat on the bench, stretching out one leg. I didn't attempt to read him. "You knew what could've happened."

"I knew exactly what could've happened," Casteel returned. "I knew the risks, and I'd do it all over again even if she had Ascended."

My heart gave a happy little wiggle, but Casteel's father looked less than impressed. "You know what that act did to our kingdom—to our people—and you were willing to risk that again?"

"If you think that what I did was a shock, then you need to understand that I will do anything and everything for *my wife*." Casteel's gaze latched on to his father's. "No risk is too great, nor is anything too sacred. Because she is my *everything*. There is nothing greater than her, and I do mean *nothing*."

My lips parted on a breathy inhale as I stared at Casteel. A messy, little ball of emotions climbed its way up my throat.

"I do not doubt that, son. I was there when you came to and realized that she was gone. I saw you, and I have never seen you like that. I will never forget it," his father said, and my head snapped in his direction. That was twice now that someone had said that. "And I can even understand your need to protect her. Gods, do I understand that." He dragged a hand over his face, stopping to scratch at the beard. "But as the King, I cannot approve of what you did."

Casteel's hand slipped from mine as several of the wolven looked at the King. A cold, utterly frightening sort of anger brewed inside the Prince—the kind of rage I knew had been one of the reasons he had come to be known as the Dark One. "I wasn't aware that I asked for your approval."

My heart stuttered as his father snorted. "I think that's obvious, considering that the deed is already done."

"And?" Casteel challenged in a voice that was too soft. Too calm.

Tiny hairs rose all over my body as my palm became damp around the hilt of the wolven dagger. A great sense of wariness rose from the wolven. They became eerily still. "Wait," I said, unsure if I was speaking to them or if I spoke to every living creature in the room. "Casteel took a huge risk, one that many would agree he shouldn't have taken, but he did. It's over. I'm not a vampry." I thought of the blood hunger I'd experienced upon awakening. "Or at the very least, I am not like the others. And while he may be deserving of the lecture—"

His father arched a brow while Casteel frowned at me. "It feels a little irrelevant right now," I stressed.

"You're right," King Valyn said after a moment. "He's lucky. Or you are. Or I and the entire kingdom are because you're not an Ascended. That much I know. If you were, my son knows what I would be obligated to do." His gaze met mine. "And I say that knowing it is highly unlikely that I would even reach you before these wolven—those I have known for hundreds of years—ripped into me." His gaze flicked to his son's. "You would've started a war, one that would've weakened us to the real threat that lies in the west. You just need to know that."

One side of Casteel's lips curled up, and I tensed at the sight of the smirk. "I know what my actions would've caused."

"And yet?"

"Here we stand," he replied.

I inhaled sharply as I felt the hot burn of anger break through the walls that his father had built. "Yes, here we all stand, apparently determined to irritate the hell out of one another. Not me. I don't want to irritate anyone—you know, the person who was attacked not once but twice and then shot in the chest with a crossbow," I snapped, and both their gazes shot to me. "And yet, I'm the one who has to tell you two to knock it the hell off."

The King blinked at me. "Why am I reminded of your mother, Cas?"

"Because that sounds like something she'd say," he replied. "Or probably has said, minus the being shot part."

I rolled my eyes. "Okay, well, as I said, I'm not an Ascended, or at least not like the others. We all can agree on that, right? So, would you happen to know what I am?" I asked, and then an awkward laugh escaped me. The sound earned a few curious stares from the wolven. "That sounded extremely weird to say out loud."

"I've heard far stranger things," Casteel commented, and that earned him a curious glance from *me*. "She does not feel like anything I've felt before," Casteel said to his father, his tone shifting from that deadly calm that was always a warning of very bad things to come. "But she's not mortal any longer."

It was very bizarre to hear that, despite already knowing it.

"No, she is not." His father studied me so intently that it was hard to stand there and not react. Especially since that kind of scrutiny had only ever accompanied someone staring at my scars. I didn't think he even saw them at the moment. "And you're not a vampry. None of them can walk in the sun or be among our kind so soon after the change and be so calm."

"I didn't think so," Casteel said. "Can you explain what happened?"

His father didn't answer for a long moment, and as I focused on him, I truly felt nothing from him. "It has to be her heritage. Her bloodline," he said. "Somehow, it played a role in this. She feels…I don't understand how she feels."

Warning bells went off, and it had everything to do with the sudden biting taste of conflict filling my mouth. Did he know more than he was saying? Instinct told me that he did. I glanced around the chamber, seeing only the wolven among us. I took a deep breath. "Alastir told me who I'm related to—"

"I can only imagine what Alastir has told you," King Valyn cut in. "Some of it may be true. Some of it might not be. And there are things my wife and I may be able to confirm for you."

There was a skip in my chest, and the warmth of Casteel's body pressed against my side as he shifted closer to me. "But?"

"But this is a conversation I won't have without Eloana present," he said, and I felt another jolt in my chest. His gaze met mine. "I know it's a lot for me to ask you to wait, but she needs to be a part of that conversation."

I was being asked to wait to find out if I was truly related to King Malec—to delay possibly discovering why I didn't become a vampry when Casteel Ascended me. Of course, I didn't want to, but I looked at Casteel. His eyes briefly met mine, and then he looked at his father. "That is asking a lot, Father."

"I know, but just like you will do anything for your wife, I will do anything to protect mine."

"What does she have to be protected from?" Casteel asked.

"A history that has haunted us for centuries," his father answered, and I shivered. He stood slowly. "So, you can push this, but I won't speak about any of it until Eloana is present. You can summon her now if you want, but I figure you have other pressing matters to deal with."

Alastir.

"And I also think you want me to talk to your mother before she finds out that you've held me here," his father continued, a wry sense of humor creeping into his tone. "Plus, it gives you time to rest—both of you. You've been traveling nonstop and dealing with a lot. But it's up to you."

Casteel's stare met mine, and it took a lot for me to nod. "You sure?" he asked, his voice low.

"I am," I confirmed, even as I wanted to shout in frustration.

His father's chest rose. "Thank you. I think we all need this extra time," he said, and tiny balls of unease took root. Alastir had said that Casteel's parents weren't involved, but there was a reason he wanted to delay this conversation—why he wanted his wife present. "I believe it would be extremely wise for us to keep this from anyone not present at the ruins," he advised. In other words, no one needed to know that Casteel had Ascended me. "And that all who were there, be sworn to secrecy."

"Agreed," Casteel stated.

"But you sense something different about me, right?" I looked between the two. "Wouldn't any who can sense that know?"

"They will only know that you are neither vampry nor mortal. What they feel will not tell them what occurred," he explained, and that was definitely a comfort to know. But what about the trees of Aios? That must have alerted the people of Atlantia that something had happened. "Am I free to go, then?" he asked of his son, and I couldn't determine if that was a serious question or not.

Casteel nodded. Kieran and the others tracked the King as he walked toward us, stopping a few feet away as he stared at his son. Neither of them spoke. I wasn't naïve enough to believe that no damage had been done to their relationship, even though I wished that wasn't the case. I only hoped it was repairable.

King Valyn's gaze shifted to mine. "I am sorry for what was done to you when you arrived and what has happened since. This is not who Atlantia is. Neither Eloana nor I would have allowed something like this to happen if we'd known what Alastir had planned," he told me as empathy pushed through the walls he'd built, reaching me. "And I also know that my apology does very little to change or rectify what has happened—what could have been the outcome of such treachery and evil. And that is what Alastir and those who conspired with him have committed."

I nodded. "It's…" I stopped myself before telling him it was okay. Because it wasn't—none of this was. So, all I could do was nod once more.

King Valyn turned to his son. "I can only assume what you plan to do with Alastir and the others who are held below, but I want your assurance that he will not survive the night. If he does, he will be executed in the morning," he told Casteel. "And while the crown still sits upon my head, it is an order I will personally ensure is carried out."

While I was glad he didn't demand leniency for Alastir, the part about the crown sent a wave of anxiety through me. I knew what he meant without him having to say it more clearly. He didn't expect to bear the weight of the crown for much longer.

"He will not survive the night," Casteel assured him. "None of them will."

King Valyn nodded and then hesitated for a moment. "Come to us when you are both ready. We will be waiting."

I watched Casteel's father make his way around us, the wolven clearing a path for him.

"Wait. Please." Aware of Casteel's stare, I turned to where his father stopped before the door. He looked back at me. "You were at the ruins in the Wastelands. Thank you for helping Casteel—for helping me," I said, hoping I wasn't proven a fool later for thanking him. "Thank you."

King Valyn's head tilted to the side. "You don't have to thank me. You're family now. Of course, I would help you."

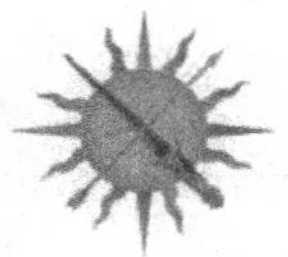

Home.

Kieran sat beside me in his wolven form as I stood between the cypresses, under the splintered beams of moonlight. The cliff's edge overlooked Saion Cove's now-dark waters, reflecting the deep blues and blacks of the night sky. From here, I could see the city lights glittering like stars coming to rest beyond the trees and valleys. It all looked like a beautiful canvas, almost unreal. It reminded me a little of

Carsodonia, but even in the middle of the night, the bay would be full of ships, transporting people and goods in and out. But it was peaceful here, with the sound of the waterfalls and distant calls of nightbirds, and I was shocked and relieved to feel the same as I had when I stood in the Chambers of Nyktos.

I still felt like I was home.

Was it my bloodline—the eather in it—recognizing the land, the air, and the sea? Was my heritage that powerful? Because I honestly hadn't believed I would feel that after the attack.

A warm breeze sent a tangled strand of hair across my face. I caught it, tucking it back as the same current caught the edges of the cloak I wore, lifting them. Would my parents—at least the one who carried Atlantian blood in them—have felt this way upon seeing Atlantia? If they had made it. My chest clenched with sorrow and anger, and it took everything in me to push it down and not let it take over. If I allowed that, the nasty ball of emotion that had settled in my chest would work its way free, and I…I couldn't allow that to happen. Not now.

Weight pressed against my leg and hip, and I looked down to find that Kieran had leaned into me. Like I often did with Delano, the urge to pet or scratch his head was hard to ignore. He'd stayed outside with me after Casteel had led me onto a stone pavilion behind the Temple of Saion and then went underground with a few others to retrieve Alastir from the crypts.

It wasn't the same one they'd kept me in, but Casteel had asked me to stay aboveground. I imagined he did that because he didn't want me to be surrounded by the dead again, to be reminded of my time spent with them. His foresight was another thing I was eternally grateful for.

I turned back to the sea as I dredged up the hope I'd felt when I realized that there was a chance that Ian was like me. If he was, then he could come here. He would love it. I already knew it after only seeing what little I had. He would feel the peace, too. And when he saw the sea, as clear as it was during the day, and as dark as it was at night? I couldn't wait to discover what stories he'd be inspired to tell. A smile tugged at my lips.

Kieran stood, ears perking as he heard the footsteps several moments before me. Maybe I was stronger, but it appeared I hadn't developed the nifty hearing abilities of the Atlantians—because, of course not.

I looked over my shoulder. Emil approached slowly, aware that

Kieran wasn't the only wolven among the trees.

"It is time?" I asked.

Emil nodded as he stopped several feet from me. "When Alastir saw that Cas was alone, he believed you to be dead. We didn't correct that assumption. Cas thought that the belief would make Alastir more inclined to speak, to incriminate any others who may be involved. But the bastard isn't saying much."

"But he is saying something?"

Emil's jaw hardened. "Nothing that needs repeating."

"Let me guess? He said that he was only doing what he needed to do to protect Atlantia and that I was a threat?" I surmised, and the Atlantian's gaze turned steely. "And I imagine he was also incredibly polite and apologetic as he said those things."

"Sounds about right," Emil sneered, and I wasn't surprised or disappointed. What else could Alastir truly say? Admit that there hadn't been anyone else there that night at the inn? It wouldn't matter if he did. There was nothing any of us needed to hear from him. At least, nothing I wanted. "Which is also why I think Casteel allowed him to believe you're dead. I think he's already amused by the look that will most likely settle upon Alastir's face when he realizes that he failed. Come." Emil started to turn. "Cas will summon us when he wants us to make our presence known."

But had he failed?

Yes.

I jerked as my heart jumped. I looked down at Kieran, my skin erupting in tiny bumps. He continued watching Emil with those blue-silver eyes. "Did I—?" I stopped myself. There was no way I had heard Kieran's voice in my mind. Casteel couldn't even communicate that way. But hadn't I heard Delano's voice earlier? I'd been asleep, though.

"Are you okay?" Emil asked, his concern evident.

"Yeah. Yes." I quickly bent, picking up the wolven dagger from where I'd placed it on the ground. "I'm ready."

Quietly, I followed Emil through the thick stand of trees, returning to the firelight of the pavilion. I stopped when Emil lifted a hand for silence. We were still several yards from the pavilion, but I could see Casteel.

He stood in the center of the structure, arms at his sides, his head cocked just a bit, revealing only the striking curve of his cheek and a tilt of full lips. Dressed in all black, he looked like a spirit of the night, one called forth to carry out vengeance.

I slipped the dagger under the fold of my cloak as I saw the Guardians lead about half a dozen men out from the back of the Temple, all of them bound with their hands tied behind their backs. Muscles stiffened as Naill led the last one. Alastir's scarred face was devoid of emotion as they lined him up with the others.

Hatred seared my soul as he and the others were forced to their knees. My parents. Casteel. His parents. Me. All of us had trusted him, and he had not only planned to hand me over to the Ascended but had also ordered my death. And in a way, he hadn't failed. I had been killed. Casteel had saved me, and I had awoken as something else.

What Alastir believes about me doesn't matter, I told myself as I watched Casteel prowl forward, moving toward the nameless men who bled the bitter taste of fear into the air. I hadn't done anything to deserve what Alastir and they had done. I had only defended myself. My parents had only trusted him. My grip tightened on the dagger.

Casteel was so incredibly fast.

I didn't even realize what he'd done until the man farthest away from Alastir toppled over. Five more followed like dominos, and I didn't see the moonlight glinting off his slick sword until it stopped a mere inch from Alastir's neck. He'd severed their heads. All of them except Alastir. In a few heartbeats.

I sucked in the breath that seemed to leave Alastir's body. The wolven was so still that it was like he was made of stone.

"You betrayed your King and Queen," Casteel said, his voice showing no emotion. And I…I felt nothing from him as he held the blood-soaked edge of the sword to Alastir's neck. "You betrayed me, and you betrayed Atlantia. But none of those are the worst of your sins."

Alastir turned his head just enough to look up at Casteel. "I did—"

"The unthinkable," Casteel said.

"The prophecy—"

"Is utter bullshit," Casteel snarled.

Alastir was silent only for a few moments. "I am sorry for the pain I have caused you, Casteel. I had to do it. She had to be dealt with. I hope you will understand that someday."

A tremor coursed through Casteel as I felt his temper rise, hot as the molten ore used to forge steel. For a moment, I thought that Casteel would do it. That he would end Alastir's life right there. And, honestly, I wouldn't have held it against him. If Alastir had done this to Casteel, I wouldn't be able to stop myself.

But Casteel did.

With awe-inspiring self-control, he pulled the sword away from Alastir's neck and lowered it, slowly using the tunic Alastir wore to wipe the weapon clean.

The insult heightened the color on Alastir's cheeks.

"You are responsible for the years of nightmares that have plagued Poppy, aren't you?" Casteel asked as he finished cleaning his sword. "And then you befriended her. Looked her in the eyes and smiled at her, all the while knowing that you left her to die a horrific death."

Alastir stared straight ahead. "I did."

"Those Craven may have been the ones to tear into her skin, but it was ultimately you who is responsible for her pain—for the scars both visible and hidden. For that alone, I should kill you." Casteel sheathed his sword. "But I won't."

"W-what?" Alastir's head jerked in his direction. "You…you offer me a reprieve?"

"I'm sorry." Casteel didn't sound even remotely apologetic. Emil was right. He *was* amused. "I think you misunderstand. I said I should kill you, but I won't. I didn't say you wouldn't die tonight." He looked over his shoulder at the trees.

To where I waited.

Emil nodded as he stepped aside.

I walked forward.

A harsh breath was the only sound as I crossed the distance. Alastir's eyes widened. Our gazes met and held. A guttural rumble of warning came from behind me. Warm fur brushed my hand as Kieran prowled forward, coming to stand beside me.

Heart strangely calm, I held the dagger under the cloak as Alastir looked up at me in shock. "How…?" His handsome, scarred face contorted as his surprise slipped away, and rage etched his features. His hatred was a tangible entity. "Do it. I dare you. It won't matter. This doesn't end with me. You'll prove me right. You will—"

Swinging my arm in a quick, sweeping arc, the bloodstone sliced deep into his throat, ending the poisonous words in a gurgle.

I knelt, catching Alastir by the shoulder before he fell forward. We were at eye-level now, the shock of the wound replacing the hatred in his eyes. I had no idea what mine showed—if they showed anything.

"I will never think of you again after this night," I promised, wiping the blade clean on the front of his tunic, just as Casteel had. "I just wanted you to know that."

His mouth opened, but nothing but blood came out. I rose as I let go of him. He toppled, jerking as his blood spilled freely.

"Well," Casteel drew out the word. "That will not be a quick death."

Watching the stone turn black in the moonlight for a moment, I looked at Casteel. "I was wrong before. Some don't deserve the honor of a quick death."

One side of his mouth quirked, hinting at a dimple as his gaze flickered over my face. "Such a stunning, vicious little creature."

I turned as Kieran stalked past me to where the body thrashed on the ground. He planted a massive paw on Alastir's back, his claws digging in as he lifted his head to the sky. A deep howl pierced the silence of the night, echoing through the valleys and over the sea. Tiny goosebumps prickled my skin. The sound was haunting, seeming to hang in the air even after he lowered his head.

A heartbeat passed.

Down below, near the dark sea, a long, keening howl answered. Farther out, there was another and another. Then, throughout the city, *hundreds* answered Kieran's call, their yips and barks only overshadowed by the pounding sound against the ground, the rush of their bodies racing among the trees. The thousands of claws digging into soil and stone.

They came.

Like one of the relentless waves crashing against the rocks below, they came in flashes of fur and teeth, both large and small. They came, and they devoured.

Chapter 14

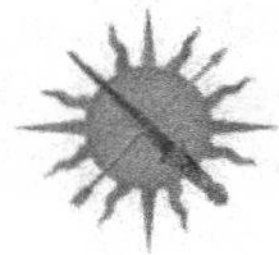

Dawn arrived in vivid streaks of pink and blue as we followed a tree-heavy path around the Temple of Saion, along with the realization that the pleasure derived from retribution was unfortunately short-lived.

It wasn't that I regretted taking Alastir's life or not ensuring that his death was a quick one. It was just that I wished it wasn't necessary. As the sun rose, I wanted it to be rising on a day not overshadowed by death.

I didn't realize that I was still clutching the wolven dagger until Casteel quietly pried it from my fingers and slipped it into the sheath at his side.

"Thank you," I whispered.

His gaze flew to mine, his eyes a glittering shade of topaz. I thought he was about to speak, but he said nothing as wolven rose from among the bushes and trees. There were so many of them, some large, and others small, barely bigger than Beckett. My chest squeezed as I watched them prowl alongside us. All of them were alert, their ears perked.

I couldn't stop thinking about what they had done to Alastir and the others—the sounds of flesh tearing and bones cracking. Tonight would stay with me for a long, long time. I wondered if such an act upset their digestion.

I didn't ask, though, because I figured that was a rather inappropriate question.

But right now, I was more focused on putting one foot in front of the other. Every step took energy I was quickly running out of. The exhaustion could've stemmed from the lack of sleep as we traveled across the Skotos for the second time, the lack of rest from our first trip, or from everything that had happened from the moment I arrived in Atlantia. It could've been a combination of all those things. Casteel had to be equally exhausted, but the good news was that I was once more exposed to sunlight, and my skin wasn't decaying or doing anything equally disturbing.

So that was a plus.

"You hanging in there?" he asked in a low voice as we approached Setti, the horse's coat a gleaming onyx in the morning sun. He grazed in the grass.

I nodded, thinking this likely wasn't the homecoming Casteel had wanted. How long had it been since he'd even seen his parents last? Years. And *this* was how he had to greet them, with an attack on him, me, and a potential wedge being driven between him and his father.

A heaviness settled in my chest as one of the Guardians led Setti to us. I looked up at the looming Skotos to see a canopy of glistening red.

The landscape of Atlantia had been forever changed, but what did it mean?

"Poppy?" Casteel's voice was quiet.

Realizing that he was waiting for me, I dragged my gaze from the mountains and reached up, grasping Setti's saddle. I didn't find out if I had the strength to pull myself up as I'd done outside the hunting cabin. Casteel lifted me and then quickly followed.

Kieran joined us, having returned to his mortal form, now dressed in the clothing Niall had brought back with us. He mounted one of the horses, and I saw the shadows gathering under his eyes. We were all tired, so it was no surprise that we rode away from the Temple in silence, followed by the wolven. I didn't see Emil or Naill when we left, nor did I catch sight of Quentyn.

It took some time for us to navigate the cliffs and come upon the field of pink and blue wildflowers. I looked at the trees at the other end of the field but couldn't see the Chambers of Nyktos from the road. I wondered what kind of shape the Temple was in. Sighing, I faced forward. My heart skipped in my chest as I looked ahead and saw the Pillars of Atlantia once again. The marble and limestone columns were so high they nearly reached the clouds. Shadowy markings etched the stone in a language I couldn't read. This was the resting place of Theon, the God of Accord and War, and his sister Lailah, the Goddess of Peace and Vengeance. The columns were connected to a wall that was as large as the Rise that surrounded the capital of Solis and continued on as far as I could see.

Home.

I still felt that way. It was the skip in my chest. The sense of rightness. I looked over my shoulder at Casteel to tell him as much, but I picked up on the anger brewing inside him. It pooled in my mouth like acid, and his concern was a too-thick cream in the back of my throat.

"I'm okay," I told him.

"I wish you'd stop saying that." His grip tightened on the reins. "You're not okay."

"Am, too," I insisted.

"You're tired." Casteel looped his arm loosely around my waist. "You've been through a lot. There's no way you're okay."

I stared at his grip on the reins. Sometimes I wondered if he could feel my emotions or read my thoughts. He couldn't, but he knew me better than those who'd known me for years. It was sort of amazing how that had happened in such a relatively short period of time. But right now, I almost wished he didn't. I blinked back the hot rush of pointless tears. I didn't even understand why I suddenly felt so emotional, but I didn't want it weighing on his mind. I started to reach for him but stopped, dropping my hand into my lap instead. "I'm sorry," I whispered.

"For what?"

I swallowed hard as I lifted my gaze to Kieran's back. "Just…for everything."

Casteel stiffened behind me. "Are you serious?"

"Yes?"

"What exactly is this *everything* you're apologizing for?"

I doubted repeating the word would suffice. "I was just thinking about how you haven't seen your parents in years, and how your homecoming should've been a good one—a happy one. Instead, all of this happened. And Alastir…" I shook my head. "You knew him far longer than me. His betrayal has to bother you. And I was also thinking about the Chambers of Nyktos and wondering how damaged it must be now. I bet the Temple has been there for thousands of years. And here I came and—"

"Poppy, I'm going to stop you right there. Part of me wants to laugh—"

"Same," Kieran commented from up front.

My eyes narrowed on the wolven.

"The other part of me finds absolutely nothing funny about you apologizing for things you have no control over."

"I also second that," Kieran tossed out.

"This conversation doesn't involve you, *Kieran*," I snapped.

The wolven shrugged a shoulder. "Just chiming in with my two cents. Carry on. My father and I will pretend we can't hear either of you."

I scowled at him as I glanced to where Jasper rode past us in his mortal form. I had no idea when he'd shifted.

"Look," Casteel said, his voice low, "we're going to need to talk about a lot when we're somewhere private, and I've had a chance to make sure your injuries have healed."

"What injuries?"

Casteel sighed behind me. "Since you apparently didn't notice, you were still covered in bruises after you *rested* in the hunting cabin."

After he'd Ascended me into…whatever I was now. "I'm—"

"Don't tell me you're fine again, Poppy."

"I wasn't," I lied.

"Uh-huh." He shifted me closer to him, so I leaned into his chest. "What you need to know now is that none of this is your fault. You did nothing wrong, Poppy. None of this is on you. You understand that? Believe that?"

"I know that. I did nothing to cause any of this," I told him, speaking the truth. I didn't blame myself for other people's actions, but I was still a disruptive presence, whether I intended to be or not. It was a different kind of guilt.

We fell silent as my gaze shifted beyond Kieran to the sprawling city of Saion's Cove. Ivory and sand-colored buildings—some square and others circular—gleamed under the fading sun, dotting the sweeping, rolling hills and valleys. Some structures were as wide as they were tall, sitting closer to the ground. Once again, it reminded me of the Temples in Solis, but these were not made out of the black, reflective stone that those were. These captured the sun, worshipped it. Other buildings were taller than even Castle Teerman, their sleek towers sweeping gracefully into the sky. And every rooftop I could see was covered in green. Trees rose from them, and vines spilled from the rooftops, all bursting with vivid pink, blue, and purple flowers.

Saion's Cove was nearly the size of Carsodonia, and this was just one of Atlantia's cities. I couldn't even begin to imagine what Evaemon, the capital of Atlantia, must look like.

The first signs of life we saw were from the farms just outside the city. Cows and fluffy sheep grazed in the fields. Goats nibbled at weeds and low-hanging branches near the road. Orchards bearing yellow fruit were mixed among various crops, and seated back from the main road, cream-colored walls of homes peeked out from behind mossy cypress trees. Many buildings were there, among the trees, all of them spaced apart and large enough to house a decent-sized family. This was nothing like Masadonia or Carsodonia, where sprawling manors and estates were prevalent, and the workers either traveled from the city or stayed in barely livable huts on the properties.

The livestock took no notice of the wolven that followed us as we passed the farms. Perhaps they were used to their presence or sensed they were of no threat to them. Had the farmers or people in the city heard the wolven in the middle of the night as they came to the Temple of Saion? That must have been a sound to wake up to.

But thoughts of the wolven's howls fell to the wayside as nervous energy jolted my system. The city suddenly appeared before us.

There were no gates, no inner walls or buildings heavily stacked upon one another. The scent of people forced to live in cramped, narrow spaces didn't stain the air. That was the first thing one smelled when entering either Masadonia or Carsodonia. It always reminded me of misery and desperation, but Saion's Cove smelled of fruit from the nearby orchards, and salt from the sea. The farmlands and moss-strewn cypresses simply transitioned into the city, and that was a statement.

There was no separation between those who fed the city and the tables that food sat on.

Seeing that brought forth a rush of faith and possibility, and I sat a little straighter. I didn't know much about Atlantian politics, and I knew the kingdom wasn't without problems. They were quickly becoming overpopulated, something Casteel hoped to alleviate through negotiations with Solis officials and by reclaiming the lands east of New Haven—a large and mostly uninhabited chunk of Solis. Some may not even notice how significant this one difference was, but it was huge. And it was proof that if Atlantia could do it, so could Solis.

But how could that happen? If Casteel and I were successful in overthrowing the Blood Crown, Solis would remain as it was, only safer for mortals because only the Ascended who agreed to control their thirst would survive. But the power remained with the wealthy. And the wealthiest were among the Ascended. They thrived in a stratified system, which would be harder to break than stopping the Rites and the murders of innocents.

And could the majority of the Ascended be trusted to change? Would the new King and Queen who replaced the ones who currently ruled the Blood Crown even agree? Would Solis really be any different? We had to try, though. It was the only way to avoid war and prevent further destruction and countless deaths. First, we had to convince Queen Ileana and King Jalara that, unlike what the Duchess had claimed about my union with the Prince, it would be the Ascended's undoing and not the downfall of Atlantia. Both the Duchess and Alastir were wrong—and dead.

In a way, the Ascended had kickstarted their downfall by creating the Maiden and convincing the people of Solis that I had been *Chosen* by the gods—gods the mortals believed were very much awake and constantly vigilant. The Ascended had made me their figurehead and a symbol of Solis to the people they controlled through manipulation. My marriage to Casteel would serve two purposes. It would prove that the Atlantians were not responsible for the plague known as the Craven—another lie the Ascended had spun to cover their evil deeds and to incite fear to make controlling people easier. And the people of Solis would believe the gods had approved of the Chosen joining with an Atlantian. Because of their lies, we held the upper hand. The only way any Ascended could remain in power was if they understood that. Because if they turned against me, their entire kingdom of lies would crack underneath them. Casteel had been right when he'd said that Queen Ileana was clever. She was. She had to agree. We would prevent a catastrophic war and maybe be able to reshape Solis in the process—for the better.

But a voice inside me, a strange one that sounded a lot like mine but wasn't and came from the same place that ancient thing in me had seemed to awaken, existed deep in the very core of my being. What that voice whispered left me unsettled and cold with dread.

Sometimes war cannot be prevented.

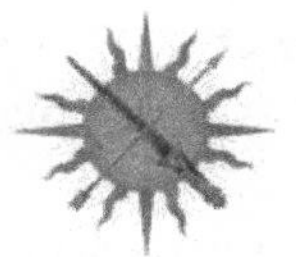

Two large coliseums sat on either side of the road we traveled on, reminding me of the ruins in Spessa's End. Statues of the gods lined the interior of the columns and the outer walls farthest from the road were higher, full of rows and rows of seats. Bouquets full of bright purple flowers sat on each of the steps leading into the structures. They were empty, as were the smaller pavilions we passed, their gold and blue canopies rippling softly in the warm breeze, and in the windowed and roofed buildings, but it didn't stay that way.

"Casteel," Kieran said, his voice carrying a tone of warning.

"I know." Casteel's arm tightened around me. "I was hoping we'd be able to make it farther before we were noticed. That's clearly not going to happen. These streets are about to fill."

That odd voice inside me and the unease it stirred quickly faded as people slowly and cautiously ventured outside. Men. Women. Children. They didn't seem to notice Jasper or Kieran, as if the sight of the former shirtless on horseback was a common occurrence. And maybe it was. Instead, they stared up at Casteel and me with wide eyes. Confusion radiated from anyone I looked at. Everyone appeared frozen, and then an older man in blue yelled, "Our Prince! Prince Casteel! Our Prince returns!"

A gasp went through the crowd like a gust of wind. Doors of shops and homes alike opened down the road. They must not have known that Casteel had recovered from the shadowshade flower. I wondered exactly what knowledge they had of what had occurred in the Chambers of Nyktos. Had the blood rain not fallen on the city? Surely, they had seen the trees of Aios, even though soaring buildings now blocked the mountains.

Shouts of excitement and cheers filled the streets as people clamored and spilled out of buildings or leaned from windows above. Arms rose and trembled as some yelled Casteel's name, and others praised the gods. An older man dropped to his knees and clasped his hands together against his chest. He *wept*. And he wasn't the only one. Women. Men. Many openly cried as they yelled his name. Casteel shifted behind me as my eyes grew to the size of the sun. I…I'd never seen anything like this. Ever.

"They…some of them are crying," I whispered.

"I think they feared I was dead," he remarked. "It has been quite some time since I've been home."

I wasn't sure if that was the reason. From what I'd seen in New Haven and Spessa's End, he was well loved and respected by his people. My throat tightened as I looked around, seeing a blur of ecstatic, smiling faces. Nothing like this happened when the Ascended rode through their towns. Not even when the Queen or King moved about in public, which if I remembered correctly, had been rare. There had always been silence.

People jerked to a stop, their cheers falling to whispers. At first, I didn't understand what the cause was.

The *wolven.*

They must've fallen back at some point, but now they returned to our sides. They prowled the street and swept over the sidewalks, moving between mortals and Atlantians alike. They didn't snarl or snap, but their bodies were clearly tense.

My skin prickled with awareness as gazes moved from Casteel to the wolven and then to me. I stiffened, feeling their stares on my bloodied and dirtied clothing and the bruises surely visible. The *scars.*

"I would've taken a different route to Jasper's home if it was possible," Casteel told me, his voice low as we turned onto a road where the buildings reached for the clouds, and the crystal-clear waters of the Seas of Saion began to peek out from behind structures. I'd forgotten the offer Jasper had made at the Chambers. It was telling that Casteel rode there and not to his family's holdings. "But this is the least populated way."

This was the least populated area? There had to be…gods, there had to be *thousands* on the streets now, appearing in windows, and coming to stand out on ivy-smothered balconies and terraces.

"I know this is a lot," he continued. "And I'm sorry we couldn't delay this."

I reached down to where his hand rested lightly on my hip. This time, I didn't stop myself. I folded my hand over his and squeezed.

Casteel turned his hand over, returning the gesture. We didn't let go of each other's hands.

Part of me wanted to look away, to not allow myself to sense what the people were feeling, but that would make me a coward. I let my senses remain open, to stretch out just enough to get the briefest glimpse of their emotions in case I lost control of…whatever I was truly capable of. My pounding heart and wild thoughts made it difficult to concentrate, but after a few moments, I tasted…the tartness of confusion, and the lighter, springy flavor of curiosity coming from the people of Atlantia.

There was no fear.

No hatred.

Just curiosity and confusion. I hadn't expected that. Not after the Temple. My body sank against Casteel's, and I rested my head against his chest. The crowd's emotions could change once they learned what I'd done, and what I may or may not be. But right now, I wasn't going to worry about that. I started to close my eyes when deep blue fabric snagged my attention.

A white-haired woman stood on a balcony of one of the high-rise buildings, the wind tugging at the blue gown she wore. Holding onto a black railing, she slowly lowered herself to one knee and placed her fist over her thin chest. Her head bowed as the wind whipped her snowy hair. On another balcony, a man with gray hair in a long, thick braid, did the same. And on the sidewalks…

Men and women whose skin and bodies bore the signs of age lowered themselves to their knees, among those who stood.

"*Liessa!*" a man shouted, slamming a hand against the sidewalk, startling me. "*Meyaah Liessa!*"

Setti's head reared as two children raced out from one of the buildings—one of them no more than five years old—their long, brown hair streaming out from behind them. One of them shifted right there, pitching forward as white-and-brown-streaked fur erupted from the skin. The wolven was so tiny as it yipped and bounced, ears flopping as the older child by only a year or so ran beside the pup.

Casteel's grip on Setti tightened as the child shouted, "*Liessa! Liessa!*"

Liessa. I had heard that before when I'd had that nightmare in the Skotos Mountains and heard Delano's voice. He'd said those words. Or I had dreamed him saying them, at least.

An older child grabbed the younger one and turned, chasing after the one who'd shifted. Younger men and women appeared on the sidewalks and above, babies held to their hips as they lowered to their knees. Shock rolled out from others in icy waves as the chant of "*Liessa*" grew in volume.

"What does that mean?" I asked Casteel as another small child shifted into a fuzzy little thing that was nudged back onto the sidewalk by one of the larger wolven following us. The little girl or guy nipped and then promptly started chasing its tail. "*Liessa?*"

"It's old Atlantian. The language of the gods," Casteel said, his voice rough. He cleared his throat as he squeezed my hand again. "*Meyaah Liessa.* It means: my Queen."

Chapter 15

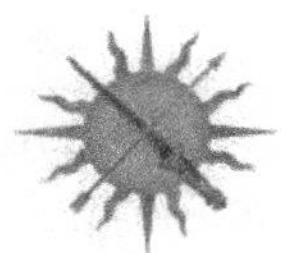

Jasper's home sat atop a bluff that overlooked the sea and a large swath of the city's homes. Only the high-rises and a palatial home on another cliff rose higher. I assumed the latter was the King and Queen's residence, and I had no idea if they had arrived in Saion's Cove yet or if they'd heard the shouts.

Meyaah Liessa.

My Queen.

That was one of those three things I had managed not to dwell on since I woke in the hunting cabin. *Queen.* I couldn't process that, and I wasn't even going to try as I scanned the hanging stems of white and violet flowers dangling from numerous woven baskets strung halfway up the walls of the courtyard. Not until I bathed, slept, and got some food in my stomach.

As we neared the stables, the center of the courtyard drew my gaze. Water splashed and spilled over tiered levels of a water fountain crafted from stone the color of midnight and even more reflective than the material used to build the Temples in Solis.

A man in tan breeches and a loose white shirt hurried from one of the stables. His gaze bounced from Jasper and Kieran to Casteel. Surprise flickered through him. He bowed deeply. "Your Highness."

"Harlan," Casteel acknowledged. "I know it's been quite a bit of time since you've seen me, but you don't have to call me that."

I couldn't help but try to imagine any of the Ascended—let alone the King or Queen—allowing such familiarity. Those who hadn't greeted Duke Teerman formally tended to disappear shortly thereafter.

Harlan nodded as Jasper dismounted. "Yes, Your—" He caught himself with a sheepish smile. "Yes, it has been a while."

As the man took Setti's reins, I saw that his eyes were a dark brown. He was either mortal or of the changeling bloodline. I wanted to ask, but that seemed like a rather impolite question. He looked up at me, his gaze briefly lingering on my face before moving on.

"Harlan, I would like to introduce you to someone extremely important to me," Casteel said as Kieran faced us. "This is my wife, Penellaphe."

My wife.

Despite everything, my heart still did a silly little leap.

"Your wife?" The male blinked once and then twice. A toothy grin spread across his face. "Congratulations, Your— Congratulations. Wow. I don't know what is more surprising. Your return or that you're married."

"He likes to go big or go home," Kieran commented as he patted his horse's side. "In case you've forgotten that."

Harlan chuckled as he scratched at his mop of blond hair. "I guess I have." He looked at me again. "It's an honor to meet you, Your Highness." He bowed then with far more flourish.

Kieran raised his brow at me as he mouthed, *Your Highness.*

If I weren't so tired and uninterested in making a second bad first impression, I would've jumped from Setti and punched the wolven in the face. Hard. Instead, I unglued my tongue from the roof of my mouth. "Thank you," I managed, hoping I didn't sound as strange to him as I did to myself. "You don't have to call me that either. Penellaphe is fine."

The male grinned, but I had a feeling my suggestion went in one ear and skipped right out the other.

"Setti has been on the road for quite some time. He could use some extra care," Casteel commented, thankfully drawing the attention away from me.

"I will make sure he and the others receive it." Harlan held onto the reins as he rubbed the side of Setti's muzzle.

Casteel leapt down with a fluid grace that made me wonder if he were a pit of endless energy and then immediately reached for me. I took his hands, and he lifted me from the saddle, placing me on the ground beside him. His hands slid to my hips and lingered there. I looked up at him, and he bent down, pressing his lips to my forehead. The sweet kiss tugged at my heart.

"Just a couple of more minutes," he murmured as he tucked several tangled strands of hair over my shoulder. "And we'll be alone."

I nodded. His arm stayed around me as we turned.

Kieran and Jasper had stopped in front of us, but the wolven not in their mortal forms caught and held my attention. They had followed us into the courtyard, and there were…gods, there had to be hundreds of them. They prowled along the stables and the estate. Dozens leapt onto the walls of the courtyard. Others climbed the wide steps of the manor and stood between the pillars. They parted, creating a path between us and the bronze doors. But before Casteel or I could move, they shifted. All of them at once. Fur thinned and gave way to flesh. Bones cracked and shrank, fusing back together. Limbs straightened and claws retracted into nails. Within seconds, they stood in their mortal forms. There was a whole lot of skin on display. More than I ever needed to see. My cheeks started to heat as I struggled not to look, well…anywhere. I started to ask Casteel what was happening, but the wolven moved simultaneously.

Right hands balled into fists. They placed them over the center of their chests and then sank onto one knee, lowering their heads as the ones on the street had done. All of them—the wolven in the courtyard, the ones on the wall, on the steps and between the pillars.

I felt a little dizzy as Jasper and Kieran turned to us and followed suit.

"They have never done that for me," Casteel remarked under his breath.

Kieran lifted his head just enough for me to see that he smirked.

"I don't know why they're doing it for me."

He glanced down at me, his brows knitted. "It's because you have the blood—"

"I know," I said, my heart starting to pound again. "I know, but…" How could I put into words how crazy this was to me? People bowed before me as the Maiden, but this was different, and it had nothing to do with the fact that *naked* people prostrated themselves before me.

Though, that seemed important, too.

Kieran rose, meeting Casteel's stare. He nodded. I had no idea how they communicated to one another if there was no bond. Hell, I had no idea how they did it when there had been one. He said something to Jasper, and his father shifted back into his wolven form. The others followed suit, and again, I was left wondering how they all acted in unison. I watched them move away from the home, spreading out through the courtyard and beyond the walls, wondering if it was some sort of instinctual drive or something beyond that.

Casteel's hand dropped to the center of my back as he started forward. "Well, that was fun, wasn't it?"

I looked up at him, my brows raised. "That was a lot of…nakedness."

A half-grin appeared as he looked down at me.

"You'll get used to it," Kieran stated as he climbed the steps.

I wasn't so sure about that.

"More like you're sort of forced to," Casteel said as Kieran walked in through the open doors. "Wolven tend to find clothing cumbersome."

I thought about all the breeches and shirts they seemed to go through, and I could sort of understand why they felt that way.

A warm breeze stirred gauzy curtains as Kieran led us past several large sitting rooms full of oversized chairs in vibrant hues. The air carried a hint of cinnamon that lingered as we followed him into a canopied breezeway. I didn't see any sign of Kieran's mother or anyone else, and I wondered if she was among the wolven who had been outside.

We ended up back inside, in a different wing of the house, walking down another long, seemingly never-ending hall. My steps slowed, and I sighed as we passed yet another door. "How many people live here?"

"Depends on the time of year," Kieran answered. "At times, every room is filled, and we have a lot who come and go, those in need of temporary housing."

"Oh," I answered, internally sobbing when we passed two more doors. "How long is this hallway?"

"Not much longer," he said, and Casteel's hand moved in a slow, comforting circle on my back. A moment later, the hall curved, and I saw the end—thank the gods. Kieran stopped in front of cream-colored double doors. "I figured you'd want to stay in your old rooms."

"You've stayed here a lot?" I asked as Casteel's hand slipped from my back. I missed the weight of it immediately.

He nodded, opening one side of the doors. "My parents don't come here a lot, and especially not after everything happened with

Malik," he answered, and I thought that made sense. "I'd rather be here than in an empty estate."

I couldn't even imagine how big his parents' home here or in the capital was if this was the size of Jasper's.

"I'll make sure your bags are brought in from the stables," Kieran offered.

"That would be amazing. Thank you." Casteel glanced at him as he reached over, taking my hand. "We're going to need some time before we have visitors."

A wry grin appeared on Kieran's face. "I'll make sure my mother understands that."

For some reason, my stomach flip-flopped at the thought of meeting Kieran's mother.

Kieran slipped away then, and he did so with impressive quickness. Maybe he was half-afraid I would start asking questions. Little did he know, he didn't have to worry about that. I shuffled into the room as Casteel nudged the door open farther.

Where was the bed?

That was all I could think as I walked across the cream-colored tile floors into the space where a pearly-hued settee and two wide chairs were situated in the middle. Behind the sitting area was a table with marble legs carved into vines, and two high-backed dining chairs upholstered in a thick gray material. A chaise lounge was positioned in front of closed, lattice doors, and above, a ceiling fan churned lazily.

"The bedroom is through here." Casteel stepped through a rounded archway to the right.

I almost tripped as I walked into the room.

"That's the largest bed ever." I stared at the four-poster bed and its gauzy white curtains.

"Is it?" he asked, tugging the curtains back on one side and securing them to the posts. "The bed in my residence in Evaemon is bigger."

"Well…" I cleared my throat. "Congratulations on that."

He tossed me a grin over his shoulder as he unsheathed my dagger, placing it on the nightstand and then removed his swords. By a large wardrobe, I recognized saddlebags—the ones from when we'd first entered Atlantia. How long had they sat here, waiting for us? I turned slightly. Several chairs were situated across from the bed. Another set of lattice doors led to what appeared to be a veranda, and there was an even larger ceiling fan, one with leaf-shaped blades that spun, moving the air about. "Wait." My gaze shot back to him. "You have your own residence?"

"I do." Having finished with the curtains on the bed, he straightened. "I have quarters at my family's home—the palace—but I also have a small townhome."

I was sure that I knew Casteel better than most, but there was still so much I had to learn about him. Things that weren't all that important, and the things that made him who he was today. We just hadn't had the time to truly discover each other's secrets yet, and I wanted that time as painfully as I wanted to hold my brother, see Tawny again, and learn that she hadn't Ascended like the Duchess had claimed. I wanted that as badly as I wanted to see Casteel reunite with his brother and for Malik to be healthy and whole.

And we'd almost lost the chance for more time.

Casteel stepped to the side, turning to me. I saw the open door behind him. Faint sunlight drenched ivory-tiled walls and glimmered off a large, porcelain soaking tub. Drawn forward, I might've stopped breathing as I realized how big the tub was and that all the bottles on the shelves were full of colored salts, creams, and lotions. What sat in the corner of the bathing chamber was what I couldn't look away from, though. Several pipes descended from the ceiling, each one with an oval-shaped head on it, and all full of tiny holes. The floor under them was sunken, and a large…drain was in the center. One side, under the window, held a tiled bench built into the wall.

"That's the shower," Casteel said from behind me. "Once turned on, the water comes from overhead."

All I could do was stare.

"The faucets at the sink are like the ones in the shower and tub. The handle painted red is hot, and the blue one is for cold water. You just turn it— Poppy?" There was a smile in his voice. "Look."

Blinking, I pulled my gaze from the shower to watch him turn the red handle. Water poured into the basin.

"Come." Casteel motioned me forward. "Feel the water. It'll be cold for a few seconds."

I went to his side, slipping my hand into the stream of water. It was cold and then cool before turning to lukewarm and then hot. Gasping, I jerked my hand back as my eyes flew to his.

The dimple in his right cheek deepened. "Welcome to the land of hot water at your fingertips."

Awe filled me. Tawny would love this chamber. She probably

would never leave it, demanding her suppers be served here. Sadness threatened to creep in and crowd out the joy, and it was hard to set it aside and allow myself to enjoy this moment. I started to dip my hand into the water again, but Casteel turned it off. "Hey—"

He took my hand. "You can play with the faucets and water all day, but let me take care of you first."

Looking up, I started to tell him there was no need, but I saw my reflection and stopped moving, stopped thinking.

It was the first time I'd seen myself since I'd awakened in the cabin. I couldn't stop staring, and it wasn't the absolute mess that was my hair. Lowering my hands to the rim of the sink, I stared at my reflection.

"What are you doing?" Casteel asked.

"I…I look the same," I said, noting the strong brow, the line of my nose, and the width of my mouth. "But I don't." I lifted a hand, touching the scar on my left cheek. His gaze followed mine to the mirror. "Do the scars look…less to you?" I asked because they did to me. They were still clearly noticeable, the one at my hairline that cut through my brow, and the other that sliced across my temple, reminding me of how close I'd come to losing an eye. The scars didn't appear to be a shade paler than my skin like before. They were the same tone of pink as the rest of my face, and the flesh didn't feel as rough, nor did it look as jagged.

"I hadn't noticed," Casteel said, and my gaze shot to his in the reflection. I…I sensed surprise from him. He spoke the truth. He truly hadn't noticed the difference because he never really noticed the scars in the first place. They had never been a *thing* to him.

I might've fallen even more in love with him right then if that were possible.

"They are a little fainter," he continued, his head cocked. "It must've been my blood—how much of it. It could've repaired some of the old wounds."

I glanced down at my arm then and looked—*really* looked. The skin was less shiny and patchy there.

"It amazes me," he commented. "That the scars are what you notice first."

"Because the scars are what everyone seems to see first when they look upon me," I stated.

"I don't think that's the first thing, Poppy. Not before," he said, brushing a clump of my hair over my shoulder. "And definitely not now."

Definitely not now.

I lifted my gaze once more and looked beyond the scars and the smattering of freckles across my nose to my eyes. They were green, just like I remembered my father's being, but they were also different. It wasn't exactly noticeable upon first glance, but I saw it now.

The silvery sheen behind my pupils.

"My eyes…"

"They've been like that since the Temple of Saion," he said.

I blinked once and then twice. They remained the same upon reopening. "This isn't what they look like when they glow, right?"

He shook his head. "That light behind your pupils seeps out into the green. It's far more intense."

"Oh," I whispered.

"I think it's the eather in you," he told me, angling his body toward mine.

"Oh," I repeated, thinking that it must be the same thing that made Casteel and the other Atlantians' eyes become luminous and churning.

He arched a brow. "That's all you have to say to seeing your eyes? Oh?"

"My eyes…they feel the same," I offered up, truly having no idea what to say.

One side of his lips quirked. "And they're still the most beautiful eyes I've ever seen."

I turned to him, looking up. "None of this bothers you? My heritage? Whatever it is that I am?"

His half-grin faded. "We had this conversation when we talked about Malec."

"Yes, we did, but…but when you met me, I was the Maiden. You thought I was mortal, and then you learned I was half-Atlantian. But now you know I'm descended from a god, and you don't even really know what I am," I pointed out. "My gifts aren't even the same. I'm *changing*."

"So?"

"*So?*"

"When you met me, you thought I was a mortal guard who'd sworn an oath to protect you. But then you learned I was an Atlantian and that I was the Prince," he countered. "Did any of that change how you saw me?"

At first it had, but… "No. It didn't."

"Then why is it so hard for you to believe that it changes nothing for me? You are still Poppy." He touched my cheek. "No matter how much more you change, you are still her in your heart."

I glanced back at the mirror, seeing a familiar face that was also unfamiliar in the smallest ways. I felt like myself in my heart…and I hoped that didn't change.

Chapter 16

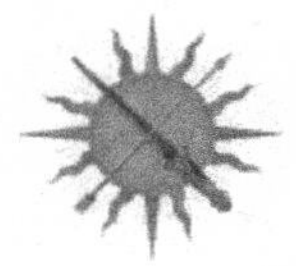

“Come,” Casteel repeated, taking my hand. “Let me look at you.”

“I told you, I’m okay.”

He led me away from the mirror and back into the bedchamber. “And I told you to stop saying that when I know you aren’t.”

“I don’t even feel those bruises you mentioned,” I said as he placed me by the side of the bed.

His ocher gaze flicked to mine. “I know there are wounds that aren’t visible to the eye, and I wish you would stop trying to hide them from me.”

I snapped my mouth shut.

“I think there is a lot we need to talk about. He reached for the hem of my tunic, lifting it. “But there’s something really important we need to talk about before we discuss anything else.” He motioned for me to lift my arms, and I did so. Air flowed over my bare arms as I watched him toss the top aside. The plain slip I wore was so much thinner and better suited for the climate, but its tiny straps and the near-sheer, cinched bodice hid very little.

He drew a finger along the strap as he eyed it, slipping it under the flimsy material. “These silly, tiny straps…” The tips of his fangs dragged across his lower lip.

“Is that what you want to talk about?” My skin tingled as he ran his finger along the bodice of the slip, over the swell of my flesh. The peaks of my breasts tightened and hardened as his gaze returned to mine.

“I think these straps are very important and extremely distracting, but they're not what we need to discuss," he replied. "Sit, Poppy. I know you're exhausted."

I glanced down at my dusty pants. "I'll dirty the bed if I sit."

"Then you'll have to take the pants off."

My brows lifted. "Are you trying to get me naked?"

"Poppy," he purred, brushing several strands of hair over my shoulder. "When am I *not* trying to get you naked?"

I laughed softly. "Good point." I reached for the flap of the breeches, knowing he was teasing and enjoying it—and relieved that I could still enjoy it despite everything that had happened. I undid the buttons.

"Boots," he reminded me. "Here. Hold onto my shoulders."

Casteel knelt before me, and the sight of him—the breadth of his shoulders, the hair that had dried in a mess of waves and loose curls, toppling over his forehead, and the thick fringe of dark lashes nearly undid me. He was beautiful. He was brave. He was intelligent. He was kind and accepting. He was ferocious.

And he was *mine*.

Hands trembling slightly, I placed them on his shoulders. He made quick work of tugging off the boots as I steadied myself. The pants came next, and then I was standing before him in nothing but a slip that reached my thighs.

Casteel remained where he was, his gaze traveling over the length of my legs. His stare lingered, not on the old scars from the night of the Craven attack, but rather on the dull blue patches of skin, bruised now from the gods only knew what. His gaze roamed over me—my arms, the skin above my breasts, my face.

His eyes were like iced-over chips of amber when they met mine. "If any of those who inflicted one second of pain on you still breathed, I would tear them apart, limb from limb. I pray that the death you dealt them was slow and painful."

"It wasn't slow for most." An image surfaced of them clutching their heads and screaming as their bodies contorted. "But it was painful for all."

"Good." His gaze held mine. "Don't spend a second on guilt or pity. None of them—and especially not Alastir—deserve that."

I nodded.

"I promise you if anyone else was involved in this, they will be found, and they will pay. The same goes for anyone else who seeks to threaten you. No matter who."

He meant those words, and instinct told me that no one was excluded. Not even his parents.

"And I promise the same to you. I will allow no one to harm you," I swore, the center of my chest thrumming.

"I know." Casteel took my hands and pulled me down so I was sitting on the edge of the soft bed. A long moment passed. "I'm your husband, right?" he asked, remaining crouched.

My brows lifted at the unexpected question. "Yes?"

"Now, I don't know a whole lot about being a husband," he said as he placed my hands in my lap, and I really had no idea where he was going with this. "Do you know what's carved into our rings? It's in old Atlantian," he told me when I shook my head. "Both say the same thing. *Always and forever*. That is us."

"Yes," I whispered, my throat tightening. "It is."

"Obviously, I don't have experience in the whole marriage department, but be that as it may, you're my wife. That means we don't pretend anymore, correct? That, always and forever, we are real with one another."

"Yes." I nodded.

"Not about anything. Not even when you don't want me to worry. I know you're strong and so resilient it's fucking unbelievable, but you don't have to always be strong with me. It's okay to not be okay when you're with me," he said, and my breath caught. "It's my duty as your husband to make sure you feel safe enough to be real. You don't have to pretend that you're okay with everything that has happened, Poppy."

Oh…

Oh, gods.

His words wrecked me. Tears scorched my throat and rushed to my eyes. I did the only mature thing possible. I smacked my hands over my face.

"Poppy," Casteel whispered, folding his fingers around my wrists. "That sounded like it hurt."

"It did." My voice was muffled. "I don't want to cry."

"Does smacking yourself in the face help with that?"

"No." I laughed, shoulders trembling as tears dampened my lashes.

"I didn't mean to make you cry." He tugged a little on my arms.

My hands stayed over my face. "Then don't say incredibly sweet and supportive things."

"Would you rather I say something mean and unsupportive?"

"Yes."

"Poppy." He drew my name out, pulling my hands away from my face. He gave me a lopsided grin, one that made him seem so incredibly young. "It's okay to cry. It's okay to be vulnerable. This was possibly the worst homecoming ever. This last week sucked, and not in a fun way."

I laughed again, and it ended in a sob. I didn't stop the onslaught of emotion this time. I broke, and just like Casteel had promised, he was there to catch those pieces, holding them together and keeping them safe until I could piece myself back together. Somehow, I ended up on the floor with him, in his lap, my arms and legs wrapped tightly around him.

And I stopped pretending.

Because I wasn't okay.

I wasn't okay with what had happened, with what it could signal and what it meant when I didn't even know what I was now. Nor was I okay with learning that my parents had been betrayed by someone they trusted—that they'd truly been attempting to escape Solis with Ian and me but never made it, risking their lives for me—for us. That betrayal hurt, and the pain throbbed intensely. All those things I tried not to think about crashed into me, and who…who would be okay?

Seconds turned into minutes, and those minutes stacked on top of one another. My tears dampened Casteel's chest. I hadn't even cried like this when I lost Vikter. That had been a harsher explosion of emotion, but Casteel…he had been there for that, too. And as he held me to him, his cheek pressed against the top of my head, his hands smoothing up and down my back, I didn't worry about being seen as weak. I didn't fear that I'd be reprimanded for showing emotion as he gently rocked us back and forth. I hadn't even allowed myself to do this with Vikter, and I knew he wouldn't have judged me. He would've let me cry it out and then told me to deal with it. And, sometimes, that was what I needed. This wasn't one of those times, and not since my parents had died and Ian had left for Carsodonia had I felt safe enough to be this vulnerable.

And I knew why I could be like this with Casteel. It was further proof of what I felt so deeply when I opened my senses to him now. I was drowning in the taste of chocolate-dipped strawberries.

Love.

Love and acceptance.

I didn't know how long we stayed like that, but it felt like a small eternity by the time the tears stopped flowing. My eyes ached a little, but I felt lighter.

Casteel turned his head, pressing a kiss to my cheek. "You up for taking your first-ever shower? Afterwards, we'll get some food in us, and eventually—unfortunately—find you some clothing. Then we'll talk about everything else."

At first, my brain got snagged on the whole *shower* part and then got hung up on the *everything else* section. Everything else was meeting with his parents, the whole Queen business, and…well, everything else.

"Or we can get some food in us first. It's up to you," he said. "What would you like?"

"I think I would like a shower, Cas." I gasped as he nipped my finger.

His eyes opened, shining like citrine jewels. "Sorry. Hearing you say that just…does things to me."

Having a relatively good idea of what those things were, warmth slid into my veins. My gaze crept over his shoulder, and excitement bubbled to life. "It's going to feel weird bathing while standing."

"You're going to love it." Casteel rose then, easily bringing me with him. His strength was always a shock, one I wasn't sure I'd ever get used to.

I followed him into the bathroom. Only the faintest light seeped in through the window above the bench. Casteel turned the knob on a lamp over the vanity, and a soft, golden glow stretched across the tiled floor. I watched him place two thick towels on a small stool between the tub and shower stall. I hadn't even noticed that before.

Casteel shucked off his clothing with an utter lack of self-consciousness that was fascinating and enviable. I couldn't take my eyes off him as he walked into the sunken stall and began fiddling with the faucets on the wall.

Water spilled out of the multiple pipes overhead, resulting in a heavy shower. I should've focused on whatever sorcery made that possible, but I was mesmerized by him—by the dusting of dark hair on his calves, the breadth of his shoulders and chest, and the lean, coiled muscles of his stomach. His body was proof of a day rarely spent idle. He enthralled me, everything from the delineated lines of his chest, the wickedness of the length of him, to the life he'd lived that played out across his bronzed skin in a smattering of pale scars.

His body was…gods, it was a masterpiece of perfection and flaws. Not even the Royal Crest brand—the circle with the arrow piercing the middle—on his right upper thigh detracted from the raw beauty of him.

"When you look at me like that, every good intention I had of letting you enjoy your first shower disappears with each passing second," he said, water sluicing over his shoulders as he crossed under the rain shower. "And is replaced by very inappropriate intentions."

Heat flushed my veins as I toyed with the hem of my slip. My gaze dipped below the tight muscles of his abdominals, lower than his navel. He'd hardened, the skin there a deeper hue. A curling motion was sharp and sudden in the pit of my stomach and then between my thighs.

His chest rose sharply. "I think you're interested in those inappropriate intentions."

"And what if I am?"

"I would find it very hard not to cave to them." His eyes brightened. "And that would be a problem."

My pulse was a heady thrum. "I'm not sure how that could be problematic."

"The problem? If I get inside of you right now, I don't think I can control myself." He stopped in front of me and dipped his head. His lips brushed the shell of my ear as he slipped a finger under the strap of the slip. "I'd have you up against that wall, my cock and fangs so deep inside you that neither of us would know where one began and the other ended."

An intense, aching pulse washed through me in tight waves. The memory of the scrape of his fangs against my skin, the bite, and the brief pain that gave way to pleasure took center stage in my mind. "I still don't see how that is a problem."

A deep, rough sound came from the back of his throat. "That's because you haven't seen me lose control."

"You were in control in that carriage? After the battle at Spessa's End?"

"Yes." His head tilted, and my entire body jerked at the feeling of a sharp fang against the side of my neck.

That tantalizing ache settled between my legs and throbbed. "What about that morning when you woke hungry and—?" I gasped as his tongue soothed the area his fang had teased.

"And I had my mouth between your thighs, and the taste of you coursing down my throat?"

I shuddered, my eyes drifting shut. "Yes. T-that morning. You weren't in control then."

"You reached me, Poppy." His fingers slipped under both straps of my slip, and he drew it down slowly, over the tingling tips of my breasts. "I didn't lose control then."

"And after...after I fed from you?" I asked, finding it difficult to swallow. "In the hunting cabin?"

"I was still in control, Poppy."

Air hitched in my throat. If he truly hadn't lost control any of those times, I wasn't sure I could imagine what it would be like if he did. As the slip gathered at my waist and then fell to the floor, I found myself shamefully wanting to know.

"I would lose control now." His fingers skated down the curve of my shoulder and over the swell of my breast. The touch was featherlight, but my back arched. He brushed his lips over my cheek as his thumb moved in maddening circles over a tingling nipple. "My mouth would be all over you. I'd drink from your throat. I'd drink from here," he whispered against my lips as he folded his hand around my breast, kneading the flesh. I gasped as I felt his other hand slip between my thighs. "I'd definitely drink from here."

He could...he could drink from *there*? "I don't have an issue with any of those things."

He made that rough, needy sound again. "Your body has been through a lot, Poppy, and in a very short period of time. You may feel fine. You might even be, but less than two days ago, you barely had a drop of blood left in you. I'm not going to risk feeding from you. Not today. So, one of us needs to be the responsible party."

A throaty laugh left me. "You're the responsible one?"

"Obviously." He skimmed a finger through the dampness gathering at my center, stroking the fire already flaming to life in my veins.

"I don't think you know what being responsible means."

"You might be right." Casteel kissed me, tugging at my lower lip. "So, you need to be the responsible one."

"I don't want to."

He chuckled against my mouth and then kissed me again, slipping his hand out from between my thighs. "Shower," he reminded me—or himself.

The level of disappointment I felt when he took my hand was quite shameful, especially when he turned, and the hard length of him brushed my thigh. Another wanton pulse rolled through me as he led me into the stall. He stepped into the shower and turned to me, water wetting his hair, coursing over his shoulders, and droplets—*warm* droplets—sprinkling my outstretched arm. His heated gaze was so intense it was like a physical caress as it swept over me.

My body trembled as I stood there, letting him look his fill. It wasn't exactly easy. I fought the urge to shield myself as he held onto my hand. It wasn't that I was uncomfortable around him or ashamed of the numerous imperfections. No matter how much I trained with weapons and my body, my waist would never be narrow, nor would my hips ever be slender like the Ladies in Wait in Solis.

I liked cheese and bacon and chocolate-covered everything too much for that.

I wasn't embarrassed by my scars, either. Not when he looked at me like he did now, as if I could very well be a deity or a goddess. Not when those scars, like his, were proof of the life I'd lived and the things I'd survived.

It was just this…openness was new to me. I'd spent the better part of my life clothed from chin to floor, and more than half of my face covered. I knew how to hide. I was only now learning how to be seen. I fought that urge, feeling a little giddy with pride and awareness, and with each second, I grew more comfortable.

"You're beautiful." Casteel's voice was like a balmy summer night. "And you're mine."

I was, completely.

And that didn't make my skin feel itchy, or my tongue burn with words of denial. It wasn't a statement of dominance or control. I knew exactly what those two things were. This was simply the truth. I *was* his.

And he was mine.

Casteel tugged me forward, and I went. Water fell over me, and I squeaked at the sensation of the spray pattering over my skin. "Did you forget you were in a shower?" he asked, letting go of my hand.

"I think so." I turned my palms up, watching the water form shallow puddles. It bordered on almost too hot, just like I liked it. Tipping my head back, I gasped as the water fell over my face and through my hair. It was like a heated rain shower. I turned in a slow circle, thrilled by how the water felt against my skin, even the raw and achy parts.

Opening my eyes, I glanced over at him. He was smiling—a real one. A rare one, both dimples on display. "Do I look foolish?"

"You look perfect."

I grinned as I moved under the next pipe, where the water fell heavier. It plastered the hair to my face, and I laughed. Shoving the strands back, I saw him grab one of the bottles from the shelf near the faucets. The liquid was clear and smelled of lemons and pine.

As I played in the water, moving between what Casteel explained were showerheads, he bathed himself. When he was finished, he came up behind me, more of that enticingly scented soap in hand.

"Close your eyes," he ordered.

I obeyed, enjoying the feeling of his fingers against my scalp as he worked the soap into a lather. "I could get used to this," I whispered.

"So could I." He moved closer, and I felt the heated brand of him against my lower back. "Tip your head back and keep your eyes closed."

I did as he requested. His lips touched mine, and I smiled. He then gathered my hair, rinsing the soap out. It was so much easier in a shower. All I had to do was stand there.

I may just move into the shower and never leave.

The idea continued to grow in its appeal as Casteel left my side briefly, returning with a soapy square. Foam followed the soft sponge as he dragged it over my arms, chest, stomach, and then to my lower back. He was careful with the small cuts the stones had left behind, and the tenderness of his care tugged at my heart. My chest swelled with all the love I felt for him and it grew achy, heavy even as the sponge seemed to vanish, replaced by the roughened glide of Casteel's soapy palms.

My eyes drifted shut once more, and my mind wandered to pure, sinful places as his hands took the same path the sponge had minutes before. I thought about what he'd said he would do with his fangs and…his cock. My blood heated as the fire roared to life inside me once more. Could he do that here, under the shower? That seemed quite slippery, but if anyone could do it, it would be Casteel.

He glided his hands over my breasts. My head fell back against his chest as they lingered there. I bit down on my lip as one of his hands coasted over my belly. My skin tightened as pleasure curled low. His fingers on the hardened peak of my breast wrung a gasp from me as his other hand made its way below my navel. My body reacted without thought, widening the space between my thighs.

"Enjoying your shower?" His voice was thick with smoke.

He knew exactly how much I was enjoying it, and the knowledge that he could scent my arousal enflamed me instead of embarrassing me. I nodded anyway. "Are you being responsible?"

"Of course." His hand slipped between my thighs. "Just being thorough," he said, swirling his thumb across the bundle of nerves there.

I gasped, rising on tiptoe. The ache twisted deeply as my lips parted. I moaned as my hips lifted to meet his hand.

He kissed my shoulder as he eased his hands away. My eyes snapped open, and I started to turn toward him. "I'm not finished," he said before I could speak. "Your legs still need to be cleaned."

My brows rose. "Seriously?"

His eyes were like pools of warm honey. "Very serious."

I couldn't care less about my legs. "Casteel—"

"I would never forgive myself if you didn't find your first shower to be as effective as a bath," he said, and I resisted the urge to roll my eyes. "But you should sit. You're looking a little…flushed."

"I wonder why."

He chuckled deeply, and I briefly considered hitting him but decided against it even though he truly deserved it for teasing me like this. I let him take me to the bench and sat, sucking in a soft breath of surprise as I realized a faint mist of water fell over the space.

Casteel added more soap to his hands and lowered himself to his knees before me. "Comfortable?"

I glanced down between his legs as I nodded. He wasn't even remotely unaffected by this.

"Good. Your comfort is my utmost concern." Water clung to his lashes as he curled one hand around an ankle. He grinned, his gaze rising to mine as he lifted my leg. My breath snagged as he placed my foot on his shoulder. The position left me…oh, gods, it left me utterly exposed to him.

A shaky breath left me as I watched him shift his gaze to my very center. A hint of fang appeared behind his parted lips, and everything inside me twisted most deliciously. My palms flattened against the smooth bench as he drew his soapy hands up my calf and then my thigh. I held my breath as his fingers reached the crease between my hip and thigh. He dragged his hand along the inside of my leg, his knuckles brushing my most sensitive area. Air punched out of my lungs.

Casteel's hand stopped there as he met my gaze. "Still comfortable?"

"Yes," I whispered.

That sensually cruel smile of his appeared, and tension gathered sweetly in my body. He dragged his hand back down as the mist of water continued wetting my skin. When he finished, he placed my foot back on the floor and then lifted my other leg. Cooler air rushed against my heated flesh. He did the same as before, sliding the soap between my toes, over the pad of my foot, and then up and up my leg. I tensed, nearly straining in anticipation, my heart pounding as his knuckles once more grazed my core. Drawing his hand back down the length of my leg, he wiped away the soap and bent his head, kissing the jagged scar on the inside of my knee.

Hooking his arm around my calf, Casteel didn't put my foot down on the floor. He moved in closer, the width of his shoulders widening my legs.

My heart stuttered as my eyes widened. A wave of taut shivers cascaded through me. Not even that morning he'd woken from the nightmare and had been close to bloodlust had I been this exposed to him. A flutter moved from my chest to my stomach.

"Are you…are you still being thorough?" I asked, my voice husky.

"Yes. I think I missed a spot." He kissed the space above the old scar. "I think I see many more spaces I missed. And you know me, I'm a perfectionist. I also wouldn't want those spots to feel left out. Do you?"

"No." My heart pounded so much that I wondered if he could see it, but when I looked down, all I saw was the turgid peaks of my breasts between soaked strands of coppery hair. I lost a bit more breath as I took in the sight of myself—my shoulders back against the tile, my breasts thrust out, and my legs open wide for Casteel. My eyes remained open as my head fell back against the wall. I watched him as his wet hair teased my skin.

"How about here?" He kissed the inside of my thigh as his palm ran up the back of my leg. "Or here?" His lips found one of those ragged scars on the insides of my thighs. He shifted his head as he brushed his lips over the pulsing flesh between my legs. I jerked. "Yeah, I think this spot is especially dirty and lonely."

I moved beyond words as his head bowed. The wet slide of his tongue over me dragged a throaty moan from me. My eyes fluttered shut and reopened only halfway when he said, "I need to pay extra special attention to this area." He made another pass with his tongue, this time swirling it around the tight bud of nerves. "It may take me a while."

I trembled as his tongue flicked the skin and then slipped inside me. A dizzying burst of pleasure shocked my senses. He tilted his head again, and his lick was deep and slow and wonderfully indecent. My hips tilted up, matching his strokes—his teasing, shallow strokes. What he was doing was decadent and not anything I had ever imagined when thinking about bathing.

I would never be able to think of anything else when I was near water now.

My hips twitched as I felt a long finger replace his tongue, trailing lightly over the swollen flesh then slipping inside me a fraction with each sweep. My body was becoming an inferno.

"Cas," I breathed, shuddering as I teetered closer and closer to the precipice.

He halted, looking up at me with eyes that were now luminous. "You should hold onto the bench."

With shaking hands, I gripped the edge of the seat.

One side of his lips curved up. "Good girl."

He dipped his head, his breath hot against me. A heartbeat passed. I felt his lips and then the erotic graze of a fang—

I cried out as the sharp, brief sting sent a shockwave through my entire body. A knotted whirl of burning pleasure shot down my legs and up my spine. My eyes were wide-open, but I swore I saw bursts of white light. Then his mouth closed over the throbbing bundle of nerves as his finger thrust inside me. He sucked deep and hard, coaxing not only my arousal but the thin bit of blood I knew he'd also drawn. My entire body reared off the bench, my grip slipping—

He placed his other hand on my stomach, pressing me back down to the seat. He feasted from me as his finger pumped in and out. He *consumed* me, and I was lost—willingly lost in the raw sensations flooding me, devoured by the groan he unleashed against my flesh. I squirmed against him in senseless desperation. The feel of him was too much, and yet, it wasn't enough. The pleasure bordered on pain wrapped in beauty. It was exhilarating and frightening as the intense heat coiled deeper and tighter inside me.

"Cas," I moaned again, not even recognizing my voice as his hand left my stomach. Tipping forward on the edge of the bench, I gained leverage with my other foot. My chin dropped as my hips lifted from the tile and rolled against his finger, against his mouth. The sight of me churning against him became branded in my mind. The sight of the muscles in his upper arm flexing and tensing as his hand moved between his legs was imprinted on my skin. His lashes swept up, and his gaze locked with mine as his arm made quick and jerky, hard movements and pushed me over the edge. I came apart, screaming his name as he gave a hoarse shout against my skin. I shattered, over and over, breaking into pleasure-wrapped shards. The release was devastating and glorious in its intensity, coming in on endless waves that left me boneless against the tile. When he eased his finger out of me, tiny bursts of pleasure still sparked through me.

His lips curled into a smile against my swollen flesh. "Honeydew."

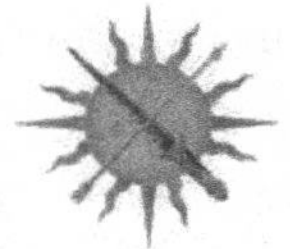

Casteel wrapped a towel around me. Before I could take one step, he lifted me into his arms.

I grasped one shoulder. "I can walk."

"I know." He carried me into the shadow-filled bedchamber.

"This is not necessary."

"Everything that has to do with you is necessary." Casteel deposited me on the bed, and within a heartbeat, he had me stretched out on my side and was seated beside me. He was fully and unabashedly naked while I was still wrapped in the fluffy towel. "So, how did you enjoy your first shower?"

My cheeks warmed as I grinned. "It was very…life-changing."

"Agreed." One side of his lips curved up as he reached over, tucking a strand of my wet hair back from my face. "Hungry?"

I nodded, smothering a yawn.

"I'll see what I can wrangle up for us." He leaned over me, capturing my lips. The kiss was soft and languid and wrapped my heart in warmth and light.

He withdrew, rising from the bed, and I watched him through half-open eyes as he walked to the oak wardrobe. He pulled on a pair of black breeches. As he made his way back to me, he unsheathed the wolven dagger. "The wolven are outside right now, patrolling."

My brows rose. "They are?" When he nodded, a sleepy frown pulled at my lips. "Why can't I feel them, and you can?"

"Because I'm special," he replied with a smirk.

I rolled my eyes.

He chuckled. "I can't feel them. I can hear them. Still makes me special," he added, and I sighed.

I thought about what I'd thought had happened with Kieran and Delano. "Do you think that Primal bond thing means that I can feel them in a different way?"

"I think you mean Primal *notam*."

"Whatever."

"But what do you mean *feel them* in a different way?"

"I don't know." I gave a half-shrug. "A couple of times since I woke up in the cabin, I thought I heard Delano and Kieran in my mind."

One eyebrow rose. "What?"

"Yeah, I heard their voices in my head." I sighed. "When I was in the Skotos, having that dream? I heard Delano answer something in that nightmare, and I heard him say that I was their…*Liessa*," I told him. "And then I swore I heard Kieran's voice when we waited outside the Temple of Saion. I didn't get a chance to ask either of them, but with Delano I also felt more than his emotions when I focused on him in the mountains. I felt, like…I don't know how to explain it, but it was like his unique imprint. His mark. I've never felt that before. I know it sounds unreal—"

"I don't think it sounds unreal," Casteel said, his brows knitting. "I think anything is possible. We should definitely ask Kieran if he heard you or if he even knows if it's possible. I know it wasn't for us when we were bonded."

Pressing my lips together, I nodded.

Casteel stared down at me for a moment. "You're utterly unique, Poppy. You know that, right?"

I gave another lazy, one-shouldered shrug.

A faint smile appeared and then disappeared. "You're safe here," he told me as he placed the dagger beside my hand. "But just in case, if anyone comes in here, stab first and ask questions later. You should be familiar with that mentality."

"Why does everyone act like I run around stabbing people?"

Casteel stared back at me and then looked pointedly at his chest.

"Whatever," I muttered. "You deserved it."

"I did." He grinned as he placed a knee on the bed and lowered the upper half of his body over mine. "I'll be right back."

"I'll be here." I picked up the dagger. "Hopefully, not stabbing anyone."

The dimple in his right cheek appeared, and he dipped his head, kissing just above my brow and then lower, over the scar. "Princess?"

My lips curved up. What had started as a nickname had become a reality. "Yes?"

His mouth moved over mine. "I love you."

The smile on my face grew as my heart did a little skip in my chest. "I love you."

He made that rough, rumbling sound. "I will never get tired of hearing that. Say it over and over, a hundred thousand times, and it will feel like I'm hearing it for the first time."

I tipped my head up, kissing him. He was slow to leave, but he finally did, and my tired gaze moved to the lattice doors. Night had fallen outside, and I strained to hear what had been so obvious to Casteel. I heard nothing but the low hum of insects and the melody of nightbirds. My grip tightened on the cool bone handle of my dagger.

Casteel didn't have to worry. If anyone came into this room, I would be ready.

Chapter 17

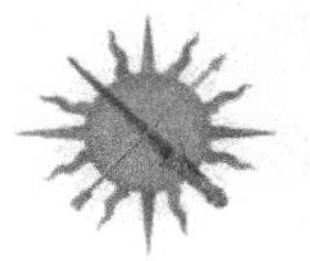

Upon his return, I figured Casteel was relieved to learn that I hadn't needed to stab anyone.

Or maybe not.

I think he liked it when I stabbed people.

Especially him.

He'd returned with a bottle of wine and a platter of sliced meats and cubed cheeses. There were also small blocks of milk chocolate, and I might've shoved three chunks into my mouth all at once. I'd changed into one of Casteel's old cream-colored tunic shirts, much like the one he wore now. He'd helped me roll up the too-long sleeves. The tunic covered more than a slip would or that indecent nightgown had. Even though there was much to discuss, the full stomach, wine, and what he'd done in that shower all worked against that. I ended up falling asleep as Casteel took the platter into the sitting room, and was only half-aware when he rejoined me in bed, curling his long body around mine and gathering me close.

I slept the kind of deep sleep where even dreams didn't follow. I woke at some point, the gray light of dawn beginning to find its way into the room, and sleepily made use of the bathing chamber. When I returned to the bed, Casteel immediately wrapped his body around mine. I didn't know how long I slept that time before I woke again, my eyes fluttering open to soft lamplight. Shifting under the light blanket, I brushed up against a leg.

"Good evening," Casteel drawled.

I rolled onto my back and looked up.

Casteel was sitting propped against the headboard, dressed in black breeches and a white shirt similar to the one I wore. He was thumbing through a leather-bound book. "I took it upon myself to unpack the bags we brought with us and hang your clothing in the wardrobe. Kirha—Kieran and Netta's mother—dropped off some additional clothing she believed would fit you and recommended a seamstress, even though I like the idea of you having limited clothing options."

I wasn't even remotely surprised to hear the last part. "What time is it?"

"It's close to eight at night." He glanced over at me. "You've slept for almost twenty-four hours."

Dear gods, it'd been a long time since I'd slept that long. "I'm sorry—"

"Don't apologize. You needed the rest. So did I," he said. "Though I was starting to get a bit lonely over here."

"How long have you been…?" My eyes started to narrow as I stared at the book he held. It looked awfully familiar. "What are you reading?"

"Your favorite book." His eyes slid to mine knowingly, and I jerked upright. "You know, I have this theory about Miss Willa Colyns."

"I can't believe you still have that damn journal."

"She mentions something here, in chapter twenty-three, that got me thinking." He cleared his throat. "'*Andre was the most uninhibited of all my lovers—*'"

"You do not need to read it to tell me your theory."

"I disagree," he replied. "*'He was quite shameless in his search of pleasure as he was with his willingness to give, but his most impressive seduction was not his manhood.'*" He looked over at me. "You do remember what manhood means?"

"Yes, Casteel. I remember."

He smirked as he returned to that damnable journal. "Where was I? Oh, yes. Something about his manhood."

"Why do you like saying that word so much?"

"Because you like hearing it."

"I do not." I shoved my hair back from my face.

"Stop interrupting me. This is a very important observation," he replied. "'*But his most impressive seduction was not his manhood. It was the dark, wicked kiss of our kind, one he was all too eager to bestow in the most scandalous locations.*'"

I realized what Casteel was getting at. The dark, wicked kiss of *our kind*. But my mind got stuck on the *bestowing the kiss in the most scandalous locations* part. Casteel hadn't bitten me in that very scandalous location in the shower, but he'd drawn blood.

"I do believe that Miss Willa was either Atlantian or of Atlantian descent. Perhaps even one of another bloodline," he noted. "I wonder if she still lives. If so, I also wonder if she's planning for a volume two." He paused. "You look very flushed, Poppy. Was it the wicked bite part? Or would you like to hear more about Andre?" He glanced back at the journal. "'*While partygoers celebrated the birthday of some young lady, Andre coaxed me out into the gardens, where he and his confidant, Torro, celebrated me.*'"

I bit down on the inside of my lip, words fizzling out on the tip of my tongue. They…celebrated her? *They*?

Casteel continued, "'*Torro took me from behind, his thick hardness already taking me to bliss while Andre knelt before me, his mouth closing over my—*'"

"That's enough." I shot forward, snatching the book from his hands. I got the book but didn't make it very far.

Casteel folded an arm around my waist, pinning me and the journal to his chest. "You shouldn't have stopped me there." His eyes warmed. "Miss Willa was in for a very exciting evening in that garden. They were about to be joined by one not-very-innocent Lady."

"I don't care—wait." Curiosity got the best of me. "What? The…the *four* of them? Together?"

He grinned as his other hand slid down my back. "Oh, yes." His palm glided over my rear, which had become exposed in my rush to grab the journal. He cupped the flesh, sending a shivery wave of awareness through me. "Four of them. Together. Lots of manhoods. Lots of scandalous lady parts."

"Lady parts?" I choked on a laugh.

He nodded as he dragged the edge of his teeth over his bottom lip. "How are you feeling?"

"I feel…uncomfortably curious," I admitted. I had questions. Like how did that even work?

Casteel's brows flew up. His surprise was like a burst of cool wind on my skin, and then something spicy and lush landed on the tip of my tongue. "Poppy," he purred, his eyes deepening to a warm honey color. "I was talking about how you felt after getting some sleep."

"Oh." Heat swept through my entire body. Scrunching my nose, I planted my face in his chest. "I feel fine." And embarrassed.

His laugh rumbled through me as his arms tightened. "I'm glad to hear that. I'm glad to hear both of those things."

"Oh, my gods," I muttered. "Please forget that I said I was curious."

"Unlikely."

"I dislike you."

"That's a lie."

"I know."

Another deep laugh came from him, and I smiled because I loved that sound. How deep and real it was. "We'll talk about your uncomfortable curiosity in great detail later, but you need to get off me and change into something that makes it less easy for my manhood to find its way to your lady parts."

I lifted my head from his chest. "You're holding me to you."

"True." His arm eased off me, and I started to rise when he lightly smacked my rear. I let out a little squeak, and those damn dimples appeared in both of his cheeks.

I stared down at him. "That was very inappropriate."

"It was, wasn't it?" He didn't feel even a hint of shame.

Still flushing to the roots of my hair, I started to move but stopped. Tension crept into my muscles, a contrasting mixture of reluctance and determination.

"What?" Casteel's gaze searched mine. "What is it?"

"I…" It was hard to explain what I felt. It was a mixture of several things. I shifted onto my knees between his legs. "I almost don't want to leave the bed. Things…everything feels different here. Like nothing outside of this place exists or matters. And I know…" I looked over to the latticed door, to the night beyond. "I know when I do, I'll have to face all the things that do matter." My gaze fell to the journal I held against my chest. "That probably makes me sound like an immature child."

"No. Not at all. I get what you're feeling." He folded his fingers under my chin, lifting my gaze to his. "When Malik and I went to the caverns, it was our way of escaping."

"What were you two escaping?" I asked. He'd never expounded on that.

"Malik and I stumbled into many conversations." A wry grin formed. "Ones that were probably more like arguments between our mother and father. My parents love each other fiercely and have always had the same goal in mind—to provide a better life for all who call Atlantia their home. To make sure that everyone is safe and well cared for. But their methods of achieving that goal don't always line up."

I thought about that. "Ruling a kingdom and actually wanting what is best for the people you're responsible for cannot be easy."

"No, it's not," he agreed. "My father has always had more of an aggressive mentality toward achieving that goal."

One of his father's more aggressive ideas was to send me back to the Queen of Solis in pieces. "And your mother truly doesn't have the same ideology?"

"I think my mother has seen enough war to last her four lifetimes," he said. "Even when Malik and I were both too young to fully understand the problems Atlantia faced with the ever-decreasing land and the threat of Solis just beyond the Skotos Mountains, we could feel the heaviness that sat on our father's shoulders, and the sadness that wore on our mother. She is an incredibly strong woman. Just like you. But she worries greatly for the people, and some days, the sadness overshadows the hope."

"Do you know if your mother loved Malec?" I asked. According to Casteel, it was rare for Atlantians to marry without love between the two, but his mother's marriage to the original King didn't sound like it had been a happy one. Part of me hoped she didn't love him, considering how the marriage had turned out. But she'd given her son a name so strikingly similar to her first husband's that I had to wonder.

Casteel appeared to think it over. "She never really talked about him. Malik and I used to think it was out of respect for our father, but he isn't the type to be affected by another who is no longer a part of her life. I think she loved him, Malec, and as crazy as this will sound, I think Malec loved her, too."

Surprise shuttled through me. "But he had numerous affairs, right? And didn't you say it was rumored that he and Isbeth were heartmates?"

Casteel nodded as he twisted a strand of my hair between his fingers. "I think Malec was in love with being in love, and he was constantly chasing that feeling instead of nourishing what he already had." He dragged his thumb over the hair he held. "If the rumor of Malec and Isbeth being heartmates is true, it could've been the first time he stopped searching and paid attention to what was in front of him."

My brows knitted. "All of that sounds incredibly sad and also hopeful. I mean, that if your mother did love Malec, she was still able to find love again. To open herself like that once more. I don't know..." I held the journal close to my chest. "I don't know if I could do that."

"I would never give you a reason to, Poppy."

My heart melted in my chest and then froze. But what if I was immortal? It seemed utterly incomprehensible to think that I would outlive Casteel, but we really had no idea what I had Ascended into. And while it would take several lifetimes for Casteel to begin even showing signs of aging, he would. And I...I didn't want to think about spending my future without him, no matter how much of one we shared together. There were the heartmate trials, but the gods slept. There was also the Joining, but I had no idea if that worked in the opposite direction, linking his lifespan to mine.

And I didn't even know why I was thinking about any of this when we had no idea what I was or what kind of lifespan I would even have. What had Casteel told me once before?

Don't borrow from tomorrow's problems?

I needed to start living that way.

"But when Malik and I went to the caverns," he continued, thankfully unaware of where my thoughts had gone, "we were able to pretend as if none of the conversations happened. The heaviness and sadness didn't follow us there. Nothing outside of that place existed."

"But you were young boys then."

"That doesn't matter. The feeling still remains, some hundred years later," he said, and my stomach dipped at the reminder of how old he was—how old I would one day become. "This bed—this room—can become our version of the caverns. When we're in here, nothing outside it matters. This will be our peace. We deserve that, don't we?"

My breath caught, and I nodded. "We do."

His gaze softened as he slid his thumb across my bottom lip. "I wish we could stay in here forever."

I smiled faintly. "I do, too."

But we wouldn't—we couldn't. Because a moment later, a knock sounded on the door. I rolled off him, standing.

Casteel sighed as he rose, too. He stopped to drop a kiss on my cheek. "Be right back."

A moment later, I heard Kieran's voice. Placing the journal on the nightstand, I roamed into the bathing chamber, quickly taking care of my personal needs but not bothering to do much with my hair. I checked my eyes in the mirror before I left, finding that they still had the silvery-white sheen behind the pupils. My stomach took a small tumble at the sight, but I reminded myself that I was still the same.

Mostly.

Casteel was entering the bedchamber when I returned, carrying a fresh platter of food and a new bottle of what appeared to be some sort of sweet wine. One look at the hard line of his jaw, and I immediately knew that whatever news Kieran had brought wasn't good. I sat on the bed. "What happened?"

"Nothing major."

"Really?" I watched him come to me.

"Yeah. It's just my father. He apparently decided to change his mind when it came to waiting for us to come to him. He wants to talk with me."

I relaxed as he popped the cork and poured a glass of wine. "Then you should talk to him. He's probably just concerned."

"Does it make me a bad son if I say I don't care?" He handed the glass to me.

A wry grin formed as I pulled my legs up, crossing them. I took a sip. The wine tasted of sugared berries. "A little."

"Oh well."

I tipped toward him. "I know that you do care, though. You love your parents. You haven't seen them in the gods know how long, and you haven't had a chance to talk to either of them under any normal circumstances. Go talk to your father, Cas. I'm fine."

"Cas." He bit down on his bottom lip as he planted his fists on the bed and bent over. "I've changed my mind about you calling me that."

"You have?" I lowered my glass.

He nodded as he leaned in, brushing his lips across mine. "Because hearing you say it makes me want to get my mouth between your thighs again, and that need is quite distracting."

Heat flooded my veins. "Sounds like that's your problem." I grinned. "*Cas*."

"Gods," he said, the word rumbling out of him. He kissed me quickly, nipping at my bottom lip as he withdrew.

Kieran appeared in the archway as Casteel straightened. He'd changed since he left us, having donned fawn-colored breeches and a sleeveless, white dress shirt that he had tucked in. "Did you actually get some rest, or did you spend hours asking Cas question after question?"

"I slept," I told him as I plucked a chocolate-glazed strawberry from the tray. "After asking a few questions."

"A few?" Kieran snorted.

"Yes, only—" Words failed me as Casteel caught my wrist. He lifted my hand, closing his mouth over my finger.

A wicked trill flooded my veins. His tongue swirled over my skin, catching the melting chocolate. Air caught in my throat as the edge of his fang pricked my skin when he drew back. I felt the languid tug of his mouth all the way through me.

The gold of his eyes turned to a heated honey. "Tasty."

Tension coiled deep inside me as I stared at him. A wolfish half-grin appeared.

"Did you two forget I was here?" Kieran asked. "Holding a conversation with you two? Or trying to."

I sort of did.

"Not at all," Casteel remarked. "Poppy did have a very relaxing evening. We did some light reading."

Light reading?

"Is that so?" Kieran's brows rose.

Wait.

"Yes, from Poppy's favorite journal, written by a Miss Willa—"

"He was reading that," I cut in, picking up a piece of cheese. "I woke up, and he was reading—"

"You know, the one I found her with on that window ledge? The scene was about a very dark sort of wicked kiss on a very inappropriate area," Casteel continued while Kieran stared at us blankly. "And foursomes."

Slowly, I looked up at Casteel. Oh, my gods. My eyes narrowed as I debated throwing the cheese in his face. I didn't. Instead, I ate it rather aggressively. He was lucky I loved cheese.

"Foursomes?" Kieran repeated, his gaze shifting to me. "I imagine you had a lot of questions about that."

"I did not," I snapped.

"I don't believe that for one second," Kieran stated, a half-grin forming. "You probably asked how it was possible."

I had totally been wondering that, but those words never once passed my lips.

"Would you like to explain it to her?" Casteel asked.

"That won't be necessary," I cut in as Kieran opened his mouth. "I have a vivid enough imagination, thank you very much."

He looked a little disappointed.

Casteel's laugh teased the top of my head as he fished out another strawberry from the bowl of fruit and offered it to me. "I am very intrigued by this imagination of yours."

"I'm sure you are," I muttered, taking the berry. "Want to know what I'm imagining now? I'm currently entertaining myself with images of kicking both of you in the throats."

Kieran's gaze swept over me, and still only in Casteel's shirt, I was sure I appeared as threatening as a sleepy kitten. "Now I'm also intrigued," he commented.

I rolled my eyes as I shoved a piece of melon into my mouth. "Whatever," I muttered around the fruit as Kieran dipped out of the room.

"I won't be gone long. Kieran will be here—and I know you don't need a guard," he added before I could say anything. "But he insisted, and it makes me feel better to know that someone else will be here. You should try to get some more rest. I'm sure it wouldn't hurt."

I swallowed the urge to tell him that I didn't need a bodyguard. "Okay."

His eyes narrowed on me. "That was a surprisingly quick submission."

"Submission?" I arched a brow as I took a drink of the wine. "I wouldn't call it that."

"You wouldn't?"

I shook my head. "I hate the idea of having a babysitter, but a group of people did try to kill me earlier, and we have no idea if there are more of like mind. So I would call my quick *agreement* common sense."

The dimple appeared in his right cheek. "Common sense. That must be a new thing for you."

"I'm really imagining kicking you in the face now."

He chuckled, kissing me quickly once more. "I won't be gone long."

"Take as long as you need."

Casteel touched my cheek and then left. I exhaled heavily as my gaze flicked to my half-full glass. I leaned over the platter of food, placing the glass on the nightstand. As I ate a few cold strips of grilled chicken breast, nothing but silence came from the living area. What was Kieran even doing out there? Probably just standing by the archway, arms crossed and looking as bored as ever.

Rolling my eyes, I sighed. "Kieran?"

"Poppy?" came the response.

"You don't have to stay out there."

"You're supposed to be resting."

"All I've done today is rest." I popped a piece of cheese into my mouth. "But you lurking on the other side of the wall is not at all restful."

"I'm not lurking," he replied dryly.

"You're standing just out of sight, keeping watch. I don't know if there could be a better example of lurking than that," I replied. "Or I could come out there. Not sure how relaxed I would be in..." I grinned as Kieran appeared in the doorway. Walking over to the corner of the room, he dropped into the chair and looked at me. I gave him a little wave. "Hi."

"Hi." He stretched out his long legs, loosely crossing them at the ankles.

I stared at him. He stared at me. I picked up the small plate from the platter. "Cheese?"

A faint grin appeared as he shook his head. "You're going to make this weird, aren't you?"

"I offered you cheese." I placed the plate back on the bed. "How is that making anything weird?"

"You waved at me."

I crossed my arms. "I was being polite."

"The fact that you're being polite is also weird."

"I am always polite."

Kieran lifted his brows, and I didn't need to read his emotions to sense the incredulity.

"I *was* going to offer you the last of the chocolate, but you can forget about that now."

He laughed as he leaned back. "So, what are you more uncomfortable with right now? The fact that you tried to feed from me, or that I saw you naked—though I saw a lot more than that—?"

"You really don't need to bring any of that up," I stated, glaring at him.

"Or is it the Primal *notam*?"

"I'm regretting inviting you in here," I muttered. "Honest? All of it makes me a bit uncomfortable."

"You don't need to worry about how you were when you woke up," Kieran told me. "It happens."

"How often have you really had someone try to eat you upon waking up?"

"You'd be surprised."

I opened my mouth to ask for details but then closed it, thinking it was probably a road I really didn't need to travel right now. "I don't know what to think about any of this."

"It's a lot. A lot has changed for you in a very short period of time. I don't think anyone would know what to think."

I peeked over at him, wanting to know how he felt about the whole thing, but I really wanted to know if we had somehow communicated without speaking. "I—"

"Let me guess," he said. "You have a question."

I frowned as I crossed my arms over my chest.

"What?" He glanced over at me.

"Nothing." I exhaled heavily. A moment passed. "Kieran?"

"Yeah?"

"I have a question."

He sighed, but there was a slight curve to his lips. "What is your question, Poppy?"

"How do you feel about the *notam*?"

He was quiet for a moment and then he asked, "How do I feel about the *notam*? What do my people think? They are amazed. They are awed."

"Really?" I whispered, picking up one of the pillows and hugging it to my chest.

"Yes." He rose and made his way to the bed, sitting so we were shoulder to shoulder. "So am I."

I could feel my face heating. "Don't be. It makes me feel weird."

He grinned as he dipped his chin. "I don't think you understand why we feel…honored to be alive when a descendant of the gods is present. Many of my kind are not old enough to have lived among them. Alastir was one of the only few, and well, fuck him, right?"

I grinned. "Yeah. Fuck him."

He smiled. "But the children of the gods have always held a special place with the wolven. We exist in this form because of them. Not because of the Atlantians."

I squeezed the pillow tightly as I wiggled down onto my side, remaining silent.

"My ancestors were wild and fierce, loyal to their packs, but the kiyou were driven only by instinct, survival, and pack mentality.

Everything was a challenge—for food, mates, pack leadership. Many didn't survive very long, and the kiyou were on the brink of extinction when Nyktos appeared before the last great pack and asked that they protect the gods' children in this realm. In return, he offered them human form so they could communicate with the deities and have long lifespans."

"He *asked* and didn't just make the kiyou wolven?"

"He could have. He is the King of Gods, after all. But he made it clear that the agreement was not servitude but a partnership between the kiyou and the deities. There cannot be equality in power if there is no choice."

He was right. "I wonder why Nyktos asked for this partnership. Was it because he is the only god who can create life? I imagine being given a mortal form was like creating new life. Or perhaps because he is the King of Gods?"

"Probably all those reasons, but also because he is one of the few gods that can change forms," he said.

"What?" I didn't know that.

He nodded. "He was able to take the shape of a wolf—a white one. You haven't seen much of Atlantia, but when you do, you will see paintings and statues of Nyktos. He's often depicted with a wolf either at his side or behind him. When the wolf is behind him, it symbolizes the shape he can take, and when the wolf is beside him, it represents the offer he made to the kiyou."

I let that sink in, and of course, my mind went to one place. "And yet I can't shift into anything."

"You're really hung up on that, aren't you?"

"Maybe," I muttered. "Anyway, did some of the kiyou refuse?"

Kieran nodded. "Some did because they did not trust the god, and others simply wanted to remain as they were. The ones who took his offer were given mortal form and became wolven. We were here before an Atlantian ever was."

It made me wonder why a wolven didn't rule then, especially considering that they were viewed as equal to the elemental Atlantians and the deities. Were other wolven in positions of power like Jasper? Like…Alastir had been? "Has a wolven ever wanted to rule Atlantia?"

"I'm sure some had the desire to, but that pack instinct from our ancestors remains inside of us. We prefer to watch over our packs to this day. A kingdom is not a pack, but several wolven are Lords and Ladies and oversee smaller cities and villages," he told me, shifting onto his side and resting his weight on an elbow so we were facing each other. "The Lords or Ladies in Atlantia are often land or business owners. They're not all from an elemental line. Some are wolven, some are half-mortal, and others are changelings. They aid in ruling alongside the Queen and King. There are no Dukes or Duchesses, nor do titles necessarily stay within families. If land or a business is sold, the title and its responsibilities transfer with it."

Hearing all of this was a stark reminder that I needed to learn a lot about Atlantia, but I wasn't exactly surprised to hear that they had similar class structures, and I felt safe assuming that this was another thing the Ascended had copied. I was, however, surprised to hear that the titles transferred. In Solis, only the Ascended were considered nobility or of a ruling class, and they held the position for life—which was basically an eternity.

"Discovering what you are doesn't mean we no longer respect the Queen and King," Kieran said after a moment. "But you…what you are is different to us. You are proof that we came from the gods."

I tilted my head. "Do some need a reminder of that?"

Kieran grinned. "There will always be people who need to be reminded of history."

"Explain," I stated.

His pale eyes warmed. "Every so many decades, an arrogant, young, elemental Atlantian demands a bonding or behaves as if he or she is better than all the others. We're more than capable of reminding them that we consider everyone equal, but at the end of the day, we are not in service to anyone."

I smiled at that, but it faded. "But there've been issues between the wolven and Atlantians of late, right?"

"A lot of it is the land issue. We lost so many of our people during the war, but our numbers are growing. Soon, it will be a problem."

"And the other issues? They have to do with Casteel's parents still ruling?"

"No one is comfortable with that, but we can sense that something has to give. Our land issues. The uncertainty about the Crown. The Ascended and Solis. I know that may sound strange, but it's a part of our instincts that remained from the time when we were kiyou. We can sense unrest," he said, and I listened intently, wanting to understand what was causing the division between the wolven and the Atlantians. "And things that have happened have aided in that sense of unease."

"What things?"

"From what I heard from my sister and father, there have been a few unexplainable incidents. Crops destroyed overnight, sheared and trampled. Homes inexplicably catching fire. Businesses vandalized."

Stunned, I lowered the pillow to the space between us. "Other than the fires, none of that sounds exactly unexplainable. Those aren't natural incidents."

"True."

"Has anyone been injured?"

"Not seriously."

Yet went unsaid. "Casteel hasn't mentioned any of this."

"I don't think he—"

"Wanted me to worry?" I finished for him, irritated. "That is going to need to change."

"In his defense, a lot has happened."

I couldn't argue with that. "Does anyone have any idea who is behind this or why?"

"No. And it is bizarre." Kieran sat up. "Everyone who lives in Atlantia believes in community, the strength and power in that."

"Obviously, someone doesn't believe in the strength and power of community," I remarked, and he nodded. We hadn't even had time to discuss what happened in the Temple. "Do you think Alastir was involved in any of that?"

"I don't know." Kieran exhaled heavily. "I've known that wolven my entire life, and I never expected him to do what he did. I haven't always agreed with him. Neither has my father. But we always thought he was a good man." He dragged a hand over his head and then looked at me again. "But if he and the others acting on his belief believed they were protecting Atlantia, I don't understand how damaging crops and businesses would help their cause."

My gaze fell to the teal-colored pillow, and I forced my grip to loosen. It didn't make sense to me either, but those actions created unrest. It would ultimately come down to what a person believed they could achieve through the disruption. Thinking of the Ascended, it seemed all too clear to me. The people of Solis lived under constant hardship, and it made them easier to manipulate and control. Alastir had basically been staging a coup, and that would have been easier to carry out if the people of Atlantia were unhappy. But with Alastir and the others gone, could there still be more out there who sought to create strife in Atlantia, and saw me as a threat? Casteel and Kieran had to believe there was a chance. That was why Casteel had handed me the dagger before he left to get food, and was why Kieran sat here now.

What the Duchess had said to me in the carriage and what Alastir had claimed resurfaced like a wraith determined to haunt me.

Kieran reached over, tugging gently on a strand of my hair. "What are you thinking about?"

I let go of the pillow. "Did Casteel tell you what the Duchess said to me before I killed her?"

"No."

That surprised me, but I didn't think it had anything to do with Casteel not wanting Kieran to know. There really hadn't been time for them to talk. "She said that Queen Ileana would be thrilled when she learned that I married Casteel and that I would be able to accomplish what she had never been able to do. That I would take Atlantia."

Kieran frowned. "That doesn't make sense."

"But it does, doesn't it? Being a descendant of the gods means I usurp the throne without force. I take Atlantia."

"Yes. You are the rightful ruler," he said, and I swallowed hard, almost reaching for the wine glass again. "But I don't see how that helps Solis at all."

"I don't either, but that is what she said, and…"

"And you think there's something to that because of the shit Alastir said to you?" he surmised.

I said nothing.

"Listen to me, Poppy." He leaned over so we were eye-to-eye and there was barely any space between us. "Every single one of us who lives within Atlantia is a potential threat to the kingdom. Our actions, our beliefs? Any of us could tear the kingdom apart. You being a descendant of the gods doesn't make you more of a threat to the kingdom than anyone else. Only you control your actions. Not your blood—not your bloodline. Alastir was wrong. So was the Duchess. And the fact that you didn't turn into a vampry when Casteel Ascended you should be evidence of that. And if you take the Crown, you're not taking it in the name of Solis."

"I can't say that's evidence of anything when we have no idea what I've become," I pointed out, but what he said made me think of what I'd told Casteel earlier. "I have another question for you."

He leaned back. "Of course, you do."

"When we were waiting outside the Temple of Saion and Emil was speaking to us, I thought something in response to what he said."

"You wondered if Alastir's plan had failed," Kieran finished for me. My breath caught as I stared at him. "But you said that out loud, Poppy."

I stilled. "No, I didn't."

The corners of his lips turned down. "Yes, you did."

"I didn't," I insisted, my heart thumping. "I only *thought* that, Kieran. And I heard you respond."

He didn't move or speak for a moment, and then he drew his legs up as he leaned forward. "I was in my wolven form."

"I know."

"I didn't speak that answer. I…"

"You thought it." I sat up. "That's what I'm trying to tell you. And that wasn't the only time that happened," I said, and then I told him about Delano. "Somehow, we communicated…telepathically."

"I…" The shock Kieran felt was like ice water. "Can you feel my imprint—my mark, like you did with Delano?"

"I don't know. I haven't tried."

"Can you?" When I nodded, he sat up, his knee pressing against mine. "Then try it."

Eager to figure out if I could, I inhaled deeply and focused on Kieran. The feel of his shock was still there, cool and slippery, but I pushed past that. The center of my chest hummed, and I felt it then, the invisible pathway that pushed past emotions and thoughts. It was like a cord connecting us, one invisible to the eye, and it fed back an earthy, woodsy sensation, one that reminded me of… "Cedar."

"What?" Kieran blinked.

"You feel like cedar."

He stared at me. "I feel like a tree?"

"Not really. I mean, that's just what your…imprint or whatever feels like to me. Something rich and woodsy, connected to the land." I shrugged. "That's the only way I know how to explain it."

"And what did Delano feel like? A featherlight sapling?"

A laugh burst from me. "No. Not a sapling. He felt like…I don't know. Like spring."

"And I feel woodsy."

"I'm beginning to think I shouldn't have said anything."

One side of his lips kicked up. "I kind of like it, though—the rich and woodsy part."

I rolled my eyes as I leaned back against the pillows. "I've never been able to feel any of that before. Or hear thoughts."

"Before you ask, no, I cannot read your thoughts. Not then or now. I only heard that one," he said, and I *had* been about to ask that. "It may have happened because you were experiencing a strong emotion."

Just like when I had summoned the wolven without realizing it.

"To be quite honest, I'm glad I can't. I imagine your mind to be a constant cyclone of questions, one fighting the other in a deathmatch to see which one has the honor of being asked."

I frowned at him. "That was kind of rude." Then I pitched forward, startling Kieran. "Can we try it now? See if I can do it on purpose?"

"Do you know how to do it?"

"No," I admitted, holding the teal pillow to my chest again. "But I think it has to do with that imprint—the singular pathway. I think I just need to follow that. I mean, that's something new, so it would make sense that it would be the way," I explained while Kieran stared at me as if I spoke in a language he didn't understand. "Okay. Just give me a second to concentrate."

"You sure you only need a second?" he quipped.

"You sure you don't want to find yourself staring down at the hilt of a dagger protruding from your chest?"

The wolven grinned at me. "That would make it hard to test out whether you can do this on purpose or not."

I shot him a look.

He laughed softly. "Go ahead. See if you can do it."

Drawing in a shallow breath, I opened my senses to read Kieran. I tasted the sugary sweetness of amusement on my tongue, and then I…I reached further, finding that earthy, woodsy sensation. I latched on to the cord. *Kieran?*

"Yeah?"

I jerked back, my eyes widening. "You heard me?"

He nodded. "It almost sounded like you spoke out loud, but I know you didn't, and it…it sounded like a whisper. Try it again. See if I can respond to you."

I focused on him, feeling the freshness of curiosity replacing the amusement. I connected to that pathway even quicker this time. *Kieran?*

The strangest thing happened, and I wasn't sure if it had happened before and I hadn't realized it, but I felt him—felt his mark brush against my mind like a woodsy, balsam-scented breeze. *You have a healthy obsession with stabbing people.*

Gasping, I gave a little jump. "I do not!"

A wide grin broke out over Kieran's face. "You heard, then?"

"I did." Dropping the pillow, I smacked his arm. "And I don't have a healthy obsession with that. I'm just surrounded by people who have an *unhealthy* obsession with annoying me."

He chuckled under his breath. "It must be the *notam*. It's the only thing I can think of. It makes sense. Sort of."

My brows lifted. "What does *sort of* mean? Could the deities communicate with the wolven like this?"

"Not that I know of," he said, looking at me so intently that it felt like he *was* trying to see into my mind. "But how do you think Nyktos communicated with the kiyou? They wouldn't have understood language. Not the spoken kind. He communicated directly with their minds."

Chapter 18

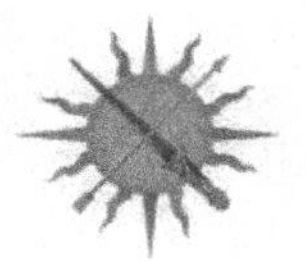

My stomach tumbled as I stared at Kieran. "But then how can I…?" I trailed off. "None of this makes sense, Kieran. I get that I carry the blood of Nyktos in me, and even Malec's if what Alastir said is true, but that doesn't explain how my abilities are so strong when as far as I can remember, neither of my parents had these gifts. Neither did Ian. And, yes, I know he might not be my full-blooded brother," I said before he could remind me of that fact. "But if I am the descendant of Malec and one of his mistresses, that had to be several generations ago. How did I end up with so much eather?"

"Good question," he said after a moment. "Perhaps your ability to communicate with us like Nyktos did with the kiyou is because you were Ascended. All your mortal blood was replaced with Atlantian. That could've…I don't know, unlocked something in you."

"Like I'm a door?"

A wry grin formed. "A better analogy would be a chest unlocking inside you, but even before Casteel Ascended you, your gifts were far stronger than they should be, so—" Kieran's head snapped around to the lattice doors, his eyes narrowing on the darkness beyond it.

I set the pillow aside. "What is it?"

"I don't know. I thought I heard something." He rose, his attention focused on the closed doors as he reached inside his boot and pulled out a narrow, long-bladed dagger. "Stay here."

Stay here? My nose wrinkled as I scrambled across the bed, nearly taking out the platter of leftover meat and cheese. Snatching the wolven dagger, I slipped it free from its sheath as I stood.

"And, of course, you are not staying put," Kieran muttered, opening one of the double doors.

"Nope." I followed behind him.

Kieran stepped out onto the veranda. The only light came from what spilled over from the bedchamber and a small lantern above a wide outdoor daybed. His gaze focused on the wall several yards away as he walked forward, brushing aside a sheer curtain.

He stiffened.

I scanned the trees and the wall beyond them, barely making out the heavy vines draped over the stone in the moonlight. "What?"

"Sage was patrolling this section of the wall. She's a wolven," he explained. "I don't see her at all."

A shout came from our left, near the stables. I twisted at the waist, stepping off the patio onto stone that was still warm from baking in the sun all day.

Kieran caught my arm. "Don't you dare."

I pulled against his hold, my gaze swinging up to him in surprise. I couldn't believe he was stopping me. "Something is happening. Casteel is—"

"Cas will be fine," he snapped, hauling me into the enclosed patio once more. "I know you can fight. You're a badass, Poppy. But not only will Casteel have my head if something happens to you, you are also our Queen."

I sucked in a sharp breath. "I am no one's Queen. I am just Poppy."

"Whether you claim the throne or not, you are still our *Liessa.*"

"So you expect me to hide, then? Is that what being a Queen means to the wolven?" I glared up at him, feeling the acidic burn of his anger, and the heavier press of his concern. It was a new experience to feel anything other than wry amusement from Kieran. "Then what kind of Queen would that make me?"

His jaw hardened. "The kind that stays alive."

"And the kind not worthy of those willing to defend her," I snapped, struggling to remind myself that his reluctance came from a place of worry. "Now let go of my arm."

"Or?"

I stopped considering all his possible good intentions. "Or I will make you."

Kieran's pale gaze burned brightly as he lowered his head so we were nearly eye-to-eye. "You are already worthy of those who protect you," he bit out. "Which is infuriating."

I tugged on my arm again. "I'm a little confused."

"If you weren't so brave, my life and Casteel's would be a hell of a lot easier," he muttered, releasing my arm. "Do not get yourself killed."

"How about you try not to get yourself killed, huh?" I retorted, and his brows furrowed as he stared at me. "By the way, you and I are going to discuss this later."

"Can't wait," Kieran muttered.

Another shout reached us before I could respond. I spun toward the sound. It was closer, quickly followed by a rumbling growl.

Without warning, lights flared across the wall, startling me. I stepped back, bumping into Kieran. His hand landed on my shoulder, steadying me as bright beams of lights cut through the trees and blossom-heavy bushes.

A shadow peeled away from a tree and stepped into a funnel of light. My entire body flashed cold. A pale, bare-chested man stood before us, his face hidden behind the familiar mask of a Descenter.

Alastir's parting words stung my skin. *You think this ends with me?* I had hoped it had, but the man across from us was proof that what Alastir had been involved in hadn't ended with his death.

"Hell," Kieran muttered under his breath as at least a dozen more drifted from behind trees and bushes in the courtyard.

"I'm guessing these aren't friendly Descenters?" I asked.

The Descenter closest to us unstrapped a dagger from his hip.

"I'm going to go with no," I answered my own question, my pulse kicking up as I stared at the blade. "And I'm also going to assume that they no longer have any intention of not outright killing me."

"That's not going to happen," Kieran promised.

"No. It won't." My grip tightened on the wolven dagger as I scanned them. From what I could tell, they all appeared to be male. They had to be part of the brotherhood Alastir had spoken of, but that couldn't mean that all Descenters were involved. Although, if any in Atlantia looked upon me as the Maiden, a tool of the Ascended, it would be them.

I allowed my senses to stretch out, and what came back to me was…cold emptiness. "I…I don't feel anything," I whispered, focusing on the one with the dark blade. Unnerved, I realized I still sensed nothing. "It's like with the Ascended."

"They are not Ascended," Kieran said, his nostrils flaring as he scented the air.

There was something…off about the men standing in the beams of light. Something that had nothing to do with my inability to read their emotions. Shivers broke out across my flesh as I stared at them. It was their skin. It appeared paper-thin and too pale as if not a drop of blood remained in their veins. My stomach squeezed tightly. "Are they…? They aren't Atlantians, are they? Or any other bloodline?"

"No," Kieran growled. "I have no idea what these *things* are."

Things?

I swallowed hard as instinct demanded that I put as much distance between myself and these things as I could. The Craven always provoked the same reaction, but I didn't run from them, and I wouldn't run now.

Kieran's chin dipped. "I have no idea what in the hell any of you are, but whatever you are planning, I strongly advise against it."

Movement along the wall caught my attention. Another masked man was crouched there, his skin carrying a pink undertone. He wasn't the shade of death. I reached out with my senses, tasting…something dry and oaky, like whiskey—almost nutty. Determination. The one on the wall was different. He was alive, for starters. My eyes narrowed on an ivory and gray-brown chain draped over his chest. Anger rushed through me like a swarm of hornets. If there had been any doubt about what they wanted, it was erased now. Those bindings would not touch my skin again.

"You have no idea what you guard, wolven," the masked male spoke, his deep voice muffled from behind the mask. "What you seek to protect."

"I know exactly who I protect," Kieran stated.

"You don't, but you will," the man replied. "We just want the Maiden."

"I am not the Maiden." I welcomed the burn of my rage. It smothered the ache of grief over the fact that others were of like mind with Alastir. I pushed it aside before the sadness could settle inside me.

"Would you rather be called the Blessed One? The Chosen?" he countered. "Or would you prefer to be addressed as the Harbinger? The Bringer of Death and Destruction?"

I stiffened. I had heard those titles before, but I'd forgotten. Jansen had called Nyktos something similar. The hum in my chest vibrated. "If you truly believe that is what I am, then you're a fool to stand there and threaten me."

"I am no fool." The man reached up, unhooking the chain from his shoulder. "You, the one foretold in the bones, should've never survived that night in Lockswood."

Tiny bumps raced across my skin as my entire body seized in shock. It had nothing to do with the so-called prophecy. *Lockswood.* I hadn't heard anyone speak the name of the small village in years. Not even Alastir had said it.

But it was clear that Alastir had shared what he had taken part in all those years ago with this man. "Who are you?"

"I am no one. I am everyone." He rose slowly. "And you will be the Queen of nothing. Kill her."

The things before us moved as one, rushing forward. The growl that came from Kieran's very mortal throat should've sent them running, but it didn't. Several surrounded us. Using a curse that would've turned Vikter's seasoned ears red, I dipped under the wide swing of an attacker. A stale floral scent hit the air as Kieran's arm swept out, dragging the sharpened edge of his blade through the throat of two of the things.

"Good gods," Kieran exclaimed as I popped up behind the things in Descenter masks and kicked out, slamming the heel of my foot into the back of a kneecap. The thing made no sound as his leg gave out. I twisted at the same instant, shoving my dagger into the chest of another. That stale scent increased as an oily, black substance sprayed out over my hand.

That was definitely not blood.

I gasped as I pulled the dagger free. The thing staggered and then broke apart—shattering into a fine dusting of dirt and black oil that gleamed purple in the light. The Royal Knights had done something similar upon being stabbed with bloodstone, but the knights' skin and bodies had cracked first. These things just exploded in a geyser of purple yuck that smelled like stale lilacs.

As the other creature started to regain his footing, I spun, wrapping my arm around his masked head. I jerked back and thrust the dagger into the weak spot at the base of his skull. I let go, jumping back before the thing erupted.

"What are these things?" I yelled, backing away from the oily stain the two had left behind.

"I have no idea." Kieran took out another as his lip curled in disgust. "Just kill them."

"Oh, well, I was thinking about keeping one." Cold, clammy fingers grazed my arm as I whirled around. "You know, as a—"

"If you say pet, I'm going to think you're more demented than Cas."

"I was going to say friend."

Kieran looked over at me, brows arched. "That's even worse."

I snapped forward, grabbing the edge of a mask. I yanked hard. Rope snapped. The mask slipped free—

"Oh, my gods!" I shrieked as I staggered back.

The thing didn't have a face.

Not really. There was no nose. No mouth. Just thin, black slits where eyes should've been. Everything else was smooth, thin, pale flesh.

I would never unsee this.

"Take it back! Here." I flung the bronze mask back at the thing. The metal bounced off its chest and hit the ground. It cocked its head to the side.

"What?" Kieran shifted toward me. "Holy shit, it's a—I think it's a Gyrm."

"A *what*?"

"Something that does not belong here."

"That's not helpful." I pointed at it with my dagger. "It has no face!"

"I can see that."

"How does it even breathe?"

"Now"—he grunted as one of the things jumped on his back. Bending, he flipped it over—"is not the time for questions, *Poppy*."

Good point, but still, how did it breathe with no mouth or nose?

The Gyrm thing came at me, and I forced myself past being creeped out. I needed to focus because the one who apparently had a mouth and could speak, knew about Lockswood. I would have to freak out about these things later. I met its attack, shoving my blade deep into the creature's chest. I wasn't as quick as before, and black liquid sprayed the front of Casteel's shirt.

Whirling around, I spotted the male on the wall. I stalked forward, ignoring the sharp stones under my bare feet.

Another Gyrm shot toward me, and I braced myself. He lifted his sword, but I struck first, jamming my dagger up under the edge of his mask. I jerked back as he fell, his body fracturing into nothing within seconds. I turned to see Kieran jerk his blade through the neck of another. Purple goo sprayed out as his gaze found mine.

"Your eyes," he uttered, dragging the back of his hand over his face. "They're glowing quite brightly."

They were?

The hum in my chest was a whisper in my blood as I turned back to the wall. The man was still there, and the energy building inside me felt like it had at the Chambers of Nyktos. My heart tripped over itself as another masked creature appeared in the bright light. I tightened my grip on the dagger, resisting the pull of that vibration. I didn't want to do that again. Not until I fully understood it and knew I could stop it.

A damp hand clamped around my arm. Letting all those early mornings and afternoons spent with Vikter take hold, I twisted inward and swept out with my leg. The Gyrm hadn't expected the move, or maybe I had simply moved faster than it could react to. I took his legs out from under him and then brought the dagger down, a direct hit to the chest. Springing to my feet, I turned to find another.

The creature lifted his sword, and I snapped forward, blocking its blow as I shoved the dagger deep into its chest. Yanking the blade free, I darted to the side as it fell apart. I lifted my gaze to the tall form that had replaced the one who'd now fallen—

I drew back a step. Casteel's father stood there, his own cream-colored shirt splattered with purplish-red liquid. How many of these things were roaming about? Surprise radiated from him in waves as his wide gaze swept over me, and that was about when I remembered that I wore nothing but Casteel's shirt—his now-ruined shirt.

Gods.

Could I not meet Casteel's family under normal circumstances?

"Hello," I murmured, straightening.

King Valyn's brows lifted, and then he lurched toward me, his sword rising. My heart stuttered as panic seized me. I froze in horrified disbelief. He was going to—

Grabbing my arm as he thrust out with his sword, he yanked me to the side. Air punched out of my lungs as I stumbled, finding a masked Gyrm impaled on the King's sword.

"T-thank you," I stuttered as the thing shattered.

Amber eyes flashed to mine. "Did you think my strike was meant for you?" he asked.

"I..." Good gods, I really had.

Casteel prowled out of the shadows then, drops of the purplish blood dotting the striking lines and angles of his face. He wasn't alone. Several guards flanked him. His gaze zeroed in on me, searching for signs of any new injury or wound. There were none, but if there had been, I knew he would've found them. He stalked right to me, his sword slick with whatever existed in those creatures lowered at his side. His star-bright eyes snagged mine and held. My breath caught as he curled his arm around my waist, drawing me hard against his chest. The heat of his body quickly seeped through our shirts. It was like no one else was in the garden as he lowered his mouth to mine—surely not his father, because the kiss was fierce and deep, making my heart race.

When Casteel's mouth left mine, my breath came out in short pants. He pressed his forehead against mine, holding me tightly. His voice was rich and smoky as he asked, "How many of them did you kill?"

"A few," I answered, curling my free hand into the front of his shirt.

His lips brushed my ear. "A few?"

"A decent amount," I amended.

Casteel kissed my cheek. "That's my girl."

A throat cleared, and I suspected it had come from Casteel's father. My cheeks heated and then caught fire as Kieran said, "You have no one to blame but yourself for Cas's inability to remember that he isn't alone."

King Valyn chuckled roughly. "Good point."

Casteel kissed the center of my forehead. "You okay?"

"Yes. You?"

"Always."

I smiled faintly at that, but it quickly faded. I wiggled free of Casteel's embrace and turned to the wall, scanning the entire length of it.

Dammit, the wall was empty.

"He's gone," I bit out.

"Who?" Casteel asked.

Frustration burned through me. "There was a man with these things. He knew about Lockswood."

"Lockswood?" Casteel's father echoed.

"It's near Niel Valley in Solis." I twisted toward Casteel. He'd gone unnaturally still, and I could sense his throbbing anger. "The inn my parents stopped at for the night—the one the Craven attacked—was in the village of Lockswood. Where my parents died. Alastir obviously told this Descenter about that night."

"That was no Descenter," King Valyn remarked, and both Casteel and I turned to him. He bent, picking up one of the masks that had fallen from the creature. "And those things wearing these masks? Gods, not only do they not belong here, the masks they were wearing have nothing to do with the Descenters."

Confused, I looked at Casteel. He frowned as he glanced down at what his father held. "The Descenters wore those masks in Solis to hide their identities," he stated.

"But they weren't the first," his father stated. "The Unseen were."

Chapter 19

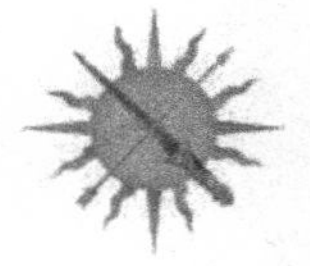

"The Unseen?" I repeated.

"You're fucking kidding me, right?" Casteel demanded. "I was under the impression that the Unseen were either disbanded or had died out long before the War of Two Kings."

"That's what we all thought," King Valyn said. "Until lately."

"What exactly are the Unseen?" I asked.

The King glanced over his shoulder, and it was then that I noticed a woman. She was tall and muscular, her skin a light brown with golden undertones, her hair jet-black in the floodlight, pulled back in a tight, singular braid much neater than the one I usually wore. She was dressed in white like the Crown Guards, but golden scrollwork crossed the center of her chest. She held a sword in one hand, and the hilt of another was visible from her back. A silent command passed between her and the King, and then she nodded. Turning, she sheathed her sword and then let out a low whistle.

Several guards drifted out of the trees' shadows, and from the spaces the floodlights didn't penetrate.

"Search the premises," she ordered. "Make sure no one is here that does not belong."

I watched the guards hurry off, splitting up and heading in different directions, passing Jasper as he prowled toward us in his wolven form. Whoever this woman was, she held a place of command. Within moments, she was the only guard remaining.

The King turned to us—to me. "Would you like to head inside?" he offered. "It appears you were caught unprepared for battle and visitors."

Mindful of the dagger I held, I crossed my arms over my chest. "Putting on more appropriate clothing won't change the fact that you've already seen me in nothing more than a shirt," I said, surprising myself. I wasn't at all used to so much exposed skin, but then again, I'd just faced down a bunch of creatures who had no face. My legs being visible didn't even make the top fifty things I was currently concerned about. "I'm fine if you are. I would like to hear about whatever the Unseen are."

Amusement radiated from both King Valyn and his son. A familiar half-grin appeared on the King's face, and damn if there wasn't a hint of dimples. "I am fine," he said, handing the mask to the female guard. He sheathed his sword. "This is Hisa Fa'Mar. She is one of my most trusted. Commander of the Crown Guard."

The woman drifted forward, and I knew the moment I saw her that she was an Atlantian, possibly even an elemental. She bowed slightly at the waist, first at the Prince and then to me.

"I do not believe we have met before," Casteel said.

"No. We have not." Her smile was quick as golden eyes shifted to me. "You are quite skilled at combat. I saw you briefly," she added. "You have been trained?"

"I have. I wasn't supposed to be, but I didn't want to be helpless like I was the night a group of Craven attacked an inn my parents and I were at," I explained, when the crisp, fresh taste of curiosity reached me, conscious that King Valyn was listening intently. "One of my personal guards trained me so I could defend myself. He did it in secret at great risk to his career and possibly even his life, but Vikter was brave like that."

"Was?" King Valyn asked quietly.

The knot of heartache lodged in my throat like it always did when I thought of Vikter. "He was killed by the Descenters in the Rite attack. A lot of people died that night—innocent people."

"I'm sorry to hear that." Empathy flowed from him. "And to know that those who support Atlantia were the cause."

"Thank you," I murmured.

He stared at me for a long moment and then said, "The Unseen were an ancient brotherhood that originated at least a thousand years ago or so, after several generations of Atlantians were born, and other bloodlines took root. Roughly around the time the…" He drew in a deep breath. "Around the time the deities began to interact more with the mortals who lived in lands far from Atlantia's original borders. The ancients began fearing that the Atlantians and the other bloodlines were not entirely supportive of their decisions regarding mortals."

"And what kind of decisions were they making?" I asked, half-afraid of the answer based on what I'd already been told.

"The deities wanted to bring all the lands, the seas, and the islands together under one kingdom," King Valyn said. That didn't sound all that bad—for a brief moment. "It didn't matter that some of those lands already had rulers. They believed they could improve the lives of others as they did with the lands just beyond the Skotos Mountains that had already been occupied by mortals. Many Atlantians and other bloodlines didn't agree with them, believing it was best to keep focus and energy on Atlantian lives. The deities feared there would be an uprising, so they created the Unseen to serve as a…network of spies and soldiers, designed to crush any type of rebellion before it started. That was done by keeping the Unseen members' identities hidden. That way, they could move undetected among the people of Atlantia like spies. And when it came time for them to be seen and heard, they wore masks carved to resemble the wolven."

"In a way, they were mimicking what Nyktos had done," Kieran added as he wiped the back of his hand across his face. "It was obviously a fairly lame attempt, but whatever."

"How did the wolven feel about that?" I wondered aloud.

"I don't think it bothered them at the time," Casteel's father answered as Jasper prowled around us, constantly searching for signs of intruders. "Both the Unseen and the wolven had the same goals then: protect the deities. Or at least that was what the wolven believed."

Had the same goals *then*. It was obvious that those goals had splintered and changed.

"The Unseen were nothing like the wolven. They were more like a group of extremists," Casteel said. "They would attack anyone they believed was a threat to the deities, even if the person was simply raising questions or disagreed with what the deities wanted."

"That reminds me of the Ascended." My bare toes curled against the stone. "You couldn't question anything. If you did, you were seen as a Descenter, and that didn't end well for you. But if the Unseen were designed to protect the deities, then why would they come after me?"

"Because that was how they started. It wasn't how they ended." His gaze briefly met mine. "The Unseen swore an oath to the Crown and to the kingdom but not the heads those crowns sat upon.

Eventually, they turned on the deities. What caused it is still unclear, but they began to believe that some of the deities' choices regarding the mortals were no longer in the best interests of Atlantia."

Immediately, I thought of Alastir and Jansen. That was what both had claimed. That what they'd done was in the best interest of their kingdom.

"So they were disbanded," King Valyn continued. "Or at least that's what everyone has believed for at least a thousand years."

"You really believe Alastir was involved with them?" Casteel asked with a sneer. "A group of men who feel emasculated by the fact that the actual Guardians of Atlantia are all female, so they desperately cling to their special, secret group?"

"Alastir said he belonged to a brotherhood of sorts," I reminded Casteel. "He called himself a Protector of Atlantia."

"I had no knowledge of Alastir's involvement in any of this before the attack at the Chambers," his father said. "But after seeing those masks at the ruins, I began to wonder if it was the Unseen. If they have returned, and if they are behind much more."

I thought of what Kieran had shared with me before. Casteel was thinking along the same lines. "You're talking about the destroyed crops, fires, and vandalism?"

His father's lips were pressed into a hard line as he nodded.

"We don't think they've been active this entire time," Hisa said. "Or if they have been practicing, they weren't acting upon any perceived notions of oaths. That's changed, however. And it changed before news of the Prince's…" She trailed off, her brow pinching as she appeared to search for how to phrase what she wanted to say next. "It changed before news of our Prince's entanglement with you."

Entanglement sounded vastly less awkward than capture, so I had to give it to her. She knew how to be tactful.

"How can you be sure they are responsible for the vandalism?" Kieran asked.

"The mask." Hisa lifted the one she still held. "We found one of them at the site of a fire that destroyed several homes near the water. We weren't sure it was connected—there is still no hard evidence. But with this?" She looked around the now-empty courtyard. "And them wearing these masks at the ruins? They have to be connected."

"I think it is," I said. "It reminds me of the Ascended. They used fear, half-truths, and outright lies to control the people of Solis. They would often create hysteria like the Duke did after the attack on the

Rise. Remember?" I glanced at Casteel, who nodded. "Placing the blame of the Craven attack on the Descenters when, in reality, they had been the ones to create those monsters. But by doing so, by creating unrest and suspicion among the people, it made them easier to control. Because the people were too busy pointing fingers at one another rather than joining together and looking toward the Ascended as the root of their woes." I tucked a strand of my hair back, unused to having so many listening—so many looking at me.

"I was just thinking that if the Unseen were behind the destruction of crops and vandalism, they could be doing it to create more unrest—to get people angry or suspicious, just in time for them to provide someone to blame for what is happening."

"That someone being you?" the King asked.

Tension crept into my muscles. "It appears that way."

King Valyn inclined his head as he studied me. "Unrest and unease are two very powerful destabilizers of any society. No matter how great one is, they can be taken apart piece by piece from the inside, often weakening the foundation to the point of collapse before anyone realizes what is happening."

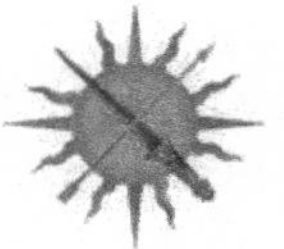

"I have a lot of questions," I announced the moment Casteel ushered me back into our room, and King Valyn left.

"Not a single person in the entirety of either kingdom would be surprised by that," Kieran stated as he closed the veranda doors behind him. "Not even remotely."

Casteel's lips twitched as my glare swung toward the wolven. "I'm sorry, but maybe faceless people is a common occurrence in Atlantia, but it's not something I'm used to."

"That is not a common occurrence," Casteel replied as he tried to lead me to the bathing chamber.

"And you and I need to have a quick chat," I continued, stopping. Casteel sighed heavily.

"We do?" Kieran raised his brows.

"Oh, yes, we need to talk about what you tried to do out there."

Casteel's head turned slowly toward the wolven. "What did you try to do?"

Kieran folded his arms across his chest. "I tried to get her to stay inside and remain safe."

A loud, rough laugh burst out of Casteel. "And how did that go?"

"As painless as you can imagine," Kieran retorted dryly. "I was only pointing out that you would prefer that she remain unharmed, and that who she is to you, to me, and—"

"Casteel has never once asked that I not engage," I cut him off. "And he is my *husband*."

Casteel dropped his head to mine as a deep, rumbling sound radiated from his chest. "Husband." He pressed his lips to my temple. "I love hearing you say that." He lifted his head to look at Kieran. "My wife can defend herself. You know that."

"I do."

My eyes narrowed. "Seems like you forgot."

"I didn't." Kieran's jaw flexed as his stare held Casteel's. "Things are different now, and you know that."

"No, they are not." I pulled free of Casteel. "I am not a Queen, but like I said before, even if I were, I would never be the kind that expects others to risk their lives while I sit back and do nothing. That will never be me, and I seriously doubt Casteel would be that kind of King."

"I wouldn't." Casteel came to stand behind me, folding his arms around my waist. "Not only can she defend herself," he repeated, "she needs to be able to defend herself. And that is why she *will* be allowed to do so, whether she is our Queen or our Princess."

My heart swelled so fast it was a wonder it didn't lift me right to the ceiling. Casteel…he just understood me. Understood my need to never be helpless.

"You're the only person I truly trust Poppy with. Only you," Casteel continued, and my breath halted a little in my chest. "I know your concern comes from a good place, and Poppy knows that, too."

My lips remained sealed.

Casteel squeezed me. "Don't you, Poppy?"

I swallowed a curse. "Yes, I do know that." And I did, but I was irritated and confused about those things that had been outside—bewildered and unsettled about everything the one on the wall had said. "I know it comes from a good place."

Kieran rubbed his jaw as his stare drifted to the terrace doors. "I know you're capable of defending yourself. Stopping you had nothing to do with that. But it's just that you're in danger here, and you shouldn't be. This is the one place you should be safe." He dropped his hand and faced me. "I know none of that means I should've told you to stand down. I'm sorry."

The sincerity in his apology was clear in his voice. It tasted of warm vanilla, but I could also taste a hint of something sour, just like I had with Casteel, which caused an ache in my chest. Neither of them was responsible for what had happened here. "It's okay," I said, looking up at him. "I will make sure it's safe for me. *We* will make sure of that."

Kieran nodded, smiling faintly. "Damn right, we will."

I grinned at that.

"Well, now that we cleared that up, I know you have a lot of questions," Casteel said, turning me toward the bathing chamber. "But let's get this stuff off you first." He paused. "And into something clean."

I glanced down at my hands, my nose wrinkling as I saw that they were spotted with purple. "Is it even blood?"

"I honestly can't say for sure." Casteel led me to the vanity in the bathing chamber and turned on the faucets. He grabbed a bottle and squirted some of that rich, pine-scented soap onto my hands. "Whatever it is, it smells weird."

I nodded as I rubbed my hands together. "It reminds me of stale lilacs."

His brows knitted as he grabbed a bar of soap. "You know, you're right." He turned, handing the soap to Kieran. In the mirror, I watched him strip off his ruined shirt and toss it aside as he turned on a faucet to the shower. One of the overhead showerheads came on. "The one you said was on the wall," Casteel said quietly, drawing my attention. "He spoke?"

I nodded as I rubbed the liquid soap up my forearms. "He wasn't like the others. He was either mortal or Atlantian."

"He wore a silver mask," Kieran said, the muscles along his back and shoulders tensing as he dipped his head under the spray as he scrubbed his face and his closely-cropped hair. "Like Jansen did at the ruins. He also had those damn bone bindings with him."

"What?" Casteel barked out.

"He did," I said, running my hands under the warm water.

"Those bones will never touch your skin again." Casteel's voice was full of smoke and blood, and eyes as cold as frozen amber met mine. "That, I can promise you."

"I promise myself that," I murmured, as a cold slice of unease pierced through me when I thought of the Unseen. "No one has spoken the name of that village in years."

Casteel's jaw clenched as he ran his palms up my forearms, washing off the soap. "I knew where the inn was located because I did some digging into your background before we met, but that wasn't readily available information." He scooped my hair back from my face as I reached for more of the soap. "We don't know how many people Alastir shared that knowledge with."

He held my hair as I quickly washed my face. When I was done, the scent of stale flowers no longer clung to my skin at least, and Kieran had turned off the water. "Thank you," I said as he handed me a towel.

"Alastir claimed there was another at the inn, correct?" Water dampened Kieran's throat and chest as his gaze met ours in the mirror. "Called him the Dark One?"

I backed away from the vanity, lowering the towel. "He did. Why?"

"Is it possible that Alastir simply shared that information with others?" Kieran answered. "Or is there the chance that he was speaking the truth? That another was there."

Anything was possible, but… "Alastir made it sound like this mystery figure led the Craven there." I watched Casteel strip off his ruined shirt. That strange, purplish blood streaked the upper part of his chest. He took the bar of soap from Kieran as I said, "Can these…Unseen control the Craven?"

Tension bracketed his mouth as he lathered the soap between his palms. "The Unseen were gone long before the first Craven was ever created—or as far as we know. Either way, the Craven can be herded in a direction, but they cannot be controlled beyond that." He looked back at Kieran. "If you want, you can grab one of my shirts."

Kieran nodded, making his way to the wardrobe just outside the bathing chamber as I placed my used towel in a hamper. "But I…"

"What?" Casteel dragged his soap-covered hands over his face and then through his hair.

It took me a moment to pull my thoughts together. "I was told that my parents left Carsodonia because they wanted a quieter life. But that was a lie. They discovered the truth, or they always knew what the Ascended were doing and decided they could no longer be a part of it,"

I said, hating to even speak those words. "He also claimed that my mother was this Handmaiden, trained to fight." I hurried over to the stool, grabbing a smaller towel like the one Kieran had used as Casteel dipped his head, washing his face, and then ran the water through his hair. "That could be true, or it could also be a lie. But what if Alastir spoke the truth? What if someone else was there and led the Craven to the inn?"

I handed Casteel the towel as I said, "I…I have these memories of that night," I said, glancing at Kieran. He'd donned a black tunic. "I know I heard Alastir's voice—I heard him talking to my father. But I…I've dreamt of someone in a dark cloak. Someone else could've been there, and Alastir didn't make it sound like it was someone who had anything to do with him. What if…what if that Craven attack had nothing to do with Alastir or the Unseen?"

"You're thinking the Ascended may have had something to do with it?" Kieran asked from the doorway. "But if they knew what you were, they would want you to stay alive."

"Agreed." Casteel dragged the towel over his chest and face. "Luring the Craven to the inn would've been too much of a risk. Those creatures cannot be controlled by anyone."

"And all that hinges on whether or not the Ascended knew what I was before my parents left—before I was attacked. I still don't know that for sure," I said. "Alastir never confirmed that."

Casteel rubbed the towel through his hair. "But if they did know, that would mean that the Ascended—the Blood Crown—knew that one of your parents was a descendant of Atlantia."

"And that leaves us with the question of why they weren't used in the same fashion as all the others descended from Atlantia," I murmured, sighing. One possible answer or question just led to another. It made my head hurt.

And my heart, too.

"Before those things showed up tonight, you asked how it was possible for your abilities to be this strong—how they were this strong even before Cas Ascended you." Kieran drew my gaze to him. "One of your parents had to be a full-blooded Atlantian."

"But how is that possible if I'm descended from Malec? His offspring with a mistress would've been mortal. And if my mother was a Handmaiden, it couldn't have been her, right?" I looked at Casteel.

"I would think not," he answered, tossing the towel into the hamper. "None I saw were, but that doesn't mean it isn't possible—

possibly implausible, but not impossible."

"And I look like my mother," I told them. "Except for my eyes."

"Your father?" Kieran asked, even though I was sure we'd had this conversation before.

"He was from Carsodonia, just like my mother was," I answered.

"I know you don't like to hear this," Kieran started, and I stiffened, knowing where he was going with this, "but that's all assuming that your parents were your birth parents. Or—" he quickly added when I opened my mouth. "Or what you remember, what you were told about who your parents were, simply wasn't the truth."

Chapter 20

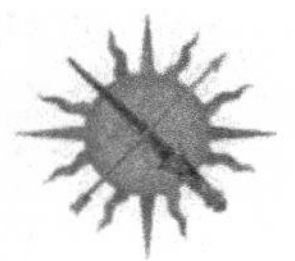

"He's right," Casteel said softly, his gaze searching mine. "I don't know why Alastir would've lied about your mother being a Handmaiden. If he was telling the truth, your mother was never a Lady in Wait, destined to Ascend. That could also mean your father wasn't a merchant's son." He paused. "It could also mean that only one—or neither of them—was your parent by blood."

And if neither of them was? Then Ian…he may not be like me at all if he Ascended. He may be like any other vampry.

Leaning against the cold tile, I tipped my head back. I started to respond and then stopped as my toes curled against the floor. "I was young. My memories of before that night are spotty at best. I just know what I was told about them, and although Ian was older, it wouldn't be like he knew any differently." I shook my head, overwhelmed. "But I look like my mother, so maybe my father was an Atlantian, and my mother a mortal descendant of Malec and his mistress. Would that explain my abilities being so strong?"

"That would be one hell of a coincidence," Kieran noted, and he was right.

Casteel and Kieran exchanged a look. "I don't know," Casteel answered. "That's a complicated bloodline to sort through, but that's also working off the assumption that you are related to Malec. You may not be. Alastir could be wrong, even if he truly believed that."

I wondered if his mother would know somehow.

Casteel's gaze met mine. "We'll figure this out."

Other than his mother, as unlikely as that may be, only one other person may know.

Queen Ileana.

Casteel turned to Kieran. "I think there's an old robe in there. Can you grab it for me?"

Kieran handed him a long piece of black clothing as he said, "There's something I need to do real quick. I'll be right back."

Watching me, Casteel nodded curtly as he hung the robe from a hook by the door. "We'll be here." He waited until Kieran disappeared. "Let's get you out of that shirt so I can burn it."

A wry grin tugged at my lips. "I guess this shirt isn't salvageable?"

"Unlikely." He came to me, curling his fingers around the hem. "You know the drill."

I did.

I lifted my arms. "I think you like taking my clothes off."

"I do." Casteel tugged the shirt up and over my head. Cool air washed over all the newly exposed skin. He dropped the tunic to the floor as he stared down at me, his lips parting just enough that I could see a hint of his fangs as his gaze swept over me in a slow, lingering perusal. Muscles tightened low in my stomach. He placed his hand on the side of my ribs and under my breast. The contact sent a sharp pulse through me. His other hand did the same on the other side of my body. "However, I do not like undressing you, only to cover you immediately."

I looked down, my toes curling even more against the tile floor at what I saw beyond the puckered, rosy-pink tips of my breasts. His golden-bronze skin was such a striking contrast to mine, and his hands were so large and strong.

"What Kieran asked of you tonight? Don't hold it against him. He cares for you. And his concern?" he said. "I have to fight my instincts when it comes to you rushing out there to battle everything and anything, too. It's not because I don't think you're capable. It's just that I fear losing you." He lowered his head, and his warm breath coasted over my chest and to the swell of a breast. "But your need to defend yourself is greater than my fear. That's the only reason I don't stop you. It will be the same for Kieran."

"I know—" I gasped as his mouth closed over my breast. My eyes widened as I stared down at the dark, damp curls of his hair. His tongue swirled over my nipple, eliciting another strangled sound from me. He looked up at me, eyes burning as he arched a brow, waiting for me to continue. "I…I won't hold it against Kieran."

A brief, pleased smile crossed his face, and then he caught the sensitive skin between the edges of his teeth and then his lips. "You know what helps me get over my fear?"

I shook my head.

"This." The pink tip of his tongue flicked over the throbbing, tightened skin. "This helps. So does your bravery, and you know what else? I get to reward you for your bravery."

My pulse had already been pounding, but now it thundered through me. "I…I get a reward?"

"You do, but I also get a reward for looking past my fear," he said, his thick lashes lifting once more. Gold churned restlessly in his eyes. "It's a good thing this reward will be mutually beneficial."

"It will be?"

He nodded, and then his mouth closed over my breast again. I felt the wet slide of his tongue and then the wicked scrape of his fangs. My breath caught at the forbidden sensation, and then he struck, sinking his sharp teeth into the flesh above my nipple. I cried out, threading my hands into his hair as my entire body jerked. The razor-sharp pain was intense, shooting through my entire body. There was a second where I wanted to pull away when the pleasure-pain was almost too much, but it was gone in a heartbeat. He sealed his lips over the tingling skin of my breast and sucked deep, drawing the sensitive peak into his mouth, taking my blood into himself.

A fire erupted inside me, heating my blood and every part of my body. My head spun, and I shuddered as his growl rumbled against my skin. I held onto his hair, shamelessly holding him there as damp heat flooded my entire being. An aching spike of pleasure darted through me. My hips twitched as he tugged at my skin.

"Cas," I breathed.

He made that sound again, that sensual, rough sound, and then he moved, pressing my back against the wall, the hard line of his thigh between my legs. I gasped at the contact of the cold tile against my bare skin and the feel of his breeches-clad thigh against my core. He dropped a hand to my hip, and as he pulled harder on my breast, he tugged my hip down and forward, rocking me against his leg. Tense, tight waves of pleasure rippled out from between my thighs and from my breasts as I stood on tiptoe, my weight mostly supported by him. The drag and pull of his mouth on my breast seemed to be connected to the intense throb at my core. My hips moved against his thigh. There was nothing slow about it. I rocked hard against him, driven by the dual sensations of him feeding from my breast and the soft friction of his leg against my swollen, tightened flesh. Tension curled and whirled, spinning tighter and faster. He feasted, and I became frenzied, tugging at his hair, sinking my nails into his skin. My legs clamped down on his thigh, and all the tension inside me erupted, lashing through me in the most delicious and stunning way. I shook, calling out his name as my release rolled through me.

I was still trembling, twitching when his tongue soothed over his bite, and he straightened, holding me tightly against his chest. His mouth closed over mine in a slow, languid, iron-rich, and musky kiss. The taste of my blood on his lips sent another wave of pleasure through me.

"You," he drawled, his voice thick. "You really liked that reward."

My forehead rested against his as I struggled to gain control of my breathing. "A little."

"A little?" His laugh was like smoke. "You came so hard, I could feel you through my pants."

"Oh, my gods." I choked on a laugh. "That is so…"

"What?" His lips dragged across mine. "Inappropriate?"

"*Yes.*"

"But it's true." He kissed me as he eased me to my feet. "You can stand? Or have I blown your mind and your muscles?"

"Your ego is ridiculous. I can stand." Barely. "And in case you're wondering, I would like more of those rewards, please and thank you."

A devastating smile appeared, and those two dimples winked to life. "Although I love hearing the word *please* spill from your lips, you never have to say it."

I grinned as he pulled away. While he turned to grab the robe, I glanced down. My cheeks heated at the sight of the two reddish-pink puncture wounds and the swollen skin around them. Goodness. The mark he left behind was indecent.

I loved it.

He held the robe for me, and I turned, slipping my arms through the sleeves. The material was unbelievably soft and yet lightweight enough that I didn't think I'd grow heated. The length was a little long, completely hiding my toes, but it smelled like him—like pine and spice.

He stepped in front of me, quickly buttoning the two sides and then tightening the sash. "This looks far better on you than it ever did on me."

"I can't even picture you wearing this." I looked at the long, flowing sleeves and flapped my arms.

"I'd rather be naked." He winked when I raised a brow. "I'd rather you were naked, too."

"Shocker," I murmured.

While Casteel went to the wardrobe to pull out fresh clothing, I quickly wrangled my hair into a braid. The pleasant haze of his wicked reward sadly faded by the time I sat on the couch in the living area and Kieran returned, a large book in his hands and his father with him.

Jasper's piercing gaze found mine, and he started to lower. I stiffened, but he seemed to stop himself before bowing. The curse he muttered garnered a small grin from me. "You are well?" he asked.

I nodded. "I am. You?"

"Peachy," he muttered, dropping into one of the chairs. "Where is—?"

"Right here." Casteel sauntered into the room as he dragged a hand over his head, brushing the still-damp strands off his face. He went to a credenza against the wall. "Drink?" he offered. Only Jasper nodded. Casteel poured two glasses as Kieran sat beside me. "So, the Unseen…?"

"Yeah," Jasper growled. "That was the first I'd heard there might be a chance they were involved, which irritates the piss out of me. No offense to your father," he tacked on halfheartedly. "But that is something he should have clued me in on, even if it had nothing to do with her."

"Agreed," Casteel muttered as he glanced over at Kieran. "Does this book you brought with you hold the answers to why my father kept that so quiet?"

"Unfortunately, no." Kieran cracked the thick book open. "Those things that were outside? I figured you had a lot of questions about them."

"Who wouldn't?" Casteel responded, handing Jasper a glass. "If that was the first time they saw one of them?"

"Exactly." I watched Kieran flip through the pages.

"Well, I figured it was best that I grab this," Kieran said. "It's an old textbook, centering around the history of Atlantia—the gods and their children."

"Oh." I leaned over, my interest more than piqued, but the moment I saw one of the pages, I sighed. "It's in a different language."

"It's in old Atlantian—the Primal language of the gods." Casteel sat on the arm of the settee. "I can barely read that now."

Jasper snorted. "Not surprised to hear that."

One side of Casteel's lips tipped up as he took a drink. "I'm hoping this book you kept for some reason tells us exactly how the Gyrms were here, in our realm, and why they were after Poppy."

Our realm? Why did that sound familiar to me?

"He kept all of his old schoolbooks," Jasper explained. "Well, his mother did. They're in one of the rooms in the back."

I had yet to meet Kirha and really hoped I got to soon. I wanted to thank her for the clothing. "Is she okay?"

"She's fine." Jasper smiled, and the rough lines of his face softened. "Slept through the whole damn thing."

My brows rose. "Really?"

He nodded. "She's always been a heavy sleeper, but with the babe on the way, she could sleep through the gods waking."

"Here it is," Kieran announced, lowering the book to his knees as he looked over at Casteel. "Did you see them without the mask?"

"That I did," he drawled. "At first, I thought my vision had gone out on me, and then I heard my father say something like, 'What the fuck?' and I knew it wasn't just me."

I got momentarily distracted by picturing the tall and ominous figure that was his father saying that. Kieran tapped on the page, and I looked down, my stomach hollowing as I saw an ink sketch of one of the creatures we'd seen outside. It was extremely realistic—the head, the thin slits for eyes, and then nothing but smooth skin. Then again, there wasn't much for this artist to capture beyond a male body's general, well-muscled shape.

"How do they breathe?" I asked again because that seemed like a fairly important question.

Casteel's lips twitched as Kieran's eyes closed. "If it was a Gyrm?" Jasper spoke, rising from the chair to look down at the drawing. "They don't need to breathe because they are not alive."

Confusion drew my brows together. "How is that possible? How can something walk around and interact with people and not be alive?"

"One could ask the same question about the Craven," Casteel said. "They react to those around them. They have mouths, and their bodies go through the motions of breathing. They hunger." He lowered his glass to his knee. "But do you think they live? Truly?"

I didn't need to think about that. "No," I said, looking back at the sketch. "Not once they turn. They're no longer alive. Nothing remains that makes them mortal, at least."

And that was sad because all of them had been mortal at one time—people who had lives and were someone's daughter or son, friend or lover—before the Ascended ripped everything away from them.

My hands curled into the soft material of the robe. The number of lives the Ascended had destroyed was utterly incalculable. They could've done that to Ian and to Tawny, devastating everything that made them who they were.

The Ascended had to be stopped.

"The difference here is that the Gyrms were never alive in the first place," Kieran explained, running a finger along sentences that looked like nothing more than scribbles on an ivory page to me. "They were created from the soil of the gods and from the eather—from magic—and used to do the bidding of the one who summoned them. Created them. They have no thoughts, no will beyond why they were summoned."

I blinked once and then twice. "They were created from dirt and magic? Seriously?"

Jasper nodded as he started pacing. "I know it sounds like something made up to scare children—"

"Like the *lamaea*?" I asked.

He stopped and looked at me, glass halfway to his mouth as Casteel coughed out a quiet laugh. His pale eyes shot to the Prince. "I don't even need to ask which one of you told her about that. Out of the things you could've shared with her, you chose that?"

"It was a passing comment in a wider, much more important conversation that she has somehow latched on to and never forgotten." Casteel took a drink. "Not my fault."

"How could I ever forget about a creature that has fins for legs and tails for arms?" I wondered out loud.

"The *lamaea* were never real. It was just a thing really twisted parents made up." Kieran shot his father a pointed look. "But the Gyrms were, and they were usually summoned to serve as soldiers or guards—protectors of sacred places. It says here that they can be killed with any puncture wound. Apparently, it shatters the magic holding them together, so one doesn't have to aim for the heart or the head."

"Good to know," I murmured.

Kieran continued scanning the page. "Once they've served their purpose, whatever holds the soil and magic used to conjure them—usually a vase or cloth of some sort—is destroyed by fire. Once nothing but ash remains, they disappear."

"They're just conjured into existence to do whatever someone needs, and then…*poof*, they're gone?" My nose wrinkled. "That seems wrong and sad. And, yes, I get that they're technically not alive. It still doesn't feel right."

"It's not," Casteel agreed, a muscle working in his jaw. "It's why that kind of magic is forbidden by Atlantians and mortals alike in this realm."

There was that word again. It tugged at the memories of my time in the crypts with Jansen. "When you say 'realm,' what are you talking about?"

"The Lands of the Gods, that realm," Casteel answered as his hand wandered to my upper back and slid under my braid. "It's called Iliseeum."

"Iliseeum?" My breath caught as what Jansen had said finally came back to me. "Jansen mentioned a place called Iliseeum—and a place called the Shadowlands. I thought he was making stuff up." I glanced around the room. "Both are real?"

"They are." Casteel reached over, straightening the collar on the robe. "Iliseeum is the Lands of the Gods. The Shadowlands are where the Abyss is located and how the Vale is accessed."

"He also…he also said that Nyktos was known as…the Asher? He said he was called the One who is Blessed, the Bringer of Death, and the Guardian of Souls," I said, frowning. "And he said that Nyktos ruled over the Land of the Dead and that he was the Primal God of Common Men and Endings."

"Technically, Nyktos is those things," Jasper answered. "As the God of Life and Death, he rules both the Shadowlands and the realms of the living, but he is not the God of Common Men. And I never heard of him being referred to as the Asher or the One who is Blessed." He looked over at me, brimming with curiosity. "Although, weren't you called that? Blessed?"

I nodded.

"Interesting," he murmured. "I think Jansen told some truths and then made things up to sound more knowledgeable and important, just like the Unseen were often known to do."

My brow rose. Jansen did have an inflated sense of self-worth. "But how have I never heard of Iliseeum until now?"

"I bet there's a lot you haven't heard of." Jasper took a drink. "Did you know that Nyktos has a Consort?"

"He does?" I stared at the older wolven.

Kieran looked at me. "How do you think he had offspring?"

"First off, he could have multiple special people in his life," I pointed out. "But most importantly, he's the God of Life. Couldn't he just *create* his children?"

"He probably could." Casteel tugged lightly on my braid. "But he didn't create his children like that. He and his Consort did it the old-fashioned way."

"What is her name?" I asked. "And why is this the first time I'm even hearing about her?"

"No one knows her name," he answered. "She has only ever been known as the Consort."

"Well, that sounds…sexist," I muttered.

"Can't disagree with that," Casteel replied. "And to answer your other question, no one knows why the Ascended decided to erase some of these bigger details from their history."

"Maybe they didn't know," Jasper pointed out. "Only the oldest of the Ascended, those first turned, would've known the real history of our lands and peoples. And most, if not all of them, were killed before the war." Queen Eloana had ordered that—the execution of all vamprys once they became too numerous and too blood-hungry to control. "It was the later ones, those turned by the Atlantians and who traveled farther east that fought back so strongly."

"Godly magic can be found here, right? Like the eather in the bones of the deities," I said, and a hot pulse of anger radiated from Casteel.

"Not just in the bones of a deity, but also in the blood of a god." Jasper stopped pacing, coming to stand near the terrace doors of the living area. He took a deep drink, finishing off the whiskey. "Of course, it's easier to visit a crypt and remove the bones of the deities than to attempt to get one's hands on the blood of a god."

I shuddered at the thought of how disruptive that act would be to the dead. It wasn't something I had really considered while in the crypts.

Casteel's fingers continued moving along the back of my neck, working out the knots in the tight muscles there. "What I don't understand, though, is how anyone would get soil from Iliseeum. How would they know where it was located and how to get there?" Casteel stated. "Especially when only those with godly blood can travel between the realms."

"That's not exactly true," Jasper said.

Casteel's and Kieran's heads jerked in his direction. "Come again?" his son said.

"Iliseeum doesn't exist in a realm that only the gods can enter," he said, setting his empty glass on the table by the doors. "And a few do know where Iliseeum is." He looked at the Prince. "What do you think exists beyond the Mountains of Nyktos?"

Casteel's hand stilled on my neck. "There's nothing but mountains and land unsuitable for building or supporting life."

"For thousands of years, that was repeated over and over until it simply became something known and never questioned. But it was a lie to sway those who were too curious," Jasper responded. "Iliseeum lies beyond the Mountains of Nyktos."

Chapter 21

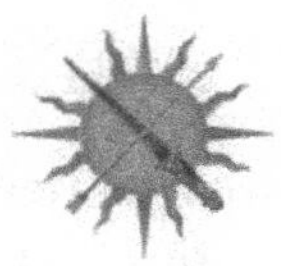

Casteel's hand slipped from my neck as shock rippled through him. For a moment, I thought he might drop his glass of whiskey. "Are you for real?"

Kieran closed the thick book. "He can't be."

"It's true," Jasper confirmed.

The room was thick with tangy confusion. "How is it possible that no one figured that out?" I asked. "That no one attempted to cross the mountain or take to the sea in a ship?"

"More than just words have hidden Iliseeum's location." Jasper tilted forward, resting his arms on his bent knees. "Iliseeum is well-protected by land and sea."

"The eather—like the mist in the Skotos Mountains?" I guessed.

Jasper nodded. "As both my son and Cas know, the sea is too rough to travel on once any ship nears Iliseeum's coast."

"It's not just rough waters." Casteel's hand returned to the base of my neck. His fingers moved in a slow, steady slide as he said, "Sea stacks around the coast can tear a ship apart in minutes if one gets close enough to even see through the mist that obscures the coastline. Just like the mist from the Skotos protects the shores of Atlantia from both the Stroud Sea and Seas of Saion."

"We tried once—Casteel and I—when we were younger. We tried to take a ship as close to the coast as we could, to see if any part of the land was habitable," Kieran said. "We damn near drowned in the process."

"That's because you're both idiots," Jasper replied, and I blinked.

Casteel took a healthy drink of his whiskey. "Can't really argue with that."

"Wait." I frowned. "The Stroud Sea reaches the coasts of Atlantia? I thought the Skotos mountain range extended into the water and—"

"Traveled to the ends of the realm?" Casteel finished for me. "No. That's why the mist is so thick. It makes it appear as if the mountains are hidden behind it, but that's only so no one attempts to travel through it."

I gave a little shake of my head and refocused. "What about traveling through the mountains?"

"The Mountains of Nyktos are impossible to cross by Atlantian or mortal. The mist there? That kind of magic is deadly." Jasper's wintry gaze flicked between his son and the Prince before returning to me. "You would possibly be the only one who could cross the mountains."

Casteel glanced down at me, and his lips twisted in a faint smile. "You are just special."

I ignored that. "So, it causes hallucinations like the mist in the Skotos?"

"No." Jasper laughed, shaking his head. "The magic in these mountains suffocates anyone who it doesn't recognize as a god."

My mouth dropped open. "Oh. Okay. That's a lot." I twisted the sash of the robe around my hand. "But I'm a descendant of a god. I'm not a god. Those two things are vastly different."

Jasper raised his brows. "I don't think we know exactly what you are, and that is a hill I am willing to crash and burn on."

I closed my mouth because he was right.

"Then how did anyone cross over to Iliseeum to obtain the soil?" Kieran veered us back on track.

"A few know how to bypass the mountains." Jasper leaned back, resting an ankle on a knee.

We all waited for him to continue.

And waited.

I stared at him. "You going to tell us how?"

Jasper eyed each of us for a long moment before settling on Casteel. "Your father and your mother have killed to keep Iliseeum's location hidden." His voice was as quiet and cold as falling snow. "So have I."

Casteel's head cocked slightly to the side as his hand stilled along the back of my neck. "And I'm inclined to kill to discover the truth."

A chill swept down my back as Jasper grinned at the Prince, either unbothered by the threat or not aware of what that too-flat tone signaled. Bloody things usually followed his usage of that tone. "I don't think there needs to be any sort of killing," I ventured.

"That's rich coming from you," Kieran commented.

My head snapped in his direction. "I'm trying to deescalate the situation."

Kieran snorted.

"What's rich is that you've all killed to keep the Lands of the Gods secret," Casteel said. "And yet, the Unseen obviously discovered how to travel to Iliseeum. That is, unless there is a bucket of Iliseeum soil I'm unaware of."

"I don't believe there's a bucket of soil lying around," Jasper advised, eyes glimmering as amusement filtered from him to me. "Most wouldn't even have the knowledge of how to use such magic—only the oldest of our kind. And I imagine the Unseen would have known when they were more prevalent. I'm guessing they must've kept records of such things."

"Other than you and my parents, I assume Alastir knew?" Casteel drew his hand down my spine. Jasper nodded. "Who else has that knowledge?"

"Very few who are still alive." Jasper drew a finger over the stubble covering his chin. "I believe Hisa knows. As does Dominik—another of the commanders."

"I remember him. He's one of the oldest elementals," Casteel told me, lifting his glass as his gaze flicked back to Jasper. "Is he in Saion's Cove?"

"He's in Evaemon, as far as I know. Or just outside of the capital," he explained. "I imagine Wilhelmina knows—" Casteel choked on his drink as my mouth dropped open. Jasper's eyes narrowed. "You okay over there?"

"Wait," Casteel coughed again, eyes watering. "Wait a godsdamn second. Wilhelmina? Who is Wilhelmina?"

Jasper frowned, clearly confused. "You never met Willa?"

Oh, my gods. There was no way.

"What is her last name?" Casteel asked.

Please don't say Colyns. Please don't say Colyns, I repeated over and over as Kieran's father stared at Casteel as if he'd lost his mind. "I think it's Colyns."

My jaw was now in my lap. Godsdamnit, Casteel's theory had been right. Miss Willa was an Atlantian. I couldn't believe it—wait. Did that mean she was here, in Atlantia?

Oh, wow, if so, I had…so many questions for her.

"Last I heard, she was in Evaemon, or nearby in Aegea," Jasper answered.

Casteel slowly turned to me, his lips curving into a smile wide enough that his dimples had already appeared. "I can't say I've met her personally, but Poppy might—"

"I have never met her!" I all but shouted as I twisted toward him, punching his thigh.

"Ouch." Leaning away from me, he rubbed his leg as he laughed.

"What is going on with you two?" Jasper asked.

"Apparently, there's a Willa who wrote a sex diary of some sort," Kieran said with a sigh. "It's Poppy's favorite book or something."

I turned to the wolven as Casteel made a choking sound again. "It is not my favorite book."

"Nothing to be ashamed of if it is," he said with an indifferent shrug, but I tasted his sugary amusement.

"A sex book?" Jasper repeated. I was going to wither up and die right here.

Kieran nodded. "Cas was just saying he thought Willa might be an Atlantian because of a—"

"Okay," I cut in before Kieran or Casteel could go into that further. "None of that is really important right now."

"Oh, I disagree." Casteel stretched over, placing his drink on a small table by the settee. "Is Willa an elemental? Something else? And you had no idea that Miss Willa Colyns is a popular biographer of a certain aspect of her life in Solis?"

Gods, I hated all of them right now. I hated myself even more for wanting to know the answers.

"She's of the changeling bloodline, I believe," Jasper answered, his forehead creasing. "Though sometimes I wonder about that. But no, I didn't know that. Explains a lot, though, now that I think about it."

Kieran's lip curled, but Casteel looked even more interested in what that meant. I held up my hand and said, "Why would she know about Iliseeum?"

"Because Willa is old," Jasper said. "She is the oldest changeling that I know of. She is one of Atlantia's Elders."

"How old is *oldest*?" I prodded.

He raised a brow. "Pushing two thousand years old."

"W-what?" I stuttered, thinking of Cillian Da'Lahon, who *The History of The War of Two Kings and the Kingdom of Solis* claimed saw over two thousand and seven hundred years before his death. "Is that common? To live that long?"

Jasper nodded. "In times of peace and prosperity, yes."

"And, yes, a wolven can live that long, too," Kieran chimed in before I could ask.

My mind was…well, it couldn't even comprehend living that long. How did one not grow tired of everything after that many years? I thought about the subject matter in Willa's book, and figured that probably explained a lot.

I shook my head, hoping it would clear. "Can she do what Jansen could? Take on others' images?"

Jasper shook his head. "No. Jansen was…gods, he had to be the last of the changelings that could do that."

As terrible as it sounded, I felt relief. "Who are the Elders of Atlantia?"

"They are a type of Council who helps to rule alongside the King and Queen when needed," Casteel explained, tugging gently on my braid. "Normally, they are never called on unless a major decision needs to be made. The last time they came together was when Malik was taken, I believe." A sharp swirl of anguish pulsed through him. "I wasn't in Evaemon when that happened. I was here."

He'd been here recovering, trying to piece himself back together. My chest ached for him.

"You better believe they've been called now," Jasper's tone was dry, and my stomach tumbled. "You just might get to ask Willa about the book you were talking about."

Oh, gods.

While I did have a lot of questions for her, I wasn't sure I could hold a conversation because I would be thinking about wicked kisses and foursomes.

But I really didn't need to focus on that. Because if a Council had been convened, I knew why—my arrival and everything that had happened.

"As much as I want to hear more about Miss Willa, we have more pressing things to deal with," Casteel stated, surprising me. "How does one enter Iliseeum if they cannot do so by land or sea?"

Jasper didn't answer for a long moment. "You know, you would've learned about it when you took the throne." His gaze touched mine for a brief moment, and I knew what he meant. That Casteel would've learned when *I* took the Crown. "You don't travel over or through the

Mountains of Nyktos. You travel *under* them."

An icy wave of surprise scuttled through Casteel. "The tunnel system?"

Jasper nodded. "The one from Evaemon leads into Iliseeum if—and that's a big *if*—you know how to navigate it."

"Damn," Kieran muttered, scrubbing a hand over his head. "All those years messing around in those tunnels and we could've ended up in the damn Lands of the Gods."

It struck me as a very odd coincidence that Casteel and Kieran had spent their childhood attempting to map out those tunnels and caverns, and this whole time, they could've taken Cas right to this Lands of the Gods. Had he or his brother been drawn to them? If so, had it been some sort of divine intervention?

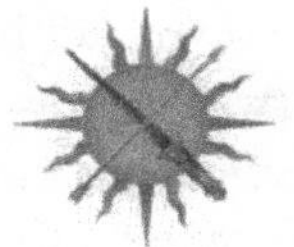

I stayed way too long in the shower the following morning, testing the limits of exactly how long the water would remain hot.

Feeling the warm water pelting my skin and washing the soapy suds away was truly too much of a magical feeling to rush. The shower felt like it cleansed more than soap, as if it were rinsing away the stickiness of confusion that prevented me from looking past the shock of everything I had discovered and learned. That could've been my imagination, but by the time I forced myself to turn off the faucets, I felt like I could face what today held.

What awaited me in Atlantia.

And maybe it wasn't just the shower, but all the hours of deep sleep I'd ended up stacking up over the last day or so. It could've been last night, when Jasper had left, and Kieran wanted to discuss the tunnel systems. Casteel had taken the seat Kieran had occupied, rearranging me so I was all but cradled against him as they spoke. I was amazed by how much they recalled regarding the tunnels, still able to remember the differences in certain underground rock formations and the scents that changed depending on which tunnel they were in. I'd only briefly been in the one that led to the beautiful, lilac-filled cavern in Spessa's End, and the other that rested below New Haven, to view the names of those who had died at the hands of the Ascended.

So many more names needed to be added to that wall.

But as they talked, I couldn't help but wonder if some kind of prophecy did exist. If hardly anyone knew that Iliseeum rested beyond the mountains, then was it possible for there to be a prophecy that no one knew about? Or was that comparing apples to oranges? I didn't know.

Before Kieran left, I'd asked about the wolven named Sage—the one who was supposed to be patrolling the wall. She had been found on the other side of the wall, having been struck from behind. The injury and the subsequent fall from the wall would've either seriously injured or killed a mortal, but according to Kieran, who had checked in on the wolven before returning to our rooms with the book, she would recover in a day or so. Hearing that and learning that there had been no casualties among the wolven or anyone else who had engaged in the battle with the Gyrms had filled me with a lot of relief. That could've aided in me not feeling so overwhelmed.

It also could've been the sweet kiss that Casteel had given me after I woke this morning and before he left to shower. Or how his eyes were pools of warm gold when he looked upon me. Before he left the bed, he'd told me that his father's visit had been borne of worry. That he hadn't liked how things had ended between them in the Temple of Saion. I was glad to hear that they'd cleared the air between them—at least a little bit before those creatures showed. I also shared with him what I had confirmed with Kieran about being able to communicate with him. Casteel…well, he took in that newest development like he had everything else. He was curious, awed, and completely unbothered by it, and that helped me be somewhat unfazed by the fact that I had done something that only Nyktos could.

Either way, it could've been one or all of those things that'd made me feel prepared for everything Casteel and I had to discuss and figure out.

I found the clothing Vonetta had given me in Spessa's End hanging among several other brightly colored garments that her mother had given Casteel for me to wear. The only visible white I saw in the entire wardrobe were two slips. A smile tugged at my lips, and I didn't stop it—didn't even have to think about concealing it like I had when I'd been the Maiden.

Casteel.

This was all him. He'd made sure there was little white to be found in my options.

Gods, I loved that man.

I started to reach for a tunic with frilly sleeves, but a stunning, cobalt blue, buttery-soft muslin drew my attention. The gown was simple, reminding me of what the Ladies in Solis called a day dress but was far better suited for the warmer climate of Saion's Cove. The bodice was layered and cinched, erasing the need for a slip. The near-sheer gown was gathered at the waist and the hips by a sky-blue chain girdle, and the material bunched at the shoulders. It was sleeveless.

My gaze shifted back to the tunics and the other dresses that featured wide, elbow-length sleeves that offered a bit of coverage. I hesitated. Normally, I preferred to wear breeches or the lighter leggings and something that hid the scars on my arms, but the color was beautiful. I'd never worn anything like it. I'd never been allowed.

And I didn't need to hide my scars.

I grabbed an undergarment and pulled the gown off the hanger. I changed into the dress, relieved that it fit well enough. I found a brush and worked out the tangles in my hair. There wasn't much I could do with it outside of braiding it, so I left it down and then found a pair of sandals in the wardrobe that tied at the ankles. I hitched up the folds of the skirt, sheathing the dagger to my thigh.

Casteel was waiting for me in the sitting room, standing before one of the open lattice doors with his arms loosely folded across his chest. A warm breeze flowed into the room and was spun about by the dual ceiling fans. He started to turn as I walked under the archway. "There is some fruit. And, of course, your favorite, cheese…" He trailed off, his lips parting until the tips of his fangs became visible.

"What?" I stopped, glancing down at myself while smoothing an imaginary wrinkle from the skirt. "Do I look foolish? The bodice is a bit tight." I fiddled with the cowl neckline. "Or is it outdated? I figure this must be one of Vonetta's older gowns since she's taller than I am, but the length is almost a perfect fit for—"

"Unworthy."

"Excuse me?"

"I am unworthy of you," he stated roughly. "You are a dream."

My fingers fell away from the neckline as I looked over at him.

Casteel's arms had fallen to his sides as his gaze swept over me. His chest rose sharply. "Your hair. That gown." His eyes heated. "You are so beautiful, Poppy."

"Thank you." I felt my throat warm as my heart swelled. "And you *are* worthy."

He smiled as he cleared his throat. "Please tell me you're wearing your dagger."

Fighting a grin, I lifted the right side of the skirt to my thigh.

Casteel groaned. "Gods, you're perfect."

"And you are demented," I said. "Worthy, *but* demented."

"I'll take that."

I laughed. "Did I hear you mention cheese?"

"You did." He extended an arm to the table. "Help yourself."

I did exactly that, seating myself at the table and immediately reaching for chunks of yumminess.

"What would you like to drink?" he asked, joining me. "There's water, wine, and whiskey—the three Ws of life."

I arched a brow. "Wine."

He smirked as he poured the faint pink liquid and then fixed himself a glass of whiskey. I tentatively tasted the wine, pleased to find that it tasted like strawberries. "What do you think about the whole Iliseeum thing?" I asked since we hadn't really talked about that.

"Honestly?" He let out a low laugh. "I really don't know. I grew up believing that Iliseeum existed in a realm beside ours but not part of ours. Just like the Vale and the Abyss. And to think my parents always knew? Alastir? Jasper?" Casteel shook his head. "But then you really didn't know Iliseeum was real at all. It had to be more of a shock to you."

"It was," I admitted, squinting. "But there is still so much I don't know. I'm kind of in a constant state of surprise, but it's amazing to think that at one time, when the gods were awake, they were right there. I wonder how often they interacted with Atlantians and mortals."

"Not often from what I've been taught. But that too may not be exactly true." He ate a piece of cheese. "The crazy thing, Poppy? Is that Malik, Kieran, and I must have gotten close to Iliseeum at some point. We traveled those tunnels heading east. We always ended up stopping, though, at some point."

"Was there ever a reason for you to stop?"

His brows lifted. "At the time, no, but looking back now? Yes. We always started to feel weird, like we needed to go back home. It was something that none of us could explain. We chalked it up to us being afraid of getting caught for being gone too long. But now I think we were being warned away by the magic that guards Iliseeum. It made sure we never got too close."

"I suppose that's a good thing. Who knows what would've

happened if you all had made it to Iliseeum?"

He grinned. "Well, if our presence woke the gods, I'm sure we would've won them over with our stunning personalities."

I laughed. "I was thinking last night that your interest in the tunnels almost feels like divine intervention."

"It does feel that way, doesn't it?"

I nodded. A few moments passed, and I peeked over at him. He was quiet as he picked through the fruit, handing me a plump grape and then a dewy slice of melon. "I know we have to talk. You don't have to delay it any longer."

"We do." Leaning back in his chair, he dragged his teeth over his lower lip as he continued rooting through the fruit. "Something I didn't go into a lot of detail on this morning was something my father shared with me last night. Every member of the Guards of the Crown, from here to Evaemon, are being checked for possible involvement or knowledge of what the others were doing."

"Have others been discovered?" I asked.

"None believed to have been directly involved so far," he said as I took the strawberry he offered, and he picked up a piece of roasted meat for himself. "But there have been a few who suspected that something was going on with those working with Alastir. And some expressed concern about your presence."

"Well that isn't that surprising, is it?"

"Not really, but it leaves me wondering exactly how much they truly knew of what the others planned." His fingers folded around his glass. "My father even believes that the ones involved with the attack may have spoken openly with those who weren't, basically infecting others with their nonsense."

Alastir's and the other's beliefs and words truly were like an infection, but was it one that could be cured? As we ate, I thought of those who had first attacked me. "The people who were at the Chambers?" I said, and Casteel stilled for a moment before picking up a napkin and wiping his fingers clean. "Once they realized what I was, one of them asked the gods to forgive them."

A cruel, tight smile formed over the rim of his glass as he took a drink. "They won't."

"I…I hope they do."

His brows lifted. "That is too kind of you, Poppy."

"They didn't kill me—"

"They wanted to."

"Thanks for the unnecessary reminder."

"It sounds like a very necessary reminder," he replied flatly.

I resisted the urge to throw the piece of cheese I held. "Just because I hope they're not wasting away in the Abyss for all eternity doesn't mean I'm okay with what they tried to do to me."

"Well, I do."

I ignored that. "They were obviously very misinformed."

"So?"

"What I'm trying to say is they weren't like Alastir or Jansen or those who wore the Descenter masks. Their minds were made up. Nothing was going to change that." I tossed the piece of cheese onto the platter. "But the ones at the Chambers? The others who may have known something was going on, or have concerns? Whatever opinions they've formed can be changed. It's not a…fatal infection. They're not the mindless Gyrms or the Craven.""

"Sounds pretty fatal to me," he commented.

I took a shallow breath. "If the people in the Chambers had changed their minds before it was too late and they had survived, I wouldn't want to see them killed now."

Casteel opened his mouth as he lowered his glass to the cream-hued linen covering the table.

"I know what you're going to say. You would see them killed. I would see them given a second chance if they were misled. And *after*," I stressed, "they were punished appropriately. It's obvious they were taught or…indoctrinated into this way of thinking. And those who may have known what the others were involved in? The ones who have concerns now? That can be changed."

He eyed me as he dragged his fingers over the rim of his glass. "You really believe that?"

"Yes. I do. People can't be killed simply because they have concerns. That is something the Ascended would do," I told him. "And if we believe that people aren't able to change the way they think and what they believe or how they behave, then what is the point of giving the Ascended a chance to change their ways? What would be the point of hoping for change in anything?"

"Touché," he murmured, tipping his glass to me.

"You don't believe that people are capable of change?" I asked.

"I do," he admitted. "I just don't care if they are if they're the people who've harmed you."

"Oh." I picked up another small cube of cheese. That wasn't

exactly surprising to hear. I moved onto something we really hadn't discussed, not even when it was brought up with Jasper. "Well, you need to start caring. I don't want people killed because they don't trust me or like me. I don't want to be a part of that."

"You're asking me to care about those who potentially had knowledge of those who have not only betrayed me but also betrayed you," he countered quietly. "I believe the technical term would be that they committed treason against me and you."

"Yes, but having beliefs or concerns that have not been acted upon does not immediately equal treason. If there is evidence that they were aware and did nothing, they should, at the very least, have a trial. Or is Atlantia no different than Solis when it comes to due process?"

"Atlantia believes in due process, but there are exceptions. Namely—you guessed it—treason."

"Still, if people have been misled, they should be given the chance to redeem themselves, Cas."

His eyes flared an intense shade of amber. "You're not playing fair, Princess, knowing how much I love hearing you call me that."

The corners of my lips curved up just the faintest bit.

He tsked softly. "Already wrapping me around your finger."

I fought the smile. "I'll only wrap you around my finger if you agree with me."

Casteel laughed at that. "I agree," he stated. "*But*…my condition is that I agree to hear them speak—to state their case. They're going to have to be really convincing if they have any hope of surviving."

My shout of victory died a little before it reached my lips. "I don't like your condition."

"Too bad."

I narrowed my eyes.

"Sorry," he demurred, not even sounding remotely apologetic. "What I meant to say is that we're compromising between our two wants. I'm meeting you halfway here. I am giving them a chance."

I wasn't sure what chance he was giving, but this was a…compromise. It was also a definite improvement. "Okay. Then I will meet you in the middle."

"You should since you're practically getting what you wanted," he remarked with a grin.

I kind of was, but I wasn't confident that many would be able to convince him.

Casteel was quiet for a long moment. "And I am serious about giving people a second chance. To allow them to prove that they will not be a concern to *us*. But if they act upon their feelings, or I suspect they will, I cannot promise I won't intercede in a non-violent manner."

"As long as your suspicion is rooted in evidence and not emotion, I can agree with that."

His lips twisted into a half-smile. "Look at us, agreeing on who to kill and who not to."

I shook my head. "Which is a conversation I truly never expected to take part in."

"But you're so good at it," Casteel murmured.

I snorted as I toyed with the stem of my glass. "Well, hopefully, it won't come to that."

"I hope the same."

"What about Alastir's or Jansen's family?"

"Jansen didn't have any family still alive, and Alastir's living members have been contacted or are in the process of being notified of his involvement," he said. "I don't believe we will have any problems with them, especially when they learn what happened to Beckett."

A sharp slice in my chest accompanied the mention of the young wolven's name. Then I thought of Alastir's great-niece. "What about Gianna? Since he hoped you'd marry her, do you think she could also be involved in this?"

"To be honest, I can't answer that for sure. I haven't seen Gianna in years. When I knew her, she was strong-willed and kind of did her own thing. But she would be a virtual stranger to me now," he explained. "She isn't here, by the way."

"Hmm?" I murmured, attempting to appear disinterested in that little piece of knowledge.

Casteel smiled at me, and the dimple winked into existence. Apparently, I hadn't been that convincing. "I asked Kirha when I saw her this morning. Gianna's in Evaemon."

I was a little relieved, but also strangely disappointed. I wanted to see her. I didn't even know why.

"There's something else we need to talk about before we inevitably meet with my parents." Casteel finished off his glass, and having a feeling of where this was going, I tensed. "We need to discuss your claim to the throne."

It felt like the floor rolled under my chair as I swallowed. A ball of uncertainty rested heavily in my stomach.

Casteel set his empty glass down and leaned back in his chair as he studied me. "You have the blood of the gods in you, Poppy. How much and what that truly means is unknown, but what is clear is that the kingdom is yours. Alastir knew it. My mother recognized it. And despite what my father said about her reacting with emotion, he realizes what it means. The bonds with the wolven breaking and shifting to you is further confirmation. The Atlantians you saw on the street when we entered Saion's Cove? Many who saw what the wolven did were confused, but word of what you are has already begun to spread. It will reach the capital before too long, especially if the Elders have been contacted."

"Do you…do you know what has been said about the trees of Aios? I'm sure it was noticed."

"It was. From what my father said, the people see it as a sign of great change."

"Not something bad?"

"No. Most do not see it as such." His eyes never left mine. "But some aren't as positive. As I'm sure you already realize, some Atlantians will be resistant to what this signals, only because they do not know you," he quickly added. "Only because they fear change and differences. They will see you as an outsider."

"And the Maiden," I pointed out.

The line of his jaw hardened. "If so, that is a misconception I will quickly rectify."

I lifted my chin. "As will I."

Casteel's smile brimmed with approval. "We will *both* rectify that quickly," he amended. "But most will see you for who you are. Which is the next Queen of Atlantia."

The breath I took went nowhere.

His steady gaze met and held mine. "Just like I see you for who you are. My Queen."

Shock flooded my senses. That was only the second time he'd called me that, and I realized then that since his mother had taken off her crown, he'd only called me Princess a handful of times. "But you don't want to be King," I exclaimed.

"This isn't about what I want."

"How can it not be? If I'm the Queen, you are the King—something you don't want to be," I reminded him.

"It was something I never believed I would need to be," he said, and so quietly, every part of my being focused on him. "It was something I *needed* to believe because it always felt like if I accepted my future, I was also accepting Malik's fate. That he was lost to us." He drew his fingers over the curve of his jaw as his gaze shifted to his empty glass. "But at some point, I began to realize the truth. I just didn't want to accept it."

My heart skipped a beat. "You…you don't believe he still lives?"

"No, I believe he does. I still believe we will free him," he stated, his brows lowering. "But I know—gods, I've known for longer than I care to admit to myself, that he won't be in the…right frame of mind to take the throne. The gods know I wasn't exactly all there when I was freed."

An ache pierced me once more. Kieran had already accepted that, too, and a part of me was relieved to know that Casteel understood the reality of what he'd face upon freeing his brother. It would still hurt, but not nearly as fiercely. "But you found yourself."

"Unfortunately, Atlantia doesn't have the luxury of waiting for him to do the same. My parents have already sat on the throne for too long," he told me. A King and Queen could only rule for four hundred years. And as he said, his parents were far past that. "There has been pushback, Poppy. It's a combination of fear of what the future holds if we can't sustain our population, and the general unease that comes with any two people ruling for too long."

"You told me there had been no challenges to the throne."

"And you also know I didn't want to tell you the truth because I didn't want to freak you out," he reminded me. "And you appear to be seconds away from—"

"Throwing a plate of cheese at you? Yes, I am seconds away from doing just that."

"Don't do that." Amusement crept into his expression, irritating me further. "You'll be upset when you don't have any more cheese to eat."

"It will be your fault," I snapped, and a dimple appeared in his right cheek. "Stop smiling. You should've told me. Just like you should've told me about the damage that was done to the crops and the vandalism."

"I only learned of the worst of it when I spoke with my father last night." His amusement faded. "I wanted to hear it from him before I shared." He tilted his head. "There haven't been any official challenges, Poppy, but pushback will eventually become that, with or without your arrival."

"My arrival has nothing—"

"Do not continue denying what you are. You're smarter and stronger than that," he interrupted, and I snapped my mouth shut. "You do not have the luxury of doing so. Neither do I, and neither does the kingdom. Your arrival changes everything."

I sat back, weighed down by the truth of his words. After I left the shower, I'd told myself that I was ready to discuss all of this—to face it all. Right now, I was proving that to be a lie. I was also proving childish. My unexpected heritage, what Casteel had done to save me, and its implications, wouldn't go away simply because I had a hard time acknowledging them. I had to face this.

A kernel of panic took root in my chest where that strange energy hummed quietly. I stared at the fruit and cheese. "When we free your brother, he won't need the extra pressure of being expected to take the throne. It wouldn't be right to thrust that upon him."

"No," Casteel agreed solemnly. "It would not."

But what if Malik *did* want what he'd grown up believing was his birthright once he did find himself? I wasn't sure the question even mattered at the moment. The bridge hadn't even been built to cross yet. I swallowed the heavy feeling in my throat. It made sense why Casteel had refused the throne. I could see what that signified to him. "So you want to be King now?"

He didn't answer for a long moment. "This would have happened eventually, even if you weren't a descendant of the gods. Malik wouldn't be ready to lead, and we would have had to make a choice. At the end of the day, I want what is best for Atlantia," he said, and I remembered then how Kieran had described him as a young boy. How many would've mistaken him for the heir and not his brother. I heard it then, the seriousness in his tone. I'd heard it moments earlier when he'd called me out on my denials. "But I also want what is best for you."

My gaze lifted to him.

"We know what we both need to do. I need to free my brother. You need to see Ian. The Queen and King of Solis must be stopped," he told me. "But after that? If you want to claim the Crown, I will support you. I will be right beside you. Together, we will learn to rule Atlantia," he said, and my stomach dipped. "If not, just tell me what you want to do, where you want to go. I will be right beside you."

"Where I want to go?" I asked, confused.

"If you decide you do not want to take the throne, we cannot stay here."

Chapter 22

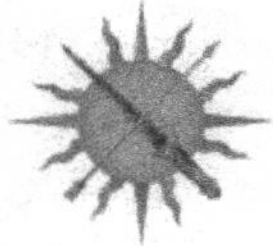

"Why not?" I pitched forward again.

"Because you usurp the throne, Poppy. No other Queen could rule with you in Atlantia. The wolven will treat you as the Queen even if you do not sit on that throne. Some Atlantians will treat you the same. Others would follow who wears the crown, whether that is my mother or someone else. It would create a division, one we haven't seen since the deities themselves ruled. I can't do that to Atlantia," he said.

"I don't want that to happen." My heart started thumping heavily as I gripped the edge of the table. "But this is your home."

"You told me that *I* was your home. That works both ways," he reminded me. "You are mine. What matters is that we're together and happy."

His words warmed me, but he would be leaving because I chose not to take the Crown. I pressed against the back of the chair, suddenly understanding what he was saying. "If I wasn't a descendant of a god, and Malik wasn't ready to rule, what would you have done if I said I didn't want to rule?"

"Then we wouldn't," he answered. There had been no hesitation.

"But then what happens to the Crown? Do your parents continue to rule?"

"They would until the Crown was challenged."

"And what happens if the Crown is challenged?"

"Several things, Poppy. None that you need to worry about—"

"Actually, I think I do." I sensed his concern then, heavy and thick. "You're holding back because you don't want me to worry."

"You shouldn't read my emotions," he countered. "It's rude."

"Casteel," I growled. "We are talking about the potential of you and me becoming King and Queen, and I cannot be Queen when my husband hides things from me because he's afraid I'll be overwhelmed.

"I wouldn't say I was hiding things—" He closed his mouth when he saw the look on my face.

"You know what that says to me? That you don't think I can handle being Queen," I told him.

"That's not at all what I'm saying." He leaned forward, placing his hands on the table. "It's not my intention to keep you in the dark. Some of what I didn't share was because I didn't have all the information, and I—" He shoved a hand through his hair. "I'm not used to sharing these kinds of things with anyone but Kieran. And I know that's not an excuse. I'm not saying that it is. To be honest, you've handled everything thrown your way better than most people would. It's not that I truly fear you'll freak out. It's just that I don't want you to be overwhelmed. But you're right. If taking the Crown is something you choose, I can't hold things back.

Sensing his contrition, I nodded.

He shifted back in his seat. "If we didn't take the throne, my parents could concede, but they would only do that if they felt the one who'd issued the challenge was fit to rule—and they could only do *that* if one challenged the throne at a time. If there's more than one, then the Elders weigh in. There could be trials where the challengers would have to prove themselves."

"Like the heartmate trials?" I asked.

"I imagine. I don't know for sure. It has never…gotten to that point before."

Another wave of disbelief swept through me. "And you'd be willing to walk away? To possibly let what has never happened before occur?"

"Yes," he said, again without even a moment of hesitation. "I do not want to be party to forcing you into yet another role you did not ask for nor desire. I will *not* replace the veil you loathed with a crown you hate. If you do not want to take the Crown, I will support you," he swore, and the intensity in his words captured me. The irrevocable oath he was making. "And if you decide you want to take what is yours, claim the throne, I will set this entire kingdom on fire and watch it burn if that ensures that the crown sits on your head."

I jolted. "You love your people—"

"But I love *you* more." Flecks of gold burned brightly in his eyes, churning restlessly. "Do not underestimate what I would or would not do to ensure your happiness. I think you know this by now. There is nothing that I wouldn't do, Poppy. *Nothing*."

I did. Gods, he'd already done the unthinkable by Ascending me, but he'd been prepared for me to become a vampry. He would've fought anyone and everyone who came near him to keep me alive, even if I became a monster. I didn't doubt him now.

"This is about you, about what you're comfortable with and what you want," he continued. "No one is going to force this choice on you. It will be your call, and then we will deal with whatever may or may not happen. Together."

A soft tremble worked its way through me. I didn't doubt what he said. I didn't underestimate him. I was at a loss for what to say as I stared at him in silence, utterly overwhelmed. That kind of devotion? His promise? It was…it was life-altering.

And maybe the truth was that I wasn't worthy of him.

I rose and walked around the table to where he sat without really understanding what I was doing. He tilted his head back, watching me silently. I didn't let myself think about what I was doing or if it was normal or acceptable. I just did what I wanted, what felt right to me. My senses were open to him, and I felt a rush of warmth and sweetness as I sat in his lap. His arms immediately wound around me, and he held me tightly as I wiggled as close to him as I could get, tucking my head under his chin.

I closed my eyes. "I hope this chair doesn't collapse on us."

Casteel chuckled as he dragged a hand over my hair. "I'll break your fall if it does."

"Stop being sweet."

"I was just pointing out that I would, indeed, break your fall if the chair broke as it would be me who hit the floor first," he said, brushing my hair back from the side of my face. "And you're the one being sweet right now." His arms tightened around me and then relaxed only slightly. "I like it."

"I like you," I murmured, pressing my fingers into his chest. "You know what it means to me, having that choice. That freedom." Emotion swelled in my chest and burned its way up my throat. "It means everything to me."

He slid his hand around to my cheek, tilting my head back.

Dipping his head, he kissed me softly. "I know."

"You are worthy of me, Cas. I need you to know that."

"With you in my arms, I feel worthy," he said, pressing his lips against mine once more. "I do."

"I want you to feel worthy of me when I'm not in your arms." I placed my fingers against his cheeks. "Why would you think you're not? After all you've done for me?"

He was quiet, and I could feel the sourness of shame as thick lashes lifted. "What about all I've done *to* you? I know you've accepted these things, but that doesn't change that I lied to you. That because of those lies, you were hurt. Because of what I did, people died—people you loved."

My heart ached. "Neither of us can change the past, Cas, but because you lied, I saw the truth of the Ascended. People were hurt—Loren, Dafina." I drew in a shaky breath. "Vikter. But how many lives have you saved? Countless, I'm sure. You saved mine in more ways than we probably even know."

A small smile appeared and then faded, and I sensed it was about more than just what had happened to me. His shame and guilt ran so much deeper than that.

"Talk to me," I whispered.

"I am."

"I mean, *really* talk to me." I smoothed my fingers along his cheeks. "What makes you think you're unworthy of me?"

His throat worked on a swallow. "Are you reading my emotions?"

"No." I sighed when he arched a brow. "Kind of."

He chuckled, the sound hoarse. "I don't know, Princess. There are things that…come into my head sometimes. Things that lived in my head when I was caged by the Ascended. I don't know how to put them into words, but even if I did, neither of us need to deal with that right now."

"I disagree," I said empathetically. "We do."

One side of his lips tipped up. "We have a lot on our plates. You have a lot on yours. I'm not going to add to that. I don't need to," he added when I opened my mouth. "I'm okay, Poppy. Trust me when I say that."

"Cas—"

He kissed me, capturing my lips in a deep, drugging sort of kiss. "I'm okay, Princess. I swear."

Sensing I would get nowhere with him right now, I nodded, then curled my hands around his wrists as he tucked my head back under his chin. This wouldn't be the last time we talked about this, I would make sure of that. We sat there in silence for several minutes as I thought about everything from the time he was held prisoner to the decisions I had to make. My natural inclination was to turn down any claim to the Crown immediately. It was the only sensible reaction. I had no idea how to be a Queen of anything, not even a pile of ashes. And while Casteel might not have been raised from birth to take the throne, he had been raised a Prince. I'd seen him with his people and already knew he would make a wonderful King. But me? I was raised as the Maiden, and very little of that upbringing would be of any use. I had no desire to govern people, determine what they could and couldn't do, and assume that kind of responsibility. Where was the freedom in that? The freedom to live my life as I saw fit? I had no hunger for power, no great ambition…

But I said nothing as I sat there, enjoying the simple feel of Casteel's hand stroking my hair. I would've enjoyed his touch even more if I hadn't realized there was an entirely different way to look at this. I had no idea how to rule, but I could learn. I would have Casteel at my side, and who would be a better teacher? Governing people did not necessarily equate to controlling them. It could mean protecting them, just as I knew Casteel would—like I knew his parents had done to the best of their ability. How they may or may not feel about me didn't change the fact that they cared for their people. That they were nothing like the Royals of Solis. That kind of responsibility was frightening, but it could also be an honor. I had no thirst for power, but maybe that was the key to being a good leader? I wasn't sure. But I knew I had great ambitions. I wanted to free the people of Solis from the tyranny of the Ascended, and what could be more ambitious than that? But how could I achieve that when I refused to bear the burden of a Crown? Who knew what kind of influence Casteel and I would be able to wield regarding Solis if we were forced to abandon Atlantia, leaving it to be ruled by someone who could have very different intentions when it came to Solis and the Ascended? Someone who may never see Ian as anything but a vampry. And maybe that was all that Ian was now. Possibly even Tawny. I didn't know, but what if my brother was different? What if other Ascended could change like Casteel had said a few had? What would happen if someone took the throne and declared war against them? I didn't know, but freedom was the choice. It was in the way I chose to live my life. And what kind of freedom would there be if I was the reason Casteel had to leave his people? His family?

That kind of knowledge carried with it a different type of cage, didn't it? Just like fear was another prison, and I was…

"I'm afraid," I admitted quietly as I stared at the sun-drenched ivy beyond the open terrace door. "I'm afraid of saying yes."

Casteel's hand stilled on my back. "Why?"

"I don't know how to be a Queen. I know I can learn, but do the people of Atlantia have the patience for that? The luxury of waiting for me to gain the same kind of experience as you? And we don't even know what I am. Has Atlantia ever had a Queen that was possibly neither mortal nor Atlantian nor deity? You don't have to answer that. I already know it's a no. And what if I'm a terrible Queen?" I asked. "What if I fail at that?"

"First and foremost, you won't be a terrible Queen, Poppy."

"You have to say that," I said, rolling my eyes. "Because you're my husband, and because you're afraid I'll stab you if you say otherwise."

"Fear is not remotely what I feel when I think you might stab me."

My nose scrunched as I shook my head. "That is twisted."

"Perhaps," he noted. "But back to what you said. How do I know you wouldn't make a terrible Queen? It's the choices you've made time and time again. Like when you sought to help those who were cursed by the Craven, risking the gods know what kind of punishment to ease their passing. That is just one example of your compassion, and that is something any ruler needs. When you went up on the Rise during the Craven attack? When you fought at Spessa's End, willing to take the same risks as those who'd taken an oath to protect the people? Those are only two examples that prove you have the courage and the willingness to do what you would ask of your people. That is something a King and a Queen should be willing to do. You have more experience than you realize. You proved that in the hunting cabin when you spoke of power and influence. You paid attention when you wore the veil. More than any of the Royals ever noticed."

He was right about that. I *had* watched and listened without being seen. From that, I had learned what not to do when in a leadership position, starting with the simplest of things.

Do not lie to your people.

Or kill them.

But the bar wasn't set very high in Solis. Atlantia was entirely different.

"And the fact that you are willing to give people who might've been involved in a plot to harm you a second chance proves you are far more suited to rule than I am."

I frowned, lifting my head. Our gazes met. "You would make a wonderful King, Cas. I've seen you with people. It's evident that they love you as much as you love them."

His eyes warmed. "But I am not nearly as generous, compassionate, or as forgiving as you—all qualities that can bring down a Crown if they're absent," he told me, pausing to brush a wisp of hair back from my face. "If we were to do this, I would need to learn some things—areas I would need *your* help with. But the fact that you are afraid of failing speaks volumes, Poppy. It should scare you. Hell, it terrifies me."

"It does?"

He nodded. "Do you think I don't fear failing the people? Making the wrong choices? Setting the entire kingdom on the wrong path? Because I do, and I know my parents still do, to this very day. My father would probably tell you that you would most likely do just that if you stopped being afraid of failing. He would also say that kind of fear keeps you brave and honest."

But couldn't that kind of fear make you indecisive, too? Stop you before you even traveled down a road? The fear of failing was powerful, just as fear of the unknown and uncharted destinies was. And I'd felt that kind of terror a hundred or so times in my life. When I went to the Red Pearl. When I smiled at the Duke, knowing what would come from doing so. When I joined Casteel under the willow. I'd been scared then. I'd been terrified when I finally admitted to myself what I felt for Casteel, but I hadn't let fear stop me then. This was different, though. So much more important than forbidden kisses.

This was more important than us.

"What about your brother? Ian? How would that be affected?"

"The only thing that would change is that we would negotiate as the Queen and King instead of the Princess and Prince," he answered.

"I doubt that would be the only thing that changed," I said wryly. "We would come to the table with far more power and authority, I imagine."

"Well, yeah, that too." Casteel's arms tightened around me. "You don't have to decide today, Poppy," he said, much to my relief. "You have time."

Some of the knots loosened in my stomach. "But not a lot."

"No," he confirmed as his gaze swept over my face. "I would've liked for you to see a little of Atlantia before you made up your mind. What happened last night—"

"Shouldn't have anything to do with me seeing Atlantia." I sat up, meeting his gaze. "It shouldn't interfere with us carrying through with our plans, or with us at all. I absolutely refuse to allow this group of people to put me in a different sort of cage. I'm not going to stop living when I just started to do so."

Casteel's eyes were as warm as the summer sun as he lifted a hand to my cheek. "You never cease to amaze me."

"I'm not sure what I said that is so amazing."

His lips curved up. The dimple appeared. "Your determination and will to live, to enjoy life no matter what is happening or how confusing things are, is one of the many things I find amazing about you. Most wouldn't be able to handle everything you have."

"There are moments when I'm not sure I can," I admitted.

"But you do." He slid his thumb over my lower lip. "And you will. No matter what."

His faith in me touched a small, insecure spot deep inside me that I wasn't sure I knew existed until that moment. A part of me that worried I asked too many questions, understood too little of this world, and that I was only stumbling from one shock to the next. But he was right. I was still standing. I was still dealing. I was strong.

I started to lean in to kiss him, but a knock on the door stopped me.

Casteel let out a low growl. "I don't normally like to be interrupted, but especially when you're about to kiss me."

Dipping my head, I kissed him quickly before hopping out of his lap. He rose, shooting me a sultry look that scalded my skin as he went to the door. Hoping I didn't look as flushed as I felt, I turned to see Delano standing there. The smile tugging at my lips froze the moment I connected with his emotions.

All I could taste was bitter, heavy cream. Sorrow and concern. I started toward the door. "What happened?" I asked as Casteel looked over his shoulder at me.

"A man is here to see you," Delano answered, and Casteel's head snapped back to the fair-haired wolven.

"For what reason?" Casteel demanded as I joined them.

"Their child has been injured in a carriage accident," he told us. "She's extremely—"

"Where is she?" My stomach dropped as I stepped forward.

"In the city. It's her father who's here," Delano began, his gaze darting between Casteel and me. "But the girl—"

At once, the talk of the Crown, the Unseen, and everything else fell to the wayside. There was no thinking about what I could do to help. I brushed past him, my heart thumping. I'd seen the results of carriage accidents in both Masadonia and Carsodonia. They almost always ended tragically for tiny bodies, and I'd never been allowed to step in and ease their pain or fright.

"Dammit, Poppy." A door slammed behind Casteel as he entered the hall.

"Don't try to stop me," I tossed over my shoulder.

"I wasn't planning to." He and Delano easily caught up with me. "I just don't think you should go rushing out there when the Unseen just tried to kill you last night."

I looked over at Delano as I kept walking. "Did the parents or the child have a face?"

His brows knitted at what definitely sounded like a weird question. "Yes."

"Then they're obviously not Gyrms."

"That doesn't mean they aren't part of the Unseen, or change the fact that you should proceed with at least a measure of caution," Casteel countered. "Which, I know, you are not on friendly terms with."

I sent him a dark look.

He ignored it as we rounded a bend in the hall. "Is it just the father?"

"Yes," Delano answered. "He appears very desperate."

"Gods," Casteel muttered. "I shouldn't be surprised that they learned of her abilities. There have been arrivals from Spessa's End over the last couple of days."

None of that mattered. "Has anyone sent for a Healer?"

"Yes." Delano's sadness thickened, and my heart skipped. "The Healer is actually with the child and mother now. The father said the Healer told them there's nothing to be done—"

Grasping the skirt of my gown, I took off running. Casteel cursed, but he didn't stop me as I ran down the never-ending hall, vaguely aware that I didn't think I had ever run this fast before. I rushed out into the warm, sunny air and started for the doors at the end of the breezeway.

Casteel caught my elbow. "This way will be quicker," he told me, guiding me out from between the pillars and onto a walkway crowded by bushy shrubs covered in tiny starbursts of yellow.

The moment we entered the courtyard, and before I could even see anyone beyond the walls, the raw and nearly out-of-control panic radiating from the man standing near a horse slammed into me.

"Harlan," Casteel called. "Bring me Setti."

"Already on it," the young man responded, leading the horse out as the man turned to us.

I sucked in a sharp breath. The entire front of his shirt and breeches were stained red. That much blood…

"Please." The man started toward us and then jerked to a stop. At first, I thought it was the sudden presence of several wolven that seemed to appear out of nowhere, but the man started to bow.

"There is no need for that." Casteel stopped him, his grip slipping to my hand as I let go of my gown. "Your child is injured?"

"Yes, Your Highness." The man's eyes—Atlantian eyes—bounced between us as Kieran stepped out of the front doors of the home, his hand on the hilt of his sword. With one look, he picked up his pace, entering the stables. "My little girl. Marji. She was right beside us," he told us, his voice cracking. "We told her to wait, but she…she just took off, and we didn't see the carriage. We didn't see her do it until it was too late. The Healer says that nothing can be done, but she still breathes, and we heard—" Wild, dilated eyes flicked to me as Harlan brought Setti forward. "We heard about what you did in Spessa's End. If you could help my little girl… Please? I beg of you."

"There's no need to beg," I told him, heart twisting as his grief tore through me. "I can try to help her."

"Thank you," the man's words came out with a rush of air. "Thank you."

"Where is she?" Casteel asked as he took Setti's reins.

As the man answered, I gripped the saddle and hoisted myself up without getting my legs tangled in the gown. No one reacted to how I was able to seat myself on Setti as Casteel swung up behind me, and Kieran joined us, already astride his horse. No one spoke as we left the courtyard, following the man onto the tree-lined road. We rode down the hill fast, accompanied by the wolven and Delano, who had shifted and was now a blur of white loping over rocks and darting between trees and then structures and horses.

We had just talked about seeing the city, but this wasn't how I imagined it happening. The ride was a blur of blue skies and a sea of faces, narrow, tight roads, and gardens nestled between sweeping buildings adorned with heavily flowered vines. I couldn't focus on any of it as the urge to help the child took center stage. And that desire…it was different. It was hard to comprehend because the need to help others with my gift had always been there, but this was more intense. As if it was an instinct that equaled breathing. And I didn't know if that had anything to do with everything that had happened or if it was borne of the need to learn if my gifts could still ease pain and heal instead of what I'd done at the Chambers.

My heart pounded as we entered a street crowded with people. They stood in front of homes and on cobblestone sidewalks, their unease and grief sinking into my skin as my gaze settled on a plain white carriage left unattended in the road.

The father drew his horse to a halt in front of a narrow, two-story home with windows that faced the glittering bay. As Casteel brought Setti to a stop, a wild mix of emotions rose from within the wrought-iron-enclosed courtyard and slammed into me, knocking the breath from my lungs. I twisted to find Kieran at our side. He reached up, grasping my arms.

"Do you have her?" Casteel demanded of Kieran.

"Always," he replied.

Casteel's grip on me slipped away, and Kieran helped me down. The moment my feet were on the ground, Casteel was beside me. I glanced at the carriage, seeing strands of hair tangled in the wheel—I quickly looked away before I saw anything else.

"Through here," the father said, his long legs carrying him over the sidewalk and through the gate.

A man dressed in gray stood at the entrance to the garden. He turned to us. A satchel hung from his shoulder, and several pouches were clipped to the belt around his waist. I knew at once that he was the Healer.

"Your Highness, I must apologize for this disruption," the man said, the sun glinting off the smoothness of his bald head. His eyes were a vivid gold. The Healer was Atlantian. "I told the parents the child was beyond our care and that she would soon enter the Vale. That there was nothing to do. But they insisted that you come h-here." He stuttered over the last word as he looked at me. His throat worked on a swallow. "They had heard that she—"

"I know what they heard about my wife," Casteel stated as Delano prowled ahead. "This is no disruption."

"But the child, Your Highness. Her injuries are significant, and her vitals are not conducive to life. Even if your wife can ease pain and heal bones with her touch," the Healer said, his rejection of such an ability clear. "The child's injuries are far beyond that."

"We shall see," Casteel answered.

I inhaled sharply as we walked through the gate. There were so many people huddled together in the small garden. My throat dried as I struggled to make sense of what I felt from them. I…I tasted bitter panic and fear. It soaked the air, but what raised the hairs on my arms was the intense, scalding pain coming through my senses, painting the blue sky a maroon, and darkening the ground, tainting the flowers so lovingly cared for. It fell in endless waves of acute agony, like dull razor blades scraping against my skin.

A pale-skinned man turned as he dragged his hands over his head, tugging at wheat-colored strands. Shock and the bitterness of horror punched through the choking pain. His panic was so potent that it was a tangible entity as he stared at Casteel.

"I didn't see her, Your Highness," the man cried, looking over his shoulder. "I didn't even see her. Gods, I'm sorry." He staggered around and then toward the group. "I'm so sorry."

Casteel spoke softly to the man as Delano moved ahead, shouldering through the crowd. I heard the sound of gulping cries, the kind of sobs that stole the breath, and most of the sound.

"I brought help," I heard the father say. "Do you hear me, Marji? I brought someone who is going to try to help you…"

My stomach lurched as I saw the limp body—a too-small form clutched to the chest of a woman on her knees, who shared the same auburn hair. The father crouched at the child's head. It was the woman making those ragged, broken sounds. Her emotions were frenzied, shifting from terror to sorrow to murky disbelief.

"Come on, baby girl, open your eyes for your papa." Her father shifted closer, carefully brushing her hair back—

The child's hair wasn't auburn.

That was blood streaking the light brown strands—hair that matched the father's. My gaze swept over the child as Delano circled the huddled group. One leg wasn't lying right, twisted at an unnatural angle. "Open your eyes for me," her father pleaded. A murmur of surprise rose from those who stood in the garden as they realized that the Prince was among them. "Open your eyes for your momma and me, baby girl. There's someone here to help."

The mother's gaze darted around those standing there. I didn't think she saw a single face when she uttered, "She won't open her eyes."

The child's lashes were dark against cheeks absent of color. I could barely feel her pain anymore, and I knew that was a bad sign. For that kind of pain to ease so quickly and totally, things were grave. Atlantians, even those of the elemental line, were basically mortal until they entered the Culling. Any number of injuries that could fatally harm a mortal could do the same to them.

The mother's gaze landed on me. "Can you help her?" she whispered, shuddering. "Can you? Please?"

Heart thumping and skin vibrating, I neared them. "I will."

At least I thought I could. I had healed Beckett's broken bones. I had no idea if that would happen now, but I knew I could pump as much warmth and happiness into her as I could. I feared that was all I could do. I worried the Healer had been right, and this child had moved beyond anyone's ability. I just prayed that my touch didn't manifest in the same way as it had in the Temple.

Casteel walked ahead, crouching beside the parents. He placed a hand on the woman's shoulder as I lowered myself while Kieran had gone still, all except for the rise and fall of his chest. His nostrils flared as Delano whimpered, sinking onto his haunches at the child's feet.

Casteel's gaze met mine, and I saw it there—the welling grief. "Poppy..."

"I can try," I insisted, kneeling across from the mother. The stone was hard under my knees as I tried not to notice how the child's head hung so limply, how it didn't seem shaped right. I started to reach for the girl, but the mother's arms tensed around her. "You can still hold her," I said gently. "You don't have to let her go."

The woman stared at me in a way that made me unsure if she understood me, but then she nodded.

"I just need to touch her," I told her, feeling their shock, their uncertainty, and even the anger I thought had come from the Healer. I shut them out as I focused on the child—the too-pale child. "That's all. I won't hurt her. I promise."

The mother didn't say anything, but she didn't move as I lifted my hands again. Inhaling deeply, I kept my attention on the child as I opened my senses wide. I felt...I felt nothing from the girl. Unease trickled through me. She could be deeply unconscious, slipping where pain couldn't follow, but what I saw on the carriage wheel and the way her head appeared caved-in…

I had only ever healed wounds and bones, and only recently. Nothing like this.

I could still try.

Curving a hand around her arm, I swallowed hard at the stillness of her skin. That was the only way I could describe the feel of her flesh. I suppressed a shudder and let instinct guide me. Gently, I placed my other hand on her forehead. My palms warmed, and a tingling sensation spread down my arms and across my fingers. The child didn't move. Her eyes remained closed. Beckett had responded almost immediately when I touched him, but there was nothing from her. My throat thickened as I looked at her chest. Either her breathing was too shallow or she didn't breathe—hadn't been breathing. A slice of pain cut through my chest.

"Poppy," Cas whispered. A moment later, I felt his hand on my shoulder.

I didn't let myself feel what he was experiencing. "Just a few more seconds," I said, my gaze returning to the child's face, to the blue pallor of her lips.

"Oh, gods," the father moaned, rocking backward. "Please. Help her."

One of the wolven brushed against my back as desperation swelled.

"This is unnecessary," the Healer stated. "That child has already gone into the Vale. You are doing nothing but giving them false hope, and I must say something—"

Casteel's head lifted, but I was faster. My chin jerked over my shoulder as my gaze met the Healer's. Static danced over my skin.

"I don't give up so quickly," I said, feeling the heat in my skin flare. "I will still try."

Whatever the Healer saw in my face—in my eyes—he shrank back from, stumbling a step as he pressed a hand to his chest. I honestly didn't care as I turned back to the child, exhaling roughly.

It couldn't be too late for this child because that wouldn't be fair, and I didn't care how unfair life could be. The girl was far too young for this to be it for her—for her life to be over, all because she'd run out into the road.

Tamping down my rising panic, I ordered myself to focus. To think about the mechanics. When I healed Beckett, I hadn't had to think about much. It just happened. Maybe this was different. She was injured far more seriously. I just needed to try harder.

I *had* to try harder.

My skin continued vibrating, and my chest hummed like a hundred birds taking flight inside me. Sharp inhales echoed around me as a faint silver glow emanated from my hands.

"Good gods," someone rasped. The sound of boots sliding over pebbles and dirt sounded.

Closing my eyes, I searched for memories—good ones. It didn't take me as long as it had before. Immediately, I recalled how I felt kneeling in the sandy dirt beside Casteel as he slipped the ring on my finger. My entire being had been wrapped in the taste of chocolate and berries, and I could feel that now. The corners of my lips turned up, and I held onto that feeling, taking that pulsing joy and happiness and picturing it as a bright light that funneled through my touch to the child, wrapping around her like a blanket. All the while, I repeated over and over that it wasn't too late, that she would live. *It's not too late. She will live. It's not too late. She will live—*

The child jerked. Or the mother did. I didn't know. My eyes flew open, and my heart stuttered. The silver light had spread, settling over the child in a fine, shimmery web that blanketed her entire body. I could only see patches of her skin underneath—her *pink* skin.

"Momma," came the soft, weak voice from under the light, and then stronger, "*Momma.*"

Gasping, I drew my hands back. The silvery light twinkled like a thousand stars before fading away. The little girl, her skin pink, and her eyes open, was sitting up, reaching for her mother.

Stunned, I leaned back as my gaze swept to Casteel. He was staring at me, golden eyes filled with wonder. "I…" He swallowed thickly. "You…you are a goddess."

"No." I folded my hands against my legs. "I'm not."

Sunlight glanced off his cheek as he tipped forward, bracing his weight on the hand he'd placed on the ground. He leaned in, brushing his nose across mine as he cupped my cheek. "To me, you are." He kissed me softly, scattering what was left of my senses. "To them, you are."

Chapter 23

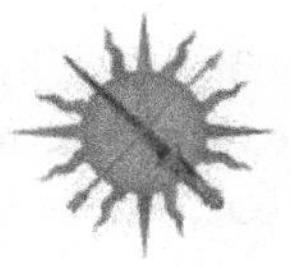

To them?

I pulled back, my gaze locking with Casteel's. He nodded, and I rose on shaky legs, looking over the now-silent garden. My gaze crept over slender, crystal wind chimes that hung from delicate branches, and yellow and white coneflowers as tall as me. My lips parted on a soft inhale. Nearly a dozen people had gathered inside the garden—not including the wolven. All of them had lowered to one knee, their heads bowed. I turned to where Kieran *had* stood.

My breath caught. He too kneeled. I stared at his bent head and then lifted my gaze to see that the Healer, who hadn't believed I could help, who had been angry that I was giving the parents false hope, had bowed, as well, one hand flat to his chest and the other against the ground. Beyond him and the iron fence, those who had been in the streets no longer stood. They kneeled, too, their hands pressed to their breasts and their palms against the ground.

Curling a hand against my stomach, I turned back to Casteel. Our gazes met and held as he shifted onto one knee, placing his right hand over his heart and his left on the ground.

The gesture…I recognized it. It was a variation of what the wolven had done when I arrived in Saion's Cove. But I'd seen it before, I realized. The Priests and Priestesses would do it when they first entered the Temples in Solis, acknowledging that they were in the presence of the gods.

You are a goddess.

My heart tripped over itself as I stared at Casteel. I wasn't a…

I couldn't even force my brain to finish that thought because I had no idea what I was. No one did. And as my gaze fell to where the little girl was still held tightly by her mother and now her father, as well, I…I couldn't disregard that possibility, even as impossible as it seemed.

"Momma." The girl's voice drew my gaze. She had wrapped her arms around her mother's neck as her father held them, kissing the top of his daughter's head and then the mother's. "I was dreaming."

"You were?" The mother's eyes were squeezed shut, but tears streaked her cheeks.

"There was a lady, Momma." The little girl snuggled closer to her mother. "She had…" Her words were muffled, but what she said next was clear. "She said I-I always had the power in me…"

You always had the power in you…

Those words were oddly familiar. It felt like I had heard them before, but I couldn't place them or remember who'd spoken them.

Casteel rose, and in a daze, I watched him walk toward me, his steps full of fluid grace. If someone said he was a god, I wouldn't question it for a second.

He stopped in front of me, and my chaotic senses fixed on him. The breath I took was full of spice and smoke, warming my blood. "Poppy," he said, his tone full of heat. His thumb slid over the scar on my cheek. "Your eyes are as bright as the moon."

I blinked. "Are they still that way?"

His grin spread, and one dimple hinted at making an appearance. "Yes."

I didn't know what was said to the others, but I did know that he spoke to them with the calm confidence of someone who'd spent their entire life in a place of authority. All I was aware of was him steering me around people, past the man who'd been in such a panic but now just rested on his knees, staring up at me as his lips moved, forming words over and over. *Thank you.*

The wolven were once again beside us as we left the garden. The people on the cobblestone sidewalk and in the street were still there. They had risen and stood as if transfixed, and they all seemed to share the same bubbling, sparking emotion. Excitement and awe as they watched Casteel and I—watched me.

Instead of taking me to where Setti waited, Casteel looked at Kieran. He didn't speak, and again, I was amazed at how they seemed to communicate or know each other so well that words weren't necessary.

They weren't now because a slow grin ticked across Kieran's face as he said, "We'll wait for you here."

"Thank you," Casteel replied, his hand firmly wrapped around mine, and then he said nothing as he turned me around and started walking.

I followed, my shock from what had just happened giving way to curiosity as he led me a few yards down the street, Casteel seemingly unaware of the wide-eyed stares, the murmurs, and the hasty bows. I wasn't all that aware of it, either, unable to feel much past the thickening, spicy taste in my mouth, and the tension growing low in the pit of my stomach.

He led me under a sand-colored archway and into a narrow alley that smelled of apples and was lined with urns overflowing with leafy ferns. Gauzy curtains danced from the open windows above as he led me farther into the passageway. The soft melody of music drifted out from above us, the deeper in we went. He made a sharp right, and through another archway was a small courtyard. Wooden beams stretched across from building to building. Baskets of trailing flowers dangled, the array of colors creating a canopy that only allowed thin fragments of sunlight through. Vine-covered trellises created a privacy hedge around hundreds and hundreds of delicate white-petaled flowers.

"This garden is beautiful," I said, starting toward one of the fragile white blossoms.

"I really don't give a fuck about the garden." Casteel stopped me, pulling me into a shadow-heavy alcove.

My eyes widened, but before I could respond, he turned, pressing me back against the stone wall. In the dim lights, his eyes were a luminous, churning honey color. "You know, don't you?" Casteel folded his hand behind my head as he leaned into me. Against my stomach, I could feel the hard, thick length of him as he brushed his lips across my temple. "What you did back there?"

Soaking up his lush, piney scent and his warmth, I let my eyes drift shut as I clutched his sides, swords and all. "I healed her."

He kissed my cheek, right along the scar, and then drew back. His eyes met mine, and I swore a fine tremor coursed through his body. "You know that's not what you did," he said. "You brought that girl back to life."

The breath I took seized in my throat as I opened my eyes. "That's not possible."

"It shouldn't be," he agreed, sliding a hand over my bare arm and then across my chest. A curl low in my stomach made itself known as his palm grazed my breast. "Not for a mortal. Not for an Atlantian, or even a deity." His hand slipped over my hip and then my thigh. I could feel the heat of his palm through the dress as he skimmed past the wolven dagger. "Only a god can do that—only one god."

"Nyktos." I bit down on my lip as his fingers gathered the material of the gown in a fist. "I'm not Nyktos."

"No shit," he said against my mouth.

"Your language is inappropriate," I told him.

He laughed darkly. "You going to deny what you did?"

"No," I whispered, my heart skipping. "I don't understand how, and I don't know if her soul had truly entered the Vale, but she…"

"She was gone." He nipped at my lower lip, drawing a gasp from me. "And you brought her back because you *tried.* Because you refused to give up. You did that, Poppy. And because of you, those parents won't be mourning their child tonight. They'll be watching her fall asleep."

"I…I just did what I could," I told him. "That's all—"

The sheer intensity of the way he claimed my lips cut off my words. That low curl in my stomach intensified as he tilted his head, deepening the kiss.

Balmy air curled its way around my legs as he drew the skirt of my gown up. Shock at his intentions warred with the elicit pulse of pleasure. "We're in public."

"Not really." The tips of his fangs grazed the underside of my jaw, and every muscle in my body seemed to clench. Up and up it went until his fingers skimmed the curve of my ass. "This is a private garden."

"There are people around—" A breathy moan escaped me as the skirt rose above the dagger. "Somewhere."

"No one is even remotely close enough to us," he said, slipping his hand out from behind my head. "The wolven made sure of that."

"I don't see them," I said.

"They're at the mouth of the alley," he told me, catching my ear between his teeth. I shuddered. "They're giving us privacy to speak."

A short giggle left me. "I'm sure that's what they think we're doing."

"Does it matter?" he questioned.

I thought about that as my pulse sped up. Did it? What had happened last night flashed before me, as did the memory of seeing Casteel prone on the Chambers' floor. Believing he'd died. In a heartbeat, I remembered what it had been like when the blood had drained from my body, realizing there would be no more new experiences, no more moments of wild abandon. That little girl had gotten a second chance, and so had I.

I wouldn't waste it.

"No," I said as his gaze lifted to mine. Heart pounding, I reached between us. The backs of my trembling fingers brushed against him, and he jerked as I undid the flap of buttons. "It doesn't."

"Thank fuck," he growled and then kissed me again, obliterating any reservations that stemmed from a lifetime of being sheltered. His tongue stroked mine as he slid an arm around my waist, lifting me. His strength never ceased to send a thrill through me. "Wrap your legs around me."

I did, moaning at the feel of his hard flesh nestled against mine.

He reached between us, and I felt the tip of him pressing into me. "Just so you know"—he raised his head, his gaze locking with mine—"I'm completely in control."

"Are you?"

"Totally," he swore, thrusting into me.

My head pushed back against the wall as the feel of him, hot and thick, consumed me. His mouth closed over mine, and I loved the way he kissed me, like my very taste was enough for him to live on.

He moved against me and in me, the twin warmth of his body and the stone blocks at my back a delicious assault on my senses. The thrusts of our tongues matched the slow plunge of his hips. Things…things didn't stay that way. Wedging his arm between my back and the wall, he rocked against me until my body became a fire he fanned with each stroke and each intoxicating kiss. He pressed in, grinding against the small bundle of nerves, only to pull back and then return with another deep thrust. When he started to retreat, I tightened my legs around his waist, locking me to him.

He chuckled against my lips. "Greedy."

"Tease," I said, mimicking his earlier act by catching his lip with my teeth.

"Fuck," he groaned, shifting his hips as he ground into me, over and over, the movements increasing in intensity until they became feverish, until it felt like I would break apart. My head spun as the bliss built. He felt like he was everywhere, and when he dropped his mouth to my throat, and I felt the scrape of his fangs, it was all too much. Spasms rocked my body in tight, slick waves, throwing me so high, I didn't think I'd ever come down as he followed me into that bliss, shuddering as my throat muffled his deep moan of release.

We stayed like that for a little bit, joined together, and both struggling to gain control of our breathing. Shaken, it took quite a few minutes for me to come to my senses while he eased himself from me and carefully lowered me to my feet.

With his arm holding me tightly against him, Casteel looked over his shoulder. "You know what? It is a beautiful garden."

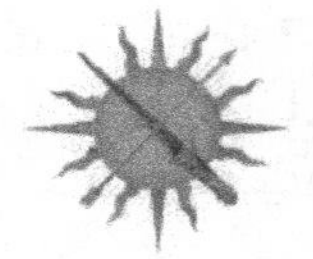

Casteel and I walked hand and hand through the city on the coast of the Seas of Saion, the sun and salty breeze warm against our skin as we stepped out of the seamstress shop, where a Miss Seleana quickly took my measurements. We weren't alone. Kieran walked on the other side of me, and Delano, along with four other wolven, followed as Casteel took me through the winding, colorful streets full of storefronts painted in yellows and greens, and homes that boasted vivid blue front doors. An orange poppy blossom was tucked in my hair, one Casteel had paid nearly triple for, even though the street vendor tried to give us a dozen for free. Our hands were sticky from the cinnamon pastries we had been given a few blocks from the florist, in front of a shop that smelled like all things sugar and was painted to match the dewy grass. And there was a smile plastered to my face that not even the brief bursts of distrust radiating on and off throughout the afternoon could erase. I only seemed to sense the cautious emotion from the mortal inhabitants and a few of the Atlantians with graying hair. Those were few and far between. Otherwise, all I felt was curiosity and surprise. No one, not even those who bowed with a sense of wariness, was rude or threatening. That could've been because of Casteel, Kieran, and the wolven. It could've also been the Guards of the Crown, dressed in white that we spotted shortly before picking up the flower, their presence evidence that Casteel's parents knew we moved about the city.

Or it could've been what they had heard about me—about what I was capable of.

Either way, I honestly couldn't give a fig. I was enjoying myself despite the unanswered questions, the shadow of the Unseen lingering over us, what I'd done for the girl in the garden, and everything that needed to be decided and done.

When Casteel had asked if I wanted to take a walk through the city, I'd hesitated. We needed to speak with his parents. Not only did we owe them that, but there was also the possibility that they held some of the answers to the questions we had. But Casteel had kissed me and said, "We have tomorrow, Poppy, and we have right now. You get to decide how you want to spend it."

I wanted those answers. I wanted to somehow ensure that his parents didn't…well, think I was a threat. But with my muscles still lax and my blood still warm from those wicked moments in the alcove, I'd decided I wanted to spend right now exploring. Enjoying myself. Living.

And so, that was what we did.

We were steadily walking toward the lower part of the city and the glistening beaches, past buildings with outdoor dining tables packed with people chatting and sharing food. Kieran had called them cafés, and I knew places like that existed in Solis, but I'd only ever seen them in Masadonia, and from a distance. I'd never been inside one.

Having just experienced an icy treat made of crushed ice and fruit, we didn't venture into any of the cafés.

Casteel stopped when we came upon a squat, windowless building, though, tugging me to the side. Stone benches sat between the pillars of a wide colonnade. "Didn't you say you were interested in museums?"

Surprise flickered through me. On our journey to Skotos when we left Spessa's End, I'd mentioned to Delano and Naill when they talked about the different conservatories in Atlantia, that I'd never been allowed to enter one in Solis. I hadn't realized that Casteel had been paying attention, nor did I expect him to remember something I'd forgotten.

I nodded as I resisted the urge to wrap my arms around him like one of the furry little creatures that hung from the trees by their tails in the forests near the Elysium Peaks. I didn't think Casteel would mind, but Kieran would probably sigh.

"Would you like to go inside?" Casteel asked.

"I would." Eager to see some of Atlantia's history, I managed to proceed up the steps beside Casteel and Kieran, moving at a sedate pace.

The inside was dimly lit and a bit stagnant, smelling faintly of camphor. As we passed a limestone sculpture of one of the goddesses, Kieran explained that there were no windows, so the light didn't fade the paintings or stones.

And there were a lot of paintings of the gods—both of them together and individually. It was easy to pick out the ones depicting Nyktos since his face was always obscured by either glowing light, or his features were simply not rendered in detail.

"Remember what I told you about how he was depicted with a wolf?" Kieran said, drawing my gaze to a painting of the King of Gods standing beside a tall, grayish-black wolf.

"This represents his relationship with the wolven?"

Kieran nodded. There were many like that, even small sculptures of Nyktos with a wolven by his side. And farther down the long wall was a sketch with a white wolf drawn behind him, symbolizing his ability to take the shape of a wolf.

"I wonder what is in the museums in Solis," I said as we stopped before a painting of the Goddess Ione, cradling a swaddled infant. "Do they have paintings like this? Did they copy them?"

"Is it true that only the upper class could enter the museums?" Kieran asked.

I nodded, stomach souring. "Yes. Only the wealthy and the Ascended. And so very few mortals are wealthy."

"That is an archaic and brutal caste system." Casteel's eyes narrowed upon a landscape of what appeared to be Saion's Cove. "One purely designed to create and strengthen oppression."

"By creating a gap between those who have access to all the resources, and those who have access to none," I said, my chest becoming heavy. "And Atlantia is really not like that? Not even a little?" The last bit I asked of Kieran, as I thought of those who needed to be reminded of who the wolven were.

"We are not like that," he said. "Atlantia has never been that way."

"That doesn't mean that we've been perfect." Casteel's hand threaded through my hair. "There has been strife, but the Council of Elders was formed to prevent anyone from making a choice or decision that could jeopardize the people of Atlantia. That doesn't mean the Crown doesn't have ultimate authority," he explained. "But the Council has a say, and it would be very unwise for their opinions to go unheard. It has only happened twice before, and the end results were not favorable."

"When Malec Ascended Isbeth, and the others started following suit?" I surmised.

Casteel nodded. "The Council was against allowing it to occur, having the opinion that Malec should apologize, make what he did right, and forbid future Ascensions."

"And what do you mean by make things right?" I had a sinking feeling I already knew.

"He was advised to rid himself of Isbeth, one way or another," he said. "He did none of those things."

"And so, here we are," Kieran murmured.

I swallowed. "And what of the other time?"

A thoughtful expression pinched Casteel's features. "It was back before Malec ruled, when there were other deities. The Council was started then, when the bloodlines began to outnumber the deities. The Council suggested that it was time for the crown to sit upon the head of one of the bloodlines. That was also ignored."

Alastir hadn't mentioned that in his cruddy history lesson. If they had listened to the Council, would the deities have survived?

A couple with two young children hastily bowed as we rounded a corner. Their shock at seeing us was evident in their widened eyes. As Casteel and Kieran greeted them with a smile and words of hello, I saw that they were most likely mortal. I followed suit with the greeting, hoping I didn't come across as stiff.

Moving onto a case containing what appeared to be some sort of clay vase, I said, "Can I ask you two a question and have you give me an honest response?"

"Can't wait to hear what this will be," Kieran murmured while Casteel nodded.

I shot the wolven a dark look. "Do I seem awkward when I meet people?" I could feel warmth suffusing my cheeks. "Like back there, when I said hello? Did it sound right?"

"You sounded like anyone saying hello." Casteel lifted a hand, tucking a strand of hair back from my face. "If anything, you seem a little shy, not awkward."

"Really?" I asked hopefully. "Because I…well, I'm not used to actually interacting with people. In Solis, people didn't really acknowledge me unless it was in a situation where it was allowed. So I feel weird, like I'm doing it wrong."

"You're not doing it wrong, Poppy." The lines of Kieran's face softened. "You sound fine."

Casteel dropped a quick kiss to the bridge of my nose. "We swear."

Kieran nodded.

Feeling a little better after hearing that, we continued on. If I were to become Queen, I supposed I'd have to get over these annoying insecurities.

Unsure of how that would happen, we slowly made our way past paintings and statues, many depicting the gods or fantastical cities that stretched into the clouds. Casteel claimed those were the cities in Iliseeum. They were all beautiful, but I stopped in front of a charcoal drawing. Some of it had faded, but it was clearly a sketch of a man seated upon a large throne. The lack of features told me it was Nyktos who sat there, but it was what sat at his feet that snagged my attention—and held it. Two extraordinarily large felines rested before him, their heads tilted in his direction. My eyes narrowed as I cocked my head to the side.

"This is a really old drawing," Casteel said as he idly ran his hand up and down my back. "Supposedly drawn by one of the deities."

It took me a moment to realize what those sketched cats reminded me of. "Are they cave cats?"

"I don't think so," Kieran answered as he stared up at the drawing.

"They look like them," I said. "I saw one of them once…" I frowned as the dream I'd had while in the crypts resurfaced. "Or maybe more than once."

Casteel glanced down at me. "Where did you see one? In a painting or drawing like this?"

"No." I shook my head. "There was one caged in the castle at Carsodonia."

Kieran's brows lifted. "I don't think that's what you saw."

"I saw a cat as large as you are in your wolven form," I told him. "Ian saw it, too."

He shook his head. "That's impossible, Poppy. Cave cats have been extinct for at least a couple of hundred years."

"What? No." I looked between them. Casteel nodded. "They roam the Wastelands."

"Who told you that?" Casteel asked.

"No one told me that. It's just…" I trailed off, my gaze returning to the drawing. It was something that was just *known*. But in reality, it was the Ascended who had said as much. The Queen had told me that when I asked about the creature I'd seen in the castle. "Why would they lie about something like that?"

Kieran snorted. "Who knows? Why have they erased entire gods and created ones that don't exist like Perus? I think they just like to make things up," he countered—and he had a good point.

I stared at the two cats. "Then what was in that cage?"

"Possibly another large wild cat," Casteel answered with a shrug. "But I think these two felines are supposed to symbolize the children of Nyktos and his Consort."

"When you say *children*, are you talking about Theon or all the gods?" I asked.

"His actual children," Casteel confirmed. "And Theon was never his actual son. That's another thing the Ascended either lied about or they simply misunderstood due to his many titles."

It was very possible it was a mistranslation. I stared at them, thinking how one of them was responsible for Malec. "Could they shift into cats?"

"Not sure," Kieran said. "Nothing that I remember reading ever said as much, and I don't believe Nyktos's ability to shift was something passed on to his children."

Of course, not. "What are their names?"

"Like with his Consort," Casteel said, "they are not known. Not even their genders."

I raised a brow. "Let me guess, Nyktos was just super-protective of their identities?"

Casteel smirked. "That's what they say."

"Sounds like he was super controlling," I muttered.

"Or maybe just really private," Kieran suggested as he reached over and tugged gently on the strand of hair Casteel had tucked back earlier. "Being the King of Gods, I'm sure he sought privacy wherever he could."

Maybe.

As we continued on through the museum, it was hard not to think back on that painting or the creature I'd seen in that cage when I was a child. I remembered the way the animal had prowled in its confines, desperate, and with a keen intelligence in its eyes.

Chapter 24

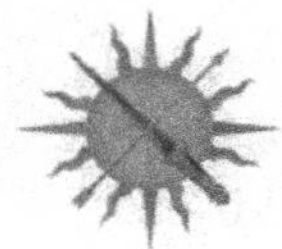

We ended up sharing a dinner of freshly grilled fish and roasted vegetables in one of the cafés closest to the water, joined by Delano, who had shifted into his mortal form at some point. I had asked if the other wolven wished to join us, but they had chosen to remain in their wolven forms, watching over any and all that ventured near us, including the Crown Guard.

It wasn't until after the sun had begun its steady descent into the horizon that we made it to the beaches. The first thing I did was unstrap my sandals. The very moment my feet sank into the gritty sand, a smile tugged at my lips as a barrage of memories rose within me—memories of my parents and Ian, walking along another beach. As my sandals dangled from my fingers, and Casteel wrapped his hand firmly around mine, I looked out at the sea, watching the clear waters turn a shade of silver as the moon rose. Those afternoons on the beaches of the Stroud Sea felt like a different lifetime, eons ago, and that saddened me. How long before they became memories that felt as if they belonged to someone else?

Delano, who walked ahead, turned to face us. "If you're not tired, there's something ahead you might enjoy, Penellaphe."

"I'm not tired." I looked up at Casteel. "Are you?"

A faint smile appeared as he shook his head.

Delano's gaze flicked from Casteel to Kieran before returning to me as he walked backwards. "There is a celebration of a wedding," he explained. "Just around the bend."

"Are we able to join? I mean, they don't know me—"

"They will welcome you," Delano cut in. "Both of you."

"You want to?" Casteel asked. Of course, I did. I nodded. He looked over his shoulder to where I knew the members of the Crown Guard followed several paces back. "Thank you for your watchful eyes. That will be all for tonight."

I turned just as I saw several guards bow and then pivot. "They're actually leaving?"

"They know they don't belong at a celebration like this," Kieran explained. "It's not personal. It just is."

Just is?

My feet sank into damp sand as we made our way around a dune, the sounds of laughter and music growing louder. There was so much to soak in—the shouts of happiness, the canopies rippling in the salty breeze, the thick blankets and cushions scattered about the sand, and the groups of people huddled about, dancing and talking. There was so much life, so much warmth and joy, that it flooded my senses, leaving me exposed like a live wire but in a way that was pleasant for the first time. In a way that I *wanted.* My gaze bounced everywhere, stopping on those moving around the flames.

"During these kinds of celebrations, only the wolven can dance around the fire," Casteel explained, following my gaze. "Though I bet they'd allow you. You're their *Liessa*."

"It's strange to be the wolven's Queen and not be a wolven," I said, watching people envelop Delano as the wolven who'd been trailing us all day rushed forward, disappearing into the crowd.

"Tonight is about celebration," Kieran told us. "You don't have to worry about anyone bowing or beating their fists off the sand tonight."

A tiny grin appeared. "Was my awkwardness the last time really that noticeable?"

"Yes," both Casteel and Kieran answered.

"Wow," I said, ducking my chin against Casteel's arm as I smiled.

But Kieran was right. As he broke away from us, joining several others who stood near a few of the canopied tents, only waves and smiles greeted us. Taking my sandals from me, Casteel dropped them onto the sand and then unstrapped his swords, lying them on a blanket—a sign that he felt it was safe to do so here. Sitting, he pulled me down so I was nestled between his legs, facing the bonfire.

I'd completely lost sight of Delano as I relaxed in Casteel's embrace, but I found Kieran a few moments later, talking with a tall, dark-haired female. That was about all I could see of her from a distance. "Who is Kieran speaking to?" I asked.

Casteel looked over the top of my head. "I think her name is Lyra. If that's who I think it is. She's a bit younger than Kieran and me, but her family is close to his."

"Oh," I whispered, watching them and thinking of what Kieran had once said about loving and losing someone. He'd never expounded on that, but what I'd felt from him when he spoke was the kind of anguish one felt when the person they loved was no longer in the realm of the living. It made me happy to see him with someone, even if they were just talking and laughing. Not that I would share that with him. He'd probably consider it a question.

"You know how you said it was weird to be a Queen to the wolven but not be a wolven?" Cas said after a few moments. "It made me think of how when I met you, I was looking for the Maiden, but I found a Princess, a Queen—my wife." He laughed, and it sounded as if it were one of awe. "I don't know. It just made me think about how you find things you never knew you needed when you're looking for something completely opposite."

"Or not looking at all," I said, my nose scrunching. "Or maybe I *was* looking. I went to the Red Pearl that night because I wanted to live. And I found you."

He curled his arms around me, tightening his embrace. A couple of additional moments passed as we watched the wolven around the fire. "What would you want to be doing right now if you could be doing anything? Barring seeing your brother or anything that has to do with what we need to do."

My brows rose at the unexpected question. Letting my senses stretch out to him, I felt a boyish sense of curiosity, one that brought a grin to my face. I didn't even have to think about it. "This. You?"

"I'm being serious," he said.

"I am, too. I would want to be doing this—all that we've done today," I said. "You?"

"The same," he said quietly, and I knew he spoke the truth. "But with you naked and more sex."

I laughed loudly at that because I also sensed that to be true. "I'm glad that I chose to spend right now this way."

"Me, too." He pressed his lips to my cheek.

I really didn't know when we would have another day like this one, or at what point there would even be time. But I didn't want to think of the reasons why it would probably be a while. That wasn't how I wanted to spend right now, so I watched those dancing around the fire with avid interest, entranced by the joyous frenzy of the dark outlines of their bodies, how they moved from one partner to the next, both male and female, with the kind of reckless abandon I'd shared with Casteel in the garden. What I felt from them could only be described as a release, as if they danced to toss away the chains of what preyed on their minds and souls, and in so doing, found freedom.

A body peeled away from the fire and moved toward us. Sweat glistened off Delano's bare shoulders as he bowed at the waist. Pale hair tumbled across his forehead as he extended an arm. "Would you like to dance?"

I started to take his hand, but uncertainty filled me. Was it appropriate for me to do so?

Casteel dipped his cheek to mine. "You can dance with him." His arm loosened around my waist. "You can do whatever you want."

Do whatever you want.

Four words I hadn't heard for most of my life. "I…I don't really know how to dance."

"No one does," Delano said, grinning. "Until they do." He wiggled his fingers. "What do you say, Penellaphe?"

Excitement bubbled up in me as my gaze darted over his shoulder to the figures moving around the bonfire. *Do whatever you want.* The breath that left me was heady. Twisting, I curled my fingers around Casteel's chin and pulled his mouth to mine. I kissed him quickly. "I love you, Cas."

His arm tightened briefly around me. "Have fun."

Turning back to Delano, I placed my hand in his. "Poppy," I told him. "Call me Poppy."

Smiling, Delano pulled me to my feet. "Then let's dance, Poppy."

Stomach skipping, I followed him toward the rippling flames. Delano turned to me as the warmth of the fire pressed against my skin.

"I really don't know how to dance," I told him apologetically.

"Look around us." Keeping his fingers wrapped around mine, he picked up my hand and placed it on his hip before resting his on my waist. "Do they look like they know how to dance? Or do they look like they're having fun?"

Glancing around, I saw nothing like what I saw when I'd snuck through the back halls to spy on the balls held in the Great Hall of Castle Teerman. There were no rigid movements, nor was everyone paired with someone. A girl with long, blonde hair danced alone, her arms stretched above her head as her hips moved with the tempo. A brown-skinned man also danced alone, his body moving with fluid grace. Couples spun around each other, and others danced so close to one another it was difficult to tell where one body ended and the other began. I spied Kieran with the dark-haired female. With her golden-brown arms twined around his neck, they were one of the couples who danced so close that tongues would've been wagging in Masadonia. Kieran lifted the female, spinning her as she threw her head back and laughed.

"What do you see?" Delano prodded.

Dragging my gaze from them, I looked up at him. "They're having fun."

He smiled. "You can do that, right?"

I peeked over to where Casteel sat on the plush blanket, one arm resting on a bent knee as he watched us. A tiny part of me wasn't sure I knew how to have fun, but I…I'd had fun today. I'd had fun when Tawny and I had snuck out together to visit the lake. I hadn't been thinking about having fun those times. I was just…*living*. And that was the key, wasn't it? To not overthink and to just live.

I looked up at Delano. "I can."

"I know." His smile widened, and then he started to move, taking small, swaying steps to our left and then the right. I followed him.

His steps were far surer, while mine were rigid, and I was sure I looked foolish, my arms stiff and cockeyed as I clutched his hand. Others moved faster around us, but as we continued dancing in our little circle, I realized that each of his steps was in tune with the steady beat of the drum. My muscles loosened, as did my grip on his hand. Delano stepped back, lifting our connected arms. The skirt of my gown billowed around my legs as he spun me. The hum in my chest sparked as my hair lifted from my shoulders when he turned me again. A quiet laugh escaped me, and then a louder one as he raised our arms once more and spun himself. His hand came back to my waist, and we moved faster in our little circle, swirling around the fire.

The hum in my chest found my blood as the hem of my gown twirled around my ankles. A new hand closed around mine as Delano let go. Whirling, I found myself held by Kieran.

I grinned up at him. "Hi."

His lips curved up. "Hello, Poppy." He stepped back, spinning me. I stumbled, laughing as he caught me. "You surprise me."

"Why?" I asked as we moved around the flames.

"I didn't think you'd dance," he said, pulling me to his damp chest. "You honor us by doing so."

Before I could even begin to question why that would be an honor, Kieran spun me out, and another hand folded around mine. I turned to find that it was Lyra who now danced with me. We were nearly as close as she and Kieran had been, her legging-clad thighs brushing mine with every sway of her hips. Taking hold of my other hand, we moved together around the fire. Strands of hair stuck to my neck and temples as we weaved in and out of those flowing with the beat around the fire, each spinning into different partners. On and on, I danced, both with people I didn't recognize and those I knew, and all the while, that buzz in my chest and my blood vibrated in my skin. My head tipped back, my face exposed to the flames and moonlight as I was whirled into Delano's arms and then into Kieran's, who lifted my feet from the sand. Grasping his shoulders, I laughed as he turned us around and around.

"Someone is jealous," he said when my feet touched the sand once more. We spun—

Kieran's chuckle tickled my cheek as Casteel snagged me by the waist. I all but fell into him as he said, "I am definitely getting jealous."

"No, you're not." All I felt from him was smoky spice. "You're…"

"What?" he asked as he led me away from the fire, the dancers, and back into the moonlight-flecked shadows.

Breathless, I followed on tingling feet. "You're turned on."

He dipped his head, pressing his forehead to mine. "When am I *not* turned on around you?"

I laughed softly. "Good question."

"Admittedly, I am more turned on than usual." He drew me down onto the thick blanket, pulling my back to his chest. "It's your fault, though."

"How is it my fault?" I wiggled back, grinning as I heard him groan.

"It's your laugh." His lips brushed the damp skin of my neck. "I'll never get used to hearing it or thinking you do it enough." His chest rose sharply against my back, and I sensed something raw and sharp from deep within him. "After everything that happened with Shea and my brother, I honest to gods never thought a laugh could wreck me like yours does. And when I say it wrecks me, I mean in the best way—in the most complete way. And I…" A shaky breath left him. "I just want to thank you for that."

"You're thanking me?" I twisted as far as I could in his embrace, searching for his gaze and finding it. "I should be thanking you. It is you who made it possible for me to laugh without recourse."

He dropped his forehead to my temple. "Yeah?"

"*Yes*," I said, curling my hand around the back of his neck. "I'm *living* because of you, Cas, and I mean that both literally and figuratively. You think you're not worthy of me? In reality, I sometimes wonder if I'm not worthy of you."

"Poppy—"

"It's true." I squeezed the back of his neck. "Nothing you say can change that, but I know. I know in *here*." I pressed my palm to my chest. "That I would do anything for you. I know you would do anything for me. You have, and nothing in this realm or any other will ever change that or how I feel about you. Nothing should ever make you forget that I laugh because of you."

Shuddering, he pressed his lips to my temple and then folded one arm around my waist, resting his hand on my hip, where his fingers traced idle circles. He didn't say anything as he rested his chin atop my head, and neither did I. Words weren't always needed, and inherently, I knew this was one of those moments.

We just *were* as I watched those dancing around the fire break into smaller groups, some drifting out toward where the waves ebbed and flowed over the sand, and others into the canopied tents. I caught sight of Kieran once more. He was with who we thought was Lyra. Or at least I thought so. I honestly couldn't be sure. His arm was around the woman's shoulders, his head bent toward hers as they walked into the shadows of the bluffs.

I looked away, watching those who were still at the fire for a couple of minutes before I glanced back toward the bluffs.

My lips parted. I had no idea how Kieran and the female had gotten from where I'd last seen them to him leaning back in the sand and her kneeling between his legs, her hands in the general vicinity of an area that would definitely be considered naughty.

"Are they…?" I sucked in a sharp breath as Kieran's head fell back. My eyes widened.

Casteel's chuckle was dark and soft. "Do you still need me to answer that question?"

I swallowed. "No."

The hand at my hip continued moving in small, distracting circles as I watched who I thought might be Lyra move her head back and forth in a way that reminded me of how I moved against Casteel.

"Are you scandalized?" Casteel whispered.

Was I? I wasn't sure. Maybe I should be because I definitely shouldn't be watching. Every single social propriety there was, demanded that I look away and pretend that I had no idea what they were doing. But I did know. I'd read about the act Lyra was engaging in now in Miss Willa's diary. My heart thumped heavily. It was like when Casteel kissed me between the thighs, except the way Willa had described it, there was less kissing and licking, and more…sucking. That whole act had confused me greatly when I first read about it, but that was before I had learned that there were all kinds of acts one could do with any number of body parts.

"I'll take your non-answer as a no?" Casteel queried.

Feeling my cheeks warm, I dragged my gaze to the fire where people sat and talked, either unaware of what was happening in the shadows or not caring. "You did say the wolven were into public displays of affection."

He laughed again. "I did, and they are very open with their…affections. They feel no shame in doing so. I'm sure at some point you will definitely see a bare ass or two."

I liked that they felt no shame, possibly never even knowing the sourness of that emotion attached to such actions. There was an enviable freedom in that, to exist and be so free and open.

"If it makes you uncomfortable, don't feel embarrassed to say so," Casteel said quietly. "We don't have to stay, and we can leave whenever you want."

His offer tugged on my heart, and I turned my head, kissing the underside of his jaw. "Thank you for saying that, but I'm not uncomfortable."

"Okay," he said, tilting his head and kissing me.

And I really wasn't as I leaned into Casteel, resting my head against his chest. If there was no shame in their actions, then there was none in my heart.

But I really shouldn't be watching, and that was exactly what I was doing, my gaze finding where Kieran and Lyra had gone with rather unerring accuracy. I saw Lyra place a hand on his chest, pushing him back as he started to sit up or…reach for her. She was in control of her actions as Kieran retreated to rest on his elbows, a confidence in her as her head moved, a hand following the movements.

I really should have kept my senses locked down when I focused on Lyra, but I felt that control I had assumed was there, mixed with warm smokiness. The warmth in my cheeks increased, flowing down my neck as I shifted, stretching out my leg. My breath caught as Casteel's fingers moved a scant couple of inches from my hip to the left, still moving in those maddening, tiny circles.

And I really, really shouldn't have left my senses open when my gaze flicked to Kieran. The spiciness gathered in the back of my throat and low in my body, the place Casteel's fingers were so dangerously close to. I closed down my senses before I pried any further, but I…

"Poppy?"

"Yes," I whispered as Lyra seemed to tilt her head, pressing in impossibly close to Kieran's body.

"Are you watching them?" Casteel asked, his voice full of smoke.

A denial rose to the tip of my tongue.

"If so, you wouldn't be the only one, nor are they the only ones being watched," he said, one of his fingers stretching over the thin material of my gown. "They find no shame in any act of affection, whether they are involved in it, casual observers…or more active watchers."

Active watchers?

My gaze wandered across the rippling canopies and the shadowy depths inside, to where a slender arm beckoned to another who had been seated in the sand outside. The man put the bottle of what he'd been drinking down and rose, bending down as he entered the space under the canopy, where the shadowy outlines of bodies moved in unison. He joined them as Casteel shifted behind me again, leaning forward to slip his hand under where the hem of my gown was gathered at my knees. My heart might have stuttered as he trailed those fingers up the length of my bare skin, somehow managing to keep the skirt of the gown in place. The fingers on his right hand continued creeping lower and lower as I saw the man lower himself behind the one who moved on top. My pulse pounded as Casteel's fingers hesitated under my gown at the vee of my legs.

A slight tremor of anticipation tinged with uncertainty ran through me, followed by a sharp twist in my very core.

"Poppy, Poppy, Poppy," Casteel murmured as a finger above the gown reached the sensitive bundle of nerves. "Does what you're seeing in that tent answer any questions you might have had about how three lovers can enjoy each other?"

Yes? No? I saw the woman who had been riding the man under her still, her back bowing as the man behind her pulled her close to his chest.

"The newcomer is either moving inside her or against her," Casteel explained as his finger moved in those damn circles above the gown and along the crease of my thigh and hip. "Did Willa's journal explain the technicalities of that?"

The heat from my skin had entered my veins, stirring up my blood as I nodded. "It did." I wet my lips. "It sounded like it could be…painful."

"It can be if not done with care," he said. "And it appears that they are taking care."

No one appeared to be in pain, and no one seemed to be paying any attention to where we sat on our blanket. A breathlessness entered me as I slowly inched my thighs apart and asked, "Are they taking part in the Joining?"

"I do not know." The fingers against my bare skin slid toward the elicit ache. A strangled sound left me as he lazily drew a finger through the gathering wetness there. "A Joining is not required for such acts."

"Have you—?" I bit down on my lip as his finger pierced my flesh. My entire body jerked, spasmed, just like the three in the tent. I really needed to stop looking.

And, of course, I found myself looking to where Kieran and Lyra were. They were kissing now, but her arm still moved at his hips in a slow rhythm.

"Have I what?"

Pulse thrumming as Cas's finger slowly plunged in and out of me as he continued worrying the sensitive flesh, I gave up on remaining still before I even started to try. I lifted my hips against his hand as I forced my brain to remember how to form words. "Have you ever done that? What they're doing under the canopy?"

His lips moved down the side of my throat, tugging gently on the column of my neck. "I have." He nipped my flesh, wringing a gasp from me. "Does that bother you?"

Some of the passion faded enough for me to ask, "Why would it?"

"The pasts of some haunt the future of others," he said, his hands stilling.

My brows lowered as my gaze flickered. "You're over two hundred years old, Cas. I imagine you've done all manner of things."

His fingers moved again. "With all manner of people?"

The way he said that made me giggle. "Yes." Though my smile faded because I wanted to ask if he'd done that with Shea. A moment later, I realized that I could simply ask the question. So, I did.

Casteel kissed my neck. "No, Poppy. We didn't."

Surprised, I started to look back at him, but he curled his finger, hitting a spot inside me that caused my legs to stiffen and my toes to curl into the blanket. "W-why not?"

"We were friends, and then we were more," he said, the tension curling deeper and deeper inside me as my gaze darted across the fire, the canopies, and the shadows. Somehow, my focus ended up on Lyra and Kieran. They were no longer kissing. Lyra's head was at his waist again, and his hand was balled in her hair, his hips moving— "But our relationship was never one of raw need. That doesn't mean I cared any less about her, but it wasn't like this. There was no constant need to be inside her in every way imaginable, and even ways not yet thought of. I never found myself constantly hungering, and I believe you need that to find yourself exploring those things with someone you're committed to," he said, and my breaths became shorter and shallower. "I never had what I have with you with her, Poppy."

I don't know if it was the things he was doing to my body, what was going on around us or his words, but I teetered on that edge and then tumbled over it, falling and crashing like the waves rolling against the beach. The shattering release left me trembling.

Once my heart slowed enough for the pleasure-induced fog to clear, I turned my head toward him. "Do you…do you want to do that with me?"

He kissed me as he eased his hand out from under my gown. "I want to do everything imaginable, and things no one has ever thought of with you," he said. "But I only *need* you, Poppy. Now. Always."

My heart skipped and then sped up as my chest swelled with so much love I felt as if I could float right to the stars. I twisted in his embrace, clasping his cheeks as I rose onto my knees. "I love you." I kissed him, hoping that everything I felt for him could be communicated with that kiss, and then decided the kiss wasn't enough. A tendril of excitement swept through me as I rocked back, grabbing his hands. "I want to go somewhere…private."

Amber glowed from within hooded, sensual eyes. "We can go back—"

"No." I didn't want to wait. If I did, I would lose my nerve. "Is there not somewhere private here?"

The tips of his fangs became visible as he bit down on his lower lip and looked over his shoulder. "Yeah," he said. "There is."

Without another word, we rose. Under the moonlight, Casteel led me farther down the beach, to where I hadn't seen the tree-heavy dunes in the darkness. He guided me around the first outcropping of trees and then stopped. It was so dark that I could barely make out his features as he looked down at me. "You're up to something, aren't you?"

"Maybe," I admitted, grateful for the heavier shadows here as I took hold of the front of his shirt and stretched up, bringing his mouth to mine.

My heart thrummed as our tongues touched and danced, much as I had around the fire. We kissed and kissed, and even though he had to know this wasn't why I'd sought privacy, he didn't rush me. He just followed *my* lead, saying nothing as I pressed tiny kisses to the base of his throat. Sliding his palms up and down my arms, he remained quiet as I drew my hands down his chest. When I reached his stomach, I sank to my knees.

His hands fell away from me, hovering at my sides as I unhooked the flap of his breeches, feeling the rigid thickness there.

The taste of smoky spice consumed my senses as I reached in, wrapping my fingers around his warm, hard skin. He was breathing heavily now, and my heart raced as I eased him out. His skin felt like heated steel encased in silk as I tipped forward, halting when I felt him spasm in my hand.

"Poppy," he ground out. I lifted my gaze, momentarily stunned by the churning flecks of bright gold in his eyes. A shudder worked its way through him. "You don't have to do this."

"I want to," I told him. "Do you want me to?"

"You can do anything to me, and I'll want it." Another tremor worked its way through him. "This? My cock in your mouth? I'd have to be dead and nothing but ash to not want that."

My lips twitched. "That's…kind of flattering."

He choked out a rough laugh. "You are—" He groaned as I glided my fingers from his base to his tip.

"Am what?"

His fingertips touched my cheek. "Everything."

Smiling, I lowered my head. The salty taste of his skin was a surprise, dancing over my tongue. Tentatively, I moved my hand down his length, exploring as I brought him deeper into my mouth like I had read about in Willa's diary.

"Poppy," Casteel groaned, his palm flattening against my cheek.

She'd written about other things, stuff that reminded me of what Casteel had done for me, and I wasn't sure if he'd enjoy that or not. But I…I wanted to do those things. I drew my tongue over his taut skin, finding a little indentation under the ridge of his head and swirling my tongue over it.

"Fuck." His body jerked. "I…I wasn't expecting that."

Fighting a smile, I did it again, and he swore. "Did you read about that in Miss Willa's book?"

I hummed out an agreement, and the act seemed to vibrate through him. His entire body flexed, and I *felt* him throb.

"Fuck," he rasped. "I love that godsdamn diary."

A laugh escaped me then, and based on the way his hips jerked, he liked how it felt. There was nothing in Miss Willa's diary about laughing while doing this, but as I curled my hand around his base, I stopped thinking about that damn journal and just let instinct take over. I flicked my tongue across the head of his cock, marveling at his reaction—at the lazy heat swamping my senses. I liked doing this. Liked knowing he enjoyed it.

His hand slid from my cheek as his fingers threaded through my hair. He cupped the back of my neck, but he didn't put any pressure there. All he did was move his thumb, gently massaging the muscles. It was a…supportive presence as he continued letting me learn what made his body move in short, shallow thrusts, what caused his breath to catch, and what made the spicy flavor intensify. I realized something. Not only did I like this but I also enjoyed the control, the way I could slow his breathing or increase the way he throbbed against my tongue just by the pressure of my mouth, or how hard or soft I sucked on his skin.

"Poppy, I'm not…gods, I'm not going to last much longer." His grip on my neck tightened as he rocked against my hand, in my mouth. "And I don't know if that diary spoke of what happens."

It had.

And I wanted that. Wanted to feel him finish, to experience that, knowing I had brought him to that point. I drew my hand up the length of him, closing my mouth over his head. He shouted my name, and then his hips stiffened as he pulsed and spasmed against my tongue.

No sooner had I finished, and before I could even feel rather proud of myself, he dropped to his knees before me, clasping my cheeks. Tilting his head to the side, his mouth was suddenly on mine, his tongue against mine. The kiss was as demanding as it was worshipping, all-consuming as it left little room for anything else.

Casteel lifted his head, his eyes locked on mine. "You," he said, his voice thick and tone reverent. "All I ever need is you. Now. Always."

Chapter 25

Casteel and I had spent the day before living, so we would spend today ensuring we had more days like yesterday.

We would meet with his parents.

But first, we needed to get out of bed, something neither of us seemed in a rush to do. While Casteel toyed with my hair, we chatted about what I had seen the day before, which included me waxing on rather poetically about the frozen treat I'd consumed.

In a lull of silence as I convinced myself it was far past time to get up, Casteel asked, "When you healed that girl yesterday, did you notice anything different about your abilities?"

"Not really," I told him as I traced figure eights across his chest. "Well, I'm not sure if that's true. When I healed Beckett's injuries, I didn't really need to think about it. It just happened. But this time, I had to do what I normally did before."

"Think of happy memories?" He twisted a strand of hair around his finger.

"Yes. I thought of when we married." I lifted my head, resting my chin on his chest. He smiled softly at me. "And I thought about how unfair the girl's injuries were, and I…"

"What?"

I drew my lip between my teeth. "It seems silly to even consider this, but I did think to myself that it wasn't too late—that she would live while my hands were on her."

His gaze coasted over my features. "Did you know that she was already gone?"

"I…" I'd started to deny it, but I stopped myself as what Casteel had said the morning before resurfaced. Denial was no longer a luxury. He spoke of the Crown, but the same logic applied here. "I can't say that she was gone for certain, but she was close."

He slowly unwound my hair. "Then you either willed her soul to remain with her, or you brought her back to life, Poppy."

My heart tripped over itself. "It's hard for me to accept that, but I think I did." Hair tumbled over my shoulders as I rose onto my knees. "It makes sense that I can do that because of who Nyktos is, but it's kind of—"

"Amazing." He carefully untangled his hand from my hair.

"I was going to go with unnerving," I said.

His brow furrowed. "You gave that child a second chance at life. How can that be anything but marvelous?"

I glanced down at my hands, unsure of how to explain what I was thinking. "It's just that kind of ability…is powerful in a frightening way."

"Explain."

Sighing, I shook my head. "I know the people who saw what happened yesterday think I am a deity—"

"I believe they think you're a goddess," he countered. "And there is a difference between the two."

"Okay. They think I'm a goddess. But we both know that isn't the case," I pointed out, and he simply raised a brow. I rolled my eyes. "Either way, doing that felt like…playing god. It feels like an ability that could be misused without even realizing it—that is if I can even do it again."

He was quiet for a moment. "Do you think it was her time, and you interfered?"

I stiffened. "I cannot believe that it was time for anyone that young to pass on to the Vale. I don't think that at all."

"Neither do I." He tapped his fingers on my hand. "But you're worried about interfering when it is someone's time, aren't you? Because if someone is hurt and dying, you won't be able to stand by and allow that."

He knew me all too well. "How do you know when it's someone's time?" I asked and then laughed at the absurdity of the question. "How would any of us know that?"

"We don't." His eyes met mine. "I think all we can do is what feels right. It felt right for you to save that girl. But maybe another time will come when it won't feel right."

I couldn't imagine a time when helping someone wouldn't feel right, but that kind of unanswerable question would have to wait. We needed to get ready for the day.

A nervous sort of energy buzzed through me that had nothing to do with our conversation as I changed into black leggings and a sleeveless wrap tunic dyed in a shade that reminded me of Jasper's hair and fur. I was surprised that the delicate silver chain held the tunic together, and I only hoped it remained that way throughout the day. The last thing I needed was to expose the nearly transparent slip I wore underneath.

Then again, considering how Casteel's father had last seen me, it probably wouldn't come as much of a shock.

But I just wanted things to go smoothly between his parents and me because I knew if they didn't, the path would be rocky between Casteel and his parents going forward.

The moment I joined him in the sitting room, his fingers found their way into the waves and curls of my hair. "I love your hair like this," he murmured. "I'm beginning to think you do this because you know I become distracted by it."

I grinned as we stepped outside the room, my nervousness easing a bit. "Maybe," I said, even though I'd totally left it down because I knew he liked it like this.

And because I'd spent years with the heavy length pinned tightly back and up.

"Did you still want to see Kirha before we leave?" he asked.

I nodded. I'd mentioned this morning that I wanted to thank her for the clothing and her hospitality before we left to meet with the current Queen and King of Atlantia. Casteel had already sent word ahead of our impending arrival. With his hand folded around mine, he led me out into the breezeway, where ceiling fans churned overhead, stirring the scent of cinnamon and cloves that seeped out from the open windows of rooms facing the pathway.

If it weren't for the faded, oily stains on the walkway and the darkening of the dirt every couple of yards, it would be hard to imagine that those faceless creatures had been here two nights before. But they had, and Casteel and I were prepared in case the Gyrms appeared once more. I carried the wolven dagger hidden beneath my tunic, and

Casteel had two short swords strapped to his sides. We also weren't alone.

A wolven with fur as dark as Stygian Bay prowled along the top of the courtyard wall, tracking our progress. I had a feeling he or she wasn't the only wolven nearby as we stepped out from the breezeway and onto an earthen path lined with tall palms. The fan-shaped leaves provided adequate shade from the late-morning sun as we followed the winding walkway. Bursts of color from tiny wildflowers and vivid pink and purple blossoms peeked out from the tangled vines that swept over the walls in some sections and blanketed most of the garden floor. The garden was nothing like the showy and wildly diverse ones in Masadonia, but I liked the earthy, natural feel of it. And I had a feeling that no matter how many times one walked the pathways, they would find something new among the foliage.

We rounded a bend, and a patio became visible. Several stone benches and wooden stools that appeared to have been crafted from the trunks of trees encircled a large fire pit. The gray stone patio led straight to the open doors of an airy, sun-drenched room.

Among the plants placed on small tables and growing from large clay pots on the tile floor, oversized chairs with thick cushions and brightly colored ottomans were situated in clusters next to wide couches and settees. Large floor pillows in every shade of blue imaginable were scattered across the floor, but Kirha Contou sat on a plush, teal rug in the center of the room, legs crossed, and her head bowed. Narrow rows of small, tight braids were swept up and pinned back from her face as she rooted around in a basket of yarn. Her son was with her.

Wearing all black, Kieran stood out rather starkly in the colorful room. He sat beside her, leaning against one of the chair backs, his long legs stretched out in front of him. He held a ball of orange yarn in one hand and a white one in the other. Several more lay in his lap, and the image of him sitting there, a faint smile softening the handsome lines of his face as he watched his mother, would be forever imprinted on my brain.

Both of them looked up as Casteel and I neared the doors. My senses were open, and their emotions immediately stretched out, the cool splash of surprise I felt from Kieran as the orange ball of yarn fell from his hand and rolled across the rug caught me a little off guard. If Kieran had been aware that Casteel and I had witnessed his…activities in the shadows, he showed no sign of it as we'd ridden back to his family home under a sky blanketed by endless stars.

Even if he did, I didn't think that was the source of the surprise. I had no idea what it was as I focused on the woman beside him.

His mother was utterly beautiful—the spitting image of Vonetta from her deep, rich brown skin and broad cheekbones to the full mouth that seemed to hint at a laugh. What I felt from her also reminded me of her daughter. The taste of smooth vanilla was as comforting as a warm blanket on a cold night.

I realized I had seen her before when I first arrived here. She'd been in the crowd of wolven and had smiled as Casteel and I bickered.

"Kieran," Casteel drawled. He squeezed my hand as we stepped through the doors and then let go. "Are you knitting me a shirt?"

The wolven's expression smoothed out. "That is exactly what I'm doing," he replied, his tone flat.

"He's actually very good with the needles," Kirha said, placing the basket aside.

The syrupy-sweet taste of embarrassment radiated from Kieran as his cheeks deepened in color. His gaze narrowed on his mother. My brows lifted as the image that had been branded in my mind was now replaced by one that included Kieran knitting a shirt.

That was something that would never leave my mind.

Kirha started to rise as Casteel rushed to say," You don't need to get up."

"Oh, but I do. I've been sitting for so long, I feel like my legs have gone numb," she replied as balls of yarn spilled from Kieran's lap and tumbled across the carpet. He took hold of his mother's arm, aiding her.

Kirha murmured her thanks as she straightened. Under the lavender, sleeveless gown she wore, her swollen stomach pulled at the light material. She pressed a hand behind her hip and stretched her back. "Good gods, this better be the last baby."

"Yeah, well, someone needs to make sure your *husband* gets that through his thick skull," Kieran muttered.

"Your *father* will when he's constantly changing diapers again. I birth them, he cleans them," she remarked, grinning when Kieran wrinkled his nose. "That's the deal."

"I'll have to remember that," Casteel murmured.

My stomach dropped so fast I almost toppled over as my wide eyes shot to Casteel. For some reason, I hadn't even thought about…*babies* since the cavern—since I had thought he didn't want to have children with me. I'd been hurt then, which had been irrationally silly, considering we hadn't even admitted our feelings to one another yet. He was still taking the herb that prevented pregnancy, and as a Maiden, I'd believed I would Ascend. Having children was never something I'd ever considered, so it wasn't something that lingered in my mind. But now it was dancing at the center. A baby. *Babies.* Casteel's and my baby. Casteel holding a small, swaddled infant. My lips parted on a thin inhale. That was really something I did not need to think about at the moment.

"Poppy looks faint." Kieran smirked.

Casteel turned to look at me, his brows lowering as concern echoed through him. "Are you all right?"

I blinked, shoving the unnecessary image out of my head as I stepped forward. "Yes. I'm fine." I plastered a big smile across my face before either of them could ferret out where my mind had gone. "We didn't mean to interrupt. I just wanted to thank you for allowing me to stay here, and for the clothing."

A ready smile appeared on Kirha's face as she clasped my arms. "No need to thank me. Our home has always been open to Cas. Therefore, it will always be open to you," she said, and the sincerity in her words was clear. "I'm glad you like the clothing. I must say, you look far too beautiful for this one over here." She jerked her chin at Cas.

"Ouch," Casteel murmured, placing a hand over his heart. "My feelings. They hurt."

Kirha laughed as she pulled me into a close hug—well, as close as I could get with the belly between us, but the embrace was warm and unexpected and so…*nice*. It was the kind of hug I hadn't felt in ages. One I secretly hoped I'd receive from Queen Eloana upon my arrival. This kind of embrace was the type a mother would give, and it brought forth a rush of bittersweet emotions. Nothing about my smile was forced when she pulled back, clasping my arms once more. "I am so happy to meet you." Her gaze swept over my face, not lingering on the scars. "I hope you are feeling well?"

I nodded. "I am."

"Good." She squeezed my arms and then let go, placing a hand on her belly. "Kieran told me you met Vonetta?"

"I have," I said as Casteel appeared at my side, resting his palm on the center of my back. "Vonetta was so kind to me. She let me borrow one of her gowns and helped me get ready for the marriage ceremony.

I hope I get to see her again soon."

"What about me?" Kieran asked, and his mother and I looked at him. "I've been kind to you."

"Someone sounds like they're already experiencing middle-child syndrome," Casteel murmured under his breath.

"And I'm also, like, standing right here," Kieran added. "In front of you."

My lips twitched as I glanced at him. "You are…okay."

"Okay?" he repeated with a huff of offense, crossing his arms.

"Don't pay him any mind," Kirha said. "He's annoyed because the Healers believe he will soon have another younger sister."

Casteel chuckled. "You and Jasper are about to be sorely outnumbered."

"Tell me about it," Kieran muttered.

"When are you due?" I asked.

"Within a month, if the gods are willing," she answered, rubbing her stomach. "And not a day too soon. I swear this child is already as large as Kieran."

"That sounds disturbing," Kieran frowned, and I had to agree with him on that. "You said you were going to see your parents?"

Casteel nodded. "We are headed there now."

"Then I will go with you." Kieran turned to his mother. "Do you need anything before I leave?"

"No."

"You sure?"

"Yes." She laughed. "Your father should be here any moment now. He can help me with this." She gestured at the yarn. "I'm sure he'll be thrilled to assist me."

The look on Kieran's face said he doubted that as Casteel and I helped gather up the wayward balls of yarn, placing them next to the basket.

"Penellaphe?" Kirha stopped us as we turned to leave. "I know you didn't meet Casteel's parents under the best of circumstances."

His expression was stoic as I glanced at him. "No, I did not."

"And for that, I am even more saddened by what was done to you," she said. "Eloana and Valyn are good people. They never would've allowed what happened if they had known. That, I know for sure. And once they get past the initial shock of everything that has occurred, I also know that Eloana will accept you just as warmly and openly as I have."

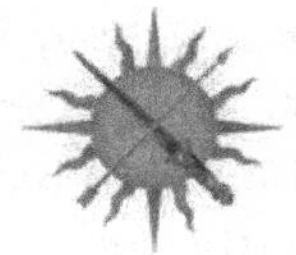

Once we were near the stables, I looked over at Kieran, still thinking about what Kirha had said before we left. "Your mother? Does she have a way of knowing things like your father?" *Like you,* went unsaid.

He frowned slightly. "At times, yes. Why?"

Well, as I had expected, that hadn't been an odd coincidence. "Nothing." I shook my head, aware of Casteel listening intently. "I was just curious."

"There were definitely some powerful changelings somewhere in both of their bloodlines," Casteel remarked as he took Setti's reins from an unfamiliar stablehand, his gaze drifting over his shoulder.

I saw three wolven in their true forms. One of them was the black one I'd spotted near the wall, but it was the mortal-looking female dressed in all black, breeches and tunic, that I focused on. I immediately recognized her, even though her pin-straight brown hair was pinned back at the nape of her neck.

It was Lyra.

I stole a glance at Kieran as she approached us, but I picked up on no real discernible emotion from either of them.

Stopping a few feet from us, Lyra dropped into a swift one-knee bow. "*Meyaah Liessa,*" she said. Behind her, the wolven lowered their heads to the ground.

Unsure of what to do with such a formal greeting after dancing around a bonfire with her the night prior, I glanced between Kieran and Casteel, the latter nodding reassuringly. Before I could say something most likely embarrassing, Lyra rose. Her pale gaze shifted to Casteel. "We will serve as your guards as you make this trip."

"Thank you, Lyra," Casteel said. "That is most appreciated."

I nodded my agreement, hoping I didn't look as ridiculous as I felt. I probably did. Lyra gave me a quick, lopsided smile as her gaze briefly connected with mine. I turned to see Casteel biting down on his lip as if he wanted to laugh, and I suspected it had nothing to do with my response to her greeting but had everything to do with what we'd watched last night. My eyes narrowed on him as I gripped the saddle, and he looked as if the struggle became even harder. I swung myself up onto Setti.

Casteel joined me, folding an arm around my waist while I stroked the side of Setti's neck. As I watched Kieran mount his horse, I asked, "Is the bowing thing going to happen often?"

"Yes," he answered, taking the reins of his horse.

"Why didn't your mother do that?" I wondered out loud. "Not that I wanted her to, but I'm curious. Is it because she's pregnant?" I doubted she would've been able to drop into such a position.

"I told her it would make you uncomfortable if she did," Kieran answered. "Just like I told my father not to do it."

My chest warmed. "You know what?"

He raised a brow as he looked down at me. "What?"

I reached over and patted his chest. "You're more than okay."

"Now that I know you think I'm more than okay, I can sleep well at night." His tone was as dry as the Wastelands, but I grinned.

"By the way, when it happens again, you can say 'You may rise,'" Casteel said as he nudged Setti into motion. "Or if you would like to use something less formal, you can simply say 'Yes' or greet them by name if you know who is before you. And before you ask them to cast the formality aside, please know that I have also asked that of many, and you've seen how well it worked for me."

Not very well at all.

Sighing, I leaned against Casteel as we rode out of the courtyard. The wolven, now four of them, followed at a discreet distance.

"We won't have to ride through the busiest parts of the city to get to the estate," Casteel told me as we veered onto a paved road surrounded by tall, lush cypress trees. The wolven quickly disappeared into the thick foliage. "We can follow the bluffs straight to it. There will be people, but nothing like when we entered the city or yesterday."

While I'd thoroughly enjoyed my all-too-quick visit to Saion's Cove, my mind was already a twisted mess, focused on the upcoming meeting with Casteel's parents. "Thank you."

He dipped his head and kissed my cheek as Kieran sent him a wry look. "Don't let him convince you that his motives are completely altruistic. He also doesn't want to be on the receiving end of shouts and long looks of admiration."

There had been a lot of them the day before.

"It makes me self-conscious," Casteel said.

"Really?" I asked, and when Casteel agreed, I looked to Kieran for confirmation. "Is he lying to me?"

"A little."

"He has no idea what he's talking about," Casteel claimed as the hand that had been resting on my hip inched across my lower stomach. His thumb moved, idly drawing circles around my navel.

"I think I'll believe Kieran," I decided.

"How dare you?" he teased, and I felt the nip of his sharp teeth against the curve of my neck. I jerked as a rush of heat flooded my system. "I am very shy."

"And very delusional," I retorted, glancing at the tall trees. With the thinness of the tunic, it felt like there was next to nothing between his hand and my skin.

It was hard not to show any reaction to his touch as glimpses of sandstone structures peeked out between the trees crowding the path. The farther we traveled, the lower his pinky finger roamed, and I began to see people behind the trees, loading carts and wagons with bushels and baskets. I wiggled a little when his finger danced lower, looking over my shoulder at him.

A look of pure innocence had settled on his features as he met my gaze. "Yes?"

I narrowed my eyes.

One side of his lips kicked up. The dimple in his right cheek appeared as a horse-drawn wagon neared the path. The driver's wide-brimmed hat obscured his features, but I felt the cool jolt of surprise as he and the younger man, who appeared barely in his teens, walked alongside the large, gray horse.

The driver waved, and the young man quickly dropped to one knee before rising to also wave.

I started to lock up but forced myself to relax and behave somewhat normally by returning the greeting, along with Casteel and Kieran.

Feeling rather proud of myself, I smiled at the wolven as they passed the two on the road. While I wondered which of the wolven was Lyra, a woman appeared between the trees several yards ahead, the bright orange tunic flattering against her deep black skin. She kept an eye on a small child who chased after a golden-winged bird that hopped along the tree's lower branches. Upon seeing us, a wide smile broke out across her face as she placed her hands on the child's shoulders and whispered to her. The little girl looked over with an excited squeal and immediately started jumping on one foot and then the other.

Casteel chuckled under his breath as the woman shook her head and bowed at the waist, patiently coaxing the child to do the same. They too waved, and this time, I wasn't frozen. I waved back like Casteel and Kieran had done, and it felt…less awkward. Like my arm wasn't as stiff as it had been before. But I quickly forgot about what my arm looked and felt like as the little girl all but rushed from her mother and nearly tackled the black-and-white wolven. Choked laughter came from Kieran as the girl wrapped tiny arms around the wolven.

"Oh, gods, Talia," the woman exclaimed. "What have I told you about randomly hugging people?"

I grinned as she gently untangled the girl from the wolven, who playfully nipped at one of her arms. A riot of giggles erupted from the child, and a second later, she was back to chasing the bird. The wolven she'd hugged trotted on, and I swore it smiled.

Once we passed, I looked back at Casteel. But before I could ask the same question as I had nearly every time we passed someone yesterday when I couldn't tell if they were of Atlantian descent or one of the bloodlines, Casteel beat me to it. "Both were Atlantian," he said, his thumb resuming the slow and utterly distracting circles. "The first were of Atlantian descent. Mortals. The last two were elemental."

"Oh," I whispered, focusing ahead. Atlantians had always been cooler toward me, with a few exceptions like Emil, Naill, and Elijah. My heart squeezed painfully as I thought of Elijah and Magda—of *all* those Atlantians, Descenters, and wolven senselessly murdered by the Ascended. Even then, I could hear Elijah's deep belly laugh.

But yesterday, the vast majority of those we came across had been warm and welcoming, just like the ones we passed now. Could it be that those of like mind as the Unseen were truly a small fraction of the populace? Just as a tiny kernel of real hope formed in my chest, Casteel's arm tightened around me.

Sometimes, I wondered if he knew where my thoughts had gone, which made me think of something else. "Do you have a changeling in your bloodline, Cas?"

"Not sure, but I can tell you something's changing in my pants right now," he murmured.

"Oh, my gods." I barked out a loud laugh as several of the nearby wolven made rough, huffing sounds. "That was so..."

"Witty?" he suggested, while Kieran snorted.

"Stupid," I said, biting down on my lip as a giggle snuck free. "I can't believe you said that."

"Neither can I," Kieran agreed, shaking his head. "But the

Da'Neer bloodline is purer than his thoughts."

I grinned as we passed small groups of people heading in and out of the narrow roads.

"It's not my fault my thoughts are less than innocent," Casteel countered, waving as someone stopped to bow. "I didn't introduce myself to the world of Miss Willa."

"Oh, my gods," I grumbled, half-distracted by my attempts to read the emotions of those we passed.

"To be honest," he continued, "I think I was more shocked about the fact that I was right, and she is Atlantian, than by anything else your father said."

"Why doesn't that surprise me?" I muttered.

Casteel laughed, and as we continued on, the nervousness from earlier returned. But then he handed over Setti's reins and let me control and guide the horse. Eventually, the trees cleared, giving way to lush green grass that flowed to the very bluffs overlooking the sea. Ahead of us, a hedge of sorts surrounded a large circular Temple set on a high podium, its white columns rising against the deep blue of the sky. Beyond it, a row of lavender-colored, trumpet-shaped blossoms of jacaranda trees struck a familiar chord inside me. I'd loved the trees that grew abundantly around the garden outside Castle Teerman. They made me think of Rylan, a guard of mine who'd been killed by Jericho—a wolven who had been working with Casteel. A heaviness settled in my chest. Rylan hadn't deserved to die like that.

And Casteel hadn't deserved everything that had been done to him.

Two wrongs never made things right or better, nor did they cancel one another out. They just were.

All thoughts about what I'd done on the road here faded to the background as the wolven appeared at our sides as we rode past the Temple and under the shade of the mildly honey-scented jacaranda trees. I could see a garden of sorts through the hedge, one that must've opened to the Temple. The other end flowed to an elegant building of limestone and marble. Gold scroll accents were painted around open windows where gauzy white curtains swayed in the salty breeze from the sea. The center was a wide structure with numerous windows and doors, several stories tall, with a domed glass ceiling and spires that I'd seen upon my arrival. Sweeping, two-story wings connected by vine-covered breezeways flanked each side. Balconies jutted from the second floors, the curtains swept to the sides and cinched to pillars.

Underneath, private verandas separated by walls covered by ivy and tiny pale blue blossoms rested. The Cove Palace wasn't half the size or nearly as tall as Castle Teerman and would be dwarfed by Wayfair Castle, where the Queen and King of Solis resided. But it was beautiful, nonetheless.

Behind me, Casteel had stiffened. "The guards are new," he said to Kieran.

Guards weren't usually posted at the entrances to where the King and Queen were currently staying?

"That they are." Kieran drew his horse closer to ours as he eyed the guards. "But not entirely a surprise."

"No, they are not," Casteel agreed.

The guards bowed deeply, but they watched the wolven with wary gazes. Suspicion tinged with curiosity radiated from them as we rode through the breezeway. I didn't pick up on any outright hostility as I guided Setti past them, but they were definitely watchful as we entered the courtyard where a tiered fountain gurgled water. Crimson roses climbed the basin, scenting the air as we dismounted from the horses. Several stable hands appeared, taking the reins.

Placing a steadying hand on my lower back, Casteel guided me toward the rounded steps. A man dressed in a golden tunic stood at the door, bowing before opening both sides. My nervousness resurfaced with a vengeance as we entered a short hall that opened to a circular chamber. The last of the sunlight shone across the numerous rows of empty benches, and light spilled from electric-powered wall sconces inside alcoves on either side of the vast chamber. The space could easily accommodate several hundred, and I couldn't help but notice how different this was from the Great Hall in Masadonia. There was little to no separation between where the people sat and the dais before them.

My eyes were trained on the white banners hanging on the back wall as Casteel led us to the left. In each banner's center was an emblem embossed in gold, shaped like the sun and its rays. And at the center of the sun was a sword lying diagonally atop an arrow. It was then when I realized that the arrow and sword were not equally crossed. They met at the top instead of the middle, and I didn't know how I hadn't noticed that before or why it stuck out to me now. But situated this way, the sword was actually longer, more prominent than the arrow.

"Has that always been the crest?" I asked.

Kieran shot me a quizzical look as we stopped before the banners. "You ask the most random things."

Honestly, I did, so I couldn't even muster up a retort.

"The crest can change with each ruler if they want." Casteel glanced at the banners. "But it always contains the three symbols—the sun, the sword, and the arrow."

"So this isn't the one your mother and father chose?"

He shook his head. "I believe this was what King Malec chose," he told me, and I was a little surprised to hear that his choice for a crest hadn't changed.

"The sun represents Atlantia?" I surmised, eyeing the crest. "And, let me guess, the sword represents Malec, and the arrow your mother?"

"You would be right," Casteel answered. "You don't like it, do you?"

I shook my head.

"What about it don't you like?"

"The sword and arrow aren't equal," I told him. "They should be equal."

One side of his lips curved up. "Yeah, they should be."

"They were equal at one time," Kieran said, now looking up at the banners. "Before Malec, and when two deities sat on the thrones. I imagine the sword is more prominent because, technically, Malec was far stronger than Queen Eloana." He sent Casteel an apologetic look. "No offense."

"Technically or not, it leaves a bad taste in my mouth," I said before Casteel could respond.

Kieran's wintery gaze met mine. "If you take the Crown, many will expect the arrow to become more prominent, as you are more powerful than Cas."

"If I take the Crown, the arrow and sword will be equal," I returned. "A King and Queen should be of equal power, no matter what blood courses through their veins."

The wolven grinned. "I would expect nothing less from you."

I opened my mouth, but he brushed past me, walking along and leaving me staring at his back. "He's annoying," I muttered to Casteel.

"But he's right." Casteel looked down at me, his eyes like warm honey. "I would expect nothing less from you, either."

I glanced back at the banners, thinking they needed to be changed, whether I took the Crown or not.

Pulling my gaze from the banners, we caught up with Kieran as we moved through a hall that opened to breezeways on either side and flowed straight into a large banquet hall. The table could seat an army, but it sat empty with only a vase of peonies in the center. We walked through a smaller room, one with a smaller, round table that appeared recently wiped down, and chairs with gray seat cushions. I caught a glimpse of my wide eyes in a mirror on the wall and quickly looked ahead. In front of us was a door, slightly ajar, and two Guards of the Crown. Both men bowed, and then one stepped aside as the other reached for the door.

The muted sounds of conversation drifted out of the room, and my heart skipped several beats. My steps slowed. What if Kirha was wrong? What if Casteel's parents had only grown angrier after their shock faded? His father hadn't been rude the night before, but we had only been in each other's presence for mere minutes.

And I had thought he'd been about to use the sword on me. His father had known that, too.

I stared at the door, heart thrumming. Who could blame them if they never accepted me? I was an outsider, the former Maiden of the Ascended, who'd taken their son and was possibly on the verge of taking more than that.

Their kingdom.

Chapter 26

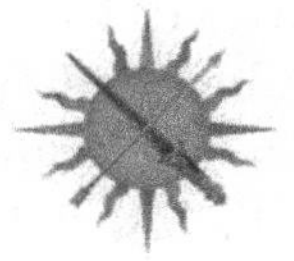

Casteel's gaze met mine. Sensing a thread of concern in him, I nodded before he could question me. A faint smile appeared, and then he motioned for the guard to open the door.

The airy, brightly-lit room smelled of coffee, and the first person I noticed was his mother. She sat on a dove gray settee, wearing a simple short-sleeved gown of pale blue. Her onyx-hued hair was once again twisted in a simple knot at the base of her neck. She had just placed a small cup on a low-profile table and appeared frozen there as she stared at Casteel with bright amber eyes. A rush of emotion poured from her— relief, joy, love, and underneath all of that was something tangy. Sorrow. There was a throbbing, steady current of grief as she rose, reminding me very much of what I'd often felt from Casteel when we first met.

My gaze inched away to where the faired-haired man stood at the back of the room, a short glass of amber liquid in his hand. Neither he nor the Queen wore their crowns, and I wasn't sure if that was common or not while in their private residences. I was almost convinced that Queen Ileana and King Jalara wore theirs to bed.

Goosebumps pimpled my flesh as Casteel's father stared directly at me. I didn't hold his stare in challenge but simply looked elsewhere. I felt barely anything from him. Casteel's father was either very reserved or knew how to block his emotions. They weren't the only people in the room.

Standing by a large window overlooking a garden was the Commander of the Crown Guard. Hisa stood quietly, her hands clasped behind her back.

"*Hawke.*" The nickname was a soft breath on the Queen's lips as she refocused on her son.

"Mother," he said, and I noticed a roughness to his voice that stung my eyes. It struck me then that they hadn't had a chance to even speak since his return.

She rushed forward, tripping over the corner of a cream rug. Casteel was there, catching her before she even really stumbled. She laughed as she threw her arms around him. "I was so glad when I heard that you planned to see us today. Look at you." Casteel's mother drew back, clasping his cheeks. She brushed at his hair. "Look at you," she repeated and then pulled him in for another hug, one tighter and longer than the first. Casteel didn't just allow it, he welcomed it.

Watching him be held by his mother softened…well, it softened every part of me. He was Casteel, the Dark One. I'd seen him remove a man's heart with barely a flicker of emotion and launch himself into trees and use his fangs to tear through throats. He was capable of great strength and terrible violence, and yet, right now, he was only a boy in his mother's arms.

"Mother." His voice was a bit rough around the edges. "You may be cracking a rib or two of mine."

Her laugh was light and happy as she pulled back. "That's doubtful." She placed a hand on his cheek again. "Have you gotten taller?"

"No, Mother."

"You sure?" she asked.

"The boy stopped growing ages ago, right around the time he stopped listening to us," his father finally spoke, and his tone was fond despite the words.

She laughed again, patting Casteel's cheek. She may have said something else because Casteel nodded and then stepped aside. He extended a hand toward me. "I would like to *properly* introduce you to my wife," he said, warm honey eyes meeting mine. "Penellaphe."

Keeping my gaze locked with his, I came forward, placing my hand in his. He squeezed my hand as the sweet taste of chocolate filled my senses. I exhaled slowly, returning the gesture as I looked at his mother. Maybe it was my years as the Maiden because instinct guided my actions and had nothing to do with the hum of awareness that seemed to vibrate through my blood. I bowed at the waist and then straightened. "It is an honor to meet you officially." The words spilled quietly from my lips. "Casteel has spoken so warmly of you."

Amusement stretched from Casteel, but from his mother, I got what felt like a cool splash of water filtered back to me, mingled with an edge of disbelief. It was almost as if she were finally looking at me. And maybe this was the first time since I'd entered the room. There was no doubt in my mind that she had learned what had happened in the Wastelands, so I couldn't exactly blame her for being shocked to see me standing before her, relatively normal and not a blood-hungry vampry.

A jolt ran through me because as unbelievable as it was, I sometimes forgot, if only for a few minutes, what had happened. When I remembered, like now, I also felt a dose of disbelief.

But Casteel's mother had gone completely still as she stared at me, the blood draining rapidly from her features.

"Mother?" Casteel started toward her. "Are you all right?"

"Yes," she said, clearing her throat as her husband came forward a step. My spine stiffened as she continued staring at me. "It's just—I'm sorry." Her golden eyes widened as a weak smile formed. "I just can't believe what I'm seeing. Valyn told me what happened—that you were Ascended."

"I couldn't let her die," Casteel stated before I could. Anger simmered from him like a riptide under still waters. "I knew exactly what I was doing and what I did is on me. Not her."

Queen Eloana's gaze flicked to her son. "I know. That is what your father said. I don't hold her responsible for what you did."

My breath caught. "You shouldn't hold Casteel responsible, either. I'm not a vampry."

"I can see that," she said, her gaze tracking over my features as if she were searching for a hint of the Ascended we all knew. "But what if you had become that?"

"What if?" Casteel challenged softly, releasing my hand.

His father took a long drink from the glass he held, and I had a feeling we were quickly veering down the same path Casteel and his father had taken about my Ascension. I truly didn't want a repeat of that.

"We can't change what was done to me or what Casteel did to save my life. It happened," I said, clasping my fingers together tightly. "And, obviously, we are all lucky that I didn't turn into a vampry. It seems rather pointless to continue discussing what could've happened when it simply did not. He understood the risk. He still took the chance, and I am still here. Not a vampry. It's over."

The anger receded in Casteel, but the coolness of his mother's surprise grew. "It's only over if what was done in those ruins remains between those who were present. If word of what happened were to ever make it out, some would possibly see you as no different than the Ascended, so it's not simply over just because it seemingly turned out well."

Her tone was level, but there was a condescending touch to it that scalded my throat and stung my eyes. Warm skin brushed against my arm. Kieran had stepped in closer to me, and the simple touch was another jolt, reminding me of how such a thing had been forbidden to me as the Maiden. And that made me think of all those years I had been forced to remain quiet. To allow anything to be said in front of me or about me or to me. To accept whatever was done to me.

And I'd been so worried about his parents accepting me, even before Casteel and I had stopped pretending and admitted that what we felt for one another was real. I still wanted their acceptance, but what was done to me had been done to both of us. We hadn't chosen to be put into that situation. Those who called Atlantia their home had. Her people had. I pushed through the burn in my throat because I had to.

Because I wore no veil now.

Some instinct told me that what happened right now could very well shape the dynamics of my relationship with Casteel's parents from here on out. The gods knew it was already on shaky ground, but they weren't the Teermans, who had been my guardians when I lived in Masadonia. They were not Queen Ileana and King Jalara. And I didn't escape one Crown only to be silenced and patronized by another.

I met and held her gaze as I shut down my senses, not allowing myself to read anyone in the room. At this moment, what *I* felt mattered. "It's over because not only is lecturing Casteel irrelevant and serves no purpose other than to imply he's guilty of something, when in reality, *your* people are the only ones who are guilty." My chin lifted a notch. "But also because it's a rather repetitive, tiresome conversation at this point."

Queen Eloana's nostrils flared as she inhaled a sharp breath. Her lips parted.

But I wasn't done. "Furthermore, regarding what happened in the Wastelands spreading beyond those who were present, I'm not sure that is a concern. As I understand it, the wolven are loyal to me and won't do anything that causes harm to come to me. Is that not correct,

Kieran?"

"That is correct," he answered.

"The Atlantians present are loyal to Casteel, and I do not believe he feels they will betray him," I said, still holding the Queen's gaze. "Am I right, Casteel?"

"You are," he confirmed, his tone not nearly as dry as Kieran's. Still, there was an undeniable smokiness to it.

"With the exception of the King, the remaining witnesses are dead, and it can be safely assumed they will not be sharing the events of the night anytime soon," I continued, my fingers beginning to ache from how tightly I clasped them. "But in the rare, off chance that what happened that night becomes widely known, I am still unsure what there is to be concerned about. The Atlantian people appear to be intelligent enough to realize that since I have no fangs and can walk in the sun, I am not a vampry. Or am I overestimating the people's common sense?"

No one responded.

It was so quiet in the room that a cricket could have sneezed, and we would have heard it.

Casteel broke the tense silence. "You have not overestimated the people, and not only is this conversation pointless, it's also offensive, considering she was attacked by our people."

"We had no knowledge of Alastir's plans or that the Unseen were active and involved in this," the Queen stated. "Nor did he give us any indication that he was plotting such a thing."

"When Alastir came with Kieran to alert us of the Ascended's arrival in Spessa's End," his father said, "he told us about your intention to marry, and his belief that it was tied to…Malik." He took a quick drink, clearing his throat. I felt it though, push through the walls around my senses, before it vanished—the burst of tangy, almost bitter agony. "He said he was unsure how committed you two truly were to each other."

"We're committed," Casteel advised as the rush of hot anger joined my irritation. "Very."

"I do not doubt that," his father drawled. "I think one would have to be blind to not notice that."

I thought of the way Casteel had kissed me in front of his father, and my cheeks warmed. "Is that all Alastir said?" I asked. "Did he know that I was a descendant of the deities?"

"Alastir told us who you were and what you could do," Queen

Eloana acknowledged. "We knew what that meant. No average mortal with Atlantian blood could have those abilities. Any of us who is old enough to remember the deities would've known—though maybe not at first. No one would even be thinking of that. But at some point, Alastir became aware of your heritage and realized who you were."

"But you knew the moment you saw me," I said, remembering the look on her face as if I had seen it yesterday. "Alastir told you that it wasn't too late."

"Because he knew what it meant for the Crown, as did I when I saw you—saw how you radiated light. I knew what you were," she told us. "I didn't understand what he meant in the Chambers when he said it wasn't too late, but after becoming aware of his plans, I imagine he believed we'd support what he hoped to accomplish."

"Which was to hand me over to the Ascended so they could kill me?" I said, suppressing the shudder that rose at how close he'd come to succeeding. "Just like those in the Chambers who attacked me before you all arrived. I tried to stop them—"

"Tried?" King Valyn said with an incredulous laugh that reminded me so much of Casteel. "I would say you succeeded, Maiden."

Casteel's head snapped toward his father, tension stiffening his broad shoulders. "Her name is Penellaphe. And if you get my *wife's* permission, you may call her that. If not, then you may call her Princess. Whatever rolls more respectfully off your tongue. But what you will *never* refer to her as is the Maiden. Do you understand me?"

I pressed my lips together. His words. His tone. I didn't know why, but I wanted to smile.

His father drew back, eyes flaring wide, but his wife held up a hand. "Your father nor I mean any disrespect, Hawke."

"You don't?" I blurted out, and her golden gaze shot to me.

"No," she stated, her delicate brow pinching. "We do not."

I stared at the Queen—at my mother-in-law. "When you first saw me, you spoke as if Casteel had brought a curse back to the kingdom instead of a wife."

"I was caught off guard by what I saw," she responded, "as I imagine anyone would have been." Her brow tightened even further. "I...I never expected you."

"And I never expected *any* of this." I held her stare, needing her to understand that I wasn't the Maiden—that I wasn't the Ascended's tool like those in the Temple had believed. "Alastir wouldn't have known this, but I was there when the Ascended delivered their *gifts* at Spessa's

End." My chest squeezed as I thought of Elijah, Magda—of all of them who had been murdered so senselessly. "I fought them alongside Casteel. I killed the Duchess of Masadonia. I healed *your* people even as some of them looked upon me as if I were some kind of monster. I didn't force *your* guards to attack me, and that's who some of those people were, weren't they? Guards of the Crown. Members of the Unseen."

The Queen remained silent as I leaned forward. It didn't go unnoticed how the King shifted as if he wished to stand and shield his wife, or how Hisa stepped forward. Maybe later, I'd feel ashamed for the savage rush of satisfaction that gave me. Or maybe I wouldn't. "I don't know what you might think of me or what Alastir shared with you, but I didn't choose to be the Maiden or to wear the veil. I didn't choose to be a descendant of some deity or come back here and break bonds or usurp any bloodlines. The only thing I have ever chosen is your son."

Casteel's head tipped back, and his chest rose with a deep breath, but he remained quiet, letting me speak for myself.

"Did Alastir tell you *that* when he arrived from Spessa's End?" I asked.

"No," his father responded quietly. "He did not."

"I didn't think so."

Casteel spoke then. "We came here in hopes that you two could help us determine what my wife Ascended into. And on a personal note, I'd hoped that you'd get to know Penellaphe a little and vice versa. But if we're going to rehash the past, then there is nothing left for us to do but take our leave."

"But we must speak of the past," his mother said, and Casteel went rigid. "Just not in the way you think," she added with a heavy exhale. I finally opened my senses, letting them stretch out toward her. The tanginess of anguish was so extreme that I almost took a step back. She smoothed a hand over her already coifed hair as her husband joined her at her side in the same silent way Casteel often moved. He placed a hand on her shoulder as she said, "I need to apologize. I truly didn't mean to cause offense, but I know that I have. My shock over the entire situation has obviously made a mess of me," she said, reaching up and folding a hand over her husband's. "But there is no excuse. Because you both are right."

Her gaze swept back to me. "Especially you. What was done was not your fault or my son's, and what I had planned to say to you was how sorry I am for what happened." There was sincerity there, tasting of contrition, and I relaxed a little. "But both Valyn and I are relieved that you are…that you stand before us with our son." There was a beat of emotion I couldn't read because it came and went so quickly. "I should've said this as soon as you walked into the room, but I…" She trailed off, shaking her head. "I am deeply sorry, Penellaphe."

I watched Casteel's father dip his chin to kiss his mother's temple, an act that tugged at my heart, reminding me of Casteel. The breath I took no longer scalded my throat, even if my skin still pricked with pent-up frustration. But Casteel's parents had been dealt a shock. I couldn't forget that she likely knew I shared the same blood as her first husband. I was a painful reminder of a past she probably wished never to think of.

And while the part of me that existed in the center of the hum in my chest wanted me to turn around and leave, I knew that would be as pointless as lecturing Casteel. Besides, I was capable of compassion, and I did feel empathy for his mother—for both of his parents. I was not what they expected. Ever.

"It's okay. You haven't had a chance to really see Casteel, let alone speak to him. And I can understand why you'd be shocked to see me as I am and not as one *should* be after an Ascension," I said. There was no missing the twin bursts of surprise from both his parents.

Queen Eloana blinked rapidly while her husband stared at me as if I'd sprouted a third arm. His mother recovered first. "Thank you for being so understanding, especially when we are the ones who have much to atone for. Please,"—she extended an arm to identical settees that sat across from the one she had been seated upon—"have a seat."

Casteel glanced back at me, the question clear in his eyes. He was leaving it up to me, whether we stayed or left. I reached out to him, welcoming the weight and feel of his fingers around mine. I nodded.

Relief was evident from both his parents. "Would either of you like something to drink? Kieran?" she asked.

We passed on the offer as we sat in the thickly cushioned settee—the kind I could easily imagine curling up in to read a book.

Just not that damn diary.

Kieran remained standing, taking up a guard position behind the settee, and it didn't escape me that that was exactly what he was doing. He was standing guard directly behind me, his hand resting on the hilt of his sheathed sword.

That had to send a rather uncomfortable message.

"I hope what you saw of Atlantia yesterday has shown you that your experiences with us so far are not who we are," King Valyn stated, his stare nearly as intense as his son's as he revealed their knowledge of how we'd spent the day before. He and his wife sat. "And those you may have met yesterday are more of a representation."

"I want nothing more than for that to be true," I admitted. "What I've seen so far of Saion's Cove has been lovely."

His father nodded. "I want to make sure that is the only truth you come to know."

"We learned last night that we owe you our gratitude, something else I should've said already." The Queen's citrine-bright gaze fixed on me. I tasted the lemon of curiosity, a tart blast of confusion, and the tangy undercurrent of sorrow. "Thank you for aiding the child who was injured in the carriage accident. You prevented a great, unnecessary tragedy."

I glanced at Casteel, unsure of how to answer. *You're welcome* seemed like an odd way to respond in this situation. His hand tightened around mine. "I…I only did what I could to help her."

The King arched a brow. "Only did what you could? You saved that child's life. That was no simple act."

I shifted in my seat, uncomfortable.

"My wife is far humbler than I am," Casteel asserted, and there was a soft, barely audible but recognizable snort from behind me. The corners of my lips turned down as Casteel's gaze slid to mine. "If I were capable of doing what she did, I would have my greatness inked on my skin."

"Really," I replied dryly. "That sounds excessive."

"But as you already know, I am excessive in all things," he told me in a voice that was all lush, decadent smoke.

Warmth crept into my cheeks as a wicked heat settled low in my belly. Immediately, I thought of what we'd done on the beach the night before. That had been…excessive.

Casteel grinned.

His father cleared his throat. "Have you always been able to do what you did with the child?"

Pulling my gaze from Casteel, and my mind from very inappropriate places, I answered. "No, I haven't," I said and then gave a brief recap of the evolution of my abilities. "They were changing before I Ascended."

"I figured it had to do with the Culling," Casteel supplied.

"The Culling would explain the change," his mother agreed.

"And this was before the Ascension? I know of no other half-Atlantian to go through the Culling." His father eyed me closely. "Or any Ascended mortal with Atlantian blood who went through a Culling and did not become a vampry. But then again, I know of no other half-Atlantian descended from the gods, who is alive today."

"Me, either," I said and then cringed. Obviously, I didn't. *Gods.*

Amusement trickled in from Casteel, and surprisingly, his father. A faint grin appeared on the King's face as Casteel said, "You said you know of no other that is alive today. Are you saying there *were* others like her before?"

I almost wanted to smack myself for not catching that earlier.

The Queen nodded. "It didn't happen often, but deities did create children with either Atlantians or mortals. When that happened, the eather of the deity often manifested in the child in one way or another. Of course, that manifestation was stronger if the other parent was Atlantian."

"The children? The ones from those who were mortal?" I asked, my need for answers great. "They were still mortal?"

She nodded as she picked up her small white cup from the table. "From what I remember, they healed faster than most mortals from injuries, and they were not often sick," she explained as she looked to her husband, taking a sip. I had always healed fast, and I rarely ever got sick. "But they remained mortal—aging the same as any other. They probably would've lived slightly longer if it weren't for their need to chase after death."

"What does that mean?" Casteel asked.

"Those who carried the blood of the gods were often warriors—the first to stop a fight, and sometimes start one," the King explained. "They were the bravest men and women I've ever known, fighting in the trenches alongside Atlantian soldiers. Most, if not all of them, died in the war or were taken captive by the Ascended once they realized the blood they carried within them."

My stomach soured. They were probably fed upon or used to create more Ascended, facing a brief but no less horrific taste of what Casteel had suffered, and his brother currently lived. My lip curled as I shook my head. "Gods." I swallowed hard as Casteel squeezed my hand. "How long have the Ascended been doing this?"

"As long as they have breathed," the King said, and I shuddered. "They have committed atrocious sins against Atlantians, mortals, and the gods."

None of what he said was an understatement.

"The thing is, though," his father continued as he rested his elbow on the settee, "not even the children of a deity and an Atlantian had abilities that manifested so strongly in them as they have for you. What you did at the Chambers is something not even the most powerful elemental Atlantian can do," he said, sliding a thumb along his jaw as he looked between Casteel and me. "You asked me in the Temple of Saion if I could explain what happened to you when Casteel Ascended you."

"And you told us that you didn't know," Casteel replied.

"That wasn't entirely a lie," he said, glancing at his wife before turning to Casteel. "The past that your mother spoke of plays a role in this—what you've become. But it doesn't explain how."

Icy fingers of unease touched the nape of my neck, sending a shiver down my spine.

"Your parents?" his mother asked as she tipped forward slightly. "You believed them both to be mortal?"

"I did," I said, shoulders tensing. "But I'm not so sure now. I don't even know if they were my birth parents."

Her throat worked on a swallow. "And you have a brother?"

Alastir had definitely informed them well. "I do. He is older by two years."

"And he Ascended?" she asked, and I nodded stiffly. She clasped her hands lightly in her lap. "Are you sure of that?"

"He has only ever been seen at night," Casteel confirmed. "Beyond that, there is no way of knowing. But he has been seen multiple times. I do not believe they are using him for blood—in the same way they intended to use Penellaphe."

I knew what his parents were thinking. That Ian was either my half-brother or not my brother by blood at all. If either were the case, I didn't care. He was still my sibling. Just as my parents, who had given their lives to protect us, would always be the only mother and father I knew.

"I believe that we can answer some of the questions you have," his mother stated, her gaze briefly meeting her husband's.

Casteel squeezed my hand as I said, "Alastir told me that I share similar abilities with—"

"Malec?" Queen Eloana interjected, her sorrow becoming a thickness that cast a pall on the room. "You do. You would. He spoke the truth."

Sucking in a sharp breath, I was stunned and even more surprised by the fact that I was so shocked. Apparently, some part of me hadn't wanted to believe it was true. I sat back, trying to pull my hand free of Casteel's grip.

He held on as he angled his body toward mine. "It doesn't matter, Poppy. I told you that before." His gaze snared mine. "It doesn't matter to me."

"And it doesn't matter to us," Kieran stated softly from behind us, bravely speaking for the entirety of the wolven.

"You actually look like him," Casteel's mother whispered, and my head swung in her direction. "Even if I hadn't seen the power radiating from you, I would've known exactly who you came from. You have many of his features and his hair—though his was a shade of red that carried more brown in it, and his skin was a little darker than yours."

I could feel the blood slowing in my veins. "I was always told that I looked like my mother—"

"By who?" she asked.

"By..." Queen Ileana had told me that. Ever since I could remember, she'd said that I was a replica of my mother when she was my age. I never once questioned that growing up, and even though I was beginning to suspect that at least one of my parents wasn't related to me by blood, I'd never truly thought it was my mother.

Casteel stared at me for a moment and then turned to his mother and father. "What are you saying?"

"What we're saying is that it's impossible for the ones you believed to be your parents to be who you remember them to be." King Valyn's tone was softer than what I even imagined him being able to accomplish. "Or they were not your parents at all. Because we know who one of them was."

The sympathy that radiated from the Queen nearly choked me. "Malec had to have been your father, Penellaphe."

Chapter 27

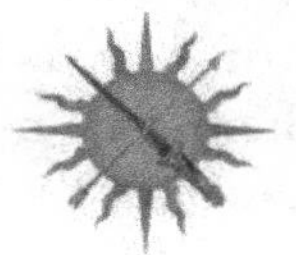

I stared at Casteel's parents, caught in a cyclone of confusion and disbelief. I wanted to stand, but Casteel still held onto my hand tightly. And where could I go?

"For you to have your abilities, you have to be the child of a deity and not just share their blood," King Valyn explained in that same gentle way. "And it also means that neither of your parents could've been mortal."

I inhaled sharply. "What?"

"There's simply no way that you were ever mortal," Queen Eloana said, her gaze searching mine. "That doesn't mean that the mother you knew isn't your mother. It just means that she was never mortal."

I shook my head as my brain rapidly tried to process this new information. "But wouldn't Alastir have known that? He met her."

Queen Eloana lowered her gaze, and I knew then that she had said what she had to lessen the impact.

My stomach hollowed. "Don't do that—don't lie to soften the blow. I appreciate it. I do." And I did. It meant that she cared in some fashion about my feelings. "But I need to know the truth. I need to face it."

A measure of respect rippled through the Queen as she nodded. "He would've known if the woman he met was not mortal."

"It also means that Leopold couldn't have been Malec." Kieran had moved to perch on the arm of the settee. "Alastir would've known and would've said as much."

I focused on taking deep, even breaths as I reminded myself that I had already suspected that at least one of my parents hadn't been related to me by blood. I'd even started to accept that, and I…I could accept this. But Malec as my father? Something didn't add up about that. But my thoughts were too much of a whirlwind to figure out what that was at the moment.

"And he would've told me if he had happened across Malec," Casteel's mother stated, snapping my attention back to her. "He would've told both of us."

Casteel's fingers slipped from mine then, and my heart stuttered at the blast of iciness that rolled off him as he stared at his parents. "Did you two know about Penellaphe before me? Did you know what Alastir took part in that night in Lockswood?"

Oh, my gods.

I…I hadn't even considered that. But I tasted it then, the sourness of shame, coming from both of them. The center of my chest hummed, and Kieran inhaled raggedly as he stretched his neck from left to right. "You…you knew?"

"We knew that he had found what he believed to be a descendant of Malec's," Queen Eloana answered as her husband reached between them, clasping her hand. "But we did not know anything else about you or your family. He didn't even know then that you were Malec's child. He only came to realize that when he met you again."

Casteel's body was impossibly rigid, and I saw Hisa inch away from the window and move toward his parents. "But you knew that he killed her parents? Left her to die?"

His father met his stare. "We only knew after the fact. There was nothing we could've done then."

A moment passed, and then Casteel started to stand. I snapped forward, grasping his arm. "He's right," I said, swallowing thickly as his head swung in my direction. His eyes reminded me of frozen topaz. "There was nothing they could've done after the fact. This is not their fault."

So focused on Casteel, I couldn't quite place the strange sensation again, a fleeting emotion that was sour yet also tangy. I had no idea who it came from or if I had really even felt it when Casteel's rage was a fire storm. "They're not to blame for what Alastir did," I told him, curling my other hand around his arm. "They're not."

He didn't move for several heartbeats and then stiffly returned to sit beside me. The muscles under my hands remained tense as Hisa stepped back to her post by the window, her hand easing away from the hilt of her sword.

"How?" Casteel demanded raggedly. "How could either of you continue a friendship with that bastard after knowing what he did?"

That...

That was an excellent question.

His father's chest rose with a heavy breath. "Because we thought that he was acting in the best interests of Atlantia."

"He allowed a child to be attacked by Craven," snarled Casteel. "How in the fuck is that in the best interests of Atlantia?"

"Because Malik was gone, you showed no interest in taking the Crown, and a descendant of Malec, raised among the Ascended, cared for by a Handmaiden of the Blood Crown, would've been able to claim the throne," his mother said, and I felt Casteel flinch. "And even not knowing the extent of the blood that she carried in her, there was no way that Alastir or either of us believed it to be a coincidence that a Handmaiden was masquerading as the mother of a child who was the heir to Atlantia."

Masquerading as the mother...

"*Gods*," Kieran muttered, dragging a hand over his face.

Casteel sat back, a muscle flexing in his jaw as he looked at me. "Poppy, I—"

"Don't. Don't you dare." Releasing his arm, I clasped the sides of his face. "Don't you dare apologize. This isn't your fault either. You were trying to find your brother then. You had no idea what Alastir would do or that I even existed. Don't you take on that kind of guilt. Please."

"She's right, son." His father cleared his throat. "This is not on you."

"And you truly think you hold no responsibility in this?" Casteel said, his eyes never leaving mine.

"No, we do," his mother said quietly. "We didn't like what was done, but we did not disagree with it. And that is something we've lived with since then and will continue to live with."

"Just like those you killed to protect the location of Iliseeum?" Casteel broke my hold as he turned to his parents. "Is that another thing you both live with?"

"It is," King Valyn confirmed, and if either were surprised that we had learned about Iliseeum's location, they didn't show it. "And if you become King, you will have to do many things that will turn your stomach, haunt your dreams, and that you'll have to live with."

The truth in that statement silenced Casteel. For a second. "I'm sure there will be, but if I discover that any of my people took part in harming or killing a child, they will find themselves in the Abyss, where they belong. That will never be blood that sits on my hands."

Sorrow pierced through the walls surrounding King Valyn. "I hope and pray that it never does."

"Prayers aren't needed," Casteel replied coolly as he picked up my hand and pressed a kiss to the center of my palm.

"Wait," Kieran blurted out, startling me. "I don't understand how Malec is her father. I know it's never been stated what happened to him, but it's been safely assumed that he's not alive, and hasn't been for centuries. After all, why wouldn't he have returned to claim the throne?"

I jerked. *That* was what hadn't made sense about Malec being my father. Yes, no one appeared to know what had happened to him or Isbeth. But how could he still be alive?

"It was a safe assumption," Casteel's mother said, rising. "And that's why it's also impossible."

I blinked once and then twice. "Come again?"

"It's impossible that Malec sired a child nineteen years ago." The skirts of her gown snapped around her ankles as Queen Eloana strode to the oak credenza, picking up a decanter of amber liquid. "Are you sure none of you wants a drink?"

Kieran looked like he needed one when he said, "I really don't understand what is happening."

"After I had the marriage annulled, and Malec was dethroned, he disappeared," she said, pouring herself a glass and placing the topper back on the decanter, her hand remaining there as she stood with her back to us. "At that time, I was otherwise occupied with the growing threat of the Ascended, and the beginnings of the war, but it wasn't until some years later, after Valyn and I married and the War of Two Kings ended, that I found him." Her shoulders were tense as she took a drink— a nice, long one.

"I knew I had to. If not, he would forever pose a risk to not only Atlantia but also to the family I was trying to build. I knew him." She looked over her shoulder as she took another drink. Her lips peeled back, revealing the tips of her fangs. "He would have sought revenge for what I'd done. So, I hunted him down, deep within Solis, and entombed him."

"You...you used the bone chains?" I asked.

She gave a curt nod. "It is extremely difficult to kill a deity. Some would say impossible without the aid of another or a god," she said, and I remembered what Alastir had said about Malec. That he had killed many of the other deities.

Not only was my…father prone to chaotic violence and was a habitual adulterer, he was also apparently a murderer.

But that was if he was my father. And that was something Queen Eloana had yet to explain.

"That was some four hundred years ago." She faced us, holding the glass to her breasts. "It would've taken more than half of those years for him to become weak enough to die, but he would've been dead by the time you were born."

Casteel's brows furrowed as he looked over at me and then back to his mother and then his father. "Then how is Malec Poppy's father?"

"Maybe you're wrong," Kieran suggested. "Maybe Malec isn't her father."

King Valyn shook his head. "There are no other deities. Malec killed the last of them when he ruled. But it's not just that." His gaze flicked to me. "You do look like him. Too much to be a child several generations removed."

I opened my mouth, but I didn't know what to say.

"And what you did for that child yesterday?" his mother said. "From what we've heard, she was too far gone to be healed. Malec could do the same."

"But he rarely did?" I said, repeating what Alastir had said.

She nodded. "He did when he was younger and less embittered and bored with life and death." She took another drink, and I noticed her glass was nearly empty. "He actually saved my life. That's how we met." Her throat worked on a swallow as I glanced at Casteel, unsure if he had known that. "No other deity could do that. Only those who carried the blood of Nyktos. And there was only ever Malec. And he was Nyktos's grandchild. That was why he was so powerful. That partially explains why you are so powerful, as Nyktos would be your great-grandfather."

"Besides that, Malec was the oldest deity." Casteel's father sat forward, rubbing his palm on his right knee. "The rest were the children of great-grandchildren, born of the gods."

Which meant that if Casteel and I had children, they would be…they would be like the deities who once ruled Atlantia. Perhaps a little less powerful due to Casteel's elemental bloodline, but still…powerful.

I couldn't even think about that at the moment. "But Nyktos had two children," I said, remembering the painting of the large, gray cats. "They only had one child between the two of them?"

She nodded.

"I still do not understand how Malec is her father, then," Kieran stated, and I was right there with him.

"Where is Malec entombed?" Casteel asked.

His mother walked over to where his father sat. "I do not know what the area would be called now, as so much of that land has changed in the years since. But it would not be hard to locate. Trees the color of blood, the likes of which grow at the Chambers of Nyktos and now flourish across the Skotos Mountains, will mark the land that entombs him."

I gasped. "The Blood Forest outside of Masadonia."

Casteel looked at me and then at Kieran. "You know something I've always wondered? Why the Blood Crown sent you to live in Masadonia when it would have been safer for you to be in the capital."

As did I.

"Because her blood would've been too much of a lure to the Ascended, and she would've been placed with someone the Crown trusted," his father said, and my stomach twisted with nausea.

"I've had serious doubts about the Blood Crown's judgement, but if they trusted the Teermans, that shows a lack of awareness that is startling," Casteel replied, smoothing his fingers down the center of my palm.

"But they never fed from me," I said. "As much as I can remember."

"No, they abused you instead." His tone hardened. "I'm not sure I see much of a difference between the two."

"I'm sorry to hear that," Queen Eloana said, lowering her now-empty glass to a table by the settee.

"I…" My stomach tumbled some more as something occurred to me. "Is it possible that Ileana or Jalara learned where Malec was entombed?"

King Valyn inhaled deeply, and every part of me tensed even further. "I imagine they did. It's the only plausible explanation as to how Malec is your father."

I stared at them.

Casteel's fingers stilled against my hand. "Are you implying that the Ascended raised him? Because I never heard them mention him."

"They would've had to have gotten to him before he died," his father said. "But even if it took only a century or two to learn that he was entombed there, it would've taken a lot of Atlantian blood to bring him into any state of consciousness. And even then, he would've been…not of the right mind. I doubt he would recover from such a thing in hundreds of years."

My gods.

I pressed my other hand against my mouth. The implications were so horrifying, I couldn't speak.

"And when did you all suspect that he had risen?" Casteel asked softly.

"When we saw her at the Chambers. Saw what Alastir claimed for ourselves," his mother said. "We would've talked to you immediately, but…"

But there hadn't been time.

A wild sense of panic rose in me, thinning each breath I took. I fought past it as my heart thundered against my chest. None of this changed who I was. None of this changed who I would grow into. At the end of the day, these were just names and stories. They were not me.

I breathed a little easier.

"The only way to know for sure if Malec has risen is to go to the Blood Forest," Kieran stated. "And that would be damn near the definition of impossible with all the Craven there and how deep within Solis it is."

"And what would be the point?" I asked, glancing at the wolven. "It would only confirm what we already know to be true."

Kieran nodded after a moment.

"Why the blood tree?" I asked, looking over at Casteel's parents. "Why do they grow where my blood spills and Malec is or was entombed? Why did they change in the mountains?"

"The…the trees of Aios once bore crimson leaves," Queen Eloana answered. "When the deities ruled over Atlantia. They changed to gold when Malec was dethroned."

"And we think that when Casteel Ascended you, it changed something in you. Perhaps…unlocking the rest of your abilities or completing some kind of cycle," Valyn explained. "Either way, we believe the trees changed to reflect that a deity was now in line for the throne."

"So…they're not a bad thing?" I asked.

A faint smile tugged at Queen Eloana's lips as she shook her head. "No. They have always represented the blood of the gods."

"And that is why I did not become an Ascended? Because of the blood of the gods, or that I…I was never truly mortal?"

"Because you were never truly mortal," King Valyn confirmed. "Who your mother is? What she is? She would've had to be of elemental descent or of another bloodline, perhaps one that died out as far as we knew. And she would've had to be old—nearly as old as Malec."

I nodded slowly, realizing that there was no way Coralena was my birth mother unless she was somehow fully aware and party to what the Ascended were doing. I doubted that was the case, as I couldn't see any Atlantian being okay with that.

Or surviving long enough in the capital if the Blood Crown had moved me away from there because I would've been too much of a lure.

"It is possible," Kieran began, looking past me to Casteel. "Isn't it? That another Atlantian was held by the Blood Crown?"

"They were usually half-Atlantians, at least that I saw or heard of," Casteel answered, his voice rough. "But it's not impossible that I just never knew or that…she was held at a different location."

If that were the case, then was my birth mother…forced into pregnancy? Raped by a deity out of his mind and somehow manipulated into the act?

Gods.

My hands trembled, and this time when Casteel released me, I pulled my hand free. I rubbed my palms over my knees.

"I hate asking this," Casteel whispered, even though everyone in the room could hear him. "But are you okay?"

"I feel like vomiting," I admitted. "But I won't."

"It's okay if you do."

A strangled laugh left me. "I also feel like I could very well become the Bringer of Death and Destruction that the masked Unseen called me." I looked at him then. "I want to destroy the Blood Crown." Tears filled my eyes. "I need to do that."

Queen Eloana watched as his gaze searched mine. He nodded. He didn't speak, but there was a silent vow there.

It took me a few moments to find my ability to talk again. "Well, at least you can stop calling me a goddess. I am just a…deity."

A heartbeat passed, and a wide smile broke out across Casteel's face. Both dimples made an appearance. "You will always be a goddess to me."

Feeling my cheeks warm, I sat back. A hundred or more questions roamed through my mind, but two came to the forefront. "Have you heard of any prophecies supposedly written in the bones of the Goddess Penellaphe that warn against a great evil that will destroy Atlantia?"

Casteel's parents stared at me as if a third arm had grown out of my forehead and waved at them. It was his mother who snapped out of her stupor first. She cleared her throat. "No. We don't have prophecies."

"But I'm kind of curious about this one," King Valyn murmured.

"It's really dumb," Kieran advised.

"It is." I glanced at Casteel before continuing. "Do you know if deities have to…if they need blood? I did when I first woke up after Casteel gave me his blood, but I haven't felt a…hunger for it since then."

King Valyn's brows lifted. "As far as I know, deities didn't need to feed." He looked at his wife, who nodded. "On the other hand, I do remember reading something long ago about gods needing to feed if they'd been wounded or physically exerted themselves too much. Your need could've stemmed from receiving so much Atlantian blood," he said, his brow furrowing. "That could've been a one-off thing or something that becomes a necessity."

Casteel smiled faintly as I nodded. The idea of drinking blood was still a strange thing for me to consider, but I could get used to it. I snuck a glance at Casteel. He would *definitely* get used to it.

His mother's gaze met mine. "Would you like to take a walk? You and I?"

Casteel stiffened beside me, and inside me, my heart turned over heavily. "I don't know about that," he said.

Sorrow spiked in his mother, bright and raw. "I only wish to get to know my daughter-in-law. There is no nefarious reason to the request, nor any other shocking news to share."

There wasn't—at least, I didn't sense hostility from her or dread, only sadness and maybe the nutty flavor of resolve. I wasn't exactly sure I was prepared to be alone with his mother. The mere idea made it feel like a hundred flesh-eating butterflies were in my chest, and that provided momentarily disturbing imagery.

"I promise," his mother said. "She has nothing to fear from me."

"I don't," I agreed, and she looked at me. "I don't fear you at all."

And that was the truth. I was nervous, but that was not the same as fear.

The Queen stared for a moment and then smiled. "I would think not. My son would only choose a bride whose bravery equaled his own."

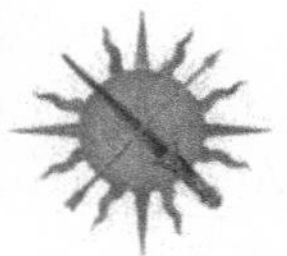

The Queen of Atlantia and I walked a path made of ivory stone and lined with soaring blossoms a bluish-purple shade. We weren't alone, although it might appear that way at first to some. Hisa and another followed at a discreet distance. Kieran also followed, and I was sure I'd spotted a flash of black when we first stepped onto the path. I believed that to have been Lyra, moving through the shrubs and trees.

"My son is…very protective of you," Queen Eloana noted.

"He is," I said. Casteel hadn't exactly been thrilled when I agreed to walk with his mother. He worried, and I think he feared that she might say something that would hurt my feelings or perhaps overwhelm me. But I didn't expect instantaneous friendship from his mother, and I had grown accustomed to existing in a near-constant state of being overwhelmed.

And, honestly, what more could be shared that would be more shocking than what I had already learned? The fact that I was able to walk and think about anything else was proof that I had most likely moved beyond being overwhelmed.

"Though I have a feeling you are more than capable of protecting yourself," she commented as she stared ahead.

"I am."

There was a faint smile on her lips when I glanced over at her. "You like gardens?" she asked, but it was more of a statement than a question.

"I do. I find them to be very—"

"Peaceful?"

"Yes." I smiled tentatively. "Do you?"

"Gods, no." She laughed, and I blinked. "I am far too…what does Valyn say? Too *frenetic* to find peace among flowers and greenery. These gardens," she said as she gestured with her arm, "are beautiful because Kirha has a green thumb and took pity on me. She enjoys spending hours removing spent blossoms, and I enjoy spending those hours distracting her."

"I finally met Kirha today," I ventured. "She has been very kind."

She nodded. "That, she is."

I took a deep breath and said, "But I don't think you wanted to speak to me about Kirha."

"No." Glancing at me, her gaze flickered over my face before returning to the pathway. Several moments passed. "I would love for us to talk about something normal and mundane, but that will not be today. I wanted you to know that we were aware of you when you were the Maiden, before Alastir returned with news of Casteel's intention to marry you. Not that you were the child he had…met all those years ago. Only that there was a girl the Blood Crown claimed was Chosen by the gods, one they called the Maiden. Admittedly, it was not news we paid much attention to. We figured it was some ploy the Ascended had created to strengthen their claims—their behaviors, like the Rite."

"There was supposedly another before me," I commented after a moment. "Her name is not known, and it is said that the Dark One killed her."

"The Dark One?" she mused. "Is that not what they call my son?"

"It is, but I know he didn't kill her. I'm not even sure she existed."

"I haven't heard of another. That doesn't mean one didn't exist," she said as we neared the jacaranda trees. "You were raised in Carsodonia?"

Clasping my hands together in front of me, I nodded. "After my parents were killed, I was."

"I'm truly sorry to learn of your parents' deaths." Empathy flooded my senses as she turned to the right. "And they were the ones who cared for you—the ones you remember. They are your parents, Penellaphe."

"Thank you." A knot formed in my throat as I glanced up at the cloudless, blue sky and then looked over at her. "I'm sure you know that I spent many years with Queen Ileana."

Tension bracketed her mouth as she echoed, "Ileana." Her nostrils flared in distaste. "The Queen of Blood and Ash."

Chapter 28

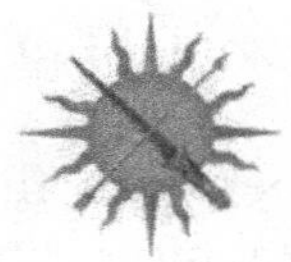

Shivers erupted over my skin as I stopped walking. "What?"

The Queen of Atlantia faced me. "She is called the Queen of Blood and Ash."

Not only had I never heard that, it didn't make sense to me. "But the Descenters and Atlantians—"

"Use that phrase? We were not the first to do so, just like the Descenters weren't the first to wear those masks," she replied. "When the Blood Crown began their dynasty, they called themselves the Queen and King of Blood and Ash, referencing the power of blood and what remains after destruction."

"I…I didn't know that," I admitted.

"Those words—that title—are important to us because it means that from the blood of those who have fallen at the hands of the Ascended, and from the ash of all they have destroyed, we will still rise." She cocked her head to the side. "To us, it says that despite what they tried to do to us, we were not defeated. And because of it, we will rise again."

I thought that over as the Queen began to walk again, and I followed her. "Do the Ascended know that is why the Descenters and Atlantians say that?"

A small smile appeared. "They do, and I'm also sure that it bothers them greatly to know that we took their title and made it mean something else." The surge of gratification coming from her made me grin. "It is why you have never heard that title. I doubt many of the mortals alive or even some of the Ascended have heard it. They stopped using it several centuries ago, around the time the first

Descenters left their mark behind, using those words. They sought to distance themselves from the title, but that is who they are." Her gaze met mine before she strode forward once more. "The attack that killed your parents and gave you those scars? You are very lucky to be alive."

It took me a moment to follow the shift in subject. "I am," I agreed, and then I thought of something. "Do you think it's because of my bloodline? Why I survived?"

"I would think so," she said. "At a young age, Atlantians are nearly mortal, but you… You are different. The deity bloodline is obviously the strongest in you, and it protected you."

"I…"

"What?" She sent me a quick glance when I didn't continue.

"It's just that I spent a lot of my life wondering how I survived that night, why I was…Chosen to be the Maiden. And now that I know why, I have more questions because I was told so many lies," I told her. "It's just a lot to process."

"But you appear to be doing just that."

"Because I have no other choice. It's not like I can deny this. It sickens me to think of what the Blood Crown may have done to create me." It also scared me to think of why they had done all of this. But that was something I couldn't focus on now. "Not only to who might have been my mother, but also to Malec. I know he wasn't a good man, but he was still a person," I said. "And yet, I feel…detached from it. I feel sorrow and sympathy for them, but they are strangers, and it doesn't change who I am. No matter what Alastir or the Unseen believe. I am not the sum of the blood that courses through my veins."

"No," she said after a few moments. "I do not think you are."

"Really?" I blurted out in surprise.

Another small smile appeared on her lips. "I remember the deities, Penellaphe. While many could be prone to all manner of misdeeds, not all of them were that way. The others? If they had gone to sleep like the gods, who's to say what would've become of the deities? We'll never know. But Malec…he wasn't a bad man, Penellaphe."

Even though I had just basically said that Malec was nothing more than a stranger to me, part of me filled with curiosity and the need to learn more about the man who was my father. That had to be natural. "He wasn't?" I asked finally.

Her hair shone a blue-black in the sunlight as she shook her head. "He wasn't a bad ruler. For a long time, he was fair and just. And he could be very generous and kind. He was never abusive toward me or intentionally cruel."

"He was unfaithful. Repeatedly," I said, and immediately wished I hadn't voiced what I was thinking. "I'm sorry. I shouldn't—"

"No need to apologize," she said with a low laugh. "He was unfaithful and, yes, repeatedly. The man had two heads, and I'm sure you can guess which one he used most."

It took me a moment to realize what she meant, and then my eyes widened.

"But he wasn't like that when we first met. It was only toward the end that I started to see this…stirring inside him. This great unrest that I came to believe, even before what he'd done with his mistress, was because he was becoming something else. I…I don't know what happened, what changed him so that he was no longer satisfied with me and the life we were trying to build. Why the generosity and kindness that had once been second nature to him faded. But I know it was no fault of mine, and I have long since stopped wondering and caring about why he sought completion and purpose in the arms of others. What I am trying to say is that your father wasn't a monster, Penellaphe. He was a deity—the most powerful one there was. But he was still a man who became lost."

My respect for her grew. It would've been all too easy for her to paint him with one brush. I wouldn't have blamed her if she had. But she wanted me to know that there was some goodness to the man. The breath I exhaled was a little looser, easier. I appreciated what she did more than she may realize.

But it also left me with another question. "You said you hunted him down because—"

"Because he would have sought revenge against me. Against Atlantia. When the Council demanded that he deal with the mistress he Ascended, he felt betrayed by them. And when I annulled the marriage, taking the throne with the support of the Council, it compounded that feeling. He couldn't believe it. That he, a deity and descendant of Nyktos, could be overruled." She brushed a wisp of hair back from her face. "And things had…greatly soured between us by the end. He would've come back, and after what he did, he was no longer fit to rule."

"And you think Casteel will be fit?" I asked, even at the risk of rehashing what I had shut down earlier. "He did the same as Malec. He had no idea that I would not become a vampry."

Her gaze slid to mine as we passed lavender and vivid red hibiscus bushes. "But I do not believe Casteel would've attempted to take the throne if you had become one. I know my son. He would've taken you and left, not risking your life or Atlantia. Malec wanted Atlantia *and* his vampry mistress. While the risk he took disturbs me, the situations are not the same."

She was right. The situations weren't the same. And she was also correct about what Casteel would've done.

Although if I had Ascended into a vampry, I imagined that Casteel would've laid waste to quite a few people before leaving.

Through the soaring spikes of purple and blue flowers, Kieran matched our movements through the garden as we fell silent. If he was trying to be inconspicuous, he was failing. Queen Eloana noted where my attention had gone. "You will need to get used to someone always a few steps away."

My gaze shifted to her. "I had many shadows when I was the Maiden."

"And my son was one of them." She stopped in front of a towering shrub of pale pink blossoms that formed an arch over a stone bench.

"He was."

"Would you mind if we sat?" she asked. "I am far older than I appear and haven't gotten much sleep the last couple of nights."

Wondering exactly how old she was, I sat.

"I have a question for you," she said once she was seated beside me. "You and Casteel…" She drew in a short breath, but I felt it. The punch of potent anguish as she slowly exhaled. "You plan to find and free Malik?"

This was why she'd wanted to speak to me in private. I started to respond when I stopped myself from lying—because I didn't have any reason to lie. Casteel and I were no longer pretending to be in love to gain what we both sought. We *were* in love, and that didn't change what we believed or wanted to achieve. However, as I focused on her emotions, her anguish was a tangy, bitter taste in the back of my throat, and I didn't want to add to that.

But if I had any hope of fostering a relationship with Casteel's mother beyond a rather antagonistic one, I couldn't build it on a foundation of lies. "We do plan to find and free Malik."

"And that is why my son took you?" she asked, her amber eyes bright—too bright. "In the beginning? He kidnapped you?"

I nodded. "He planned to use me as a bargaining chip, and that is why we initially agreed to marry."

Her head tilted slightly. "Why would you agree to that?"

"Because I need to see my brother, to learn what he has become. And I would've had better luck achieving that with Casteel at my side than alone," I confessed. "That's why I originally agreed to marry him, and it doesn't matter to me if Ian is a brother by blood or not. He's my brother. That's all that matters."

"You're right. He is your brother, just as the ones you remember as your parents are that." A moment passed. "What do you think you will find once you see your brother?"

Her question was so similar to Casteel's, I had to smile a little. "I hope to find my brother as I remember him—kind, nurturing, patient, and funny. Full of life and love."

"And if that is not what you find?"

I briefly closed my eyes. "I know Ian. If he's been turned into something cold and immoral—something that preys upon children and innocents? That would slowly kill him—kill whatever part of who he really is that remains inside him. If that is what he's become, I will give him peace."

Queen Eloana stared at me as something that reminded me of respect pierced through her grief. It was accompanied by the warm, vanilla taste of empathy. "You could do that?" she asked quietly.

"It's not something that I want to do." I watched the breeze stir the towers of blossoms. "But it's something I have to do."

"And now? This is still your plan?"

"It is," I told her, but I didn't stop there. "But we aren't pretending to be in love to accomplish our goals, Your Majesty. I do love your son, and I know he loves me. When I said that he was the first thing I'd ever chosen for myself, that wasn't a lie. He is…" I smiled through the knot of emotion swelling in my throat. "He is my everything, and I would do anything for him. I don't know when it changed for us exactly, but we were both falling for each other long before I knew that Hawke wasn't his first name. None of that changes how we got here—the lies or the betrayals. But we are here now, and that's what matters."

Her throat worked on a swallow. "You've truly forgiven him for that betrayal?"

I thought about that for a moment. "I think too much value is given to forgiveness when it's easier to forgive but far harder to forget. That understanding and acceptance is far more important than forgiving someone," I said. "I understand why he lied. That doesn't mean I agree with it or that it's okay, but I have accepted it, and I've moved on. We've moved on."

She inclined her head, nodding. I had no idea if that meant she believed me. Her internal pain overshadowed anything else she may be feeling. Several moments passed. "Do you think Malik lives?"

"Casteel believes that he does."

Her gaze sharpened on me. "I asked if you believe Malik lives. Not if my son believes it."

I stiffened, glancing through the garden to where Kieran stood with his back to us. "He…he has to be alive. Not because I want him to be alive for Casteel and for your family's sake, but how else would my brother have Ascended? We're not entirely sure that they have another Atlantian held captive," I said, thinking of the unnamed and faceless woman who could possibly be my birth mother. "And Duchess Teerman claimed that Malik was. She wasn't the most trustworthy of sources, but I think she spoke the truth. I just don't…"

"What?" she prodded when I fell silent, sensing a small measure of hope from her.

"I just don't know what kind of…state he will be in." I twisted my fingers together in my lap, bracing myself for the raw wave of pain that came from her. Tears pricked my eyes as I glanced at her. Her lips trembled as she pressed them together. "I'm sorry. I can't imagine how you feel. Knowing that they turned my brother and possibly my dearest friend is hard enough. But this is different. I'm so sorry."

She breathed as if the air were full of shards of glass. "If he is alive and they've had him this long?" Her gaze touched mine and then flicked to the sky. "It would almost be better if he…"

She didn't finish her sentence, but she didn't need to. "If he were dead?"

Her shoulders jerked as she blinked rapidly. "That is a terrible thing to think, isn't it?" She pressed a hand to her chest as she swallowed several times. "Especially as a mother, it's a terrible thing to wish for your child."

"No. It's just…real," I said, and her eyes flew to mine. "Feeling that way doesn't mean you don't love or care for him or even hope that he's not still alive."

"How can you say that when you know that a part of me wishes he had passed on to the Vale?"

"You know that I can sense emotions," I stated, and tension

bracketed her mouth. "I can feel your anguish, but I also felt your hope and your love for your son. I know that's real," I repeated, searching her gaze. "And I think wishing that any loved one was at peace isn't wrong. I love my brother. What I may have to do doesn't change that."

"No," she agreed softly. "It just proves how much you do love him."

I nodded. "The same goes for you and Malik."

She stared at me for several seconds and then a small, trembling smile appeared. "Thank you," she whispered, reaching between us and patting my arm. "Thank you."

I didn't know what to say to that, so I said nothing. I simply watched her pull herself together. Queen Eloana swallowed once more and then let out a deep, slow breath. Her anguish eased off then, returning to levels that reminded me of how Casteel had felt when I first met him. Her features smoothed out as she cleared her throat, lifting her chin ever so slightly. And, frankly, it was an awe-inspiring thing to witness because I knew just how deep and how terrible her pain was.

Casteel's mother may never care deeply for me, and we may never grow close, but that didn't change the fact that she was an incredibly strong woman, one to be respected and admired.

"So," she began, folding her hands in her lap, "how is it that you and my son plan to achieve this?"

"We will offer the Blood Crown an ultimatum. They will release his brother, agree to stop making more vamprys and killing those who are willing to feed them, and they must relinquish control of the lands east of New Haven to Atlantia." I was unsure how much of this she may already know. "If they refuse, there will be war."

She watched a tiny, blue-winged bird jump from branch to branch on a nearby rose bush. "And you think that the Blood Crown will agree to this?"

"I think the Ascended are smart, and I think they know that their control of Solis has been built upon nothing but lies and fear. They told the people of Solis that I was Blessed and Chosen by the gods. And they've also told the people that Atlantia was forsaken by those very same gods. I'm sure you know what the people of Solis are told about Atlantians—about how your kiss is a curse that creates the Craven." I watched her roll her eyes and couldn't stop my smile. "My union with the Prince of Atlantia will prove that to be untrue. It will serve as a crack in the lies. The people of Solis believe what they've been told because they've never been allowed to see any other truth. We will change that. The Ascended won't have a choice."

"But will it be enough for them to give up power? To stop feeding and turning others?"

Telling her that I hoped so probably wouldn't come across as very reassuring. "If any Ascended hope to live, they will."

"Including the Queen and King?" she questioned. "Will they live and retain power?"

"No. They will not, no matter if they agree," I said, studying her profile. I didn't know if she knew of my past with the Queen of Solis. "Ileana raised me for many years. It was she who changed my bandages and held me when I had nightmares. She was the closest thing I had to a mother then, and I cared for her very much," I shared, forcing my hands to relax. "It has been hard to reconcile the Queen I knew and the monster she obviously is. I don't know if I ever will, but I don't need to reconcile who she was to me with who she truly is to know that she nor King Jalara can live. Not after what they did to Casteel—to Malik, my brother, and everyone else."

"And to you?"

I nodded.

Queen Eloana watched me quietly for several heartbeats. "You mean that."

What she said wasn't a question, but I answered anyway. "I do."

Her gaze swept over my face, touching briefly on the scars. "My son said you were brave and strong. I see that is no exaggeration."

Hearing that from Casteel's mother meant a lot, but knowing how much strength and grit were inside her made it mean even more. There was a good chance that I might do something silly like run around the garden…or hug her.

I managed to remain seated and keep my arms to myself.

"What my son failed to mention though, is that you're also incredibly logical," she added.

A laugh burst from me. I couldn't help it, and it was loud enough that Kieran looked over his shoulder at us with a questioning raise of his brows. "I'm sorry," I said, smothering a giggle. "It's just that Casteel would argue that logic isn't one of my strong suits."

There was a faint curve of her lips. "That doesn't surprise me. Most men wouldn't know logic if it smacked them in the face."

This time, my laugh was a lot softer, partly due to her response and Kieran's reactive frown.

"But because you do appear to be logical, even when emotions are involved, I feel that I can be blunt," she continued, and my humor shriveled up. "And that I can admit that I did have yet another agenda for speaking with you privately. My husband wants to go to war with the Ascended—with Solis. There are many who wish the same."

"The…the Council of Elders?"

A shadow flickered across her face. "Most of them want to see Solis destroyed. The Lords and Ladies of Atlantia? Very many of them, as well. It's more than just what has been done to our sons. It is what has been done over and over to Atlantia. They want blood."

Casteel had said as much. "I can understand that."

"You said inside that you wanted to bring death and destruction to Solis," she pointed out, and I shivered despite the warmth. "Valyn was probably pleased to hear that he may have a supporter in you, but I don't believe you understand what that truly means or what has already begun."

I flattened my hands in my lap. "What has already begun?"

"Casteel hasn't been home to see that we've been training our armies daily outside of Evaemon, nor does he know that we have already moved a sizable unit to the northern foothills of the Skotos Mountains," she told me, and I sensed Kieran's cool surprise even from where he stood. "I'm sure he's being told this now or will be shortly, but we are already on the line of war. And if we cross it, we will go after every Ascended. There will be no chances for them to prove they can control their bloodlust, that they can rule without tyranny and oppression." Her steady gaze held mine as I stiffened. "Your brother? Ian? Your friend you spoke of? If either proves to be what you hope, they will still be destroyed along with the rest. All will be killed."

Chapter 29

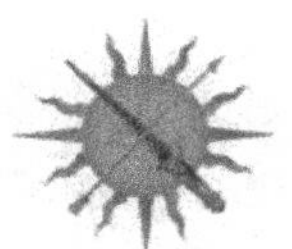

I inhaled sharply. "But—"

"We gave them a chance before," Queen Eloana interrupted as she reached out, touching one of the roses. "The entire kingdom of Atlantia did. We allowed the vamprys to grow and flourish, believing that it would be the best for all, as long as they could control themselves. We were foolish to believe that. That choice—that optimism—will not be made again by the generation who already lived through that heartbreaking failure."

Every part of me focused on her words as anger hummed in my chest. "And you? Do you want to make war?"

"Very few men don't want to make war, while nearly every woman wants to end it. Most would believe the former causes the most bloodshed," she said, running a finger over the ruby petal. "They'd be wrong. The latter is always the bloodiest, and always requires a great sacrifice. But, sometimes, no matter how many measures one takes, or how much they are willing to compromise, war cannot always be prevented."

I stilled—every part of me going quiet. What she said was so similar to the voice—that strange, smoky voice—I had heard when we neared the city limits of Saion's Cove. It had to be a coincidence because that voice had not been hers. "But what measures has Atlantia taken to compromise since the end of the last war?"

"Some would say allowing Solis to exist would be the greatest compromise we ever offered," she returned.

"I would say that doesn't sound like a compromise at all," I stated. "It sounds like Atlantia basically closed their borders and spent centuries preparing for war, biding their time instead of trying to negotiate with Solis, despite the failures of the past. Meanwhile, the Ascended continued to grow, to kill, and to terrorize. So, no, that doesn't sound like a compromise. It sounds like complicity to me. And trust me, I would know since I was complicit for years. The only difference is that I didn't know the truth—and that is a poor excuse when all I had to do was open my eyes to what was really happening. However, those within Atlantia always knew the truth and did nothing, allowing the Ascended to take root."

A sense of wariness radiated from Kieran as Queen Eloana left the blossom alone and looked at me. But if my words angered or upset the Queen, I truly did not care at the moment. She had basically just told me that my brother would be killed—that it didn't matter if any of the Ascended were capable of change. And yes, I had my doubts, but that didn't mean they *couldn't*. And the innocent people who would die were sure as hell worth at least trying.

"Brave," the Queen murmured. "You are very brave."

I shook my head. "I don't know if it's bravery or not. I know that Atlantia's involvement would've been complicated, but neither Casteel nor I want war."

"But you said—"

"I said I wanted to see the Ascended destroyed," I cut in. "And I do. I want to see the Blood Crown destroyed, but that does not mean I want an all-out war. I may not have been alive during the last war, but I know the innocent will suffer the most—the people of Solis and the Atlantians. Maybe those within Atlantia cannot feel sympathy for those in Solis, but they are not the enemy here. They are also victims."

"Part of what you said is correct. We have been biding our time," she said after a pause of silence. "But what you are wrong about is our lack of empathy toward the people of Solis. We know that they are victims. At least, the vast majority of us know that."

"I hope that is true."

"But?"

I said nothing.

One side of her lips curled up. "You haven't had the greatest experiences with the people of Atlantia. I can't blame you for doubting that."

That did factor into my disbelief, but it wasn't the only reason. "If the Atlantians are sympathetic to the people of Solis, then they should be willing to try to prevent war."

"But again, the ones who make that decision are those who have lived through the last war or grew up in its aftermath. Their thirst for retribution is as strong as an Ascended's hunger for blood," she countered, and once more, her word choice snagged my attention.

"What are you really saying to me, Your Majesty?" I asked.

"Call me Eloana," she offered, and I blinked, not exactly understanding at what point in our conversation we'd gone from formal titles to intimate names. "What if your ultimatum fails?"

The fact that she didn't answer my question didn't go unnoticed. "Then, like you said, sometimes war cannot be prevented." A chill that was hard to ignore swept over me as I said those words. "But at least we tried. We didn't just take our armies into Solis and set the kingdom on fire."

"And that's what you think we will do?"

"Isn't it?"

"We want to be able to make use of those lands, Penellaphe. We do not want a dozen more Wastelands on our hands," she pointed out. "But we would burn Carsodonia. Cut the head off the snake. It is the only way."

I stared at her, aghast. "Millions of people live in Carsodonia."

"And millions could die," she agreed, exhaling softly. I felt a spike of anguish, one I didn't think had anything to do with Malik. "I don't want that. Neither does Valyn. Gods know we have both seen enough blood—spilled enough of it. But we have decided, as have the Elders, to go to war. It is done," she advised. My heart thumped heavily in my chest. I hadn't expected to hear this today. I could sense that Kieran hadn't either. His shock was just as potent as mine as Eloana's jaw clenched and then relaxed. "Only the King and Queen can stop war from happening now."

"Then stop it," I exclaimed.

Slowly, she turned her head to me, and the next breath I took hitched in my throat. I knew what she was saying without vocalizing the words—I knew what she meant when she continued saying that her generation wouldn't give the Ascended the chance to negotiate—that neither she nor King Valyn could do that again.

Whereas Casteel and I could.

Her focus returned to the roses. "I love my kingdom almost as much as I love my sons and my husband. I love each and every Atlantian, no matter how much Atlantian blood courses through their veins. I would do anything to keep my people safe, healthy, and whole. I know what war will do to them, as does Valyn. I also know that war is not the only thing my people have to fear or worry about. A different kind of battle will be brewing soon within the Pillars of Atlantia, between those who cannot trust a stranger ruling over them and those who see you as the rightful Queen—the only Queen."

My hands clenched in my lap once more.

"It wouldn't matter if you absconded. The divisiveness will be as destructive as war, and it will only serve to weaken Atlantia," she continued, confirming what Casteel had said and then proving just how well she knew her son. "Casteel loves as fiercely as his father and I do, and given what little I know of your past, he will not force this choice onto you. I also know what that means. I could potentially lose both of my sons."

My heart twisted sharply in my chest.

"And I do not bring this up for you to carry that burden. From what I can tell, you already carry enough. I have a feeling if you were asked to take the Crown today, you would refuse."

I stared at her. "Would you want me to accept it?"

"I want what is best for my kingdom."

I almost laughed again. "And you think that's me? I'm not even nineteen. I barely know who I am or understand what I am. And I don't know a single thing about ruling a kingdom."

"What I think will be best for my kingdom is my son and you." Amber eyes met mine. "Yes, you are young, but so was I when I became Queen. And when mortals ruled the lands before our kingdoms existed, there were Kings and Queens younger than you. You're a deity, descended from the King of Gods. That is who you are now, and no rules prevent you from discovering who you will become while you rule."

She made it sound so simple, and yet she had to know it wasn't.

"I also have to disagree with you saying that you know nothing about ruling a kingdom," she continued. "You have proven that is not the case in just this conversation with me."

"Just because I don't want to make war doesn't mean I am fit to rule."

"Because you are willing to think of the people, speak your mind, and do what is necessary even if it kills a tender part of you, means you are fit enough to wear the crown," she returned. "Ruling a kingdom can be learned."

All I could do was stare at her. I was willing to consider taking the Crown, but I hadn't expected her to support it.

"Why do you not want to be Queen?" she asked.

"It's not that I don't want to. I just never considered such a thing." *I'm afraid.* But I didn't say that. Sharing that with Casteel was one thing. "It's not what I chose."

"I'm going to be blunt once more," she advised, and I wondered when she'd stopped. "I am sorry for everything that was forced upon you in your life. I can imagine that your need for freedom and to have control over your life is as great as the need many have for retribution. But I honestly do not care."

Oh. Okay. That was really blunt.

"That may sound cruel, but many have had horrific things forced upon them throughout their lives—their freedoms, their choices, and their lives unfairly stripped away from them. Their tragedies are no greater than yours, and yours is no greater than theirs. I am empathetic to what you have suffered, but you are a descendant of a god, and because of what you have experienced in your short life, you of all people can wear the weight of a crown." She didn't mince words. Not once. "But if you do decide to take what is yours by birthright, then all I ask is that you do it for the right reasons."

It took me a moment to gather enough of my wits to respond. "What do you consider to be the right reasons?""

"I don't want you to take the Crown just to find my son or your brother. I don't want you to take the Crown just so you can save lives or even stop the Ascended," she said. I was thoroughly confused now since they all seemed like excellent reasons to take the Crown. "I want you to take the Crown because you love Atlantia, because you love her people and her land. I want you to love Atlantia as much as Casteel does, as much as his father and I do. That is what I want."

I leaned back, a little surprised that I didn't fall off the bench.

"If you don't love Atlantia now, I don't blame you. Like I said, you haven't had the greatest of experiences, and I fear that you will not have the time to fall in love before you must make your choice." Concern broke through the grief. She was worried about this—gravely so.

I felt like my heart was beating too fast. "How long do I have?"

"Days, maybe. A little over a week, if you're lucky."

"If I'm lucky?" I laughed, and it sounded as dry as bones. Casteel had insinuated that we didn't have long. But days?

"News of your arrival and who you are has already reached the capital. The Elders know. There are questions and concerns. I'm sure some doubt your heritage, but after yesterday—after what you did for that little girl—that will change," she told me, and I tensed. Her eyes narrowed. "Do you regret what you did? Because of what it confirms?"

"Gods, no," I asserted. "I will never regret using my gifts to help someone. The Ascended wouldn't allow me to use them, giving me excuses, but I now know why they didn't want me to use my abilities. What I could do revealed too much. I hated it—hated being unable to help someone when I could."

"But did you? Did you find ways to help people without being caught?"

I nodded. "I did. If I could find a way, I helped people—eased their pain. Most never knew what was happening."

Approval drifted through her, reminding me of buttery cakes, and a quick smile appeared. "We cannot leave the people of Atlantia hanging in limbo for too long."

"In other words, the plans to enter Solis with your armies will happen in a few days?"

"Yes," she confirmed. "Unless…"

Unless Casteel and I stopped it.

Good gods.

"I know you got to see a little of Atlantia yesterday, but you didn't meet nearly enough people. You don't have long, but you can leave today for Evaemon. You'd arrive tomorrow morning and could then take as many days as we have to explore what you can of Atlantia. To talk to the people. Hear their voices. See them with your eyes. Learn that not all of them would've taken part in what happened at the Chambers or would stand by Alastir and the Unseen." She reached over, placing her hand over mine. "You don't have much time, but you can take what you do have to give the people of Atlantia the chance you are willing to give our enemies. My son's plans and yours can wait a few days, can they not?"

Casteel was definitely his mother's son.

I looked at the gently swaying spikes of purple and blue flowers. I wanted to see more of Atlantia, and not just because I was curious to see the capital. I needed to because I had a choice to make—one I'd never planned on, but one I had to come to terms with sooner rather than later. I swallowed, turning back to the Queen.

Before I could speak, the sound of footsteps reached us. We both turned to the path we'd followed and stood. My hand drifted to the hem of my tunic as Kieran stepped out from the tall cones of blossoms, only a few feet from me.

"It's Casteel and his father," he told me.

"Well," the Queen said, smoothing her hands over the waist of her dress, "I doubt they grew bored enough to interrupt us."

Neither did I.

A moment later, they rounded the corner, the sun turning Casteel's hair a blue-black. A heavy, thick feeling followed by a tart taste reached me. He was concerned. And conflicted.

It was not just him and his father who came down the cobbled pathway. A tall, striking figure was behind them, her skin the beautiful shade of night-blooming roses and thin, narrow braids hanging to her waist.

Vonetta.

Confusion rose as I glanced at her brother. He appeared just as surprised as I was by her presence. She had remained in Spessa's End to help protect and build the city, only planning to return when her mother gave birth.

My gaze shot back to Casteel. Muscles tensing with awareness, I drew in a deep breath. Visions of the Duchess's *gifts* filled my mind, along with the fires they'd set at Pompay. "What happened?"

"A convoy of Ascended has arrived at Spessa's End," he answered.

"Does it still stand?" I asked, fighting back the horror his response triggered.

He nodded, his eyes locked with mine. "They have not attacked. They wait," he said as a different kind of dread filled me. "For us. They have requested an audience."

"Is that so?" His mother's hands lowered to her sides as she let out a short, harsh laugh. "A random Ascended thinks they have the right to ask for such a thing?"

"It wasn't a random Ascended," Vonetta spoke as she stepped forward. Casteel's jaw flexed. Unease coated her skin, and I knew that whatever she was about to say, she didn't want to. "He claims to be your brother. Ian Balfour."

Chapter 30

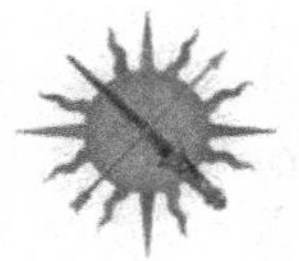

I was moving before I realized it, coming to stand in front of Vonetta. "Did you—?" I stopped myself, willing my heart to slow. I had no idea if Vonetta had traveled here by horse or in her wolven form. Either way, I knew she hadn't stopped. A thread of weariness clung to her. I reached for her, clasping her hands. "Are you all right?"

"I'm fine," she stated. "You?"

"I don't know," I admitted, feeling as if my heart were about to come out of my chest. "Did you see him?"

There was a moment of hesitation before she nodded, and every part of my being zeroed in on that second. "You spoke to him? Did he look okay?" I asked as Casteel placed a hand on my shoulder. "Did he look happy?"

Her throat worked on a swallow as she sent a quick glance over my shoulder to Casteel. "I don't know if he was happy, but he was there and appeared in good health."

Of course—how would she know if he was happy? And, seriously, I doubted it was a warm introduction between the two. I opened my mouth, closed it, and then tried again. "And he was…he was Ascended?"

"He showed at night." Vonetta turned her hands, grasping mine as she exhaled roughly. "He was…" She tried again. "We can sense the vampry. He was Ascended."

No.

Even though I should've known better—should've expected this—who I was at my very core rebelled against what she said as a shudder worked its way through me.

Casteel slid his hand across my upper chest, curling his arm around me from behind as he bowed his head to mine. "Poppy," he whispered.

No.

My chest tightened as sorrow sank its claws so deeply into me, I could taste the bitterness in my throat. I knew better. Casteel had told me that he believed Ian had Ascended. This shouldn't be news to me, but a part of me had hoped...had *prayed* that Ian hadn't. It had absolutely nothing to do with the fact that it confirmed we either shared one parent—our nameless birth mother—or possibly none at all. I didn't care about that because he was still my brother. I'd just wanted him to be like me, to have Ascended into something else. Or that he simply hadn't become a vampry. Then I wouldn't have to make that choice I'd just spoken to Queen Eloana about.

"I'm sorry," Vonetta whispered.

The back of my throat burned as I closed my eyes. Images of Ian and me flashed rapidly behind my lids—us collecting shells along the glistening beaches of the Stroud Sea, him older and sitting with me in my bare room in Masadonia, telling me stories of tiny creatures with gossamer wings who lived in the trees. Ian hugging me goodbye before he left for the capital—

And all of that was gone now? Replaced by something that preyed upon others?

Anger and grief rushed through me like a river swelling over its banks. Off in the distance, I heard a wolven's mournful howl—

Vonetta dropped my hands as another keening wail tore through the air, closer this time. The anger inside me grew. My skin began to hum. That cellular need from earlier, when I realized what could have been done to my birth parents, returned. I wanted to utterly and completely *destroy* something. I *wanted* to see those armies that Queen Eloana had spoken of unleashed. I *wanted* to watch them crest the Skotos Mountains and descend upon Solis, sweeping across the lands, burning everything down. I *wanted* to be there, beside them—

"Poppy." Kieran's voice sounded wrong, scratchy and full of rocks as he touched my arm and then my cheek.

Casteel's arm tightened around me as he pressed his front to my back. "It's okay." He folded his other arm around my waist. "It's all right. Just take a deep breath," he ordered quietly. "You're calling the wolven." A pause. "And you're starting to glow."

It took a moment for Casteel's voice to reach me, for his words to make sense. The wolven…they were reacting to me—to the rage seeping into my every pore. My heart tripped over itself as the need for retribution gnawed at my insides. That feeling—that *power* it invoked…it terrified me.

I did what Casteel had ordered, forcing myself to take a deep breath and breathe through the way it scalded my throat and lungs. I didn't want that, to see anything burn. I just wanted my brother, and I wanted the Ascended unable to do this to another person.

The deep breaths cleared the blood-drenched fog from my thoughts. As clarity arrived, so did the realization that there was still a chance that Ian wasn't completely lost. He was likely only two years into his Ascension, and they trusted him to travel from Carsodonia to Spessa's End? That had to mean something. That who he was before the Ascension hadn't been completely erased. The Ascended could control their bloodlust. They could also refuse to feed from those who were unwilling. Ian could be one of them. He could've maintained control. There was still hope.

I latched on to that. I had to because it was the only thing that tamped down the rage—the ugly want and need that nearly boiled over inside me. When I opened my eyes to see Vonetta staring at me, her mouth pressed into a thin, tight line, some semblance of calm returned. "I...I didn't hurt you?" I glanced at Kieran, seeing that he, too, was paler than usual. I didn't hear the wolven, but I saw Lyra and the other three wolven crouched behind Casteel's parents as if they were waiting for a command. My gaze swept back to Vonetta. "Did I?"

She shook her head. "No. No. I just…" She let out a ragged breath. "That was wild."

The tense lines of Kieran's features eased. "You were very angry."

"You could feel that?" Casteel asked over the top of my head. "What she was feeling?"

The brother and sister nodded. "Yeah," Vonetta said, and my stomach flipped. I knew the wolven could sense my emotions, that it could call them, but it had seemed like Lyra and the other wolven were waiting to act. Luckily, I didn't think Casteel's parents had been aware of what was happening. "I felt that a couple of days ago. All of us wolven in Spessa's End did." Vonetta's gaze flicked over us while I looked at Lyra. She and the other wolven had relaxed. "I have a lot of questions."

"Great," Kieran muttered, and Vonetta shot her brother a dark look.

Casteel lowered his chin to my cheek. "You doing okay?"

I nodded, even though I wasn't right then. But I would have to be. I placed a hand on his forearm. "I didn't mean to do that—call to the wolven." My gaze found Casteel's parents. Both stood unnaturally still, and at that moment, I couldn't bring myself to even wonder what they were feeling or thinking. I refocused on Vonetta. "My brother is there? Waiting?"

She nodded. "Him and a group of soldiers."

"How many?" Casteel's arms eased from around me, but he kept a hand on my shoulder.

"About a hundred," she answered. "There were also Royal Knights among them."

Meaning there were Ascended trained to fight among the mortal soldiers. That also meant that Ian was well protected in case any in Spessa's End decided to act. I hated the relief I felt. It was wrong, but I couldn't help it.

"He said he had a message from the Blood Crown," Vonetta told us. "But that he would only speak with his sister."

His sister.

My breath caught.

"Did he say anything else?" King Valyn asked.

"He swore that they weren't there to create more bloodshed," she explained. "That doing so would start a war that he had come to prevent."

"That is highly unlikely," Casteel's father growled, even as a spark of hope blossomed in me—a tiny, overly optimistic spark of hope.

But I turned to Casteel. "We have to go to Spessa's End."

"Wait," Eloana said, stepping forward. "This needs to be thought over."

I shook my head. "There is nothing to think about."

Her gaze found mine. "But there is a lot to think about, Penellaphe."

I didn't know if she was talking about the kingdom, the Unseen, or even Casteel and me. It didn't matter. "No. There is not," I told her. "My brother is there. I need to see him, and we need to know whatever message the Blood Crown may have for us."

"I understand your need to see your brother. I do," she said, and I could feel the truth behind those words—and the empathy that fueled them. "But this isn't just about you and your needs anymore—"

"That's where you're wrong," Casteel cut in, his eyes hardening to chips of amber. "It is about her needs, and they come first."

"Son," his father began, "I can respect your desire to care for your wife's needs, but the kingdom always comes first whether you're the Prince or the King."

"It's a damn shame if you really believe that," Casteel replied, looking over his shoulder at his father. "Because to me, attending to each other's needs ensures that the kingdom's needs can be met. One cannot happen without the other."

I stared at Casteel. He...gods, there were times I couldn't believe I'd actually stabbed him in the heart.

This was one of them.

"Spoken like a man in love and not someone who has ever ruled a kingdom," his father retorted. "Who has very little experience—"

"None of that matters," his mother interrupted, her irritation nearly as strong as her grief. "This is likely a trap designed to lure not only one but both of you out."

"It very well could be, but my brother is just beyond the Skotos Mountains with a message from the Blood Crown. I cannot think of anything else until I see him." My gaze sought out Casteel's. "We need to go," I told him. "I need to go."

A muscle along Casteel's jaw ticked. I couldn't pick up any emotion from him, but he nodded curtly. "We will leave for Spessa's End," he announced, and his father cursed. He sent the King a look that brooked no room for argument. "Immediately."

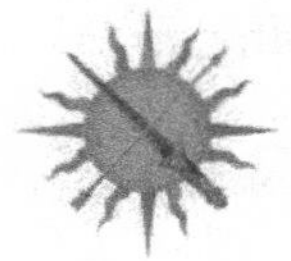

Casteel's parents protested—loudly and strongly—but neither of us would be swayed. They weren't even remotely thrilled when we left the estate, and I didn't blame them for that. My arrival had pushed the Crown to the edge of chaos, and we would lose vital time by going to Spessa's End. But there was no way I could have done what the Queen had asked of me if I remained. I wanted to see all I could of Atlantia, but my brother was more important than a gilded crown or a kingdom.

Casteel's parents would return to the capital, and we would join them there once we returned from Spessa's End. I knew their decision to go to Evaemon meant that I would have to make my decision then, based on what little I'd seen of Atlantia.

I couldn't think of any of that now.

As soon as we arrived at the Contous' home, Kieran and Vonetta went to their parents. Both Jasper and Kirha came to our room, while I quickly braided my hair before shoving a sweater and a heavier tunic into a saddlebag for both Casteel and I, remembering how cold it could get in the Skotos Mountains. On the way out, I stopped at the wardrobe, grabbing an extra shirt for both of us, each in black, and another pair of breeches for him just in case our clothing became soiled…or bloodied.

Which seemed to happen a lot.

"The wolven will travel with you," Kirha said as I entered the sitting room. She sat in the chair Jasper had occupied the night before. He now stood behind his wife. "That's the only way to ensure the trap fails—if this is a trap."

"How many?" Casteel asked as he took the saddlebag from me. His brows flew up as he glanced down at the leather bag. "What did you pack in here? A small child?"

I frowned. "Only a change of clothing." He looked at me doubtfully. "Or two."

A lopsided grin appeared.

"At least a dozen and a half can be ready to leave immediately. Maybe a little more. Kieran is wrangling them now," Jasper said. "And that's not including my children and me."

"You're coming with us?" I turned to them. "And Vonetta? She just arrived, didn't she?"

"I told her she could stay," Kirha said, shifting in the seat as if she sought a more comfortable position. "That she could sit this one out. But she refused. Spessa's End has become a part of her heart, and she doesn't want to be away while the Ascended are camped outside their walls. She is showering now, just so, you know, she can become filthy all over again."

I cracked a grin at that. I didn't know how she could make that trip again. I honestly didn't know how Kieran had done it twice when Spessa's End had been under siege, but I was still surprised that Jasper would make the trip. I was unsure of how to tactfully point out that his wife was super pregnant.

"Do not worry about me. I will be fine," Kirha said, winking when my eyes widened. "I'm not going to have this baby in the next week or so. Jasper will be here for the birth."

The silver-haired wolven nodded. "Besides, I don't think we will be gone all that long. I'm guessing we will travel straight through the mountains."

I looked at Casteel. He nodded. "Doing so would mean we'd arrive a few hours before nightfall tomorrow. It will give us some time to check out what they potentially have planned and for us to rest."

"It's going to be a hard and fast journey but more than doable," Jasper stated. "Meet you at the stables in a few?"

Casteel agreed, and I watched Jasper help his wife stand. When the door closed behind them, I said, "I wish Jasper didn't feel like he has to go with us—not when Kirha is so close to giving birth."

"If he believed for one second that she would have that baby in the next couple of days, he wouldn't leave," Casteel explained. "I wouldn't worry about that or Vonetta. She wouldn't make the trip again if she didn't think she could handle it." The sound of a saddlebag snapping closed sounded. "What did my mother want to discuss with you?"

"The future of the kingdom," I said, turning to him. Knowing that we only had a handful of minutes to discuss things, I gave him a quick rundown. "She said that the Atlantian armies were preparing to enter Solis. Did your father tell you that?"

"He did." That muscle flexed in his jaw again. "I knew he was planning this. However, I didn't know how advanced those plans had become. From what I could gather from speaking with him, half of the Elders are in agreement. It's not that he wants to go to war. It's that he sees no other choice."

Crossing my arms, I stared out the terrace doors. "And you still do?"

"I believe it's worth a shot. I believe it is more than that."

I was relieved to hear that. "Your mother wanted me to take the next couple of days to travel to Evaemon and see the city before I made my choice about the Crown. She told me that her generation is incapable of giving the Ascended a chance because of what they've lived through. That it would have to be us who took that risk. She seemed...supportive of me taking the Crown. That it would be what is best for the kingdom," I said, looking back at him. He watched me closely, and I registered no shock from him. "This doesn't surprise you?"

"No." A lock of wavy hair fell over his forehead. "She has always put the kingdom first, over her own needs."

"And you truly believe that isn't what makes a good King and Queen?"

"My parents have ruled Atlantia fairly and have done the best they can—better than anyone else could have. Maybe I'm biased in believing that, but whatever. Personally, I don't believe that an unhappy or distracted King or Queen makes for a good ruler," he told me. "And you wouldn't have been able to enjoy any of your time spent exploring Atlantia if you chose not to go to your brother. It would be the same for me if I learned that Malik was near. I would have to go to him."

How well he knew me never failed to amaze me, and he couldn't read my emotions.

"Besides," he continued, "we plan to negotiate with the Blood Crown. If they have a message, we need to hear it."

Nodding, I turned back to the terrace doors, watching the vines move gently in the salty breeze. "What does your father think of us—of us and the Crown?"

"He doesn't know what to think. He's more…reserved than my mother when it comes to revealing what he is thinking," Casteel said. "Always has been, but he knows that if you claim the Crown, there is little he or the Elders can do."

Chapter 31

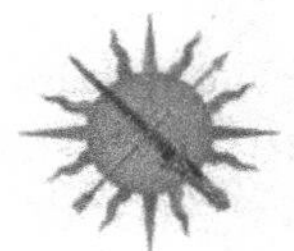

As we left Saion's Cove and passed through the Pillars of Atlantia once more, we caught Vonetta up on all that had happened since we'd last seen her. The sorrow she felt for Beckett lingered long after she'd taken her wolven form, and we crossed the meadow of flowers.

The journey to Spessa's End was as hard and fast as Jasper had warned, much more brutal than when we'd crossed over from the Wastelands. Under the canopy of red leaves, we stopped only to take care of personal needs and allow Setti and the wolven to rest and eat.

I busied myself by seeking out each wolven I caught sight of and reading their imprints. Vonetta reminded me of her brother, woodsy. But instead of cedar, her imprint was like white oak—and vanilla. Her father reminded me of rich soil and cut grass—an earthy, minty feeling. Others were similar, reminding me of cold mountains and warm waters. I followed each of their imprints, repeating it over and over until all I needed to do was look at one of them to find their imprint. When I spoke to Vonetta through the cord the first time, I might've given her a small heart attack.

We crested the mountains as night fell, and the mist…it was different. Only thin vapors trailed along the moss-blanketed ground instead of the thick mist that obscured the trees and the steep drops.

"I think it's you," Casteel had said as Setti rushed on. "You said you thought the mist reacted to you before. You were right. It must've recognized your blood."

In the darkness, I'd looked for Kieran, hoping he was close enough to hear that I had been right about the mist when we traveled through it the first time.

Because the mist didn't slow us down, we were able to continue through the night, making it farther than we'd thought we would by the time gray light filtered through the leaves.

The muscles in my legs ached as we cleared the Skotos, following Vonetta as we traveled through the valley. I couldn't imagine how any of the wolven or Setti were still able to keep going. I couldn't even figure out how Casteel's hold on me hadn't slackened even once during the trip. His grip and the anxiety of knowing I would see my brother soon were the only things keeping me sitting upright.

We reached Spessa's End several hours before nightfall. Riding through the heavily wooded area skirting the east wall, we entered the town through a hidden gate, unknown to anyone who may be camped outside the northern wall.

My stomach began to twist and roil with anxiety as the sun followed us across the courtyard, where Coulton ambled out of the stables, dragging a white handkerchief over his bald head. The older wolven gave us a grimace of a smile as he caught hold of Setti's halter. "I wish I was seeing you two under better circumstances."

"As do I," Casteel agreed, and I spotted several Guardians garbed in black among others stationed on the wall. Those who were attempting to make a home at Spessa's End were on the wall.

Shoving the handkerchief into his back pocket, Coulton offered his hand in assistance. I took it, noting the slight widening of the man's nostrils. "Now I know why I felt that zap," he said, squinting up at me. "*Meyaah Liessa.*"

"How did you know?" I asked as he helped me down. It wasn't something we had gotten a chance to ask Vonetta.

"All of us felt something several days ago," he explained as Casteel dismounted. "Hard to explain, but it was like this wave of awareness. None of us was sure exactly what it was, but now that I see you, I know. Makes sense," he said as if the fact that I was a deity wasn't remotely shocking or a big deal at all.

I kind of liked that. "By the way, you don't have to call me that."

"I know." Coulton grinned, and I had a feeling he would continue calling me that. "Keeping our Prince in line?"

"I try." I smiled at him as I walked to Setti's head on legs weak from such a long journey.

The wolven chuckled as I stroked Setti's nostrils. "I imagine it's a full-time job."

"I'm offended." Casteel dragged a hand through his windblown hair as he squinted up at the wall. "How is everyone doing with the unexpected guests?"

"Nervous, but okay and prepared," Coulton answered, and my fingers curled into Setti's mane. "Once I get Setti taken care of, you all want some food sent to your rooms?"

"That would be good," Casteel said, lifting the saddlebag over a shoulder as the weary wolven streamed across the courtyard, many of them panting, even Delano.

Concern blossomed as I watched Vonetta lower her belly to the ground, her fawn-colored fur identical to her brother's. Jasper sat beside her as he scanned the courtyard, his large body hunched slightly. I searched for Kieran and found him nudging a smaller wolven with deep brown fur. Opening my senses, I focused on the wolven. The grittiness of exhaustion came back to me. I pushed past that as my chest hummed, finding the individual pathway. Through the cord, I felt the…warm, rolling waters. Lyra was the brown wolven. I shifted my attention to Kieran, searching until the phantom scent of cedar reached me. Having no idea if this would work, I followed the individual cord, pushing my thoughts through it. *Are you all okay?*

Kieran's head jerked in my direction as Coulton began leading a tired Setti to the stables, where I hoped they showered him with carrots and fresh, green hay. A heartbeat passed, and then I felt the whisper of Kieran's voice. *We are tired but okay.*

I shivered at the unnerving sensation of *feeling* his words. *You all will rest*, I sent back to him. It wasn't a question, more a demand. I had a feeling they would all remain on guard with the Ascended near.

We will. His presence retreated briefly, and then I felt the brush of his thoughts against mine. *Meyaah Liessa.*

My eyes narrowed.

"Are you communicating with one of the wolven?" Casteel asked as he slid an arm around my shoulders, his gaze following mine to where Kieran playfully nipped at Lyra.

"I was." I let him steer me toward the east corner of the Stygian Fortress. "I wanted to make sure they rested and didn't patrol."

He squeezed my shoulder as we walked under the covered breezeway, past several closed-off rooms. "I'm extremely envious of that ability."

"You're not worried that we could be talking about you without you knowing?" I teased as we neared the terrace at the end. It was as I remembered, the chaise lounge and low-to-the-floor chairs inviting.

"Why would I be?" Casteel opened the door, and the scent of lemon and vanilla greeted us. "I'm sure you only have amazing things to say."

I laughed at that. "Your confidence is an extremely envious ability."

He snorted as he closed the door behind us. "You should rest until food arrives."

"I can't rest." I walked through the familiar sitting area, easily able to see Alastir seated there on the couch. I stopped at the entrance to the bedchamber, and for a moment, I was swept back to the night that felt like forever ago, when Casteel and I had finally stopped pretending. "I don't think I can eat."

"You should try." Casteel was close behind me.

"*You* should try," I murmured.

"I would, but I can't unless you do," he said. "But since neither of us is going to rest right now, we might as well talk about tonight."

I faced him. He was in the process of tugging off his boots. "Okay. What do you want to talk about?"

He arched a brow as he placed his boots near one of the chairs. "We need to be careful of what is said to your brother. Obviously, there's a damn good chance they know what your blood is, but they may not know how your gifts have changed. He shouldn't be told. The less they know about us, the better. It gives us the upper hand."

I sat on the edge of the chair, slowly toeing off my boots. "That makes sense." And because it did, it made me feel a little ill. "And what if Ian…if he is as I remember?"

"Even then, we don't want to give them any information they do not already know." He quieted for a moment as he unstrapped the sword on his left side and then the one on his right, lying them upon an old wooden chest. "I hope that he is as you remember, but even if he is, you need to keep in mind that he is here on behalf of the Blood Crown."

"It's not like I'm going to forget that." I tugged off my socks, leaving them in a ball beside my shoes while Casteel had draped his over his boots.

He eyed me for a few seconds. "My mother and father could be right. Tonight may be a trap."

I rose, beginning to pace in front of the terrace doors. "I know that, but that doesn't change that my brother is here."

"It should, Poppy," he countered. "The Ascended want you, and they know exactly how to draw you out."

"Do I really need to repeat myself?" I snapped as I walked past him into the sitting room. He followed. "I *know* that this could be a trap, but as I said, my brother is here." I pivoted, prowling back toward the bedchamber. "He has a message from the Blood Crown. We are going to see him. And if you're trying to stop me now, after we came all this way, you're going to be very disappointed."

"I'm not trying to stop you."

"Then what are you getting at?" I demanded.

"Are you going to look at me and listen?"

My head shot in his direction. "I'm looking at you right now. What?"

His eyes burned a fiery gold. "But are you listening?"

"Unfortunately," I retorted.

"That was rude, but I'm going to ignore that." A muscle ticked along his jaw as he tilted his head. "You know that what we're doing is a risk."

"Of course, I know that. I'm not foolish."

His brows rose "You're not?"

My eyes narrowed. "I understand the risks, Casteel. Just like you understood them when you decided to masquerade as a mortal guard."

"That's different."

"Really? Seriously? At any moment, you could've been discovered and captured. Then what?" I shot back. "But you did it nonetheless because you were doing it for your brother."

"Okay. You're right." He stepped into me, eyes churning with flecks of heated amber. "I was willing to take those risks with my life—"

"I swear to the gods if you say you're not willing to allow me to take those same risks, I'm going to hurt you," I warned.

One side of his lips kicked up. "If that's a threat, it's my favorite kind."

"It will not be in a way you like." I glanced pointedly below his waist. "Trust me." I turned from him and took a step. Without warning, he was suddenly in front of me. I jerked back. "Damn it. I hate when you do that!"

"You know I will never stop you from defending yourself—from picking up a sword or bow and fighting," he said, coming forward. I held my ground. "But I also won't let you walk right into a trap, arms open."

"And if it is a trap, do you think I will just give up and say 'You got me?'" I challenged. "You said it yourself. I can defend myself. I will not let anyone take you or me, and based on what I can do, I'm confident I can ensure that."

"You were really hesitant about using your power not that long ago," he reminded me. "You changed your mind?"

"Yes!" And I had, without a doubt. "I would use everything in me to make sure that I and those I love aren't taken again by the Ascended."

"That is a relief to hear," he said.

"Well, I'm glad you're relieved. If you're not trying to stop me, then why are we even having this discussion?"

"All I am trying to suggest is that you hold back until we make sure it's safe for you—"

"No." I waved a hand, cutting him off. "Not going to happen. I'm not staying back. Would you if this were your brother?" I demanded. "Would those risks outweigh your need to go to him, and would you stand back?"

He dropped his head back, inhaling sharply. A long moment passed. "No, those risks would not outweigh my need."

"Then why are you trying to stop me?" I honestly didn't know why he was being like this. "You of all people should understand."

"I do." He reached out, curving his hands around my shoulders. A static charge of energy passed from his skin to mine. "I told you that I believed Ian had Ascended, but deep down, you hadn't accepted that, and I understood why. You needed to believe that there was still a chance that he was mortal or like you."

The air I breathed stung. I couldn't deny anything he'd said. "What does that have to do with this?"

"Because when you learned he was an Ascended, you got so upset, you lost control of your emotions. You began to glow and call the wolven to you," he said, lowering his chin so we were at eye-level. "They felt your anger, and I don't know if you noticed or not, but I'm pretty sure if you had commanded them to attack, they would've done so without hesitation."

I had noticed that.

"And while I have to admit that is a rather impressive ability, I also fear what will happen when you see Ian, and you no longer recognize him," he said, and my heart seized. "And I don't fear your anger or what you do with that wealth of power in you. I don't fear that at all. I fear what it will do *to* you—the knowledge that your brother is truly gone."

I sucked in a shuddering breath as I briefly squeezed my eyes shut. His concern warmed me. It came from such a beautiful place.

"Are you truly ready for that?" he asked, moving his hands to my cheeks. "Are you really ready to do what you believe is necessary if you find that he has become something unrecognizable?"

The air I breathed continued to hurt as I placed my hands on his chest, feeling his heart beat strongly under my palm. I looked up at him, seeing the flecks of amber. "You know I hope to find a part of him still inside there, but I know I have to be ready for what I find. I have to be ready if nothing of Ian remains."

Casteel smoothed his thumbs over my skin. "And if you're not ready when it comes to releasing him from this curse?"

"I am willing to shoulder whatever pain comes from giving my brother peace," I told him.

A fine tremor coursed through him. "I have to see my brother."

"I know, and I swear, I'm not going to hold you back. That isn't what this is about. Yes, I am worried about this being a trap. Like I said, they know exactly how to draw you out. But not for one second do I want to prevent you from going to see Ian. I just—I want to stop you from feeling that kind of pain if I can. I was hoping…" He shook his head. "I don't know. That you wouldn't have to deal with that on top of everything else," he said. "But I should've known better. Life doesn't wait to hand you a new puzzle until you've figured out the last one."

"It would be nice if it did, though." I exhaled roughly. "I can handle this, no matter what happens."

Casteel touched his forehead to mine. "But you have no idea what the weight of that kind of pain is like. I do," he whispered. "I know what it feels like to kill someone I once loved and respected. That pain is always there."

Knowing he was talking about Shea, I resisted the urge to take his pain. "It lessened, though, didn't it?"

"It did. A little with each passing year, and even more so when I found you," he confided. "And that's no lie."

I curled my fingers into his shirt. "And it will lessen for me because I have you."

He swallowed and then pulled me to his chest, wrapping his arms around me. "I know it's selfish of me to not want you to bear that pain."

"You not wanting that is one of the reasons I love you." I lifted my mouth to his because saying it wasn't enough.

And that kiss of gratitude and affection quickly turned into something needier, more demanding. The one kiss quickly spun out of control, or maybe that was the thing about kisses. They weren't meant to be controlled.

I didn't know how he got me undressed so quickly, but I was completely nude by the time I managed to pull his shirt off over his head. He caged me in, my back flush with the wall and my front against his. My senses nearly shorted out at the feel of his warm, hard skin.

Scraping a fang over the side of my throat, his hands skimmed down, one stopping on my breast and the other gliding between them, lingering where the bolt had entered me. There was no sign of that now, but I knew he would never forget the exact spot of the wound. His hand continued on over the softness of my stomach and the scars, slipping between the vee of my thighs. His fingers spread out, the pads of his fingertips brushing against the very center of me, sending a jolt through my body.

"You know what I've been craving?" He captured my lips in a quick, scorching kiss as his other hand teased the aching peak of my breast. "Poppy?"

I swallowed as his hair tickled my cheek. "What?"

"Are you even listening to me?" He nipped at my throat. I shuddered as he said, "Or are you not capable of listening?"

"Totally." My entire being focused on how his fingers curled around my nipple, how his other hand stroked lazily between my thighs. "I'm totally capable of—" I gasped, clutching his shoulders as he slipped one finger inside me. "Of…of listening."

He chuckled against my neck as he slowly moved his finger in and out, over and over until I was breathless. "So?" Do you know what I'm craving?"

Truthfully, how quickly he distracted me utterly astonished me. Pleasure curled, stirring something deep. "What?"

"Honeydew," he whispered against my lips, picking up the pace as he tipped his head down. "I could live on the taste of you. I swear to you."

My pulse rocketed as his decadent oath wove its way through me. He lifted his head, working another finger inside as his eyes became bright and full of more wicked promises. He watched, soaking in every soft gasp and flutter of my eyelashes as his fingers pumped in and out, his gaze latched on to mine, refusing to allow me to look away, to escape the maddening rush of feelings he created.

Not that I ever wanted to.

A dimple appeared in his right cheek as he brushed his thumb over the sensitive part of me, his eyes alight as I sucked in a shrill breath. He began tracing an idle circle around the tightened bud, coming close to touching it but always straying away at the last moment.

"Cas," I panted.

"I love the way you say that." Golden flecks sparked to life, churning. "I love the way you look right now."

"I know." My hips moved forward, but he pressed in.

"Stay still," he ordered gruffly. His thumb made another enticingly close circle. "I'm not finished looking at you. Do you know how beautiful you are? Have I told you that today?" he asked, and I was almost sure he had. "How stunning? With your cheeks flushed and lips swollen? *Beautiful.*"

How could I not feel that way when I could *feel* that he believed what he said. I felt like I was burning up inside, catching fire. My hands slipped down his chest. Awed by the way his heart pounded against my palm, I strained against his hold, brushing my lips against his. He leaned into me, his arousal pressing against my hip as he kissed me.

"I have to do something about that craving," he told me, and that was the only warning I had.

Before I could protest the absence of his hand between my legs, he was kneeling. "I could spend an eternity on my knees before you," he vowed, his eyes amber jewels.

"That would be painful."

Casteel pressed his thumb down on the bundle of nerves, and I cried out, my hips arching into his hand. "Never."

His mouth closed over me, and he did something truly devious with his tongue. I cried out, driven to the edge with his sensual assault. My back arched as far as he'd allow it.

I wanted more.

And I wanted this to be about both of us. Not just me.

Maybe it was everything that had happened and what I could soon face. Maybe it was the heat of his mouth against me. It could've simply been the fact that I *needed* him—*needed* to remind both of us that no matter how tonight ended, we were alive, we were here, together. And nothing could ever change that.

All of those reasons could have fueled my actions. Given me the strength to take control of my desires, the situation, and of Casteel—and prove that I could handle him at his calmest and at his wildest, his most loving and his most indecent.

I pushed off the wall, clasping the back of his neck. I wasn't sure if I just surprised him or if I had overpowered him. It didn't matter. Curling my hand around the back of his neck, I urged him to stand, bringing his mouth to mine. I tasted him on my lips. I tasted me and us. Slipping my hands into his breeches, I undid them as I walked him backward, helping him get rid of them. When his legs hit the bed, I pushed him.

Casteel sat, his brows lifting as he stared up at me. "Poppy," he breathed.

Placing my hands on his shoulders, I planted my knees on either side of his thighs. "I want you, Casteel."

He shuddered. "You have me. You will always have me."

And I did have him as he shifted under me. I lowered myself onto him, the air seizing in my throat as we became one.

Pulse fluttering, I curled my arm around his neck, sinking my fingers into his hair as I dropped my forehead to his, clutching his arm with my other hand. I began to move, rocking against him slowly. I gasped as heat filled my chest and settled between my thighs in a tight, hot ache. My breath touched his lips. "Prove it," I ordered. "Prove that you're mine."

There wasn't even a moment of hesitation. His mouth crashed onto mine, and the kiss was stunning in its intensity, stealing my breath. My entire body tensed as I lifted myself and brought my body back down, drinking as deeply from his lips as he did from mine. The fine, rough hairs on his chest teased the aching tips of my breasts as I rode him.

"Yours." Stark need shone through the slits of his eyes. "Now. Forever. Always."

My fingers tightened around his hair. With each roll of my hips, he reached that spot inside me, the one that sent pleasure bounding through every limb. I moved faster, moaning as I angled my body toward his. I shuddered, letting go of his arm and dragging my hand over his chest. A wildness entered my veins as the friction of the hard length of him ignited a fire. I kissed him greedily, sucking on his lip, his tongue. His hands gripped my hips as he lifted his, meeting my thrusts.

"Should have known," he said, his breath coming in shorter, faster pants. "You'd love doing it like this."

"I love…I just love doing it," I whispered. "With you."

His hands slid to my rear, cupping it as he rocked me harder against him. "Yeah, you do." He squeezed, holding me tightly against him until there wasn't a breath of space between us. "Promise me."

All the throbbing tension in me curled tightly. I tried to lift myself but he held me in place. "Anything," I rasped, my nails digging into his skin. "Anything, Cas."

"If Ian is what you fear and giving him peace is something you cannot safely carry out…" he said, his words causing my already stuttering heart to skip. He dragged his hand up my back, fisting his fingers in my hair. He tugged my head to his. "Promise me that if it puts you at risk, you won't attempt it. That you will wait until it's safe. Promise me that."

The words spilled from me. "I promise."

Casteel moved at once, lifting me from his lap and onto my belly. Before I had a chance to take a breath, he thrust deeply into me. My back arched as I kicked my head back, his name a hoarse shout on my lips. He rolled into me, grinding his hips against my rear.

I cried out, and a word snuck out, a demand that scalded my cheeks. "Harder."

"Harder?"

"Yes." I curled my upper body around, reaching back and clasping his hips. "Please."

"Fuck," he growled, and I felt him jerk deep inside me. "I love you."

There was no chance to tell him the same. He forced an arm under me, curling it just below my breasts. His chest came down on my back, his weight supported by the arm propped by my head. Then he gave me what I wanted, thrusting into me *hard.*

Casteel was relentless, his body pounding against mine. We became twin flames, burning bright and uncontrollable, lost to the fire. It was a welcomed madness, the frenzy in our blood and our bodies, and it went beyond sex and finding pleasure. It was all about us taking and giving from one another, falling and letting go together, being swept away in trembling waves of rippling pleasure.

But when the tremors subsided and Casteel eased us onto our sides, my promise to him returned like a vengeful ghost, there to warn me that I might not be able to keep it.

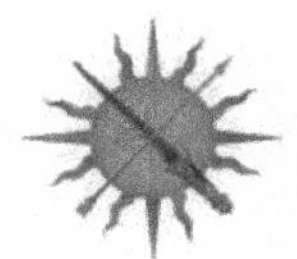

Casteel and I dressed as the last traces of sunlight slipped over the floor, both of us donning the extra black tunics I'd packed. I did manage to eat some of the roasted chicken that had been delivered to the room, and we were able to freshen up. I took my time smoothing my hair into a braid.

Vonetta arrived shortly after, her striking features tense. "They're here."

Chapter 32

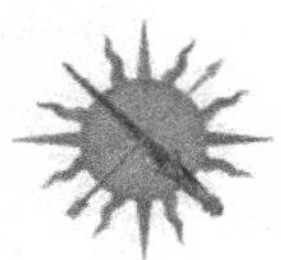

"There's just the one carriage and four guards," Vonetta told us as we walked across the courtyard, passing the spot where Casteel and I had knelt and exchanged vows. She had her braids swept up in a tight bun, and her hand rested on the golden short sword at her hip. "The remaining Ascended have stayed back."

"Are they Royal Knights?" Casteel asked.

Vonetta nodded as the lit torches along the wall rippled from the breeze.

Spying the Guardians on the wall, I spotted the thick, blonde braid in the moonlight. Nova stood there, two swords in hand. Beside her, another Guardian held a bow at her side. "My brother?"

"He hasn't been seen, but we believe he remains in the carriage."

The endless roiling of my stomach threatened to return, but I forced myself to stay calm. The last thing I needed was to start glowing.

As we neared the gates, I saw several men armed with swords and crossbows. I recognized a few as those I'd aided after the siege. They bowed as we approached. Kieran and Delano prowled out of the shadows in their wolven forms. "Did you all rest?" I asked Vonetta.

She nodded as we caught sight of her father and several other wolven. "We did. I hope you two did."

There was a ghost of a smile on Casteel's face, one I hoped Vonetta didn't notice. "I'm sorry about this," I said to her. "This stress is the last thing the people of Spessa's End need."

"It's not your fault, Your Highness," she started.

"Poppy," I corrected her. "We're…friends, right?" A flush crept up my neck. "I mean, I did wear your gown to my wedding, and—" I trailed off as old insecurities reared their bitchy heads. Vonetta had been nothing but kind and welcoming to me, but she was friends with Casteel, and she'd met me when I was positioned to become a Princess. And now that I was their *Liessa*? It felt like Tawny all over again, and I felt even more foolish. Because, seriously, this was not the time for this. "Just ignore me. I don't even know why I'm thinking about this when there are Ascended waiting for us beyond the gate."

"I think some would call that avoidance," Casteel murmured.

I shot him a look of warning, and a dimple appeared.

"We're friends," Vonetta said, grinning. "At least, I thought we were. So I'm glad to hear you think so, too, because boy, it would've been awkward if not."

Relief swept through me. "I think it's already awkward. At least, for me," I said as amusement radiated from the general direction of where Kieran waited. Jerk.

"Don't worry about it." She reached over, squeezing my arm. If she felt the weird static charge, she didn't show it. "And don't apologize for what is happening tonight. Everyone here knows the risks. The Ascended could come at any time. We're prepared."

Based on how quickly they'd come together before the Ascended attempted to overtake Spessa's End with the Duchess, it was obvious that they truly were.

Having come down from the wall, Nova joined us. The blonde Guardian placed a fist over her heart and bowed at the waist, the moonlight glinting off the golden band around her upper arm. "What is the plan?"

Casteel glanced at me. I remained quiet because I believed she was looking for a more detailed plan beyond me not losing control of my emotions.

"Kieran and Delano will go with us," Casteel decided. "Netta, I know you're quick with a blade, so I want you with us. You, too, Nova."

Both of the women nodded, and then Nova advised, "We have archers on the wall, and several wolven already beyond the gate, hidden in the woods."

"Perfect," Casteel replied, and I started to speak but stopped. Cas took note of it. "What?"

"I'm just…I'm curious about why you chose only Kieran and Delano in their wolven forms, and Vonetta and Nova," I admitted, cheeks warming as I looked between the two women. "Not that I doubt you two are skilled. I know for a fact that you both are, so please don't take my question that way. I'm just curious to understand the strategy." And that was the truth. I wanted to know why he would approach the Ascended without the entirety of the wolven present and every armed soldier we had.

"There are two reasons," Casteel explained as I quickly reached out with my gifts, relieved that I didn't feel anger or irritation from Nova and Vonetta. "They don't need to know how well-organized we are. The less they see, the better. It gives us the element of surprise if needed."

I nodded. "That makes sense."

"And as you know, the Ascended nor the people of Solis expect females to be as skilled as men when it comes to battle," he continued. "That's something so inherently ingrained in them that even those who have heard of the Guardians' fighting skills still won't view them as a threat."

I should've realized that. "They'd be sadly mistaken to hold that belief."

"And that is a mistake we intend to exploit," Nova stated, and I hoped the Guardian no longer viewed me as a possible distraction to Casteel or a weakness.

"Thank you for explaining," I said, filing the information away.

Casteel nodded. "You ready?"

Drawing in a shallow breath, I nodded, even though I wasn't—because I had to be. "Yes."

"Your promise." He stepped closer to me, lowering his chin. "Don't forget it."

"I haven't," I whispered, the wolven dagger strapped to my thigh suddenly becoming a heavy weight. It would be nearly impossible to walk away from Ian if he'd become what I feared, not knowing when I'd get the chance again.

"You can do this," he told me. Kissing the center of my forehead, he then took my hand and turned to the men at the gate. With a nod, the heavy doors opened with a groan of stone against stone.

Torches had been lit on both sides of the road, casting an eerie glow over the crimson, windowless carriage that waited, the side embossed with a circle with an arrow piercing the center. The Royal

Crest.

Ian traveled in a carriage used by the Blood Crown. Nausea rose in my throat.

Two guards in black armor with matching mantles swept over their shoulders stood beside the carriage's horses. Another two stood by the closed door, their grips on their swords firm. These knights had a new piece of attire. Their helmets were adorned with combs made of horsehair and shone red in the moonlight. Red-painted masks with slits for eyes fitted tightly to the upper parts of the knights' faces and hid their identities. It reminded me of the masks worn during the Rite.

"The masks," Vonetta murmured from behind us. "Are an interesting choice."

"The Ascended are dramatic in all things," Casteel said, and he was right.

My heart thumped crazy-fast as Casteel threaded his fingers through mine, and we walked forward, joined by Kieran and Delano and flanked by Vonetta and Nova.

I sensed nothing from the Royal Knights as pebbles crunched under our boots. We stopped several feet from the carriage. Having taken a vow of silence, the knights didn't speak. At least, these didn't. The ones who'd come to New Haven had had a lot to say.

"You called," Casteel spoke first, an air of nonchalance oozing from his tone. "We answered."

A beat of silence passed, and then a soft rap came from inside the carriage. My breath seized as one of the knights reached forward, opening the door.

Time seemed to slow as one cloak-covered arm extended from the carriage, and a pale hand clasped the door. My heart seemed to stop as a long, lean body unfolded from the interior, stepping out onto the road. The black cloak settled around legs wrapped in dark breeches. A white shirt peeked out from the folds of the cloak. I ceased to breathe as the body turned to where I stood, and I lifted my gaze. Hair a reddish brown in the firelight. A handsome, oval-shaped face and smooth jaw. Full lips not tilted up in a boyish smile like I remembered but settled in a flat line.

Ian.

Oh, gods, it was my brother. But as my gaze continued tracking up to settle on his face, I saw the eyes that'd often shifted from brown to green depending on the light were now a fathomless, pitch-black.

The eyes of an Ascended.

He said nothing as he stared at me, his expression utterly unreadable, and the strained silence stretched between us like a widening gulf.

I felt a crack widening in my chest. My fingers went limp, but Casteel's hold on my hand didn't falter. His grip tightened, reminding me that I wasn't alone, that he believed I could handle this because I could. I forced air into my lungs.

I can do this.

Lifting my chin, I heard myself speak. "Ian."

There was a twitch of movement around his mouth that could have almost been a flinch as he blinked. "Poppy," he said. And there went another tear in my heart. His voice was soft and light as air. It was his voice. The corners of his lips tipped up in an almost familiar smile. "I have been so worried."

Had he? Truly? "I am fine," I said, surprised by how level my voice sounded. "But you? You're not."

His head cocked to the side. "I am more than well, Poppy. It is not I who has been taken by the Dark One and held hostage—"

"I am not a hostage," I interrupted as a red-hot arrow of anger pierced me. I latched on to it, as it was far better than the rising grief. "I am here with my husband, Prince Casteel."

"Husband?" Ian's voice roughened, but the inflection was forced. It had to be. The Ascended may be prone to extreme emotion like anger or lust, but concern? Sympathy? No. He stepped forward. "If this is a farce, I—"

A rumble of warning came from my right as Kieran inched forward. Ian halted, his eyes widening on the fawn-colored wolven. "Good gods," he exclaimed, and he really did sound surprised…maybe even awed. "They really are huge."

Kieran's lips peeled back in a snarl as his body tensed. I focused on him, opening that cord—our connection. *It's okay.*

I feared Kieran couldn't hear me and would launch himself at Ian, but the growling faded.

"My *wife* is here of her own free will," Casteel spoke then, his tone losing its hint of boredom. "And while I entertained this meeting, I will not tolerate insinuations regarding the legitimacy of our marriage."

"Of course, not." Ian's dark stare slid its way to the Prince. There was a hardness to his features that had never been there before. "What does Atlantia truly hope to gain by taking my sister?"

A wave of awareness curled down my spine as the knight to Ian's left turned his head toward him. I was surprised that he didn't refer to me as all the Ascended did. As the Maiden. A tiny spark of hope returned.

"Atlantia has many things to gain from it," Casteel responded. "But I have gained everything from the union."

Ian stared at him, his brows knitted. He then looked at me, tentatively taking several steps forward. The wolven allowed it. "Am I supposed to believe you willingly married the monster responsible for our parents' deaths?"

"I happily married the Prince, who you and I both know had nothing to do with our parents' deaths."

Ian shook his head, his brows raised. "I can only imagine what you have been told that led you to stand beside the enemy—those responsible for such terror and pain. I will not hold it against you," he said. "Neither will the Crown. The Queen and King are so very worried about you, and we had so much hope that we would free you in the Wastelands."

"I do not need to be freed." Wrapping myself around the anger I felt, I smirked. "I'm sure they're very concerned to have lost their blood bag."

"Poppy, that's not—"

"Don't," I interrupted him, sliding my hand free from Casteel's. "I know the truth about the Ascended. I know how the Craven are made, and I know why they are holding Prince Malik and what they planned to use me for. So, let's not pretend that I don't know the truth. That you don't. The Blood Crown is the root of the evil plaguing the people of Solis. They are the oppressors, not the heroes."

A heartbeat passed. "The villain is always the hero in their story, aren't they?"

"Not in this one," I retorted.

He didn't speak for a long moment and then said, "I would like to speak with you." His dark eyes flicked to the storm brewing beside me. "Alone."

"That's not going to happen," I said, my heart cracking a little more.

"Because you don't trust me?" A muscle twitched near Ian's mouth. "Or because the Dark One will not allow it?"

A midnight laugh rumbled from Casteel. "You don't know your sister all that well if you believe anyone can stop her from doing what she wants."

That was the thing, though. Another fissure streaked across my heart. Ian only knew me as his baby sister and then as the Maiden. He only knew me back when I did what I was told. And, gods, I wanted him to know me now—know the real me.

But seeing that inhuman coldness etched into his features, I knew that would never happen.

I wanted to cry.

I wanted to sit down right there and crack wide-open. It wouldn't change what was standing in front of me, but it would make me feel better. At least temporarily. But I couldn't do that. Not here. Not anytime soon. So, I thought of Casteel's mother, and I did what she had done in front of me. I stitched myself back together so tightly that only a thread of grief coursed through me.

Once I was sure I had it under control, I took a step toward Ian. "You are my brother. I will always love you." My voice caught. "But you have to know what they do to those children given over to the Rite. They serve no gods. How can you be okay with that? The Ian I knew would've been horrified to know that children are murdered—that innocent people are slaughtered in their sleep—all so the Ascended can feed."

Something flickered across his face, but it was gone too quickly for me to know if it was really even there. His features smoothed out. "But I am an Ascended, Poppy."

I drew in a ragged inhale as I stiffened. The warmth of Casteel's body pressed against my back. "And Tawny?" I rasped.

"Tawny is safe," he stated flatly. "As is the Dark One's brother. Both are well taken care of and provided for."

"Do you truly expect us to believe that?" Casteel demanded, his anger rising to the surface.

"You don't have to. Both of you can see for yourselves," Ian replied. His words fell like frozen rain. "That is why I am here."

I suppressed a shudder as the spark of hope died. There was nothing familiar about Ian's tone now, and his words meant more than what was spoken. He wasn't here out of concern. "The message from the Blood Crown?" I managed.

He nodded. "The true Queen has requested a meeting with the Prince and Princess of Atlantia."

True Queen? I almost laughed. I was surprised that Casteel didn't. I glanced at him. His striking features had sharpened. "Funny, we wish to speak to the *false* Queen, as well."

"Then she will be pleased to hear that you will meet with her in a fortnight to discuss the future. At the Royal Seat in Oak Ambler," Ian told us, referencing a small port city just before the Wastelands. "Of course, she extends this offer with a promise that no harm will come to either of you in hopes that you will honor her offer and leave the armies you have gathered to the north."

My stomach dropped as a cool shower of surprise echoed from the wolven and Casteel. How did they know?

"Yes." Ian smiled then, and it killed me a little when I saw the hint of fangs along both rows of teeth. "The King and Queen know of the armies gathering. They hope that this meeting can prevent unnecessary bloodshed. He glanced to where Vonetta stood. "You are more than welcome to join."

My brows crept up on my forehead. Ian had been a bit of a flirt growing up, but wasn't he married now? Then again, he'd barely spoken of his wife, and it wasn't like I'd seen a loving relationship between an Ascended pair before.

"Thanks, but I'll pass," Vonetta replied dryly as I sensed a rise in Kieran's annoyance.

"Shame," Ian murmured. "I had hoped to continue our conversation."

"Not me," she muttered, and I so wondered what conversation he was referencing.

"Why, in either kingdom, would we trust that offer?" Casteel had silently moved to stand beside me once more, something that caused the knights to start forward.

Ian held up a hand, halting the knights. "Because the Blood Crown has no desire to start another war," he responded. "One I hope you realize you will not win."

"We're going to have to disagree on that," Casteel bit out.

"So we shall." Ian inclined his head. "But you should also know that if you come with ill will, not only will you be destroyed, but so will Atlantia—starting with Spessa's End."

Rage coated the back of my throat, and I reached out, curling a hand around Casteel's arm. A slight tremor coursed through him. His chin had dipped, his features becoming sharp angles. I squeezed his arm, and he briefly glanced down at my hand as if he didn't know who touched him. It took several seconds for him to wrangle his anger.

"The Blood Crown is rather confident," I said, taking on the same tone of nonchalance Casteel had had in the beginning. Dark eyes met mine. "Which tells me that the Queen has no real knowledge of what armies are gathering to the north." Considering that I had no real idea, it was nothing more than a bluff.

"Sister," Ian purred, turning my stomach. "You could have hundreds of thousands of soldiers, half of them wolven larger than the ones before me, and you would not defeat what the Queen has created."

Unsettled, I stared at him. "What has the Queen created, Ian?"

"Let's hope you never need to find out."

"I want to find out," I insisted.

"Do you speak of more knights?" Casteel cast a sneer in the direction of those standing behind him. "Because if so, we're not worried."

"No." Ian continued to smile, while the knights showed no reaction to Casteel's taunt. "The Revenants are not knights. They are not Ascended, mortal, nor Atlantian. They are something far more…unique than that."

Revenant? I had no idea what that could even be.

"I must take my leave now. It is a long journey back to the capital. I look forward to seeing you in Oak Ambler." His gaze shifted to me. "I wish to hug you, Poppy. I hope you can look past our differences and grant this favor."

I locked up as the weight of the wolven dagger reminded me of the oath I'd made to myself and what I'd promised Casteel. Ian was…he was no longer my brother. There were moments when I saw him, but those seconds truly meant nothing. He was no longer in there.

My gaze snapped to the knights. They were shifting uneasily, obviously not excited about Ian's request or how far away he was now standing from them, and I could feel the wariness coming from all those around me, especially Casteel.

This…this could be my chance. I would be more than close enough to use the dagger. I didn't think he'd expect it. I could do it. And in my heart, I knew that to be true. But at what risk? Casteel and the others could easily take the four knights. I didn't doubt that for one second, but what if the Blood Crown took that as an act of war and Ian had spoken the truth about these Revenants? What if my one act spawned the war that Casteel and I were trying to prevent?

I…I didn't want that.

Relief warred with disappointment so potent that it felt like I'd taken the dagger and used it on myself. However, I would rather carry the guilt of allowing my brother to continue on this way than shoulder the regret of causing countless people to lose their lives.

"It's okay," I told Casteel as I stepped forward. "He won't hurt me."

Ian frowned slightly, but I hoped Casteel understood what I said. Wariness throbbed from all those behind me, and I swore the wolven dagger did the same. But I ignored both things as I stopped in front of Ian. He didn't smell like the sea and sun anymore. Instead, I caught the floral musk of an expensive cologne. Ian's skin was cold, even through his shirt, and it all felt wrong as he folded me in his arms. I closed my eyes and let myself imagine just for a second that this was the Ian I remembered—that I was hugging my brother, and he was okay.

"Poppy, listen to me," he whispered, and my eyes opened. "I know the truth. Wake Nyktos. Only his guards can stop the Blood Crown."

Chapter 33

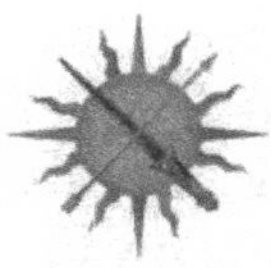

"Well…" Jasper drew out the word from where he sat in one of the closed-off rooms beyond the Great Hall of the fortress. Delano and Lyra were trailing the Ascended to make sure they left, but the rest of us were here. "That was unexpected."

I almost laughed, but I didn't think that was appropriate. I was already wearing a path in the stone floor, pacing the length of the room. I couldn't sit. Not with how my mind was racing. Not with my emotions all over the place, bouncing from sorrow to hope to disbelief.

Ian was still in there.

For him to say what he had, he *had* to be. And I…I could've stabbed him. My stomach roiled and then lurched. Ian was still in there. Good gods, I wanted to shout with joy and also sink to my knees and sob because that meant he was himself while surrounded by Ascended. What he must deal with. I couldn't let myself think about that. He was smart and clever. Obviously, he was stronger than I ever realized for him to survive as he had.

But the implications of Ian remaining himself? Being able to put on a convincing act to survive so young in his Ascension? There could be others—many more.

"What do you think he meant by Nyktos's guards?" I asked.

"That, I am not sure." Casteel watched me from where he sat. "It would be hard to imagine that his guards would leave him."

Nova frowned from where she stood by the door. "You think he spoke the truth? That this is not a trap of sorts?"

"He said he knew the truth," I told her—told the room. Casteel had been close enough to overhear my brother's whisper. The rest hadn't. "He had to be talking about the Ascended."

"He didn't sound like he knew the truth about the Ascended," Jasper remarked with a scowl. "He sounded like every Ascended I've come across."

"That had to be an act," I said.

"Then he's one hell of an actor," the older wolven retorted.

It was a good act, but we were thinking about two different situations. "Growing up, Ian made up these stories and then told them to me. He did it because he knew I was…I was often lonely and bored." I started walking again, fiddling with the edge of my braid. "Anyway, when he told me those stories, he acted them out, adopting different accents and mannerisms. He was good at it—good enough that he'd be at home on a stage."

"And I barely heard what he whispered to Poppy," Casteel commented. "There's no way the knights did."

I nodded. "He made sure they couldn't hear. That's why he moved so far from them—something I could tell made them uncomfortable."

"Truth or not, the fact that Ian even brought up Nyktos makes me think that he knows about your heritage," Kieran began, leaning against the table beside where his sister sat perched on the edge, her feet resting on a chair. "And that means the Blood Crown likely does, as well. Which isn't exactly a surprise, but it could mean they have some understanding of your abilities."

"They may." I stopped playing with my braid and instead started worrying the skin of my thumb. "I mean, it sounded like they orchestrated my creation," I said without going into too much detail. It was strange how twenty-four hours ago, I had been caught up in the knowledge that Malec was my father. Now, replaced by something far more important, it felt like a non-issue. "Then they probably have a good idea of what my gifts could grow into. But these Revenant things? I've never heard of them before."

"Neither have I," Casteel said, which was unsettling since he'd spent time in the capital far more recently than I had.

"But whatever they are, they must be bad for Ian to say a large army couldn't beat them."

"That is if what he said is true," Kieran pointed out.

"It may not be. It just might be." Casteel squinted as he drew his thumb along his lower lip, watching me. "Wake Nyktos."

Our gazes connected. What my brother told me to do sounded too bizarre to even consider, but…

"I doubt any god would be all that happy with being awakened, let alone Nyktos," Vonetta said. "What if he said that in hopes the god takes you out?"

My stomach tumbled at the thought. Angering a god would be a surefire way to remove me from the picture. But I also thought about what the Duchess had said. That I had succeeded where she couldn't. Could waking Nyktos be a part of that?

I didn't think so. Duchess Teerman referenced Atlantia, and I truly believed that Ian was trying to help us.

"But the Blood Crown wants Poppy alive," Casteel pointed out. "And they want her at this meeting. If the plan is to get her killed by waking Nyktos, why set up the meeting?"

"Good point." Vonetta's fingers tapped on her bent knees as she glanced between Casteel and me. "You two are seriously thinking about it, aren't you? Waking Nyktos?"

Casteel still held my gaze. "If what Ian said is true, we may need Nyktos's guards. Either way, Atlantia has lost the element of surprise when it comes to our armies."

I nodded in agreement. "Are you familiar with Oak Ambler?"

A smoky smile appeared as he shared a quick glance with Kieran. "We've been to and infiltrated Castle Redrock."

My brows lifted. "Do I want to know why you did that and what the outcome was?"

His gaze sharpened, burned. "Probably not."

"Let's just say some Ascended there won't be missed by those who call Oak Ambler home," Kieran commented. "It's probably best if you don't know more."

"It would be wise for us to arrive before they expect us," Casteel said, and I nodded.

"I can agree with that. I can also say for sure that your father will be pissed when he hears that the Blood Crown knows that Atlantia has been gathering forces to the north," Jasper muttered, dragging a hand down his face as he looked at Casteel. "Hell."

I stilled, my gaze finding Casteel's once more. When Ian had dropped that unexpected tidbit, I couldn't understand how they knew. Now, I did. "Alastir."

Casteel's jaw hardened. "From what my father said, only the Council was aware of the true purpose behind the armies being moved to the north. The public believes it's a training exercise, but Alastir knew."

"And he'd been communicating with the Ascended." I shook my head. "How in the world could he have justified sharing that kind of information with the Ascended as something that would've benefited Atlantia?"

Jasper snorted. "I think Alastir had a lot of beliefs that didn't make sense, but maybe he did that in hopes that Solis would strike first, forcing Atlantia's hand. A backup plan in case all else failed."

That made unfortunate sense. "Who knows what else he could've told them?"

That quieted the room, and in the silence, my mind returned to bouncing between Ian and what it meant for the Ascended before finally settling on something I hadn't really allowed myself to think about.

The Crown.

The plans already in place wouldn't change with the news that Ian wasn't evil incarnate—and it was possible that other Ascended were the same. Once the King learned that Solis was aware of the Atlantian armies, it would spur an attack. Ian and any Ascended like him may die if the Atlantian armies were successful. If not, and these Revenants were something terrible and powerful, able to devastate the Atlantian armies? Not only would Spessa's End fall, but the entire kingdom of Atlantia could. Either way, innocent people would die on both sides. I stopped as I neared Casteel's chair. He looked up at me, his gaze searching my face.

Casteel and I could stop this.

That meant only I could stop it.

My pulse picked up as I stared down at him. I knew what we had to do—what *I* had to do. It felt like the floor shifted under my feet. A kernel of panic bloomed, and I used everything in me to shut it down.

Casteel reached out, extending a hand. I placed mine in it. "What?" he said quietly.

"Can we talk?"

He rose at once, sending the group a quick glance. "We'll be back."

No one said anything as we slipped from the room and then moved through the empty Great Hall where the Atlantian banners hung on the walls.

"Where do you want to go?" Casteel asked.

"The bay?" I suggested.

And that's where we went, Casteel leading the way around the half stone wall that remained. Under the bright light of the moon and in the much cooler air of nighttime, the grass and dirt gave way to sand as the scent of lavender surrounded us.

We stopped on the edge of the midnight bay, the waters so dark they captured the stars above. Stygian Bay was the rumored gateway to the Temples of Eternity. I suppressed a shudder at the thought that the God of Common Men and Endings slept under the still waters.

"You doing okay?" Casteel asked.

Knowing he was talking about Ian, I nodded. "It's strange. When I decided not to give Ian peace, I was both relieved and disappointed."

"What made you decide not to do it?" Casteel pulled his gaze from the bay and looked over at me. "Because I really thought you were going to do it."

"I was. It was the perfect chance. I knew you all would've been able to handle the knights. But besides the fact that we have no idea what these Revenants are, we're also trying to prevent a war. If I'd ended Ian, the Blood Crown could have taken that as an act of war against them and struck at Spessa's End. I couldn't risk that."

He reached over, rubbing his hand down my back. "I'm proud of you."

"Shut up."

"No. Seriously." A faint smile appeared. "You made the call before Ian spoke to you, when you thought he was truly lost to you. You didn't think of what you wanted, but what was best for the people of both Solis and Atlantia. Many wouldn't have done that."

"Would you?"

His forehead creased as his attention returned to the bay. "I'm not sure. I'd like to think I would have, but I think it's something you really can't know for sure until you're in that position."

Silvery moonlight glanced off the curve of his cheek and jaw as if the light of the moon were drawn to him. "So, you believe that Ian isn't like the others? That what he said is true?"

He didn't answer for a long moment. "I believe in things that make sense, Poppy. Him telling you to wake Nyktos because his guards can defeat the Blood Crown only makes sense if he was trying to help us. I cannot think of how that would help the Blood Crown. Like I said in there, they have not indicated that they want you dead. I do think he's trying to help you—help us—at great risk to himself. For him to be willing to do that to help his sister has to mean that he's still in there. A normal Ascended would be looking out for only themselves.

He's not like them."

I briefly closed my eyes, nodding. Hearing that Casteel believed that Ian was still in there erased the tiny doubts I still had and made what we needed to talk about easier. "And that could mean that some Ascended, young ones like Ian, who might not have had years and years to control their bloodlust, aren't a lost cause."

"It could."

"And Atlantia is preparing for war—to kill all the Ascended. Your mother told me it wouldn't matter if Ian wasn't like the others. They wouldn't take that risk." I moved to what was left of a pier, sitting on a stone post. "I can't let that happen. We can't let that happen."

Casteel turned to me, remaining quiet.

I took a deep breath as I looked up at him. "It's not just about my brother. Yes, he's a big reason. I know your mother wants me to choose the Crown because I love Atlantia, but there isn't enough time for me to feel that way. I…I don't know if I need to right now. Because I am already protective of Atlantia and her people. I don't want to see them used by the Ascended or harmed during a war. I also don't want to see Solis ravaged. I know you don't either."

"I don't."

My hands started to tremble, so I folded them between my knees. "I have no idea how to rule a kingdom, but I know that can be learned. You said so. Your mother said so. I don't know if I'm ready for that, or if I would ultimately make a good Queen, but I want to make things better for the people in Solis and in Atlantia. I keep thinking about how the Ascended need to be stopped. I know that needs to happen, and that has to mean something, right? And I have to believe that being able to possibly prevent war is worth figuring that out. People's lives are worth that, including my brother's. You'd be by my side. We'd rule together, and we'd have your parents to help us." And maybe I would come to love Atlantia as deeply as he and his parents did. It already felt like home to me, so it was possible. But there was also a little guilt. I wanted his mother to approve of why I decided to take the Crown. I swallowed, but a knot remained in my throat. "That is if you want this. If you can be happy with this. I don't want you to feel forced into it," I said as he took a quiet step toward me. "I know you said that part of you knew it would happen eventually, but I want you to know for sure that this is what you want and not…not do it just because I'm choosing this," I finished, watching him and waiting for a response. When he stopped before me, saying nothing, the knot expanded in my throat.

"Are you going to say something?"

Casteel knelt in front of me, resting a knee in the sand. "I told you before that if you wanted the Crown, I would support it. I would be right there with you. That hasn't changed."

"But what do you want?" I insisted.

He placed his hands on my knees. "This isn't about me or what I want."

"Bullshit," I exclaimed.

Casteel laughed. "I'm sorry." He dipped his chin, grinning. "You're just adorable when you curse."

"That's weird, but whatever. It's not just about me."

"It's about you because I know what ruling a kingdom entails. I grew up with a Queen as a mother and a King as a father. I also grew up knowing that I could ascend to the throne." Golden eyes met mine. "Even though I've held off assuming the role, it wasn't because I didn't want to be King."

"I know," I said quietly. "It was because of your brother."

"I know I can do this. I know you can. But it's not such a shock to me." Casteel worked his fingers between my knees, releasing my hands. He held them loosely in his. "I want to protect my people and the kingdom, and if sitting on that throne will do that, then it's what I want. *But*," he stressed, "I want you to have the choice—the freedom. I also want you to know that you don't have to justify or explain your reasons for taking the Crown. Not to me. Not to my mother. And there is no one right reason, as long as it is your choice. So," he said, running his thumbs over my knuckles, "is it your choice to take the Crown?"

My heart skipped a beat. "It is," I whispered. It was only two words, but they were life-altering and terrifying, and it was strange. To think that before I could remember being called the Maiden, forces had been at play that strove to stop this very moment from happening. There was a bittersweetness to this, but there was also a sense of…*rightness* that buzzed through my veins, in the blood of the gods. Like what I felt when I first stood at the Chambers. I almost expected the ground to tremble and the skies to open.

All that happened was Casteel bowing his head as he drew our joined hands to his heart. "My Queen," he murmured, lashes sweeping up as his eyes met mine. And that connection—the one tied to my heart and soul was just as life-changing. "I guess I will have to stop calling you Princess."

My lips twitched. "You've barely called me that since we got here."

"You noticed?" His brows rose as he kissed my hands. "Didn't feel right calling a Queen a Princess. Didn't matter if you never took the Crown."

"You're being sweet again."

"Are you going to cry?"

"I don't know."

Chuckling, he let go of my hands and stretched up, cupping my cheeks. "You're sure about this?"

My heart gave another leap. "I am." Something occurred to me. "I want the crest changed. I want the arrow and sword to be equal."

His dimples appeared then. "I like the sound of that."

I took a deep breath and let it out slowly. "Okay."

"Okay," he repeated, nodding. "We need to rest here for the night, but I'll send someone ahead of us to Evaemon. Tomorrow, we will leave for the capital."

Where we would take the Crown.

And then we would travel to Iliseeum and wake the King of Gods.

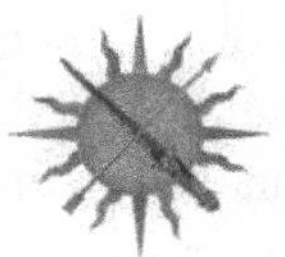

"You've got to let go, baby. You need to hide, Poppy—" Momma stilled, and then she wrenched her arm free, reaching inside her boot. She pulled something out, something black as night and slender and sharp. She moved so fast—faster than I'd ever seen her move, spinning around as she rose, the black spike in her hand.

"How could you do this?" Momma demanded as I scooted to the edge of the cupboard.

A…a man stood a few feet from her, cloaked in scary shadows. "I'm sorry."

"So am I." Momma swung out, but the shadow man caught her arm.

"Momma!" I screamed, and glass cracked.

Her head jerked around. "Run. Run—"

Glass shattered, and the night spilled into the kitchen, tumbling down the wall and hitting the floor. I froze, unable to move as the gray-skinned creatures rose, their sunken bodies and red-smeared mouths scaring me. They swarmed the kitchen, and I couldn't see her. "Momma!"

Bodies snapped in my direction. Mouths dropped open. Shrill howls ripped through the air. Bony, cold fingers pressed into my leg. I screamed as I scrambled back inside the cupboard—

"Shit," the dark man cursed, and a spray of something rotten hit my face. The thing let go of my leg. I started to twist away, but the shadow man reached inside the cupboard, grabbing my arm. "Gods, help me," he muttered, yanking me out.

Panicked, I pulled at his grip as those things came at him. He swept out an arm. I twisted, struggling. My foot slipped in the wetness. I turned sideways—

Momma was there, her face streaked with red. She thrust that black spike into the center of the shadow man's chest. He grunted out a bad word. His grip loosened and slipped away as he fell backward. "Run, Poppy," Momma gasped. "Run."

I ran. I ran toward her—

"Momma—" Claws caught my hair, scratched my skin, burning me like the time I'd reached for the kettle. I screamed, straining for Momma, but I couldn't see her in the twining mass on the floor. Teeth sank into my arm as Papa's friend silently backed away. Fiery pain roared through me, seizing my lungs and my body—

What a pretty little flower.

What a pretty poppy.

Pick it and watch it bleed.

Not so pretty any longer...

I jerked awake, a scream burning the back of my throat as my wide-eyed gaze swept across the dark bedchamber.

"Poppy," Casteel called, his voice thick with sleep. A second later, his chest pressed into my back as he folded an arm around my waist. "It's okay. You're safe. You're here."

Heart pounding, I stared into the darkness, telling myself that I was in Spessa's End. I wasn't trapped in Lockswood, alone and—

My breath caught. "I wasn't alone."

"What?"

I swallowed, my throat sore. "There was someone else in that kitchen where I was hiding in the cupboard. Someone my mother knew. I know she did."

"Alastir—"

"No," I whispered hoarsely, shaking my head. "It was someone else. He was like…like a shadow, dressed in black." I twisted in Casteel's embrace, barely making out his features in the darkness. "He was dressed like the Dark One."

Chapter 34

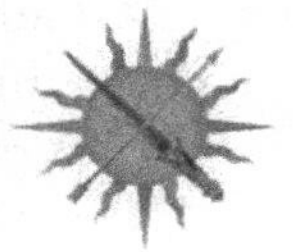

Casteel had sent Arden, a wolven from Spessa's End, ahead of us. He would travel first to Saion's Cove and then to Evaemon to alert the King and Queen of our impending arrival.

Casteel let me handle Setti's reins and guide the horse until we encountered more treacherous terrain. It took us a day and a half to reach the Cove this time, having stopped halfway through the Skotos Mountains to rest. We stayed the night at Jasper and Kirha's. The seamstress that we'd visited while we explored the city had been able to create several pairs of leggings, tunics, and even a gauzy dress in emerald for me, along with some underclothing. Those items were now packed carefully, and the remaining pieces she worked on would be sent to Evaemon. That night, we shared supper with the Contous, several of the wolven, and Naill and Emil. It had been so normal that it was almost hard to believe that we had just met with Ian and were planning to enter Iliseeum.

And wake the King of Gods.

Or that Casteel and I were about to become King and Queen.

We'd discussed everything with Kirha and Jasper at length when we arrived. We would need to travel to Iliseeum as soon as we could if we hoped to make it to Oak Ambler before we were expected. A group would travel with us—not a large one as Casteel and Kieran had explained that the tunnels could be narrow and cramped. And then from there? Well, we hoped that one of the Elders knew where Nyktos slumbered and that my blood would help us enter unharmed.

But during dinner, we didn't talk about any of that, even though everyone present knew what was about to happen. Instead, Kirha and Jasper had entertained us with stories about their children and Casteel when they were younger—much to their annoyance and reluctant amusement. I didn't think I'd ever laughed as much as I had that night. And later, when Casteel and I were alone, I didn't think it was possible to be loved more thoroughly than I was.

I held onto those two things as we left Saion's Cove early the next morning, dressed in buttery-soft black leggings and a matching, quarter-length-sleeve tunic that hugged my chest and then flared at the hips. I'd grinned when I saw that she'd left a slit in the right side for me to easily reach my dagger. Jasper remained behind with Kirha, and I was pleasantly surprised to learn that Vonetta would travel with us to Evaemon. I had expected her to stay with her parents or return to Spessa's End, but she'd said that she wanted to see Casteel's and my coronation.

She wasn't the only one.

Dozens of wolven traveled with us, many that I hadn't met yet, and a few, like Lyra, that I was just getting to know. Emil and Naill were also with us, and listening to those two bicker about everything from the best-tasting whiskey to whether a sword or an arrow was a better weapon was quite entertaining. All were alert, though, just in case the Unseen made an appearance.

The content feeling kept everything at bay, as did my continuous practice with speaking to the wolven through their imprints. Even the nightmare that, if true, possibly confirmed what Alastir had claimed.

That he hadn't killed my parents.

I couldn't focus on that as we traveled north through Atlantia. There would be time later to deal with that possibility, but if I'd learned anything in the last several months, it was how to compartmentalize. Or maybe it was just Casteel's advice not to borrow tomorrow's problems.

Either way, it wasn't all that hard to just exist in the hours it took to reach Evaemon because I got a little lost in the beauty of Atlantia—the limestone homes with their terracotta roofs filling the rolling hills, the small farming villages, and the running streams that split the land, rushing from the cloud-capped Mountains of Nyktos that eventually became visible in the distance. One thing quickly became clear as we traveled.

With wooded, untouched land few and far between, no piece of land within the Pillars of Atlantia went unused.

Whether it was the fields plowed for crops or the land used for housing and commerce, Atlantia was running out of space…

Or already had.

Still, the land was beautiful—the homes, shops, and farms. It was all open, from village to city, with no walls separating them nor keeping monstrous creatures at bay. It was how I imagined Solis had once been.

Casteel had once again handed over control of Setti to me, and we continued on that way until we were halfway to Evaemon. We stopped in Tadous for the night, a town that reminded me very much of New Haven. Near the inn, young Atlantian children waved from the windows of a building I learned was similar to that of the schools in Carsodonia, where they learned their history, letters, and numbers in groups according to their age. The difference here was that all children attended, no matter what their parents did for a living. Whereas in Solis, only the children of means could afford to attend.

The temperatures were cooler here. Nothing that required a heavy cloak, but the faint trace of woodsmoke was in the air. We gathered that evening for dinner, ordering from a menu the friendly innkeeper and his wife provided.

Sitting in between Casteel and Kieran at a long banquet table, I scanned the menu while Vonetta sat across from me, laughing at something Delano said to her.

"Would you like to try a casserole?" Kieran offered as he looked over my shoulder. "That's something we can share."

"What's a…casserole?"

Casteel looked over at me, a slow grin spreading across his lips. "Poppy…"

"What?"

"You've never had a casserole before?"

My eyes narrowed. "Obviously, not."

"It's good," Kieran explained. "I think you'll like it."

"It is," Vonetta chimed in.

Casteel tugged on a loose strand of my hair. "Especially if there's a lot of…*meat* in it."

I stared at him, immediately suspicious. "Why are you saying it that way?"

"Like what?" he asked.

"Don't try to play innocent."

"Me?" He pressed his hand to his heart. "I'm always innocent. I'm just saying I think you will enjoy a meat casserole."

I didn't trust him for one second. I twisted toward Kieran. "What is he talking about?"

Kieran frowned. "A meat casserole."

I looked over at Vonetta and Delano. "Is that true?"

Dark brows lifted as Vonetta glanced at Casteel. "I honestly don't know what this one is referring to, but I was thinking about a green bean casserole."

"Oh, man, I haven't had one of those in forever," Naill murmured.

Sitting back, I folded my arms across my chest. "I don't want it."

"Shame," Casteel murmured.

"I have a feeling I'm going to want to stab you by the end of the night."

Kieran snorted. "And how is that different from any other night?"

I sighed. "True."

Leaning over, Casteel kissed my cheek and then looked at the menu. We ended up settling on roasted vegetables and duck. With my stomach happily full, I moved closer to the empty fireplace and one of the overstuffed chairs with a tall back while Casteel argued with Vonetta about…well, I wasn't sure what they were arguing about now. Earlier, it had been whether or not yams could be considered sweet potatoes, which was a strange argument, but I had a feeling it wasn't the most bizarre one they'd had.

They acted like a brother and sister, no matter if they shared blood. Watching them caused my heart to ache with envy. Ian and I could've had that, arguing about vegetables. If we'd had a normal life.

But that had been taken from us.

All because I was Malec's child and carried the blood of the gods in me. It was why I'd been forced to wear the veil and was caged for half of my life under the pretense of being Chosen. In reality, I had been, just not in the way I'd thought.

I no longer believed that there had been another Maiden. That had only been a lie to keep up the ruse. What I didn't know was what Queen Ileana hoped to gain through this. In a few days shy of a fortnight, I would know. Unease slithered through me like a snake.

But at least some part of the Ian I knew remained. We could still have that normal life where we argued about vegetables.

Kieran dropped into the chair beside me. "What are you sitting over here thinking about?"

"Nothing," I replied, and he shot me a knowing look. "Everything."

He chuckled. "You having second thoughts about your decision?"

"No." Surprisingly, I wasn't. Going to Iliseeum? Maybe a little. "Do you think going to Iliseeum is a bad life choice?" I asked as Casteel caught what I thought was a cheese ball thrown by Vonetta.

"If you'd asked me that a year ago and I knew how to enter Iliseeum?" He laughed as he drew his fingers over his forehead. "I would've said yes. But now? Ever since my father told us how Iliseeum could be accessed through the tunnels, I've been thinking how that is one hell of a coincidence—all those years we spent in them."

"I have, too," I admitted, letting my head fall back against the soft cushion of the chair as I looked at him. "It's just too convenient that you were led there."

He nodded. "Then that got me thinking about fate. About how all these little things—and the big ones—happened and could've been…preordained. As if they were all leading up to this."

"To me becoming Queen?" I laughed. "I hope you mean something else because that's a lot of pressure."

He sent me a grin. "Being Queen *is* a lot of pressure," he pointed out.

"Yeah, it is." I bit down on my lip. "Do you think that's a bad life choice?"

"If you asked me a year ago—"

"You didn't know me a year ago, Kieran."

Dipping his chin, he chuckled and then looked over at me. "Honest to the gods? I think it's the best choice for you—and for the future of Atlantia and Solis."

"Well, that makes me feel even more pressured."

"Sorry." He slouched in the chair. "But, seriously. Like I was saying earlier, I think things were pointing to this—to something major. You're doing the right thing." His gaze found Casteel. "Both of you are."

Inhaling deeply, I nodded. It felt like the right thing—terrifying, but right. "I just hope I'm not expected to walk around wearing a crown all day," I murmured.

Kieran barked out a loud laugh, one that drew both Casteel's and Lyra's attention. The former raised his brows. I sank a little lower in my seat. "You have the weirdest mind, I swear," Kieran said, shaking his head.

"Crowns look heavy," I retorted as Lyra continued staring at Kieran, a faint smile on her pretty face. "And irreplaceable if you break or misplace them."

Kieran was silent, but I could feel his stare on me.

"Lyra seems to like you," I said, swiftly changing the subject.

"She seems to like you."

"Glad to know, but I think we're talking about two different types of liking someone."

He lifted a shoulder.

"Do you like her?"

"I like her." He propped a boot on the leg of another chair. "She's fun. A good person."

My brows lifted as I snuck a peek at Lyra. She was speaking with Delano and Naill. Fun? A good person? Kieran was often as transparent as a brick wall, but that wasn't how I would talk about Casteel if someone asked me what I thought of him. I'd probably wax on poetically for quite some time…and also list all the ways he was utterly infuriating.

I studied Kieran's profile, thinking of what he'd said while we sat along Stygian Bay. "I want to be nosy."

"Like when you watched Lyra and I on the beach?"

I choked on my breath—my actual breath—as my face flamed red. "That is *not* what I was referencing."

He was grinning so hard, I was surprised his face didn't crack. "You're not going to deny it?"

"What is the point?" I muttered.

Kieran eyed me. "Intriguing."

"Shut up."

He laughed. "What do you want to be nosy about?"

I looked down, running my finger over my ring. "The person you spoke about loving and losing? What happened to them?"

Kieran was quiet for so long, I didn't think he'd answer. But then he did. "She died."

My chest twisted. "I'm sorry."

He nodded, and another long moment passed. "It was quite some time ago."

"How…how did it happen?" I cringed at the question.

"Wolven are relatively healthy, just like Atlantians and other bloodlines, but there are a few diseases we're susceptible to. All inherent," he said. "Elashya was born with one—a wasting disease traced all the way back to the kiyou. It attacks the body and then shuts everything down." He scratched his chin, squinting. "She knew her family carried the disease, but it doesn't affect everyone, so she was hopeful. But her grandmother had it, and it commonly shows up every generation or two. The problem is that someone will be healthy for a hundred or so years, and then it just hits them. Starts with involuntary twitches and spasms of the muscles, almost so small you wouldn't notice them. But then within days…that's it. Over."

My finger stilled over the ring. "You…you fell in love with her knowing you could lose her?"

"The heart doesn't care how long you may have with someone." Kieran looked over at me, his eyes sheltered. "It just cares that you have the person for as long as you can."

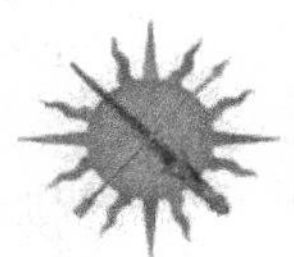

The following morning, I approached Casteel with a request as we left the inn. "I have a favor to ask."

"Anything," he replied.

I grinned. "Is it possible for us to obtain another horse?" I asked as we neared where Emil and Naill were readying their mounts. Two saddled horses traveled with us, but they belonged to Kieran and Delano, who had shifted into their mortal forms and were now astride the two steeds. "I would…I would like to ride my own horse into the capital. I remember what you taught me," I added when Casteel looked down at me. Vonetta had stopped, and even in her wolven form, she sent a look in Casteel's direction as if she were warning him not to argue. "I think I am ready—that I can control a rather calm one."

His eyes warmed in the fading afternoon sun. "I think you're ready, too," he said, and I beamed up at him. "Although, I will miss having you in front of me."

"I will miss that, too," I admitted, feeling my cheeks warm. "But I…"

"I know," he said quietly, and I think he really did understand why I wanted to ride into the capital on my own horse. What it meant for me. He pressed a kiss to my forehead and then looked over his shoulder.

"Already on it," Emil said, bowing with a flourish. "I will find you a steed worthy of your beauty and strength, Your Highness," he added with a wink and a smile.

I grinned.

"Every time he smiles at you, I want to rip his lips from his face."

My brows lifted as I looked at Casteel. "That's excessive."

"Not nearly excessive enough," he grumbled, eyeing where the Atlantian had disappeared into the nearby stable.

"Sometimes," Naill began as he hoisted himself onto his horse, "I do believe Emil has a death wish."

"Same," Casteel muttered, and I rolled my eyes.

Emil returned with a very beautiful gray mare that he'd been assured was even-tempered. Setti gave his approval by nudging the mare with his nose as I thanked Emil. "Does she have a name?"

"Storm," he answered as Casteel checked the straps on the saddle. "Named by the innkeeper's daughter."

I grinned as I stroked the fine hairs of the mare's neck. "It's nice to meet you, Storm."

Casteel raised his brows at me from the other side of the horse, but at least he wasn't ripping Emil's heart out.

Telling myself that this wasn't a bad idea, I hoisted myself onto Storm's back. My stomach flipped and flopped all over the place. I had no idea if Casteel somehow saw my nervousness, but he took the reins, holding them for a bit. Once I got used to the movement and being alone, I took them. Since we weren't doing anything beyond a quick trot, I felt rather confident that I wouldn't fall off.

Though, both Casteel and Kieran stayed close to me, riding to my left and right.

"What are you thinking about for the coronation?" Casteel asked as we rode through a wooded area. "Typically, it's an all-day celebration—a feast along with a ball."

A feast? Ball? Excitement bubbled up in me. For so many years, I'd wanted nothing more than to join the balls held at Castle Teerman, fascinated by the sounds and laughter, the dresses and artful makeup, and how the anticipation permeated the crowds. It was a reckless sort of happiness. I…I wanted that. To be in a pretty dress, have my hair done, my face painted, and to…to dance with Casteel.

But balls took weeks to plan, and I imagined coronations took even longer. And we didn't have days to spare to plan such an event.

"I would enjoy a ball," I said. "But I don't think we have time for that."

Casteel nodded. "I think you're right."

"Is it something that can be done later?" I wondered. "I mean, after we're crowned officially and have dealt with the Blood Crown and everything with that?"

A dimple appeared in his right cheek. "Poppy, you will be Queen. You will be able to do whatever you want."

"Oh," I murmured as Delano chuckled. I could…I could do whatever I wanted? I blinked as I focused on the road ahead. Anything? That was a unique feeling. A shocking one. I exhaled raggedly. "Then I would—"

An arrow whizzed past my head. I gasped, jerking to the side as Casteel reached over.

"Grab her reins," he bit out, encircling an arm around my waist.

Cursing, Kieran leaned over, grabbing Storm's reins as Casteel dragged me onto Setti. Another arrow flew over our heads.

"Motherfuckers." Naill grunted. Over his shoulder, I saw him glance down at his arm.

"Are you okay?" I shouted as Casteel wheeled Setti to the side, angling himself so his body shielded mine.

"Barely a flesh wound," the Atlantian growled, baring fangs. "Won't be able to say the same for those dead fucks."

I twisted in the saddle. All I saw were bronze masks.

The Unseen.

Dozens of them stood in the road, some armed with bows, and others with swords. *Gyrms.* The skin of their bare chests carried the grayish pallor of something that had never lived.

Then I saw nothing but wolven, streaking over the paved road and through the reedy grass, taking down those who held bows. Their screams were cut short as teeth sank deep into throats. Naill flew past us, shoving his sword deep into the chest of a Gyrm as Vonetta leapt over a fallen Unseen, crashing into the back of another. Several Gyrms breached the wolven, racing toward us as Emil rode past us, throwing a dagger. The blade pierced a mask, sending the Unseen falling backward. There wasn't even time to feel disappointment over what was happening—that this signified that there were still Unseen hell-bent on preventing me from taking the Crown.

That as Alastir had promised and had proven the night in Saion's Cove, it hadn't ended with his death.

"Hold on." Casteel twisted sharply, swinging his leg off Setti's back. I held on as he jumped from the horse. He landed without stumbling and then lowered me to the ground. Grasping the back of my head, he tipped his head down. "Kill as many as you can." Then his mouth was on mine, the kiss quick and raw, a clash of teeth and tongues.

The moment he let go, I reached for the wolven dagger and spun just as Kieran led Setti and Storm off the road—and hopefully out of harm's way.

Unstrapping his short swords, Casteel stalked forward. "You assholes interrupted a very charming conversation." He leaned to the side so fast that an arrow aimed for him flew harmlessly beyond him. "And that was incredibly rude."

Dagger in hand, I shot toward the closest Gyrm. I dipped low as it swung its sword. Popping up behind the creature, I thrust the blade deep into its back and then jumped back to avoid the inevitable gross poof. I whirled around as Delano relieved a Gyrm of its head with his sword. An Unseen rushed from the trees, weapon held high. I waited and then snapped forward, twisting as I kicked out, catching him in the knee. Bone cracked and gave. A muffled scream came from the man as I spun, slamming my dagger into the side of his neck. I jerked, dragging the wickedly sharp blade as I did. The man toppled forward. I turned, scanning those still standing and seeing none in a silver mask or any that carried the bone chain with them.

It was clear that they had no intention of taking me alive.

Another rushed from the trees. It wasn't a Gyrm. He was smarter—darting to the left and then the right. He swung the sword around as I danced to my right, slamming the blade into a nearby tree. "If I get blood on my new clothing," I warned as I sprang forward, shoving the dagger into the man's chest, "I'm going to be very upset."

"I'll get you new clothing," Casteel said, gripping an Unseen's shoulder as he thrust his sword into his gut.

I jumped back. "But I like this tunic."

"Holy shit," Emil grunted from several feet away, facing the woods.

Turning around, my stomach dropped. At least two dozen attackers drifted from the thick shadows of the trees, half Unseen and half Gyrms. The wolven and the others were making quick work of the ones on the road, but there were many, and one of ours was likely to get hurt or worse.

And I didn't want that.

There would be time later to wonder how the Unseen had learned that we'd be on the road to Evaemon. And at some point, I might think back on how easily and quickly I'd decided to tap into the hum of power building in my chest. About how I didn't stop to fear whether or not I'd be able to control myself. I just reacted, allowing instinct to take over.

Maybe later, I would even think back to the conversation I'd had with Casteel—the one where I had said I'd give those who stood against me a second chance, and how this was the exact opposite of what I'd said.

Then again, these men and creatures were actively trying to kill me, so maybe not.

I opened my senses wide and let the other side of my gift out, the half that took life instead of giving it. It was a lot like when I healed someone, but in reverse, I realized. My skin began to vibrate as the taste of metal filled the back of my throat. The hot, acidic burn of anger from the Unseen and the stark, frightening nothingness from the Gyrms reached out to me, and I took it—the hatred and even the void, letting it enter my veins and pour into my chest where it joined the eather. Under me, I felt the ground begin to faintly tremble as my gaze swept over those in masks. The primal power of the gods invaded my every sense.

My flesh sparked.

Silvery-white embers erupted over my skin, and out of the corner of my eye, I saw Casteel step back, and the wolven retreat. "Get 'em, girl."

I smiled as wispy, crackling cords stretched out from me. Someone gasped, likely an Unseen as glistening spiderwebs of light stretched out from me, crawling across the ground in a network of radiant veins. Several Unseen whirled, started to run, but they wouldn't make it. I would ensure that.

In my mind, I saw the webs of light falling upon the Unseen and Gyrms, their bodies breaking and crumbling, their weapons dropping and falling to the ground. I focused on that image as I took all the hate and fear and nothingness I held in my chest and fed it back through the many cords.

The rush of power swept over the trees, rattling the leaves until several fell. The webs of light lifted and then dropped over the Unseen and the Gyrms, those standing in the road, the ones running toward us, and even those who'd fled.

Bones cracked like thunder, arms and legs snapping and backs twisting. Bodies of inhuman creatures collapsed into themselves, shattering and sifting like dirt. One after another, they either broke or crumbled until they were just things on the ground, and then I pictured the remains turning to ash to match the piles of dirt.

After all, it seemed unsanitary to leave the bodies behind.

Silvery-white flames erupted over the still, twisted things on the ground, swallowing them and fading until all that remained was ash. The silvery webbing thrummed as the ancient, raw power pulsed through me.

"Poppy."

Static crackled through the air as I turned my head to where Casteel stood on the bank of the road, his chin lifted and hair tousled. What I felt from him wasn't acidic or empty. It was warm and sultry, spicy and sweet.

"That was incredibly hot," he remarked.

A husky, echoing laugh left me. His comment—as twisted and wrong as it was—helped me pull all that power back inside. I pictured the shimmering web fading, and when it did, I shut down my senses, and the silvery-white glow faded from my skin.

I stared at what was left of the attackers, searching for any sign of remorse, but all I found was a sense of sadness for a life wasted. These people, the members of the Unseen, could've chosen anything for themselves, and they had chosen this—actions based on one-sided beliefs of bloodlines and a fake prophecy.

"You okay?" Delano's soft question intruded on my thoughts.

I looked over at him and nodded. "You?"

His pale eyes searched mine. "Yes."

"Gods." Emil's lip curled as he dragged a hand over his face, wiping away the greasy blood as he stared down at the ashes and piles of oily dirt. "What did they really hope to accomplish?"

It was clear to me what they wanted.

Seeking out Casteel, my gaze locked with his. His eyes, like vibrant chips of glacial topaz, held mine. "They don't want me to take the Crown," I said. "They failed. So will anyone else who thinks they can stop me."

A razor-thin smile appeared on Casteel's face. "Damn straight."

Chapter 35

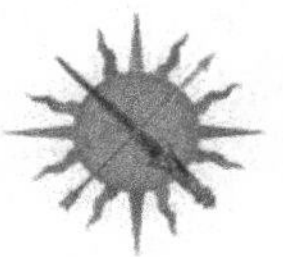

"It could've been someone in the inn at Tadous," Emil said as we rode on, watchful for more attacks. He and Naill were now in front of us, which I found…strangely amusing. They rode in a manner to protect me—Casteel and I—and I thought that perhaps I should be riding in front of *them*. "Or it could've been someone who saw Arden on his way to Evaemon and assumed he was bringing word to the capital of our arrival."

I hoped that Arden had made it to the palace safely.

"Hey," Casteel said quietly. I looked over to where he rode beside me, noticing then that Kieran and Delano had spread out a bit, giving us space. "What you did back there? You did the right thing."

"I know." And I did. "We could've kept fighting them, but someone would've gotten hurt, and I wasn't going to allow that."

"You're amazing," he replied, and I laughed softly. "I mean that, Poppy. Actually, you may be a deity, but you looked like a goddess."

"Well, thank you." I smiled at him. "I'm just glad that I did and could control it."

"Same." One side of his lip curved up. "That kind of ability will come in handy down the road."

I thought of the Blood Queen.

Yes, it would.

A moment passed. "Those Unseen? They don't represent Atlantia. What they think or want is not who the kingdom is."

Our gazes met. "I know." And that was…well, I wasn't sure if that was true or not. I'd met many Atlantians who'd been welcoming, friendly even. I'd met some who'd been wary and reserved. But there had been at least two dozen Unseen among the Gyrms. How many were out there? How many people could they have infected with their beliefs that I would destroy Atlantia?

I didn't know. But like before, I tucked those concerns away because, like I'd said back in the woods, they weren't going to stop me.

They wouldn't stop Casteel.

We rode on, and somewhere around midday, I knew that we were nearing the capital when we crested a hill, and large, broad trees appeared, each full of crimson leaves. Blood trees dotted the landscape and lined the wide, paved road leading into Evaemon—trees I now knew represented the blood of the gods and not evil or something to be afraid of.

The blood trees spread out on either side of the road. I sat straighter as Evaemon came into view.

My lips parted as my eyes widened.

Towering, ivory-hued structures with whirling, sharp spires stretched into the sky, flanking stone bridges that rose on tall pillars above a wide, crescent-shaped canal of water as blue as the sky. I could see three bridges, one to the east and one to the west, which led to islands that were nearly the size of Saion's Cove, full of soaring buildings that scraped the sky. Each bridge connected to dome-shaped structures that bore suns carved from stone, which rose above the belfries, and the bridge we rode across led to the heart of Evaemon.

Square, squat buildings with colonnades as wide as a city block gave way to gray and ivory buildings built far closer together than they had been at the Cove, but they rose higher into the sky, forming elegant towers and spires. Like Saion's Cove, there were patches of green wherever you looked, strips surrounding the graceful, sweeping structures, or covering the roofs of smaller, shorter buildings. Throughout the city, Temples shimmered, reflecting the afternoon sun. My throat dried as my gaze settled on the west end of the city, where a massive structure made of shiny black stone sat upon a raised hill, the wings of the building ending in circular porticos. Numerous domed-glass ceilings and spires shone brightly in the sun as the center wing flowed into a Temple constructed of the same midnight stone as the ones in Solis. Kneeling along the Temple's steeple were stone soldiers, their sable heads bowed as they held shields to their chests and swords stretched out, the stone blades streaks of black against the sky.

Stunned, I dragged my gaze from what I could only imagine was the palace and looked out over Evaemon. My nostrils burned, along with my eyes, as I soaked in what I had once believed had fallen.

Where Saion's Cove was nearly the size of Solis's capital, Evaemon was triple the size, stretching on as far as I could see to the west and to the east, where specks of white grazed in open pastures. Past the heavily wooded area that followed the Mountains of Nyktos, and in the face of that mountain, were eleven statues taller than the Atheneum in Masadonia. Each figure held a lit torch in his or her outstretched arm, the flames burning as bright as the setting sun. When I asked who the eleventh statue was, I learned that it was Nyktos's Consort.

They were the gods—all of them—watching over the city or standing guard.

I couldn't even begin to imagine how those statues had been built to that size and raised onto the mountain. Or even how those torches were lit—how they remained burning.

"Beautiful, isn't it?" Casteel didn't need to ask. It was the most beautiful city I'd ever seen. "Nearly all of the buildings you see before you were built by the deities."

Gods, that had to mean they were thousands of years old. How anything lasted that long was beyond me. How a city could be so stunning and intimidating was also beyond my realm of understanding.

White-winged birds flew overhead as we crossed the bridge, soaring over the wolven who prowled in front of us. I glanced at the large wheels in the water, wondering if that was how they fed electricity to the city. Carsodonia used a similar technique, but not on such a grand scale. Ahead, I could see sails of small ships in the canal.

"I have so many questions," I whispered.

"Not a single person is surprised to hear that," Kieran remarked, and Delano chuckled.

"But I can't even formulate words at the moment," I admitted, clearing my throat.

Casteel drew Setti closer as he looked over at me. "Are you…crying?"

"No," I lied, blinking the tears from my eyes. "Maybe? I don't even know why. It's just…I've never seen anything like this."

A bell tolled, startling me and sending birds flying from the belfry as it rang in a quick succession of three—which was different than the bells that tolled in Saion's Cove to tell the time.

"They're just alerting the city to our arrival," Casteel reassured me, and I nodded.

Emil looked back at us, his gaze finding Casteel over my shoulder. He nodded, guiding his horse to the front. Nudging his mount on, he galloped ahead, passing through the structure at the end of the bridge.

"Where is he going?" I asked.

"Ahead to the palace to let them know we've arrived," Casteel informed me. "We're going to take a far more discreet path. There will be people, but nothing like the route Emil is taking."

Needless to say, I was grateful for that. My senses were already overwhelmed, and I really didn't want to greet the citizens of Evaemon as a blubbering mess.

The wolven remained with us, along with Naill. Soldiers among the Guardians waited in the shadows of the entry building, bowing at their waists as we passed. My heart thumped heavily as we turned to the east, entering an empty road outside the long colonnades I'd spotted at the mouth of the bridge.

"What are these buildings used for?" I asked.

"They house the machinery that converts the water into electricity," Casteel explained, keeping Setti close. "You'll see several of these throughout the city."

"That's amazing," I murmured as, across the street, where doors slowly opened from sandstone buildings, curious faces appeared.

"And boringly complicated," Naill stated from behind us.

"But you could recite each piece of equipment and what the purpose of it is," Kieran replied.

"True." Naill smiled when I glanced over my shoulder at him. "My father is one of many who oversees the mills."

"Oversees?" Casteel snorted. "More like he's the heart of the mills. His father is mostly responsible for keeping these ancient wheels working so that everyone has access to everything electricity can provide."

"Your father must be very smart," I said, my gaze flicking over the faces that appeared in the windows. There were no hostile looks or feelings. Most seemed more focused on the mass of wolven converging on the street.

"That he is," Naill answered, his pride as warm as the sun.

About a half-dozen wolven, along with Delano, had fallen back. I reached out to him in concern, finding the springy freshness of his imprint.

All is well, he assured me after a moment, his response tentative as if he were still getting used to communicating this way. *We're just making sure you and the Prince are protected from all fronts.*

Were they worried about the Unseen or something else? I focused on the road we traveled. Eventually, we passed under the bridge that led to the east, a district of Evaemon that Casteel had said was called the Vineyards.

"Wine," he explained as we rode near the bank of the main canal. Ships with white and gold sails were docked at the numerous piers. People hustled on and off vessels, carrying crates. "The district gets its name from the vineyards."

The other district was called The Splendor for its cache of museums, art, and some of the oldest buildings in all of Atlantia. I couldn't wait to explore the enclave, but that would have to wait.

We traveled along the thicket of glossy blood trees, climbing the rolling pasture hills. My breathing became short as the trees thinned out, and smooth, jet-colored stone became visible through them.

"Why is the palace so different from the rest of the buildings in Atlantia?" I asked, forcing my grip to remain loose on Storm's reins.

"It didn't always look like this. Malec renovated it when he took the throne," Casteel explained, and I felt my stomach dip. "He said that it was to honor Nyktos, claiming it was more in line with the Temples in Iliseeum, from what I recall."

I thought that over. "Do you think he traveled to Iliseeum?"

"I don't know, but it's possible." The cooler breeze lifted the wavy strands of Casteel's hair. "Otherwise, how would he know what the Temples looked like there?"

"Good point," I murmured. "Priestess Analia once told me that the Temples in Solis were the oldest buildings, there long before the Ascended ruled."

"For once, that bitch spoke the truth," Casteel replied, and there wasn't a single thing about what he called her that offended me. Analia *was* a bitch. "Those Temples are made of shadowstone, a material that was mined in the Shadowlands and transported over to this realm ages ago by the gods, depositing some of it in the Elysium Peaks."

I hadn't known that.

Then again, I hadn't realized the Shadowlands even existed until recently. But it was just odd to me that the Ascended would change so much of the true history of the gods, and yet leave the Temples as they were. Maybe that was a line they wouldn't cross.

Either way, thoughts of shadowstone and ancient Temples fell to the wayside as we cleared the trees, and the back of the palace came into view.

We could see down into the city from our vantage point, homes and businesses staggered over the hills and valleys and in between the canals. The Evaemon Palace was built into the hillside, the gleaming black structure a formidable sight with numerous windows lining the towers and along the lower floors. But something immediately stood out.

No walls surrounded the palace, none along the back nor the front courtyard that led to the Temple. Several ebony pillars connected a catwalk from the palace to the Temple and surrounded most of the palace, now patrolled by Guards of the Crown. It struck me then that there hadn't been any walls around the estate in Saion's Cove, either.

Several Crown Guards, adorned in white and gold, stood under the archway and by doors a shade darker than the mare I sat astride as we rode through.

I couldn't believe how open the palace was. In every city of Solis where a Royal was seated, their homes were guarded by walls nearly half the size of the Rise that protected the city. No one could even come close to the castles or any of the Royal keeps or manors as there were always vast courtyards separating the home from the inner walls. But here? One could potentially walk right to the very entry points of the palace.

It was clear that the ruling class welcomed interaction with their citizens. Yet another stark difference from how the Ascended ruled Solis.

I almost dropped Storm's reins at my first sight of the courtyard. "Night-blooming roses," I whispered. Velvety black petals, now closed against the rays of the sun, climbed the pillars at the front of the palace, creeping across the onyx walls and up over the towers and spires.

Casteel's gaze followed mine. "I wanted to tell you about them when you mentioned that they were your favorite, but I couldn't." His brow creased. "They kind of slipped my mind since then."

I blinked, a bit shook by the sight of them. What a coincidence that the flowers I had always been drawn to covered the palace walls I would now call home.

"Cas!" a voice called out, drawing my attention to the stables. A young man strode across the courtyard, dressed in fawn-colored breeches and a white shirt like Casteel's but untucked. A wide smile broke out across the rich brown of his face. The smile only halted a fraction of a heartbeat when the wolven noticed him. "Is that really you? Or some bizarre hallucination?"

The casual use of Casteel's name signalized that this man must be a friend—someone Casteel trusted. As he grew closer, I saw that his eyes were a clear amber. He was an elemental Atlantian, and he was quite handsome, his features broad and warm, hair cropped close to his head much like Kieran's.

"That would be a strange hallucination," Casteel joked as he reached down, clasping the man's hand while I urged Storm to slow and then stop. "It's been too long, Perry."

The Atlantian nodded as a tan wolven crept close, watching the man closely. Luckily, Storm had shown no real reaction to so many wolven being close by. "It truly has been. I was surprised to hear that you'd come home. Almost didn't believe it was true when word reached us."

"I imagine many were surprised," Casteel answered smoothly. "How have you been?"

"Staying in the best kind of trouble." Perry's curious gaze flicked over to me as Casteel chuckled, lingering for a moment before moving to Kieran. "But not nearly as much as when you two are around."

My brows rose at that as Kieran asked, "What are you doing out here?"

"Engaging Raul in my stimulating and entertaining conversational skills."

"More like annoying the shit out of me," came a gravelly voice. An older man with hair the color of clouds and a beard of the same shade but streaked with black strode out from the stables with a slight limp, wiping his hands on a cloth he shoved into the front pocket of his brown tunic.

"Well, damn. Is it really the wayward Prince returned home?" the older man said. "I must be seeing things."

Perry's grin kicked up a notch. "That's just your failing eyes, Raul."

"Well, that would go along nicely with my failing body," he answered.

"Speaking of failing bodies, I'm surprised you're still alive," Kieran commented as he swung off his horse, and I blinked.

Casteel snorted. "What are you talking about? Raul will outlive us all."

"I fucking hope not—shit." Raul stopped beside Perry, squinting hazel eyes as he stared up. "Here I am, cursing up a storm, and you have a lady with you."

"A lady he hasn't introduced us to yet," Perry informed, his look a bit coy. My senses reached out to the Atlantian, and I felt nothing but amusement and curiosity. "A very quiet lady I've never seen before but believe I have heard about."

"That's because you don't know many ladies," Raul retorted as he reached for Storm's reins, scratching the horse's neck.

Perry nodded with a laugh. "Can't argue with that. But I have heard about this particular lady. That is if the rumors are true." He paused, looking over to where the wolven watched him. "And I'm thinking the rumors are very true."

"This is Princess Penellaphe. My wife," Casteel announced, and my heart gave a happy little skip in response to his words. "If that is the rumor you speak of, then it is true."

"Part of the rumor," Perry answered.

Raul muttered, "Well, shit."

I had no idea if their response was common or a harbinger, but then Perry started to step forward. A fawn-colored wolven appeared in front of Storm, its ears pinned back. Perry raised his brows. "Is that you, Vonetta?"

It was.

But the wolven gave no response, only continued staring at the Atlantian, her body tense and still. If Vonetta and Perry had been on familiar terms before, it no longer appeared to matter. But if Perry was allowed to call the Prince, "Cas," then I knew he was trusted.

I followed the vanilla-oak of Vonetta's imprint. *It's okay. He is a friend of Casteel's, right?*

There was a moment of silence, and then Vonetta's whisper found my thoughts. *Friends of Cas have betrayed him.*

Well, she had a good point there. *Let's give him a chance, though.*

Vonetta shot me a rather arch look for a wolven, but she backed off several feet.

"Shit," Raul repeated.

"Well, if that isn't confirmation of the other rumor, then I don't know what would be." The smile returned to Perry's handsome face as he looked up at me. A bubbly, fresh taste coated the inside of my mouth. Perry was curious…and still amused. "Should I call you Princess or Queen?"

No one answered for me. "You may call me Penellaphe," I decided.

Perry's smile increased, and the hint of fangs became visible.

"Well, Penellaphe, may I help you down?"

I nodded. Raul steadied Storm as Perry helped me down. "Thank you," I said.

"Pleasure is all mine." He glanced at Casteel as he held my hands. "Leave it to you to show up after years of absence with a pretty wife at your side."

Casteel dismounted with annoying ease. "I do love to make an entrance." He came around my back, slipping my hands free from Perry's.

Perry glanced at Kieran. "Since this fool is with you, does that mean Delano has returned? I haven't seen him."

"He has." Casteel threaded his fingers through mine. "He should be arriving shortly."

Perry's smile made such a quick return that I doubted he was often *not* smiling, but the smoky taste of attraction accompanied the curve of his lips now.

"Any idea where my parents are?" Casteel asked.

Perry nodded toward the building with the kneeling, stone soldiers encircling the cupola.

"I'll catch up with you later," Casteel told Perry before speaking to Raul. "You're going to take care of the horses for me?"

"Isn't that my job?" Raul retorted, and a startled laugh left me, earning a gentle hand squeeze from Casteel. "At least it was the last time I checked. If I've been fired, no one has decided to let me know."

"As if we would ever think of doing such a thing," Casteel replied, grinning.

"As if you spend much time thinking about anything," Raul snapped back.

Liking the old, somewhat crotchety man, my lips curved into a smile.

"Are you seriously smiling at him after he just suggested that I don't have a brain?" Casteel demanded in mock-offense.

"I am under the impression he suggested you don't use your brain often," I told him. "Not that you don't have one. And, yes, I am smiling at him. I like him."

"Her Highness has good taste." Raul nodded in my direction. "Not counting the taste that got you standing next to that one."

I laughed again. "Trust me, I have questioned that."

Perry laughed, and then came a rough chuckle from the old man. "I like her, Cas," said the Atlantian.

"Of course, you do," muttered Casteel. "Can you give Setti and Storm some extra sugar cubes? They deserve it."

"Will do."

We parted ways then, walking across the courtyard, followed by the wolven. I opened my mouth—

"Let me guess," Kieran cut in. "You have questions."

I ignored him. "Does Perry live here? At the palace?"

"He has quarters here, but he has his own home with his family in Evaemon." Casteel brushed the hair out of his eyes with his free hand. "We basically grew up together."

"Why does he have quarters here if he has his own home?"

"Because he is a Lord, much like his father, Sven," he advised, "who is an Elder. All the Elders have rooms here."

Considering that the palace appeared large enough to house a small village, I wasn't surprised to hear that.

"I'm also betting that the Council has been called and are awaiting our arrival," Casteel continued.

My heart tripped over itself a little. Although the wolven we'd sent ahead wouldn't have told Casteel's parents of our decision, nor did I think Emil would, I imagined his parents sensed that we'd made a decision.

Although this was the Temple, a wicked sense of deja vu swept over me as we neared the semicircular steps, and two guards opened the door. This time was different, though, because I wasn't entering as a Princess uncertain about her future.

I was entering as one who was about to become Queen.

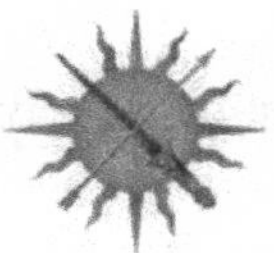

Emil waited for us just inside the Temple entryway, standing under an Atlantian banner that hung from the ceiling. My gaze locked on the closed doors beyond him, where at least ten guards were positioned. Wariness radiated from them, coming from what was probably a very unexpected sight of several dozen wolven climbing the steps beside us.

My heart tripped in my chest even as I walked forward. My hand trembled even enclosed in Casteel's. I knew I was making the best choice. I was as ready as I would ever be, but it felt like a dozen flesh-eating carrions had taken flight in my chest. This was…this would be huge. I would enter as Poppy and leave as a Queen—Queen to people who didn't know me and who may not trust me.

Casteel stopped, turning to me. His fingers touched my cheek, just below the scars. He guided my gaze to his. "You've faced Craven and vamprys, men wearing masks of human flesh, creatures without faces, and stared down Atlantians who wanted to harm you with the kind of strength and bravery most lack," he whispered. "Remember what you are. Fearless."

Fingers touched the other side of my cheek, and Kieran's pale eyes locked with mine. "You are a descendant of the gods, Poppy. You run from no one and nothing."

My breath caught as my gaze held Kieran's and then shifted to Casteel. The center of my chest hummed. A heartbeat passed, and then I looked at the closed doors. It was okay to be nervous. Who wouldn't be in my situation? But I wasn't afraid.

Because they were right.

I was brave.

I was fearless.

And I ran from no one and nothing—and that included a crown.

My gaze flickered over the wolven, stopping on Vonetta. Exhaling slowly, I nodded. We turned to the doors as they opened to an area lit by the sun coming from the dome's glass sides.

Rows of semicircular benches sat on either side of the aisle, offering enough seating for what had to be several thousand—possibly more. Above, a balcony area where even more people could attend jutted out, and under them stood ten statues of the gods, five on each side. They held unlit torches against their black stone chests. Ahead of us, the statue of who I could only assume was Nyktos stood in the center of the dais. Beyond him was another set of doors as large as the ones we'd entered through, where guards stood now. I recognized Hisa. The thrones sat before the statue of Nyktos.

They were both made of pearlescent shadowstone, streaked with thick veins of gold. Their shape fascinated me. The backs were circular and spiked, shaped like the sun and its rays, and at the center of the top, carved out of the same stone, was a sword and arrow crossing each other.

The current Queen and King of Atlantia stood beside their thrones, and as their son and I walked forward with the wolven trailing and spreading out among the rows of benches, I realized that both wore their crowns.

The crown upon the King's head was twisted, bleached bone, but the one that sat upon the Queen's head was golden, shining bone. I hadn't seen the crown since the Chambers of Nyktos. Eloana and Valyn stood in silence as we approached them, Casteel's mother's hands clasped at her waist.

"Mother," Casteel said as we stopped before the steps of the dais. Kieran and the others hung back several feet. "Father."

"We are glad to see that you have both returned," his father replied, one hand resting on the hilt of his sword.

"Not without interruptions." Casteel tilted his head. "We were accosted by members of the Unseen."

"Were there any injuries?" his mother asked.

"No." Casteel looked at me. "My wife made sure of that."

"We all made sure of that," I added.

"I'm relieved to hear that," she said. "But it shouldn't have happened."

No, it shouldn't have.

But it did.

"Arden arrived safely, I assume?" Casteel queried.

His father nodded. "Yes. He is resting in one of the rooms. All the wolven told us was that the meeting went well."

"Your brother?" His mother's gaze touched mine, the crown such a stark contrast to her dark hair. "Was he how you remembered?"

"He wasn't," I said. "And yet, he was. But he's not like other Ascended."

Her chest rose sharply behind the ivory gown she wore. "I don't know if that is a good or a bad thing."

"I don't either," I admitted.

"There must be much that you both need to share with us," his father began, and I saw movement out of the corner of my eye. In the shadowy alcoves of the dais, several people stood. My senses stretched out, finding an array of emotions, everything from curiosity to faint distrust. "But we assume that you're here to discuss more than your meeting with the Ascended."

Irritation sparked at him referring to Ian as *the Ascended* even though he was…an Ascended. I could recognize the irrationality of that, but it still didn't stop the burn of annoyance.

"You're correct," Casteel replied and then looked at me. Our gazes met. "We have come for more than that."

I focused only on Casteel, not allowing myself to read his parents or the shadows standing in the alcoves. The taste of chocolate-dipped berries calmed my nerves, and the steadiness in his golden eyes eased the tension gathering in my neck.

I was brave.

I was fearless.

Squeezing Casteel's hand, I turned back to his parents. "We have come to claim what is mine—the Crown and the kingdom."

Chapter 36

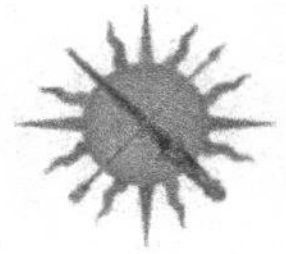

Eloana unclasped her hands, letting them fall to her sides. A heavy breath left her, one I hoped was of relief or at the very least acceptance.

His father stepped forward. "And if we contest your claim?"

My head shot in his direction. "You can," I said before Casteel had a chance to respond. "But it won't change the inevitable." Vonetta brushed against my leg as she prowled forward. Lyra had leapt onto one of the stone benches, and without looking, I knew the others had also moved in closer. I slipped my hand free of Casteel's and stepped forward, looking at his father. "The only people I will ever know as my parents were killed to prevent this moment. I was left dead and scarred because of my birthright and forced to wear the veil because of my bloodline. My brother was Ascended because of it. I've had years of controlling my own life taken away from me. Innocent people have died because of what is owed to me. I almost died. And on the way here, we were attacked. None of that has stopped this moment from coming. The Crown belongs to me and my husband, and I believe you already know that."

Valyn stared down at me, his expression unreadable, and I doubted I would succeed if I tried to read his emotions. His gaze flicked to where his son stood. "Do you have anything to add?"

"Not really." A shadow of a smile filled his tone. "She pretty much summed it up. You know that the Crown belongs to her. To us. We will need your help—both of you—when it comes to ruling Atlantia. But we don't need unnecessary drama."

I fought a smile as his father's eyes narrowed. "I apologize, son. I wouldn't want to cause any unnecessary *drama*," his father replied dryly.

"Apology accepted," Casteel murmured, and I heard the huffing sound of a wolven laughing behind me. Valyn's eyes narrowed.

"He's right," I agreed. "We do need your help. There is much for me to learn, and there is a lot that Casteel and I have to do."

"And your reason for coming to this decision?" Eloana asked.

Thinking of what Casteel had said to me, I met her stare. "My reasons don't matter as long as they're my reasons."

She stared at me for a moment, and then one side of her lips curved up. With a nod, she looked at her husband. "It's time," she said. "It's been time."

"I know," his father said with a heavy sigh. "I just hope you both understand that this responsibility doesn't end when you accomplish what you seek."

"We know," Casteel answered, coming to stand beside me once more.

I nodded. "We do."

Valyn and his wife came to the edge of the dais. "I have a suspicion that neither of you will want to go the traditional route?"

Casteel looked over at me. Assuming the *traditional route* meant balls and feasts, I said, "Once we have handled the threat to the west, we would like for there to be a…more elaborate coronation. Neither of us feels the timing is appropriate to do so now."

Eloana nodded. "The coronation celebration can be held whenever, upon your discretion."

A tremor coursed through me. I reached over, and within a heartbeat, Casteel's hand folded over mine. "So, what happens now?"

"It's fairly simple," his father answered. "In front of the Council of Elders, we will relinquish the crowns and the control to you and my son. And then we announce to the citizens the changing of the Crown."

My heart skipped a beat as I glanced at the shadowy alcoves. "Does that happen now since the Council is already present?"

Valyn smiled faintly. "It can."

Casteel eyed the alcoves. "And do any of them stand in opposition?"

There was silence, and then to our left, a tall man stepped out from the shadows. His eyes were a bright yellow, and his dark hair was turning silver at the temples, meaning he was a very, very old Atlantian.

"Lord Gregori." Casteel inclined his head, apparently recognizing the man. "You have something to say?"

"I do, Your Highness." The man bowed while Eloana sent her husband a wry look. "I know there is nothing we can say to suspend what is about to occur, but as one of the oldest Elders on the Council, I feel that I must speak for myself and others who are concerned about this development."

If he was one of the oldest members of the Council, then I suspected he was a changeling. My gifts pressed against my skin, and I let my senses open just enough to get a read on him. The stringent taste of distrust dried my mouth but wasn't at all surprising considering his words.

"Your concerns are noted," Casteel observed. "But as you suspected, they will not delay this."

The acidic burst of irritation rose from Lord Gregori. He started to step back.

"What are your concerns?" I asked, genuinely curious.

Lord Gregori's gaze skipped to me. His features showed none of the wariness he felt. "We are on the brink of war, and some of us feel that this is not the time to transfer power."

Anxiety hummed in my chest as I studied him. A year ago, I wouldn't have had the opportunity to find the courage to ask such a question. Six months ago, I might've accepted that what I knew was only half the answer. Today, I didn't. "And that is all?"

Lord Gregori stared back at me, his spine rigid. "No. We do not know you," he stated coolly. "You may share the blood of the gods—"

"She is a deity," Valyn corrected sternly, surprising me. "Descended from the King of Gods, and is Malec's child. She is not one who simply shares the blood of the gods. You know that."

My eyes grew wide.

Pink spotted Lord Gregori's cheeks. "My apologies," he murmured. "You are a deity, but you are still a foreigner to our lands."

"And one raised by the enemy as the Maiden?" I finished for him, wondering if it was too much of a leap to consider that he may sympathize with the Unseen, possibly even support them. "Our enemies are the same, Lord Gregori, as are our loyalties. I hope you give me a chance to prove that to be true."

Approval flickered through Casteel's father, and I'd be lying if I said that it didn't feel good.

"I pray to the gods that you do." Lord Gregori bowed stiffly before stepping back into the shadows.

"Anyone else feel the need to share their opinion?" Casteel asked. There was no movement from the alcoves, but obviously, others shared Lord Gregori's concerns. "Good." Casteel smiled tightly. "Because there is much we need to discuss with the Council."

"They are eager to hear what you must share," Eloana replied. "We can relinquish the crowns now, and while you meet with the Council, we will send word to the people throughout Evaemon that their new King and Queen will greet them," she said, turning and extending a hand to the tall doors beyond the statue of Nyktos. "From the balconies of the Temple of Nyktos."

A shiver skated over my skin as I stared at the smooth, reflective black stone of the floor, a little unnerved to realize that I stood in his Temple. Swallowing, I looked up. "All of this can be done today? The exchange of power? Speaking with the Council and then greeting the people?"

"Yes," Eloana confirmed.

Casteel squeezed my hand. "Then let's do this."

A fondness settled in his mother's features as she motioned for us to join them. "Come. You should not stand below us but before us."

Drawing in a deep breath, Casteel and I climbed the short set of steps. What happened next was surreal. My heart slowed and calmed. The faint tremor faded as the hum in my chest spread throughout my body, seeming to wash away and replace the nervousness with a keen sense of rightness. I looked down at the hand that held Casteel's, half-expecting to find that it was glowing, but my skin appeared normal.

"Bow," the Queen ordered softly.

Following Casteel's lead, I lowered to one knee before his mother. Our hands remained joined as his father stood directly before him. I looked over my shoulder. The wolven had sunk to the floor throughout the Temple, heads bowed but eyes open and fixed on the dais. Kieran, Naill, and Emil had done the same, and I saw that Delano had joined us in his mortal form, bowing alongside them.

"As we stand in the Temple of the King of Gods and before the Council of Elders who bear witness, we relinquish the crowns and the thrones of Atlantia," Valyn announced, "and all the power and sovereignty of the Crown. We do this of our own free will, to pave the way for the peaceful and rightful ascension of Princess Penellaphe and her husband, Prince Casteel."

Shock splashed through me in response to my title being stated before Casteel's.

Eloana reached up, removing the gilded crown. Beside her, Valyn did the same with his. They placed them on the floor of the dais.

A whirl of air swept through the Temple, lifting the strands of my hair. Before us, the bleached bones of the crown Valyn had placed on the floor cracked and slipped away, revealing the gilded bone beneath. Both crowns shimmered, a light from within them pulsing intently and then fading until they glimmered in the sunlight.

A rattled breath left Valyn as he and his wife picked up the crowns once more. His voice was steady as he said, "Do you, Casteel Hawkethrone Da'Neer, swear to watch over Atlantia and her people with kindness and strength and lead with compassion and justice, from this moment to your last moment?"

Those words. *From this moment to your last moment.* My throat tightened.

"I swear to watch over Atlantia and her people," Casteel answered, his voice thick. "With kindness and strength, and to lead with compassion and justice, from this moment to my last moment."

"Then so be it." His father placed the golden crown atop Casteel's head.

"Do you, Penellaphe Balfour Da'Neer," Eloana spoke, and a rush went through me at hearing his last name attached to mine, "swear to watch over Atlantia and her people with kindness and strength and lead with compassion and justice, from this moment to your last moment?"

My skin vibrated as I once again followed Casteel's lead. "I swear to watch over Atlantia and her people with kindness and strength, and to lead with compassion and justice, from this moment to my last moment."

"So be it," Eloana answered, lowering the crown she held to the top of my head.

Flames sparked to life in the once-barren torches of the gods that stood to either side, one after another, until fire erupted from the torch that Nyktos held. The flames that crackled and flickered above the torches were silvery-white.

"Rise," Eloana ordered softly, her eyes glistening with bright tears when I looked up. She smiled. "Rise as the Queen and King of Atlantia."

Chapter 37

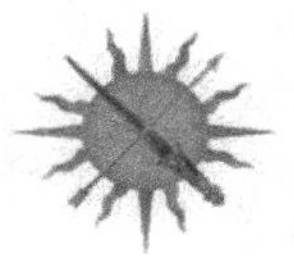

The weight of the gilded crown was unexpected, lighter than I imagined but only in the physical sense. An intangible heaviness came with it, one that spoke of thousands of years of decisions, choices, sacrifices, and gains.

But I would bear the weight because I'd sworn to, just like Casteel had.

He looked rather striking with the crown resting upon his head.

I looked over at him as we stood just inside the palace foyer before a row of banners that hung from the ceiling to rest a scant inch or two from the floor. The palace staff had been called and briefly introduced to us by Eloana and Valyn. There had been hundreds of them, from kitchen staff to housekeeping to the stable hands and those responsible for the grounds. My head had spun from all the faces and names, and now they were filing out from the foyer while my gaze swept over Casteel.

He wore the crown as if he'd been born to.

Eloana approached us, along with an older woman wearing a long-sleeved gown of gold—the color that all the staff wore. I'd learned that many lived within the palace on the floors above, while some maintained homes offsite with family. I'd been shocked to learn that they held quarters among the Lords and Ladies. In Solis, the staff was considered servants, and they shared bare rooms lined with cots and very little personal items.

"I would like to introduce you to Rose," Casteel's mother said, touching the woman's arm. "She is the palace manager—or the magician of the palace. Whatever you need or would like done, she is your woman."

Rose bowed as warmth and bubbly happiness radiated from her. "It will be an honor to serve Your Majesties."

"It will be an honor to have you continue on as the magician of the palace," Casteel replied smoothly.

A bright smile broke out across Rose's face. "The Royal Chambers are being cleared as we speak, and I took it upon myself to have some of your personal items moved, Your Majesty." This was said to Casteel, and I was curious to discover what these *personal items* were. "I have already had refreshments sent to the State Room for your session with the Council of Elders. Is there anything else that you would like?"

I couldn't think of anything.

"There is one thing." Casteel looked over at me, his eyes twinkling. "I believe my wife and I would like to make a change."

My gaze flew to the banners. "The crest," I blurted out, and both Rose and Casteel's mother turned to look at the banners. "I mean, I would like to change the Atlantian Crest. I was told that we could."

"You can." Eloana turned back to us.

"Yes." Rose nodded. "What change would you like to make?"

I glanced at Casteel, grinning when he winked. "I would like the arrow and sword to be crossed equally over one another so that neither is longer than the other."

"We can do that," Rose conferred while I felt a splash of surprise from Casteel's mother. "I will have the banners pulled down at once and send word to the steel workers, seamstresses, and leather shops that they can expect an influx of work—which they will be happy to hear," she added quickly and brightly. "There are saddles and stamps, shields and flags which will need to be changed. The banners we could have completed within the week, the shields will take a bit longer. And the rest—"

"There is no rush," I assured her. "Whenever it can be done is fine."

Her look turned perplexed. "It will be done at once. Anything else?"

"I…I don't think so?" I said.

Casteel shook his head. "That should be all for now."

"Perfect." She bowed and then spun, hurrying off as she motioned to several staff members who waited by the walls.

"She is mortal. I know you were going to ask," Casteel stated before I could do just that. "I don't think she has any Atlantian blood in her. Does she, Mother?"

Eloana shook her head. "Many generations ago, her family did, but by now, she is of a mortal line. I was surprised by your request," she admitted, turning to me. "The sword represents the strongest one in the union. That would be you, Your Majesty."

Casteel was utterly unfazed by the blunt statement. "I believe that Casteel and I are of equal strength," I reasoned, a little surprised that she would even question it. "I want the people of Atlantia to see us as such."

Eloana held my gaze for several moments and then nodded. "I think that is a wise choice," she said finally.

"And, please, just call me Penellaphe," I said.

Her smile widened as she nodded. "I will join you all shortly in the State Room." She started to turn and then faced Casteel. Her gaze roamed over his face. "I am so very proud of you today." Stretching up, she pressed a kiss to his cheek.

Casteel cleared his throat. "Thank you."

His mother smiled and then left, heading down the same hall that Rose had disappeared down. She was leaving to make sure the announcements were sent out.

"Ready?" he asked.

I nodded.

Taking my hand, we walked forward under the banners and into a hall straight ahead. Evaemon Palace was a surprise. Based on the exterior alone, I would've imagined that the inside would be cold and unwelcoming, but only the floors were made of the crisp black I now knew was shadowstone. The walls were covered with a cream-hued type of plaster, and all the windows and glass ceilings let in a surprising amount of natural light.

Staff hurried along the sides of the corridor near the walls, stopping to bow hastily before disappearing into other wider halls. I caught sight of a sparse atrium, one full of night-blooming roses, and the hall we entered had numerous closed doors.

"These are meeting spaces," Casteel explained, his hand wrapped firmly around mine. Kieran, Delano, Emil, and Naill walked with us. Some of the wolven had remained in the foyer while Vonetta and Lyra followed with a dozen or so wolven.

They weren't the only ones who trailed behind us. From the moment the crowns had been placed on our heads, Hisa and several

Crown Guards followed. I wondered if it was strange for them to switch who they protected so quickly, and if it was also odd for Casteel's parents to suddenly be lacking familiar shadows—although at least two guards had flanked Eloana when she parted ways with us in the foyer.

The hall we traveled down spilled into another foyer, one where a grand staircase spiraled up to the second floor and several above it. "Guest rooms are above, along with the staff rooms."

I resisted the urge to break from Casteel and rush over to the staircase to see if the black stone of the banister was as smooth as it looked. "What—what about our rooms?"

"They are the east wing," he answered, nodding at an older male who descended the stairs, carrying a platter of empty glasses.

"Oh," I murmured and then frowned. "Wait. They're *in* the east wing, right?"

A smirk appeared as Kieran said, "His and Her Majesty's quarters *are* the east wing."

I…

Well, I had nothing to say to that as we entered the hall beyond the staircase, passing several paintings I would have to stop and look at later when I wasn't thinking about the fact that the Royal Chambers were an entire wing of the palace. "Where will your parents live?" I blurted out the thought as it occurred to me.

Casteel grinned. "They will probably remain here for a bit while the transition is made, and then they'll either stay or move to one of the estates."

"Oh," I repeated.

We entered a circular chamber where the breezeways connected the east and west wings. A goddess statue stood in the middle, her arms stretched above her head and palms tilted upward. I had no idea which goddess she was, but she was definitely…ample in the hips and chest areas.

We passed a family room, a rather inviting space with couches and thick carpets and a glass ceiling, and then continued on through the Great Hall and past a dining area large enough to seat dozens.

The State Room was more than one space, situated toward the west wing of the palace. Cream settees lined the walls of the reception hall, placed in between large potted plants with leafy palms. Staff lingered near the banquet tables, where people I assumed were members of the Council helped themselves to drinks and finger foods.

At the back of the hall, two open doors led to a chamber that was long and oval, set with a table that stretched nearly the length of the room.

We'd taken perhaps two steps into the Hall when the Elders turned from the table. Along with the staff, they all bowed deeply, even Gregori—the only one I recognized.

"As you were," Casteel issued with a nod, and I committed that phrase to memory as the staff and Elders immediately straightened.

His father broke away from where he'd stood with a woman with deep brown skin, and a man with long, reddish-brown hair.

"We are still waiting on a few to return from their rooms, but they should be here shortly," Valyn said, clasping his hand on Casteel's shoulder. His voice lowered. "You will be expected to choose an advisor. Both of you. It doesn't have to happen today, but you should choose one soon."

"I already know who I will choose." Casteel looked at me, and I could only think of one person. I glanced to where Kieran now stood just inside the door, his head tilted as Delano spoke quietly to him. I nodded in agreement. "I will want to speak with him first."

Valyn's gaze flicked to Kieran. "He is a good choice." He squeezed Casteel's shoulder, and I was relieved to see the gesture. "For both of you." There was a pause as he looked at his son, clearing his throat.

Opening myself up, I could…taste what reminded me of vanilla—sincerity—but there was also a warm, cinnamon flavor. *Pride*. Emotions seeped through the cracks in the walls his father had built around himself, and even without my gift, I could sense that he probably wished to speak with his son alone. The gods only knew how long Valyn had waited for this moment, having gone from expecting one son to assume the role and then hoping the other would eventually take the throne.

My gaze skittered over to where Naill and Emil had roamed into the chamber. "I'll be right back," I said, and Casteel's gaze shot to me. I smiled at him and then his father. "Excuse me."

Vonetta prowled alongside me as I walked into the chamber, aware of the eyes that followed. I let my senses open wide, and once again, I tasted the springy freshness of curiosity and the undertone of concern, thick like buttermilk. As I continued on, my chin lifted, my gaze moving from Naill and Emil to the round windows spaced between similar-shaped mirrors throughout the chamber. I could see just the steel gray and ivory of buildings. Eager to see more of Evaemon, I almost didn't catch my reflection in the mirror just inside the room.

But I did.

My steps faltered. My eyes appeared brighter than normal, the silvery sheen behind my pupils more noticeable. There was a faint pink blush to my cheeks. I didn't really notice the scars. The crown of twisted bone that sat upon my head drew my attention.

And the fact that my hair was a bit of a mess. It was braided, but the ride here and the skirmish with the Unseen had caused many strands to sneak free.

Realizing that I was still in clothing dusty from the road and probably stained with blood during my crowning and my first Council meeting, I swallowed a sigh and glanced out into the reception hall. My head tilted as I scanned the Elders. It wasn't until then that I realized they were dressed similarly to Casteel and me. They were all dressed in either black or gray tunics and pants trimmed in gold—even the women. There were no fancy, gauzy gowns made of rich, supple material. The clothing was pragmatic. I suspected that all of them were fighters in one way or another.

I glanced at my reflection once more, still a bit startled to see the golden crown. Gods, what would Tawny think if she saw this? She'd probably laugh in surprise and then fall into stunned silence. A sad smile tugged at my lips. And Vikter? Gods, he…

Blowing out a sharp breath, I managed to resist the urge to reach up and touch the crown and forced myself to walk past the mirror. I was sure that Vonetta probably wondered how long I would stare at my reflection.

"I see you found sanctuary and more."

That throaty, smoky voice stopped me. A wave of tiny bumps pimpled my skin. I turned around and felt as if the floor fell out from under my feet. A woman stood there, her hair a deep black and thickly curled, hanging loosely to frame deep, rich brown skin. Full, red lips curved into an impish smile as she dipped in a bow that was subtle even in a gray tunic and pants.

My lips parted. I couldn't believe who I was staring at. "You were at the Red Pearl," I exclaimed as Vonetta looked up, cocking her head to the side. "You sent me to the room Casteel was in."

The woman before me's smile grew as she straightened, the soft scent of jasmine surrounding us as she whispered, "I was right, wasn't I? About what you found in that room."

"You were, but how…?" Was she a changeling? I knew they could know things by speaking or touching someone. Others simply knew things. So many questions rose to the tip of my tongue, starting with why she'd done that and what she had been doing at the Red Pearl. She had been dressed as one of the employees—

Casteel slid his arm along my lower back as he came to stand by my side. He lowered his head, pressing his lips against my cheek as he said, "I grew lonely and came to find you."

In any other situation, I would've pointed out that he hadn't been alone, and I also would've been secretly thrilled with his willingness to say such a thing in front of another, but this was not a normal situation. I stared at the woman before us.

"Ah, the last of you have arrived," Valyn announced as he joined us, stopping beside the woman from the Red Pearl. Over his shoulder, I saw Eloana. He smiled at the woman. "I don't think you've had a chance to meet before."

"We haven't," Casteel confirmed, as I kept my mouth shut, and the woman smiled at me.

"This is Wilhelmina Colyns," Valyn announced, and every single part of my body flashed hot and then cold. "She joined the Council after you…"

Valyn was speaking, but my heart was pounding so fast that I couldn't be sure if he even spoke a language I understood. Oh, my gods, it was *Miss Willa.*

The Miss Willa.

Standing in front of us.

How could I have forgotten that she was a member of the Council?

A wild wave of amusement rolled off Casteel so strong that I almost laughed. "Wilhelmina," Casteel drawled, and I looked at him.

And then I remembered that this was Casteel, and he could say anything in front of his father—and his mother. And, oh my gods—

"We have not met," I said quickly, reaching down and placing my hand on his arm. I squeezed hard. "It is an honor to meet you."

"A huge honor," Casteel added while confusion pinched his father's features.

Miss Willa smiled. "The honor is all mine."

"Are you all ready?" Eloana asked, thankfully interrupting.

I could've hugged and kissed the woman. "Yes." I squeezed Casteel's arm, just *knowing* he was about to say something else. "We are."

"Perfect." Eloana glanced at Willa. "Would you like something to drink?"

"Whiskey, if you have it," Willa answered.

Eloana laughed. "Now you know we always have that on hand."

The remaining Elders entered the room, taking seats at the table. Only Vonetta remained inside with us, the rest of the wolven standing guard outside the closed doors. Willa joined the Elders, whiskey in hand. Casteel's parents did not take seats at the table but took two against the wall where Naill, Delano, and Emil stood with Kieran and Hisa. No other guards were in the room. There were two seats left at the head of the table, reserved for the King and Queen.

For us.

Taking those seats felt as surreal as the crowning had, and thoughts of Willa faded as introductions were made. There were eight members in attendance. We were missing only Jasper, who had remained in Saion's Cove. Another wolven had taken his place, a Lady Cambria, whose blonde hair was sprinkled with silver strands. In the aftermath of all that was happening, I knew it would be difficult to remember most of the names, but I would remember Sven, who looked very much like the son I had met by the stables. There were three others, two males I suspected were mortal, and a female Atlantian.

And they all sat in silence, staring at Casteel, their combined ages and experience wholly intimidating. Muscles tightened in my neck and shoulders, and suddenly, the crown felt heavier. An urge to shrink in the chair, to make myself as small and invisible as possible swept through me, but it was brief because I was neither small nor invisible.

And I would never be that again.

"I'm not sure what the formalities of such meetings are, but those of you who already know me are well aware that I'm not one for formalities," Casteel announced as he looked over at me. "And neither is my wife, Penellaphe. So, we may as well get to the point. There is a lot to discuss, and very little time to waste."

"If I may speak," a pale-skinned man with golden eyes sitting near the middle of the table said. All I could think about was the last time I had sat at a table with Casteel, and similar words had been uttered. This man hadn't been in the reception hall. I would've recognized his icy-blond hair.

"Of course, Lord Ambrose." Casteel leaned back, resting his hands on the arms of the chair.

"Lord Gregori spoke for those of us who have concerns," the

Atlantian began, and my senses zeroed in on him. Distrust coated him. "We understand that there was nothing that could stop the ascension of the Crown, but we do feel that we must address those concerns."

Across from him, Willa took a drink of her whiskey and not-so-discreetly rolled her eyes.

"Didn't Lord Gregori address them in the Temple?" Casteel questioned, head tilted. "I believe he stated them as succinctly as possible. Or rather your Queen stated them as succinctly as possible."

Ambrose glanced in my direction. "She did, and she was right. We do not know her, and she was raised by the enemy. That was stated but not discussed."

"There's nothing to discuss beyond what was already stated," I spoke up, meeting Ambrose's stare. "I understand your concerns, but I also know that nothing I say will change them. All I can do is prove that you have nothing to fear."

"Then, if you wish to prove that there is nothing to fear, you should have no issue with us voicing our concerns," Ambrose countered.

"I don't," I replied as Casteel began tapping his finger on the arm of the chair, his ring making soft thuds against the wood. "I've been told that it is wise to heed the advice of the Council, and that when it hasn't been, nothing good has come from it—advice Casteel and I plan to follow. But I already know how you feel, Lord Ambrose. I already know how several of you feel." My gaze swept around the table. Gregori's lips thinned. A woman with dark hair sat back. Lady Cambria's smirk matched Willa's. Sven appeared bored. "There is too much to discuss to sit here and talk about what cannot be changed in a discussion, nor will I sit here and answer for crimes or choices or decisions that the Ascended or the deities made before me. I have already paid dearly for their sins." My gaze returned to Ambrose. "I will not entertain doing so again."

The Atlantian swallowed. "We have heard of the resurgence of the Unseen and the attack on you. We condemn it and do not stand for such actions." His hand flattened on the table. "But—"

"There is no but," Casteel interrupted, his tone soft but full of smoke.

Ambrose's mouth tightened, but he nodded stiffly. "Understood."

I started to relax, but Casteel's head tilted. "You were not in the reception hall when we arrived."

"I was not, Your Majesty."

"You did not bow upon entering the room," he continued, and I glanced at him.

"Cas," I started softly.

"It's a common courtesy," Casteel said, his gaze trained on the Atlantian. "The most basic of them. Nor have you once referred to your Queen as 'Your Majesty' or even 'Your Highness' as you spoke to her. Again, the most basic of common courtesies and respect." Silence fell throughout the room. "Am I not right, Father? Mother?"

"You are right," Eloana answered. "Those who did not greet either of you as such in the hall should have done so once within sight."

"Lord Ambrose, you did bow to my son," Valyn added.

Anger simmered in Lord Ambrose, as did embarrassment. He said nothing.

"You will bow before your Queen." Casteel eyed the Atlantian coolly. "Or you will bleed before her. It is your choice."

A low growl of agreement echoed from where Vonetta was crouched beside me.

I tensed. I wanted to intervene, to put a stop to this before something unnecessarily bloody happened during our very first Council meeting as rulers, but instinct warned that an example was being made—one that would indicate whether or not Casteel or I would tolerate disrespect. And respect was important. If we didn't have the Elders' respect, how would we have the kingdom's respect? Still, the threat made my skin itchy.

Wood scraped against stone as Ambrose rose. He bowed stiffly. "I apologize, Your Majesty," he said to me. "I meant no offense."

I nodded, and as he straightened, I called on what Casteel had said before. "You may sit."

Ambrose did just that, and the thread of tension eased from the room.

"Now, can we get started?" Casteel asked as he scanned the Elders and was met with several nods. "Good, because we want to stop a war before one starts."

Sven leaned forward. "This, I am very interested in hearing."

Others seemed to share his sentiment, and some didn't, but they all listened to our plan to meet with the Blood Crown in Oak Ambler and offer our ultimatum, explaining why we believed it would work.

"It could," Lady Cambria stated, brows pinched. "You're ripping out the foundation that holds all their lies together. The Ascended are a lot of things, but they are not stupid. They know what that will do to their people."

I glanced at Valyn. "It will lessen, if not destroy, their control over the people of Solis and destabilize their society. I do not believe they will risk that."

"None of us want war," Lord Gregori stated, looking around the table. "Those who were alive during the War of Two Kings are still haunted by those horrors. But you're asking for us to agree to give the Ascended a second chance? To prove they control their bloodlust? We've been down that road before."

"We know. Right now, we are asking that you understand our decision to keep the soldiers in the north at bay," Casteel said, making it clear he was not asking for their permission. "Once we meet with the Blood Crown and have their answer, then we can reconvene and discuss whether or not you feel that you can give any of them a second chance. But we haven't crossed that bridge yet, and we have no intention to burn it before we do."

"I have innumerable reasons for why I want to see the Ascended killed," a female Atlantian stated. Her sand-colored skin was without a trace of wrinkles and her brown hair was free of any gray or white. I believed her name to be Josahlynn. "But I only need one. My husband and son died in that war."

My heart clenched. "I'm sorry to hear that."

"Thank you, Your Majesty." Her chest rose with a deep breath. "As the rest of you know, I've been on the fence about what to do. If we can prevent more husbands and wives, sons and daughters from dying, we should."

There were many nods of agreement, but Lady Cambria leaned forward, resting her arm on the table. "But it is far too dangerous for you two to be the ones to meet with the Blood Crown. You are the King and Queen—our *Liessa.* Someone else should be sent in your place. I will gladly go."

"As will I," Sven announced, and so did many others.

I felt Kieran's wry amusement the moment our gazes touched. "Neither of us will ask any of you to do what we are not willing to risk ourselves," I said. "Plus, it will be far safer for us than it will be for any of you. The Blood Crown does not want us dead."

"We will also enter the city before we're expected," Casteel explained. "Giving us time to see what they may have in store for us."

"And who set up this meeting?" Ambrose asked.

I braced myself. "My brother, who was Ascended."

As expected, this created several outbursts and questions. Once they quieted, I explained who Ian was to me, and that even if we shared no blood, he was still my brother. Throughout the discussion, Casteel had extended his arm, placing his hand on the back of my neck where his fingers moved in slow, soothing circles. There were echoes of empathy from around the table, mingled with blunt pity. "Before we left, Ian told me that the only way we could defeat the Blood Crown—force them into taking our ultimatum—was by waking Nyktos and gaining the assistance of his guards."

"We plan to travel to Iliseeum in the morning," Casteel explained.

"Travel to Iliseeum? To wake Nyktos?" a mortal Elder exclaimed. "I mean no offense by saying this, but are you two out of your minds? Wake the King of Gods? And I truly mean no offense," he quickly repeated when Casteel's gaze fixed on him. "But we will be having another coronation before you even leave to meet with the Blood Crown."

"Well, that was highly encouraging," Casteel murmured, and I cracked a grin.

"The resting place of the gods is well protected, either by Primal magic or guards," Lord Ambrose stated, his brows raised. "I imagine the King of Gods is surrounded by both."

"Yes, but Pennelaphe is of his bloodline," Willa noted. "What is guarding him should be able to sense that." She paused. "Hopefully."

The *hopefully* part was really reassuring.

"Or he could become extraordinarily angered by such an intrusion and kill any who dare to wake him," another Elder pointed out.

"There is that." Willa lifted her drink.

"Do you need to travel to Iliseeum?" Casteel's father asked. "We do not know if you will need Nyktos's guards. It may be an unnecessary risk."

"Or it could be what forces the Blood Crown's hand," Eloana countered.

Casteel's fingers continued moving along the nape of my neck as his gaze shifted to mine. "What do you think, my Queen? The plan isn't set in stone."

It wasn't, but I believed my brother. Whatever these Revenants were, we needed all the help we could get.

"He's slept long enough, hasn't he?" I said, and approval flashed in those amber eyes despite the insanity of what we were considering.

"We will wake him."

"How would you even begin to locate his resting place?" asked Lady Josahlynn.

That was a good question. I started to look at Casteel, but Willa spoke. "I imagine he slumbers in his Temple. It shouldn't be hard to find, as it looks like the palace and the Temple of Nyktos here, but larger."

Well, I supposed Malec had been correct in his belief that his renovations were more in line with the Temples in Iliseeum.

Casteel raised a brow as he leaned into me and murmured, "Now we know where to find him."

I nodded, wondering how Willa knew. Had she been to Iliseeum? Then again, she had sent me to Casteel's room without his knowledge. The Atlantians didn't believe in prophecies, but they *did* believe in Seers.

"You're willing to do this—all of this?" Ambrose asked with a shake of his head. "Because of what an Ascended said? When we know you cannot trust an Ascended?"

Willa rolled her eyes with a delicate snort. "Anyone who has lived long enough and can look past their own asses knows that not even the vamprys are inherently evil."

Mutters of derision rose from other Elders. Glancing at Casteel, I saw a slight frown tug at his lips as I leaned forward. "You mean those who have managed to control their bloodlust?"

"Those who have managed have been few and far between," Gregori countered. "At this point, they are more legend than reality."

"Legend or not, when they are first turned, vamprys are consumed by bloodlust. That is correct." Willa's eyes met mine with a look that made me think of my Ascension. "And it can take time for them to find their way out of that, but it is who they are in their hearts and souls that determines whether or not they can be trusted."

My breath caught. Could that be why a part of Ian remained? Because he had been a good person before his Ascension? If so, then there was hope for Tawny and how many others?

"That is an extremely optimistic and naïve outlook on the Ascended," Gregori asserted.

Willa looked at the Elder. "I'd rather be optimistic than bigoted and close-minded, but I am never naïve. I have more than a thousand years on you," she said softly, and I blinked. "Consider that before you speak so ignorantly, and maybe you will save yourself future embarrassment."

I...I really liked Willa.

And it had nothing to do with her diary.

She held Gregori's stare until he looked away, a muscle flexing in his jaw. Then she turned to Casteel and me. "You have my support, even if you do not require it. You also have my advice. I've never been to Iliseeum. Obviously," she told us, finishing off her glass of whiskey. "But I know those who have."

A thought I really didn't want to entertain entered my mind. Malec apparently knew what the Temples in Iliseeum looked like, and my *father* had a lot of mistresses.

And Willa had had a lot of partners.

What if she'd written about him in— Nope, I stopped myself from going there. I did not want to think about that.

Willa's gaze met mine and then Casteel's. "Whatever you do, do not enter Dalos, the City of the Gods. You will know it when you see it. If you enter, you will never return."

Chapter 38

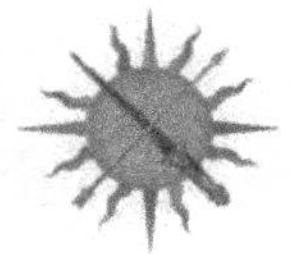

After Willa's unsettling warning, the Elders gave their reluctant support of our plans to travel to Iliseeum and then meet with the Blood Crown. The cautious backing mostly came from those concerned about our safety, but I could sense a few simply didn't agree with any of that.

Those who thought war was inevitable.

Lord Ambrose and Lord Gregori were two of them.

But I didn't think they truly wanted war. It was just that they couldn't see a way around it, and I hoped we proved them wrong.

The meeting was adjourned, and there was one thing left to do. We were to greet the public, along with the Elders and Casteel's parents. Their presence would be a show of support and approval.

And then Casteel and I would be alone. Of course, we still needed to speak with Kieran, but we would have to process everything, and maybe even live a little before we embarked on our journey to Iliseeum.

I lingered as everyone filed out of the room, making their way back toward the Temple of Nyktos. I wanted to speak to Willa, who had taken her time rising from the table.

Or she simply knew I wanted to speak with her.

Either way, I had many questions and only a handful of minutes to speak to her with only Vonetta waiting by the door.

"May I ask you a question?" I said.

Willa looked over at me, her golden-brown eyes alight with the same strange, knowing glint that had been present when I first met her. "You are the Queen. You can ask whatever you like."

I didn't think being Queen gave me carte blanche for questions—which I had many I wanted to ask. "Why were you at the Red Pearl?" I asked.

"I have a wandering soul that has a thirst for exploration," she answered, and based on her diary, I could agree with that.

"But isn't it dangerous for you?"

Her laugh was throaty. "The best kind of adventures always carry a hint of danger, as I'm sure you know," she said, and my cheeks warmed. "And it had been many years since I'd been to Masadonia. I had the strangest urge to travel there."

Her strange urge roused my suspicions about exactly what she was. "Why did you send me to the room Casteel was in?"

Her red lips curved upward in a slight smile. "It simply…felt right to do so."

"That is all?"

She nodded as she approached me. "One's instinct should always be trusted."

"You're a changeling, aren't you?" When she nodded, I asked, "So, your instinct is far more…accurate than others?"

A soft laugh left her. "Some would say that. Some would even say that instinctual accuracy has led me to become one of the greatest Seers Atlantia has ever known."

A Seer. I knew it!

"When I saw you in the Red Pearl, I knew you wore a mask. Not the one that hid your identity, but one you were forced to wear for many years beneath the veil. One you didn't know you even wore. I saw you, and I knew you were the Maiden." Willa's eyes searched mine as tiny bumps rose all over my skin. "I knew you were a second daughter, one who shared the blood of the gods." Her gaze flicked over my shoulder to the door. "And I knew *he* was seeking the same thing that led you to the Red Pearl that night."

My brows knitted. "He was there to discuss his plans."

Thick curls swayed as she shook her head. "That was one of the reasons, but deep inside, he was searching for the same as you." She paused. "To live."

Air lodged in my throat.

"Can I share something with you?" Willa leaned in, touching my arm. A faint charge of energy danced over my skin. "You weren't the only one seeking sanctuary that night. He was in need of shelter—one that could bear the weight of his desires, his love, and his pain. And he found it. He may have given you freedom, but you have given him more than you could ever know."

Emotion clogged my throat, stealing whatever words I had to

speak.

"Don't forget that," she said.

"I won't," I managed.

Willa smiled.

"Penellaphe," Eloana called from the doorway. "Are you ready?"

Inhaling deeply, I nodded. "I am," I replied and then lowered my voice. "Thank you for answering my questions."

She inclined her head. "Always. And if you become…curious enough to ask those other questions I'm sure are brewing in your head, I'll be more than happy to answer them or refer you to a certain…chapter."

Oh.

Oh, my.

"T-thank you," I stuttered out and then started to turn.

"Your Majesty," Willa stopped me, and when I faced her, her smile was gone. "A Seer cannot always know things about another, nor can most close their eyes and look past the now into tomorrow and the days that come after. I cannot," she told me, and those tiny bumps returned. "Atlantians can be superstitious, even if they don't believe in prophecies. Do you know why they don't?"

My skin chilled. "No."

"Because we believe that the days yet to be seen are not foretold. That even what the gods may have in store for us is not written in stone," Willa said, the golden flecks in her eyes burning brightly. "But what is written in bone is different, and what is not believed should not be ignored."

Heart thumping and aware that Eloana was waiting, I stepped in closer to Willa. "Are you speaking of the prophecy the Unseen believe in?"

Willa touched my arm once more, and that same charge of energy swirled over my skin. "Your namesake was so wise, she could see beyond the day before her, but what she saw is not what they believe. You are not the great conspirator, but one of two who will stand between what has awakened and the retribution it seeks to reap against man and god."

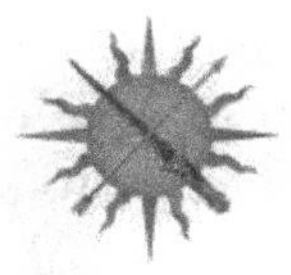

Willa's words haunted my steps through the palace and the Temple of Nyktos. While the logical part of me wanted to rebel at the idea of any part of the prophecy being true, I felt some measure of relief hearing her say that I wasn't the great conspirator the Unseen believed me to be.

But if what she spoke was true—and how could it not be when she knew so much else—she had to be speaking of the Blood Crown and Casteel and me. I imagined the Ascended sought retribution for a lot, but what could've awakened? All I could think of was Malec. Obviously, for me to be here, he had to have risen.

The low murmur of voices drew me from my thoughts as we passed the statue of Nyktos and his silver-white flames. Hisa stood at the doors. The Elders had already stepped outside onto the balcony, joined by Willa. Casteel's parents waited with the commander.

Eloana had asked if Casteel or I wanted to change before we greeted the people of Evaemon. While there had been a brief moment where I'd pictured myself in a pretty gown, I'd declined, only taking enough time to tame the strands of hair that had slipped free from my braid. It was unlikely that the people would see me in anything other than what I wore today—or things like it—for some time, and it seemed rather pointless to present myself in another fashion.

Besides, it only delayed us speaking with Kieran, and me talking with Casteel about what Willa had shared. So, we stood there as we had been when we first rode into Atlantia earlier.

It had truly been a long day.

"You two ready?" Valyn asked.

Casteel glanced at me, and I nodded. "We are."

I looked to my side, where Vonetta remained in her wolven form, and Kieran stood in his mortal one. The remaining wolven, including Delano, flanked us. Naill and Emil were among them. I refocused on Casteel's parents. "Will you introduce us?"

Eloana shook her head. "We will stand beside you, but the eldest member of the Council will introduce you and Casteel."

Remembering who the oldest Elder was, I said, "Willa?"

Valyn nodded as he eyed his son, who grinned. "I feel like I'm missing something," Valyn murmured.

"You're not," I said when Casteel opened his mouth, having no idea how no one in Atlantia appeared to know about Willa's journal. "I promise."

Casteel shot me a look, which I ignored.

"This won't take very long," Eloana said, a thread of weariness in her voice. It had been a long day for them, too. "And then you two can retire…or do whatever you please."

"A bed would be nice," Casteel said, and I really hoped he didn't elaborate on that thought.

"Will you two remain in the palace?" I asked. "I hope you will."

"As do I," Casteel agreed.

Valyn looked at Eloana before nodding. "We plan to stay—at least until you have returned from Iliseeum and your meeting with the Blood Crown. We figured you would want us as your surrogates until then."

"They will handle minor issues that arise during the time we're absent," Casteel explained quickly. "Usually, the advisor, or in rare cases the Council, steps in."

I nodded.

Eloana's gaze moved between us, and I knew it was time. Hisa and another guard stepped forward, each grasping the handle of a door. Kieran's gaze met mine and then Casteel's. He grinned as he joined Emil and Naill.

My heart started pounding as the doors began to inch open. The sound of the crowd grew louder as the last of the sunlight shone through the ceiling and seeped through the opening in the doors.

The balcony was rounded and long enough that each of the Elders stood to the left and right, against the black, stone railing. Willa had been waiting toward the back of the balcony, but now she walked forward, her curls a blue-black in the faint sunlight. She spoke, and a hush traveled throughout the crowd. I couldn't be sure what she said because my blood thumped in my ears, and my chest hummed. All I was aware of was that Casteel's parents had moved to stand on either side of us, and the utter surrealness of Miss Willa—*the* Miss Willa—about to introduce us to the kingdom as King and Queen.

Never in a thousand years could I have ever dreamt up this moment.

A laugh bubbled up, but I managed to squash it. Now was not the time for hysterical giggles.

Casteel reached between us and took my hand. My gaze snapped to his. Those eyes of his were like endless pools of warm honey, and when I breathed in, all I tasted was chocolate and berries.

"I love you," I whispered, tears stinging my eyes.

Casteel smiled. Two dimples appeared, one after the other. I saw a hint of fang, and a wholly inappropriate twist started up low in my stomach.

And then we were walking forward, out into what remained of the evening sun and the breezy air, to stand above a crowd that nearly stopped my heart.

There had to be *thousands*—tens of thousands. There was a sea of people in the courtyard below the Temple, some standing on the rolling green hill and beyond, on the nearby buildings' balconies, and in open windows. People even stood on the roofs of the shorter buildings. As far as I could see, the streets of Evaemon were filled.

"With the support and respect of the Council of Elders and the former King and Queen of Atlantia, the abdication and ascension of the Crown have taken place." Willa's voice carried from the balcony, falling upon the people like soft summer rain. "It is a great honor that I introduce He who is born of the First Kingdom, created from the blood and ash of those who fell before him, the second son of the former King Valyn and Queen Eloana—Casteel Hawkthrone Da'Neer, the King of Blood and Ash."

My breath caught at the title that belonged to the Ascended— to the Blood Crown. Casteel stiffened beside me, but the crowd erupted in shouts and cheers, roaring applause that echoed throughout the valleys and the streets like thunder.

Willa held up her fist, and silence fell. "He is joined by She who carries the blood of the King of Gods, the *Liessa*, and the true heir of Atlantia—Penellaphe Balfour Da'Neer, the Queen of Flesh and Fire."

I jolted, my heart stuttering. There was silence, acute and so intimidating—

Howls came from behind, startling me. Long, keening calls that were answered throughout the city. Below and farther out, men and women, the old and young in mortal form, answered in deep, throaty howls ending in high-pitched whoops.

Then a loud thump came from the yard. A man had slammed his foot into the dirt. The woman beside him followed, and then another and another, just like the day I'd arrived in Saion's Cove. But these were not just wolven. They were Atlantian and mortal, their feet pounding the dirt, and their fists striking stone, the sound reverberating through the yard, the streets, the balconies, and from the terraces. Many were on their knees, slamming their hands down.

"This…this is good, right?" I asked.

"They're sending a message," Eloana said from behind us.

"What kind?"

Casteel smiled down at me. "That they are *yours*. And that, if need be, they will go to war for you."

War was what we were trying to prevent, but…I supposed their willingness was good to know. "You mean that they are *ours*."

His smile grew, but he didn't answer.

The slamming of fists and feet ceased, and silence fell around us. Tiny hairs rose all over my body as I slowly looked out at the city. Tens of thousands of heads were lifted now, watching us—or me—expectantly.

Casteel squeezed my hand. "They are waiting for your response."

My response? "I have a feeling that a *thank you* would not suffice."

Casteel choked on what sounded an awful lot like a laugh. I looked at him, my brows raised.

"Sorry."

My eyes narrowed. "You don't sound sorry."

He bit down on his lower lip, but the corners of his mouth curved up. Not one but two stupid dimples appeared.

"You're so annoying," I muttered.

"*Endearingly* annoying," he corrected, and his father sighed.

"More like it's a good thing you're pretty," I grumbled under my breath.

Casteel tugged me back to his side, folding an arm around me. Before I could protest, he lowered his mouth until it was only an inch or so from mine. "More like it's a good thing you love me unconditionally."

"That, too." I sighed.

Casteel lowered his head, kissing me, and there was nothing quick or chaste about the way his lips claimed mine. It might've even been a little inappropriate—or a lot—but so was the way I sank against the length of his body.

I jerked as howls and cheers erupted from the wolven and the Atlantians in the yard and from the city, mingling with catcalls and hoots.

Casteel chuckled against my lips as he pressed his forehead to mine. "Our people are really into displays of public affection, in case you haven't noticed."

"I noticed." Face surely the color of a blood tree, I looked out at the city—to *our* people.

Willa turned back to the crowd, which had quieted once more.

"From the Blood and Ash and the Kingdom of Flesh and Fire, our King and Queen have ascended the throne, sworn to defend Atlantia from enemies known and unseen. To rule with kindness and strength, and to lead with compassion and justice. From this moment to their last moments, they are your protectors."

Casteel's brilliant amber eyes caught mine. He took our joined hands and lifted them high into the air, and the people…the people *celebrated.*

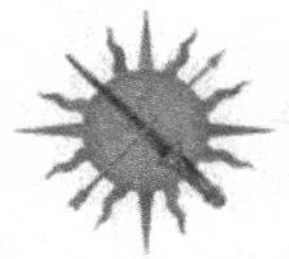

The people of Atlantia were still celebrating the ascension of the Crown based on the joyous noise that could be heard faintly from within the Royal Chambers.

And Kieran had not been joking when he'd said that our rooms were the entirety of the east wing. The foyer opened into a sitting area, and on either side, doors led to his and her spaces. I wasn't sure why they needed both, but there was also a private dining room furnished with a round table still large enough to seat several people. An atrium outfitted with comfortable chairs and settees was also present, with plush rugs and night-blooming roses that had opened their delicate petals at the first sign of the moon.

The bedchamber was…excessive.

A canopy bed sat in the center of the room, and it took up nearly the entirety of the space. The curtains were tied back, revealing fresh linens and a mound of soft pillows. There were only two chaises situated in front of the doors that led to a private terrace and garden, and a large wooden chest sat just inside the bedchamber. The wardrobes were housed in a room the size of my bedchamber in Masadonia. Casteel had explained it was called a walk-in closet, and I thought it could very well be a live-in closet.

The bathing chamber…well, it made the one in Saion's Cove appear paltry in comparison. The toilet was hidden behind a wall, and there were two vanities, an indecently large soaking tub, and the life-changing shower stall that boasted multiple showerheads and stone benches.

And there were many *indecent* things I could think of taking place in there.

From the main entryway, a door opened to the staff hallway and the private stairs that led upstairs to rooms reserved for guests of the King and Queen. Those who had traveled with us were now settling in, and Casteel's parents had just left after advising that if there was anything we wished to change about the quarters, we only needed to let Rose know.

Since very few items in the space could've belonged to either Eloana or Valyn, I had a feeling that many of the things already in the rooms were new and that they had planned for this moment from the second they returned to Evaemon.

While Casteel spoke with one of the staff members to have food sent to our quarters, I roamed the rooms, searching for the personal items that had been sent over in advance.

I found them sprinkled throughout: an adorable stuffed bear that had surely seen better days rested on a shelf. Several leather-bound books lined the shelves in the main sitting area—some were children's books, and the rest appeared to be a collection of fables. There were no textbooks to be found. Grinning, I discovered two training swords hanging in the hall between the sitting room and the dining area, their blades dull. Several paintings hung in the dining room, and the one of lilacs, gray stone, and clear blue waters had to be Casteel's.

It was the cavern.

In the walk-in closet, I found the clothing we'd brought with us, and the things that had been sent ahead, already hung up and folded. Inside the chest was a trove of weapons that pierced flesh and stone, some made of a golden metal, some steel, and others bloodstone. On the other side, between the doors to the bathing chamber and the closet, were two raised, stone podiums with a thin ledge. Inherently, I knew what they were for, having a wispy memory of spotting something similar in Wayfair Castle.

Reaching up, I lifted the crown from my head. The gilded bone was smooth and cool to the touch, reminding me of the wolven bone in my dagger. Carefully, I placed it on the podium, letting it rest on the ledge.

The Queen of Flesh and Fire.

Flesh and Fire. I had heard that phrase twice before. Casteel's mother had said it when she first saw me, and it had been mentioned in the prophecy that Alastir had recited.

But I wasn't the great conspirator.

And the title…well, it sounded badass.

Grinning, I turned from the crown and wandered over to the nightstand. I found a wooden toy horse. I picked it up, marveling at the intricacy. No detail had been spared. I turned it over, surprised to see Malik's name carved underneath. I ran my thumb over the strokes in the wood.

"Malik made that," Casteel said from the doorway. I turned, watching him remove the crown and place it on the pedestal next to mine. "It was for my birthday. My sixth, I believe. Gods, that was forever ago." He paused. "Which reminds me, I don't think we know each other's birthdays, do we?"

"I'm sure we—" I laughed as I realized that he was correct. I placed the horse back where I found it. There was so much we knew about each other, and yet so many things we didn't. "When is your birthday?"

He grinned as he leaned against the wall. "I was born on the first day of the sixth month. You?"

My smile started to fade. "I was born in the fourth month."

"And?" An eyebrow rose.

I drifted forward. "I…I don't know. I mean, I don't remember. I have these vague memories of celebrating a birthday when I was younger, but after my parents died, neither Ian nor I really celebrated." I lifted a shoulder. "And I guess over the years, we sort of forgot the date, so we'd pick a random day in April for me and December for him."

His grin had disappeared. "Pick a day."

"For what?"

"Your birthday. Pick a day in April, and that will be your birthday."

A pang of sadness lanced my heart. "Vikter asked me once when my birthday was. He said the same thing. Pick a day in April." I let out a low breath. "I picked the twentieth day, and that was when he gave me the wolven dagger."

"Perfect." The smile returned but it didn't reach his eyes. "How are you holding up?"

"I'm okay. Like I don't feel…different. I mean, maybe I do? I don't know." I laughed self-consciously as I approached him. He pushed off the wall. "I feel calm, though. How about you?"

"I feel the same." He opened his arms, and I went to him, looping mine around his waist. Pressing my cheek to his chest, I closed my eyes and sank into his embrace, taking in his spicy, piney scent. "Though I have to admit when that crown turned gold, I was relieved. I wanted a crown as spiffy as yours."

I laughed. "I talked to Willa."

"I noticed." His lips brushed the top of my head. "I was very curious about what you two were talking about—and sort of jealous."

Grinning, I stretched up and kissed the corner of his lips. "Nothing your dirty mind will approve of."

He pouted.

It looked ridiculous and yet adorable, *endearingly* so. I told him that she was the woman who'd been at the Red Pearl and had sent me to his room, much to his surprise. He'd had no idea that any of the Elders traveled to Solis, but considering her diary, it made sense. I didn't tell him what she'd said about him. I didn't think he'd want someone knowing the innerworkings of his heart, but I shared with him what she'd said about the prophecy.

Casteel was still a bit doubtful as we walked back toward the sitting area. "It's not that I can't believe in it," he said, his arm draped over my shoulders. "I just find it hard to believe that if there is one that may be true, how can there not be others? Ones we haven't heard of?"

"I don't know," I said. "Maybe prophecies aren't meant to be known."

"That sounds like something a Seer would say."

I giggled. "It does."

One dimple appeared as he smoothed a hand over my cheek, tucking back a strand of wayward hair. "The food should be here soon, and I know you're probably tired and have already been eyeing that shower. I know I have been, but I wanted to talk to Kieran first. You up for that?"

"Of course."

"Good. Because he'll be down here in a few minutes," he said, and I laughed again. I saw it—the churning of vivid, golden sparks in his eyes. His lips parted until the tips of his fangs appeared. "I love that sound. I love how much more you laugh now."

"I do, too," I admitted quietly. "And it's because of you."

His eyes closed briefly as he dipped his forehead to mine, and a long moment passed with us just standing there. "Before Kieran gets here, I wanted to ask you something."

"That sounds serious."

"It kind of is." He lifted his head. "Have you felt any hunger?"

"For food?" I drew out the question.

His lips twitched. "Not the kind you're thinking of."

"Oh." My eyes widened. "For blood?"

He grinned then. "You don't have to whisper it."

"I didn't."

"You totally did."

"Whatever." I bit down on my lip. "I don't think so? I mean, I haven't felt that gnawing ache again. I think I would know if I had."

"It's not always like that, my Queen."

My Queen. I liked that. Almost as much as I liked it when he called me Princess. Not that I'd admit that to him. "How does it feel?"

"You'll feel inexplicably tired, even after sleeping. You'll eat, but you'll still feel hunger. Food will eventually lose its appeal," he told me. "You'll be easier to irritate, which wouldn't be new for you."

"Hey!" I smacked his arm.

"Perhaps you do need to feed now," he teased, eyes glittering. "Once you get to the point where food no longer eases your hunger, you'll need to feed."

I nodded. "Okay."

"You probably wouldn't need to feed by now, anyway. If we're basing it on when Atlantians need to feed," he said. "But you may be different. You may not even need to, but I wanted to check in."

I searched to find even a flicker of unease at the possibility of feeding and found none, when a knock sounded.

Casteel let Kieran in. The wolven appeared to have managed a shower and a change of clothing. A fresh white shirt and black breeches had replaced what he'd worn earlier. I was jealous.

"We won't keep you long," Casteel said, coming to join me. "But there is something important we wanted to ask you."

Kieran raised a brow as he glanced between us. "Is it about the Joining?"

For the second time in twenty-four hours, I choked on my breath. "*What?*"

"Am I wrong?" Kieran crossed his arms.

"Yeah." I nodded while Casteel appeared to do his best not to burst into laughter. "That so wasn't where we were going with that, and by the way, the Joining isn't necessary, right? I'm a deity. I have an incomprehensible lifespan now."

"Well," Casteel drew out the word.

I looked over at him, and then it struck me—what I'd worried about when I first learned that I could be immortal or the closest thing to it. "I'll outlive you, won't I?"

"Deities have double the lifespan of Atlantians, maybe even longer if they take the deep sleep," Casteel explained. I didn't feel a single ounce of worry coming from him while I was five seconds away from throwing myself onto the floor. "But we have a very long time before we have to stress over that."

"I'm stressing over it now."

"Obviously," stated Kieran. "I'm bonded to you—all the wolven are. Not in the same way the bonds worked with the elemental lines, but a wolven would still be the connecting piece that fuses two lifelines together." He frowned. "Or three, I suppose. It's just your life that his would be bonded to."

I stared at him.

"Anyway, it could be any wolven." Kieran shrugged.

I continued staring at him.

"Okay. That's good to know." Casteel patted my shoulder, and I sat down on the thick, black cushion of a chair. "But that really wasn't what we wanted to discuss with you."

"No shit," Kieran said.

Blinking, I shook my head. We were about to ask him to be our advisor. Tomorrow, we would travel to Iliseeum and then into Solis. I so did not need to think about any of that right now.

"We wanted to ask if you would do us the honor of being the Advisor to the Crown," Casteel began. "I had this whole speech planned in my head about how you have been a brother to me and that there is no one I trust more, but now things are just kind of awkward, so…yeah. We would like for you to be our advisor."

Now it was Kieran who stared at us, his eyes wide, and I felt the coolness of shock from him—something I didn't think he often felt.

"You're…you're surprised," I said. "How can that be? You have to know that Casteel trusts you. As do I."

"Yeah, but…" Kieran rubbed the heel of his palm down the center of his chest. "The Advisor to the Crown is usually someone far older than me, with more experience and connections."

"The King and Queen are usually people far older than us," Casteel replied dryly.

"I know, but…why wouldn't you choose my father?" he asked. "He would serve you well."

"But not as good as you," Casteel told him. "You don't have to accept—"

"No, I accept," Kieran confirmed. "It would be an honor." His wide, pale blue eyes darted between us. "I just…I really thought you'd ask my father."

I was shocked that he'd thought that.

"Literally no one else entered my mind." Casteel stepped forward, clasping the back of Kieran's neck. "It would always have been you."

What I felt from Kieran warmed my chest. He was surprised but proud and swimming in that warmth. I swore tears glimmered in his eyes as he said, "It will be my honor to serve as advisor to both of you," he repeated. "From this moment to the last moment."

"It is *our* honor," Casteel said, pulling him in for a one-armed hug. "Seriously."

Kieran returned the embrace. Seeing them hug it out brought a smile to my face. Friendship was a far stronger bond than even something the gods could create. "Okay." Kieran cleared his throat as he stepped back.

"I know there's normally a ceremony," Casteel said, glancing over at me. "It's like the one we did in the throne room of the Temple." He turned back to Kieran. "We could do it when we have the larger coronation."

Kieran nodded. "I would like for my parents and my sisters to be there."

Sisters. My smile grew. He was already thinking of his baby sister.

"As would I," Casteel said.

He dragged a hand over his head. "I feel like I need a drink. Or five."

Casteel chuckled. "I think all of us could use one after today." He turned to the credenza where several bottles and crystal glasses with vines carved into them sat. "What would you like?" he asked of me.

"Whatever you're having."

An eyebrow rose. "Intriguing."

I shook my head.

"You know," Kieran said, looking over at me as he sat in an identical chair, "I've never heard of a response like that to a crowning before. The people are happy. That's what they're celebrating."

"I imagine they're relieved that there'll be no more tension over how long Cas's parents have ruled." I sat back as Casteel sent me a heated look while pouring three glasses of something I would probably regret later.

"I think it has more to do with you," Casteel said.

"Because I'm special." I rested my chin on my fist and rolled my eyes. "A unique snowflake."

He laughed deeply. "Hell, yeah, you are."

Still not as special as those who could shift forms. I would never get over that, but the reaction was probably also in response to the fact that their Prince Ascended—

My eyes widened as I sat up straight. "Oh, my gods. I just thought of something."

"Can't wait to hear this," Kieran murmured.

"Nyktos is protected by guards," I said, remembering what had been said during the Council meeting. That wasn't exactly breaking news. "The…draken either went to sleep or protect the resting place of the gods, right?"

Kieran took the drink that Casteel offered him. "Yes."

My stomach dropped to my toes. "And the guards that Ian told us we need? Would they happen to be the ones protecting Nyktos's resting place?"

Casteel put my drink in my hand. "Are you just now realizing who and what Nyktos's guards are?"

Yes.

Yes, I totally was.

"We're supposed to get the draken to help us?" I exclaimed. "Those who are basically able to take the form of a *dragon*?"

Casteel stared at me, nodding slowly. "I thought you realized that."

"No!" I shouted, and Kieran's brows flew up. "Yeah, I remember being told that, but I've also been told a lot of things since then, and…good gods, I'm going to get to see a draken?"

"Yes, my Queen." Casteel sat on the arm of my chair. "You may get to see a draken."

"I don't know why you look so excited," Kieran remarked. "The draken were a notoriously…unfriendly bloodline, with temperaments that would make yours look like a small, cuddly animal's."

I lifted my right hand and extended my middle finger. He smirked. "But I have the blood of Nyktos in me," I pointed out.

"And they can also breathe fire." Kieran tipped his glass at me. "So, let's hope none of us pisses them off."

Chapter 39

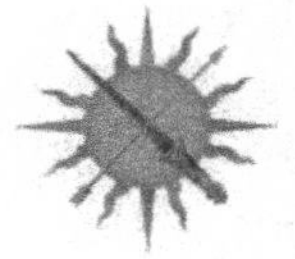

The following morning, I stood in the foyer of the Temple of Nyktos beside Casteel, fiddling with the chest strap I'd found among Casteel's weapons. I'd also helped myself to the iron dagger I'd found in the depths of the chest, and it was now secured to my harness. The bloodstone dagger was strapped to my thigh. Neither of us wore the crowns, having left them in the bedchamber. We stood with Kieran and his sister, Emil, and Delano. Naill was sitting this one out, opting to spend time with his father. As I watched Delano adjust the strap holding his swords to his sides, I hoped he'd found time to let Perry know that he had returned to the capital.

"Kieran and I are pretty confident that the tunnel that leads to the mountains is the one underneath," Casteel said. "It's a narrow one with nothing really exciting."

By *really exciting*, I assumed he meant the lilac-filled cavern.

"You guys did really weird things as kids." Vonetta stood between her brother and Emil, her arms crossed. Two short swords were secured at her hips. She'd swept her long braids back from her face, and they hung down her back. "Just thought I'd share that."

I grinned.

"I didn't even know there were tunnels." Emil glanced at the jet-black floors.

"There are." Hisa strode forward, two guards flanking her. "They're accessed by the crypts."

Crypts.

I shuddered.

"Sorry." Casteel gently squeezed the back of my neck. "The good news is that it's nothing like what you were kept in."

"It's okay," I told him, and it would be. It wasn't like we'd be spending any amount of time in them.

Carrying a heavy ring of keys, Hisa continued toward a narrow door. Turning the key as she twisted the handle, the door creaked open.

Faint light lit our way down a staircase that made awful sounds under our weight. The temperature dropped at least five degrees with each step, and the familiar musky scent turned my stomach.

Hisa proceeded forward, passing several stone tombs. Casteel stuck close to me, his hand slipping to my shoulder. He was right. The crypt was clean and well-kept, flower garlands piled on the lids of the tombs.

"Are you sure about this?" Hisa had stopped in front of another door as she thumbed through the keys.

"We are," I answered.

She nodded and then proceeded to unlock the second door. "These tunnels were once used to move goods from different areas of the city, and then they were solely used to transport the dead," she told us, and Emil's lip curled. "But they haven't been accessed in several decades. I have no idea what kind of shape they're in.

"It's unlikely that there has been any type of collapse," she continued. "But hopefully, the route you seek is still open."

"From what I remember, it's a pretty straight path with only a few turns." Casteel picked up a torch. Delano stepped forward, striking flint against the top. Sparks gave way to fire. He handed the torch to Kieran. "It should only take an hour to reach the mountains."

"And then?" I asked as he picked up another torch. Flames flared to life.

"That, I don't know." Casteel looked at Kieran. "We never went farther than the mountains."

"The mountains are tall but not particularly wide through this area," Hisa said, frowning. "We're at the foothills here, so I imagine it would be a half-day's journey. Farther north or south, it would probably take several days."

"How far have you traveled into the mountains?" Vonetta asked, and I thought it was probably a good idea that we'd stuffed the bag strapped to Emil's back with as much food as possible. Each of us carried our own canteens. It wasn't a lot of water, but we would have to make it last.

"To where the mist mingles with the clouds in scouting missions. I know we reached the mist faster here than in other areas," she answered. She glanced at the door. "If I had any idea what waited in that mist…" She trailed off with a shake of her head. "Please, be safe. All of you." To Casteel and me, she added, "The people want to get to know their Queen and become reacquainted with their King."

"And they will," Casteel promised.

Hisa blew out a deep breath as she opened the door, and a void of darkness beckoned. "We will wait for your return."

I watched the commander join the guards toward the entrance of the crypts. "Thank you all for doing this with us."

Vonetta grinned. "It's not like any of us would turn down an offer to see Iliseeum."

"Only because none of us have any common sense," Emil said.

"That, too." Delano grinned.

"I, for one, am glad that I'm surrounded by those who have more loyalty and thirst for adventure than common sense," Casteel remarked. "And now for the rules."

"Yawn," Vonetta tossed out.

I laughed. "Well, these rules will hopefully keep everyone alive. Casteel and I talked some things over this morning—"

"Is that what you two were doing?" Kieran asked.

"Yes," I snapped, cheeks flushing because that wasn't *all* we'd been doing. "Anyway, if anyone sees a hint of mist, back away and let me go first."

"I didn't exactly agree to this," Casteel muttered.

"Yes. You did. The mist cleared for me in the Skotos Mountains. I would think it would do the same thing here," I said. "That way, none of you will walk into it and suffocate to death."

"Yeah, I want to avoid that," Emil said.

"And if we encounter anything, I should probably hold off on using the eather," I said, remembering what Kieran had said about the gods being able to sense when eather is used. "I don't know what it will do in Iliseeum, if it will be any different or if the gods can sense it. I'm not sure that's how we want to wake Nyktos."

"How are we going to wake him?" Delano asked.

"Well," I glanced at Casteel, "we thought we'd cross that bridge when we came to it."

Vonetta lifted her brows. A moment passed. "That sounds like a wonderfully detailed plan."

Casteel smirked. "Aren't you glad you signed up?"

"Totally," Vonetta replied, sounding so much like her brother.

"Ready?" Casteel asked, his eyes meeting mine.

I wasn't exactly sure, but there was no point in delaying this, so I nodded, and we followed Casteel into the nothingness.

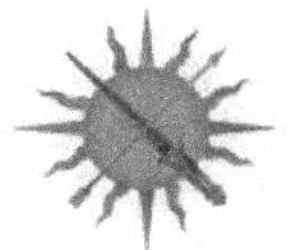

Time was a strange thing in the tunnels. With no light but that of the torches, we only knew hours had passed when hunger stirred. We stopped only to meet that need and handle personal ones in earthen rooms I convinced myself weren't full of six-legged insects. We could've been in the twisting, cramped tunnels for hours—or longer—and I didn't think we'd know.

"Careful," Casteel warned at some point in the never-ending tunnel, holding the torch ahead of him. "The floor feels weak through this section. Stay close to the wall."

I wasn't sure how he could tell that, but I did as he requested, pressing my body against the cool stone. The canteen dug into my back as I crept along, Kieran close behind me. My chest tightened as I realized that the tunnel had narrowed once more. I'd never had a problem with enclosed spaces, but I had a feeling I would now. I reached out, gripping the back of Casteel's shirt without really thinking about it. I'd gotten into the habit of doing so whenever the walls or ceiling pressed in.

"Poppy," Casteel whispered.

"What?" I focused on the reddish glow beyond him.

"You know what I should've brought with us?" he asked.

More food? Maybe a little pouch of cheese? I was hungry again. "No," I answered.

"Miss Willa's journal."

I stopped momentarily, and Kieran bumped into me. Thank the gods, he'd given the torch to Delano, or my hair would currently be on fire. "Really?"

"Yeah." Casteel continued forward. "We could've passed the time taking turns reading from your favorite chapters."

"Are we talking about the same Willa?" Vonetta asked from

somewhere behind me.

"Yes. You see, there's this extremely popular book in Solis. It's actually Poppy's favorite—"

"It is not my favorite, you jerk," I snapped.

"Please don't stab him in this tunnel," Delano called out.

My eyes rolled. "I cannot promise that."

Casteel chuckled.

"What is in this book? I have a feeling I'd be interested in it," Vonetta said, and I heard Kieran groan. "What is—?" A loud crack cut off her words, and then the entire floor of the cavern seemed to rumble beneath us.

I spun around just in time to see Vonetta step to the other side of the wall and then disappear in a plume of dust. Horror seized me.

"Netta!" Kieran shouted, his fear sticky against my skin as it mixed with mine.

"I got her!" Emil yelled back. "Sort of."

Whatever relief I felt from his words was short-lived. Delano moved forward, holding out the torch. The orange glow cast light over the partial collapse and the floor around it. Emil was on his stomach, one arm stretched into the opening. How the Atlantian had been able to move so fast that he'd caught Vonetta was beyond me.

"I'm still here," Vonetta called out as her brother scrambled to the other side. "I think."

Casteel caught the back of my shirt as I started toward them. "Too much weight on that section," he cautioned as Delano scanned the floor. The wolven stepped to the side that remained intact.

He was right, and I hated it because all I could do was stand and watch as Kieran reached inside.

"Give me your other hand," Kieran ordered. "We'll pull you out together."

"If either of you two drops me," Vonetta's voice trailed out of the darkness, "I'm going to be so pissed."

"Netta, if we drop you, I'm going to throw myself in after you," Emil advised. "And then we're both going to find out what's below these tunnels."

"We're both going to be dead then," Vonetta hissed.

"Semantics," Emil replied. "I've got you. Let go of whatever the hell you're holding onto."

"I think it's a root."

"Thanks for sharing," Emil said. "Let go of the root and reach for

Kieran."

There was a soft grunt, and then Kieran cursed. "I can't reach him," she gasped out.

"Try again." Emil shifted as if he were trying to position himself to grab her one hand with both of his, which would enable him to pull her up on his own, but I could sense his fear and worry.

My heart lurched. I could totally understand Vonetta's hesitation. I shifted restlessly, hands opening and closing at my sides.

Casteel folded an arm around me from behind. He squeezed. "She's going to be fine. They've got her."

I nodded as I glanced to where Delano was looking at the floor once more. His concern tripled, and I had a feeling the section near him wouldn't remain much longer. Frustration rose within me. What good were my gifts right now? I could harness the eather to ease pain, to heal, and to harm. Why couldn't I use it now, when help was so desperately needed?

Why couldn't I? Better yet, who said I couldn't?

Another crack sent a jolt of fear through me as pieces of the tunnel under Emil began to break. Casteel cursed. If the section went, not only would we lose them, we'd be unable to return.

I had to do something.

I had to try.

Forcing myself to calm enough to focus on the image I was building in my mind. I closed my eyes, pouring all good thoughts into what I was creating. I didn't want the eather to harm. My chest hummed as I saw the webbing of shimmery light seeping over the floor. I pictured it slipping into the hole and surrounding Vonetta. I saw it lifting her—

Vonetta gasped. My eyes flew open. A silvery glow crept along the walls of the cavern. Kieran pitched forward, reaching into the tear as strings of light lifted Vonetta. He grasped his sister's hand, pulling her up as I pulled the eather toward me. Emil let go, scuttling back on his belly as Kieran and Vonetta collapsed to the side.

Letting out a ragged breath, I pulled the eather back toward me as I sank against Casteel. The radiance retreated and then disappeared.

"Are you okay, Netta?" Casteel demanded.

"Peachy." Vonetta rolled onto her back, breathing heavily. She tilted her head back toward Casteel and me. "That…that felt weird."

"You could feel it?" I asked.

"Yeah, it felt…warm and tingly." She dragged her arm over her forehead. "Thank you. All of you."

"How did you do that?" Casteel asked as Emil stood.

"I pictured it. Like you said." My heart still hadn't slowed. "And I just hoped it didn't…you know, break her bones."

Vonetta halted in the process of rising, her gaze finding mine in the dim firelight. "You didn't know if it wouldn't do that?"

"No," I admitted sheepishly.

She put her hands on her hips. "Gods, I think I need to lay down again."

Chapter 40

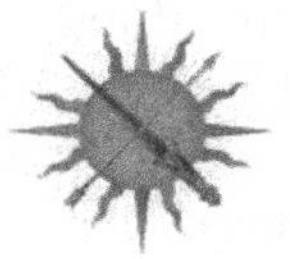

We traveled on, wary of the stability of the tunnel. Again, it felt as if we continued on for a small eternity, but the sudden and familiar scent of lilac sent a bolt of hope through me. Pressing through the narrow turn, a pinprick of light appeared in the darkness.

We had reached the end of the tunnel and Iliseeum.

"Mist," Casteel announced. "I can see it coming through the opening."

I tapped his shoulder when he didn't move. "Cas."

He growled low in his throat but flattened himself against the wall, holding the torch high. As I passed him, I pressed a quick kiss to his cheek.

"That doesn't help," he grumbled.

I would've smiled, but I saw it—tendrils of thick mist seeping into the opening in the tunnel, drifting toward us. I moved forward, sending up a prayer that Jasper had been right about my ability to pass through the mist and that my suspicion that it would not only allow me to do so but also scatter, making it safe for the others, was true.

The Primal magic rose from the floor of the cavern, forming wispy fingers as it stretched out toward me. I lifted my hand.

"I don't like this," Casteel muttered from behind me.

"It shouldn't hurt her," Kieran reminded him, but concern bled into his words.

The mist brushed against my skin, the feel of it cool and damp and *alive*. The eather retracted, lowering to the ground and then disappearing.

I exhaled roughly, looking over my shoulder. "It's okay."

Casteel nodded, and I moved ahead. The opening wasn't all that large, only about three feet high and two feet wide. "You'll have to crawl through."

"Just go slowly," Casteel advised. "We have no idea what is on the other end."

"Hopefully, not a draken looking to serve up some flame-broiled red meat," Emil muttered from somewhere in the darkness.

"Well, that put a pleasant image in my mind," Delano replied.

Hoping for the exact same thing as Emil, I went down on my knees and inched through. "Hold on," I told them. There was more mist, so thick it was like the clouds had descended to the ground. I reached out tentatively, and the magic scattered and thinned as bright sunlight penetrated what remained of the fog. Squinting at the sudden light after being in the dark for so long, I slid out, my knees and hands skimming from stone to sandy, loose dirt.

One hand going to the blade at my chest, and the other to the wolven dagger on my thigh, I stood and took a step forward.

The ground trembled faintly under my feet. I froze, looking down to see tiny rocks and clumps of sand and dirt shiver. After a heartbeat, the trembling ceased, and I lifted my gaze. The mist had completely disappeared, and I was able to take my first look at Iliseeum.

My lips parted as my hands fell away from my daggers. The sky was a shade of blue that reminded me of the wolven's eyes, pale and wintry, but the air was warm and smelled of lilacs. My gaze swept over the landscape. "Gods," I whispered, lifting my chin as my gaze crawled up and up the massive statues carved out of what I assumed was shadowstone. They were as tall as the ones I'd seen in Evaemon, those that had appeared to scrape the sky, and there had to be hundreds of them standing in line, continuing on to the left and right as far as I could see. Maybe even thousands.

The statues were of women, their heads lowered. Each hand held a stone sword that jutted forward. The stone women had wings sprouting from their backs, splayed wide, each touching the wings of the ones standing on either side of them. They formed a chain of sorts, blocking whatever resided beyond. You could only pass through under the wings.

They were beautiful.

"Poppy?" Casteel's voice neared the opening. "You okay out there?"

"Yeah. Sorry." I cleared my throat. "It's safe."

Within a handful of moments, Casteel and the rest made their way out, coming to stand beside me in silence. They all stared at the statues, their wonder bubbly and sugary.

"Are they supposed to represent the draken?" I asked.

"I don't know." Casteel's hand touched my lower back. "They're stunning, though."

They truly were. "I guess we walk ahead and see if what they're guarding is what we're looking for."

We started to cross the barren land, searching for any signs of life. There was nothing. No sound. Not even a breeze or the distant call of a bird.

"This is kind of creepy," I murmured, looking around. "The silence."

"Agreed. Perhaps this should be called the Land of the Dead," Delano said as he walked under the shadowed wing of a stone woman.

A faint tremble stirred the ground under our feet. Casteel threw out a hand. We all stopped. "This happened before," I told them. "It stopped—"

The ground erupted in several geysers all around us, sending clouds of dirt into the air and spewing small rocks in every direction.

"I'm assuming *that* didn't happen last time," Vonetta remarked.

"Nope." I threw up a hand as clumps of dirt pelted my face and arm, and the ground burst open between Casteel and me.

Another funnel of dirt exploded directly in front of Emil, forcing him back several steps. He coughed. "That was rude."

The ground steadied as the dust and dirt fell back to the earth. "Is everyone still with us?" Delano asked, wiping at his face.

We were.

"Careful." Casteel knelt near the opening between us. "This is one hell of a hole." He looked up, meeting my gaze and then Kieran's. He rose slowly. "I have a feeling we may have triggered something."

"Triggered what?" Emil asked, peering over the edge, squinting. "Wait." His head tilted to the side. "I think I—holy shit!" Jumping back, he stumbled over his feet, catching himself a second before he landed on his ass.

"What?" Vonetta demanded, reaching for her swords. "*Details.* They would be helpful at the—"

Between Casteel and I, the bleached bones of a hand appeared, fingers digging into the loose soil.

"What in the world of nightmare fuel is this?" Casteel muttered.

Those fingers were connected to an arm—an arm that was nothing more than a skeleton. The top of a skull appeared. My eyes widened in horror. Dirt poured out of empty eye sockets.

"Skeletons!" Vonetta shouted, unsheathing her swords. "Couldn't you have said that you saw skeletons in the hole?"

Casteel cursed as another bony hand appeared, this one clutching a sword in its grip.

"Armed skeletons!" Vonetta yelled. "Couldn't you have said you saw *armed* skeletons in the hole?"

"Sorry." Emil unhooked his swords. "I was kind of taken aback by the sight of fully functional, fucking skeletons *with* weapons. My apologies."

I stared at the sword—the blade was as black as the statues. The same kind of blades I'd seen in the crypts with the deities. "*Shadowstone.*" An image of my mother flashed before me, of her pulling a slender, black blade from her boot. "Their blades are like the one my mother had. That had to be a real memory."

"Poppy, I'm glad you know it was real." Casteel withdrew his swords. "But we should probably discuss that later, like when we're not facing an army of the dead?"

"Question," Delano called out, blade in hand as the top of a skull appeared from the hole nearest him. "How exactly does one kill what is presumably already dead?"

"Like super dead," Vonetta clarified as the one before her was now halfway out of the hole, a ragged, dull brown tunic draped over the skeleton's shoulder. Through the torn clothing, I saw a twisted mass of dirt beat behind its ribs.

Casteel moved as fast as bottled lightning, thrusting his sword into the chest of the skeleton and piercing the lump of dirt. The skeleton shattered, sword and all, breaking apart into dust. "Like that?"

"Oh," Vonetta replied. "All right, then."

I turned as Kieran shoved his sword into the chest of one. There were about a dozen holes behind us—a dozen skeleton guards halfway out of the ground. Another image filled my mind, one not of my mother but of a woman with silvery-white hair—the one I'd seen in my mind while I stood in the Chambers of Nyktos. She'd slammed her hands into the dirt, and the ground had cracked open, bone fingers digging their way out.

"Her soldiers," I whispered.

"What?" Casteel demanded.

"These are *her*—"

Free from whatever hole it had literally crawled out of, one of the skeleton soldiers rushed toward me, lifting its sword. Slipping the dagger free from my chest harness, I snapped forward, thrusting the blade into the mess of throbbing dirt. The skeleton exploded as another took its place. Behind it, another skeleton soldier lifted its sword. Kicking out, I planted my boot in the soldier's chest, pushing it back into another. Casteel shot forward, stabbing his sword into the dirt heart of the one closest to him. I spun, slamming my dagger into the chest of the skeleton, wincing as the blade nicked bone before hitting the heart.

"Cutting off the head does not work," Emil shouted, and I turned to see a…a headless skeleton tracking the dumbfounded Atlantian. "I repeat. It does not work!"

Vonetta whirled, thrusting one sword through the chest of a soldier, and her other blade through the headless skeleton. "You," she said to Emil, "are a mess."

"And you are beautiful," he replied with a grin.

The female wolven rolled her eyes as she spun, taking down another as Emil shoved his sword into the chest of one coming at him.

Casteel shoved a soldier back as he jabbed the sword through its ribs. Behind him, a soldier raced toward him. I shot past Casteel, stabbing the creature in the chest—

The ground trembled once more. New geysers of dirt erupted, streaking into the air. "You have got to be kidding me," Kieran growled.

I spun around, heart thudding as…*hundreds* of eruptions happened across the barren ground, from the side of the Mountains of Nyktos, all the way to the stone women. These soldiers were faster, tearing out of the holes in a matter of heartbeats.

"Good gods." Vonetta stumbled back into Emil. He steadied her before they turned to stand back-to-back.

A skeleton soldier ran forward on bony feet, sword raised. Its jaws unhinged, opening wide to reveal nothing but a black void and the sound of screaming wind. The force blew my braid back and tugged at my tunic.

"Rude," I muttered, nearly choking on the scent of stale lilacs.

Black, oily smoke spilled from the skeleton's mouth, thickening and solidifying as it poured to the ground, forming thick ropes that *slithered* forward—

"Oh, my gods!" I shrieked. "Not ropes! Not ropes! Snakes!"

"Holy shit," Delano gasped as Casteel shoved his sword through the back of the screaming skeleton. "That is so not right."

"I regret the decision to join you all," Emil announced. "I regret this decision very much."

Snakes. Gods. I hated snakes. Bile rose in my throat as I danced out of the way of the serpents. My scream built in my throat as several of the other skeletons howled. More black smoke followed. More *snakes.*

Twisting, I shoved my dagger into a soldier's chest. I would have to table what I was seeing and deal with the lifetime of nightmares later.

Casteel took out a soldier as he slammed his boot down on a snake. The smoke-serpent flattened into an oily stain, turning my stomach.

I'd also have to vomit about that later.

"Poppy." His head jerked up. "I know you said you didn't think you should use the eather, but I really think now would be a good time to go full deity on these fuckers."

"Second that," Vonetta called as she kicked a serpent away from her. It landed near her brother, who shot her a dirty look.

I had to agree as I thrust my dagger into the chest of a soldier. The freaking smoke serpents outweighed whatever risks using the eather in Iliseeum introduced. I sheathed my daggers. Focusing on the hum in my chest, I let it come to the surface of my skin. *No,* I realized. I *summoned* it to the surface. Silvery-white light crowded the sides of my vision as it sparked over my skin—

The skeleton soldiers turned toward me. All of them. Their mouths opened as they screamed. Smoke poured from the voids, falling to the ground.

"Oh." Kieran straightened. "*Shit.*"

That didn't remotely articulate what I felt as hundreds of serpents slithered over the earth, around the holes. Cursing violently, Casteel stomped his boot down again. The soldiers moved in unison, sprinting toward me—

In my mind, I didn't picture the fine webbing. I needed something faster, more intense. Something final. And I didn't even know why, but I thought of the torches inside the Temple of Nyktos and their silvery flames.

Fire.

Gods, if I was wrong, I wouldn't be the only one regretting this, but I pictured the flames in my mind, silvery white and intense. My hands warmed and tingled. My entire body throbbed with heat—heat and *power*. I didn't know if it was instinct or if it was because the serpents were so close, but I lifted my hands.

Silver-white flames spiraled down my arms and erupted from my palms—erupted from *me*. Someone gasped. It could've been me. The fire roared, licking the ground and catching the serpents. The creatures hissed and screeched as the flames consumed them. The inferno rolled across the land, hitting the skeletons with a wave of flames. Crackling, fiery light streaked between Casteel and Kieran, washing over the soldiers there and then spread out from me, following exactly what I saw in my mind, burning only the skeletons and serpents, leaving everything else untouched. And then I pulled back the eather, picturing it receding and returning to me. The fire pulsed intensely, straining toward Casteel and the others as if it wanted to consume them, too, but I didn't want that. The flames turned bright white, spitting sparks high into the air and then fizzling out until only faint wisps of pale smoke remained.

Everyone was staring at me.

"I…I didn't know if that would work or not," I admitted.

"Well…" Vonetta drew the word out, her pale eyes wide. "I'm sure I'm not the only one who is grateful that it did."

I looked down at my hands and then up, finding Casteel. "I guess I am the Queen of Flesh and Fire."

Casteel nodded as he stalked toward me, his eyes a heated amber. "I know you're the Queen of my heart."

Blinking, I lowered my hands as he stopped in front of me. "Did you seriously just say that?"

One dimple appeared as he clasped the back of my head and lowered his head to mine. "I sure as fuck did."

"That was so…cheesy," I said.

"I know." Casteel kissed me, and there was nothing ridiculous about that. His tongue parted my lips, and I welcomed his taste.

"This is a little awkward," Vonetta observed.

"They do this all the time," Kieran sighed. "You'll get used to it."

"Better than them fighting," Delano remarked.

Casteel grinned against my lips. "You're extraordinary," he murmured. "Don't ever forget that."

I kissed him in response, and then unfortunately, pulled free. "We should probably get moving. More could come."

"Let's hope not," Emil said, sheathing his swords.

"Everyone okay?" Casteel asked as we started walking. "No snake bites?"

Luckily, everyone was fine, but as we neared the shadows of the stone women, I said, "Maybe I should go first."

Delano bowed, extending an arm as Vonetta shook dust from her braids. "Be my guest."

My grin froze as I tentatively stepped into the shadow of a wing. The ground did tremor, but it was the holes, filling back with dirt. The landscape was once again flat and whole. "Okay," I breathed. "That's a good sign."

Casteel was the first to join me and then the others. We continued on, passing under the wing. The sandy dirt hardened under our feet. Patches of grass appeared, giving way to a lush meadow of bright orange flowers.

"Poppies," Delano whispered.

Lips parting, I looked over at Casteel. He shook his head in slight disbelief. The flowers we walked through could've just been a coincidence, but…

My steps slowed as we realized we were coming to the crest of a gently sloping hill and were finally able to see what the stone women and those skeleton soldiers had been guarding.

A sweeping Temple sat in the valley. Pillars constructed of shadowstone lined the wide, crescent-shaped steps and the colonnade. The structure was massive, nearly double the size of the palace in Evaemon, even without the additional wings. It rose against the blue sky in soaring towers and spires as if the fingers of night were reaching up from the land to touch daylight. Smaller shapes were situated around the temple, possibly mounds or statues. I couldn't make out what they were from this distance, but it wasn't the only thing that had been protected. It was what rested in the hills and valleys miles beyond the Temple.

It was Dalos, the City of the Gods.

Warm beams of sunlight reflected off the diamond-bright sides of buildings sprawled across the hills. Crystalline towers rose into the sky in graceful arcs, parting the wispy, white clouds sprinkled over the city and extending beyond them, glittering as if a thousand stars had kissed them. An awed silence fell over us as we gazed upon the city.

Several long moments of silence passed before Emil spoke, his voice thick. "I have to believe that this is what the Vale looks like."

It really could be. Nothing could be more beautiful.

"Do you think anyone in the city is awake?" Vonetta asked quietly.

My heart skipped a beat. "Could there be?"

Casteel shook his head. "It's possible, but we…we won't find out." His gaze touched mine. "Remember Willa's warning."

I swallowed, nodding. "We can't go into the city," I reminded everyone. "Maybe gods are awake there, and that's why we can't." I looked at Emil. "Or maybe Dalos is a part of the Vale."

Clearing his throat, Emil nodded. "Yeah."

If gods were awake in the city, I had to wonder if they were unaware of what was happening past the Mountains of Nyktos. Or if they simply didn't care.

"You think that's the Temple where Nyktos may sleep?" Delano asked.

Kieran inhaled deeply. "We might as well find out."

We started down the hill, the grass reaching our knees. The air smelled of fresh lilacs and…something I couldn't place. It was a woodsy scent but a sweet one. A more-than-pleasant smell. I tried to figure it out but couldn't by the time we reached the bottom of the hill.

The grass became white soil that reminded me of sand, but there was no beach that I could see, and it was brighter than sand. It sparkled in the sun and crunched under our—

"Are we walking on diamonds?" Vonetta stared at the ground, disbelief echoing from her. "I think we're actually walking on diamonds."

"I have no words for this," Casteel commented as Delano bent and picked up a piece. "But diamonds are birthed from the joyous tears of the gods—of gods in love."

My gaze shifted to the Temple, and I thought of Nyktos and the Consort that he was so protective of. No one even knew her name.

"You all are staring at diamonds," Kieran stated, his wariness pressing against my skin. "Meanwhile, I'm just waiting for you all to realize what this giant-ass statue is."

I looked at what Kieran stared at, and my stomach dropped. The mounds I'd seen from the top of the hill weren't several small statues but one very large one of…of what appeared to be a slumbering dragon at the steps of the Temple, just off to the right. It looked like the sketches I'd seen in books containing fables, except its neck wasn't nearly as long, and even with the wings carved to be tucked against the body, it was so much bigger.

"Whoa," Vonetta murmured as we neared the statue and the steps of the Temple.

"Let's take slow steps," Casteel advised. "If this is Nyktos's resting place, his guards may be nearby—and not stone ones."

Draken.

"If this thing comes to life, I am out of here," Emil grumbled. "You will never see an Atlantian run faster."

A wry grin tugged at my lips as I slowly approached the statue, marveling at the sculpture. From the nostrils to the frill of spikes around the beast's head, to the claws and the horns on the tips of its wings, every intricate detail had been captured. How long would it have taken someone to carve something this large? I reached out, running my fingers over the side of the face. The stone was rough and bumpy, surprisingly—

"Poppy." Casteel snagged my wrist. "The whole proceed-with-caution thing also included not randomly touching things." Lifting my hand to his mouth, he pressed a kiss to my fingers. "Okay?"

I nodded, letting him guide me away. "The stone was really warm, though. Isn't that kind of—"

A crack of thunder sounded, reverberating through the valley. I looked down, half-expecting the ground to open up.

"Uh." Kieran started to back up as he stared behind us. "Guys…"

I whipped around, my lips parting as a piece of the stone shattered over the side of the beast's face and fell away, revealing a deeper shade of gray and—

An eye.

An actual open eye of vivid blue with an aura of luminous white behind a thin, vertical pupil.

"Oh, shit," Emil whispered. "Shit. Shit. *Run*—"

A deep rumbling sound came from within the statue, causing icy fear to drench my skin. Fissures raced through the stone. Sections both large and small fell away, thumping off the ground.

I was frozen where I stood. No one ran. They too had locked up. Maybe it was out of disbelief or an intuitive knowledge that running wouldn't save us. This wasn't a stone dragon.

It was a *draken* in its true form, rising from where it had been resting against the ground, its large, muscular body shaking off the dust and tiny pieces of stone.

I might've stopped breathing.

The deep, rumbling sound continued as the draken swung its head toward us, its thick, spiked tail sweeping across the diamonds. Two vibrant blue eyes locked with mine.

"Stay completely still," Casteel ordered quietly. "Please, Poppy. Do not move."

Like I could do anything else?

A low snarled vibrated from the draken as its lips peeled back, revealing a row of large teeth sharper than any blade. The draken lowered its head toward me.

My heart might've stopped.

I was staring at a draken—a real, live draken, and it was magnificent and frightening and beautiful.

The draken's nostril's flared as it sniffed the air—sniffed *me*. The snarling eased as it continued staring with eyes so full of intelligence, it awed me. It tilted its head. A soft, whirring trill came from its throat, and I had no idea what that meant, but it had to be better than the snarling. A thin membrane fluttered across its eyes, and then its gaze shifted past me—past where Casteel and the others stood—to the Temple.

A wave of awareness shivered through me, raising the tiny hairs all over my body. Pressure pushed against the nape of my neck, boring into the center of my back. I turned around without really having made a conscious decision to do so. Casteel did the same. I didn't know if any of the others followed because all I could now see was the man standing on the Temple steps between two pillars.

He was tall—taller than even Casteel. Mid-length brown hair fell to his shoulders, glinting a coppery red in the sunlight. The dusky wheatish skin of his features was all planes and angles, pieced together with the same beautiful mastery as the stone shell that had encased the draken. He would've been the most beautiful being I'd ever seen if it weren't for the infinite coldness of his features and his luminous eyes the color of the brightest moon. I knew who he was even though his face had never been painted or carved.

It was Nyktos.

Chapter 41

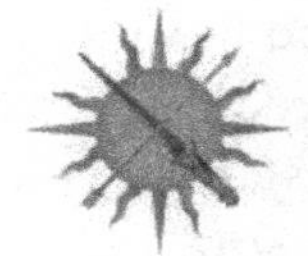

The King of Gods stood before us, dressed in a white tunic that he wore over loose black pants.

He was also barefoot.

I didn't know why I focused on that, but I did.

It was also why I was a little behind everyone else who had already lowered themselves to one knee, placing a hand over their hearts and their palms to the ground.

"*Poppy*," Casteel whispered, his head bowed.

I dropped so fast I nearly face-planted. The sharp ridges of the diamonds dug into my knee, but I barely felt them as I placed my right hand over my heart and my left palm to the rocky surface. Hot breath stirred the wisps of hair at the back of my neck, sending a bolt of unease down my spine. A rough, chuffing sound followed, reminding me an awful lot of laughter.

"Interesting," came a voice so laden with power and authority that it pressed upon my skull. "You've awakened Nektas and still breathe. That can only mean one thing. My blood kneels before me."

Silence echoed around me as I lifted my head. There were several feet between the god and me, but his silver-eyed stare pierced straight through me. "It is I."

"That I know," he answered. "I saw you in my sleep, kneeling beside the one you kneel behind now."

"It was when we married," Casteel spoke, his head still bowed.

"And I gave you two my blessing," Nyktos added. "Yet, you dare to enter Iliseeum and wake me. What a way to show your gratitude. Should I kill all of you before I learn why, or do I even care enough to discover the reasons?"

It could've been everything I'd experienced in my life that'd led to this moment. It could've been the bitter fear that punched through Casteel—fear for me and not him. It could've been *my* fear for him and my friends. It was probably all those things that drove me to my feet and loosened my tongue. "How about you don't kill any of us, considering you've been asleep for eons, and we came here seeking your aid?"

The King of Gods came down a step. "How about I just kill *you*?"

Casteel moved so fast, I barely saw him do so until he was standing in front of me, using his body as a shield. "She means no disrespect."

"But she has disrespected me."

My stomach twisted as Kieran's fingers dug into the diamonds. I knew that not even the wolven would protect me in this situation. I may represent the deities to them, but Nyktos was the god that gave them mortal form. "I'm sorry," I said, attempting to step to the side, but Casteel moved, too, keeping me behind him.

"Then should I kill him?" Nyktos suggested, and terror turned my blood to ice. "I have a feeling that would serve as a better lesson than your death. I'm sure you'd mind your manners then."

Real fear for Casteel seized me, reaching deep inside and sinking its vicious claws into my chest. Nyktos could do it with a thought, and that knowledge severed whatever self-control I had. Heat rolled through me, turning the ice to slush in my blood. Anger flooded every part of my body, and it felt as potent as the power in the god's voice. "No."

Casteel stiffened.

"No?" the King of Gods repeated.

Fury and resolve mingled with the hum in my chest. Eather throbbed throughout my body, and this time, when I side-stepped Casteel, he wasn't fast enough to block me.

I stood in front of him, hands at my sides and feet spread wide. Silvery-white light crackled over my skin, and I knew I couldn't stop Nyktos. If he wanted us dead, we would die, but that didn't mean I would stand by. I would die a thousand deaths before I allowed that. I would—

Without warning, an image flashed in my mind. The silver-haired woman standing before another as the stars fell from the sky, her hands balled into fists. Her words came from my lips, "I will not let you harm him or any of my friends."

Nyktos's head tilted to the side as his eyes widened slightly. "Interesting," he murmured, his gaze flicking over me. "Now I understand why sleep has been so hard lately—why we dream so intensely." A brief pause. "And you do not need anyone to stand before you in defense."

His statement shook me enough that the eather fizzled out.

"Though," he continued, his gaze sliding to where Casteel stood, "it's admirable of you to do so. I see that my approval of the union was not a mistake."

The breath that left me was one of ragged relief, but then Nyktos turned away. He started walking up the stairs. Where was he going? I stepped forward, and the god stopped, looking over his shoulder. "You wanted to speak. Come. But only you. No one else can enter, or they will die."

Heart thundering, I twisted toward Casteel. His features were sharp as crystal-bright eyes locked with mine. A desperate sense of helplessness echoed throughout him. He didn't want me to enter that Temple, but he knew I had to. "Do not get yourself killed," he ordered. "I will be very angry if you do."

"I won't," I promised. At least, I hoped I didn't. The draken named Nektas made that gravelly chuckling sound again. "I love you."

"Prove it to me later."

Drawing in a shallow breath, I nodded and then turned, following the King of Gods. He stood before the open doors, extending a hand toward the shadowy interior. Hoping I walked back out, I entered.

"Make sure they behave, Nektas," the god requested.

I turned to see Casteel and the others rise while the draken thumped its tail off the diamond-strewn ground. The doors closed without sound, and I was suddenly alone with the King of Gods. Whatever idiotic bravery had invaded me earlier quickly vanished as Nyktos said nothing and simply stared at me. I did what I hadn't allowed since I first saw him. I opened my senses, letting them stretch—

"I wouldn't do that."

I sucked in a startled breath.

"It would be very unwise." Nyktos dipped his chin. His eyes

burned a bright silver. "And very impolite."

Air tightened in my throat as I wrangled my senses back in. My gaze quickly flicked around, looking for another exit without turning my back to him. There was nothing but black walls and sconces. But who was I kidding? I knew running would do no good.

Nyktos moved then, striding forward. I tensed, and a smile appeared. "Minding your manners now?"

"Yes," I whispered.

He chuckled, and the sound…it was like the wind on a warm day. "Bravery is a fleeting beast, isn't it? Always there to get you into trouble, but quick to disappear once you're where you want to be."

No truer words had ever been spoken.

The scent of sandalwood brushed over me as he passed. I turned, finally seeing the rest of the chamber. Two large doors were closed. Winding shadowstone staircases rose on either side.

"Sit," he offered, gesturing to the two white chairs in the center of the chamber. A round table sat between them—a table made of bone. On top sat a bottle and two glasses.

My brow furrowed as I tore my gaze from the table and the chairs to the god. "You were expecting us."

"No." He sat in the chair and reached for the bottle. "I was expecting *you*."

I stood there. "Then we didn't wake you."

"Oh, you woke me quite some time ago," he replied, pouring what looked like red wine into a delicate, stemmed glass. "I wasn't sure exactly why, but I'm beginning to understand."

My thoughts spun. "Then why did you threaten to kill us?"

"Let's make one thing clear, Queen of Flesh and Fire," he said, and a shudder worked its way through me as he looked over at me. "I do not threaten death. I make death happen. I was simply curious to see what you and your chosen were made of." He smiled slightly, pouring wine into the other glass. "Sit."

I forced my legs to move. My boots made no sound as I walked across the floor. I sat stiffly as I told myself not to ask any of the thousand questions brewing. It was best that I get to the point and then get the hell out of there as fast as possible.

That was not what happened.

"Are any other gods awake? Your Consort?" I blurted out.

An eyebrow rose as he placed the bottle back on the table. "You know the answer to that. You saw one yourself."

My breath caught. Aios *had* appeared while we'd been in the Skotos Mountains, stopping me from what would've been a very messy death.

"Some have stirred enough to be aware of the realm outside of others. Others have remained in a semi-lucid state. A few are still in the deepest sleep," he answered. "My Consort sleeps now, but she does so fitfully."

"How long have you been awake? The others?"

"Hard to say." He slid the glass toward me. "It's been on and off for centuries, but more frequent in the last two decades."

I didn't touch the glass. "And you know what has happened in Atlantia? Solis?"

"I am the King of Gods." He leaned back, crossing a leg over the other. The repose and everything about him was relaxed. It rattled me because there was a thread of intensity under the looseness. "What do you think?"

My lips parted in disbelief. "Then you know about the Ascended—what they've done to people. To mortals. Your children. How have you not intervened? Why haven't any of the gods stepped in to do something to stop them?" The moment my demands left my mouth, my entire body seized with dread. He was most certainly going to kill me now, shared blood or not.

But he smiled. "You are so much like her." He laughed. "She will be thrilled to learn this."

My shoulders tightened. "Who?"

"Do you know that most of the gods who sleep now were not the first gods?" Nyktos asked instead of answering, sipping his wine. "There were others known as the Primal. They were the ones who created the air we breathe, the land we reap, the seas that surround us, the realms and all in between."

"No, I didn't know that," I admitted, thinking of what Jansen had said about Nyktos once being the God of Death and the Primal God of Common Men and Endings.

"Most do not. They were once great rulers and protectors of man. That did not last. Much like with the children of those who sleep now, they became tainted and twisted, corrupt and uncontrollable," he told me, his gaze moving to his drink. "If you knew what they had become, the kind of wrath and evil they spread upon the lands and man, you would be haunted till the end of your days. We had to stop them. We did." That one eyebrow, his right one, rose again. "But not before we ended the mortal lands as those who survived remembered, sending them into the Dark Ages that it took centuries and centuries for them to claw out of. I bet you didn't know that either."

I shook my head.

"You wouldn't. The history of all that was before has been destroyed. Only a handful of structures survived," he stated, swishing the red liquid in his glass. "Unthinkable sacrifices were made to ensure that their sickness could never infect the world again, but obviously, mortals were rightfully wary of the gods. We entered into a blood treaty with them, one that ensured that only gods born within the mortal realm could retain their powers there." Quicksilver eyes lifted to mine once more. "None of the gods can enter the mortal realm without weakening greatly…and resorting to what is forbidden to ensure their strength. That is why we have not intervened. That is why my Consort sleeps fitfully, Poppy."

I jerked at the sound of my nickname. All of that sounded like a reasonable explanation for why they hadn't become involved, but something stood out to me. "How…how is a god born in the mortal realm?"

"Good question." He smiled behind his wine glass. "They should not be."

I frowned.

His smile kicked up a notch.

And then it occurred to me—what he had said about only a few Primal gods being among those who slept now. If what Jansen had claimed was true, and Nyktos was already a god before he became this… "Are you a Primal?"

"I am." He stared at me. "And that means you have Primal blood in you. That is what fuels that bravery of yours. That is why you are so powerful."

I took a drink then, swallowing a mouthful of the sweet wine. "Does that mean my mother could've been mortal?"

"Your mother could've been from any blood, and you would be who you are today, regardless. Unexpected, but…welcomed nonetheless," he said, and before I had a chance to even process what that could mean, what that could signify, he continued. "But that's not what you came to talk to me about, is it? And I bet you have a lot of questions." One side of his lips tipped up as a somewhat…fond look crept into his otherwise cold features. "Is your brother who you want him to be? Is the mother who you remember yours?" His eyes drilled into mine as goosebumps spread across my skin. "Are your dreams a reality or your imagination? Who truly killed the ones you called Mother and Father? But you don't have long to ask those questions. You have time for only one. These lands are not meant for your friends, nor your lover. If they stay much longer, they will not be able to leave."

I stiffened. "None of us has entered Dalos."

"It doesn't matter. You came to ask for my aid? There is nothing I can do for you."

"I don't need your aid," I clarified, placing my glass on the table. Gods knew how many questions I wanted to ask about Ian, about my parents and the memories, but this trip wasn't about me. It was about those waiting outside and all those I had yet to meet. "I need the aid of your guards."

Nyktos's brow rose. "You know who my guards are."

"Now I do," I mumbled under my breath. His head tilted, and I cleared my throat. "You're aware of what the Ascended are doing, right? They're using Atlantians to make more of them, and they're feeding upon innocent mortals. We need to stop them. I've learned that the Ascended have created something that I was told only your guards can help us stop. Something called a Revenant."

The change that swept over the god was instant and final. The façade of ease vanished. Streaks of white bled across his irises, luminous and crackling. Everything about him hardened, and every instinct in me went on high-alert.

"What?" I ventured. "Do you know what the Revenants are?"

A muscle ticked in his jaw. "An abomination of life and of death." He stood abruptly, eyes settling to a pearly shade of steel. "What you face is a greater evil that should not be, and I…I am sorry that you will see what is to come."

Well, that didn't bode well at all.

"You need to leave, Queen." The doors behind me swung open.

I stood. "But your guards—"

"You were born of flesh with the fire of the gods in your blood. You are a Bringer of Life and a Bringer of Death," Nyktos interrupted. "You *are* the Queen of Flesh and Fire, due more than one Crown, one kingdom. What you seek, you already have. You always had the power in you."

Chapter 42

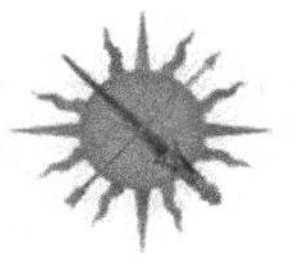

You always had the power in you.

The words echoed through me as I roamed the halls of the Evaemon Palace several days later, trying to learn where all the many halls led and the purpose of all the rooms while Casteel spent time with his father and mother in the brightly lit family room.

An unrelenting malaise nipped at my heels, following my steps just as Arden, the silver-and-white wolven, and Hisa and another Crown Guard did. Except they were far quieter than my thoughts.

I couldn't shake the feeling that my friends' lives had been risked. And for what? To learn that whatever these Revenants were, was a greater evil than we knew? Which, by the way, meant that was all we knew. No one, not even Casteel's parents, could hazard a guess as to what a Revenant could be and how it would warrant such a warning.

I traveled the back hall of the west wing where the staff offices were located, as were the laundry and the kitchens. Warmth crowded the area, along with the aromas of fresh linen and roasted meat as I admitted that the trip to Iliseeum hadn't been a complete and utter waste. I had learned that Nyktos was a Primal god, something Valyn vaguely remembered hearing his grandfather mention once. And until now, he'd believed that his grandfather had been speaking of the gods we'd always known. Discovering that I had Primal blood explained why my abilities were so powerful. It also meant that the mother I remembered—the one Alastir had claimed was a Handmaiden—could very well have been my real mother. And, once again, I was back to the possibility that Ian could be my half-brother. That we shared the same mother but different fathers. Discovering that was huge and important to me, but only to me. It wasn't what we'd gone for.

Which was to gain the aid of Nyktos's guards—the draken.

At least, I'd gotten to see one, so there was that. Sighing, I tucked a strand of hair behind my ear. I'd left the crown in the bedchamber, and I wished I'd left my brain there, as well, where Casteel had managed to pull my thoughts from the trip to Iliseeum multiple times in the ensuing days.

Since we'd returned, Casteel and I had barely had any time alone. There were meetings with the Council. Time spent with Eloana and Valyn, where I was taught the different laws of the kingdom at a head-spinning speed. Sessions held where the people of Atlantia could approach us to ask for aid or offer their services for various needs throughout the kingdom. Dinners had been late, and we mostly spent them with Kieran, strategizing the best way to enter Oak Ambler without being seen. Entering Castle Redrock wouldn't be a problem. Slipping into the city's Rise unseen would be, and it hadn't been until the prior night that Kieran had come up with a plan.

I had yet to venture off the palace grounds, but it was just Casteel and me at night. We spent the time talking. I learned more about his brother and what it had been like growing up in Atlantia as the second son his father once expected to lead the Atlantian armies.

"That is how you became so skilled at fighting," I'd said as we lay together in bed, facing one another.

He'd nodded. "Malik trained alongside me for years, but when it came time for him to learn to rule, it became time for me to learn how to lead an army and kill."

"And to defend," I'd amended softly, tracing small circles on his chest. "You learned how to defend your people and those you care about."

"True."

"Did you want to be that?" I'd asked. "A commander?"

"*The* commander," he'd corrected with a teasing kiss. "It was the only skill I really knew, and I wanted to be able to serve my brother when he took the throne someday. I didn't really question it."

"At all?"

He'd fallen quiet for few minutes and then laughed. "Actually, that is not entirely true. I was fascinated with the science behind farming as a child—how the farmers grew to learn what time of year was best to plant certain crops, how they set up their irrigation systems. And there was something about seeing all that hard work come to fruition when it came time to harvest."

A farmer.

Part of me hadn't expected that, but then I thought of what he'd claimed his father did when I spoke with him in the Red Pearl. I'd grinned as I kissed him, and he then proved that fighting hadn't been the only skill he'd learned.

Another night, when his body was curled around mine and after a long day of meetings, he'd asked, "There's something I've been wondering and keep forgetting to ask. When we entered Iliseeum, and you saw the skeleton soldiers, you said they were hers. What did you mean?"

I'd realized then that I hadn't shared that image with him. I'd told him what I saw when I was in the Chambers of Nyktos. "I saw her again when I was sleeping after the attack—after you saved me. It felt like a dream…but not. Anyway, I saw her touch the ground, and I saw bone hands digging their way out." I'd looked over my shoulder at him. "Who do you think she could be? If she is or was real?"

"I don't know. You said she had silver hair?"

"Her hair was a silvery blonde."

"I can't think of any of the gods that resembles her, but maybe she was one of the Primals Nyktos spoke of."

"Maybe," I murmured.

We'd also spent the time using our mouths and tongues to speak words of the flesh. I enjoyed each thoroughly and equally.

But Casteel didn't feel as if the trip was a waste. While I found Nyktos's parting words to be generally unhelpful at the end of the day, Casteel took them to mean that I would one day rule both Solis and Atlantia. But those words made me think of what the Duchess had claimed.

That Queen Ileana was my grandmother. That was highly impossible, but it was the only way I would have a true claim to the throne—succession instead of conquering. Or maybe Nyktos meant that we would take the Blood Crown that way? I didn't know, and the pressure to convince the Blood Crown in our upcoming meeting was even greater. We couldn't let this become a war including these Revenants. I had a horrible feeling there would only be one way to stop this. Maybe that was what Nyktos had meant. That I had the power in me to stop this.

Icy fingers drifted across the nape of my neck. I'd heard those words before, spoken by the little girl who'd been so grievously wounded, but when she'd spoken them, they had struck a chord of familiarity in me. Over the last several days, I'd tried to remember, but they were like a dream you tried to retain hours after waking.

Passing the entrances to the busy kitchens, I rounded the bend in the hall and nearly walked right into Lord Gregori. I took a startled step back. The dark-haired Atlantian wasn't alone.

"My apologies." A slight frown appeared as he noted the absence of my crown.

It did not go unnoticed that he didn't acknowledge my title. Neither had Lord Ambrose when I passed him the other day in the halls as I'd left to explore the grounds with Vonetta. "It is I who should apologize. I wasn't paying attention to where I was walking." My gaze darted to the young woman behind him. She appeared to be around my age, but I knew immediately she was a wolven, so she could be dozens or even hundreds of years older than me.

The pale, wintery eyes were a striking contrast to the golden hue of her skin, and the warm blonde hair that fell over her shoulders in loose waves. Her features were a mix of traits you would've found on different people. Her eyes were wideset and yet hooded, softening the sharp angles of her cheeks and the blade of her nose. Her brows were thick and several shades darker than her hair. Her mouth was small, but her lips were full. She was short, several inches shorter than me, but the cut of her tunic showed off the curves of her breasts and the lushness of her hips that would've seemed at odds with someone of her stature. Nothing about her made sense, and yet everything about her lined up so imperfectly that any artist would likely be driven to commit her image to canvas with charcoal or oil. She was perhaps the most uniquely beautiful person I'd ever seen, and I couldn't stop staring at her.

And I was sure I was probably creeping her out a little based on her growing unease.

"I was actually looking for the King," Lord Gregori announced. "But I see that he is not with you."

Pulling my gaze from the unfamiliar wolven, I focused on the Atlantian. The thread of distrust was apparent, even if I wasn't able to read his emotions. Either the Atlantian kept forgetting that I could do that, or he simply didn't care. "He is with his parents. Is there something I can help you with?"

Amusement flickered through him, the mean kind. "No," he said, his smile simpering, his tone overly conciliatory. "That will not be necessary. If you'll excuse me."

He hadn't been excused, but he still brushed past me. I turned as Arden flattened his ears, watching the Lord as he nodded at Hisa and the other guard. The striking image of Arden rushing off and biting the Lord's leg filled my mind, and I smothered a giggle at the ridiculousness. Arden's head swung to me, and then he looked at the one who remained.

Remembering the female wolven, I turned back to her. "I'm sorry. I thought you were with him."

"Oh, gods, no, *meyaah Liessa.* We just happened to enter the hall at the same time," she said, and I grinned at the shamelessness of her response. "I was actually looking for someone I hadn't seen in a while."

"Who? Perhaps I could help you locate them?"

Her smile faded a bit, and unease returned. "You probably can. I was looking for Kieran."

Surprised, my brows lifted. "He is with his sister. I think they were in…" I frowned, going through the many different doors and rooms in my head. "One of the five hundred thousand rooms here. Sorry."

The wolven laughed. "It's okay." She looked up and around, taking in the vaulted ceilings and skylights. "This place is a lot to get used to."

"That it is." My curiosity took over. "I don't think we've met."

"We haven't. I was in Aegea with my family when you and Cas—you and the King—were crowned," she said, and I zeroed in on her words. She'd either almost called him by his first name or his nickname, which wasn't all that surprising since she was looking for Kieran. If she was friends with one, I was sure she was friends with the other. "And if we'd met, I'm sure you would remember."

Her nervousness itched at the back of my throat, stroking my wariness. "What do you mean by that?"

The wolven's shoulder's leveled. "My name is Gianna Davenwell."

I inhaled sharply. Her unease made sense now on several levels. I swallowed as my gaze swept over her features again. Of course, the one Casteel's father had wanted him to marry would have to be so fascinatingly beautiful and not resemble a Craven.

And, of course, I wouldn't be dressed in any of the pretty gowns that had arrived from Spessa's End. My hair was braided, and I wore leggings and a tunic—a pretty one the shade of amethyst that I had thought flattered my figure before I saw Gianna and realized she was the woman Casteel could've married.

Now I wished I'd worn the crown.

"I am so sorry for what my great-uncle took part in and orchestrated," she added quickly, her anxiety now edged with the bitterness of fear. "We had no idea. My family was shocked and horrified to learn—"

"It's okay," I said, and surprise rolled through her—through *me* as I yanked my head out of a very unmentionable place. "If you and your family didn't know what Alastir planned, then you have nothing to apologize for." And that was true. One was not guilty because of who they were related to. "I am sorry for what happened to your cousin. I met Beckett. He was kind and entirely too young to have died."

Grief darted through Gianna as she drew in a shaky breath. "Yes, he was far too young." She swallowed. "I planned on coming to you and the King, but I…I thought it was better if I spoke with Kieran first. To see if he thought…"

If it would be wise for her to approach me went unsaid. I could understand that concern. "Neither of us hold Alastir's family responsible. We hold him and the others who conspired with him responsible."

Gianna nodded, her gaze skittering to where Arden sat, and the guards waited. What went unspoken between us strained the silence to an almost painful level of awkwardness.

I decided to address that head-on like I imagined Casteel's mother would have done. Like I knew even Queen Ileana would do. "I know that Alastir and Casteel's father had hopes that you would marry Casteel."

Gianna's already large eyes widened as Arden softly grumbled. I realized then that she reminded me of one of those porcelain dolls Ileana had given me as a child. Pink infused her cheeks. "I… Okay, to be honest, I was hoping you didn't know that."

"Me, too," I admitted wryly, and her lips formed a perfect oval shape. "Only because you are very beautiful and don't resemble a barrat," I continued, and her mouth closed. "And because I like you after just speaking with you for a few moments. I would prefer not to like the person my father-in-law wished his son had married. But here we are."

Gianna blinked.

The sugary amusement I felt now definitely came from Hisa, and I thought that maybe I shouldn't have been so honest. But Arden and the guards were about to be entertained by even more blunt honesty. "Casteel told me that you two are friends, but that you had never shown any inclination towards being interested in marrying him. Is that true?"

It took Gianna a moment to respond. "I am sure few *wouldn't* be honored to be married to him," she began, and I started to feel my chest hum. "And, yes, we are friends—or we were. I haven't seen him in ages." Her brows knitted. "I'm not sure if he will even recognize me."

That was highly unlikely.

"But it wasn't like that between us," she continued. "At least, it didn't feel that way, and he…he was engaged to Shea, and that just kind of weirded me out."

The vibration settled. "Then we are in agreement about the latter."

Relief started to seep through her. "I have no feelings for your husband," she said. "Not before, and definitely not now."

"Good." I met her gaze, smiling. "Because if you did, I would probably tear you apart, limb by limb, and then feed what remained to a pack of hungry barrats," I said. "Now, would you like to find Kieran? I think I remember which room he's in."

"I met Gianna today," I announced later that evening as we took our seats in the State Room.

Casteel choked on his drink as Kieran took his seat beside us, the latter attempting and failing to hide a smile.

"She is quite beautiful," I said, watching the door. Very few would be joining us tonight, but at the moment, only Hisa and Delano stood at the entrance. "Something you failed to mention."

Setting his drink down, he looked over at me. "It's something I've forgotten if it is true."

I hid my smile as I took a sip of my wine. "She is very nice, though."

Casteel eyed me. "What did you talk about?"

"She apologized for Alastir, and I told her she and her family had nothing to apologize for," I told him. "And then I told her that I knew about Alastir's and your father's plans."

"That is not all you said."

I shot Kieran a look. "How do you know?" I demanded. When we ended up finding Kieran and his sister, nothing of my conversation with Gianna had been mentioned. I also hadn't lingered long afterwards, and I seriously doubted that Gianna would've repeated what I said.

"How do you think?" Kieran remarked. "Arden couldn't wait to tell everyone and anyone who would listen, what you said."

I frowned.

"What else did you say?" Casteel asked.

I lifted my shoulders. "Nothing, really. Just that if she had any interest in you, I would…"

Casteel dipped his head closer to mine. "What?"

My lips pursed. "I might've said something like I'd tear her apart limb by limb and feed her to barrats."

He stared at me.

I sighed. "It wasn't one of my finer moments, I admit."

"Damn." Casteel broke the silence, his gaze the shade of heated honey. "I wish we weren't about to have this meeting because I really want to fuck you on this table right now."

My eyes widened.

"*Gods*," Kieran muttered, sitting back as he dragged a hand over his face.

"Is everything fine?" Casteel's mother asked as she strode into the room, his father beside her.

My face heated as Casteel dragged his gaze from mine. "Everything is delightfully perfect," he told them, sitting back in his chair.

I turned to Kieran and whispered, "Thanks for that."

A closed-lip smile appeared. "You're welcome."

Resisting the urge to punch him, I looked over as Hisa closed the doors. Lord Sven and Lady Cambria had joined us, along with Emil, Delano, and Vonetta. Lyra, in her mortal form, had also come in, along with Naill. In the last several days, I'd learned that both Sven and Cambria assisted with the security of the kingdom and held positions within the Atlantian armies. No other Elder was present.

It was Kieran who spoke once Hisa had taken her seat on his other side. "We're all set to leave for Oak Ambler tomorrow," he announced. "A small group will travel with the King and Queen. It will just be

Delano and me."

Valyn inhaled deeply as he sat back in his chair. "That is not nearly enough."

"I have to agree," Hisa spoke up. "You will be entering Solis, meeting with the Blood Crown. It is unlikely that their armies will not have a substantial presence. Four of you is not nearly enough if something were to go wrong."

"It's not," Casteel agreed. "But that is just one group."

Hisa raised a brow. "I'm listening."

"They will be expecting us to arrive via horse," Kieran said. "Entering through the eastern gates of the Rise, but we don't want to do what they expect."

"That's where you will come in," I said. "You, along with Emil, Vonetta, and Lyra will leave in the morning, taking a small contingent of guards with you to arrive at the eastern gates. They have to expect that we would not come without some sort of convoy, even if they remain outside the Rise."

Hisa nodded. "And you all?"

"We will travel by sea." Kieran glanced at Sven. "Thanks to you, we have a ship."

Sven smiled. "More like thanks to my son, who is currently loading several crates of wine—well, mostly wine bottles full of water and horse piss," he said, and my lip curled. "We aren't going to just give the Blood Crown several hundred bottles of our wine."

Eloana placed a hand over her mouth, but not quickly enough to hide her smile.

"As most know, we monitor many of the shipments in and out of nearby ports," Lord Sven continued. "And since Oak Ambler is the closest, we know that wine and other goods are infrequently shipped into the city. The shipment will not be questioned."

"They won't be expecting us from the sea." Casteel picked up his chalice. "Not with the mist that comes off the Skotos Mountains. As far as people know, both mortal and vampry alike, the mountains continue into the sea. That is what the mist leads them to believe."

"I can confirm that," I noted. "We believed that the Stroud Sea ended at the Skotos."

"That doesn't mean the Blood Crown believes that," Valyn pointed out. "They could've gotten that information from any number of Atlantians they captured over the years."

"True." Casteel nodded. "But I'm also sure they will have scouts on the road leading to Oak Ambler. The group traveling by land will be spotted. Lyra and Emil will travel with their identities hidden. Vonetta will be in her wolven form, and Naill will be at Emil's side."

"It takes, what? Four days by land to arrive at Oak Ambler?" Lady Cambria inclined her head. "How many by sea?"

"With our ships?" Sven grinned. "Faster than anything Solis will have, but you will have to go slow through the mist. So, you're looking at roughly the same time."

Understanding flickered on Hisa's face as she smiled tightly. "It will take us about two days to clear the Skotos and enter the Wastelands. We would be spotted before you arrive."

"Meaning they will turn their attentions to you," Kieran stated. "Emil and Lyra, along with Vonetta and Naill, will enter and travel to Castle Redrock."

"Hopefully, that is what occurs," Eloana said, shifting in her seat, uneasy. "There is still a chance that you could be discovered."

"There will always be a risk," Casteel confirmed. "But we have a better chance this way."

"And then?" Valyn queried. "Once you're in front of the Blood Crown, how do you plan to get out if things do not go as planned? If it is a trap? I will go to the north to await word with the armies, but what will you do if it is a trap?"

My mind went to what I'd believed Nyktos had been referring to regarding the power already residing in me. I lifted my gaze to Casteel's.

"What are you thinking, my Queen?" he asked.

The way those two words rolled off his tongue caused a wicked curl to start up low in my stomach. The way his eyes heated as they held mine told me he knew exactly what they did.

He was…incorrigible.

I took a drink. "I was unable to gain the aid of Nyktos's guards," I stated, and I could feel Casteel gearing up to deny that, so I rushed on. "And with what he and my brother said about the Revenants, we do not want to go to war with Solis. So, I was thinking that if this is a trap, or if the Blood Crown doesn't take our ultimatum, we are left with only one recourse."

The room fell silent with understanding. "And what if that provokes what you're attempting to avoid?" Lord Sven asked.

"The King and Queen wouldn't have survived even if they agreed," Casteel said after a moment. "If we have an agreement, we would be careful about ensuring that neither Ileana nor Jalara are a threat any longer—once we were sure that the remaining Blood Crown is in agreement with what we have set forth." One of his fingers drew idle circles on the bottom of his chalice as his attention flicked back to me. "But I don't think that's what you're talking about."

I shook my head. "If they don't agree, the only option we will be left with is one that ensures the Revenants can't be used or can be dealt with. And there is only one way we can do that." I sought out Eloana's gaze in the room. "We cut the head off the snake. We destroy the Blood Crown in its entirety, and I…I can do that."

Chapter 43

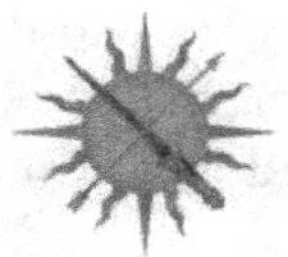

Clutching the rails of the quarterdeck, I kept my eyes open as I stared at the choppy steel-blue waters of the Stroud Sea. It hadn't been bad when the ship first left the shores of Atlantia and drifted seamlessly through the mist. The gentle swaying of the ship had been kind of a fun experience.

But then we'd cleared the mist, and all there was were the deep blue waters that stretched for as far as I could see. It looked as if the sea kissed the sky. I'd thought closing my eyes would help.

Nope.

That was much worse because without my eyes open to confirm that I was indeed standing straight and steady, I felt like I was falling.

What had Perry claimed not too long ago? That I would gain my sea legs in no time? I didn't think that would happen at all. The small crew who worked the riggings of the masts made it all seem so easy.

"Please don't vomit," Kieran said.

I glanced over at him, my eyes narrowing. He'd joined me the moment Casteel had left my side to speak with Delano and Perry on the helm. "I cannot make that promise."

He chuckled as he turned his face to the sky and the last of the sun. "Well, if you do, please aim for over the railing."

"I'll make sure I aim for your face," I retorted.

That got another laugh from the wolven. My grip on the railing tightened as I turned back to the sea. "You know," he started, "it might help if you stopped looking at the water."

"I've tried that." I forced a dry swallow. "It did not help."

"Then you need to be distracted," he replied.

"And it's a good thing I excel at the art of distraction," Casteel said, striding up behind us. He reached around, peeling my death grip from the railing. "Come," he said, leading me away as the breeze rippled across his loose white shirt and tossed about the waves of his hair.

"Have fun," Kieran called out.

"Shut up," I snapped, walking stiffly beside Casteel.

Perry and Delano waved at us as Casteel guided me to the stairs that led down into the cabins. It was dimly lit belowdecks, and I'd only been below for a short period of time earlier to try and eat something, but I had found the floors of the stately cabin we'd been given just as unsteady as the ones above.

Casteel opened the door, and I inched my way in. Everything was bolted down. The table and two chairs. The bare surface of a wide, wooden desk. The wardrobe. The wide bed in the center of the cabin. The clawfoot tub. The standing dressing mirror and vanity. Even the gas lamps were secured. He led me to the desk.

"Take a seat," he said, and I started to sit in the chair in front of the desk, but he tsked softly under his breath. Letting go of my hand, he grasped my hips and lifted me onto the desk.

My heart gave a silly little tumble at the show of strength as he opened one of the cabin windows. I was neither small nor dainty, but he often made me feel that way. I watched him pick up one of the bags we'd brought with us and place it by the desk.

"You were about to take my seat." He returned, taking the chair directly in front of me.

I raised an eyebrow as I gripped the edge of the desk, and he tapped my booted calf, motioning for me to lift my leg. "What are you up to?" I asked.

"Distracting you." He tugged off the boot, letting it fall with a thump to the floor.

I watched him remove my other boot and then my thick socks. "I think I know what you're up to, but not even that will distract me from the fact that everything feels like it's swaying, and we could capsize at any second."

His brows lifted as he looked up at me. "First off, you should have way more faith in my skills when it comes to distracting you," he said, and I immediately thought of the night in the Blood Forest. My skin flushed. "And the boat capsizing is not what is going to happen next."

"What is?" I asked as his palms slid up my legs.

"I'm going to do what I wanted to last evening and fuck you on this desk," he told me, and muscles low in my stomach clenched.

"This isn't a table."

"It'll work." He gripped the waist of my breeches. "But first, I'm hungry."

The breath I took caught. "Then you should retrieve something to eat."

"I have."

My face caught fire.

Blazing, golden eyes locked with mine. "Lift your ass, my Queen."

A giggle crept free. "That is a sentence that sounds wholly inappropriate."

He grinned, and a hint of a dimple appeared. "I'm sorry. Let me rephrase that. Please lift your ass, my Queen."

The ship rocked, jostling me. My ass did lift, and Casteel seized the opportunity. He pulled off my breeches, letting them join the boots on the floor. Cool air swirled around my legs, stirring the edges of my slip.

"You're going to have to let go of the desk." He curled his fingers around the hem of the long-sleeved shirt.

I forced my fingers to ease, and my stomach lurched as the ship rocked again. I started to grab the desk, but he was faster, pulling the shirt up and over my head. The moment my arms were free, I grabbed hold of the desk once more.

"Pretty," he murmured, toying with the tiny strap on the slip and then the lace of the cinched bodice. His deft fingers loosened the buttons with shocking and impressive ease. The material parted, exposing my skin to the salty night air seeping in through the cabin window. He dragged his thumb over the rosy tip of one breast, causing me to gasp. "Not as pretty as these, though."

My heart thudded, and I wasn't sure if it was due to the ship's motions or the intent in his words.

He eased the straps down my arms, stopping when they fell against my wrists. Then he stretched up, reaching around to pick up my braid. He pulled the leather thong from the end and slowly began to unwind the hair.

"I'm going to make you re-braid my hair," I told him.

"I can do that." He spread the lengths over my shoulders, then he caught the edge of the slip, pushing it up my hips to where the material gathered at my waist. Those callused palms swept down my legs once more as he leaned back. Gripping my ankles, he spread my legs and placed my feet so they dangled off the arms of the chair. I'd never been more exposed in my life.

He dragged a finger along his lower lip as his gaze swept over me. "I've never seen a more tantalizing dinner. It makes me want to rush to the main course." His gaze lingered on the shadowy area between my thighs. "But I do love a good appetizer."

Oh…gods.

Casteel looked up at me, a secretive little grin playing across his lips as his arousal washed over me, mixing with mine. "I almost forgot. The next best thing to a good conversation while enjoying dinner is reading a good book."

My eyes widened as he bent, reaching into the bag. "You did not—"

"Don't move." Casteel shot me a heated look, and I froze. He withdrew the all-too-familiar leather-bound book. Straightening, he cracked it open. "Pick a page, my Queen."

Was he going to read to me? "I…I don't know. 238."

"238, it is." He found the page and then turned the book over to me. "Read to me. Please?"

I stared at him.

"It would be so very difficult for me to enjoy my dinner and read at the same time," he coaxed, eyes glimmering. "Or is reading this out loud too scandalous for you?"

It was, but the challenge in his tone provoked me. Letting go of the desk, I snatched the damnable book from his hand. "You really want me to read this to you?"

"You have no idea how badly I want to hear you say words like *cock*." His hands settled on my knees.

I glanced at the page, quickly searching for the word and found it. Damn it. Damn him, and—I gasped as his lips skated over the scar on my inner thigh.

"You're not reading." He kissed the rough skin. "Or are you that distracted already?"

I sort of was, but I forced myself to focus on the first line and immediately regretted it. "'*His…his manhood was thick and proud as he stroked it, enjoying the feeling of his own hand, but not as much as*—'" I jerked as his lips danced over my very center.

"Keep reading," he ordered, his words sending a dark and hot shiver through my core.

My gaze darted back to the page. "'*But not as much as I enjoyed watching him pleasure himself. He worked himself until the tip of his…*'" My entire body trembled as his hot, wet tongue slipped over me. "'*Until the tip of his proud, his… his proud cock glistened.*'"

A deep sound rumbled from him, causing my toes to curl. "I'm sure there's more." His tongue danced over my flesh. "What does he do with that proud, glistening cock of his, Poppy?"

Pulse pounding, I scanned the page. "He…" A breathy moan left me as he pierced the flesh there. "He eventually stops stroking himself."

"And?"

The words didn't make any sense for a moment. "And he pleasures her with it."

"Don't tell me." He nipped at the skin, dragging a ragged sound from me. "Read it to me."

"You are…wicked," I told him.

"And also very curious to discover how he pleasures her," he replied. "I may learn something."

My laugh ended in another moan as he returned to his dinner. "'*He grasped my hips with those large hands of his and held me there, between him and the wall, as he slid into me. I tried to keep quiet, but no—*'" I cried out as his mouth closed on the bundle of nerves, and he suckled deeply.

The scrape of his fang sent an intense bolt of pleasure through me. My legs attempted to close reflexively, but he caught an ankle, preventing it as he tugged on the skin there. Tension tightened and curled and throbbed—

His mouth left me. "Keep reading, Poppy."

Struggling to breathe, I wasn't sure if I could read, but I managed to find where I'd stopped. "'*But no one…fucked as passionately as a soldier on the eve of battle.*'"

The chuckle that left Casteel was sensual and dark. "Keep going." He flicked his tongue over the pulsing pinnacle. "And I'll keep enjoying my appetizer."

I blinked several times. "'*He took me…hard and furiously, and I knew I would bear the marks of such on the morrow, but I…*'" My hips lifted as he worked a finger into me. He wasn't slow. He didn't need to be. I was as primed as I imagined Miss Willa had been. "'*I will wear those marks with more than fond memories. I will think of how his hips pounded against mine, how his…his cock stretched and filled me…*'" As I read from the indecent diary, Casteel enjoyed his appetizer with his fingers and his mouth, until I no longer knew what I read. Until I couldn't make sense of the words, and the journal slipped from my grip, falling closed on the desk, and I shamelessly writhed against his mouth and hand. The release came all at once, rushing over me in stunning, crashing waves.

I was still trembling when he rose above me, tearing at his breeches. His…his cock was just as hard as the one I'd read about, just as proud and…glistening with a bead of liquid.

"Poppy?" he breathed as his lips danced over my jaw, down my throat.

"Cas?"

The sound he made nearly sent me over the edge all over again. "I just want you to know one thing." His mouth hovered over my wildly beating pulse before he eased me onto my back. He gripped my hips, tugging me to the edge of the desk. My feet slipped free of the arms of the chair. I curled my legs around his waist as his lips skated down my throat, over my chest, and to the aching tip of a breast. "I'm still in complete control."

He thrust into me at the same moment his fangs pierced my skin. Twin bursts of fiery pain lanced my breast, stunning me for a brief second, and then my entire body spasmed at the deep, staggering pull of his mouth. He devoured, and he fucked, just as he'd said he wanted to. Heat flowed through my body, igniting a fire that couldn't be controlled. He drank from me as his body moved in and out of me, and when he lifted his head from the tingling skin of my breast and bit into his wrist, I didn't look away from the bright red liquid welling on his skin.

"Just in case you need it," he rasped, lips smeared crimson with my blood, with his.

I didn't think about it. Maybe later I would wonder why it felt so natural to sit up and close my mouth over the wound, and what that could signify for later, but I was beyond thinking.

I drew his blood into me, struck first by the citrus-in-the-snow scent and then the luscious, dark taste of him. My mouth and then throat tingled as he filled me, thick and warm. I drank as images of pine and snow-draped limbs flashed, and the feel of the cold snow against my skin surfaced. I knew he was thinking about us in the woods. I let myself fall into that memory, into the taste of him and the power that was his blood. I didn't know how he moved us to the bed, but we were suddenly there, and his mouth was on mine, and our combined taste was in me. Casteel moved slowly, tenderly, and this…this was different than what we had done on that desk. In this moment, I felt bonded to him. It was more than just sex, more than two bodies enjoying each other. It was us, living and loving one another.

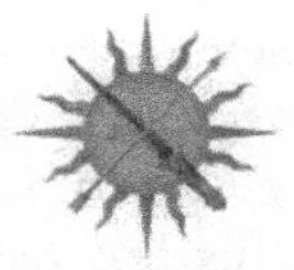

Casteel and I lay there, our skin cooling in the breeze coming in from the opening of the small cabin window as the ship gently rocked on the waters of the Stroud Sea. His chest was pressed to my back as he traced idle circles down my arm, and I toyed with his other hand. He'd shucked off his clothing at some point, and the soft fur of the blanket lay pooled at our feet. There would've been a time when I would've balked at the idea of being so exposed, but not with Casteel. Never with him.

"You're worthy," I said, just because I wanted him to know that. I lifted his hand, kissing the backs of his knuckles.

He pressed his lips to the back of my shoulder. "And you're being sweet."

"I'm being real," I told him. His hand stilled on my arm, and he fell quiet. I looked over my shoulder at him. Several emotions rolled through him. The sweet and spicy flavor of what he felt for me, but also the tangy-bitterness of agony that stole my breath. "What?" I shifted onto my back, my gaze searching his. "What is wrong?"

"Nothing." His throat worked on a swallow.

"Don't." I rose onto my elbow so we were face-to-face. "Don't tell me nothing. I can feel that it is something."

His lashes swept down, shielding his eyes, but I saw the dark shadows there. Ghosts. "Hiding one's innermost feelings isn't exactly easy around you."

"I know. I would say I'm sorry."

"But you're not?" One side of his lips tipped up.

"Yes, and no. I don't like to pry when I know it's not wanted." I spoke into the breath between our lips. "Talk to me, Cas."

"Cas." He shuddered, and then his lashes lifted. "Do you know why I love hearing you say that?" He swallowed again as he touched my cheek with the tips of his fingers. A long moment passed. "When I was held by the Ascended, there were times I feared I would forget my name—forget who I was. I did, actually—when I was starved. When I was used. I was a thing. Not a person. Not even an animal. A thing."

I bit down on the inside of my lip as my heart twisted. I didn't say a word. I didn't dare move or breathe too heavily. I didn't want to do anything that would make him stop talking.

"Even after I was freed, I sometimes felt that way. That I was nothing more than this thing without a name or autonomy," he admitted hoarsely. "It would just…creep up on me, and I'd have to remind myself that I wasn't. Sometimes, that didn't work, and it was always Kieran and Netta or Delano—Naill, or even Emil—who would snap me out of it. As would my parents. They didn't even know. None of them did, other than maybe Kieran." His fingers trailed down my arm, to where my hand rested on his hip, above the brand of the Royal Crest. "It was just someone saying, 'Cas.' Or my mother calling me Hawke that reminded me I wasn't a thing."

Tears of pain and anger filled my eyes. I wanted to hug him. I wanted to launch myself from the ship and swim to the shore to find the Queen and King and kill them right now. But I held myself still.

"That I was a person," he whispered. "That I wasn't that thing in the cage or that thing that couldn't control anything around me—not even what was done to me or how my body was used. Hearing them just say 'Cas' pulled me out of that hellscape." His fingers slid all the way up my arm to cup my cheek. He tilted my head back. "When you call me Cas, it reminds me that I'm real."

"Cas," I whispered, blinking back tears.

"Don't," he pleaded softly. "Don't cry."

"I'm sorry. It's just that I want…" Gods, there was so much I wanted for him. I wanted him to never have experienced any of that, but I couldn't undo the past. "I want you to know that you are always Cas. You were never a thing, and you aren't one now." I rose, easing him onto his back. The buttery light of the gas lamp flowed over the striking lines of his face. "You are Casteel Hawkethrone Da'Neer. A son. A brother. A friend. A husband." I leaned over him, and there was no mistaking the deepening of the color of his eyes as his gaze dropped to my breasts. Clasping his cheek, I guided his gaze back to mine. "You are a King. *My* King. And you will always be my everything, but never will you be a thing."

Casteel moved fast, pinning my back to the bed with the warm weight of his body. "I love you."

And I showed him that I loved him, with my words, my lips, my hands, and then my body, over and over until the beautiful amber eyes were clear of any and all shadows.

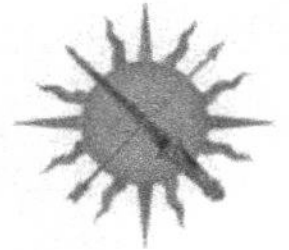

I had been…thoroughly and repeatedly distracted from the constant sway of the ship throughout the journey to Oak Ambler, but I hadn't gained my sea legs by the time the sea gave way to land, and the burnt-red stone of Castle Redrock loomed over the city and the village just outside the Rise. The bright, late-morning sun shone overhead as Casteel and I made our way back into the cabin. It would be safer for us to move about during the day. We had arrived two days before we were expected, which meant that Vonetta and the group should be arriving at the same time, or perhaps a little earlier.

The goal was to blend in and go unnoticed. My scars would make that difficult, but thankfully, cooler temperatures meant donning a cloak with its hood up wouldn't draw too much attention. I was wearing an old pair of breeches that Casteel had wrangled for me, ones worn at the knees. The clothing I'd acquired in Saion's Cove would have been too fine for someone not Ascended or of a wealthy class.

And the wealthy in Solis did not walk the streets of any city. They rode in carriages, even if they were traveling a block. I donned a simple white shirt, one with loose sleeves fitted at the wrists. It was strangely…freeing that the white shirt didn't affect me—that I'd barely even thought of it as I slipped the sleeveless bodice over the shirt, cinching it tightly at the waist and the breast with front-lace stays like many of the women of the working class in Solis were wont to do. I was securing the chest harness when I looked up to find Casteel staring at me.

He was dressed as he usually was, cutting a striking figure in black breeches and a long-sleeved tunic. Blending in was far easier for males. "What?"

His gaze swept over me, lingering on the curves of the bodice along my chest. "I like what you're wearing," he said. "A lot."

Feeling my cheeks warm, I picked up a dagger and secured it to the chest harness, and then sheathed the wolven dagger at my thigh.

"Now I really like what you're wearing." He strode toward me.

"You're demented."

"Only slightly." He tossed my braid over my shoulder. Dipping his head, he kissed me and then straightened the bow on the stays of the bodice. "I cannot wait to untie these later."

I smiled as a curling motion swept low in my stomach. The smile faded too quickly as my heart tripped over itself. *Later isn't guaranteed*, whispered an annoying voice, and if that voice had a body that wasn't mine, I'd punch it.

There would be a later.

We would make sure of that.

A knock sounded on the door just as Casteel finished strapping his swords to his sides.

Perry stepped inside, a cap in his hand. "We're about to dock."

"Perfect," Casteel replied while tension crept into my muscles. "As soon as you offload the crates, I want you out of here and back to Atlantia."

"I can stay nearby." Perry offered. "You can send a signal, and I can come and take you all back to Atlantia."

"That will be too much of a risk," I told him. "And we're already risking too many lives as it is."

Casteel slid me a knowing half-grin. "That, and Poppy probably doesn't want to spend four more days on a ship."

I said nothing as I shot him a glare. He was also right.

Perry grinned at me. "It can take longer for some people to get used to travelling by sea."

"I think some people are just not cut out for sailing," I said. "And by some people, I mean me."

He chuckled. A call came from above—a greeting. His gaze returned to us. "May I ask a favor of you two?"

"Anything," Casteel said as he tossed the cloak to me.

Perry dragged his fingers around the rim of his cap. "Keep an eye on Delano for me," he said, and I looked up at him as I started on the row of buttons across the chest of the cloak. "Sometimes, he's a little too brave."

"Delano will return to you," Casteel said as he slipped on his cloak, and I nodded.

"Thank you." He gave us a brief smile. "I will see you both up there."

When he was gone, I turned to Casteel. "Are Perry and Delano together?"

"They have been." He came over to me, tucking my braid under the back of my cloak before sliding a cap over my head. "On and off for the last couple of years, I think."

I grinned, thinking of them at the helm, smiling and laughing at whatever the other said. "They're cute together."

"You're cute." Casteel tugged on the brim of my cap and then lifted the hood of the cloak so it draped over the hat. "Though I prefer to be able to see your face." He tugged on his own cap, and somehow, the shadows it created along the lower half of his face made him appear all the more mysterious. Once his hood was in place, he said, "We got this."

My heart lurched. "I know. We do."

"You're ready, then?"

I knew he wasn't just talking about leaving the ship. "I am ready to do whatever needs to be done."

He nodded, and then we left the cabin, leaving our belongings behind. Perry and his crew would take what we'd brought with us, including that damn journal, back to Atlantia. The group that had traveled with Hisa carried extra supplies.

We climbed the stairs and made our way over to where Kieran and Delano stood by the crates. They and the crew were dressed similar to us, cloaks and caps shielding their faces. I looked over my shoulder to where ramps had been placed on the deck of the ship, connecting it to the pier. With a cap pulled low over his face, Perry spoke with someone dressed in black. They were guards from the Rise. Beyond them, the pier was a mass of controlled chaos. Men hurried from ships to the brick warehouses and wagons. Street vendors hocked food and other goods. My gaze swept up to the deep gray walls of the Rise, constructed of limestone and iron. Guards patrolled the wall, stood on the battlements, and were perched in their nests like birds of prey. I saw no black mantles, but there were…*a lot* of guards. More than one would expect to see at Oak Ambler on a normal day.

But today was not any other day.

The Blood Crown was within those walls.

Chapter 44

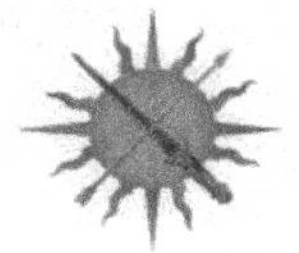

"Come on now, you lazy bastards," Perry shouted, and I raised an eyebrow as he stalked across the deck, smacking his hands together. "Get a move on."

"He's really enjoying this far too much," Delano muttered under his breath, and I stifled a giggle.

Casteel and I lifted a crate and started moving toward the pier. The wooden ramp wobbled under our feet, causing me to gasp as I glanced down at the churning dirty waters.

"Easy now," Casteel murmured.

I nodded as Perry led us to a wagon. Kieran and Delano were right behind us. My heart pounded as we passed the guards, but the men weren't paying us any mind, their attention drawn to the few women who were catcalling at the men still on ships, their faces heavily painted.

Thank the gods for some men's inability to focus on anything else if a pretty face was nearby.

"What in the hell are you all doing?" a man demanded as he rounded the side of the wagon, a severe frown set in the heavy jowls of his face. "This isn't—"

"Quiet." Casteel spun toward the man, and the power, the slickness in that one word stole my breath.

The man went silent as he stared into Casteel's eyes. His entire body had gone stiff as he was held there, suspended by invisible strings of compulsion. I was fixated myself as it was so rare to see Casteel use compulsion.

"You will not say a word—any word—while these crates are

loaded into your wagon. You will not make a single sound," Casteel said, his voice soft and fluid. "Once the crates are loaded, you will take them to wherever it is you're going. Understand?"

The man nodded, blinking slowly, and then he just stood there as the other crew surrounded us with their crates. I couldn't help but stare at the blank expression on the man's face.

"Go," Perry whispered under his breath as he leaned in between us. Bottles rattled from the crate Delano and Kieran placed in the wagon. "And may the gods be watching over you."

"May the gods be watching over *you*," Casteel replied, slipping around Perry.

Casteel nudged my shoulder as he brushed past. I turned, glancing briefly at Perry. "Be careful."

"I will, my Queen."

Turning, I kept pace with Casteel as we quickly slipped into the cloaked and jacketed mass of workers streaming in and out of the Rise gate. Scanning the crowd, I knew better than to look behind us for Delano and Kieran. They would find us. I focused ahead.

The closer I got, the…worse the smell became. Sweat and oil mixed with the scent of spoiled fish. I knew it would only grow, increasing due to all those forced to live in the small homes below the Rise, nearly stacked on top of each other, where the sun didn't seem to penetrate. The stomach-churning smell wasn't the only thing I noticed. The condition of the Rise caught my attention. There were tiny…fissures throughout the massive, thick structure. I'd never seen anything like it and couldn't quite think of what could have done that kind of damage.

"Look at the Rise," I said under my breath, and Casteel's head lifted the slightest bit.

He said nothing as we crossed through the gate with the throng of workers entering the city. He led us toward the narrow streets of the business district, where markets crowded the road covered with the waste that horses and mortals alike had left behind. Awareness pressed against my back, and I knew that Kieran and Delano had found us.

A horse-drawn wagon passed, the driver hunched over and unaware of the small child racing along the cobblestone sidewalk, carrying a stack of papers. His red-cheeked face was stained with soot, and his blond hair was slick and unkempt as he rushed into the street—

Casteel's hand snapped out, catching the child by the scruff of the neck and hauling him back.

"Hey! Let go of me, sir!" the boy shouted, holding onto the newspapers with everything in him. "I ain't done—" He quieted as the powerful hooves of the horses and wagon wheels pounded by inches from his face. "Shit," the child whispered.

"You're welcome," Casteel replied, placing the child on the sidewalk.

The kid whirled around, his eyes wide. "Thank you, sir! I would've been flattened like me momma's bread." He turned wide eyes to the street.

"Flattened like his momma's bread?" Delano whispered behind me, and I fought a laugh.

"You can thank me by telling me what happened to the Rise," Casteel said, his hand slipping inside his cloak. "To cause the cracks in it."

The child's brows knitted as he stared up at the shadowy area of Casteel's face. "It was the ground, sir. It rocked here, and I heard from Telly at the fish stand that the ground shook all the way to the capital. My momma said it was the gods. That they'd been angered."

I didn't know what would cause such a quake, but I knew it hadn't been the gods.

"When did this happen?" Casteel asked.

"I don't know. Like a month or so ago." The boy shifted from one foot to the other. "How do you not know when everything was shaking?"

"I suppose I was sleeping," Casteel replied, and I rolled my eyes.

The boy stared at him in disbelief, but the look quickly turned to wonder as Casteel withdrew his hand from his cloak, dropping several coins atop the stack of papers. The child's little eyes widened.

"Next time, try looking both ways before running out into the street," Casteel said, stepping around the kid.

"Thank you!" the little boy yelled and then took off.

"Just so you know," Kieran drawled a few seconds later, "he did not look both ways."

"Of course, not," Casteel replied, walking so his body was between mine and the street.

"What do you think caused the quake?" I asked as we moved deeper into the city, cutting down an alley overflowing with trash. I tried not to breathe.

"I really don't know." Casteel glanced at me. "I've never heard of a quake that extended from here to Carsodonia."

"Well, if the gods were awake and had to smell this alley," Kieran began, "I understand why they'd make the ground shake."

"It's not all like this," I reminded them. "The people who live here don't have a choice, other than to make do with what they have."

"We know," Casteel said quietly, leading us onto another packed, filthy street.

Our pace was quick as we navigated the congested streets and neighborhoods, working our way around vendors, others hurrying about their daily tasks, and those who appeared to shuffle aimlessly in their ragged, limp clothing, their faces drawn, and skin ghostly pale. They reminded me so much of the Craven that my stomach turned. I wondered and then feared that they were suffering from a wasting sickness that often arrived in the night to steal the lives of those sleeping.

A sickness I now knew stemmed from the Ascended's blood hunger.

I wasn't the only one who stared at the poor souls. They also caught Kieran's and Delano's attention. The wolven's dismay and suspicion clouded the already stifling streets.

Casteel and I ditched our hats but kept our hoods up as we reached the inner parts of the city, while Delano and Kieran left their cloaks behind for whoever needed them. Dressed in all black and equipped with bloodstone short swords, they looked like any guard one would see in a city within the Kingdom of Solis.

The difference between the district near the Rise and the area which sat nestled below Castle Redrock was striking. This was where air flowed between spaced-out houses, and alleys gave way to winding courtyards and gardens. Where electricity powered restaurants and homes instead of oil, and fewer wagons and more carriages occupied paved, even streets free of waste and litter. The air was cleaner, the sidewalks and lawns maintained. We were forced to slow our steps here unless we wanted to attract the attention of the guards who patrolled, keeping those who did not need protection safe from those who did. Passing couples dressed in fur-lined cloaks and jeweled gowns headed into shops and climbing into carriages, Casteel folded an arm around my waist as I hunched my shoulders. I imagined with a cursory glance, it looked as if Casteel were trying to keep me warm while out for a stroll under the canopies of bushy ferns and overhead walkways.

Ahead, the castle resembled dried blood caked in the daylight as we crossed the wide, tree-lined road and entered a heavily forested park at the foot of the secondary wall that surrounded Castle Redrock. Once shielded by the woods, Casteel and Kieran led us through the maze of trees and wild berry bushes. No more than half an hour later, the outer wall of Redrock became visible.

"Are we going to scale the wall?" I asked.

Casteel chuckled. "That won't be necessary, my Queen. We will simply walk through it and into one of the old passageways underneath."

I glanced at him and then at Kieran, thinking of the inner wall around Castle Teerman and the section near the jacaranda trees. My head snapped back to Casteel. "Are you seriously telling me a part of the wall is down here, too?"

Grinning, Casteel tugged on the lapel of my cloak as he passed, heading for several low-hanging branches. "The Ascended are known for spending extravagant sums on rich gowns and sparkling stones. But do you know what else they are known for?" He lifted one of the branches, and through the remaining thin, bare limbs was a pile of gray rock at the foot of a narrow opening in the wall. "Their unwillingness to spend any of that coin on the most fundamental upkeep of their cities and even their castles."

"Gods," I muttered, shaking my head.

Casteel winked.

"Really is shameful." Delano knocked several pale shades of hair back from his face. One side of his lips kicked up. "And also very beneficial to us."

Casteel led the way, lifting the branches as he passed under them and holding them up for me. The earthy, musty scent that greeted us as we entered the tear in the wall and eased into a dark space reminded me too much of the tunnels that led to Iliseeum. I forced my mind to focus on the plan at hand. According to Casteel and Kieran, the courtyards could be accessed from underground walkways and chambers. From there, we would be able to get an idea of what kind of forces we were dealing with.

And then? Well, we were going to walk right into the heart of Castle Redrock, into the Great Hall, and announce that we were earlier than expected. We would catch them off guard, and that would surely mess with the heads of the guards and the Blood Crown alike, that we had been able to come in right under their noses. And being caught off guard was often a fatal weakness.

"Careful." Casteel found my hand in the darkness. "The ground slopes."

"What did the Ascended create this for?" I asked as I tried to make sense of the area we were in.

"It was here before the Ascended," Casteel said as he moved like a shadow through the nothingness. He stopped, shouldering a door that creaked softly. A torch-lit earthen tunnel awaited. "The woods led to a path straight to the bluffs. I imagine it was once used for smuggling of some sort."

"And I can tell you that the Ascended who once stayed here used it for smuggling of a different sort," Kieran commented from behind me.

People.

They could use it to smuggle mortals in and out of the castle without them ever being seen entering the grounds.

I shuddered as we walked between the damp stone walls of a passageway, my hand on the wolven dagger's hilt. We came upon a short set of steps, where the hallway split in two. Casteel headed right.

"As your advisor," Kieran began in a low voice as we passed rooms, some with old, wooden doors now barred, and others open to reveal racks of dusty bottles of what I imagined—or hoped—was wine. "I would like to formally suggest the placement of guards at the entrances of any and all tunnels at any of the residences you two may end up staying in."

Casteel snorted. "I think that is an excellent suggestion."

A sense of wariness rose in Delano, drawing my attention. "What is it?"

His pale eyes were sharp and alert as he scanned the rooms we passed. "They know we're coming. You would think that someone in their guard would have thought to station guards in these tunnels just in case, especially since the castle was breached in the past."

"Yeah, but they didn't know this would be how we came in," Kieran told him.

Delano had a point, but the Blood Crown rarely left the capital as far as I knew. Would they have known of these tunnels? Would whoever had been placed in the Royal Seat have discovered them? I imagined they had because of how easy it would be to bring people in or to…dispose of bodies.

Unease prickled my skin as we walked on, crossing another set of short steps. My gaze swept down another narrow hall that Casteel and Kieran passed, their attention focused ahead. There was a chamber to the side, one lit with several torches. I stopped suddenly, nearly causing Delano to walk into me.

"What is…?" Surprise rocked him as he saw what I did. "Holy shit."

"What?" Casteel turned as I pivoted, heading for the chamber. "What are you doing?"

"The cage—look at what's in the cage in that room." I hurried forward, not quite believing what I saw.

In the center of the small room, a large gray feline struggled to its feet behind bleached-white bars. A wicked sense of deja vu filtered through me.

"Look," I repeated, shaking my head. It couldn't be the same one, but… "This looks just like the cave cat I saw when I was a child."

"What the fuck?" muttered Kieran as he stopped at the mouth of the chamber while Casteel strode toward me.

"That…really does look like a cave cat," Casteel murmured. The large cat now prowled restlessly, its muscles tensing and bunching under its sleek coat as it peered out from between the bars with vibrant green eyes. Intelligent eyes. Knowing ones. "Why in the hell would they keep this here?"

"Or bring it with them?" Delano added softly, his eyes narrowed on the creature. "The damn thing looks underfed."

It really did.

I started toward it. The cat stopped, watching me.

"Poppy," Casteel whispered. "We need to hurry."

"I know. I just…" I didn't know how to explain what I felt. Why the eather in my chest hummed so violently now.

"Okay. So you were right. They have a cave cat." Tension crowded Kieran's voice. "But we don't have time to free the castle pets."

I knew we didn't have time, and I also doubted that a cave cat or any wild animal could be kept alive this long in a cage. But I…I couldn't stop myself. I knelt before the cage, the cat's unblinking stare capturing mine. I reached through the bars—

"Poppy! Don't you dare stick your hand—" Casteel shot forward.

Too late.

The tips of my fingers brushed soft fur as Casteel's hand wrapped around my arm. He jerked my hand back as the cat shuddered and—and kept shuddering.

"What's happening?" Panic exploded as Casteel dragged me to my feet. "Did I hurt it? I didn't mean to—"

I stopped.

We all stopped and stared.

Even Kieran.

The feline's fur stood up as it sank to its haunches, shaking fiercely. Silvery white light seeped across its eyes, spitting and crackling. Under the glossy fur, the cat's skin began to glow—

"Oh, gods," Delano groaned. "You really need to stop touching things, Poppy."

The fur retracted into skin that smoothed and became a golden, wheatish tone. Long, russet-colored hair fell forward, brushing the floor of the cage, shielding much of the nude man kneeling behind the bars, his upper body tucked close to his lower half. The sharp definition of the bones and muscles along his shoulders and legs showed how frail he was, but through the matted hair, vivid green eyes locked with mine once more.

The man shuddered again, and as quickly as he'd appeared mortal, he was once more a large feline. The cat was flat on his belly now, trembling and shivering, his head lowered.

"I'll ask again," Kieran said. "What in the actual fuck?"

"Maybe he's a wivern," Delano murmured, referencing one of the bloodlines believed to be extinct. "Or maybe a changeling? Some of the older ones could take on the form of an animal."

"I don't know." Casteel swallowed, shaken as he stared at the creature. "But we…we have to keep going."

"What?" I spun toward him. "We can't leave him."

"We have to, Poppy." He clasped my arms. "You see what kind of bars they are?" he asked, and I looked again, my stomach hollowing. "They're bone, and I doubt they're the bones of a mortal. Your abilities won't work on them, and we're not going to be able to break through them without causing a shit ton of noise."

"But—"

"And even if we did, what would we do with him?" Casteel asked, his eyes searching mine. He took a breath, lifting his hands to clasp my cheeks. "Listen to me. I know you don't want to leave him here. Neither do I. But there is nothing we can do right now."

"He's right," Kieran said, glancing back out into the hall. "We're not abandoning him."

"We're not?" I questioned.

"We know he's here. We'll ask for his freedom," Casteel explained. "That becomes a part of our deal."

"That...that is a smart idea," I said, glancing at the cat. His eyes were closed, and his sides rose and fell rapidly.

"That's because I'm smart." Casteel dipped his head, kissing my brow. "I love your compassion, Poppy," he whispered. "I really do. But we must continue."

Heart sinking, I nodded as I stared at the creature. "We'll be back," I promised him, unsure if he could understand what I said or if he was even aware that we were still there.

It took everything in me to leave the room, the man's intense stare taking up space in my mind. I didn't think he was a wivern or a changeling, because why would the bones of a deity be needed to cage one of them?

Surely that couldn't be... "Could Malec change forms?" I asked as we entered a narrow stairwell.

"No," Casteel answered from in front of me. "I know what you're thinking. That's not him. He was not the kind of deity that could shift forms."

Somehow, that didn't relieve me as it should. We rounded a bend in the stairs, and Casteel opened the door slowly. "Clear," he murmured.

We stepped out into the first floor of the castle, in a back hall. Based on the bare walls and minimal lighting, I'd bet only the servants ever used it. Quietly, we made our way toward the end of the hall where a crimson banner hung with the Royal Crest in gold. We were a few feet from the opening when Casteel cursed low and grasped my hand, hauling me behind him as he stepped forward, withdrawing a sword.

A figure stepped into the opening, coming to stand in front of the banner—a young woman with midnight hair combed back from her face and into one thick braid. Lacy black material covered her arms, upper chest, and neck, the cloth transparent except for the thicker material that ran through the lace like vines. Her tunic was fitted to her chest and stomach and flared out at her rounded hips. There were slits on either side, revealing black pants and boots that laced up to her knees.

She was no servant. If the clothing hadn't given that fact away, the crescent-shaped blades she held at her sides would have—blades the shiny black of shadowstone.

It was also the mask painted—or inked—in a deep reddish-black. A disguise that obscured most of her features as it traveled above her eyebrows, reaching her hair, and then swept below her eyes—eyes that were such an unbelievably pale shade of silver-blue, they appeared nearly leached of color—before stretching nearly to her jaw on either side. Wings. The mask looked like the wings of a bird of prey across the olive skin of her face.

Was she a…a Handmaiden? I wasn't sure, but I knew she was no vampry. She had emotions. I could feel them behind thick mental walls.

"Hello," she said rather politely. "We've been waiting for you."

I reached for the wolven dagger as Delano shot forward, thrusting out with his bloodstone sword—

The young woman was ungodly quick, a blur of lacy black and deep crimson as she spun under Delano's arm, snapping up to trap his arm between hers and his body as she twisted, hooking one leg around his waist. She spun again, forcing his body to turn away from her. Within a heartbeat, she had one crescent-shaped blade under his chin and the other pressed against his stomach.

None of us moved.

I think we were all a bit stunned by what we had just witnessed.

"Let him go," Casteel spoke in that powerful, commanding voice, the one that compelled a response. "Now."

She looked at him. "I will when I'm good and ready."

Shock flickered through Casteel and me. This woman wasn't susceptible to compulsion. My heart turned over heavily.

"Now, I was ordered to not shed blood unnecessarily, something I admit I have a tiny bad habit of doing," she told us, looking up at the hardened lines of Delano's face as he strained against her, unable to break free of her grip—the hold of a painted woman who had to be several inches shorter than me. She held Delano in place while standing on the tips of her toes. "So, please do not even think about shifting and forcing me to make bloodshed an unfortunately necessary thing."

"What in the hell are you?" Delano growled.

"A Handmaiden?" I suggested, thinking of the woman I knew as my mother—who could very well have been my mother by blood.

"Yes. That, and many other things." Unpainted lips curved up in a tight smile as her gaze flicked to us. "But right now, I'm simply your friendly escort." Her stare was unflinching as the sound of many footfalls echoed from both sides of the hall. "One of many escorts, that is."

Within seconds, Royal Guards filled both sides of the windowless hallway, swords drawn. Among them were armored knights. There were *dozens*, and the knights appeared as they had in Spessa's End. The comb atop their helmets was dyed crimson, and they wore the red-painted masks that covered the upper parts of their faces.

I exhaled raggedly.

"Let him go," Casteel demanded, his chin dipping low. "And we'll behave if you behave."

Those eerie eyes focused on him, and I sensed a quick burst of tartness—a great unease—from the woman. But it was brief, and she smiled broadly then, revealing two rows of…fangless teeth. "Of course," she replied quite cheerfully. "I excel at behaving."

I had a feeling that was a lie.

We waited, hearts pounding, and the eather in my chest straining against my skin. I could take them all out, just like I had with the Unseen on the road to Evaemon.

"You're going to let me go?" Delano asked, and the woman nodded. "Then you have to actually let me go."

"I will," she said, those eyes shifting back to me. "But you see, you have all already misbehaved, sneaking in underground." She tsked softly under her breath, and energy pulsed through me, beneath my skin. "Going where you should not have gone." Her flat eyes bored into mine. "Seeing what you should not have seen."

"The man in the cage?"

Her smile faded. "Our Queen will not be very pleased by that, but I am willing to give all of you the benefit of the doubt. Especially you," she said to me. "Do not try anything. If you do, it will not be your lives you forfeit. It will be the lives of those who were riding toward our east gates."

I stiffened as disbelief echoed through me. Vonetta and the others wouldn't have made it to the gates yet. "How?"

"We saw them and expedited their arrival," she replied, the blades at Delano's throat and stomach steady. "This morning, to be exact."

Gods.

"Where are they?" Casteel demanded through gritted teeth.

"They are safe and currently waiting for you all to join them."

"And we're supposed to believe you?" Kieran accused.

"She speaks the truth," came a familiar voice from our right.

My breath caught as I turned, and Casteel tensed as if prepared to launch himself at me. Ian stepped out from the hall, his gaze moving from us to the woman and Delano. He looked...tense, his paler-than-should-be features strained.

"You were told no unnecessary bloodshed," Ian spoke quietly.

"See?" The woman raised her brows at us. "And I haven't spilled any. Not even a drop." Without warning, she released Delano and stepped back, lowering her blades.

Delano spun around, his chest rising and falling as he glared at the young woman. She winked at him.

"She has told you all the truth. Your friends are fine." Ian's gaze touched mine. "I can take you to them, and the Queen will meet us there. You may keep your weapons."

I looked over at Casteel. His jaw flexed as he nodded curtly. "Well, we might as well. We are here to see the Blood Crown."

And it wasn't like we had a choice.

Gods, this was why there'd been no guards underneath. It could've also been why we'd had no problem entering the city. They already knew we were coming in using a different route, and earlier than expected. We'd lost the upper hand before we even realized it, and *we* were the ones caught off guard.

The guards waited until we started walking, led by the strange woman. Casteel stuck close to my side as Ian fell into step beside me.

He stared straight ahead as we traveled the windowless hall. "I hope you're well, sister," he said, and I looked up at him, staying silent. "And that your travels after we last met went well."

My gaze sharpened on him, and he glanced briefly at me. I could read nothing from those fathomless eyes or from him, but was he trying to ask about Nyktos's guards without giving anything away?

"They did," I lied.

His features eased in the slightest, and I swore it was relief. "Good."

"You're in—" I stopped myself from blurting out what I suspected. The woman in front of us looked over her shoulder. "You're alone? Where is your wife?"

"Lady Claudeya remains in the capital."

Casteel's hand brushed mine as we entered the Great Hall. Like the hallway, there was no sunlight. Heavy, deep crimson drapes covered the windows, and a knight was stationed in front of each one. Several small tables of untouched food and drinks were situated between a handful of seats and settees before a raised dais. The chairs were occupied. Vonetta rose, followed by Emil, Lyra, and Hisa. Naill was already standing behind them. None of them looked entirely thrilled, but I could feel relief coming from them and us. Someone else remained seated in one of the chairs, partially blocked by—

Vonetta caught my stare and stepped aside.

Air punched out of my lungs as Tawny rose, a beautiful sight in a simple rose-hued gown with long, fluttering sleeves.

"Poppy?" she whispered, stepping forward as she glanced at Vonetta and Emil. "You're really—"

"It is my sister," Ian cut her off, and a look passed between my brother and her, one that might have been of warning, but a knot expanded and tripled in my throat because Tawny wasn't…

She hadn't Ascended.

I started toward her, but Casteel caught my hand.

"It's okay," Ian stated quietly, and the look Casteel shot him said that he didn't think much of anything my brother said.

But Emil nodded. "It is."

Casteel's jaw worked, but he released my hand, and I rushed forward at the same moment Tawny swept past Emil, her mass of brown and gold curls as wild and beautiful as ever. The moment I reached her, I wrapped my arms around her, and when I felt her warm skin under her dress, I shook. I trembled even harder when she curled her arms around me, holding me as tightly as I held her, and I could feel that she was shaking just as badly—I could also feel her emotions. Bubbly and sugary wonder. Earthy and woodsy relief, and the bitter taste of—

"The Queen isn't what she seems," Tawny whispered in my ear as her fear coated the back of my throat. "You need—"

"Poppy looks so different," Ian interrupted, having come up behind us. "Doesn't she?"

I pulled back, my eyes searching Tawny's as she nodded. I spared a quick look at Ian and saw that the Handmaiden was eyeing us as she moved slowly behind Casteel and Kieran. Both of them had crept closer. Tawny…she knew the truth about the Queen and the Ascended, and Ian was trying to protect her.

"I *know*," I said, meeting Tawny's gaze. "I do look different without the veil."

Tawny's lips trembled, but she forced a smile as she looked between Ian and me. "You look beautiful without the veil."

I slid my hands to her arms. "I'm so happy to see you. I've missed you so much. And I've been so worried."

"As I've missed you," Tawny replied, aware of the guards circling the room. "But there is no reason to worry." She swallowed as she looked up at where Casteel had come to stand at my side. "Hello." She paused, eyes narrowing slightly. "*Hawke*."

How she said his name and the look she gave him was so Tawny, I almost started crying.

"Hello, Tawny." Casteel bowed his head. "I am relieved to see that you are well. Although I wish we were confirming that under different circumstances."

"As do we all," Ian murmured under his breath.

The young woman drifted closer, her still gaze seeming to miss nothing. Tawny started to glance back at her, but then the Handmaiden's gaze flicked to the entrance of the Great Hall.

Awareness pressed against the nape of my neck and my back, erupting in icy shivers. Ian stepped back, using his arm to guide Tawny to do the same. I knew before I turned what I would find, but I still moved as if I were caught in thick, cold slush. I looked past the line of guards with their black mantles.

Crimson and black silk skirts flowed like water across the stone floor. The gown's deep vee cut between the swells of breasts, reaching the impossibly narrow waist encased in rows of rubies chained together. Red-tipped fingers clasped together. Garnets strung and clasped tightly around slender wrists and a pale neck. Lush, red lips tipped up in a faint smile. A turned-up nose pierced with an onyx stone. High cheekbones flushed artfully with rouge. Black eyes glimmered under the golden chandeliers, outlined and winged in black. Arched, deep brown brows. Hair that shone a dark auburn was swept up and back so the mass spilled over an elegant shoulder in thick, loose curls that brushed the rows of rubies at the waist. Carved from pure, polished ruby and consisting of twelve hoops connected by oval pieces of onyx and topped with diamonds crafted into spires, the Blood Crown was one of the most beautiful and horrendous works of art that had ever been created.

As was the woman who wore it.

Queen Ileana looked just like I remembered—beautiful in a sultry way few could ever achieve and carrying a warmth to her features even fewer Ascended had ever been able to master. Our gazes locked, and I couldn't look away as memories of her brushing my hair back from the ruined side of my face, of reading to me when I couldn't sleep, of holding me when I cried for my mother and father, rushed into me, over and over.

And maybe that was why I didn't see who stood just behind her, to her right. Maybe that was why it took more than a moment for me to register the sudden explosion of icy shock rolling off Casteel, and that he'd jerked back a step. My gaze shifted to the man who stood there. It wasn't King Jalara.

This man's hair nearly reached his shoulders and was a light brown that showed hints of blond, but the sharp cheekbones, the straight nose, and the proud line of his jaw were uncannily familiar. And then his full mouth curved upward, as he stared up at us. And a…a *dimple* appeared in his left cheek. The smile, though, it was all wrong, lacking warmth and any trace of humanity.

"Brother," the stranger said, and a rolling tide of shivers shot straight down my side at the deep, gritty sound of his voice. "It has been far too long."

Casteel had stiffened beside me. "Malik."

Chapter 45

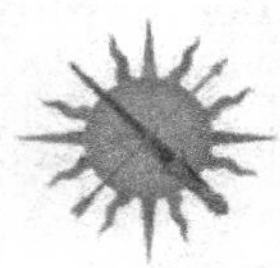

"What a happy reunion," Queen Ileana announced, her smile tight as she took in the two brothers staring at each other.

I hardly heard her—was barely aware of the Handmaiden drifting in and out from between us like a wraith, coming to stand on the other side of the Queen.

What I was staring at didn't make sense.

And I wasn't the only one who appeared frozen in shock as we stared at Prince Malik Da'Neer. How was he even free? Standing beside the Blood Queen, seemingly healthy and whole? He looked nothing like the emaciated, frail man we'd seen in the cage below. His golden bronze skin lacked the haggardness of starvation. His hair gleamed, and the polished shine of his boots, the cut of his breeches, and the tailored shirt and deep grey vest he wore dripped with wealth and privilege.

It didn't make sense.

Or it couldn't, because the only reason he'd be here was unfathomable.

"Gods," Kieran uttered, lifting a hand and then halting.

"Malik." Casteel's voice was hoarse, and the agony slicing through him stole my breath. I reached out, grasping his hand. His gaze swung between his brother and the Blood Queen. His—and all the others'—shock pelted me like icy rain. "No."

His brother's head tilted as his gaze flicked to where my hand was wrapped around Casteel's. "I see you've gotten yourself married, Cas," he said, and Casteel flinched as the breath he took punched from him. "Wish I could've been there." Bright, golden eyes met mine, and I felt Kieran shudder from where he stood beside me. "Congratulations."

"What has she done to you?" Casteel demanded, rattled to his very core.

"Opened my eyes," Malik replied.

"To what?" Casteel choked.

"To the truth." His head straightened, and I reached out with my senses, finding a thick wall shielding his emotions. "Just as she will open all your eyes."

Casteel took a step back, his disbelief as potent as his sorrow. "This can't be real." His head swung toward the Queen. He started toward her, but I tightened my grip on his hand as several of the knights stepped forward. They weren't my concern. It was the Handmaiden, whose gaze sharpened on Casteel. "What in the fuck have you done to him?"

"*Casteel.*" Her voice reached us like a snake in the grass.

His entire body went rigid beside mine, and her red lips curved up as she extended a hand toward him.

I reacted without thought, grabbing her arm. The silk of her sleeve wrinkled under my grip. "You will never lay a finger on him again."

The Handmaiden stepped forward, but Queen Ileana held up a hand as her dark gaze slid to mine. "Penellaphe." Those dark eyes roamed my face, touching briefly on the scars and then continuing on. And I thought…gods, I thought her features softened and warmed. "I have no interest in laying a hand on your husband. That would be incredibly disrespectful."

"As if you care for what is respectful," I shot back.

Her brows rose, and then she laughed softly. "Ian," she called, and I saw my brother stiffen from the corner of my eye. "You didn't tell me that our dear Penellaphe not only found her tongue but also sharpened it."

Ian said nothing.

Queen Ileana tugged on her arm, but I held on for a moment more. I didn't know why. Maybe just to prove I could, that my tongue wasn't the only thing about me that now had sharpened edges. I slowly let go, lifting one finger at a time.

An eyebrow rose as she stared at me. Then she leaned her head in, and the scents of rose and vanilla reached me. "Poppy," she said softly, holding my gaze. As close as she was, I thought her eyes…weren't as dark as an Ascended's normally were. I could see her pupils. I opened my senses, but I felt nothing from her, which wasn't a surprise. "How quickly you've turned on me, after all the years I protected you, cared for you, and kept you safe."

Her words did nothing to my heart. "You mean after spending years lying to me and keeping me in a cage?"

"You were not caged, child. I am sure your dear Prince can tell you that."

Casteel's head whipped in her direction, and his fury blasted my skin. "A room and a life of lies is still a cage," I bit out, refusing to look away. "And I am not a child, nor is he a Prince."

Queen Ileana's brows knitted and then smoothed out as she glanced at Casteel. Another soft laugh left her as she pulled back. "Well, that explains so much." She looked over her shoulder at Malik. "The younger brother surpasses the eldest." She turned back to us. "And the Maiden becomes the Queen." The corners of her lips lifted again. "Just as I had always hoped for you."

Warning bells rang, but they'd been ringing since she entered the room with Prince Malik at her side, as if he were her Consort. "Where is the King?" I asked.

"In the capital," she answered, eyeing Kieran. She reached to straighten the collar of his tunic but caught my move toward her. "Territorial, aren't you? Never would've expected that. I have a question for you, dear. One that may make Ian very uncomfortable." Her crown glimmered as she tipped her head back. "Are you Joined to this wolven? Or is it the pretty blond one? Or one of those oh-so-gorgeous females?"

The fact that she knew of the Joining didn't escape any of us. "I'm bonded to them," I answered, waiting for her gaze to settle on me. "To all of them."

Her eyes widened slightly, and then she clapped her hands together, surprising me. Casteel shot me a quick glance as the Queen looked over her shoulder at Malik. "Look at what you've missed out on."

"I'm looking," he replied dryly. "And I'm seeing."

"What in the hell is that supposed to mean?" Casteel snarled, his shock at seeing his brother—at the betrayal— giving way to fury that tasted of blood instead of anger.

"You see, I've always seen my dear Penellaphe as the future Queen of Atlantia." Queen Ileana turned to Delano, her grin resurfacing as his lip curled in disgust. She raised a hand and snapped her fingers. I tensed, but it was a small horde of servants who answered her summons, filtering into the room, carrying trays of glasses. "Just married to the wrong brother."

I choked on my breath as Casteel stared at her. "What?" I couldn't have heard her right.

"Drinks anyone?" Queen Ileana offered, and none of us accepted, not even Emil or Naill, who both looked as if they could use an entire bottle at the moment. One shoulder lifted in a delicate shrug in response to their refusal.

"What was that supposed to mean?" Casteel pressed.

"I had planned for my Penellaphe to marry Malik," she answered, and yes, I had heard her correctly the first time.

"It's true," Malik confirmed, plucking up a glass of what I sincerely hoped was red wine. He lifted it toward me. "I was your Ascension." His lips curved into a smirk. "Or at least that's what we could call it." He winked and took a drink. "But I suppose it could be considered an Ascension of the…flesh?"

Casteel exploded.

He shot toward his brother, lips peeled back, and fangs bared. He was fast, but Kieran launched himself at Casteel, wrapping both arms around his waist. "That's what they want," Kieran said. "Don't give it to them, brother. Don't."

Queen Ileana's laughter was like tinkling windchimes as she helped herself to a glass. "Please, do," she said, and I saw the knights and guards back away from Malik and Casteel. "I'm curious to know who would win this fight. My bet is on Casteel. He has always been a fighter." She grinned as she lifted one of Vonetta's braids as she drifted past her. Vonetta's lips peeled back in a silent snarl. "Even when he was on the verge of being broken."

My head jerked to her. "Shut the fuck up."

Her laughter died in a hush as she turned to me. The Handmaiden stepped back while Malik took another drink of his wine, one eyebrow arched. Ian edged toward me as Tawny paled. Casteel stopped struggling to get at his brother as he and Kieran turned to where I stood, my chest humming with eather and rage, rising and falling rapidly with my breaths.

"I am being kind, *Queen* Penellaphe, and hospitable. Because I will always have a great fondness for you, no matter where we stand," she said, her voice cool as she smiled at Naill. "I've invited you to speak with me, so we could hopefully come to an agreement about what the future holds. I assume that's why you two agreed."

"It is," I bit out.

"I've even had drinks brought in and offered food to your friends, even though they attempted to trick me into believing that it was you instead of her." Queen Ileana gestured at Lyra with her glass, and the wolven snarled at her. "But do not mistake my fondness for weakness or for permission to speak to me as if I am nothing more than gutter trash. I am *the* Queen, so show some damn respect."

I opened my mouth to tell her exactly what I thought of showing her respect, but Casteel spoke. "You are right about why we're here. We are here to talk about the future. Yours."

Standing before the dais, she faced us as the Handmaiden shadowed her on one side of the room and Malik from the other. "Then speak."

Casteel had managed to get his anger under control while I was quickly losing my grip on mine. "We came with—"

"An ultimatum? I know," she said, and Casteel snapped his mouth shut. "Release your brother and allow Atlantia to take back the lands east of New Haven? Or you will reveal the truth about the Ascended and Atlantia by using the once-Maiden as proof? Destroy us by collapsing our foundation of lies? Is that correct?"

I stilled.

All of us did.

"How?" growled Casteel. "How do you know that?"

"You have…or *had* an advisor who was very eager to rid Atlantia of the rightful heir to the throne," she answered. "So eager, in fact, that he told several of my protégés of your plans."

Alastir.

"That son of a bitch," Naill muttered.

I could barely breathe through my anger. "I want to kill him all over again," I seethed.

"He's dead?" Queen Ileana smiled. "Gods, you have no idea how happy that makes me. Thank you."

"Your gratitude is unwanted," Casteel snapped.

She shrugged again. "Anyway, your plan is clever. If you two waltzed into Solis, loving and happy together, it would shake our control. It could even topple the—what do you call it? The Blood Crown? After all, they do believe the Maiden was Chosen by the gods.

But you see, that would only work if you thought that any of us would simply relinquish Solis. I'd see the whole godsdamn kingdom burn before I ever allowed Atlantia to seize even one single acre of land."

I inhaled sharply as Ian closed his eyes, lowering his chin.

"So that's it?" Casteel stepped forward. "You really want war?"

"I want Atlantia," she replied.

"Then it's war," I stated.

The ruby crown glinted as she shook her head. "Not necessarily."

"I don't see how there is any other option," Casteel returned. "You've rejected our offer."

"But you haven't rejected mine."

Casteel laughed darkly. "It'll be a no."

"You haven't heard what I have to say." The Blood Queen held her glass with both hands. "You will claim Atlantia in my name and swear sovereignty to me. You may retain your titles of Prince and Princess, but you will ensure that several of my Dukes and Duchesses are able to safely cross the Skotos to establish Royal Seats throughout Atlantia. You will dismantle your armies and convince the people of Atlantia that this is for the best, of course." Her head cocked to the side. "Oh, and I want the former King and Queen brought to the capital, where they will be tried for treason."

Malik showed no response as he now stood beside the Handmaiden. Not a flicker of emotion for what would be a death sentence for his parents.

"You're out of your mind," Casteel breathed, and he was right. There was no other explanation for why she would think we'd ever agree to that.

"If you refuse, then war is inevitable," she continued as if Casteel hadn't spoken. "But first, I do believe you should understand what you'll be up against if your armies cross the Skotos. We have over a hundred thousand guards who have sworn an oath to the Royal Crown. They may be mortal, but they want coin and a lifetime of riches—which I can provide. They're more than willing to fight and die for that, than hedge their bets on Atlantia being any different than what they have now," she told us. "We have several thousand knights, and they will not be nearly as easy for you to fight in combat as you think. But that's not all we have."

"The Revenants?" I finished for her.

Queen Ileana's brows lifted and then smoothed out. "Interesting," she murmured, and my heart skipped a beat. I didn't dare look at Ian.

"But do you know what a Revenant is?" When none of us answered, she shifted her glass to one hand and summoned the Handmaiden forward.

Malik's jaw hardened as the Handmaiden went to join the Queen. It was brief, and I wasn't even sure if his reaction had anything to do with the summoning or not. The Handmaiden sheathed her swords along her thighs and stood perfectly still beside the Queen.

"A Revenant is an amazing thing." Queen Ileana angled her body toward the Handmaiden. "A very old thing that fell out of favor all the way back when the gods walked among man," she said, picking up the young woman's braid and draping it over her shoulder. "They are faster than most Atlantians could hope to be. Perhaps even faster than a wolven. They are incredibly strong, even those vertically challenged as this one beside me."

The young woman had said that she was many things when I'd questioned if she was a Handmaiden. She was also a Revenant, and we'd seen just how fast and strong she was.

And she didn't look even remotely pleased at her height being referenced.

"They are exceptionally trained fighters, born with inherent skill. They are good for one thing." The Queen smiled as she drew a thumb across the red-painted mask. "And that is killing."

The Revenant's strange eyes remained open, fixed on some point beyond us.

"Any mortal can become skilled at killing, can they not?" Queen Ileana asked. "But a Revenant isn't really mortal. They are something else entirely."

Queen Ileana nodded at a nearby knight. He strode forward, unsheathing a long-bladed knife. I stiffened as a sudden rush of desperation burned through me, leaving behind the choking smoke of hopelessness. It came from her—the Revenant—even as she stood there, expressionless, her gaze vacant. She didn't want—

Malik jerked as if he were about to take a step forward but stopped himself a second before the knight thrust the knife into the female's chest—into her heart.

Tawny cried out, smacking her hand over her mouth as I stepped back out of shock, bumping into Casteel. His eyes were wide as he watched the knight yank the knife free. Ian had turned his head away as the knight stepped aside. The lace of the Handmaiden's tunic quickly became wet as she stumbled to the side and then went down on one knee.

Blood trickled out of her mouth as she stretched her neck back. "Ouch," she rasped and then toppled to her side.

"She's a fighter, too," the Queen commented as a pool of red rapidly spread out from under her prone body. She looked up at Vonetta. "You. Check to see if she lives for me?"

Vonetta glanced at us and then started forward. She knelt and pressed her fingers against the side of the young woman's neck. Swallowing, she shook her head as she pulled her hand back. "There's no pulse, and I…I can smell it. Death."

I had a feeling they weren't talking about the same kind of scent they picked up from me.

Vonetta rose and quickly rejoined Emil and the others. "She's dead."

"Good gods," Kieran uttered, staring at the young woman on the floor. Her blood filled the crevices between the tiles, stretching toward us. "What was the point in that?"

"Patience," Ileana said, taking a sip.

Casteel's hand flattened against my back as my gaze darted from the Revenant to the Queen and then to Malik, whose gaze hadn't once left the still body.

"What is…?" I forced out a ragged breath. "What is wrong with you?" I asked of the Queen as I stared at the woman, at the blood spreading under her hand—

A finger twitched.

I gasped, and Casteel leaned forward, his eyes narrowed. Another finger spasmed, and then the arm. A second passed, and her entire body moved, her back bowing as her mouth opened. Dragging in deep, gulping breaths, she pressed her hand over where the wound should be, where her heart had been pierced. She sat up, blinking, and then rose to her feet and looked at us with those lifeless eyes.

"Ta-da," the Queen exclaimed with a snap of her fingers.

Kieran drew back. "What in the actual fuck?"

"The actual fuck you're asking about is a Revenant," the Queen replied. "They cannot easily be killed. You can stab them with bloodstone or any stone. Cut their throats. Set them on fire. Slice their limbs from their body, and let them bleed out, and they will come back whole." She smiled almost warmly at the Revenant. "They always come back."

They always come back.

I shuddered as I stared at the young woman, unable to process how that was even possible, because it wasn't the same as healing someone or even snatching them from the grasp of death. I didn't think my touch could… regrow severed limbs.

"What about their heads?" Casteel asked. "Do they regrow one of them?"

The Queen's smile grew as she nodded.

"Impossible," breathed Delano.

"Do you want me to show you?" she offered.

"No," I said quickly, the Revenant's desperation still an echo in my soul. "That won't be necessary."

The Queen actually looked a little disappointed as Emil rubbed his palm against the center of his chest. "That is…that is an abomination to the gods."

The Revenant said nothing, but the Queen did. "To some, they are."

And I thought of what Nyktos had said. He was right. They were an abomination of life and death.

"How?" I forced out. "How are they created?"

"They aren't simply created. They are born, the third sons and daughters of two mortal parents. Not all carry this…trait, but those who do remain unremarkable unless discovered," she said, and a sickening knowledge rolled through me. The children given to the Rite. This is what became of some of them. "The blood of a King or one destined is needed to ensure that they reach their full potential, but apparently…" She looked over at Prince Malik. "I don't have that anymore."

Malik smiled apologetically.

"And, well, the rest isn't all that important," she stated. "I have many of them, enough to become an army that you have no hope of ever defeating."

Ian…he hadn't been exaggerating. How could one fight an army that would just continuously rise after falling? Could Nyktos's guards even defeat them?

"So…" Queen Ileana drew the word out. "This is what you would go to war against." Her dark eyes settled on me. "The War of Two Kings never ended," she said. "There has just been a strained truce. That is all. And now you must see how hopeless it would be to believe that you could fight against Solis."

"Then why haven't you just seized Atlantia?" Casteel demanded.

"Half of my armies would die or become lost crossing the Skotos. Even the Revenants wouldn't fare well in the mist," she stated. "Besides, I do not want the Atlantian people to hate me. I want their respect. Their loyalty. Not their loathing."

"Well," Casteel started. "That ship has already sailed."

"Feelings can be changed," she said dismissively. "Especially when their Queen is the daughter of the Queen of Solis."

"My *mother*?" I laughed hoarsely. "I thought you were my grandmother."

"I don't know why that silly bitch told you that," she replied. "Duchess Teerman was loyal but not exactly the most intelligent."

I shook my head in utter disbelief. "Your claim of being my mother is such a ridiculous lie, I cannot believe you would even think that I would entertain such a statement."

"Oh, please do not tell me that you still believe Coralena is your mother. That treacherous bitch did not carry you for nine months and then spend hours screaming in pain to bring you into this world," she spat, climbing the wide, short steps that circled the entire chamber and led to the alcove of the curtained windows.

"Neither did you," I growled.

"Is that so?" she replied.

"You're a vampry." Casteel's hand pressed against my lower back. "You cannot have children."

"She is not a vampry," Ian said, looking at me. His features were drawn. "And she speaks the truth. She is your mother."

"Coralena was Ian's mother. Leopold was his father," Queen Ileana said, placing her empty glass on a marble podium. It was then when I realized that there were no more servants in the room. "And Cora was my most favorite Handmaiden—my most trusted. I had her care for you so that none of those who sought to gain what I had could use you, my child, against me—and many would be foolish enough to try. I trusted her, and she betrayed me. She and her worthless husband thought they could steal you away. Apparently, she discovered my intention to marry you to Prince Malik, finally bringing the two kingdoms together, and she didn't approve of it."

My heart thudded as she spoke. "Coralena survived the attack, by the way. She was a Revenant, after all." She smoothed her hands over the ruby chains at her waist. "However, she did not survive my wrath."

I shuddered, and Casteel curled his arm around my waist.

"I didn't want to do it. That hurt me more than you will ever believe. She was like a daughter to me, and she betrayed me." The Queen drew in a deep breath and then motioned the knight away from the curtained window. "I am not a vampry. Nor is Ileana my name—my first name that is." She curled her fingers around the edges of the curtain, and I reached down, gripping Casteel's arm. "The first name I was born with is one you've probably heard. It was Isbeth."

Chapter 46

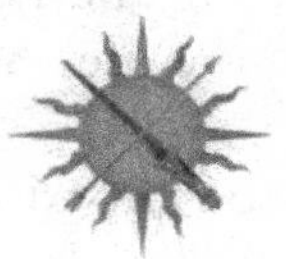

The shock that echoed through the room was contagious.

"Yes, *that* Isbeth," she continued, dragging her hand down the length of the curtain. "I was King Malec's lover—his confidante, his friend, and his…his everything. And your mother…" She looked over her shoulder at Casteel, her grip on the curtain tightening. "She took that away. She poisoned me with belladonna. Can you believe that? Tacky." Her lip curled. "If Malec hadn't found me in time, I wouldn't be standing here, but he did. He just…knew something was wrong." She pressed her hand against her chest as she held us all in suspended silence. "We were heartmates. He would have done anything for me."

Queen Ileana—no, if what she was saying was true, Queen *Isbeth* tipped her head back. "He gave me his blood, unsure of what would happen. He was just desperate and refused to allow me to die."

I thought of Casteel—what he'd done to save me.

"But he didn't make me into a vampry. I wasn't the first. You see, deities aren't like Atlantians. Their blood is far more powerful than that."

I looked at Casteel. "Is that true?"

"It is," his brother answered. "When deities Ascend a mortal, they do not become a vampry. They become something without the pesky limitations the Ascended have."

Casteel let out a harsh breath, and I knew he was thinking the same as I was. That his parents *had* to know this entire time that Queen Ileana was…that she was Isbeth.

Just then, the Blood Queen tore down the curtain, letting bright sunlight flow in through the window. The knights scattered back from where the sunlight crept across the floor. Ian moved quickly, avoiding contact, but she…

She stood in the flood of sunlight, the crown and the jewels at her throat, wrists, and waist twinkling. She did not begin screaming in pain, twisting in agony or decaying.

Nothing happened.

Just like nothing had happened when I walked into the sunlight.

I stared at her, my chest rising and falling. "What…what are you?"

"I've been many things in my life. A daughter. A friend. A whore. A mistress."

"That's a hell of a list to be proud of," Casteel growled as I saw Naill grip the back of a chair as he shook his head. "The mistress of King Malec. Congratulations."

"Malec?" She smirked at him as the guards shifted in closer, replacing the knights who now stood in the shadowy alcoves. "I was his mistress. I loved him. I still do. That is no lie. And then your mother had to go and ruin him. But, no. I am no longer the mistress of any man—mortal or god."

"God?" I coughed out. "Malec was—"

"A god," Isbeth cut me off. "He was Nyktos's son, and Nyktos is no normal god. He is a Primal, something far older and more powerful," she said, and I knew that part to be true. "Any that carry his blood would be a god. But Eloana never knew that, did she? I did. I knew exactly who and what he was. A deity cannot make a vampry, and neither can a god."

Casteel's hand slipped away from me. "You lie."

"Why would I lie about that?" She shook her head as she followed the trail of light to the steps. "Malec was a god."

"Why would he pretend to be a deity if he was a god?" Casteel demanded.

"Because he grew tired of being held in Iliseeum while the children, generations removed, were allowed to explore beyond the Mountains of Nyktos, and he could do just that. Nyktos's children were born in the mortal realm, just as his Consort was."

I jolted, remembering what Nyktos had said about the Primals' powers in the realm beyond Iliseeum. Only those born within the realm could retain their powers here.

I spared a brief glance at Casteel as she said, "Come now, you do know your own history? I lived it, Casteel. How do you think Malec managed to kill the other deities? Seize power like he did? A deity couldn't have done that, not even one descended from Nyktos. And there were no deities of that line. There has only ever been the two sons."

A long moment of silence passed, one where I could feel the chains of disbelief loosening and falling away as we stared at the Blood Queen, who clearly was not a vampry.

"Did my mother know what he really was?" Casteel forced out.

"That is at least one lie she didn't tell. And as I said, I am not a vampry, and I am not a deity." Her gaze focused back on me. "Because a god Ascended me, I became one."

"That is not how that works," Casteel growled, and while I didn't know much about the gods, I had to believe he was right. One couldn't just be made into a god.

She raised a brow. "It's not?"

Vonetta and Lyra inched toward Casteel and me, just as Naill and the others were also doing—and had been attempting for several minutes. Their loathing and fear matched that of Delano and Kieran, and that said something. If she truly was a god, wouldn't they be drawn to her like they were to me?

"But back then, many of the Atlantians didn't know that, and when they started Ascending others, they just assumed that I was the same." Her eyes were closed. "Malec told me his plans. That he would pretend to side with Eloana and the Council and help eradicate the Ascended. Said that it was the only way. Because you see, he couldn't let the Ascended continue. He understood their threat better than most did." She laughed then, the sound without humor. "Even exiled, he would stay behind and fight because he had honor. But I bet no one speaks of that, do they?"

Eloana had, in a way. She had said that Malec was a good man and King for the most part. Just not a good husband.

"So, he snuck me out of Atlantia when the war had just begun, but I had to leave alone. It would've been too risky to bring anyone with me, even our son."

My heart turned over as Casteel asked hoarsely, "A son?"

She nodded. "I had him before I was poisoned, and he was…he was like you, Penellaphe. A blessing. He was the most beautiful baby boy there ever was. And even as a small child, he had the touch. The *gift*." A fine tremor ran through her. "Malec would find me. He promised that once he was able to leave, he would. He would keep our son safe and bring him to me, and we would simply spend an eternity together—just the three of us, no Crown and no kingdom. He promised to take us to Iliseeum."

Her eyes opened, and they…they glistened with tears. "Years went by, and the war spread across the lands. I had to…I had to hide what I was. With my dark eyes, the other Ascended never questioned what I was, so I hid from the daylight and stayed among the Ascended, still believing that Malec would come for me. I never lost faith. I met many who sheltered me, and it was Jalara of Vodina Isles who I discovered would be gathering his forces outside of Pompay, where a sizable Atlantian force had gathered. I knew that was my chance to learn what'd happened to Malec and my son." Her nostrils flared. "He would've been on the cusp of manhood by then, and he probably wouldn't have recognized me, but I didn't care. I knew I would help him remember."

She came down a step. "So, I joined Jalara at Pompay, and you know what I saw? The newly crowned King Valyn Da'Neer, leading the Atlantian army. And I knew." Her hands closed into fists as her voice quavered. "I knew then that my son was gone. That he had probably been gone since the moment I left Atlantia, and they would've only been able to get to him if they'd done something to Malec. For years, I waited for them, never giving up, and they took that from me! He was all I ever wanted," she screamed, and I shuddered at her words. Her chest strained the gown as she inhaled deeply. "They took *everything* from me. My *son*. My Malec, and I did nothing wrong but love, and gods, I will *never* love like that again. That was all. That was it." She sliced her hand through the air. "They could've stopped this at any point. They just had to tell the truth about Malec and I. That I was not a vampry. That he was exiled wrongly. But in doing that, they'd have to confess what *they'd* done. Tell all their lies. Admit to murdering *children*," she hissed, and I flinched then because I…I knew that they had. "And they would have to give back the Crown if that was what Malec wanted. So, of course, they didn't. And here we are," she said quietly. "All of this?" She lifted her hands and spread her arms wide. "All of this is because of them. They created this fire and fanned it, and now it's out of control because I am the fire, and I will take everything from them."

From them.

Not Atlantia.

Not even them, really. From *her*, was what she meant. From Eloana.

The breath I took lodged in my throat. The lies… So many damn lies soaked in blood. Both kingdoms were at fault for this mess.

Both Queens.

"All of this for revenge?" I whispered. "You've created this kingdom of blood and lies for revenge?"

"In the beginning, yes, but it's so much bigger than that now. Now, it's more than me." Isbeth's eyes met mine. My mother's eyes met mine. "You were going to take it all back for me. You'd marry Malik, and through you, I would seize Atlantia."

I shuddered. "That's why you made me the Maiden? Was there even another Maiden?"

"That doesn't matter," she said, pressing her hands together. "You had to be protected. That was how I kept you safe until it was time."

"Time to marry a man you've kept prisoner for how many years?" I exclaimed.

"Does he look like a prisoner to you?" Queen Isbeth looked to where Malik stood beside the Revenant.

"I know what you did to Casteel. I am not foolish or naïve enough to be convinced that you didn't do the same thing to Malik," I said, voice low as I stepped in front of Casteel as if I could shield him from the words I'd just spoken. "No matter what either of you claim, and I am sorry, gods, I cannot believe I'm even saying this, but I am sorry for what was done to you and your son."

"Who would've been your brother," she said, eyes widening.

"*He* is my brother." I pointed at Ian. "He is my brother," I repeated. "What was done to you was wrong. What was done to your son was horrible."

"It was," she murmured. "It truly was."

"But you are no better," I said. "What you've done to children? To those given to the Temples that don't have this Revenant trait. What about the ones who died of the wasting sicknesses—those fed on by vamprys that you helped create? What of the second sons and daughters that you conned into believing that the Ascension was an act bestowed on them by the gods? What about the people of Solis, who live in fear of the gods who aren't even asleep? Who can barely fend for their families while being forced to give their children away? What about the Craven, *Isbeth*?" I demanded. "What about me? I'm your daughter, and you sent me off to live with a man whose favorite pastime was whipping me and humiliating me."

Her chin lifted on a sharp inhale. "I didn't know about that. I would've flayed the skin from his body and left him alive to be eaten by buzzards if I had known."

"That doesn't matter!" I shouted, tears clouding my eyes because this—all of this was so messed up. So wrong. "You can't blame Eloana or Valyn or Atlantia for anything else. This was you. All you. You became this."

Casteel side-stepped me then, forcing me back until I felt Kieran's hands on my shoulders. "I think it's safe to say that we do not agree to your terms."

"You don't really have that authority, do you?" Queen Isbeth said, her lips thinning. "I know what she is. She is the true ruler of Atlantia. You're just a pretty accessory."

"Oh, I'm pretty, all right." Casteel's chin dipped. "And I'm also a very deadly accessory. Don't forget that."

The Blood Queen smirked. "I haven't. Trust me."

Sickened by the knowledge—by the implications and the reality of what…what my mother had done to Casteel—to so many people—I nearly doubled over. "No," I forced out. "No, we do not now, nor will we ever agree to your demands."

"You won't like what happens if you refuse me," she said softly. "Don't do this, Penellaphe. Give me what I want and end this."

"How will giving you Atlantia end this?" I asked, genuinely curious. "Would it mean you will stop the Ascended from feeding on innocents? Will you stop the Rite? How will giving you Atlantia change what you did to them?"

Dark eyes met mine. "It won't, but you're not in a position to negotiate." She shook her head. "I can't believe you're making me do this."

"I'm not making you do anything."

"But you are." Queen Isbeth's shoulders went back as her gaze remained fixed on mine. "Kill him."

My entire body jerked as I reached out to grab Casteel because she had to be talking about him, but no guard or knight moved toward us. Neither did the Revenant. I scanned the room—

Casteel shouted. "No!"

I locked eyes with Ian. A knight had stalked up behind him, sword already unsheathed. The knight was fast, sweeping the blade through the air and then slicing it through tissue, muscle, and bone. Ending life.

Chapter 47

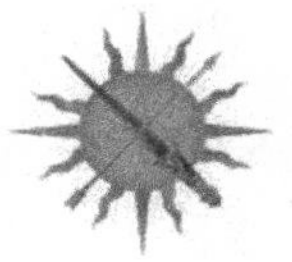

Time slowed, and I couldn't make sense of what I was seeing. That Ian was no longer whole. That there was so much red everywhere—on the ground, on me. That it was his body falling, and it was his head rolling across the floor. It didn't make sense.

Neither did the way I saw the Handmaiden lift her hand, her lips parted on a shocked gasp. Or how Prince Malik jerked back a step, the smug impassivity slipping from his handsome face as the wall around his emotions cracked just enough for me to feel the pulse of disbelief echoing through him. I didn't understand Tawny's screams as she backed away, why Emil's eyes were so wide, or how quickly the blood drained from Kieran's face, and the silent scream that etched itself onto Vonetta's features. I didn't get why Naill had closed his eyes or why Casteel was wrapping his arm around my waist, trying to turn me away, but I couldn't be moved. I wouldn't be moved. Agony ripped into my heart and chewed its way through my skull. Images of Ian and I flashed over and over in my mind, every single memory of him rapidly taking form.

"I loved him. I loved him as if he were my own flesh and blood!" Isbeth screamed, and then she calmed. "Look at what you made me do."

Everything stopped as the entirety of the kingdom seemed to close in on me. I lifted my gaze from Ian.

Casteel's arms tightened around me. "You vindictive bitch," he snarled.

Her dark eyes glistened with tears as she shuddered. "It's not my fault." She turned to me. "I warned you. You didn't listen."

And then…and then everything sped up.

What came out of my throat was a sound I'd never made before. My chest cracked open, and what poured out of it was pure, untapped rage. There was no thinking. There was no understanding. There would be no ultimatums. All that mattered was that she'd taken him from me—she'd killed him, and I let that ancient instinct take over. It knew what to do with all the rage and pain.

I threw out my arms, breaking Casteel's hold as the wave of energy pulsed out of me and rolled through the chamber. Casteel skidded back as Kieran turned. Royal Guards and knights rushed forward. They slammed into Tawny, where she stood frozen, her mouth open as she stared at me. I lost sight of her in the crush of men and shields and drawn swords as they circled the Blood Queen. And I saw the flicker of surprise on Isbeth's face just as the covered windows along the walls cracked and shattered. Intense silvery-white light crowded my vision and formed in my mind, a thick webbing that stretched out from me as I took a step forward. I took out the Royal Guards first, shattering their shields and swords, and in the next breath, them.

Casteel unsheathed his swords as guards spilled into the chamber, but there was no one between Isbeth and me. Drawing in the anger and fear throbbing around me, I pulled on my hatred, funneling it through the cords snapping and streaming toward her. I was going to tear apart the walls around her mind like I had wanted to do with Casteel's father. I wouldn't stop this time. I would peel apart her mind, one section at a time as I broke every single godsdamn bone in her body. The silvery-white light pulsed over her and—

Isbeth laughed.

She threw back her head and laughed. I lost control of my will as Casteel whipped around, staring up at the Blood Queen. "Did you not believe what I said, dear child?" She reached out, flicking a red-painted nail against the thrumming wall of power. The light flared and then collapsed into shimmery dust. "That has always been one of your greatest weaknesses, Penellaphe. Your doubt in what you see with your own eyes and what you know with your heart. If you had truly believed in what I said, you wouldn't have dared such a reckless thing. You would know that we are gods, and you don't fight a god like that."

She lifted a hand. Icy-cold fingers gripped my throat, digging into my windpipe. I reached for the hands—hands that weren't there. A razor-thin bit of air worked its way into my throat as my eyes widened and then…nothing. I stumbled back, scratching at my neck.

"Poppy!" Casteel shouted, dropping a sword as he grasped me around the waist. I stared up at him, my mouth moving but without air to give my words life. His head twisted toward the Blood Queen. "What are you doing to her?"

"Teaching her yet another valuable lesson—"

Out of the corner of my eye, I saw Lyra shift, heard her clothing rip. It was so fast. She'd been mortal one moment, wolven the next, and…

Isbeth turned her head toward her.

Kieran shouted a warning, and then Lyra's high-pitched yelp and thick, snapping and crunching sounds followed. I tried to turn my head but I couldn't. The grip on my throat tightened.

"A lesson that will get worse if another single wolven who's eyeing me like I'm dinner takes another step toward me. The same goes for the Atlantians," she said, and I wheezed pitifully, damp sweat coating my skin. "I will snap her neck."

"Stop!" Casteel yelled. "Stand down. Now!"

I dug at my throat, panic blossoming in my chest. I couldn't breathe. Pain streaked down my throat as my nails drew blood.

"Let her go," Casteel said, dropping his other sword as he clasped my wrist. "Damn it, let her go!"

"I don't think I will. You see, she needs to understand the same lesson you were so resistant to," Isbeth said. "She has no choice. She never has, and I can tell she still believes otherwise. Perhaps she is a perfect fit for you, and she'll never learn. Your brother has been far more accommodating."

My lungs burned as sharp, stabbing pinpricks attacked my hands and arms—my legs. Black dotted my vision. Pressure clamped down on my skull. Those icy fingers sank into my head, into my mind. Pain sliced through me—the kind that seized control of my entire body, and this—oh, gods, this was what I had planned to do to her but hadn't been quick enough or known how. It felt like she was tearing me apart from the inside, scattering my brain. I jerked, straining against Casteel as I clasped the sides of my head. I twisted, only aware that I breathed because I could *scream*.

"Poppy!" Casteel gripped my arm as I clutched at my head, tore at my hair as those claws kept digging in. Panic filled his eyes as wet warmth gushed from my nose, from my ears. "No. No. No." He pulled me to his chest as he twisted toward her. "Please. I beg you. Stop.

Please, godsdamn it. *Stop*! I'll do anything. You want Atlantia? It's yours—"

"You are not the true heir," she cut him off. "You cannot give me what I want."

"She can't give it to you if you kill her," he shouted as my *teeth* bled. "You want to control her? You want me, then. Take me. I won't fight you. I swear. I won't. Just stop. *Please*." His voice cracked.

Consciousness was slipping away as I fell further and further into the soul-shredding pain. I could barely hear their words or understand them. I was losing the ability to make…thoughts, but I heard that—heard Casteel begging, and through the torrential pain, I shook my head. I took those screams roaring through me and all those frayed slivers of thought to form one word, over and over. "No. No. No," I whispered and screamed as all the light went out around me because I would rather be dead. I'd rather be—

"You're killing her. Please," Casteel pleaded. "*Please*, stop."

"You. Oh, you have always been my favorite pet. And when she wakes, she'll know how to keep you alive," she replied, her voice fading and draining away until I wasn't sure that what I heard was real. "Malik. Retrieve your brother."

And then there was nothing.

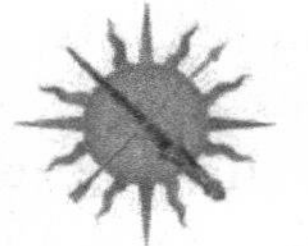

My head throbbed endlessly, and there was a metallic taste in my mouth when I opened my eyes. Fragments of sunlight drifted through the thick branches of an elm.

"Poppy?" Kieran's face leaned over mine. My head…my head was in his lap. "You there?"

I swallowed, wincing at the pain. "I think so." I started to sit up. "Where are we?"

"In the woods just outside of Oak Ambler," Hisa answered as Kieran helped me up. I rubbed my aching head as I squinted. Hisa's features were stark.

I kept looking as my mind slowly cleared away the fog. Delano sat beside Naill, who stood with a hand over his heart. Emil and Vonetta knelt beside the…beside a prone body. "Tawny?"

"She's alive." Emil looked up quickly, his eyes haunted. "But she's been wounded." He stepped aside, and I saw the darkness staining the rose color of her gown around the shoulder. "The bleeding has stopped, but…"

Vonetta pulled the collar of Tawny's gown aside, and I inhaled a shaky breath. Her veins stood out under the rich brown skin, thick and black. "I don't know what this is."

I rose, unsteady. My clothing was stiff with blood. Some was mine, but most of it had belonged to Ian. "I can help her."

"I think you should just sit back down for a little bit." Kieran was on his feet beside me.

Pressing a hand to my head, I kept looking and kept…searching the patchy memories. The sound of crunching, breaking bones came back to me. "Lyra?"

Kieran shook his head.

My heart started thumping as I slid my hand to my sore throat. *Isbeth*. "Where is Casteel?"

Vonetta turned back to Tawny, her shoulders tight—too tight.

Silence.

A tremor rippled through me. The hum in my chest pushed and expanded, and my heart—my *soul*—twisted because I already knew. Oh, gods, deep down, I already knew the answer. I cracked as I drew in a too-shallow breath.

I stumbled around in a circle. My eyes locked with Kieran's as I felt my broken heart crack even more. "No," I whispered, stepping back and then toward Tawny. I needed to help her, but I bent, doubled over. "No. He didn't."

"Poppy," Kieran whispered. "There was nothing we could do. Cas…he handed himself over. We had to leave. Isbeth said Tawny was a gift—a sign of her goodwill. One that she said she hoped you would return."

"*No*." Tears rushed my eyes as I tried to make myself go to Tawny. My stomach dropped as I jerked straight and looked at my left palm. The imprint was still there. I closed my hand and then my eyes, and I saw Ian…I saw him falling. I heard *her* laughing. I heard him begging. "No. No." I gripped the hair that had come free, pulling until I felt my scalp burn. I could hear Casteel saying: "*I was nothing more than this thing without a name*." That was what she'd done to him. What she would try to do again. "No. This wasn't supposed to happen."

"Poppy," Delano said, and I hated how he said my name, how

softly he spoke it. I hated the sorrow pouring into the air around him, soaking my skin. I shook my head, twisting toward Vonetta.

"We'll get him back," Vonetta promised, but she…she couldn't make that promise. "We will, Poppy."

Kieran inched closer, his hands at his sides. "Look at me, Poppy. "

Still shaking my head, I backed up. I couldn't catch my breath. I couldn't breathe again as my chest throbbed with eather. The pain tore through me—the pain and fear because Ian was gone, and I knew what would happen to Casteel. I knew what they would do to him—I knew what *she* would do because I knew what she had already done to him, to Malik, and to Ian.

Ian.

My gaze fell on Tawny, and I…

Throwing back my head, I screamed as the rage erupted from me. Over and over, I saw Ian falling. Over and over, I heard Casteel shouting—begging for her to stop. Lightning ripped through the sky, heating the air. A deafening boom of thunder exploded, rattling the trees and sending birds flying in every direction. Hisa and the guards froze. Delano pressed back, bumping into Naill. They began to back up slowly—away from me as my fury charged the air, whipping up a storm. And in the distant parts of my mind, I realized it had always been me. It hadn't been the gods that'd caused the storms. It hadn't been Nyktos. The blood rain had been them, but this…this was *me*—the violent stir of energy colliding with the world around me. It had always been me—this absolute power.

But I…I wasn't me.

I wasn't the Queen of Flesh and Fire.

My chest rose and fell as my fingers spread wide. I was vengeance and wrath given form, and in the moment, I was exactly what Alastir and the Unseen feared. I was the Bringer of Death and Destruction, and I would tear down the walls they sought to protect themselves with. I would rip apart their homes, scorch their lands, and fill their streets with blood until there was nowhere to run or hide.

And then I would destroy them all.

Streaks of silver-white energy crackled off my skin as I turned back to the edges of the woods, toward the city.

"Poppy. Please—" Vonetta shouted, leaping in front of me.

I threw out my hand, and she skidded through the tall grass. I stalked forward, the wind whipping overhead. Leaves snapped and fell. Trees bent under the weight of the rage pouring out of me, their limbs slamming into the ground all around me.

"Poppy!" Vonetta's scream was caught in the wind. "Don't do this!"

I kept walking, the ground trembling under my feet, the image of Ian collapsing, of Lyra being struck down, playing over and over to the sound of Casteel begging—begging *her*.

Kieran darted around one of the branches as it slammed down, kicking up dirt. "Listen to us," he shouted, the force of my anger tearing at his clothing. "You don't—"

I sent him back, his feet slipping out from under him as I screamed. Another pulse of energy reverberated through the forest. The trees in front of me shattered, and I saw the black wall of the smaller Rise surrounding the village outside of Oak Ambler. The guards saw me coming forward—coming for them. Several unsheathed swords of bloodstone as others raced through the gate. In my mind, the silvery webbing fell over the wall and seeped into it, finding those cracks I'd seen in the larger Rise. I latched on to those weak spots and tore the wall apart from the inside. Stone exploded, mowing down the guards.

A cloud of grayish dust blanketed the air as screams of panic rang out, and I smiled. Screams tore through the air, and I felt something gruesome curling the corners of my lips. I stalked forward, silvery-white light crackling between my fingers.

In the thick dust, an immobile shadow took form. It was her. The Handmaiden. She was the only still thing among the smoke, the screams and panicked shouts, her dark hair hanging in a thick braid over one shoulder.

"These people had nothing to do with what happened back there. They are innocent. Stop her." The young woman lifted the bow, completely unfazed by the gathering energy and the streaks of lightning. Not a single muscle trembled as she took unwavering aim at me. "Or I will."

I cocked my head, seeing the silvery-white light stretch out toward her—

"Sorry," she said. "That doesn't work on me."

The energy recoiled from the Revenant. I pushed harder, but the eather shrank back, crackling and spitting.

"Keep trying." The glow of silvery-white light shone brightly across her face. "In the meantime, do you know what will work on you? Shadowstone, which is what each of my arrows is tipped with. I put one of them through your head, you may get back up, but it won't be anytime soon."

My chest rose and fell rapidly as I zeroed in on the tip of the arrow. The fading sunlight reflected off the shiny black surface.

"So, I'll repeat myself," she continued, walking forward as she raised her voice. "These people have nothing to do with what was done. They are innocent. Stop this, or I will stop you."

Innocent.

Behind her, people scattered into the dirty streets, rushing toward the Rise. They carried nothing but themselves and screaming, red-faced children. They were just mortals caught between the Blood Crown and me, and I could see from where I stood, that the gate to the city was closed.

And I knew that the Ascended who still remained within wouldn't open it. They would've already done that if any of them had been like…like Ian. I sucked in a broken breath as I stared at the people crowding the gates of the larger Rise, their fear a pulsing mass.

I was not what Alastir and the Unseen claimed.

I was nothing like the deities they feared.

And I sure as hell wasn't like my mother.

"I'm sorry," the Handmaiden said, and my gaze snapped back to her as a jagged tremor rocked me. "I really am. I knew Ian. I liked him. He wasn't like…a lot of the others."

Despite the grief and the rage tearing its way through me, I focused on her, opening my senses. *That* ability still worked as it had before because I knew I was reading her emotions. I could taste them—the tartness of uncertainty and the bitterness of sorrow.

"But you need to leave. The Blood Crown has already left here. No one remains who played a role in what happened."

"Except for you," I countered.

There was a slight wince. "Did you have a choice when you were the Maiden?"

I stared at the Handmaiden. She could've struck me with one of the shadowstone arrows at any point, and I doubted she would've missed. But she hadn't. She stood between me and the villagers outside the city, the poorest among those who called Solis home. Not between me and the Ascended.

My...Coralena had been different, hadn't she? She'd been a Handmaiden—one of those Revenant things—but she had taken Ian and I away from Isbeth. She'd loved Leopold. I *remembered* how they'd looked at each other. I thought of the look on this Handmaiden's face when she'd been summoned to prove what a Revenant was—the wave of hopeless desperation and then the feeling of surrender. Emotions I had been painfully well-acquainted with. And I thought of how Prince Malik had behaved when Isbeth had called her forth. He'd stepped forward and then seemed to stop himself. I wondered how many times she'd been used for show and tell, and then I decided I didn't care.

It took every ounce of my self-control, but I pulled the energy back to me. The static charge of power faded from the air around me. The wind eased, and the trees stopped groaning behind me. "Where is she taking him?" I demanded, taking a step forward. The Handmaiden's eyes narrowed. "If you're thinking about firing the arrow, you'd better aim true," I warned. "I don't need eather to fight you. I imagine that regrowing sliced limbs and a head is quite the painful process."

Her lips twisted in a brittle, thin smile. "Don't worry. I will strike true."

I returned her grin. "Tell me where they are taking him. If you don't, you'd better kill me when you take me down because I will come back. And I will kill you."

"Do you really think that is a threat? That I fear dying? After doing it as many times as I have?" She laughed, and the sound was as crumbling as the grimace of a smile. "I welcome the final death."

"Do you welcome the death of the people you seek to protect right now?" I challenged, ignoring the spike of empathy I felt for her. "Because if you don't fear your end, then maybe you'll fear theirs."

Her nostrils flared. "You all are no better than them."

"You're wrong. I stopped," I said. "Would any of them have stopped? Would your Queen?"

She said nothing.

"I have no desire to kill innocents. I want to help the people of Solis—free them from the Blood Crown. That is what we wanted to do," I told her. "But they killed my brother and took the one person who means the world to me. I will do anything to get him back. No matter how badly it stains my soul."

"Then you know how to get him back," she snapped. "Submit to her and take Atlantia in her name."

I shook my head.

"So, you won't do anything for him, then?"

"Because once she has what she wants, she will kill him," I said.

"She will kill me."

"Then I guess you're screwed."

"No. Because I won't let either of those two things happen," I said. "I'm going to give her what she wants, but not in the way she thinks."

Curiosity flickered through the Handmaiden, but then her attention shifted just the slightest to my shoulder.

"Poppy," Kieran called quietly as several archers on the Rise scrambled into their nests.

Her chest rose with a shallow breath. "She'll take him to the capital. I don't know where. No one knows where she keeps her…pets."

A shiver of rage brushed my skin, stroking the throbbing in my chest, and her lip curled in disgust. It was brief. I wasn't sure that she was even aware of it, but I saw it.

"But it doesn't matter," she continued. "She'll have every Revenant on hand guarding him. She'll have *him* watching over your King," she told me, and I knew that she spoke of the Prince. "You won't get near him." She lowered her bow, her shoulders settling. "Unless you can bring the fire of the gods with you, none of you stands a chance."

A chill swept through me as I stared at her. Fire of the gods? Her gaze met mine as she took a step back. "I'm sure we will meet again," she said.

"We will."

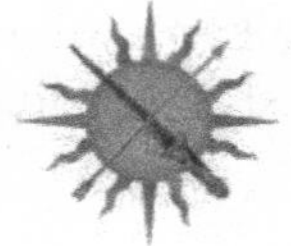

I sat in the wooden chair of the hunting cabin Casteel had brought me to, after he'd saved my life and risked so much in the process, and stared at the bed.

Tawny lay there, her face too pale, her breathing too shallow. I'd tried to heal her. I'd tried once when I went back to the woods. My gift had flared to life then, and the wound had closed, but she didn't wake. I tried again when we stopped halfway here, after we'd mounted the horses that Hisa had brought. I placed my hands on her too-warm skin as soon as we arrived at the cabin, but she didn't wake, and those dark veins had spread up her throat.

We'd traveled straight through the Wastelands and had reached the hunting cabin as night descended. We had to stop. Everyone was tired, and Tawny… I didn't know what was wrong with her or what had pierced her flesh to cause this—for my gift to not do much beyond closing her skin.

The arrow the Handmaiden had held resurfaced. It had been fashioned from shadowstone. The same weapon my mother had had the night the Craven came to the inn. The same kind of weapon the deities had been buried with and the skeleton soldiers had held. I couldn't remember seeing what kind of weapons the guards had. I'd…I'd obliterated the ones who stood in front of me, but the Handmaiden had said it would put me down for a while. I glanced at Tawny. Could it have been shadowstone? Was that why my gifts had only worked to a certain point?

My gaze lowered to my hand. I turned it palm up and, in the glow of the candlelight, saw the marriage imprint shimmer. I closed my hand, squeezing my eyes shut against the burn.

I hadn't cried.

I wanted to. I wanted to cry for Ian. I wanted to cry for Lyra. I wanted to cry for Tawny because I feared she'd never open her eyes again. I wanted to cry for Casteel because I knew what he faced, even if I could imagine what he must be thinking or feeling to know that his brother had not only betrayed him but would also become one of his prison keepers.

Anger had grown with each mile we got closer to Atlantia. If we had known the truth about who the Queen really was, we could've better prepared. We would've known it was impossible for her to be an Ascended. We would've known that anything was possible. Instead, we'd gone into the meeting hobbled by lies. No part of me believed for even one second that Eloana hadn't known the truth. Possibly even Valyn had known. The knowledge they'd withheld could've changed everything.

Because it already had.

A soft knock drew me from my thoughts. I rose and stiffly walked to the door.

Kieran stood there. "Can't sleep. None of us can." Beyond him, I saw several shapes sitting around a small fire. He looked over my shoulder. "How is she?"

"Still asleep."

"I know you haven't slept."

I shook my head as I stepped out into the cool night air, closing the door behind me. I glanced over at the bent and bowed trees as I walked with Kieran over to where the others sat.

Vonetta glanced up as I sat beside her. She offered me a flask, but I shook my head. I'd apologized to her and to Kieran, but I felt like I needed to do it again. I opened my mouth.

"Don't," she cut me off. "I know what you're going to say. It's not necessary. I understand. We all understand."

There were several murmurs of agreement from around the fire. My gaze briefly met Hisa's and then Delano's and finally Naill's. "He's still alive," I said roughly. "She won't kill him. Not when she thinks she can use him to control me—control Atlantia."

They nodded, but I sensed relief. They had needed to hear that. I'd needed to say that. "Does anyone know anything about shadowstone? That was what the Handmaiden had."

"I heard what she said," Kieran said.

"Do you think that could be what's causing Tawny's injuries?" I asked.

"I don't know." Hisa dragged a hand over her head. "She's mortal. I've never seen a mortal wounded by shadowstone before. A lot of Healers in Evaemon and some of the older Elders may have seen something like this."

I thought of Willa and then her diary, and the next breath I took *hurt.*

"What is the plan?" Emil asked as Vonetta handed him the flask. He took a drink.

We hadn't really spoken on the ride away from Oak Ambler. Not about anything, but I had done a lot of thinking—about what Isbeth had said, what even the Duchess had claimed in Spessa's End, and what the Handmaiden had told me.

Even though I'd refused Isbeth, she believed that everything was falling into place. She had the Prince and now the King of Atlantia. She had found a way to control me, and in her mind, she therefore controlled Atlantia. Just like Duchess Teerman had claimed, I would succeed where the Queen had failed.

But they were wrong.

I looked down at my hands—at the marriage imprint. *You always had the power in you.* That was something I had also thought about. I now knew where I'd first heard it. The silvery-blonde I'd seen when I had been so close to dying. That is what she had said to me.

You always had the power in you.

And it was what Nyktos had said. A part of me wondered if the woman I'd seen was his Consort. That, in her sleep, she'd reached out to me, to either warn or help me. It would make sense that she would.

After all, I was her granddaughter, if she was who I believed.

My fingers curled into my palms. The center of my chest hummed with power—the eather of the King of Gods. The kind that should've been powerful enough to destroy whatever the hell Isbeth believed she was. But I hadn't been prepared. I hadn't fought like a god because I did not believe I was one.

But Casteel had, hadn't he? Did he ever really believe I was a deity?

I exhaled roughly. "She was right."

Vonetta looked over at me. "Who?"

"The Queen. I am a god," I stated.

Her brows rose as she glanced over at Emil and Naill. "Um—"

"No. Wait." Kieran rose, understanding flickering through him. "If what she claimed is true and Malec is one of Nyktos and his Consort's sons—and you're their grandchild—you are a god," he reiterated what I'd just been thinking.

Delano nodded slowly. "It doesn't matter what in the hell Ileana—Isbeth—is. You are the grandchild of Nyktos—of a Primal God. *That* is why your bloodline is so potent. You are a god, not a deity."

"Shit," Emil muttered, taking another drink before Vonetta snatched the flask from him.

"That's what Nyktos meant," I said, swallowing. "I never needed his permission."

"For what?" Naill asked.

"To use his guards," I said, knowing that's what the Handmaiden had meant by the fire of the gods. "To summon the draken."

Chapter 48

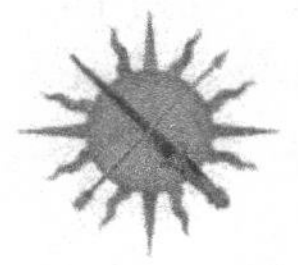

I stalked through the palace halls in Evaemon, the dust from the road and blood still staining my breeches and tunic. I headed for the sun-drenched atrium in the center, followed by Kieran and his sister still in their wolven forms. Naill and Hisa followed, their hands on their swords. Delano was with Tawny, having taken her to one of the rooms above mine. Healers and Elders were being summoned.

Crown Guards bowed stiffly as we passed, the heels of my boots clicking off the tile floor as sharply as the wolven's claws.

Vonetta was one giant ball of stress. I didn't know if she was more worried that I would obliterate Casteel's mother or if it was the plans we'd discussed on the way back to Evaemon. I, on the other hand, was strangely calm. I wasn't worried about what I was about to say to Eloana or what I would carry out next. I felt only determination and anger, so much anger, it seeped out of my bones and coated my skin, but I was calm. I didn't know one could feel such wrath and yet feel such *silence.*

The doors to the family room were open, and the scent of coffee and freshly baked bread stretched out to me, turning my stomach instead of inciting my hunger.

Eloana wasn't alone.

She sat across from Lord Sven and Lord Gregori. Several Crown Guards stood in the back of the room, but my focus was on her.

His mother looked at me, and then her gaze flicked behind me, searching for what she would not find. And she knew. The moment she didn't see Casteel, her agony was sharp and pungent. A hand fluttered against her breast as she reached for the empty space beside her, seeming to realize then that her husband wasn't there.

The two Elders stood hastily. "Your Majesty," Sven said, bowing. Concern rippled from him as he glanced at the wolven siblings. "Are you okay, Your Majesty?"

No. I wasn't. I wouldn't be okay until Casteel was by my side, and the Blood Crown was nothing but a pile of ashes. But my sorrow and fear gave way to anger as I stared at Casteel's mother. I latched on to it, letting it wrap around the hum in my chest, filling the hollowness of where my heart beat.

And that anger tasted of power and death, a lot like it had when I walked toward Oak Ambler, but I was in control this time.

Barely.

"You knew." I stared at his mother. "You knew what she was and what she *wasn't.*"

Blood drained rapidly from Eloana's face as she jerked back. "Penellaphe—"

"Where is the King?" Gregori demanded, stepping forward.

The wolven let out a low rumble of warning as my head snapped toward him. Words fell from my lips like poison-dipped daggers. "Where is the King, *Your Majesty?*" I corrected softly in a tone eerily similar to the one Casteel had used when he was but a second away from relieving someone of their heart.

Gregori stiffened. "Where is the King, *Your Majesty,*" he repeated, his irritation acid on my tongue and his dislike of me hot against my skin.

My head tilted to the side as everything came to a head. Something happened then, tearing open from deep within. It had rattled with all the lies and then had shaken loose when Casteel had saved my life. It had cracked open when I stood before Nyktos and told him that he would not hurt my friends. The locks that held it back had been blown to pieces when I saw Ian fall and then awoke to find that Casteel had been taken. It was a whole new awakening.

I wasn't the Maiden.

I wasn't a Princess or even a Queen.

I was a god.

And I was so over *this.*

"You don't like me, do you?" I queried softly.

An icy splash of shock rolled through him, but he quickly masked it. His chin lifted. "I think you know the answer to that."

"I do. And you know what?" I asked, my skin humming as the air charged around me. A silvery-white glow seeped from my skin, crowding the sides of my vision as Sven inched away from Gregori. "In the entirety of the two kingdoms, I couldn't give a fuck if you or any other member of the Council likes me. It does not change that I am your Queen, and your tone and the manner in which you address me is highly inappropriate." I watched pink seep into the man's cheeks, and I smiled tightly. "Not just because I'm your Queen, but because I am the grandchild of Nyktos, and you speak to a *god* with such disrespect."

Eloana sucked in a sharp breath as I let the restless vibration from within the center of my chest come to the surface. Silvery-white light spilled across the room, reflecting off the walls and turning the glass to shimmering diamonds. Sven tripped over the corner of the striped carpet, catching himself on the edge of a chair. The furniture and windows rattled as I took a step forward. Silver dripped from my fingertips, forming webs of iridescent light that fell to the floor, disappearing into the stone, and that beautiful light could give life. It could also take it.

Hisa was the first to move, dropping to a knee, one hand pressed over her heart, the other flattened to the floor. The other guards followed, as did Sven. Gregori remained standing, his eyes wide.

"Try me," I whispered, and those two words echoed throughout the room.

A tremor coursed through Gregori as he slowly lowered himself to one knee, bowing his head. "I'm sorry," he uttered, placing a hand to his chest and the other to the floor. "Please forgive me."

In the hidden, darkest corners of my being, the urge to lash out was a tempting force. To unleash all the sorrow and anger I felt, and let it flay open Gregori's skin and rip out each bone. I could—with just a thought, a single will. He would be no more, and he would be the last to speak to me in such a way.

Isbeth would do it.

But I wasn't her.

I reined in the eather, and pulled the power deep within me. The radiance retreated, seeping back into my skin. "Leave," I ordered the Elder. "Now."

He rose, stumbling around me and the wolven. I heard Naill's soft snicker as the Elder rushed past him. My gaze flicked to Sven. "You should leave, too," I said. "And the guards. Leave."

Sven nodded, exiting the room with far more grace than his predecessor. A few of the Crown Guards lingered, obviously still loyal to Eloana—or afraid for her. I turned to where I saw that she had lowered herself to the floor.

I fought a cruel smile, stopping it from reaching my lips as she looked up at me. "I do not believe you want many to hear what I have to say."

The skin around the corners of her eyes puckered as she closed them. "Listen to your Queen," she whispered hoarsely. "Leave."

Vonetta and Kieran tracked the guards' progress. It wasn't until Naill and Hisa had closed the door that I said, "You may rise."

Eloana rose, collapsing onto the settee, her glistening amber eyes fixed on me as I strode forward, gripping the back of a chair. The legs scraped against the floor as I dragged it so it was before her.

Slowly, I lowered myself to the chair, my eyes meeting hers as Kieran and Vonetta moved so they crouched on either side of me. Naill and Hisa remained at the door. "Ask me whose blood stains my clothing."

Eloana's lips trembled. "Whose blood—?" Her voice cracked as she glanced at the wolven. "Whose blood stains your clothing?"

"My brother's." I flattened my palms against my knees. "He was slaughtered when I refused to join the Blood Crown, uniting the kingdoms under the sovereignty of Solis. He didn't even see it coming. They cut his head from his shoulders, and he did nothing to deserve that. Nothing. *She* did it because she could." My fingers curled into my knees, where the material was stiff with dried blood. "Now ask me where your son is."

Her eyes started to close—

"No." I tipped forward. "Don't you dare close your eyes. I didn't when I watched a sword slice through my brother's throat. Don't you dare close your eyes. You're stronger than that."

Her chest rose with a heavy breath as her eyes remained open. "Where is my son?"

"She took him," I forced out, the words cutting into my skin. "And you know why? You know exactly why she wanted *your* sons. It's not just to make more Ascended. It's personal."

Her lips moved, but no sound came out.

"You knew. This whole time. You knew who Queen Ileana really was." Rage heated my blood, sparked off my skin. She leaned back an inch. "You knew she was Isbeth and that she was never a vampry."

"I..."

"Malec gave her his blood when you poisoned her." I reclaimed what distance she'd gathered. "He couldn't make a vampry with his blood. Isbeth was never the first Ascended."

"I didn't know that at first," Eloana spoke. "I swear to you. I had no idea that she wasn't a vampry. She had black eyes just like the others that were made after her—"

"Because her eyes are black but not like the Ascended," I interrupted. "They've always been black."

"I didn't know," she repeated, one of her hands curling into a fist. "I didn't know until I found Malec and entombed him. That is when I learned that Isbeth had never been a vampry, that she had Ascended into something else—"

"Something like him," I cut her off, not even truly caring if she spoke the truth at this point. "When you learned the truth doesn't matter. What does is that you knew Ileana was Isbeth, and you didn't tell us. You didn't prepare us for the fact that we weren't dealing with a vampry but with something far more powerful than that. That is why your son is not with me."

"I..." She shook her head, her features beginning to crumble. "Is my son alive?"

"Which one?"

Her eyes widened. "W-what do you mean?"

"Are you asking about Malik or Casteel?" I said. "Malik is alive. He's actually doing just fine, all cozied up with Isbeth."

She didn't move. I didn't think she even breathed. I could've broken the news to her in a far kinder way, but she could've also told us the whole truth.

"No," she whispered.

"Yes." I nodded as Isbeth's voice haunted my thoughts. "It was him who retrieved Casteel."

A tear fell from her eye, streaking across her cheek. "Is Casteel alive?"

I lifted my left hand, showing her the glimmering marriage imprint. "He is." I swallowed hard. "But I'm sure you understand that means very little at this point."

She shuddered, and I didn't know if it was from relief or fear. A long moment passed. "Oh, gods," she whispered on a ragged breath, closing her hands over her face. Her shoulders shook.

Forcing myself to sit back, I waited until she'd pulled herself together...and she did, just like I knew she would. It took a couple of minutes, but her shoulders stilled, and her hands lowered. Puffy, glassy eyes stared out from behind tear-soaked lashes. "It's my fault."

"No shit," I snapped. At least, partially, it was. Because I…I had lost control. I'd given Isbeth the opening she needed.

She flinched. "I…I didn't want people to know she'd won."

I stilled. Everything in me stilled. "What?"

"It was…it was my ego. There's no other way for me to say it. I loved Malec once upon a time. I thought the moon and sun set and rose with him. And she wasn't like the other women. She sank her claws into him, and I knew…I *knew* he loved her—loved her more than he loved me. I didn't want people to know that in the end, even with Malec entombed, she didn't just win, she became a Queen," she admitted hoarsely. "Became the Crown that forced us to remain behind the Skotos Mountains, used our people to make monsters, and took—took my children. I didn't want Casteel to know that the same woman who'd taken my first husband was who'd held him and then his brother. She won in the end, and…she's still managing to tear my family and kingdom apart."

Now I was the one struck speechless.

"I was embarrassed," she continued. "And I didn't…I know it's no excuse. It just became something that was never spoken. A lie that became a reality after hundreds of years. Only Valyn and Alastir knew the truth."

Alastir.

Of course.

"And their son?" I said. "What did you do with Isbeth and Malec's son? Did you have him killed? Was it Alastir who carried it out?"

Pressing her lips together, she looked up at the ceiling. "Alastir did. He knew of the child before I even did. Valyn doesn't know about the child at all."

I stared at her. "Is that why you didn't want to go to war? Because doing so would mean that Ileana's real identity would be revealed, along with everything else?"

"Partly," she admitted as she wiped the heels of her hands under her eyes. "But also because I didn't want to see more Atlantians and mortals die." She lowered trembling hands. "Malik is…is well and—" She cleared her throat. "He's with her?"

"He appeared well, and he supports the Blood Crown. That is all I know," I told her, sinking farther into the chair. I didn't know how much of what she said was the truth now, but I did know that the agony I felt from her hadn't just been sorrow. I recognized that the agony was partly shame now, something she'd carried for hundreds of years and would continue to shoulder. To be honest, I didn't know what I would've done if I had been in her place. The war between her and Isbeth had started long before the first vampry had been created, and it'd never ended. "Malec wasn't a deity."

"I…I can see that." She sniffed. "I mean, I saw that when you showed Gregori what you were. But I don't understand. Malec —"

"He lied to you," I said, spreading my hands along the arms of the chair. "I don't know why, but he is one of Nyktos's sons. He's a god."

Her surprise couldn't be fabricated, and it cooled some of my anger. "I didn't know—"

"I know." I curled my fingers around the edges of the arms. "Malec confided in Isbeth. She knew."

Eloana flinched as she let out a low whistle. "That stings more than it should."

"Maybe you never stopped loving Malec."

"Maybe," she whispered, staring at her lap now. "I love Valyn. I love him dearly and fiercely. I also loved Malec, even though I don't think I…knew anything about him. But I think Malec will always own a part of my heart."

And the part owned by Malec would always belong to him, and that was…that was just sad.

"Isbeth is my mother," I told her, and her eyes shot to mine. "I'm the daughter of her and Malec. And I married your son."

She paled once more.

"It was a part of her plan," I continued as Vonetta leaned into my leg. "That I would marry Malik and take Atlantia. With my bloodline and a Prince at my side, there would be absolutely nothing that could be done. But in a twist of fate, I married Casteel instead."

"Her plan worked, then," she rasped.

"No, it hasn't," I replied. "I will not take Atlantia in her name."

"She has Malik and Casteel," she countered, her tone hardening. "How has she not won?"

"She won't kill them. Malik is helping her, and she can use Casteel against me like she used your sons against Atlantia," I told her.

Her lips thinned. "I still don't see how she hasn't won."

"Because I'm not you." I noted the faint wince, and I didn't even want to feel bad for inflicting it. "I have been used my entire life in one way or another, and I will not be used again. I know what I am now. I know what it means to have had the power in me this whole time. My brother's death wasn't in vain. Neither was Lyra's. I understand now."

Eloana's brows puckered. "What are you saying?"

"I can summon Nyktos's guards, and I will. Isbeth may have her Revenants, her knights, soldiers, and those who support her." My grip tightened. "But I will have the draken."

Visibly shaken, it took Eloana a few moments to respond. "Can you even—? I'm sorry. You can. You are a god." She smoothed a hand over her gown, a nervous habit, I realized. "But are you sure? The draken are a fierce bloodline. There is a reason they went to sleep with Nyktos. Only he can control them."

"I am his grandchild," I reasoned, but I really had no idea how the draken would respond. I could only assume that what Nyktos had said also meant that they'd do so favorably. "And I don't seek to control them. I just need their help."

Understanding flickered through her. "I thought you and Casteel wanted to prevent war. You won't once the draken are awakened."

"By holding Casteel, she thinks she can stay my hand. But, sometimes, war cannot be prevented," I said, echoing her words—ones I knew the Consort had whispered to me before when I first entered Saion's Cove.

And that was something I'd realized on the journey back to Atlantia. There would be no more talks or ultimatums. What was to come couldn't be stopped. It never could be. And in a way, the War of Two Kings had never ended. There had just been a strained truce, like Isbeth had said. All the years Casteel sought to move pieces behind the scenes, to free his brother and gain land for Atlantia hadn't been wasted. It had given Atlantia time to gain what they didn't have before.

"No," Eloana agreed quietly, sadly. "Sometimes, it cannot."

I glanced to where Hisa stood beside Naill. "Can you please send word to the Blood Crown that I will meet with them in the woods outside of Oak Ambler by the end of next week?" I told her. "Make sure they understand that whoever they send had better be fit to receive a Queen. That I will only speak to her or to the King."

The corners of the commander's lips curved up as she bowed at the waist. "Yes, Your Majesty."

"A message?" Eloana asked. "What are you planning?"

"First, I brought my friend back from Solis. The one I believed to have Ascended. She hasn't, but she was wounded with what I believe was shadowstone, and my abilities aren't working on her." I dragged my palms over my knees. "Delano took Tawny to one of the rooms and summoned a Healer. I would ask that you look after her. She is…" I inhaled deeply. "She was my first friend."

Eloana nodded. "Of course. I will do all that I can to help her."

"Thank you." I cleared my throat. "I'm going to take a bath." A shower was… I couldn't do that and not think of Casteel, and the only way I was surviving currently was by *not* thinking of him. "I'm going to Iliseeum. Once I return, I will send the Blood Queen the kind of message only Casteel would be proud of."

"Knowing what my son would be proud of," she said, voice thickening, "I can only imagine what kind of message that will be."

I felt my lips curve up in a tight, savage smile. "And then I'm going to finish what you started centuries ago. I will return these lands to Atlantia, and I will return with my King at my side."

Golden eyes locked with mine. "And if you fail?"

"I won't."

Chapter 49

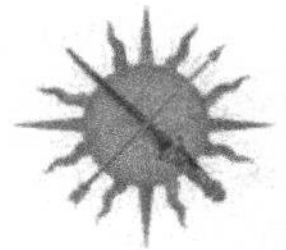

I slept for a few hours and ate a couple of mouthfuls of food only because I had to. Then I dressed in breeches and a simple white shirt that belonged to Casteel. It was far too large, but the black bodice worn over the shirt kept me from swimming in it.

Many tunics and shirts of mine now lined the walk-in wardrobe, but it felt good to have Casteel's shirt against my skin. And he'd liked it when I wore the bodice like this the…the last time I'd seen him.

I stopped at the bed, my gaze straying to the nightstand, to the little wooden horse. My heart squeezed. I hurried over to it, taking the toy in my hands. In the chest by the doorway, I found a pouch. Placing the horse in it, I left the bedchamber and then the quarters as I tied the bag to my waist.

I checked on Tawny, finding her the way I'd left her—asleep and far too still. The dark veins had traveled to the curve of her chin. Eloana sat at her side. "I summoned Willa," she said, and the breath I took was painful. "She will bring one of the oldest Healers. He will know how to treat her."

"Thank you," I said, inhaling and exhaling slowly.

She nodded. "Be careful, Penellaphe."

"Always," I whispered and then left the room, my chest aching.

Kieran waited for me in the foyer, and from there, we joined Hisa in the Temple of Nyktos. It would only be the two of us who made the trip this time. Vonetta would remain as their parents were en route to Evaemon with their new sibling. I'd told Kieran that he should stay, but that had gone in one ear and out the other, even when I pulled the Queen card and then the I-am-a-god-obey-me line. He insisted on accompanying me, claiming that none of the others would remember the path we'd taken last time. Maybe he was right. Maybe he just couldn't sleep or stay still either, his thoughts swirling from one horrific possibility to another. What if my plan failed? What if the draken refused? What if *she* hurt Casteel? What if he needed to feed? What if *I* needed…to feed? What would I do? I couldn't even think about drinking another's blood. What if I lost him? What if he lost himself again?

And I knew this wasn't easy for Kieran. Before, he had been able to tell how Casteel was doing because of the bond. He didn't have that now. He just had all the what-ifs I had.

"Kieran?" I asked as we made our way down the narrow tunnel.

"Poppy?"

I swallowed, my throat dry. "Are you…are you doing okay?"

He didn't answer right away, and I thought the hand he held the torch with trembled. "No."

I briefly closed my eyes.

"Are you?"

"No," I whispered.

We traveled the windy underground tunnels, mostly in silence after that. There were no jokes, no real conversation at all. We passed the area of the partial collapse hours before we had the first time, and I moved ahead of him when we saw the pinprick of light. I worked my way out, and then we crossed the barren land. Making our way, I made sure it was I who stepped under the shadow of the winged women. The ground didn't tremble. What I believed were the Consort's guards remained under our feet. The city of Dalos shimmered in the distance as we walked toward the shadowstone Temple.

The first thing I noticed was there was no slumbering stone draken. "Where is….?"

"There." Kieran's steps slowed as I followed his gaze to the Temple stairs. A man with black hair streaked with silver stood in the center of them, dressed in black pants and nothing else. "You think that's Nektas?" he asked, his voice low. "In his mortal form?"

"Maybe." Shards of diamonds crunched under my boots.

"The wolven is correct," the man spoke, and my brows lifted. The draken's hearing was extraordinary. "You have returned several members less than the last time. That does not bode well."

I stiffened as I stopped many yards from the Temple.

"If you are seeking Nyktos, you are not in luck," Nektas

continued. "He has joined his Consort once more in sleep."

"I'm not here to see Nyktos," I said, taking in the fine ridges all along his back. They looked like…scales.

"I understand." A heartbeat of silence. "Or is it that you now understand the power you wield?"

Wanting to know how the draken was aware of my epiphany, I glanced at Kieran. He sent me a look that said he knew I was about to ask a rather irrelevant question.

I fought the urge and won. "I understand."

His head tilted, but he still did not look at us. "Before you speak, you must be sure, for these words cannot be rescinded. Once you summon the flesh and fire of the gods, to protect and serve you, to keep you safe, they will be cast in fire and carved in flesh."

My mouth dried. "I'm sure."

"What makes you so sure?"

"The Blood Crown took what is mine. They took everything from me, and they will continue taking everything."

"And?" he queried quietly. "You seek to use us to take everything from the Blood Crown, then? To destroy them, the cities they protect themselves in, and those who stand between you and them?"

I pressed the marriage imprint against the pouch that held the toy horse. "I seek the *aid* of the draken to fight the Revenants and the Ascended—to fight beside Atlantia. I do not seek to destroy the cities or kill those caught between them and me. For the most part, the people of Solis are innocent."

"You seek to fight with the guards of the gods at your side, but you do not expect cities to fall?" He barked out a short laugh. "You are not ready for war."

"You misunderstand," I stated carefully. "Or I misspoke. I do not seek to do those things, but I understand that they may be necessary. I am ready for war. I would not be here if I wasn't. But I do not plan to soak the lands with blood and leave nothing but ruins behind."

There was a beat of silence. "Then you plan to take what is owed you and bear the weight of two Crowns?"

I forced my hands to loosen. "Yes."

His head bowed slightly. "And will you help bring back what was ours to protect? What will allow the Consort to wake?"

Kieran sent me a glance of concern, and I really had no idea what Nektas was speaking of or what would happen if the Consort awakened. But I asked, "What is it that I need to help bring back?"

"Your father."

I opened my mouth, but it took several moments for me to find the ability to speak. "Malec?"

"Malec is lost to us. He was lost to us long before any of us realized."

Confusion swept through both Kieran and me. "I don't understand," I started. "Malec is—"

"Malec is not your father," Nektas said. "The blood that courses through you is that of Ires, his twin."

Shock rolled through me as I stared at the draken's back. Isbeth…she hadn't confirmed that Malec was my father…and she had spoken of Malec in the past tense, as if she believed that he was gone. Oh my gods, Isbeth didn't know where Malec was, and…

"Ires was lured from Iliseeum some time ago," Nektas said. "Drawn into the realm with my daughter while we slept. We have not been able to look for Ires. Not without being summoned, and he…he has not called for us. But we know he lives."

My thoughts raced, settling on the painting I'd seen in the museum of Nyktos and the two…the two large cats. "Oh, gods…"

"What?" Kieran looked at me.

I swallowed, almost afraid to ask. "Could Ires shift forms?"

"He, like his father, could take other forms. While Nyktos preferred that of a white wolf, Ires was often fond of taking the shape of a large gray cat, much like Malec."

"Fuck," Kieran whispered.

I…I could only stand there while it felt like my heart had dropped out of my body. "I saw him," I uttered. "We both did."

The muscles along Nektas's back rippled and flexed. "How?"

"He was…he was caged by the one who took Casteel," I said. I had only briefly considered that the creature I'd seen in the cage had been Malec, but at that time, we'd believed Malec to be a deity. Not Nyktos's son. Not a twin. "The Blood Queen," I rasped, reeling. "She…she says she's a god because Malec Ascended her."

"A god?" A rough, dark laugh left the ancient draken. "A god is born. Not created. What she is…she, like the Revenants, are an abomination of all that is godly."

Casteel…he had been right.

Nektas's hands closed into fists. "Then your enemy is truly an enemy of ours."

Shaken by the revelation, I pressed the heel of my palm to my chest. How had Isbeth lured a god? Had Malec shared something with her? "Your daughter? Do you know if she lives?"

Nektas did not answer for a long time. "I do not know. She was young when we went to sleep, into statas. She was barely on the cusp of adulthood when Ires woke her."

"What is her name?" Kieran asked.

"Jadis."

"That's a pretty name," I said, briefly closing my eyes. I wished I hadn't. I saw the too-thin man behind the bone bars, his features mirroring the chaos of his mind. I saw the far-too-intelligent eyes of the cat. My father. And I had left him there. I shuddered.

I couldn't…I couldn't let myself go there.

The possibility that Isbeth had a draken locked away somewhere was something I would have to file away for the moment, right along with the knowledge of who my father was and the questions surrounding how he and Isbeth had come together. All I could focus on was what I knew now.

That my father was a victim of Isbeth's, too.

And I thought of Malec, entombed beneath the Blood Forest. "If a god of Primal blood was entombed, what happens to them?"

"Entombed by the bones of the deities? They would simply waste away, day by day, year by year, but they would not die," he answered. "They would just exist in a place between dying and death, alive but trapped."

Gods.

That was an even more horrifying outcome than the deities slowly starving to death, but that meant that Malec was still alive, and Isbeth still loved him.

Nektas's skin had hardened into scales. "Are you ready, daughter of Ires, the son of Nyktos and his Consort?"

A tremble coursed through me. "Yes."

"Then speak the words and receive what you've come for."

My skin tingled, and my chest throbbed. Kieran's hand closed around mine. He squeezed. A soft breeze came from nowhere, swirling across the diamonds. The scent of lilacs reached me, and then I heard *her* voice among my thoughts—heard the Consort speaking the words Nektas waited for. "I...I summon the flesh and fire of the gods, to protect me and those I care for. To ride at my side and stand guard at my back. I call upon the bloodline birthed of flesh and fire to awaken."

Nektas turned his head to the side, the vibrant blue of his irises a stark contrast to the pitch-black of the vertical pupil.

The ground trembled and gave a low rumble. Kieran's grip on my hand tightened as we took several steps back. Dirt and small diamonds spilled into the air around the base of the Temple. Chunks of crystal exploded out to the sides. Gleaming talons stretched out from the dust, sinking into the black stone. A large, leathery shape cut through the cloud of debris, arcing high as dozens of claws carved into the tower from all sides. They erupted from the earth below, pulling their scaled, winged bodies out of the soil. They climbed the sides of the tallest spire, one after another, their grayish-black tails whipping through the air. The first reached the top— its deep-purple-black scales glimmering under the sun as it shook the dirt from its body. Stretching out its long neck, frills of spikes opened around its head as its wide mouth dropped open, and a deafening roar rattled my bones.

Nektas faced me. "From this moment to the last moment, they are yours, Queen of Flesh and Fire."

My breath caught, burning my throat as wisps of smoke wafted from the purple-black creature's nostrils. It opened its jaws and let out another rumbling roar. Flames spilled from its mouth, a rolling tide of silvery-white flames. It launched from the obsidian tower, rocketing into the sky, its wings unfurling and sending a gust of wind over the ground. The others called out, their shrieks turning into keening calls. Awakened from their deep sleep, dozens of draken followed, leaping from the tower and taking flight, one after the other. They flew toward the Mountains of Nyktos and then, eventually, they would take flight for Solis.

For Carsodonia.

Chapter 50

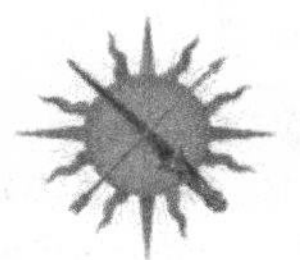

"You need to wake soon. There are draken here," I told Tawny. "Actual draken."

She didn't awaken, but the blackness in her veins had stopped spreading. Whatever the Healer Willa had brought with her had given Tawny was working. It was also changing her.

Her golden bronze curls were now bone-white. Somehow, the snowy hair made her all the more stunning.

"The draken are beautiful." I smoothed back a curl. "If a bit…temperamental. They have been asleep for a very long time, so I suppose they're allowed to be grumpy."

"Grumpy?" Kieran snorted, surprising me. I hadn't heard him come in. He'd been with Vonetta, spending time with their parents and their new sister. If he was here, I knew what that meant. "More like *bitey.*"

"You deserved it," I reminded him as I fixed the blanket around Tawny. "He got too close to one while he was resting. Almost lost a hand."

"More like an arm," he muttered.

I looked over my shoulder. "I don't think *bitey* is a word, by the way."

"It's not?" Kieran murmured, looking past me, to where Tawny lay. "She looks better."

"She does." I faced her. "It's time?"

"Yes."

Giving her hand one last squeeze, I placed it on the bed. I rose and smoothed a hand over a similar outfit to the one I'd worn to Iliseeum. The bodice was of thicker fleece material, though. Colder weather had arrived in much of Solis.

"I'll be back…." I leaned over, pressing my lips to her warm forehead. "I'll just be back. I promise."

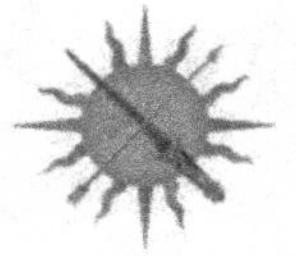

It took less than half a day to travel to the northern-most point of Atlantia, to the wall which ran all the way to the Pillars of Atlantia outside of Saion's Cove. There, I was reunited with Setti. I stroked his nose and scratched his ear. I hoped he took it easy with me. My horsemanship was seriously lacking, and he, well, there was a reason he was named after the God of War's warhorse.

"Incoming," Kieran murmured.

Over my shoulder, I saw Casteel's father approaching, his chest and shoulders covered in gold and silver armor, a helmet tucked under his arm. My stomach tightened. I had only seen him once since I initially returned to Evaemon, and that was brief, a passing in the halls. He'd immediately returned to the northern part of the kingdom.

Wolven stirred from the grass, lifting their heads as he neared. Valyn bowed, and they went back to napping or daydreaming or whatever it was that they had been doing.

"You still plan to send your message?" Valyn asked, his gaze flickering to where the crown rested on my head. I didn't know what made me decide to wear it, but it was there and it felt right.

I nodded. "It is what Casteel would do." And I knew that was true.

Valyn made a sound of agreement, and several moments of silence passed. I took a deep breath. "I'll get him back," I promised. "We will get him back. I swear."

Swallowing thickly, he nodded as he looked over at me. "I know you will." He paused. "My son is a very lucky man to have found you and made himself yours."

His words embraced my wounded heart, and the acceptance behind them choked me. It took me a moment to speak. "It is I who is lucky to have been found by your son and to have become his."

Valyn reached over, cupping my cheek with his gloved hand. "And Eloana and I are even more lucky to have you as our daughter-in-law."

Tears filled my eyes. I hadn't cried, and I told myself I wouldn't cry now. If I did, I wouldn't stop. "Thank you."

He nodded and then lowered his hand, his gaze fixed on the wall. "I have a favor to ask of you."

I searched his profile as I opened my senses. I didn't need to search long to feel the agony pounding through him. "What is it?"

Under the gold and steel armor, his shoulders tightened. "If you see my other son before I do, all that I ask is that you make his death as quick and painless as possible."

I blew out a thin breath as the knot expanded in my throat. The two words I spoke hurt. "I will."

"Thank you." Valyn nodded as he shifted his helmet to his other hand. "We will await your return in the foothills of the Skotos, from the cusp of the Wastelands to the walls of Spessa's End, Your Majesty." He bowed and took his leave.

I watched him as he strode back to where his horse waited. I would see him after I sent my message.

"That took a lot for him to ask," Kieran said, already mounted on his horse.

"I know." Holding onto Setti's reins, I swung myself up as Vonetta prowled forward in her wolven form beside Delano.

Several dozen wolven rose from where they rested in the plush grass and the warm rays of the afternoon sun as the gates of the northern wall opened, one after another. Led by Valyn and the Guardians, they rode out in groups of several hundred, their gold and silver armor shining under the morning sun. The sound of a thousand hooves clacked off stone and echoed around us as banners were lifted all the way down the line. My breath caught as I saw the Atlantian Crest. The arrow and sword now crossed over the center.

I inhaled sharply, eyes stinging as the banners rippled in the Atlantian sun. I closed my eyes, telling myself that Casteel would see them.

A low rumble came, a sound similar to thunder. Another higher-pitched, keening call followed. I opened my eyes as the wolven stopped, lifting their heads to the sky. Their ears perked. My one-handed grip on the reins tightened as Setti pranced nervously beneath me as I reached down, placing my hand over the small pouch at my hip. The ridges of the small toy horse pressed against my palm. I stared at the banners, at the crest that represented Casteel and I, as large, winged shadows fell over the armies of Atlantia as they rode west.

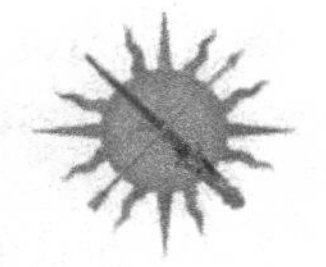

Four days later, we waited in the forest outside of Oak Ambler, among the bowed trees. When the last of the sun reached us, and stars came to life in the night sky, I slipped the horse into the pouch and rose from where I'd been sitting on the raised, flat surface of a rock.

"You should've slept some," Delano murmured as he came over to me.

"I did."

Concern seeped from every one of his pores. I hadn't lied. Not really. I had slept for an hour or so, and then I was awake and spent those hours like I spent all the hours when we took breaks to rest or eat.

I practiced fighting like a god.

Picking up the short sword, I sheathed it as I looked around with a slight frown. "Where are…?"

"The draken?" Delano's eyes glimmered with amusement as he nodded to where the cluster of trees still stood straight and proud. "Reaver is over there, currently engaged in an epic stare down with Kieran."

A faint grin tugged at my lips as I squinted. I could just make out the form of Kieran, lying low on his belly. Several feet from him, a relatively large-sized draken, idly picked at its front teeth with its claws. The draken wasn't as big as Nektas, but he was the length of five Settis and about three times the width.

Reaver was the one who'd almost bitten Kieran.

I arched a brow. I hadn't even seen Reaver in his mortal form. Nektas, who'd remained behind in Iliseeum, was the only one I'd seen for any length of time in their mortal form. I'd only learned Reaver's name because another, a female draken called Aurelia who'd been in her mortal form briefly, had given me their names. She and another were the only two females who'd awakened. Apparently, female draken were rare.

"It's time," I called out, securing the hook on my cloak. "Remember the plan."

A huffing sound came from Reaver as he rose, stretching his large, purplish-black body as he lifted his wings. That made me a wee bit concerned that he would not follow said plan. Kieran rose, and I half-expected him to flounce away from the draken, but he managed a rather sedate prance over to me.

I turned to where Vonetta and the remaining wolven waited with Naill and Emil. "Be safe."

Steely determination rose from them as I turned and began walking toward the city with Delano at my side, in his mortal form. If things went the way I hoped, there would be no risk to most of the wolven. The crunch of dried leaves alerted me to the progress Kieran made and the rattle of branches above told me that Reaver had taken flight.

Traces of moonlight cut through the bent trees as I glanced down at my left palm. The marriage imprint glowed softly. Closing my hand, I lifted the hood on the cloak just enough that the crown was hidden. I slid my right hand inside my cloak as I saw a row of torches through the bowed limbs.

"I see them," Delano said quietly. "There's about a dozen."

Less than I thought there would be, which was kind of offensive.

Kieran hung back as Delano and I neared the edges of the trees. I could see a line of guards, their mantles blending into the night, even in the moonlight. Knights. My opened senses confirmed as much, but there was another—one who stood off to the side, dressed in black. A younger male with dark hair. I sensed…nothing from him, but it wasn't the utter emptiness of an Ascended. The one with his arms crossed was not a vampry, and I was willing to bet it was a Revenant.

The knights moved in unison before Delano and I stepped out of the trees, lifting shields with the Royal Crest carved into the metal. Swords were held at their sides. I stared at the crest—a circle with an arrow piercing the center. It symbolized infinity and power, but I realized that I was the arrow on the Atlantian Crest. Not the sword. I now saw the Royal Crest in a whole new light. I smiled.

"I don't know why you're smiling," the Revenant spoke. "I don't believe things went well for you the last time you were here."

I flicked a brief glance in his direction. "I truly hope it is not you that they sent to speak with me. If so, I can assure you that tonight will not end well for you."

The Revenant lifted a dark brow. "Ouch."

"Stand aside," came a voice from behind the knights. A voice I hadn't heard in *years*.

The knights parted, lowering their shields, and I saw who stood behind them.

The golden hair was longer than I remembered, brushing the tips of his ears, but I recognized the features of a good-looking man—the heavy brow, the straight nose, the square jaw, and the thin lips that I'd rarely ever seen curved into a smile. The ruby crown glinted darkly in the moonlight.

I almost couldn't believe that I was staring at the Blood King, dressed in a white cloak trimmed in red and black with crimson crisscrossing his chest. She had answered my request and sent the King to meet with me. Laughter rose so quickly, it almost burst free from me, but then I realized that there was only one Revenant among a handful of knights to protect the actual King of Solis. It was obvious that the Blood Crown truly saw me as no threat.

And, well, now I truly *was* offended.

"Maiden," King Jalara spoke, and I stiffened. "It has been quite some time, has it not?"

"It has," I answered, aware of the rise of anger from Delano and where Kieran remained hidden in the shadows of the trees. "A lot has changed, starting with the fact that I am no longer the Maiden." I lifted my left hand, tugging down the cloak's hood. "But you already know that."

There was a slight widening of his eyes. "The gilded crown," King Jalara murmured, sounding as awed as I'd ever heard an Ascended, which was a lukewarm reaction at best. His jeweled hand winked in the moonlight as his grip on his sword increased. "My, my, my, Penellaphe," he murmured, eyeing the crown as he stepped forward. "Look at you."

Delano withdrew his sword, his features sharpening to a deadly thinness. "You will address her as Queen Penellaphe or Your Majesty."

Slowly, the King turned his head to the wolven, the mannerism serpent-like. "The one beside you?" He sniffed the air. "Nothing more than a heathen. An overgrown dog." The King sneered. "Disgusting."

"Disgusting?" I repeated. "The one beside me comes from the line of those given mortal form by Nyktos himself. The one who stands to your left reeks of decay and rot."

The Revenant frowned. "I do not." He plucked at the front of his tunic. "Rude."

"Oh, I'm sorry." I stared up at the Blood King. "Is it you who taints the air instead?"

There was a sugary burst of amusement from the Revenant as a muscle flexed in King Jalara's jaw. "I would watch your tongue, *Maiden*."

I held up my left hand as a low snarl rumbled from Delano.

King Jalara smirked. "Or maybe not. Every word you speak that irritates me, I will be sure to take it out on the one you call your husband."

Every part of me screamed in rage—screamed for blood and pain, even as I showed no emotion and looked up at the Blood King. The Ascended who had never been cruel to me as a child. Who had just been there, in the background.

"You do know that he has found his stay with us to be less than pleasant. Dear Ileana almost had him convinced that you had been captured in spite of his sacrifice. His screams of rage were a serenade for the ages."

My jaw clenched.

A smug look settled onto his features. "What? You have nothing to say? You do not ask about his well-being? No begging?" His head tilted. "No threatening? I at least expected one threat from you after hearing Ileana wax poetically about her—"

"Call her by her real name," I interrupted. "I'm sure you know it is Isbeth."

His eyes narrowed. "She is no longer Isbeth."

"And what do you think she is? Ileana, the goddess?"

"What do you think?" he challenged.

"I know a god cannot be made," I said. "She is nothing more than a twisted mess of bitterness and greed made manifest."

"And what does that make you?"

"An actual god," I replied as flatly as Casteel would've.

"And yet you couldn't defeat her?" He laughed coldly. "You may be born of Nyktos's blood, but you and I both know what you are and what you will always be. The Maiden who is part beauty and part disaster."

I said nothing. I felt nothing.

His chin dipped as he drew closer. "You should do as she requests. She is your mother."

"And yet, I couldn't care less." I held his stare. "Believe it or not, I didn't come here to spend time insulting the Blood Queen."

King Jalara inhaled sharply. "You came to surrender? To submit?"

"I came to send a message to the Blood Queen."

His brows flew up so fast and so far, I was surprised they didn't topple his precious crown. "A message? I came all the way out to this godsforsaken place on the edge of the Wastelands to deliver a message for you?"

I nodded as my right hand moved under the cloak, crossing my stomach.

"You have to be out of your mind. You are, aren't you?" King Jalara's smile was grotesque, revealing his fangs. "The only message I will deliver for you is one of submission."

"I'm sorry. I misspoke," I said, forcing a silly little laugh. "It's *you* that's the message."

"What—?" His twisted smile froze. His gaze shot over my shoulder—

Kieran exploded from the shadows, slamming into him. He stumbled, lips peeling back in a snarl as Kieran latched on to his arm, not letting him get far. I pulled the sword from my cloak and spun, sweeping out wide and high.

Only a few things in my entire life were as satisfying as the feeling of the blade meeting King Jalara's flesh, the resistance of bone, and then the shocking ease with which it gave way. The blade sliced deep into his throat and through the spinal column, separating his head from the body.

My gaze lifted to where the knights had frozen, to where the Revenant stood in utter shock, either held immobile by the sight of their King's head winging in the opposite direction of his body, or by the sight of the other wolven prowling out from the darkness.

And then I fought *like a god.*

I didn't summon the eather. I didn't visualize it. I didn't take the time to let the power ramp up inside me. I didn't need to because it was always there. I simply willed it.

The shields exploded, and then the swords. The necks of the knights twisted sideways, silencing their screams before they even formed. Their arms broke. Bones cracked throughout the bodies. Their legs bent backwards, and then I tore them apart from the *inside.*

In the mist of blood, the Revenant quickly withdrew two black, crescent-shaped swords. He held them as the wolven growled and snapped. "That won't work on me."

"No. It won't," I said as a rush of wind whipped from above. The light of the moon was suddenly obscured.

The Revenant glanced up. "What the—?"

Reaver landed before me, rocking the ground and the trees. His tail whipped around, sliding between the wolven as he stretched out his head and opened his mouth. A deafening roar erupted from deep within his throat as a wisp of smoke floated above the frills.

"But this will," I finished, sheathing the sword. "Fire of the gods, right? That will kill you."

"Good fucking gods, is that—?" The Revenant stumbled, tripping over his feet. He caught himself just as Reaver's spiked tail slammed into his chest.

Well, that was not a part of the plan, I thought as I watched the Revenant fly sideways, crashing into rock. He hit it with a fleshy smack. Sliding onto his knees, he pitched forward onto his hands with a groan.

Slowly, I looked over at Reaver. "Really?"

He made a chuffing sound as he swung his tail back, narrowly missing taking out Kieran in the process. The wolven's ears flattened as he growled.

"Calm," I warned him as I stepped over Reaver's tail. "That's not a battle you're going to win."

Everything about Kieran's stance said he'd like to try as I approached the moaning Revenant. He quieted as I knelt in front of him, clutching his chest.

"*That* was part of the message that I want you to deliver to your Queen," I said, and it was the kind of message Casteel would send.

The Revenant looked up, blood leaking from his mouth. His gaze only left me long enough to see what Delano had dropped at his feet.

It was King Jalara's head.

"Fuck," the Revenant groaned.

I took the ruby crown Delano handed me. "I want you to deliver that to her. Let her know that I have his crown. It's mine now. I want you to thank her for me, for teaching me to fight like a god. Tell her that was for Ian."

The Revenent's flat eyes met mine.

"Now this is the really important part. I need you to make sure she understands that I'm coming for her. That I will burn every Revenant that stands between her and me. I will strike down every Ascended who defends her. I will topple every castle she seeks to hide in. Make sure she understands that her survival hinges on Casteel. She will release him, or she will see each and every one of her cities *leveled*. If she touches him again, I will destroy her precious Malec, and I can. I know where to find him. He lives. For now. And if she kills Casteel? If *anyone* kills him?" I tilted my head, catching his gaze as he tried to find where the draken had flown off to. "I will make sure her death is a slow one that will take hundreds of years to complete. If not thousands. You understand?"

"Yes," he wheezed.

"Good." I rose then, the ruby crown dangling from my fingers. "Make sure she knows that I am the Chosen, the One who is Blessed, and I carry the blood of the King of Gods in me. I am the *Liessa* to the wolven, the second daughter, the true heir, owed the crowns of Atlantia *and* Solis. I am the Queen of Flesh and Fire, and the gods' guards ride with me. Tell the Blood Queen to prepare for war."

**To see a full color version of the world map, visit https://TheBlueBoxPress.com/books/tcogbmap/

Coming October 19, 2021

A SHADOW IN THE EMBER

Book one of the all-new, compelling
Flesh and Fire series.

Set in the beloved Blood and Ash world.

The story of Nyktos and his Consort.
And how their love shaped
the realms for all time.

Available in hardcover, e-book, and trade paperback.
https://theblueboxpress.com/books/jennifer-l-armentrout-a-shadow-in-the-ember/

Coming March 15, 2022

THE WAR OF TWO QUEENS

From #1 New York Times bestselling author Jennifer L. Armentrout
comes book four in her Blood and Ash series.

War is only the beginning…

Discover The Summer King Trilogy

The Prince: A Wicked Novella

She's everything he wants....

Cold. Heartless. Deadly. Whispers of his name alone bring fear to fae and mortals alike. *The Prince.* There is nothing in the mortal world more dangerous than him. Haunted by a past he couldn't control, all Caden desires is revenge against those who'd wronged him, trapping him in never-ending nightmare. And there is one person he knows can help him.

She's everything he can't have...

Raised within the Order, Brighton Jussier knows just how dangerous the Prince is, reformed or not. She'd seen firsthand what atrocities he could be capable of. The last thing she wants to do is help him, but he leaves her little choice. Forced to work alongside him, she begins to see the man under the bitter ice. Yearning for him feels like the definition of insanity, but there's no denying the heat in his touch and the wicked promise is his stare.

She's everything he'll take....

But there's someone out there who wants to return the Prince to his former self. A walking, breathing nightmare that is hell bent on destroying the world and everyone close to him. The last thing either of them needs is a distraction, but with the attraction growing between them each now, the one thing he wants more than anything may be the one thing that will be his undoing.

She's everything he'd die for....

* * * *

The King: A Wicked Novella

From #1 *New York Times* and *USA Today* bestselling author Jennifer L. Armentrout comes the next installment in her Wicked series.

As Caden and Brighton's attraction grows despite the odds stacked against a happily ever after, they must work together to stop an Ancient fae from releasing the Queen, who wants nothing more than to see Caden become the evil Prince once feared by fae and mortals alike.

* * * *

***The Queen*: A Wicked Novella**

The King must have his Queen....

Bestowed the forbidden Summer's Kiss by the King of the Summer fae, Brighton Jussier is no longer *just* human. What she is, what she will become, no one knows for sure, but that isn't her biggest concern at the moment. Now Caden, the King, refuses to let her go, even at the cost of his Court. When the doorway to the Otherworld is breached, both Brighton and Caden must do the unthinkable—not just to survive themselves, but also to save mankind from the evil that threatens the world.

TIFFANY&CO.

Discover 1001 Dark Nights Collection Eight

DRAGON REVEALED by Donna Grant
A Dragon Kings Novella

CAPTURED IN INK by Carrie Ann Ryan
A Montgomery Ink: Boulder Novella

SECURING JANE by Susan Stoker
A SEAL of Protection: Legacy Series Novella

WILD WIND by Kristen Ashley
A Chaos Novella

DARE TO TEASE by Carly Phillips
A Dare Nation Novella

VAMPIRE by Rebecca Zanetti
A Dark Protectors/Rebels Novella

MAFIA KING by Rachel Van Dyken
A Mafia Royals Novella

THE GRAVEDIGGER'S SON by Darynda Jones
A Charley Davidson Novella

FINALE by Skye Warren
A North Security Novella

MEMORIES OF YOU by J. Kenner
A Stark Securities Novella

SLAYED BY DARKNESS by Alexandra Ivy
A Guardians of Eternity Novella

TREASURED by Lexi Blake
A Masters and Mercenaries Novella

THE DAREDEVIL by Dylan Allen
A Rivers Wilde Novella

BOND OF DESTINY by Larissa Ione
A Demonica Novella

THE CLOSE-UP by Kennedy Ryan
A Hollywood Renaissance Novella

MORE THAN POSSESS YOU by Shayla Black
A More Than Words Novella

HAUNTED HOUSE by Heather Graham
A Krewe of Hunters Novella

MAN FOR ME by Laurelin Paige
A Man In Charge Novella

THE RHYTHM METHOD by Kylie Scott
A Stage Dive Novella

JONAH BENNETT by Tijan
A Bennett Mafia Novella

CHANGE WITH ME by Kristen Proby
A With Me In Seattle Novella

THE DARKEST DESTINY by Gena Showalter
A Lords of the Underworld Novella

About Jennifer L. Armentrout

1 New York Times and International Bestselling author Jennifer lives in Shepherdstown, West Virginia. All the rumors you've heard about her state aren't true. When she's not hard at work writing. she spends her time reading, watching really bad zombie movies, pretending to write, and hanging out with her husband, their retired K-9 police dog Diesel, a crazy Border Jack puppy named Apollo, six judgmental alpacas, four fluffy sheep, and two goats.

Her dreams of becoming an author started in algebra class, where she spent most of her time writing short stories…which explains her dismal grades in math. Jennifer writes young adult paranormal, science fiction, fantasy, and contemporary romance. She is published with Tor Teen, Entangled Teen and Brazen, Disney/Hyperion and Harlequin Teen. Her book *Wicked* has been optioned by Passionflix and slated to begin filming in late 2018. Her young adult romantic suspense novel *DONT LOOK BACK* was a 2014 nominated Best in Young Adult Fiction by YALSA and her novel *THE PROBLEM WITH FOREVER* is a 2017 RITA Award winning novel.

She also writes Adult and New Adult contemporary and paranormal romance under the name J. Lynn. She is published by Entangled Brazen and HarperCollins.

On Behalf of Blue Box Press,

Liz Berry, M.J. Rose, and Jillian Stein would like to thank ~

Steve Berry
Doug Scofield
Benjamin Stein
Kim Guidroz
Social Butterfly PR
Ashley Wells
Chelle Olson
Hang Le
Stephanie Brown
Chris Graham
Jessica Johns
Dylan Stockton
Celia Taylor Mobley
Richard Blake
and Simon Lipskar

Printed in the USA
CPSIA information can be obtained
at www.ICGtesting.com
LVHW040143260823
756274LV00001B/12

9 781952 457784